COLLECTED STORIES

COLLECTED STORIES

Bernard MacLaverty

JONATHAN CAPE
LONDON

Published by Jonathan Cape 2013

Secrets:
Some of these stories first appeared in *The Irish Press, The Honest
Ulsterman, Caret, Fortnight*, BBC Radio and TV, RTE Radio; *Winter's Tales
from Ireland 2*, Gill and MacMillan; *New Irish Writers*, Dtv Zweisprachig;
Soundings 3, Blackstaff Press and *Scottish Short Stories*, Collins.

A Time to Dance:
The following stories in this collection appeared previously, as listed: 'The Beginnings of a Sin'
(*In Dublin*, 1981); 'Father and Son' (*Scottish Short Stories*, Collins, 1978); 'Life Drawing'
(*Firebird* I, Penguin, 1982); 'My Dear Palestrina' (BBC Radio 4, 1980; BBC Television, 1980);
'Phonefun Limited' (Glasgow Theatre Club, Tron Theatre, 1981; BBC Radio, Northern Ireland, 1982);
'A Time to Dance' (*Scottish Short Stories*, Collins, 1980).

The author and publishers are grateful to ATV Music Ltd for permission to quote the extract from
the song 'Two Brothers' by Irving Gordon on pp. 32–33.

The Great Profundo:
Versions of 'The Break' and 'Across the Street' first appeared in the
Irish Times; 'More than just the Disease' in *Scottish Short Stories*,
Collins; 'End of Season' in *Firebird 3*, Penguin;
and 'Remote' in the *Sunday Tribune*.

Walking the Dog:
'Walking the Dog' was originally published in *Story* magazine,
'The Wake House' in the American edition of *GQ* and
'A Foreign Dignitary' in the *New Statesman*.

Matters of Life & Death:
Permission to quote from 'Cheek to Cheek'; Words & Music by Irving
Berlin © 1935 Irving Berlin Music Corp. All rights administered
by Warner/Chappell Music Ltd, London, W6 8BS.
Reproduced by permission.

First published in Great Britain in 2013 by
Jonathan Cape
Random House, 20 Vauxhall Bridge Road, London SW1V 2SA

Addresses for companies within The Random House Group Limited can be found at:
www.randomhouse.co.uk/offices.htm

The Random House Group Limited Reg. No. 954009

A CIP catalogue record for this book is available from the British Library
ISBN 9780224097802

The Random House Group Limited supports the Forest Stewardship Council®
(FSC®), the leading international forest-certification organisation. Our books
carrying the FSC label are printed on FSC®-certified paper. FSC is the only
forest-certification scheme supported by the leading environmental organisations,
including Greenpeace. Our paper procurement policy can be found
at www.randomhouse.co.uk/environment

Typeset in Sabon LT Std by Palimpsest Book Production Limited, Falkirk, Stirlingshire
Printed and bound in Great Britain by CPI Group (UK) Ltd, Croydon CR0 4YY

for Madeline

CONTENTS

INTRODUCTION

Writing essays is not what fiction writers are necessarily good at so writing an introduction to this volume of my *Collected Stories* is not easy. I can't praise the stories or point out weaknesses. I suppose the easy answer is to ask you to skip this bit and go on and read the stories. The other way is to tell you bits of my life and how I first came to writing.

I remember my mother, after watching a TV play of mine, saying to me with an incredulous and worried shake of the head, 'Where did all this come from?'

She was partly responsible, having married an artist. It was a surprising choice given that she was so full of notions of correctness. She was a good and kind woman, fastidious in the practice of her religion, who was concerned about the properness of how to talk, how to walk, how to eat. In the bus she would say to my five-year-old self, 'Sit nicely'. Everything had to be done nicely – except that you can't do creative things nicely. If you do them nicely then they cease to be any good.

My childhood was spent in a Victorian red-brick terraced house in Atlantic Avenue, Belfast. The rooms had leftover bell handles for my brother and I to summon the staff: my mother, father, grandfather, grandmother and great aunt. Across the street was another grandfather and yet another aunt. I thought that everybody grew up surrounded by old people. When you had a fight in one house you could always run to the other – and make your demands on different servants.

In our house the elders would sit round the fire making toast on the end of a long custom-made wire fork, clandestinely wrought in the shipyard by an uncle. It went in and out like a telescope. They also used to eat thinly sliced orange sandwiches and wonder aloud if it was the kind of thing the Queen ate and, if so, did she eat them at the same time of day as they did. The air was full, always and everywhere, with the sound of the old ones talking. At one time I was ill and feverish, lying on a sofa in front of the fire happed in blankets. The way the hushed conversational tones faded *diminuendo* into sleep is one of my best childhood memories.

Another is of starting a notebook to record some of the things Aunty Betty said – she had such a quirky way with words. I must have been in my mid to late teens and I see this as one of the first stepping stones to being interested in writing. Aunty Betty had four boys and one day she was down on her hands and knees wiping round the floor of the toilet and shouting, 'All you wains must have crooked flutes.'

Nowadays people who aspire to write get themselves into their nearest creative-writing class. In my day there was no such thing but I am grateful to the folk who encouraged me: teachers, neighbours, friends. The first one to draw my attention to the importance of written words was my primary-school teacher. He looked like the kind of man who could bend lamp-posts or bite through dictionaries. But he was very gentle. He set a homework to describe 'A rainy day'. When he returned our corrected jotters he gave me a sweet and a sixpence and read my effort out to the class. I think my mother liked it better than anything I ever wrote after. She kept it in a box with the insurance and other important documents until the day she died. She said to me once, 'Son, I pray every night you'll not write anything dirty.'

My primary-school teacher was an eccentric. He also told us stories that scared the wits out of us. One was his version of the man who sold his soul to the devil so's he could become the best accordion player in Ireland. But you don't get irony at that age; all that comes across is stomach-churning fear. In his telling of the story he suggested that the would-be accordionist could briefly escape from the fires of hell, and ask you for help. Don't think of it as a dream or a nightmare because the proof will be there in the scorch-marks in the wood at the foot of your bed.

In grammar school at senior level I had a great and inspirational teacher – a priest nicknamed 'the wee Dean'. He taught us about poetry, Gerard Manley Hopkins, *Macbeth*, D.H. Lawrence and much more. Each class he'd rush in with a stack of freshly Gestetnered sheets in his arms. He'd tell us how late he'd sat up preparing these. Each page was spattered with blackened 'o's like it had been hit by buckshot. The plastic centre of each 'o' had fallen out, so enthusiastically had he typed it. After I left school I met the wee Dean on the street one day. I had just borrowed a book from the library – a novel of some import. It could have been one of my discoveries of that time – Dostoyevsky or Kafka, Tolstoy or Thomas Mann – and because I might be thought a pseudo-intellectual I carried the book with the title hidden against my chest. However when I saw my former teacher approaching I turned the book face outwards – much to my shame. But he engaged with it, 'Ah I see your reading such n' such by so n' so. Great book; wonderful writer.'

It must have been around this time – coinciding with the onset of occasional shaving – I started writing: deeply embarrassing poetry, mostly in the sprung rhythms of Gerard Manley Hopkins. Then, when these so obviously failed, I made attempts at the short story. I wrote these on blank examination booklets stolen from exam rooms policed by careless invigilators. We had a neighbour – a Mrs Theo McCrudden – an English teacher (Theodora was her first name) from a few doors away who read and encouraged my first hesitant efforts. Looking back I'm glad my neighbour was not the wonderful Flannery O'Connor who, when she was asked if she thought universities stifled young writers, said that they didn't stifle half enough of them.

Religion both terrified and elevated me. It dominated my childhood. The fact that I don't believe a word of it now doesn't diminish the effect it had on me then. It elevated me because of the intimacy I had with the maker of all things – the most important personage in the Universe. We were on the best of terms, able to chat day or night. It was only much later that I realised the workshop was empty. But at that time I believed in the Church's acres of symbolism, knew without thinking that vestments were colour-coded – red for martyrs, black for death, purple for penance, green for hope, white for grace or purity. Indeed all ceremonies were layered with meaning

– at Easter the passing from one person to another of the flame of a candle in a darkened church; the cleansing nature of the waters of Baptism, the secrecy of the Confessional, the reverberations of the altar bell, the scarlet glow of the sanctuary lamp, the gym shoes we wore as altar boys so as not to be too noisy in the presence of God (although why God should want the place quiet I never knew). So I grew up knowing things represented other things. This can only be good for someone who is going to be a writer.

It is difficult to be precise when an awareness of words first began for me. There was always a time when I repeated a word so frequently that it lost all meaning and the black swamp closed over my head. The meaning of words and the meaning of the universe sat very close.

Seamus Heaney puts it well – as he puts so many things well – in *Preoccupations*: 'Maybe it began with the exotic listing on the wireless dial. Stuttgart, Leipzig, Oslo, Hilversum. Maybe it was stirred by the beautiful sprung rhythms of the old BBC weather forecast: Dogger, Rockall, Malin, Shetland, Faroes, Finisterre; or with the gorgeous and inane phraseology of the catechism; or with the Litany of the Blessed Virgin that was part of the enforced poetry of our household: Tower of Gold, Ark of the Covenant, Gate of Heaven, Morning Star, Health of the Sick, Refuge of Sinners, Comforter of the Afflicted.'

I am able to say 'snap' to all of these and add the word-induced nausea of the response to the Litany. After each item the response was 'Pray for us' which blurred into 'prefrus', 'prefrus', 'prefrus'. And the black swamp closed again.

Heaney goes on to observe, 'None of these things was consciously savoured at the time but I think the fact that I can still recall them with ease, and can delight in them as verbal music means that they were bedding the ear with a kind of linguistic hard core that could be built on someday.'

In the same vein there was the Latin we parroted as altar boys. Not having a clue what it meant we were in love with the sound of it – and the grandeur it lent to our Belfast accents.

In the missal, kneeling beside my mother at mass, I came across the word 'concupiscence'. At eight or nine I hadn't realised that the young James Joyce had a similar problem with the word 'simony'. I rolled the word 'concupiscence' round my mouth like a gobstopper and asked my poor mother what it meant but she shook her head from side to side. What did she know about the yearnings of lust and the desires of the flesh?

In an essay, early in secondary school, shortly after reading a passage of D.H. Lawrence I used the phrase 'the fecund darkness'. My Great Aunt Mary, looking over my shoulder, gave a little sniff and said there was something 'not quite right' about that word. She had been a school teacher herself but she mustn't have read much Lawrence because she nearly collapsed when she caught me reading the school set text of Thomas Hardy's adult tale *The Woodlanders*.

This fascination with words became worrying when I found myself enjoying Roget's *Thesaurus*. It was like opening a gold mine.

Another thing which might have been part of my 'linguistic hard core' was – I hate to admit it in public – being sent to elocution. It was just another bullet in my mother's bandoleer of 'doing things nicely.' Maybe that was because the other cultural nightmare was not an option – the piano. In our house there was one which had not been tuned for years and half of the notes, when pressed down, played silent. 'A dust-gatherer', my mother called it. So it was my job to stand up straight and try to speak like a BBC child. The only advantage was an early contact with poetry – particularly that of James Stephens – its sounds and rhythms. I can't remember what age I was but I was young enough to be unskilled about blowing my nose. Before going on to do my recitation at a competition my mother would give me a clean, freshly ironed hanky and tell me to get somebody backstage, preferably a woman, to do the needful before I went on.

One of the best learning experiences was long after leaving school when Philip Hobsbaum, an English lecturer at Queen's University, after reading a short story of mine in a medical magazine, invited me to come along to the 'Group'. I was an employee of the university at the time – a medical laboratory technician in the Anatomy Department. There were an amazing number of talented people in the Group, none of whom had published anything. It included the poets Seamus Heaney, Michael Longley, Frank Ormsby, Paul Muldoon, Jimmy Simmons, Joan Newman and Ciarán Carson, the playwright Stewart Parker and many others. Hobsbaum chaired the meetings and always took the part of the writer against those who were being critical, waggling his pencil as he did so.

What happened was that you submitted a story or a sheet of poems or whatever, and they would be typed up and copies would be run off and posted out to members. On Monday night the author would read his contribution aloud to the other writers, all slumped in armchairs in Philip's flat. Then people would either make helpful suggestions or, if they were feeling aggressive, unhelpful ones. The only formality was that there was no alcohol – coffee was the drink – writers, alcohol and criticism do not go together.

But the thing which amazed me about the Group was that my attempts at writing were being taken seriously. And this seriousness encouraged me to send stories to more permanent publications like *The Honest Ulsterman* and David Marcus's 'New Irish Writing' page in the *Irish Press*. The latter paid a small fee. The first money I earned as a writer was from the BBC's 'Morning Story'. I was very excited when invited into the BBC to discuss the piece I had submitted. I was told 'Morning Story' was two thousand eight hundred words and that my story was too long. At first I was indignant. Then, back at home, I discovered that the more words you took out the better the story became. Up to a point. If you went too far down that road you'd end up writing nothing.

Much later I was frightened by Wittgenstein's 'In art it is hard to say anything as good as saying nothing.'

Ours was not a great reading family. Like most things, the activity was subjugated to religion. The only reason you would read a book was if it kept you out of hell or made your entry into heaven easier. Books of this nature were kept in a glass-fronted bureau bookcase. I know the names of the authors and can recall the colours of the spines – D.K. Broster, H.V. Morton, A.J. Cronin – the initials making me think of a literary cricket team. I once talked to a man in a pub about books and he told me that I should read those *Reader's Digest* Classics. 'They cut out all the rubbish and you're left with pure classic.' The only reason a book was owned, rather than borrowed from the library, was because it had been a present bought for Christmas. Then it ended up in the glass-fronted bureau book-case. I only read one of them, it was the first grown-up book I'd ever read – essays by the humorous Irish writer John D. Sheridan. I was about ten years of age and was returning the book to where I'd found it. Whether it was 'The Right Time' or 'My Hat Blew Off' I can't remember. What I do recall was my father's interest: that I was leaving behind the Just William and Biggles books. He must have asked me why I liked the John D. Sheridan and I told him that it made me laugh – those people on the street who always asked the author for the *right* time – nothing else was any good to them. We were alone in the room standing by the window and when the issue of books was raised he sat down on the arm of a sofa to carry on the conversation. I remember that with clarity – because conversations with adults never happened.

My grandmother or my Great Aunt Mary used to read to my brother and I: a chapter a night – mostly of Enid Blyton – once *Coral Island* and *Kidnapped*. The magazines and papers which came into the house were religious – the only English newspaper allowed across the threshold was the parochially named *The Universe*. All other English newspapers had views and reported things which could damage young minds – especially the *News of the World*. We took one magazine called *The Far East* – an Irish missionary publication – and it was full of photos of smiling priests in white soutanes surrounded by 'black babies'. There was a nice story going the rounds much later – of the woman in the Falls Road post office:

How much would it be to post clothes to the Far East?

Whereabouts in the Far East?

Where do'you think, the Far East in Dublin.

I suppose the end of my childhood came with the death of my father. I did not know he was going to die. I was twelve at the time. He had been to Lourdes but I thought it was just another of his 'good works', helping with the sick – instead of being one of them. My last vivid memory, after his return, was of walking with him in Alexander Park – going round the back of the pond, the darkness under the trees, the blackness of the water – but it's as if the sound is missing. Although it was a summer's day he wore his heavy navy overcoat. His yellowed complexion I thought the result of French sunshine.

Looking back over the early stories I could not resist the urge to correct where there were mistakes and clarify where there was fog. Where clumsiness embarrassed me I rearranged. Flannery O'Connor writes somewhere that she has spent all day removing 'like' and 'as if' phrases from her manuscript. Then adds, 'it was like getting ticks off a dog' – dryly condemning the device with a brilliant use of an example of it. But mostly I let things stand as they were, and forgave myself for writing these stories of an inexperienced young man. Some stories I dropped as they jostled for space. Also, in a very few places, the meaning of words has changed and what was in the original is now offensive. So I rewrote.

It's impossible to name all the people to whom I owe a debt of gratitude but I would like to thank my agent Gill Coleridge, Anne Tannahill of Blackstaff Press, Xandra Bingley of Jonathan Cape and Robin Robertson for all their friendship and advice. And, of course, Madeline – for everything.

Bernard MacLaverty, 2013

I

SECRETS

1977

THE EXERCISE

'We never got the chance,' his mother would say to him. 'It wouldn't have done me much good but your father could have bettered himself. He'd be teaching or something now instead of serving behind a bar. He could stand up with the best of them.'

Now that he had started grammar school Kevin's father joined him in his work, helping him when he had the time, sometimes doing the exercises out of the text books on his own before he went to bed. He worked mainly from examples in the Maths and Language books or from previously corrected work of Kevin's. Often his wife took a hand out of him saying, 'Do you think you'll pass your Christmas Tests?'

When he concentrated he sat hunched at the kitchen table, his non-writing hand shoved down the back of his trousers and his tongue stuck out.

'Put that thing back in your mouth,' Kevin's mother would say, laughing. 'You've a tongue on you like a cow.'

His father smelt strongly of tobacco for he smoked both a pipe and cigarettes. When he gave Kevin money for sweets he'd say, 'You'll get sixpence in my coat pocket on the banisters.'

Kevin would dig into the pocket deep down almost to his elbow and pull out a handful of coins speckled with bits of yellow and black tobacco. His father also smelt of porter, not his breath, for he never drank but from his clothes and Kevin thought it mixed nicely with his grown up smell. He loved to smell his pyjama jacket and the shirts he left off for washing.

Once in a while Kevin's father would come in at six o'clock, sit in his armchair and say, 'Slippers'.

'You're not staying in, are you?' The three boys shouted and danced around, the youngest pulling off his big boots, falling back on the floor as they came away from his feet, Kevin, the eldest, standing on the arm of the chair to get the slippers down from the cupboard.

'Some one of you get a good shovel of coal for that fire,' and they sat in the warm kitchen doing their homework, their father reading the paper or moving about doing some job their mother had been at him to do for months. Before their bedtime he would read the younger ones a story or if there were no books in the house at the time he would choose a piece from the paper. Kevin listened with the others although he pretended to be doing something else.

But it was not one of those nights. His father stood shaving with his overcoat on, a very heavy navy overcoat, in a great hurry, his face creamed thick with white lather. Kevin knelt on the cold lino of the bathroom floor, one elbow leaning on the padded seat of the green wicker chair trying to get help with his Latin. It was one of those exercises which asked for the nominative and genitive of: an evil deed, a wise father and so on.

'What's the Latin for "evil"?'

His father towered above him trying to get at the mirror, pointing his chin upwards scraping underneath.

'Look it up at the back.'

Kevin sucked the end of his pencil and fumbled through the vocabularies. His father finished shaving, humped his back and spluttered in the basin. Kevin heard him pull the plug and the final gasp as the water escaped. He groped for the towel then genuflected beside him drying his face.

'Where is it?' He looked down still drying slower and slower, meditatively until he stopped.

'I'll tell you just this once because I'm in a hurry.'

Kevin stopped sucking the pencil and held it poised, ready and wrote the answers with great speed into his jotter as his father called them out.

'Is that them all?' his father asked, draping the towel over the side of the bath. He leaned forward to kiss Kevin but the boy lowered his head to look at something in the book. As his father rushed down the stairs he shouted back over his shoulder.

'Don't ever ask me to do that again. You'll have to work them out for yourself.'

He was away leaving Kevin sitting at the chair. The towel edged its way slowly down the side of the bath and fell on the floor. He got up and looked in the wash-hand basin. The bottom was covered in short black hairs, shavings. He drew a white path through them with his finger. Then he turned and went down the stairs to copy the answers in ink.

Of all the teachers in the school Waldo was the one who commanded the most respect. In his presence nobody talked, with the result that he walked the corridors in a moat of silence. Boys seeing him approach would drop their voices to a whisper and only when he was out of earshot would they speak normally again. Between classes there was always five minutes uproar. The boys wrestled over desks, shouted, whistled, flung books while some tried to learn their nouns, eyes closed, feet tapping to the rhythm of declensions. Others put frantic finishing touches to last night's exercise. Some minutes before Waldo's punctual arrival, the class quietened. Three rows of boys, all by now strumming nouns, sat hunched and waiting.

Waldo's entrance was theatrical. He strode in with strides as long as his soutane would permit, his books clenched in his left hand and pressed tightly against his chest. With his right hand he swung the door behind him, closing it with a crash. His eyes raked the class. If, as occasionally happened, it did not close properly he did not turn from the class but backed slowly against the door snapping it shut with his behind. Two strides brought him to the rostrum. He cracked his books down with an explosion and made a swift palm upward gesture.

Waldo was very tall, his height being emphasised by the soutane, narrow and tight-fitting at the shoulders, sweeping down like a bell to the floor. A row of black gleaming buttons bisected him from floor to throat. When he talked his Adam's apple hit against the hard, white Roman collar and created in Kevin the same sensation as a fingernail scraping down the blackboard. His face was sallow and immobile. (There was a rumour that he had a glass eye but no-one knew which. Nobody could look at him long enough because to meet his stare was to invite a question.) He abhorred slovenliness. Once when presented with an untidy exercise book, dog-eared with a tea ring on the cover, he picked it up, the corner of one leaf between his finger and thumb, the pages splaying out like a fan, opened the window and dropped it three floors to the ground. His own neatness became exaggerated when he was at the board, writing in copperplate script just large enough for the boy in the back row to read – geometrical columns of declined nouns defined by exact, invisible margins. When he had finished he would set the chalk down and rub the used finger and thumb together with the same action he used after handling the host over the paten.

The palm upward gesture brought the class to its feet and they said the Hail Mary in Latin. While it was being said all eyes looked down because they knew if they looked up Waldo was bound to be staring at them.

'Exercises.'

When Waldo was in a hurry he corrected the exercises verbally, asking one boy for the answers and then asking all those who got it right to put up their hands. It was four for anyone who lied about his answer and now and then he would take spot checks to find out the liars.

'Hold it, hold it there,' he would say and leap from the rostrum, moving through the forest of hands and look at each boy's book, tracing out the answer with the tip of his cane. Before the end of the round and while his attention was on one book a few hands would be lowered quietly. Today he was in a hurry. The atmosphere was tense as he looked from one boy to another, deciding who would start.

'Sweeny, we'll begin with you.' Kevin rose to his feet, his finger trembling under the place in the book. He read the first answer and looked up. Waldo remained impassive. He would let someone while translating unseens ramble on and on with great imagination until he faltered, stopped and admitted that he didn't know. Then and only then would he be slapped.

'Two, nominative. *Sapienter Pater.*' Kevin went on haltingly through the whole ten and stopped, waiting for a comment from Waldo. It was a long time before he spoke. When he did it was with bored annoyance.

'Every last one of them is wrong.'

'But sir, Father, they couldn't be wr . . .' Kevin said it with such conviction, blurted it out so quickly that Waldo looked at him in surprise.

'Why not?'

'Because my . . .' Kevin stopped.

'Well?' Waldo's stone face resting on his knuckles. 'Because my what?'

It was too late to turn back now.

'Because my father said so,' he mumbled very low, chin on chest.

'Speak up, let us all hear you.' Some of the boys had heard and he thought they sniggered.

'Because my father said so.' This time the commotion in the class was obvious.

'And where does your father teach Latin?' There was no escape. Waldo had him. He knew now there would be an exhibition for the class. Kevin placed his weight on his arm and felt his tremble communicated to the desk.

'He doesn't, Father.'

'And what does he do?'

Kevin hesitated, stammering,

'He's a barman.'

'A barman!' Waldo mimicked and the class roared loudly.

'*Quiet.*' He wheeled on them. 'You, Sweeny. Come out here.' He reached inside the breast of his soutane and with a flourish produced a thin yellow cane, whipping it back and forth, testing it.

Kevin walked out to the front of the class, his face fiery red, the blood throbbing in his ears. He held out his hand. Waldo raised it higher, more to his liking, with the tip of the cane touching the underside of the upturned palm. He held it there for some time.

'If your brilliant father continues to do your homework for you, Sweeny, you'll end up a barman yourself.' Then he whipped the cane down expertly across the tips of his fingers and again just as the blood began to surge back into them. Each time the cane in its follow-through cracked loudly against the skirts of his soutane.

'You could have made a better job of it yourself. Other hand.' The same ritual of raising and lowering the left hand with the tip of the cane to the desired height. 'After all, I have taught you some Latin.' *Crack.* 'It would be hard to do any worse.'

Kevin went back to his place resisting a desire to hug his hands under his armpits and stumbled on a schoolbag jutting into the aisle as he pushed into his desk. Again Waldo looked round the class and said, 'Now we'll have it *right* from someone.'

The class continued and Kevin nursed his fingers, out of the fray.

As the bell rang Waldo gathered up his books and said, 'Sweeny, I want a word with you outside. Ave Maria, gratia plena . . .' It was not until the end of the corridor that Waldo turned to face him. He looked at Kevin and maintained his silence for a moment.

'Sweeny, I must apologise to you.' Kevin bowed his head. 'I meant your father no harm – he's probably a good man, a very good man.'

'Yes, sir,' said Kevin. The pain in his fingers had gone.

'Look at me when I'm talking, please.' Kevin looked at his collar, his Adam's apple, then his face. It relaxed for a fraction and Kevin thought he was almost going to smile, but he became efficient, abrupt again.

'All right, very good, you may go back to your class.'

'Yes Father,' Kevin nodded and moved back along the empty corridor.

Some nights when he had finished his homework early he would go down to meet his father coming home from work. It was dark, October, and he stood close against the high wall at the bus-stop trying to shelter from the cutting wind. His thin black blazer with the school emblem on the breast pocket and his short grey trousers, both new for starting grammar school, did little to keep him warm. He stood shivering, his hands in his trouser pockets and looked down at his knees which were blue and marbled, quivering uncontrollably. It was six o'clock when he left the house and he had been standing for fifteen minutes. Traffic began to thin out and the buses became less regular, carrying fewer and fewer passengers. There was a moment of silence when there was no traffic and he heard a piece of paper scraping along on pointed edges. He kicked it as it passed him. He thought of what had happened, of Waldo and his father. On the first day in class Waldo had picked out many boys by their names.

'Yes, I know your father well,' or 'I taught your elder brother. A fine priest he's made. Next.'

'Sweeny, Father.'

'Sweeny? Sweeny? – You're not Dr John's son, are you?'

'No Father.'

'Or anything to do with the milk people?'

'No Father.'

'Next.' He passed on without further comment.

Twenty-five past six. Another bus turned the corner and Kevin saw his father standing on the platform. He moved forward to the stop as the bus slowed down. His father jumped lightly off and saw Kevin waiting for him. He clipped him over the head with the tightly rolled newspaper he was carrying.

'How are you big lad?'

'All right,' said Kevin shivering. He humped his shoulders and set off beside his father, bumping into him uncertainly as he walked.

'How did it go today?' his father asked.

'All right.' They kept silent until they reached the corner of their own street.

'What about the Latin?'

Kevin faltered, feeling a babyish desire to cry.

'How was it?'

'OK. Fine.'

'Good. I was a bit worried about it. It was done in a bit of a rush. Son, your Da's a genius.' He smacked him with the paper again. Kevin laughed and slipped his hand into the warmth of his father's overcoat pocket, deep to the elbow.

A RAT AND SOME RENOVATIONS

Almost every one in Ireland must have experienced American visitors or, as we called them, 'The Yanks'. Just before we were visited for the first time, my mother decided to have the working kitchen modernised. We lived in a terrace of dilapidated Victorian houses whose front gardens measured two feet by the breadth of the house. The scullery, separated from the kitchen by a wall, was the same size as the garden, and just as arable. When we pulled out the vegetable cupboard we found three or four potatoes which had fallen down behind and taken root. Ma said, 'God, if the Yanks had seen that.'

She engaged the workmen early so the job would be finished and the newness worn off by the time the Yanks arrived. She said she wouldn't like them to think that she got it done up just for them.

The first day the workmen came they demolished the wall, ripped up the floor and left the cold water tap hanging four feet above a bucket. We didn't see them again for three weeks. Grandma kept trying to make excuses for them, saying that it was very strenuous work. My mother however managed to get them back and they worked for three days, erecting a sink unit and leaving a hole for the outlet pipe. It must have been through this hole that the rat got in.

The first signs were discovered by Ma in the drawer of the new unit. She called me and said, 'What's those?' I looked and saw six hard brown ovals trundling about the drawer.

'Ratshit,' I said. Ma backed disbelievingly away, her hands over her mouth, repeating, 'It's mouse, it's mouse, it must be mouse.'

The man from next door, a Mr Frank Twoomey, who had lived most of his life in the country, was called – he said from the size of them, it could well be a horse. At this my mother took her nightdress and toothbrush and moved in with an aunt across the street, leaving the brother and myself with the problem. Armed with a hatchet and shovel we banged and brattled the cupboards, then, when we felt sure it was gone, we blocked the hole with hardboard and sent word to Ma to return, that all was well.

It was after two days safety that she discovered the small brown bombs again. I met her with her nightdress under her arm, in the path. She just said, 'I found more,' and headed for her sister's.

That evening it was Grandma's suggestion that we should borrow the Grimleys' cat. The brother was sent and had to pull it from beneath the side-board because it was very shy of strangers. He carried it across the road and the rat-killer was so terrified of the traffic and Peter squeezing it that it peed all down his front. By this time Ma's curiosity had got the better of her and she ventured from her sister's to stand pale and nervous in our path. The brother set the cat down and turned to look for a cloth to wipe himself. The cat shot past him down the hall, past Ma who screamed, 'Jesus, the rat', and leapt into the hedge. The cat ran until a bus stopped it with a thud. The Grimleys haven't spoken to us since.

Ma had begun to despair. 'What age do rats live to?' she asked. 'And what'll we do if it's still here when the Yanks come?' Peter said that they loved pigs in the kitchen.

The next day we bought stuff, pungent like phosphorous and spread it on cubes of bread. The idea of this stuff was to roast the rat inside when he ate it so that he would drink himself to death.

'Just like Uncle Matt,' said Peter. He tactlessly read out the instructions to Grandma who then came out in sympathy with the rat. Ma thought it may have gone outside, so to make sure, we littered the yard with pieces of bread as well. In case it didn't work Ma decided to do a novena of masses so she got up the next morning and on the driveway to the chapel which runs along the back of our house she noticed six birds with their feet in the air, stone dead.

Later that day the rat was found in the same condition on the kitchen floor. It was quickly buried in the dust-bin using the shovel as a hearse. The next day the workmen came, finished the job, and the Yanks arrived just as the paint was drying.

They looked strangely out of place with their brown, leathery faces, rimless glasses and hat brims flamboyantly large, as we met them at the boat . . . Too summery by half, against the dripping eaves of the sheds at the dock-yard. At home by a roaring fire on a July day, after having laughed a little at the quaintness of the taxi, they exchanged greetings, talked about family likenesses, jobs, and then dried up. For the next half hour the conversation had to be manufactured, except for a comparison of education systems which was confusing and therefore lasted longer. Then everything stopped.

The brother said, 'I wouldn't call this an embarrassing silence.'

They all laughed, nervously dispelling the silence but not the embarrassment.

Ma tried to cover up. 'Would yous like another cup of cawfee?' Already she had begun to pick up the accent. They agreed and the oldish one with the blue hair followed her out to the kitchen.

'Gee, isn't this madern,' she said.

Ma, untacking her hand from the paint on the drawer, said, 'Yeah, we done it up last year.'

ST PAUL COULD HIT THE NAIL
ON THE HEAD

All that afternoon Mary's world seemed to be falling apart at the seams. Each time she slipped out of the room she rolled the whites of her eyes to heaven. She kept rushing into the kitchen and talking in spikey whispers to the children, buttoning up their overcoats or giving them biscuits and drinks of water. She had managed to push the two boys, Rodney and John, out on to the street to play but the girls still hung about, afraid they would miss something. Now she came out to the kitchen again and stopped at the threshold. Deirdre, at two the youngest, said she was making the dinner out of cornflakes and HP sauce, sitting on her behind slopping the mess over the lip of the dish onto the floor. Mary whipped the dish from her and shook her by the shoulders, then tried to drown her screeches by shushing her.

'Patricia, take that Deirdre out of my sight, up the stairs, anywhere . . . and wash her face while you're there.'

Patricia, seven years old and the eldest, led her snivelling sister up the stairs. Mary walking down the hall saw Deirdre's white knickers, flannel grey from sitting on the floor, disappear round the stair head. She went into the front room balancing the scones on a plate.

Father Malachy, a distant cousin, who had a parish somewhere in the depths of Co Monaghan, sat firmly in the chair in the corner sipping his tea from a china cup which rattled every time he replaced it on the matching china saucer. He came to Belfast every year in early summer, would visit Mary for about an hour then go on to stay with Jimmy Brankin for the rest of the week. He had arrived sometime just before dinner and Mary had opened the door to him, squinting against the sun.

'Ach, it's you Father Malachy, come in, come in.'

13

The old priest removed his hat politely as he stepped into the hallway. He had a small navy blue suitcase worn through to the brown cardboard at a point on its flank where his leg constantly rubbed against it as he walked. He set it down on the quiet carpet of the hallway and shuffled into the front room. There were clothes strewn over the floor, on the backs of chairs. A pair of trousers partially obscured the face of the morning-dead TV.

'Sit down here, Father,' said Mary, clearing a chair and throwing the things onto the floor. 'The place is in a mess. Why didn't you drop me a line to say you were coming. O God, what a mess.'

'Now, you know as well as I do there's no need to worry about that. Where do you think I was reared?'

Just then Mary noticed the pot with Deirdre's load in it and got it out of the room as fast as she could, shielding it from him with her body and saying that he must want a cup of tea after the long journey. While the kettle was coming to the boil she took off her apron, combed her hair and took time to wash her face for the first time that day. She paraded in with the tea on the tray feeling a changed woman.

'I'm sorry, Father, I never even asked you to take off your coat.'

'No, no, I'll not stay that long,' he said.

That was three hours ago. In the meantime he had refused dinner but took two bowls of soup with several potatoes 'smashed' in it. He was now in his third bout of tea drinking and had asked for another scone with raspberry jam. Mary offered him one from the plate and he ate it noisily, not bothering to close his mouth when he chewed. He had picked a spot somewhere about the level of the pelmet and stared fixedly at it most of the day. He seemed to use it as an excuse for not talking, as if it were a TV programme and he didn't like to interrupt. It meant Mary could stare at him without being offensive. He had sunk deeper into the chair, his coat ruffling up at the back. Dandruff speckled his clerical black yet he had lost little of his white hair. His hands, except for the two yellow-brown nicotine fingers, had the whiteness of someone who had been in bed sick for a long time. Dusting the scone flour from his fingers, he steadied their tremor by joining them firmly at the tips and said, 'While you were out I was noseying around. It's a nice house you've bought. This room is lovely.'

'Oh God, what a mess it was in this morning. I'm inclined to let things slide.'

'Everything you have is good,' he said, his white hands searching the texture of the leather arms of his chair.

'Good?'

'Yes,' said Father Malachy. 'Expensive . . . The contracting must be going well with Sam.'

'Oh yes. He's doing well. Demolition's the thing at the moment. They're knocking down the half of Belfast.'

'Is that right now?'

'Slum clearance.'

They lapsed into silence again.

Mary had gone down one day with the boys to see Sam and had watched the business of devastation. Bulldozers snarled in, crashing through kitchen walls, teetering staircases, leaving bedrooms exposed. They took great bites of the house then spilled the gulp into the back of a waiting lorry, the mandible unhinging at the back rather than the front. Mary felt she shouldn't look, seeing the choice of wallpapers: pink rosebuds, scorned in her own family, faded flowers, patterns modern a generation ago. She felt it was too private. She rounded up the boys, 'Come on, come on, this is no sight for children,' and went home, remaining depressed for the rest of the day, snapping at the children unnecessarily. Since that day she had never gone back. She even disliked Sam in his large muddied boots as he clumped about the wood floor of the site hut, a yellow helmet tipped to the back of his head. While she was there Sam had shouted at one old workman, shouted so much that the spit had spun out of his mouth, then when the man had scurried away he turned and talked normally to her and the boys again.

'How *is* Sam?' Father Malachy asked, as if peering into her mind.

'He's fine,' she said. 'He's a hard man to deal with sometimes.'

'Sure, don't I know that from the wedding,' said Father Malachy.

Mary laughed remembering, then said, 'He fairly laid into the church that day.'

''Tis sad all the same.'

'But he was only joking,' Mary protested.

'I know, but it's sad anyway. Does he cause you any trouble . . . about your faith?' he asked.

'Ach, no, sure I've . . . we never talk about it.'

Father Malachy persisted. 'He's never shown any desire to join has he?'

'No Father, he's not interested in religion of any breed.'

Father Malachy cracked the stiffening joints of his fingers and stared again at the pelmet.

'Perhaps seeing your good example, he may, someday. You've no idea how it impresses non-believers to see us Catholics getting up out of our beds for early mass every morning.'

'I don't go to mass any more, Father . . . on weekdays.'

'Oh, but you still go on Sundays,' he said smiling.

'Yes Father.'

Father Malachy put the cup to his head and drank all but the tea leaves and set the rattling cup and saucer over on the sideboard.

'Last Sunday's epistle was the boy eh? St Paul could always hit the nail on the head.'

'Indeed Father. There's more tea in the pot,' she said aiming the spout at him like a duelling pistol.

'No, no more for me,' he said writhing in his chair, hunting his pockets for cigarettes. As he did so he made hollow clumping noises with his false teeth prior to smoking. He produced an untipped brand that he had been smoking since his days in the seminary, a brand that Mary had only seen in the Republic on holidays. He lit one and while inhaling picked the specks of tobacco off his tongue with finger and thumb.

'And there's no more family on the way?' he said suddenly as if continuing from something.

'No Father, why? Should there be?'

'No . . . no,' he said lightly.

'We had the children we wanted. Then Deirdre was a mis . . . Deirdre was a mistake.'

Father Malachy looked at her, almost smiling, through the triangle formed by his fingers.

'We use the rhythm method, Father, that's allowed by the church isn't it?'

'I'm not prying Mary. I know you well enough and I know the difficulties, especially when you're married to a man who has no . . . well, let's just say he's not in agreement with the Church.'

'What does the Church know about sex anyway. They're in no position to judge.'

'We can be unemotional about it, at least.'

Mary, not wanting to get involved, did not reply and the afternoon progressed made up of great slabs of silence. During the silences she would think of something to do in the kitchen, or when she actually ran out of chores she excused herself and went out, folded her arms, leaned against the sink unit and flashed her eyes to heaven.

At one stage she remembered about the children upstairs and knew they were too quiet. She said this to Father Malachy then opened the door and shouted, 'What are you two doing up there?'

She cocked her head to one side, awaiting the reply. Patricia's voice came clear down the stairs.

'We found Mammy's clock with the tablets in.'

Mary rushed out snapping the door shut behind her. She came back after some minutes, flushed and carrying Deirdre. Patricia's cries from upstairs pierced the air for a long time. Father Malachy smiling from ear to dentured ear said, 'Children can be an awful nuisance at times.'

He leaned forward and tried to tickle Deirdre under the chin, but she girned and put her head under Mary's arm.

'When will this lady be going to the nuns?' he said in a baby voice which didn't suit him.

'She's only two! Don't talk to me about nuns.'

'I don't like them either but they certainly gave *you* a grounding in your faith that'll stand by you. Your mother and father, God rest them, gave them a great foundation to build on. That's why you're strong enough to survive, Mary.'

'I know Father, it's not their religious teaching, but the way they pried that I hated.'

Then she told him how Sister Benedict had found the social

position of every girl in the class after one Maths lesson. She gave sums on how long it would take a girl to clean a house of ten fifty square feet at such and such a pace. Hands up how many girls have detached houses, semi-detached houses, terrace houses? How many girls have maids to help with the cleaning? Another sum of distance travelled per gallon of petrol ended in a classification of those girls with or without cars and if they had a car what type it was. Rolls, Jag, Ford, Austin and so on. Sister Benedict was the girl. After this lesson the rows in the class were rearranged.

Father Malachy laughed, his hands up in defence saying, 'Charity, Mary, charity.'

Mary felt a bit spent after her outburst and there followed another period of silence. She was glad that Deirdre was there at her knee, because she could croon over her, making childish conversation to fill the gaps. Then she explained to Father Malachy that the child usually slept for a while in the afternoons. While she was up the stairs putting her into her cot she heard the front door slam. 'Who's that?' she shouted.

It was the boys.

Patricia had gone out to the garden to sulk.

The boys were talking and mumbling in the hallway, again too quiet for Mary's liking. She hung over the banisters and looked down. The two boys were crouched on the carpet, Father Malachy's case open in front of them, exploring. Mary rushed down the stairs, her voice compressed with anger hissing, 'Get out, you nosey brats.'

She smacked Rodney hard on the back of his head with her bony hand but John was away before she could draw back and hit him. Rodney ran, his mouth hanging black and open in a cry which had not yet been translated into sound. She slammed the door after them and hunkered down to fix the case. She squatted for what seemed a long time looking into the case, expecting the front door to open at any second. A pair of striped pyjamas, grey and maroon, more old fashioned than her father had worn when he was alive, long cream woollen combinations, a tin of powder for cleaning dentures, a jar of yellow capsules, a handful of holy pictures, only the gold haloes catching the light like a scatter of coins. She lifted the combinations, trying to look underneath without disturbing them. A breviary and a paperback detective. She pulled back the elasticated pocket at the side, saw only an old cigarette, a dry white arc, then she put all the clothes back as she thought they should have been. She was conscious of a throbbing bruise beneath her wedding ring, where she had hit the thick bone of Rodney's skull for doing what she was now doing herself. She closed the case and as quietly as she could snapped the lock shut. Brushing down the folds of her dress, she rose and went in to Father Malachy feeling a slight shake in her knees as she walked.

After a while he asked her: 'What time does Sam come in at?'

'Oh, you can never tell with Sam.' Then she added, 'I suppose you'll be going up to see Jimmy Brankin as usual, Father.'

It was a long time before he replied.

'Poor Jimmy's dead, God rest him.' Then his mouth turned downwards at the corners, like a fish mouth. His face seemed to crumble and collapse but he rubbed his cheeks hard with the palms of his hands and prevented himself from crying.

'Oh, I didn't know,' said Mary, her mouth remaining in the 'O' position. He seemed not to hear her but went on talking.

'In December. He was stupid too, to be an oul bachelor, when he had the choice. A wife and children take the cold out of the air. But he's away.'

He rubbed his cheeks vigorously again so that his speech was deformed. Mary heard him say something about new friends being hard to make. She became embarrassed and went forward to sweep the hearth. Without looking at him she tried to comfort, saying, 'But you're holy. What about God?' *£225,674*

'Of the spirit, little comfort, little comfort.'

Then he jumped up, surprisingly sprightly, and said, 'I must get to Smithfield before it closes. Belfast would be nothing without a visit to Smithfield.'

He bent backwards to get the stiffness out of his bones, for it was the first time he had been out of the chair since he arrived. Mary followed him into the hall and as he picked up his case, heard the handle squeak. He opened the catch on the door and extended his hand to Mary.

19

'Goodbye Mary, please God I'll see you next year.'

'But where will you stay, now that Jimmy's . . .'.

'I know a hotel that's good in University Road. My curate has stayed . . .'.

'You'll do no such thing,' said Mary sharply. 'You'll stay here in the spare room.'

He refused and blustered for some time, then quietly let Mary take his case from him.

'But I'll go on down the town anyway. You can tell Sam before I get back. God bless you.'

He turned to go, then remembered something. He sunk his hand deep into his pocket. 'Here, there's a few wee medals I got from Lourdes. You can pin them on the children's vests.' He said it in a tone that belittled the present as he pressed them into her hand.

'Oh you *shouldn't*, you really shouldn't.'

He waved his hand over his shoulder as he walked away. 'The wee bits of religion about the children does them no harm.'

Mary closed the door and sighed to herself, 'Oh Jesus, Sam,' then put the case in the alcove under the stairs. She went to the front room and left the medals, almost too light for metal, on the mantelpiece. She cleared the tea things and washed them. Back in the front room again she stood for a moment at the fireplace, then scraped the medals off the mantelpiece as she had seen Sam draw a pool to him at poker and put them in her handbag where they wouldn't be seen.

A HAPPY BIRTHDAY

Sammy adjusted his tie in front of the mirror and tucked in the frayed cuffs of his shirt sleeves. He whistled a few bars of something and whatever way he was holding his mouth he noticed he had missed a few copper-coloured hairs at the angle of his lip. He got out his razor again and dipped in his mug of now luke-warm water. He opened his mouth in a mock yawn and nicked off the remaining hairs. Next he combed his hair, shading it so low at the side of his head that it covered at least half the bald area. He sang aloud as he did so. His mother spoke out from the kitchen.

'You're in the quare mood to-day.'

Sammy carried his mug out to the kitchen and offered it to his mother, saying, 'Like a nice cup of warm hairs, Ma?'

She made a face, calling him a dirty baste as he threw them down the sink.

'Why shouldn't I be in the quare mood?' said Sammy. 'Fifty to-day and they're paying out on the dole too.' His mother wiped her hands nervously on her apron.

'Don't be drinking, son, sure you won't?' Sammy said he wouldn't.

'Promise me,' she said and he nodded, while making another attempt to spread the hairs more evenly over the skin of his head at the mirror in the kitchen.

'Have you any bus fare Ma?'

'What's wrong with your legs?' she asked. Sammy stooped very low trying to see the sky above the backyard wall.

'Looks a bit like rain,' he said. His mother shuffled into the room.

'Where's my purse?' she said, stooping into the corner for her bag. 'Do you think I'm made of money, eh? The pension doesn't go too far when you're around.' Sammy slipped the two bob into his pocket and said he would pay her back when he got his money.

'I've heard that before,' said his mother. Sammy left the house and walked slowly into town.

On his way down the road he called into Forsythe's and bought four cigarettes. The girl rolled them across the counter to him and he examined them, checking the brand. He asked for a packet and the girl sorted one out from beneath the counter, and slipped the cigarettes into it. Sammy patted them happily in his pocket. On the street he asked a man for a light and inhaled deeply the first of the day. He reached the town half an hour before he had to sign on so he went into the library to read the newspapers. Nothing but bloody explosions and robberies again. Something would have to be done. The IRA was getting the run of the country without one to say boo to them. *Something* would have to be done. He made his way to the bureau at about five to eleven. It was the cheeky wee bitch who was paying out. When he got his money he peeled off two pounds for his mother and stuck them in his top pocket out of the way. Then he headed for the pub where he knew all the boys would be.

When Sammy came out the bright sunlight was a great shock to him. As he walked along the street the walls seemed to come at him and nudge him. People deliberately went out of their way to veer into his path. The bus driver smiled at him for no reason and some young ones clapped after he had sung a song. He got off the bus and walked past a line of soldiers at the main gate. He stopped with the last one and put his hand on his arm and said,

'Yis are doing a grand job.'

'Wot?' said the soldier.

'Yis are the boys.' The soldier's gun as he leaned over to try and hear pointed to the middle of Sammy's chest.

'Wot?' he said.

'Forget it,' said Sammy. He moved off through the gates towards the exhibition hall. A group of student demonstrators paraded silently weaving their way in and out of the domes. They carried placards – 'ULSTER 71 WHITEWASH', 'EXPOSE 71'. Sammy made his way in front of one with long hair and stopped him with his hand. He held him at arm's length, focusing the writing on the card. 'TELL THE TRUTH, 40,000 UNEMPLOYED'. Sammy leaned closer to him.

'Why don't yis catch yourselves on?' The student began to move forward. 'Who do you think is paying your grants for you, eh? You'll get no work coming to the country with the likes of you parading about making trouble.' The first student had pushed past him but he continued speaking to the next in line.

'Yis have never done a day's work in your lives. You don't know what ye're talking about. So-called civil rights. Why don't yis go down south where yis belong?' A policeman came up behind him and guided him away. Sammy went past the exhibition hall and found the blue igloo of the bar tent. He fingered into his top pocket and pulled out the two pounds. He had more stout, he didn't know how many, and now that he was in his own company he had a whiskey with each one. After a time he heard squealing coming from outside the tent and went out to see what it was about.

A crowd of girls were on the Hurricane Waltzer. Sammy talked to the man operating it until the session finished, then he paid his money and climbed up into a seat, being guided by hands from behind. The attendant locked him in with a bar. Sammy called to the girls who were paying their money for another turn, but the words came out all wrong. The machine started, clanking and grinding, spinning slowly. It gathered speed and began to loop and dip. The noise of the Waltzer was reaching a crescendo but at each sudden drop the squealing of the girls rose above it. Sammy's hand tightened convulsively on the bar in front of him. He saw the upturned watching faces streak into one and other. Then he opened his mouth and it all came out.

Below people screamed and ran, covering their heads. One woman quickly put up her umbrella. The student demonstrators sheltered beneath their placards. It came out of him like sparks from a catherine wheel. An emulsion of minestrone stout. Spraying on the multi-coloured domes of the exhibition. Exclamation marks, yellow and buff bird-dung streaks flecking the canvas. Sparking off the tarmac paths, soaking spots in people's Sunday best. Children slipped and fell. The machine operator and his mate stayed in their hut throughout. People signalled frantically, pointing to the revolving figure.

When the Waltzer came to a halt Sammy's mouth was still open. As the operator was unlocking the safety bar Sammy belched and the operator dived to one side. As Sammy staggered away, the operator said to his mate, 'There's not a spot of boke on him.'

'He's probably the only one in the park.'

Sammy walked in a great arc and arrived back to the operator. His flap of hair hung by his ear and his head shone. 'What's there to see here?' he asked. His elbow slipped off the edge of the counter and he belched loudly again.

The operator pointed. 'Do you see that wee girl over there?' Sammy looked at the pointing finger but not at its direction. 'She'll tell you all you want to know.'

He turned Sammy by the shoulders and aimed him in the direction of the information kiosk. When he asked the same question the girl with the skill of a thousand rehearsals told him all there was to see. Sammy swayed looking at her, blinking, then he looked down at his toes. His fingers fished for his last pound.

'Thanks,' he said. 'I'll maybe go for a drink first. It's my birthday.'

SECRETS

He had been called to be there at the end. His Great Aunt Mary had been dying for some days now and the house was full of relatives. He had just left his girlfriend home – they had been studying for 'A' levels together – and had come back to the house to find all the lights spilling onto the lawn and a sense of purpose which had been absent from the last few days.

He knelt at the bedroom door to join in the prayers. His knees were on the wooden threshold and he edged them forward onto the carpet. They had tried to wrap her fingers around a crucifix but they kept loosening. She lay low on the pillow and her face seemed to have shrunk by half since he had gone out earlier in the night. Her white hair was damped and pushed back from her forehead. She twisted her head, from side to side, her eyes closed. The prayers chorused on, trying to cover the sound she was making deep in her throat. Someone said about her teeth and his mother leaned over her and said, 'That's the pet', and took her dentures from her mouth. Her lower face seemed to collapse. She half opened her eyes but could not raise her eyelids enough and showed only crescents of white.

'Hail Mary full of grace . . .' the prayers went on. He closed his hands over his face so that he would not have to look but smelt the trace of his girlfriend's handcream from his hands. The noise, deep and guttural, that his aunt was making became intolerable to him. It was as if she were drowning. She had lost all the dignity he knew her to have. He got up from the floor and stepped between the others who were kneeling and went into her sitting-room off the same landing.

He was trembling with anger or sorrow, he didn't know which. He sat in the brightness of her big sitting-room at the oval table and waited for something to happen. On the table was a cut-glass vase of irises, dying because she had been in bed for over a week. He sat staring at them. They were withering from the tips inward, scrolling themselves delicately, brown and neat. Clearing up after themselves. He stared at them for a long time until he heard the sounds of women weeping from the next room.

His aunt had been small – her head on a level with his when she sat at her table – and she seemed to get smaller each year. Her skin fresh, her hair white and waved and always well washed. She wore no jewelry except a cameo ring on the third finger of her right hand and, around her neck, a gold locket on a chain. The white classical profile on the ring was almost worn through and had become translucent and indistinct. The boy had noticed the ring when she had read to him as a child. In the beginning fairy tales, then as he got older extracts from famous novels, *Lorna Doone*, *Persuasion*, *Wuthering Heights* and her favourite extract, because she read it so often, Pip's meeting with Miss Havisham from *Great Expectations*. She would sit with him on her knee, her arms around him, holding the page flat with her hand. When he was bored he would interrupt her and ask about the ring. He loved hearing her tell of how her grandmother had given it to her as a brooch and she had had a ring made from it. He would try to count back to see how old it was. Had her grandmother got it from *her* grandmother? And if so what had she turned it into? She would nod her head from side to side and say, 'How would I know a thing like that?' keeping her place in the closed book with her finger.

'Don't be so inquisitive,' she'd say. 'Let's see what happens next in the story.'

One day she was sitting copying figures into a long narrow book with a dip pen when he came into her room. She didn't look up but when he asked her a question she just said, 'Mm?' and went on writing. The vase of irises on the oval table vibrated slightly as she wrote.

'What is it?' She wiped the nib on blotting paper and looked up at him over her reading glasses.

'I've started collecting stamps and Mamma says you might have some.'

'Does she now –?'

She got up from the table and went to the tall walnut bureau-bookcase standing in the alcove. From a shelf of the bookcase she took a small wallet of keys and selected one for the lock. There was a harsh metal shearing sound as she pulled the desk flap down. The writing area was covered with green leather which had dog-eared at the corners. The inner part was divided into pigeon holes, all bulging with papers. Some of them, envelopes, were gathered in batches nipped at the waist with elastic bands. There were postcards and bills and cash-books. She pointed to the postcards.

'You may have the stamps on those,' she said. 'But don't tear them. Steam them off.'

She went back to the oval table and continued writing. He sat on the arm of the chair looking through the picture postcards – torchlight processions at Lourdes, brown photographs of town centres, dull black and whites of beaches backed by faded hotels. Then he turned them over and began to sort the stamps. Spanish, with a bald man, French with a rooster, German with funny jerky print, some Italian with what looked like a chimney-sweep's bundle and a hatchet.

'These are great,' he said. 'I haven't got any of them.'

'Just be careful how you take them off.'

'Can I take them downstairs?'

'Is your mother there?'

'Yes.'

'Then perhaps it's best if you bring the kettle up here.'

He went down to the kitchen. His mother was in the morning room polishing silver. He took the kettle and the flex upstairs. Except for the dipping and scratching of his aunt's pen the room was silent. It was at the back of the house overlooking the orchard and the sound of traffic from the main road was distant and muted. A tiny rattle began as the kettle warmed up, then it bubbled and steam gushed quietly from its spout. The cards began to curl slightly in the jet of steam but she didn't seem to be watching. The stamps peeled moistly off and he put them in a saucer of water to flatten them.

'Who is Brother Benignus?' he asked. She seemed not to hear. He asked again and she looked over her glasses.

'He was a friend.'

His flourishing signature appeared again and again. Sometimes Bro Benignus, sometimes Benignus and once Iggy.

'Is he alive?'

'No, he's dead now. Watch the kettle doesn't run dry.'

When he had all the stamps off he put the postcards together and replaced them in the pigeon-hole. He reached over towards the letters but before his hand touched them his aunt's voice, harsh for once, warned.

'A-A-A,' she moved her pen from side to side.' Do-not-touch,' she said and smiled. 'Anything else, yes! That section, no!' She resumed her writing.

The boy went through some other papers and found some photographs. One was of a beautiful girl. It was very old-fashioned but he could see that she was beautiful. The picture was a pale brown oval set on a white square of card. The edges of the oval were misty. The girl in the photograph was young and had dark, dark hair scraped severely back and tied like a knotted rope on the top of her head – high arched eyebrows, her nose straight and thin, her mouth slightly smiling, yet not smiling – the way a mouth is after smiling. Her eyes looked out at him dark and knowing and beautiful.

'Who is that?' he asked.

'Why? What do you think of her?'

'She's all right.'

'Do you think she is beautiful?' The boy nodded.

'That's me,' she said. The boy was glad he had pleased her in return for the stamps.

Other photographs were there, not posed ones like Aunt Mary's but Brownie snaps of laughing groups of girls in bucket hats like German helmets and coats to their ankles. They seemed tiny faces covered in clothes. There was a photograph of a young man smoking a cigarette, his hair combed one way by the wind against a background of sea.

'Who is that in the uniform?' the boy asked.

'He's a soldier,' she answered without looking up.

'Oh,' said the boy. 'But who is he?'

'He was a friend of mine before you were born,' she said. Then added, 'Do I smell something cooking? Take your stamps and off you go. That's the boy.'

The boy looked at the back of the picture of the man and saw in black spidery ink, 'John, Aug '15 Ballintoy'.

'I thought maybe it was Brother Benignus,' he said. She looked at him not answering.

'Was your friend killed in the war?'

At first she said no, but then she changed her mind.

'Perhaps he was,' she said, then smiled. 'You are far too inquisitive. Put it to use and go and see what is for tea. Your mother will need the kettle.' She came over to the bureau and helped tidy the photographs away. Then she locked it and put the keys on the shelf.

'Will you bring me up my tray?'

The boy nodded and left.

It was a Sunday evening, bright and summery. He was doing his homework and his mother was sitting on the carpet in one of her periodic fits of tidying out the drawers of the mahogany sideboard. On one side of her was a heap of paper scraps torn in quarters and bits of rubbish, on the other the useful items that had to be kept. The boy heard the bottom stair creak under Aunt Mary's light footstep. She knocked and put her head round the door and said that she was walking to Devotions. She was dressed in her good coat and hat and was just easing her fingers into her second glove. The boy saw her stop and pat her hair into place before the mirror in the hallway. His mother stretched over and slammed the door shut. It vibrated, then he heard the deeper sound of the outside door closing and her first few steps on the gravelled driveway. He sat for a long time wondering if he would have time or not. Devotions could take anything from twenty minutes to three quarters of an hour, depending on who was saying it.

Ten minutes must have passed, then the boy left his homework and went upstairs and into his aunt's sitting room. He stood in front of the bureau wondering, then he reached for the keys. He tried several before he got the right one. The desk flap screeched as he pulled it down. He pretended to look at the postcards again in case there were any stamps he had missed. Then he put them away and reached for the bundle of letters. The elastic band was thick and old, brittle almost and when he took it off its track remained on the wad of letters. He carefully opened one and took out the letter and unfolded it, frail, khaki-coloured.

> My dearest Mary, it began. I am so tired I can hardly write to you. I have spent what seems like all day censoring letters (there is a howitzer about 100 yds away firing every 2 minutes). The letters are heart-rending in their attempt to express what they cannot. Some of the men are illiterate, others almost so. I know that they feel as much as we do, yet they do not have the words to express it. That is your job in the schoolroom to give us generations who can read and write well. They have . . .

The boy's eye skipped down the page and over the next. He read the last paragraph.

> Mary I love you as much as ever – more so that we cannot be together. I do not know which is worse, the hurt of this war or being separated from you. Give all my love to Brendan and all at home.

It was signed, scribbled with what he took to be John. He folded the paper carefully into its original creases and put it in the envelope. He opened another.

> My love, it is thinking of you that keeps me sane. When I get a moment I open my memories of you as if I were reading. Your long dark hair – I always imagine you wearing the blouse with the tiny roses, the white one that opened down the back – your eyes that said so much without words, the way you lowered your head when I said anything that embarrassed you, and the clean nape of your neck.
>
> The day I think about most was the day we climbed the

head at Ballycastle. In a hollow, out of the wind, the air full of pollen and the sound of insects, the grass warm and dry and you lying beside me your hair undone, between me and the sun. You remember that that was where I first kissed you and the look of disbelief in your eyes that made me laugh afterwards.

It makes me laugh now to see myself savouring these memories standing alone up to my thighs in muck. It is everywhere, two, three feet deep. To walk ten yards leaves you quite breathless.

I haven't time to write more today so I leave you with my feet in the clay and my head in the clouds. I love you, John.

He did not bother to put the letter back into the envelope but opened another.

My dearest, I am so cold that I find it difficult to keep my hand steady enough to write. You remember when we swam the last two fingers of your hand went the colour and texture of candles with the cold. Well that is how I am all over. It is almost four days since I had any real sensation in my feet or legs. Everything is frozen. The ground is like steel.

Forgive me telling you this but I feel I have to say it to someone. The worst thing is the dead. They sit or lie frozen in the position they died. You can distinguish them from the living because their faces are the colour of slate. God help us when the thaw comes . . . This war is beginning to have an effect on me. I have lost all sense of feeling. The only emotion I have experienced lately is one of anger. Sheer white trembling anger. I have no pity or sorrow for the dead and injured. I thank God it is not me but I am enraged that it had to be them. If I live through this experience I will be a different person.

The only thing that remains constant is my love for you.

Today a man died beside me. A piece of shrapnel had pierced his neck as we were moving under fire. I pulled him into a crater and stayed with him until he died. I watched him choke and then drown in his blood.

I am full of anger which has no direction.

He sorted through the pile and read half of some, all of others. The sun had fallen low in the sky and shone directly into the room onto the pages he was reading making the paper glare. He selected a letter from the back of the pile and shaded it with his hand as he read.

Dearest Mary, I am writing this to you from my hospital bed. I hope that you were not too worried about not hearing from me. I have been here, so they tell me, for two weeks and it took another two weeks before I could bring myself to write this letter.

I have been thinking a lot as I lie here about the war and about myself and about you. I do not know how to say this but I feel deeply that I must do something, must sacrifice something to make up for the horror of the past year. In some strange way Christ has spoken to me through the carnage . . .

Suddenly the boy heard the creak of the stair and he frantically tried to slip the letter back into its envelope but it crumpled and would not fit. He bundled them all together. He could hear his aunt's familiar puffing on the short stairs to her room. He spread the elastic band wide with his fingers. It snapped and the letters scattered. He pushed them into their pigeon hole and quickly closed the desk flap. The brass screeched loudly and clicked shut. At that moment his aunt came into the room.

'What are you doing, boy?'

'Nothing.' He stood with the keys in his hand. She walked to the bureau and opened it. The letters sprung out in an untidy heap.

'You have been reading my letters,' she said quietly. Her mouth was tight with the words and her eyes blazed. The boy could say nothing. She struck him across the side of the face.

'Get out,' she said. 'Get out of my room.'

The boy, the side of his face stinging and red, put the keys on the table on his way out. When he reached the door she called to him. He stopped, his hand on the handle.

'You are dirt,' she hissed, 'and always will be dirt. I shall remember this till the day I die.'

Even though it was a warm evening there was a fire in the large fireplace. His mother had asked him to light it so that she could clear out Aunt Mary's stuff. The room could then be his study, she said. She came in and seeing him at the table said, 'I hope I'm not disturbing you.'

'No.'

She took the keys from her pocket, opened the bureau and began burning papers and cards. She glanced quickly at each one before she flicked it onto the fire.

'Who was Brother Benignus?' he asked.

His mother stopped sorting and said, 'I don't know. Your aunt kept herself very much to herself. She got books from him through the post occasionally. That much I do know.'

She went on burning the cards. They built into strata, glowing red and black. Now and again she broke up the pile with the poker, sending showers of sparks up the chimney. He saw her come to the letters. She took off the elastic band and put it to one side with the useful things and began dealing the envelopes into the fire. She opened one and read quickly through it, then threw it on top of the burning pile.

'Mama,' he said.

'Yes?'

'Did Aunt Mary say anything about me?'

'What do you mean?'

'Before she died – did she say anything?'

'Not that I know of – the poor thing was too far gone to speak, God rest her.' She went on burning, lifting the corners of the letters with the poker to let the flames underneath them.

When he felt a hardness in his throat he put his head down on his books. Tears came into his eyes for the first time since she had died and he cried silently into the crook of his arm for the woman who had been his maiden aunt, his teller of tales, that she might forgive him.

THE MIRACULOUS CANDIDATE

At the age of fourteen John began to worry about the effects of his sanctity. The first thing had been a tingling, painful sensation in the palms of his hands and the soles of his feet. But an even more alarming symptom was the night when, as he fervently prayed himself to sleep, he felt himself being lifted up a full foot and a half above the bed – bedclothes and all. The next morning when he thought about it he dismissed it as a dream or the result of examination nerves.

Now on the morning of his Science exam he felt his stomach light and woolly, as if he had eaten feathers for breakfast. Outside the gym some of the boys fenced with new yellow rulers or sat drumming them on their knees. The elder ones, doing Senior and 'A' levels, stood in groups all looking very pale, one turning now and again to spit over his shoulder to show he didn't care. John checked for his examination card which his grandmother had carefully put in his inside pocket the night before. She had also pinned a Holy Ghost medal beneath his lapel where it wouldn't be seen and made him wear his blazer while she brushed it. She had asked him what Science was about and when John tried to explain she had interrupted him saying, 'If y'can blether as well with your pen – you'll do all right.'

One of the Seniors said it was nearly half-past and they all began to shuffle towards the door of the gym. John had been promised a watch if he passed his Junior.

The doors were opened and they all filed quietly to their places. John's desk was at the back with his number chalked on the top right-hand corner. He sat down, unclipped his fountain-pen and set it in the groove. All the desks had an empty hole for an ink-well. During the Maths exam one of the boys opposite who couldn't do any of the questions drew a face in biro on his finger and put it up through the hole and waggled it at John. He didn't seem to care whether he failed or not.

John sat looking at the wall-bars which lined the gym. The invigilator held up a brown paper parcel and pointed to the unbroken seal, then opened it, tearing off the paper noisily. He had a bad foot and some sort of high boot which squeaked every time he took a step. His face was pale and full of suspicion. He was always jumping up suddenly as if he had caught somebody on, flicking back his stringy hair as he did so. When he ate the tea and biscuits left at the door for him at eleven his eyes kept darting backwards and forwards. John noticed that he 'gullied', a term his grandmother used for chewing and drinking tea at the same time. When reading, he never held the newspaper up but laid it flat on the table and stood propped on his arms, his big boot balanced on its toe to take the weight off it.

'If you ever meet the devil you'll know him by his cloven hoof,' his Granny had told him. A very holy woman, she had made it her business to read to him every Sunday night from the lives of the Saints, making him sit at her feet as she did so. While she read she let her glasses slip down to the end of her long nose and would look over them every so often, to see if he was listening. She had a mole on her chin with a hair like a watch-spring growing out of it. She read in a serious voice, very different to her ordinary one, and always blew on the fine tissuey pages to separate them before turning over with her trembling fingers. She had great faith and had a particular saint for every difficulty. 'St Blaise is good for throats and if you've ever lost anything St Anthony'll find it for you.' She always kept a sixpence under the statue of the Child of Prague because then, she said, she'd never be without. Above all there was St Joseph of Cupertino. For examinations he was your man. Often she read his bit out of the book to John.

'Don't sit with your back to the fire or you'll melt the marrow of your bones,' and he'd change his position at her feet and listen intently.

St Joseph was so close to God that sometimes when he prayed he was lifted up off the ground. Other times when he'd be carrying plates – he was only smart enough to work in the kitchen – he would go into a holy trance and break every dish on the tiled floor. He wanted to become a priest but he was very stupid so he learned off just one line of the Bible. But here – and this was the best part of the story – when his exam came didn't God make the bishop ask him the one line he knew and he came through with flying colours. When the story was finished his Granny always said, 'It was all he was fit for, God help him – the one line.'

The ingivilator squeaked his way down towards John and flicked a pink exam paper onto his desk. John steadied it with his hand. His eyes raced across the lines looking for the familiar questions. The feathers whirlpooled almost into his throat. He panicked. There was not a single question – *not one* – he knew anything about. He tried to settle himself and concentrated to read the first question.

> State Newton's Universal Law of Gravitation. Give arguments for or against the statement that 'the only reason an apple falls downwards to meet the earth instead of the earth falling upwards to meet the apple is that the earth, being much more massive exerts the greater pull.' The mass of the moon is one eighty-first, and its radius one quarter that of the earth. What is the acceleration of gravity at its surface if . . .

It was no use. He couldn't figure out what was wrong. He had been to mass and communion every day for the past year – he had prayed hard for the right questions. The whole family had prayed hard for the right questions. What sort of return was this? He suppressed the thought because it was . . . it was God's will. Perhaps a watch would lead him into sin somehow or other?

He looked round at the rest of the boys. Most of them were writing frantically. Others sat sucking their pens or doodling on their rough-work sheets. John looked at the big clock hung on the wall-bars with its second hand slowly spinning. Twenty minutes had gone already and he hadn't put pen to paper. He must do *something*.

He closed his eyes very tight and clenching his fists to the sides of his head he placed himself in God's hands and began to pray. His Granny's voice came to him. 'The Patron Saint of Examinations. Pray to him if you're really stuck.' He saw the shining damp of his palms, then pressed them to his face. Now he summoned up his whole being, focused it to a point of white heat. All the good that he had ever done, that he ever would do, all his prayers, the sum total of himself, he concentrated into the name of the saint. He clenched his eyes so hard there was a roaring in his ears. His finger-nails bit into his cheeks. His lips moved and he said, 'Saint Joseph of Cupertino, help me.'

He opened his eyes and saw that somehow he was above his desk. Not far – he was raised up about a foot and a half, his body still in a sitting position. The invigilator looked up from his paper and John tried to lower himself back down into his seat. But he had no control over his limbs. The invigilator came round his desk quickly and walked towards him over the coconut matting, his boot creaking as he came.

'What are you up to?' he hissed between his teeth.

'Nothing,' whispered John. He could feel his cheeks becoming more and more red, until his whole face throbbed with blushing.

'Are you trying to copy?' The invigilator's face was on a level with the boy's. 'You can see every word the boy in front of you is writing, can't you?'

'No sir, I'm not trying to . . .' stammered John. 'I was just praying and . . .' The man looked like a Protestant. The Ministry brought in teachers from other schools. Protestant schools. He wouldn't understand about saints.

'I don't care what you say you were doing. I think you are trying to copy and if you don't come down from there I'll have you disqualified.' The little man was getting as red in the face as John.

'I can't sir.'

'Very well then.' The invigilator clicked his tongue angrily and walked creak-padding away to his desk.

John again concentrated his whole being, focused it to a prayer of white heat.

'Saint Joseph of Cupertino. *Get me down please.*' But nothing happened. The invigilator lifted his clip-board with the candidates' names and started back towards John. Some of the boys in the back row had stopped writing and were laughing. The invigilator reached him.

'Are you going to come down from there or not?'

'I can't.' The tears welled up in John's eyes.

'Then I shall have to ask you to leave.'

'I can't,' said John.

The invigilator leaned forward and tapped the boy in front of John on the shoulder.

'Do you mind for a moment?' he said and turned the boy's answer paper face downwards on the desk. While he was turned away John frantically tried to think of a way out. His prayer hadn't worked . . . maybe a sin would . . . the invigilator turned to him.

'For the last time I'm . . .'

'Fuck the Pope,' said John and as he did so, he plumped back down into his seat skinning his shin on the tubular frame of the desk.

'Pardon. What did you say?'

'Nothing sir. It's all right now. I'm sorry sir.'

'What *is* wrong with you boy?'

'I can't do it, sir – any of it.' John pointed to the paper. The invigilator spun it round with his finger.

'You should have thought of that some months ago . . .' The words faded away. 'I'm very sorry. Just a minute,' he said, limping very quickly down to his desk. He came back with a white exam paper which he put in front of John.

'Very sorry,' he repeated. 'It does happen sometimes.'

John looked for the first time at the head of the pink paper. ADVANCED LEVEL PHYSICS. Now he read quickly through the questions on the white paper the invigilator had brought him. They were all there. Archimedes in his bath, properties of NaCl, allotropes of sulphur, the anatomy of the buttercup. The invigilator smiled with his spade-like teeth.

'Is that any better?' he asked. John nodded. '. . . and if you need some extra time to make up, you can have it.'

'Thank you sir,' said John. The invigilator hunkered down beside him and whispered confidentially.

'This wee mix-up'll not go any farther than between ourselves, will it . . .' He looked down at his clip-board. '. . . Johnny?'

'No sir.'

He gave John a pat on the back and creaked away over the coconut matting. John put his head down on the desk and uttered a prayer of thanksgiving to St Joseph of Cupertino, this time making sure to keep his fervour within bounds.

BETWEEN TWO SHORES

It was dark and he sat with his knees tucked up to his chin, knowing there was a long night ahead of him. He had arrived early for the boat and sat alone in a row of seats wishing he had bought a paper or a magazine of some sort. He heard a noise like a pulse from somewhere deep in the boat. Later he changed his position and put his feet on the floor.

For something to do he opened his case and looked again at the presents he had for the children. A painting by numbers set for the eldest boy of the 'Laughing Cavalier', for the three girls, dolls, horizontal with their eyes closed, a blonde, a red-head and a brunette to prevent fighting over who owned which. He had also bought a trick pack of cards. He bought these for himself but he didn't like to admit it. He saw himself amazing his incredulous, laughing father after dinner by turning the whole pack into the seven of clubs or whatever else he liked by just tapping them as the man in the shop had done.

The trick cards would be a nice way to start a conversation if anybody sat down beside him, so he put them on top of his clothes in the case. He locked it and slipped it off the seat, leaving it vacant. Other people were beginning to come into the lounge lugging heavy cases. When they saw him sitting in the middle of the row they moved on. He found their Irish accents grating and flat.

He lit a cigarette and as he put the matches back in his pocket his fingers closed around his wife's present. He took it out, a small jeweller's box, black with a domed top. As he clicked back the lid he saw again the gold against the red satin and thought it beautiful. A locket was something permanent, something she could keep for ever. Suddenly his stomach reeled at the thought. He tried to put it out of his mind, snapping the box shut and putting it in his breast pocket. He got up and was about to go to the bar when he saw how the place was filling up. It was Thursday and the Easter rush had started. He would sit his ground until the boat moved out. If he kept his seat and got a few pints inside him he might sleep. It would be a long night.

A middle-aged couple moved into the row – they sounded like they were from Belfast. Later an old couple with a Down's syndrome girl sat almost opposite him. It was difficult to tell her age – anywhere between twenty and thirty. He thought of moving away to another seat to be away from the moist, open mouth and the beak nose but it might have hurt the grey haired parents. It would be too obvious, so he nodded a smile and just sat on.

The note of the throbbing engine changed and the lights on the docks began to move slowly past. He had a free seat in front of him and he tried to put his feet up but it was just out of reach. The parents took their daughter 'to see the big ship going out' and he then felt free to move. He found the act of walking strange on the moving ship.

He went to the bar and bought a pint of stout and took it out onto the deck. Every time he travelled he was amazed at the way they edged the huge boat out of the narrow channel – a foot to spare on each side. Then the long wait at the lock gates. Inside, the water flat, roughed only by the wind – out there the waves leaping and chopping, black and slate grey in the light of the moon. Eventually they were away, the boat swinging out to sea and the wind rising, cuffing him on the side of the head. It was cold now and he turned to go in. On a small bench on the open deck he saw a bloke laying out his sleeping bag and sliding down inside it.

He had several more pints in the bar sitting on his own, moving his glass round the four metal indentations. There were men and boys with short hair, obviously British soldiers. He thought how sick they must be having to go back to Ireland at Easter. There was a nice looking girl sitting alone reading with a rucksack at her feet. She looked like a student. He wondered how he could start to talk to her. His trick cards were in the case and he had nothing with him. She seemed very interested in her book because she didn't even lift her eyes from it as she sipped her beer. She was nice looking, dark hair tied back, large dark eyes following the lines back and forth on the page. He looked at her body, then felt himself recoil as if someone had clanged a handbell in his ear and shouted 'unclean'. Talk was what he wanted. Talk stopped him thinking. When he was alone he felt frightened and unsure. He blamed his trouble on this.

In the beginning London had been a terrible place. During the day he had worked himself to the point of exhaustion. Back at the digs he would wash and shave and after a meal he would drag himself to the pub with the other Irish boys rather than sit at home. He drank at half the pace the others did and would have full pints on the table in front of him when closing time came. Invariably somebody else would drain them, rather than let them go to waste. Everyone but himself was drunk and they would roar home, some of them being sick on the way against a gable wall or up an entry. Some nights, rather than endure this, he sat in his bedroom even though the landlady had said he could come down and watch TV. But it would have meant having to sit with her English husband and their horrible son. Nights like these many times he thought his watch had stopped and he wished he had gone out.

Then one night he'd been taken by ambulance from the digs after vomiting all day with a pain in his gut. When he wakened they had removed his appendix. The man in the next bed was small, dark-haired, friendly. The rest of the ward had nick-named him 'Mephisto' because of the hours he spent trying to do the crossword in *The Times*. He had never yet completed it. His attention had first been drawn to Nurse Mitchell's legs by this little man who enthused about the shortness of her skirt, the black stockings with the seams, clenching and unclenching his fist. The little man's mind wandered higher and he rolled his small eyes in delight.

In the following days in hospital he fell in love with this Nurse Helen Mitchell. When he asked her about the funny way she talked she said she was from New Zealand. He thought she gave him special treatment. She nursed him back to health, letting him put his arm around her when he got out of bed for the first time. He smelt her perfume and felt her firmness. He was astonished at how small she was, having only looked up at her until this. She fitted the crook of his arm like a crutch. Before he left he bought her a present from the hospital shop, of the biggest box of chocolates they had in stock. Each time she came to his bed it was on the tip of his tongue to ask her out but he didn't have the courage. He had skirted round the question as she made the bed, asking her what she did when she was off duty. She had mentioned the name of a place where she and her friends went for a drink and sometimes a meal.

He had gone home to Donegal for a fortnight at Christmas to recover but on his first night back in London he went to this place and sat drinking alone. On the third night she came in with two other girls. The sight of her out of uniform made him ache to touch her. They sat in the corner not seeing him sitting at the bar. After a couple of whiskeys he went over to them. She looked up, startled almost. He started by saying, 'Maybe you don't remember me . . .'

'Yes, yes I do,' she said laying her hand on his arm. Her two friends smiled at him then went on talking to each other. He said he just happened to be in that district and remembered the name of the place and thought he would have liked to see her again. She said yes, he was the man who bought the *huge* box of chocolates. Her two friends laughed behind their hands. He bought them all a drink. And then insisted again. She said, 'look I'm sorry I've forgotten your name,' and he told her and she introduced him to the others. When time was called he isolated her from the others and asked her if she would like to go out for a meal some night and she said she'd love to.

On the Tuesday after careful shaving and dressing he took her out and afterwards they went back to the flat she shared with the others. He was randy helping her on with her coat at the restaurant, smelling again her perfume, but he intended to play his cards with care and not rush things. But there was no need, because she refused no move he made and her hand was sliding down past his scar before he knew where he was. He was not in control of either himself or her. She changed as he touched her. She bit his tongue and hurt his body with her nails. Dealing with the pain she caused him saved him from coming too soon and disgracing himself.

Afterwards he told her that he was married and she said that she knew but that it made no difference. They both needed something. He asked her if she had done it with many men.

43

'Many, many men,' she had replied, her New Zealand vowels thin and hard like knives. Tracks of elastic banded her body where her underwear had been. He felt sour and empty and wanted to go back to his digs. She dressed and he liked her better, then she made tea and they were talking again.

Through the next months he saw her many times and they always ended up on the rug before the electric fire and each time his seed left him he thought the loss permanent and irreplaceable.

This girl across the bar reminded him of her, the way she was absorbed in her reading. His nurse, he always called her that, had tried to force him to read books but he had never read a whole book in his life. He had started several for her but he couldn't finish them. He told lies to please her until one day she asked him what he thought of the ending of one she had given him. He felt embarrassed and childish about being found out.

There were some young girls, hardly more than children, drinking at the table across the bar from the soldiers. They were eyeing them and giggling into their vodkas. They had thick Belfast accents. The soldiers wanted nothing to do with them. Soldiers before them had chased it and ended up dead or maimed for life.

An old man had got himself a padded alcove and was in the process of kicking off his shoes and putting his feet up on his case. There was a hole in the toe of his sock and he crossed his other foot over it to hide it. He remembered an old man telling him on his first trip always to take his shoes off when he slept. Your feet swell when you sleep, he had explained.

The first time leaving had been the worst. He felt somehow it was for good, even though he knew he would be home in two or three months. He had been up since dark getting ready. His wife was frying him bacon and eggs, tip-toeing back and forth putting the things on the table, trying not to wake the children too early. He came up behind her and put his arms round her waist, then moved his hands up to her breasts. She leaned her head back against his shoulder and he saw that she was crying, biting her lip to stop. He knew she would do this, cry in private but she would hold back in front of the others when the mini-bus came.

'Don't,' she said. 'I hear Daddy up.'

That first time the children had to be wakened to see their father off. They appeared outside the house tousleheaded and confused. A mini-bus full of people had pulled into their yard and their Granny and Granda were crying. Handshaking and endless hugging watched by his wife, chalk pale, her forearms folded against the early morning cold. He kissed her once. The people in the mini-bus didn't like to watch. His case went on the pyramid of other cases and the mini-bus bumped over the yard away from the figures grouped around the doorway.

The stout had gone through him and he got up to go to the lavatory. The slight swaying of the boat made it difficult to walk but it was not so bad that he had to use the handles above the urinals. Someone had been sick on the floor, Guinness sick. He looked at his slack flesh held between his fingers at the place where the sore had been. It had all but disappeared. Then a week ago his nurse had noticed it. He had thought nothing of it because it was not painful. She asked him who else he had been sleeping with – insulting him. He had sworn he had been with no one. She explained to him how they were like minute corkscrews going through the whole body. Then she admitted that it must have been her who had picked it up from someone else.

'If not me, then who?' he had asked.

'Never you mind,' she replied. 'My life is my own.'

It was the first time he had seen her concerned. She came after him as he ran down the stairs and implored him to go to a clinic, if not with her, then on his own. But the thought of it terrified him. He had listened to stories on the site of rods being inserted, burning needles and worst of all a thing which opened inside like an umbrella and was forcibly dragged out again. On Wednesday the landlady had said someone had called at the digs looking for him and said he would call back. But he made sure he was out that night and this morning he was up and away early buying presents before getting on the train.

He zipped up his fly and stood looking at himself in the mirror. He looked tired – the long train journey, the sandwiches, smoking too many cigarettes to pass the time. A coppery growth was beginning on his chin. He remembered her biting his tongue, the tearing of her nails, the way she changed. He had not seen her since.

Only once or twice had his wife been like that – changing that way. He knew she would be like that tomorrow night. It was always the same the first night home. But afterwards he knew that it was her, his wife. Even though it was taut with lovemaking her face had something of her care for his children, of the girl and woman, of the kitchen, of dances, of their walks together. He knew who she was as they devoured each other on the creaking bed. In the Bible they knew each other.

Again his mind shied away from the thought. He went out onto the deck to get the smell of sick from about him. Beyond the rail it was black night. He looked down and could see the white bow wave crashing away off into the dark. Spray tipped his face and the wind roared in his ears. He took a deep breath but it did no good. Someone threw a bottle from the deck above. It flashed past him and landed in the water. He saw the white of the splash but heard nothing above the throbbing of the ship. The damp came through to his elbows where he leaned on the rail and he shivered.

He had thought of not going home, of writing to his wife to say that he was sick. But it seemed impossible for him not to do what he had always done. Besides she might have come to see him if he had been too sick to travel. Now he wanted to be at home among the sounds that he knew. Crows, hens clearing their throats and picking in the yard, the distant bleating of sheep on the hill, the rattle of a bucket handle, the slam of the back door. Above all he wanted to see the children. The baby, his favourite, sitting on her mother's knee, her tulle nightdress ripped at the back, happy and chatting at not having to compete with the others. Midnight and she the centre of attention. Her voice, hoarse and precious after wakening, talking as they turned the pages of the catalogue of toys they had sent for, using bigger words than she did during the day.

A man with a woollen cap came out onto the deck and leaned on the rail not far away. A sentence began to form in his mind, something to start a conversation. You couldn't talk about the dark. The cold, he could say how cold it was. He waited for the right moment but when he looked round the man was away, high stepping through the doorway.

He followed him in and went to the bar to get a drink before it closed. The girl was still there reading. The other girls were falling about and squawking with laughter at the slightest thing. They were telling in loud voices about former nights and about how much they could drink. Exaggerations. Ten vodkas, fifteen gin and tonic. He sat down opposite the girl reading and when she looked up from her book he smiled at her. She acknowledged the smile and looked quickly down at her book again. He could think of nothing important enough to say to interrupt her reading. Eventually when the bar closed she got up and left without looking at him. He watched the indentation in the cushioned moquette return slowly to normal.

He went back to his seat in the lounge. The place was smoke-filled and hot and smelt faintly of feet. The Down's syndrome girl was now asleep. With his eyes closed he became conscious of the heaving motion of the boat as it climbed the swell. She had said they were like tiny corkscrews. He thought of them boring into his wife's womb. He opened his eyes. A young woman's voice was calling incessantly. He looked to see. A toddler was running up and down the aisles playing.

'Ann-Marie, Ann-Marie, Ann-Marie! Come you back here!'

Her voice rose annoyingly, sliding up to the end of the name. He couldn't see where the mother was sitting. Just a voice annoying him. He reached out his feet again to the vacant seat opposite and found he was still too short. To reach he would have to lie on his back. He crossed his legs and cradled his chin in the heart of his hand.

Although they were from opposite ends of the earth he was amazed that her own childhood in New Zealand should have sounded so like his own. The small farm, the greenness, the bleat of sheep, the rain. She had talked to him, seemed interested in him, how he felt, what he did, why he could not do something better. He was intelligent – sometimes. He had liked the praise but was hurt by its following jibe. She had a lot of friends who came to her flat – arty crafty ones, and when he stayed to listen to them he felt left outside. Sometimes in

England his Irishness made him feel like a leper. They talked about books, about people he had never heard of and whose names he couldn't pronounce, about God and the Government.

One night at a party with ultra-violet lights someone with rings on his fingers had called him 'a noble savage'. He didn't know how to take it. His first impulse was to punch him, but up till that he had been so friendly and talkative – besides it was too Irish a thing to do. His nurse had come to his rescue and later in bed she had told him he must *think*. She had playfully struck his forehead with her knuckles at each syllable.

'Your values all belong to somebody else,' she had said.

He felt uncomfortable. He was sure he hadn't slept. He changed his position but then went back to cupping his chin. He must sleep.

'Ann-Marie, Ann-Marie.' She was loose again. By now they had turned the lights down in the lounge. The place was full of slumped bodies. The rows were back to back and some hitch-hikers had crawled onto the flat floor beneath the apex. He took his raincoat for a pillow and crawled into the free space behind his own row. Horizontal he might sleep. It was like a tent and he felt nicely cut off. In the next row some girls sat, not yet asleep. One was just at the level of his head and when she leaned forward to whisper her sweater rode up and bared a pale crescent of her lower back. Pale downy hairs moving into a seam at her backbone. He closed his eyes but the box containing the locket bit into his side. He turned and tried to sleep on his other side.

One night when neither of them could sleep his wife had said to him, 'Do you miss me when you're away?'

He said yes.

'What do you do?'

'Miss you.'

'I don't mean that. Do you do anything about it? Your missing me.'

'No.'

'If you ever do, don't tell me about it. I don't want to know.'

'I never have.'

He looked once or twice to see the girl's back but she was huddled up now sleeping. As he lay the floor increased in hardness. He lay for what seemed all night, his eyes gritty and tense, conscious of his discomfort each time he changed his position. The heat became intolerable. He sweated and felt it thick like blood on his brow. He wiped it dry with a handkerchief and looked at it to see. He was sure it must be morning. When he looked at his watch it said three o'clock. He listened to it to hear if it had stopped. The loud tick seemed to chuckle at him. His nurse had told him this was the time people died. Three o'clock in the morning. The dead hour. Life at its lowest ebb. He believed her. Walking the dimly lit wards she found the dead.

Suddenly he felt claustrophobic. The back of the seats closed over his head like a tomb. He eased himself out. His back ached and his bladder was bursting. As he walked he felt the boat rise and fall perceptibly. In the toilet he had to use the handrail. The smell of sick was still there.

How could his values belong to someone else? He knew what was right and what was wrong. He went out onto the deck again. The wind had changed or else the ship was moving at a different angle. The man who had rolled himself in his sleeping bag earlier in the night had disappeared. The wind and the spray lashed the seat where he had been sleeping. Tiny lights on the coast of Ireland winked on and off. He moved round to the leeward side for a smoke. The girl who had earlier been reading came out on deck. She mustn't have been able to sleep either. All he wanted was someone to sit and talk to for an hour. Her hair was untied now and she let it blow in the wind, shaking her head from side to side to get it away from her face. He sheltered his glowing cigarette in the heart of his hand. Talk would shorten the night. For the first time in his life he felt his age, felt older than he was. He was conscious of the droop in his shoulders, his unshaven chin, his smoker's cough. Who would talk to him – even for an hour? She held her white raincoat tightly round herself, her hands in her pockets. The tail flapped furiously against her legs. She walked towards the prow, her head tilted back. As he followed her, in a sheltered alcove he saw the man in the sleeping bag, snoring, the drawstring of his hood knotted round his chin. The girl turned and came back. They drew level.

'That's a cold one,' he said.

'Indeed it is,' she said, not stopping. She was English. He had to continue to walk towards the prow and when he looked over his shoulder she was gone. He sat on an empty seat and began to shiver. He did not know how long he sat but it was better than the stifling heat of the lounge. Occasionally he walked up and down to keep the life in his feet. Much later going back in he passed an image of himself in a mirror, shivering and blue lipped, his hair wet and stringy.

In the lounge the heat was like a curtain. The sight reminded him of a graveyard. People were meant to be straight, not tilted and angled like this. He sat down determined to sleep. He heard the tremble of the boat, snoring, hushed voices. Ann-Marie must have gone to sleep – finally. That guy in the sleeping bag had it all worked out – right from the start. He had a night's sleep over him already. He tilted his watch in the dim light. The agony of the night must soon end. Dawn would come. His mouth felt dry and his stomach tight and empty. He had last eaten on the train. It was now six o'clock.

Once he had arranged to meet his nurse in the Gardens. It was early morning and she was coming off duty. She came to him starched and white, holding out her hands as she would to a child. Someone tapped him on the shoulder but he didn't want to look round. She sat beside him and began to stroke the inside of his thigh. He looked around to see if anyone was watching. There were two old ladies close by but they seemed not to notice. The park bell began to clang and the keepers blew their whistles. They must be closing early. He put his hand inside her starched apron to touch her breasts. He felt warm moistness, revolting to the touch. His hand was in her entrails. The bell clanged incessantly and became a voice over the Tannoy.

'Good morning, ladies and gentlemen. The time is seven o'clock. We dock at Belfast in approximately half an hour's time. Tea and sandwiches will be on sale until that time. We hope you have enjoyed your . . .'

He sat up and rubbed his face. The woman opposite said good morning. Had he screamed out? He got up and bought himself a plastic cup of tea, tepid and weak, and some sandwiches, dog-eared from sitting overnight.

It was still dark outside but now the ship was full of the bustle of people refreshed by sleep, coming from the bathrooms with toilet bags and towels, whistling, slamming doors. He saw one man take a tin of polish from his case and begin to shine his shoes. He sat watching him, stale crusts in his hand. He went out to throw them to the gulls and watch the dawn come up.

He hadn't long to go now. His hour had come. It was funny the way time worked. If time stopped he would never reach home and yet he loathed the ticking, second by second slowness of the night. The sun would soon be up, the sky was bleaching at the horizon. What could he do? Jesus what could he do? If he could turn into spray and scatter himself on the sea he would never be found. Suddenly it occurred to him that he *could* throw himself over the side. That would end it. He watched the water sluicing past the dark hull forty feet below. 'The spirit is willing but the flesh is weak.' If only someone would take the whole thing away how happy he would be. For a moment his spirits jumped at the possibility of the whole thing disappearing – then it was back in his stomach heavier than ever. He put his face in his hands. Somehow it had all got to be hammered out. He wondered if books would solve it. Read books and maybe the problems won't seem the same.

The dark was becoming grey light. They must have entered the Lough because he could see land now on both sides, like arms or legs. He lit a cigarette. The first of the day – more like the sixty-first of yesterday. He coughed deeply, held it a moment then spat towards Ireland but the wind turned it back in the direction of England. He smiled. His face felt unusual.

He felt an old man broken and tired and unshaven at the end of his days. If only he could close his eyes and sleep and forget. His life was over. Objects on the shore began to become distinct through the mist. Gasometers, chimney-stacks, railway trucks. They looked washed out, a putty grey against the pale lumps of the hills. Cars were moving and then he made out people hurrying to work. He closed his eyes and put his head down on his arms. Indistinctly at first, but with growing clarity, he heard the sound of an ambulance.

WHERE THE TIDES MEET

We arrive at Torr Head about an hour before dusk and get out of the car. Three men, Christopher the boy, and the dog. Michael and Martin stand, their guns broken, loading them with bright, brick-red cartridges from their pockets. We have lost the dog's lead and I use a makeshift choker. It is an ordinary lead but I form a noose with the loop of the handle so that when he pulls too hard the noose tightens.

'For God's sake don't let him go,' they tell me. He is too eager and pulls me at a run when I want to walk. They tell me to tap him on the nose and shout 'heel' and he will respond. He is too eager. They keep their guns broken and climb the fence. The boy Christopher is excited and anxious and edges ahead to try and see. He is on tip-toe trying to see over the next rise. Michael, his father, hisses at him, 'Keep behind the line of the guns.' I walk behind all three with the dog. It is a black labrador called Ikabod. His tongue hangs out as he strains forward. I must be leaning at an angle of forty-five degrees trying to hold him. The makeshift lead is so embedded into the black folds of his neck that the only part of it visible is the taut line to my hand. The chain at my end bites deeply.

Suddenly Martin shouts, not a loud shout, but a quiet urgent one, 'Mickey, to your right.'

Michael brings the gun up to his cheek, leans slightly forward, all balance. The sound is half way between a crack and a thud. The barrel jerks slightly as he fires. Both barrels. It is only then that I see the white scuts of two rabbits disappearing into some bushes on our right. At the sound of the gun Ikabod goes mad. He pulls me running and sliding down the hill. On the point of falling I decide to let him go. If Michael has hit one of the rabbits it must be the dog's job to retrieve. Ikabod disappears into the bushes, the lead whipping after him loosely. It is only then that I hear Michael shouting, 'Hold on to him.' I hear two more shots and my head ducks down into my coat, thinking Martin is shooting over my head at the same two rabbits, but when I look round he is shooting up the hill. I don't see what he is shooting at. I go down and look over the bush. It is a sloping cliff of rocks covered in bushes and grasses. Ikabod runs hither and thither looking for the rabbits. I whistle at him and he comes back. He is a good dog. Christopher is beside me looking over, 'Did he get one? Did he get one?' We catch up with the others.

I say defending myself, 'If you don't let him off after you shoot when *do* you let him off?'

'You don't,' says Michael.

'What did we bring him for then?' He doesn't answer. 'I thought he was supposed to be a retriever.'

'For birds,' says Michael and everybody laughs. Both men are pushing cartridges into their guns. We stand a while and talk, scanning the hillside yet knowing we have scared everything within earshot.

'You don't expect to see something that soon,' says Martin. Michael, who has been here many times before, points out the sea where the tides meet. Just beyond Torr Head the sea is white and swirling. Waves leap and crash together as if onto rocks but there are no rocks. This is about two hundred yards off-shore. They tell me it is the Irish sea coming up and the Gulf Stream coming down. In a boat they say you would have no chance.

We double back to a field on the actual Torr itself where they have seen rabbits before. Each fence they break their guns. Each fence Ikabod tries to go through the wire and me over it so that there is an elaborate disentangling and tugging each time. We have reached the field now and they walk in front of me, spread out, Christopher nearer to his father than Martin. The grass is coarse and long but flattened by the wind which must be constant in this place. It has the appearance of grass by a river in flood. The men walk with their guns at the ready, chest high. They stride, but stride quietly, their head turning from side to side sweeping the landscape. I think to myself that they are like hunters and only then realise that that is what they are. We reach the Torr itself without seeing anything or a shot being fired. We stop and talk. Michael asks me if I would like a shot. I say yes, I let the dog off the lead, he runs mad.

'What is there to shoot at?' He points out an old fence post, a railway sleeper, at the edge of the cliff. He shows me the safety catch. I click it off and take aim. It has begun to get dark and the sea behind the post is slate grey. Flints of white from where the tides meet distract me. The butt seems remarkably close to my cheek and I know to expect the recoil of the gun. I am afraid of it and when I shoot I miss completely. We inspect the post. The noise of the explosion pinging still in my ears.

'I did hit it,' I say.

Michael looks closer. 'It's fucking woodworm.' He keeps his voice low so that the boy will not hear. The few small holes do look like woodworm. I go back and shoot the other barrel. I miss again. Martin has gone off looking for more rabbits. We hear a shot from over the brow of the hill. It sounds distorted, plucked away by the wind. Michael loads the gun and fires at the post. It gouges a small crater in the dead wood. Around the periphery when I look closely there are some holes like woodworm.

'Mine's a pint.'

It must be two fields before we notice that Ikabod isn't with us. We stand whistling and shouting but he does not come. We go back to the fence post and look all round, calling.

'Would he have gone over the cliff?' We climb the small fence edging very carefully down the slippy grass.

'Ik-a-bod, Ik-a-bod.' Then we hear a definite dog noise from below.

'He's there somewhere.' We do not know whether it is a cliff like the last one with bushes and outcrops and paths so we inch forward with care. I get to the edge first. It is a sheer drop. Emptiness for about two hundred feet. A rook sails past on a level with us. There is a rubble of rocks below on the beach. I see Ikabod lying on his side at the bottom. From then on we do not talk. To our right there is an accessible way down to the beach and we run. By now the boy and Martin have caught up with us. We half slide, half run down the slope holding onto the tussocky grass. When we get to the dog it is dead. I put my hand on its side and find it still warm. There is no heartbeat. Christopher talks incessantly asking, 'Is it dead, Daddy. Is it dead?' He brushes against a tall weed and seeds fall from it onto the dog's fur. I take my hand away quickly, irrationally thinking of fleas leaving their dead host. Michael stands looking down at the dead dog. I look up to tell him that it is dead and see that he is crying. The wind is cuffing his hair, blowing it about his face. He cannot answer Christopher's questions.

He hunkers down beside the dog and I hear him saying, 'Fuck it,' again and again. There is no blood, just a string of saliva which has touched on some rocks. He reaches over and undoes the dog's collar, then begins to put rocks on top of the dog. In silence everybody helps. The skin seems mobile when heavy stones are placed on it. Eventually the dog is covered with a cairn and we stand back feeling a ridiculous need for prayer. Christopher does not cry but keeps watching his father, doing everything he does except cry. As we turn away Michael says, 'You get very attached to a hound,' almost by way of apology for his crying.

On the way back to the car in darkness, we string out, a single file, about ten yards between each of us, coming together only to help one another over fences.

HUGO

'I'm sure you're walking on air,' my mother said to Paul at his wedding. He was indeed in a joyful mood and he seemed to communicate it to all those around him. 'But isn't it sad Hugo couldn't be here.'

Paul shrugged. The remark produced a sobering effect on him.

'Mother,' I said. 'This is neither the time nor the place.' The curtness of my remark, combined with an empty sherry glass, sent my mother away. Together Paul and I began to talk of old times and this led inevitably to Hugo's tragic end. Between us we fruitlessly tried to arrive at some sort of explanation. Paul seemed to see it only in terms of a simple sadness, nodding his head partly in sympathy, partly in disbelief, whereas I knew it to be a tragedy of a different order. Eventually Paul had to rise and excuse himself and go and look after his other guests.

Hugo's life and mine had intersected briefly and this had had an effect on me out of all proportion to its duration.

My father died when I was eight and it was only at about the age of fourteen that I felt the need of him. I wanted someone I could talk to, someone who would, with wisdom, answer the questions which racked me at this particular time. Someone who would give me confidence to overcome my stammering, someone whom I could ask about the complexities of love and the horrors of sex, someone who could tell me how to dress properly, someone who knew what it was right to like in Art.

My father had an old gramophone on which he played Schubert piano with pine needles. Huge shellac records, with a red circle and a white dog singing into a horn, which whirred with static but which induced a calm in me, as a child, which I have not known since. When they were finished, after about two minutes, the tick of the over-run seemed the vilest sound in the world. The clack of teeth after divine music.

Ever since I could remember there had hung on the parlour wall two framed pen and wash drawings of people unknown to me, signed by my father. I thought them good but they lacked something. Alone I would stare at them for hours and try to find words for their short-comings. Between these two drawings was a tiny picture, sent from the missions, of an oriental Madonna whose robe was made of butterfly wings – deep changing torquoise. I used to think how perfect the natural colour was, surrounded as it was by the gauche, cutout form of the madonna. Nature achieves what is right without knowing.

We lived in a large old terrace house with four bedrooms in an area of the city which had seen better days, judging by the handles in the bedrooms for calling the maids. I was an only child and used a bedroom and a playroom, which was later to become the study. Shortly after my father died Mother decided, not being qualified to do anything else, to take in boarders to try and supplement her widow's pension.

We then had a succession of faceless men, bank clerks in blue suits, an insurance man who was granted the special privilege of leaving his bike in the hallway, a bald teacher whom mother asked to leave one day after some difficulty she had in making his bed. The bathroom shelf held an array of shaving brushes and razors and the house smelt of sweat and cigarette smoke.

Then Paul arrived, a pharmacy student, and became a favourite of my mother's. He had charm and the good looks and height of a Gregory Peck. He would bring her small presents from the country after he had been home for a week-end, a dozen new laid eggs wrapped in twists of newspaper with the hen's dirt still on them or a few pots of home-made gooseberry jam, labelled and dated. My mother really appreciated these gestures.

'A bank clerk,' she said, 'would never think of it in a thousand years.' He had a mouth-organ which he played with some skill, although I did not agree with his choice of music, popular melodies and country and western tunes.

After about a year of Paul's stay one of our bank-clerks decided to get married to a girl with thick legs whom I had pushed past many nights, *in flagrante*, at the doorway. Paul asked my mother if, as a special favour, she would take in one of his friends who was at that time living in dreadful digs with a harridan of a landlady. Mother flinched a little at the words 'digs' and 'landlady' but she could refuse Paul nothing.

'If he's anything like you Paul, he'll do,' she said. Paul laughed and said he wasn't a bit like him because he would cause her no trouble.

This was Hugo. I first saw him in the kitchen on the day he arrived. He was small, much smaller than Paul, slope shouldered, wearing a good Sunday suit, sitting with his knees together. His eyes darted behind his thick-lensed glasses at me as I came through the door. His face was narrow, twig-like, his nose like tweaked out plasticine and a thin neck with a large Adam's apple which jerked when he swallowed. 'Fatten him up,' were Paul's orders to my mother. Afterwards, when I became interested in such things, I found that he bore a facial resemblance to James Joyce.

'Have you met Hugo?' my mother said. 'He's come to stay with us for a while.' I set my schoolbag in the corner and hung up my blazer.

'Hugo is a pharmacy student too,' Mother said. 'Paul told him what a good house this was to stay in. Wasn't that nice of him?' I nodded.

'Any homework?' she asked. 'Well, get it done then – before you start any nonsense.'

I cut myself a slab of bread, spread it with jam and bit a half moon out of it. I started my Maths. Hugo sat, still in the same position. He looked as if he was waiting for his tea.

'What is it?' he asked from the corner. I held up the book to show him. He came over to the table and looked at the problem. I have always found integration difficult. He sat in the chair beside me and guided me through the exercise in half the time I would normally have taken. Crumbs gathered in the spine of the exercise book and I blew them away before closing it. He proceeded to help me with my Latin, French and Physics homework, always explaining and illuminating.

He turned out to be quiet and thoughtful with a great sense of the ridiculous. He spoke in a thick regional accent, almost always self-deprecatingly. When he laughed it wasn't a guffaw like Paul's, the head thrown back. Actually his head bent forward onto his chest and he shook quietly as if suppressing a laugh. I have consulted Roget on this point and cannot find a suitable word to describe Hugo's laugh. Words for quiet laughter carry with them associations of sleaziness – 'snigger', 'snicker'. Roget also gives 'giggle' and 'titter' but these are frivolous. 'Chuckle' is the nearest but it is so inaccurate as to be almost useless. So I must content myself with 'laugh'.

It was shortly after he arrived that I saw it demonstrated. Paul was beginning to worry about being flabby and out of condition and had invested in a book on Yoga. My mother had looked at the pictures in the book and had kidded him that he wouldn't be able to do a single one. After tea Paul, Hugo and I went into the parlour to see if we could do some of the poses. I was able for some of them, probably because of my age and suppleness, but Paul rolled about the carpet grunting and gasping and twisting himself. Finally with some help from Hugo, who pushed his legs into position, he managed to complete 'the plough'. He was lying on his back with his legs, at the ankle, touching behind his head. The seat of his trousers was taut and shining. Paul, in a strangled voice, gasped to me to go and get my mother. She came, drying her hands on her apron, to see the feat. By this time Paul's face was almost purple, clamped as it was between his ankles.

'Bet you can't hold it for another thirty seconds,' my mother said.

'I can,' gasped Paul. Everyone waited, watching him. Then suddenly and quite distinctly he farted, a small piping accidental note. Laughing deafeningly his body sprung back and he lay exhausted and convulsed on the floor. Mother was screeching mock horror and abuse at him. Hugo fell into the armchair, his chin on his chest, and shook helplessly. When we had all recovered, my mother wiping her eyes with the tail of her apron and Paul shaking his head in disbelief that it should have happened to him, we noticed Hugo still laughing silently and uncontrollably in his armchair. This started us all off again. Even at supper-time Hugo was seen to be still laughing uproariously into himself.

About two months after this someone called at the door for Paul and I ran upstairs to the bedroom to see if he was in. He wasn't but Hugo was sitting in the middle of the floor in his underpants in the position of complete repose, index fingers and thumbs joined, hands relaxed and upturned, legs crossed. His head was bent down and he seemed to be barely breathing. I tend to move quietly about the house and he did not notice me. I said nothing to him and went back down the stairs to the door.

I have looked long and hard at this early period to try and read something into it of the tragedy that was to follow, but can find nothing. No prefiguring whatsoever. The only thing, looking back on it with hindsight, I took to be an indication of his state of mind – and even this is scientifically suspect – was the nature of his sleep.

Our last remaining bank clerk, Harry Carey, would occasionally decide to go home for the week-end. That would leave a bed free in the room with Paul and Hugo and I used to plague my mother to let me sleep with the boys. At first she steadfastly refused, then one day Paul over-heard me asking, when Harry had gone home, and he persuaded her.

'Sure. Let him sleep in our room if he enjoys the crack,' he said.

'Well then, if *you* don't mind. It's just for one night now. It's not to be a regular occurrence.'

But it was. Every time that Harry went home I moved in with Paul and Hugo and would lie awake until they would come to bed – even if they were out at a dance – and listen to their talk far into the small hours of the morning. Paul would sit up wearing no pyjama jacket and smoke in bed. In the dark each time he drew on his cigarette his chin and nose would be lit by a red glow. The room smelt great and grown up.

'That blonde had her eye on you, Qugo,' said Paul.

'Which one?' said Hugo. Apart from the implied self-aggrandisement in the remark it seemed there had been a shapely blonde whom Hugo had tapped on the shoulder and asked to dance. When she turned round she had a terrible squint.

I heard the crackle of sweet papers mixed with Hugo's wheezing laugh. He asked me if I'd like one. Paul struck a match and by its light I caught the sweet thrown to me. Between crunchings Hugo tried to answer the question Paul had just put to him. What would he look for in his ideal woman? Often I fell asleep to the sound of his voice.

One of the nights I slept with them I was awakened for some reason and could not get back to sleep again. Suddenly I heard a noise which terrified me. A mixture of grating and squeaking, a wild sound, not loud, which created a nausea in me as a sharp tin edge scraping along marble or brick. The room went quiet again. I thought the sound came from the direction of Hugo's bed. It came again, this time louder. I crept from bed trying to trace the sound. In the dark it came again and again. I switched on the bedside light and looked at Hugo's face. A knot of muscle gathered at the elbow of his jaw and vibrated, then his whole lower jaw moved slowly from side to side and the noise came. Hugo was grinding his teeth as he slept. Flints in a slow rub of terrible pressure. It was a sound quite unlike anything I have heard before or since. He looked pale and unrecognizable without his glasses, his hair tousled. It was only after what seemed like hours that he stopped this gnashing and I was able to sleep.

He told me later that he had very bad teeth, half rotten he said, but seemed pleased that Joyce had suffered from the same complaint.

It was at about this time that Hugo began to help me to conquer my stammer. My mother had sent me to elocution and speech therapy but it had done little good. I still got stuck. I hated the woman who taught me, with her red mouth pulsing like a sea anenome.

'Watch my lips. Now say oo . . . oo . . . oo.' She wore thick scarlet lipstick. I did not want to do things well for her so I failed.

I was hoovering the stairs one day and singing at the same time. Even though I got pocket money for it, it was a task that I enjoyed. The hoover created a two tone base note, one when idling, the other a fraction higher when the sucking end was pressed into the carpet. Around this base I would sing songs. One that was accompanied pretty well was 'I know that my Redeemer liveth' from the *Messiah* and I was singing it at the top of my voice, which incidentally was just beginning to break, when Hugo came up behind me. He mimed applause over the noise of the hoover when I had finished.

When the cleaning was over he asked me what was the first line of the aria I was singing.

'N . . . N . . . N . . . I know thu . . . thu . . . that my Redeemer l . . . le . . . le.'

'Y'see,' he interrupted me. 'You can sing it perfectly but you can't say it.'

I was embarrassed. No one had ever said this to me before. Only my mother and my speech therapist ever spoke openly about it. Everyone else waited or, what was worse, helped me out. I got up to try and leave the room.

'Wait a minute,' Hugo called after me. 'C'mere.' I stopped.

'If you're going to be a man of ideas you must be able to articulate in some way. At the moment, with the stammering, you're only giving yourself half a chance. I know it's not your problem but you know these people who tell you that they're full up to here of *something*, ideas, emotions, feelings. Ask them to put a name on it and they just shrug and look intense. You must be able to speak it or write it – and if you can't it's not a thought. It's an urge – like dogs have. Look at Paul,' he said and went into kinks of laughter, 'he can speak from both ends. So, lad, we must get you speaking.'

He treated my problem simply and openly and told me he had devised a therapy which might help me. He claimed that he was trying to cure me by the 'rhythm method', which he seemed to think funny. Firstly he got me to sing the line. Then he would get me to establish a slow rhythm by tapping my finger on the table and breaking the words up into syllables which corresponded to the beat. Gradually I would speed the rhythm and the word would come with it. Later in these lessons, in which I showed considerable improvement, I dispensed with beating on the table and would secretly tap my foot as if to music. As the months went by my performance became more and more *presto*. Then all outward signs of rhythm disappeared and by the following Christmas I could talk for long periods without stoppage – two or three sentences at a time, even though they sounded monotonous and had little cadence. Even today when I am nervous before giving a lecture to my students I take several deep breaths and behind the secrecy of the tilted lectern establish a tapping rhythm with my finger, then I start.

*

Let me pause for a moment, now that I have my story launched, to try and explain both what I am trying to do and why I am doing it. For a start, it is not a story. What has happened cannot in the truest sense be said to be fiction, but the telling of a life, which is biography. At this point I must admit to having had great difficulty writing the foregoing pages. I have never experienced this before in writing but then I have never tried to write anything like this. When I sit down to write a critical article or a lecture the words seem to flow from my pen. Indeed my first job is to limit them. To enshrine my ideas in as few words as possible is my aim. Here I am doing the opposite, trying to swell a few fragments into something substantial. I am not entirely new in this field of course. My publication on Sir Aubrey de Vere (1788–1846) is biography of a sort, but there the family gave me access to all the papers, letters, diaries and unpublished poems. Now I have nothing but some memories to work on.

One of the most difficult adjustments I have had to make is with regard to the way I write. I find it awkward to attenuate my normal style. For me to write simply is unnatural and as arduous as thinning a forest.

Why should I write it at all? Perhaps to show something of my respect, perhaps to assuage my guilt. I owe it to Hugo. If it had not been for the novel he had written I don't believe I would be trying to articulate what I think.

I know what a doubtful quality sincerity is when I find it in a piece of literature. The critic in me screams, 'It is unimportant' – now a voice in me says equally loudly, 'If I am not sincere what I am doing is worthless.' Similarly in literature adherence to the truth, the facts as they actually happened, is of no value and yet I intend to be as close to truth as my memory will permit. I must be honest.

One day when Paul and Hugo were studying for their final exams they decided to take the afternoon off and go for a walk. When I asked them they agreed to take me along, telling my mother it was no bother. We walked over the Cave Hill which dominates the town, a forested place, and the two men talked. Then after a while Paul turned to me and said, 'And what are you going to do with your life? They say you're a boy genius.'

'I d . . . d . . . don't know,' I said. 'I think I want to go to you . . . you . . . university.'

'Ah, but what will you do? Which particular branch do you intend to honour with your presence?' I was a bit embarrassed by the way he spoke to me but I answered him nonetheless.

'I think I want to do something in . . . in . . . the Humanities. I'm curious . . .'

'You're mad. Science is the only thing with any future. Like it or not, boy, in the world you've got to earn your living,' said Paul. 'And the best way to do it is with a BSc under your belt. If you have curiosity how could you be anything *but* a scientist?'

'I will wait and see what subjects I do well in. I'm doing 'A' le . . . le . . . le . . .'

'Levels,' said Paul.

A bird sang in the wood 'ch . . . ch . . . ch . . .' mocking me.

'In English, L . . . L . . . Latin, Physics and Chemistry – so I can still shoose.'

'Who's that fella to say. Don't heed him,' said Hugo. 'Science looks at the surface of things. If you have any real curiosity read Philosophy or Literature. Paul, there, has a headful of cells – mine is slightly different,' and here he laughed. 'Besides, the academic world of Science can be very vicious and narrow-minded. They'd cut your throat to publish a paper. I've seen them at work.'

'Where would the world be today without its scientists?' cried Paul.

'You're not often right, Paul,' said Hugo, 'but you're wrong this time. Look at those trees.' The sun tilted into the depths of the forest to our right, flecking the ground with yellow and brown. The remains of bluebells covered the forest floor with a film of petrol blue. 'Just look. A scientist can tell us about *phloem* and *xylem* and tap roots and chromosomes but he can't tell us what it looks like or feels like. This is rubbish anyway. There is no argument between the Arts and Sciences. That's over long ago. What we're talking about is the lad here. What is best for him. Which subject are you happiest at?'

'I thought you were a pharmacist,' I said to Hugo.

'So I am.'

'Then why do you talk as if you knew all about the Humanities?'

Paul answered for him. 'Hugo has a lot of skeletons hanging in his cupboard.' Here he cupped his hand over his mouth and hissed, 'Qugo reads books.' When Paul wanted to tease him he pronounced his name with a Q. Hugo responded by ignoring him.

'Literature is the science of feeling. The artist analyses what feelings are, then in some way or other he tries to reproduce in the reader those same feelings. How much more subtle an experiment than overflowing an oul' bath. How many feelings are there to reproduce, d'ye think? Is there a periodic classification of feelings? Nuances. That's the secret. The lines in the spectrum between pity and sympathy. Literature is the space between words. It fills the gaps that language leaves. English has only one word for love and yet how many different types of love are there in Literature?'

Paul laughed and put his arm around Hugo's shoulders as if offering him to me.

'This is Hugo at his best,' he said. 'Take him or leave him. There's not another idiot like him.'

When Hugo had been talking his face had been serious and intense. He kept adjusting his glasses on the bridge of his nose. Now when Paul presented him he laughed and the conversation turned away from my future to something else.

In all the time I knew him Hugo never collected books. He had no bookshelf – no, that is wrong – he had a bookshelf but it contained only his pharmacy textbooks, great thick volumes honeycombed with benzene rings with their pendant NH_2's and their off shoots of OH's and HPO_4's. Afterwards I discovered that the public library was the source for his vast reading. It was rare to mention a book he had not read. Sometimes, when I was tracking down something for an essay not available in our own university library I would see him ensconced in a corner of the reference section, reading. I made it a point of always going over and having a few words with him.

*

It was shortly after the conversation in the woods that we discovered that Paul had failed his finals. Hugo had passed with high commendation. There was a palpable atmosphere of depression pervading the house. It was the first time I had ever seen Paul gloomy. He sat in the chair, his handsome face unshaven, smoking and staring out the kitchen window at the tip of the backyard wall. Hugo had to control his elation at doing so well, but he was genuinely sorry for Paul. I had just finished my 'A' levels and felt confident of doing well.

'Next year for sure,' Hugo said to Paul.

'That's what gets me – doing that boring stuff all over again.'

'Yeah, I know,' said Hugo.

'Failing stinks,' said Paul. 'When I saw that board my guts just fell on the ground. It's almost as if it's personal. They're saying you're not good enough. Christ and I worked so *hard*.'

'I know – but there's worse things you could fail at,' said Hugo.

'I don't know what they are.' Paul paused to bite his nails. 'But it's great about you. I'm really pleased for you. What are you going to do?'

'Taggart says he'll keep me on, so I have a job. I think I'll stay on here as well and give you a hand next year.'

I ran out excited to tell Mother that Hugo and Paul would be staying on a further year.

On reading over what I have written so far I feel I have created a false picture of Hugo. Because I wanted to record, as exactly as I could remember, what he said I give the impression that he was talkative and gregarious. This was not so. For long periods – weeks on end – I would never hear him say a word, apart from what was required by good manners. He would seem morose, eating his meals and disappearing into the bedroom or going out for long walks on his own. At times like these I noticed that Paul left him alone, would talk if required but would not initiate any conversation to resurrect Hugo from his mood. During the year after he passed his finals this isolation happened with increasing frequency. Paul told me, many years afterwards, that this was when Hugo was working flat out on the novel. My mother even began to remark his taciturnity.

'That lad hasn't a word to throw to a dog, this weather. I'll be glad to see the back of him when he goes.'

She hadn't long to wait because the following spring Hugo announced he was moving out. Now that he was earning he had managed to get himself a mortgage and he had bought a house, not too far from where we lived. He said that he was bringing his family there to live. I was surprised at him having a family because he had never really mentioned them. It was something with which I hadn't really associated him. When he left he bought Mother a pearl necklace and she took back all that she had said about him.

'A queer fish but a good hearted lad.'

By this time I was in my first year at University, studying English Literature and before he left we had some good talks about Joyce. *The Portrait of the Artist* was one of the books I was studying. It transpired that he knew a tremendous amount about Joyce, had read every word that he had written and almost every word that had been written about him. At the time one problem that seemed to occupy him more than any other was Joyce's daughter who was now in a mad house somewhere in England. He claimed Joyce had made a sacrificial victim of her for the cause of Art. He had dragged her around the Continent from Paris to Trieste to Zurich, giving her no security, no home, no life until eventually she went mad. Joyce blamed himself for her state for ever afterwards.

'But then, d'ye think,' said Hugo, 'would it have been better if Joyce had settled in Rathgar and never written a word? His wee girl might have been normal. Would the world be a richer or a poorer place? Would you rather have Joyce with a normal daughter or *Ulysses*?'

'I know what answer you would get,' I said, 'if you asked Joyce's daughter that question.'

'A good point,' he laughed, then became serious. 'There is no doubt in my mind which I would choose.'

He helped me considerably with *The Portrait*, giving me insights into the book which, I think, my tutors and lecturers would have been incapable of.

'May I come and see you sometime in your house?' I asked.

'We could meet in a pub some night, if you like. D'ye drink yet?'

'Sure,' I said, although two pints was about my limit. 'But don't tell my mother.'

I didn't see him again until the night of Paul's celebration on passing his finals but did not get talking seriously to him because the room was crowded and noisy and everybody was tipsy.

Some months later I had volunteered to do a seminar on 'A Painful Case', one of Joyce's stories from *Dubliners* and I thought I would get Hugo's views on the subject. I got his address, which he had left with my mother for forwarding his mail, and went round one evening after tea.

It was a smallish house in a terrace. Paper blinds were pulled on all the windows like a dead house. I rang the bell and an oldish woman answered. Her grey hair stood out from her head like she'd had an electric shock. She smiled broadly.

'Is Hugo there?' I asked. She closed the door over, leaving me standing on the step, and went away. Hugo came to the door nervously pulling at the waist of his Fairisle jumper.

'Come in, come in,' he said. He seemed confused and embarrassed. He stopped in the hallway and leaned against the wall. 'What can I do for you?'

'I just thought we could have that drink. Something else about Joyce has come up. I'd like your opinion on it.'

'I'll have to shave,' he said rubbing his chin. 'Come in and wait.' Then he turned conspiratorially and whispered, 'In here.'

At that moment the woman with the electric hair opened the door of the other room and said, 'Who's your little friend, Hugo? Am I not going to meet him?'

Hugo introduced me to his mother and going out said he would be as quick as he could. It was the end of a summer day and a chill was in the air. Hugo's mother was kneeling trying to light the fire. On the side-board and pinned to the wall I could just see in the gloom unframed paintings. Childish abstracts and several crude attempts to paint what I took to be Don Quixote and Sancho Panza.

'So your mother looked after my Hugo for three years?' she said.

'That's r . . . r . . . r . . . right.'

'Very well she did it too. He was never happier. He's losing weight now. I can't look after him.' She said all these quick sentences over her shoulder.

'Are you any good at fires? No, I suppose not.' The fire had gone out at the first attempt. Now she was spoonfulling sugar from a bowl over the top of the coals. She bundled papers and put them on top of the coal and lit them.

'I think it is easier to light if the coal is warm,' she said. The flames from the papers roared up the chimney and went out. The sugar melted and bubbled a bit, then went brown. Quixote's white horse was stick-like and flat. Sancho's mule was even more badly drawn, if that was possible, and its colour had gone all muddy.

'Firelighters are great,' said the old woman. 'But we haven't got any. I think they stink the house.'

Suddenly the door opened and with relief I looked round expecting to see Hugo, but it was someone else – a boy of about my own age, wearing the exact same Fairisle jumper as Hugo had on two minutes ago. The boy looked subnormal, blunted features, eyes vacant and twitching. He spoke in a thick, unrecognizable speech. 'Oo da.'

The mother introduced me to Hugo's brother and I shook hands with him. He laughed, spittle shining on his chin, and seemed delighted to see me. Hugo seemed to take hours shaving. I was damp with sweat and the minute he came into the room I stood up, ready to go. Hugo's brother reached out his arms and said something which I couldn't begin to interpret. Hugo went over to him and ruffled his hair and hugged him kindly with one arm.

'Sure, Bobby, sure,' he said. When we left, the fire was still unlit. Outside the evening was fresh and clear.

'What did your brother want?' I asked.

'I'd promised him we'd paint.'

'Did he do the Quixotes on the wall?'

'No, they're mine,' said Hugo. I felt very embarrassed but he did not seem to mind at all that I should have ascribed his paintings to his subnormal brother.

'You're a primitive,' I said, trying to get out of the situation gracefully.

'If you say so. Bobby likes to paint. It's a kind of therapy for him as well. When I paint I encourage him to paint with me. He's improving.'

'Yes.'

'You'll have to forgive my mother. She's a bit odd. She's had a lot to put up with in her life, what with Bobby and things.'

One of the things, I later found out from Paul, was that Hugo's father had committed suicide by putting his head in the gas oven.

In the pub we sat down to pints.

'How's the job?' I asked.

'Which one?'

Taggart had given him the sack. He had got a job in another chemist's shop but had left it. Now he was just doing locums.

'There's more money in it,' he said. 'I've realised I just hate the public. They come into the shop snivelling and coughing with their eyes on the ground. Nothing is important for them. They're so stupid. I hate when you make a joke – you know, intentionally – and you are serving a fool who thinks you haven't been aware of what you've said. Then he tries to underline it with some remark and claims the joke for his own. Do you know what I mean? It's like a fully grown man being proud of finding the six sweeties hidden in the picture. I can't think of an example off-hand, yet it happens a hundred times a day. They have no intelligence themselves so they don't expect to find it in others.'

'A job's a job,' I said.

'I can't be smooth and charming like Paul. People think I am dour. Taggart just thought I was insolent, the bastard. I've applied for a job in a hospital pharmacy. You don't have to meet people there.'

As we drank he became more and more talkative. He told me things about himself which I never knew. He had gone away for a time to study for the priesthood. He had been a journalist for a year on a small provincial paper. Then he confessed to having written a novel. I was very excited by this news.

'You must let me read it.'

'I might someday. It's about 250,000 words but I'm not sure if it's finished yet.'

'Wow, that's some size. What is it about?'

'I don't like to talk about it. But if I do let you read it you'll have to be honest.' I nodded that I would be. 'I don't want just to be good. I want my book to be *great*. It has to be.' He laughed and said, 'That's the drink talking now.'

'Will you not tell me what it is about?' I asked again.

'No. But I might give you a clue.'

I bought a drink for him but none for myself. I was becoming groggy and wanted to listen to what he had to say.

'It's all a matter of juxtapositions. Intersections might be a better word. Two things happen together and we get more than double the result.'

'Like Joyce's Epiphanies?'

'Yes, a bit like that, but not the same. One recent one was – I was in the grounds of a monastery at this open air mass and there was a pop group playing the hymns very badly and just in front of me was a rose bush. It hadn't flowered but the buds were green and covered with greenfly. The leaves were riddled with holes and there were rust spots all over them. That's the kind of thing I mean. Both flawed but something different arising out of the joining of the experiences.'

'I think I see,' I said.

'You don't sound convinced.' He laughed into his beer. 'The one unforgettable one – and this one is in the novel – happened to me on a train once in England. I was in a seat opposite what looked like two soldiers, short haircuts sandpapered up the back, tattoos on their arms. It was a long journey and I was reading this book, a thing called *Good Morning Midnight*. Have you read it?'

'No.'

'All the time I was trying to concentrate, not to listen to the soldiers' conversation. They were drinking beer and the table was crowded with bottles and they were getting louder all the time. I reached this part in the book – ahh, she's a beautiful writer – there's this point in the book where the woman loses her baby at birth. This totally lonely person, without one belonging to her in the world, loses her baby, the only thing that gave her any hope – and I just choked up reading it. You know the way tears well up but don't spill and then you can't read?'

Although I have a real love of literature I have never experienced what he talked about and, even though a bit suspicious of that kind of reaction, I nodded in agreement.

'To stop the tears I just put my head back and one soldier said to the other, "What's a five letter word for gristle?"' Hugo paused to watch me. 'It's all there in the juxtaposition,' he said.

There was nothing I could say.

'Of course that's not what the novel is about. It's the *kind* of thing I hope is happening all through it.' He was still nodding his head as if in disbelief that such a perfect thing could have happened and he was the partaker and witness of it. After this and some more drink either he became incoherent or I ceased to take in what he was saying.

On the way home, dizzy with drink and Hugo's novel under my arm I was annoyed at myself for trying to think of a five letter word for 'gristle'.

That night I did not dare read the book because I knew I was in no fit state to make a judgement. I did, however, look at it. It was a huge fat cash accounts ledger ruled in red and blue covered in Hugo's tiny copperplate handwriting. The colour of the ink varied from page to page, some black, some blue, some red. Occasionally there were words crossed out and corrections inserted above but I did not permit myself to read these. I left the book at my bedside and went to sleep.

I was tempted to quote some passages of the novel here but after deep consideration I have decided against it. It was all too embarrassingly bad. He had not even grasped the first principles of good writing. I would be doing him a further disservice to parade them before the public to laugh at. Some of his ideas were good enough but the way he expressed them was lamentable. One could not even say that it was avant-garde and that I was too stodgy a critic to see it. I know enough about literature not to make a mistake like that.

My problem, over the next weeks, grew into an obsession of what to say to Hugo. I had promised him to be honest yet had not the heart to be cruel. Neither could I be dishonest. This, to me, would have been a far greater cruelty. So I compromised.

After I told him, as kindly as I could, what I thought of his novel, suggesting possible ways to improve it, he seemed to shun my company. Every time I called he was not in. Once or twice I spotted him at a distance in the centre of town but he would slip away like a ghost before I could catch him.

A year must have passed before I talked to him again. I was on my usual Saturday afternoon browse through the bookshops. I was in Green's second-hand department, feeling my usual annoyance at the lack of classification of their books. My eyes skimmed from one shelf to another, ton upon ton of print, none of it – not a single name familiar to me. Then suddenly through the shelves I saw Hugo and our eyes met for a fraction of a second. When I went round the other side he was just on the point of leaving. I called him and he stopped. He seemed affable enough but somehow detached from all that was going on around him. He told me that he had left his job in the hospital. They were always picking on him and did not give him his rightful status so he told them what they could do with their job. I asked him to go for a drink but he refused, saying that he no longer indulged. I myself think it was because he had no money.

I had been lecturing for several years when I saw him for the last time. Again he could not avoid me. I saw his familiar gaberdine ahead of me in a crowd of shoppers. His shape had slumped and he walked as if looking for something on the pavement. He walked slower than the crowd so that they flowed past him on either side. I came up behind him – I felt I should – and greeted him. He looked up startled that someone from the crowd should address him. Then, recognizing me, he smiled.

'How's things?' I asked.

'Not so bad, struggling on.'

He looked terrible – dirty, unshaven. His shirt was filthy and the collar wings curled. His glasses were mended at the bridge of his nose with sticking plaster.

'Are you working?' I knew the answer but felt I had to ask the question.

'No. Not just at the moment.'

I walked along with him and asked him what he was doing now.

'Making raspberry ruffles.'

'What?'

Something of his old intensity returned as he told me about his new hobby of sweet-making. Toffees, macaroons, yellowman and now he was looking for the ingredients to make raspberry ruffles. Did I know where he could buy loose coconut? No, I said, I didn't. We stood facing each other in the street with nothing to say.

'Doing any writing this weather?' I asked him. He laughed, scoffed almost.

'No – I'm finished with all that long ago.' He made to move away from me.

'But you shouldn't,' I said. 'By all means keep it up. You shouldn't throw a gift away. The last thing I wanted to do was to discourage you.'

He looked at me straight, his eyes hard and needle-like. 'If you say so,' and he walked away into the crowd.

It was about a year after this, as well as I can calculate, that I was sitting reading in my study. Distantly I heard the phone ring and my mother answer it. She came up the stairs and knocked lightly on the door.

'Come in.'

'I've just heard bad news,' she said. She was on the verge of tears.

'What's happened?'

'Poor Hugo is dead.' I was silent for a long time looking at my book, the print jumping before my eyes.

'What happened?'

'The poor thing took his own life. He was found hung in a barn – somewhere outside Dungannon.'

'Jesus. When's th . . . th . . . the funeral?'

'All this happened a couple of months ago. He was dead a fortnight when they found him.'

I closed the book and tried to comfort my mother who was very upset and was now crying openly.

*

I still experience a sense of shock when I remember that day. Of not eating, of being unable to read. I couldn't help feeling that I could have done something to avert the tragedy. I could have called on him, sought him out, perhaps even given him some hope. My only consolation was that during our talk on Paul's wedding day, Paul said that he felt exactly the same way, but he too had done nothing about it. When I asked him if he had ever seen the novel he said no – so far as he knew Hugo had never showed it to anyone. We drank our beer and talked, more like people at a funeral than a wedding, laughing but not loudly enough to betray ourselves to each other.

A PORNOGRAPHER WOOS

I am sitting on the warm sand with my back to a rock watching you, my love. You have just come from a swim and the water is still in beads all over you, immiscible with the suntan oil. There are specks of sand on the thickening folds of your waist. The fine hairs on your legs below the knee are black and slicked all the one way with the sea. Now your body is open to the sun, willing itself to a deeper brown. You tan well by the sea. Your head is turned away from the sun into the shade of your shoulder and occasionally you open one eye to check on the children. You are wearing a black bikini. Your mother says nothing but it is obvious that she doesn't approve. Stretch-marks, pale lightning flashes, descend into your groin.

Your mother sits rustic between us in a print dress. She wears heavy brogue shoes and those thick lisle stockings. When she crosses her legs I can see she is wearing pink bloomers. She has never had a holiday before and finds it difficult to know how to act. She is trying to read the paper but what little breeze there is keeps blowing and turning the pages. Eventually she folds the paper into a small square and reads it like that. She holds the square with one hand and shades her glasses with the other.

Two of the children come running up the beach with that curious quickness they have when they run barefoot over ribbed sand. They are very brown and stark naked, something we know again is disapproved of, by reading their grandmother's silence. They have come for their bucket and spade because they have found a brown ogee thing and they want to bring it and show it to me. The eldest girl, Maeve, runs away becoming incredibly small until she reaches the water's edge. Anne, a year younger, stands beside me with her sticky-out tummy. She has forgotten the brown ogee and is examining something on the rock behind my head. She says 'blood-suckers' and

I turn round. I see one, then look to the side and see another and another. They are all over the rock, minute, pin-point, scarlet spiders.

Maeve comes back with the brown ogee covered with sea-water in the bucket. It is a sea-mat and I tell her its name. She contorts and says it is horrible. It is about the size of a child's hand, an elliptical mound covered with spiky hairs. I carry it over to you and you open one eye. I say, 'Look.' Your mother becomes curious and says, 'What is it?' I show it to you, winking with the eye farthest from her but you don't get the allusion because you too ask, 'What is it?' I tell you it is a sea mat. Maeve goes off waving her spade in the air.

I have disturbed you because you sit up on your towel, gathering your knees up to your chest. I catch your eye and it holds for infinitesmally longer than as if you were just looking. You rise and come over to me and stoop to look in the bucket. I see the whiteness deep between your breasts. Leaning over, your hands on your knees, you raise just your eyes and look at me from between the hanging of your hair. I pretend to talk, watching your mother, who turns away. You squat by the bucket opening your thighs towards me and purse your mouth. You say, 'It is hot,' and smile, then go maddeningly back to lie on your towel.

I reach over into your basket. There is an assortment of children's clothes, your underwear bundled secretly, a squash-bottle, sun-tan lotion and at last – my jotter and biro. It is a small jotter, the pages held by a wire spiral across the top. I watch you lying in front of me shining with oil. When you lie your breasts almost disappear. There are some hairs peeping at your crotch. Others, lower, have been coyly shaved. On the inside of your right foot is the dark varicose patch which came up after the third baby.

I begin to write what we should, at that minute, be doing. I have never written pornography before and I feel a conspicuous bump appearing in my bathing trunks. I laugh and cross my legs and continue writing. As I come to the end of the second page I have got the couple (with our own names) as far as the hotel room. They begin to strip and caress. I look up and your mother is looking straight at me. She smiles and I smile back at her. She knows I write for a living. I am working. I have just peeled your pants beneath your knees. I proceed to make us do the most fantastical things. My mind is pages ahead of my pen. I can hardly write quickly enough.

At five pages the deed is done and I tear the pages off from the spiral and hand them to you. You turn over and begin to read.

This flurry of movement must have stirred your mother because she comes across to the basket and scrabbles at the bottom for a packet of mints. She sits beside me on the rock, offers me one which I refuse, then pops one into her mouth. For the first time on the holiday she has overcome her shyness to talk to me on her own. She talks of how much she is enjoying herself. The holiday, she says, is taking her out of herself. Her hair is steel-grey darkening at the roots. After your father's death left her on her own we knew that she should get away. I have found her a woman who hides her emotion as much as she can. The most she would allow herself was to tell us how, several times, when she got up in the morning she had put two eggs in the pot. It's the length of the day, she says, that gets her. I knew she was terrified at first in the dining room but now she is getting used to it and even criticises the slowness of the service. She has struck up an aquaintance with an old priest whom she met in the sitting-room. He walks the beach at low tide, always wearing his hat and carries a rolled Pakamac in one hand.

I look at you and you are still reading the pages. You lean on your elbows, your shoulders high and, I see, shaking with laughter. When you are finished you fold the pages smaller and smaller, then turn on your back and close your eyes without so much as a look in our direction.

Your mother decides to go to the water's edge to see the children. She walks with arms folded, unused to having nothing to carry. I go over to you. Without opening your eyes you tell me I am filthy, whispered even though your mother is fifty yards away. You tell me to burn it, tearing it up would not be safe enough. I feel annoyed that you haven't taken it in the spirit in which it was given. I unfold the pages and begin to read it again. The bump reinstates itself. I laugh at some of my artistic attempts – 'the chittering noise of the venetian blinds', 'luminous pulsing tide' – I put the pages in my trousers pocket on the rock.

Suddenly Anne comes running. Her mouth is open and screaming. Someone has thrown sand in her face. You sit upright, your voice incredulous that such a thing should happen to your child. Anne, standing, comes to your shoulder. You wrap your arms round her nakedness and call her 'Lamb' and 'Angel' but the child still cries. You take a tissue from your bag and lick one corner of it and begin to wipe the sticking sand from round her eyes. I watch your face as you do this. Intent, skilful, a beautiful face focused on other-than-me. This, the mother of my children. Your tongue licks out again wetting the tissue. The crying goes on and you begin to scold lightly giving the child enough confidence to stop. 'A big girl like you?' You take the child's cleaned face into the softness of your neck and the tears subside. From the basket miraculously you produce a mint and then you are both away walking, you stooping at the waist to laugh on a level with your child's face.

You stand talking to your mother where the glare of the sand and the sea meet. You are much taller than she. You come back to me covering half the distance in a stiff-legged run. When you reach the rock you point your feet and begin pulling on your jeans. I ask where you are going. You smile at me out of the head hole of your T-shirt, your midriff bare and say that we are going back to the hotel.

'Mammy will be along with the children in an hour or so.'

'What did you tell her?'

'I told her you were dying for a drink before tea.'

We walk quickly back to the hotel. At first we have an arm around each other's waist but it is awkward, like a three-legged race, so we break and just hold hands. In the hotel room there are no venetian blinds but the white net curtains belly and fold in the breeze of the open window. It is hot enough to lie on the coverlet.

It has that special smell by the sea-side and afterwards in the bar as we sit, slaked from the waist down, I tell you so. You smile and we await the return of your mother and our children.

ANODYNE

James Delargy sat in the corner at the small table with the one place-setting which the girl had indicated. She set the typed menu in its plastic casing in front of him and went off to lean against the sideboard. There was a typing error, a percentage mark between '19' and 'July'. He propped the menu against the silver milk jug, dented and worn through to the yellow brass. When the waitress came back he ordered a mixed grill. She had a nice face when she smiled. The table cloth was white starched linen, clean except for one small stain with tomato seeds embedded in it. He picked up a knife and scraped the seeds from the cloth.

Three elderly priests or Christian Brothers came in, men with thin collars, and sat at a table in an alcove. At least one of them must be interesting, thought James. The eldest one with white hair looked a bit like Auden – his face all cracked and wrinkled. But he had been sadly disappointed in priests before. Not all of them were well read. His mixed grill came.

'Do you do this all year round?' James asked her.

'Ach no, just for the summer,' she said. Her accent was pleasant and lilting.

'Are you a student?' he asked.

'Are you daft? Me, a student. I can hardly add two and two.'

'Oh I see.'

'There is no work around here in the winter. I go to Scotland to the factories. There is plenty of work there.' As she went back to the kitchen James noticed that her legs were very thick and that half an inch of her slip was showing beneath her black dress.

After tea he took a raincoat and walked out to explore the town. It wasn't much more than one street with a few smaller ones running off it. Most of the shop windows were full of holiday trinkets and picture postcards. He called in the biggest of these to see if there were any books. He had been foolish enough not to bring anything with him and the only reading he could get at the station had been *Howards End*. It had been a long time since he had read it. The shop was dark, hung about with Aran sweaters and bales of Irish tweed. There was a glass counter full of gnomes and shamrock-covered ashtrays. A rack of postcards that swung round. Against the back of the shop was a small book shelf. He moved to it and began to read the titles on the spines of the books. A girl of about eight came out of the curtain covered kitchen.

'Yes?' she said.

'I'm just looking.' The girl stood on as if he wasn't to be trusted. There was nothing but Dennis Wheatleys and Agatha Christies, science fiction and love paperbacks. There was another copy of *Howards End* and he smiled to himself. The only thing he could get was a Hemingway. He paid the girl who waited till he was out of the shop before she went back into the kitchen.

He walked the length of the beach but was stopped by a large triangular outcrop of rock jutting into the sea. He sat down and watched the water come sluicing in, higher and higher up the beach until it was at his feet. He liked what he had seen of the place – not bad for having been picked at random. The only place the doctor had told him to avoid was the place his mother had brought him for the past twenty years. He said there would be too many memories. 'Go away – get yourself a nice girl. Fall in love and then come back and see me.' The doctor said what he had to do was not to forget, but to use discretion and reason in remembering her. He must begin to build a new life for himself which his mother would have no part in. He must begin to see himself as an adult. He had protested that nursing his mother through that last terrible year would make an adult of anybody. Teaching through the day, sitting up most of the night, putting her on the commode, feeding her, caring for her, watching death insinuate itself into her face. Her nose sharpened like a pencil, her mouth caved in without her teeth those last four days she took to die. The only time he cried was the night she died. It was her total helplessness, hardly able to grip his hand, her sagging jaw, her total lack of dignity as she grunted and gasped for each breath. He thought of her as she was when he was a child and he crushed her slack yellow head against his cheek and cried. He tried to remember the name of the character in Camus' book who went to the pictures the day his mother died. Later he killed an Arab. But he couldn't remember – even now as he sat on the rock he couldn't remember. He was feeling too hot again and he bent to the sea at his feet and splashed his sweating forehead with water. A wave came in and covered his shoes.

He saw that soon the sea would cut him off so he moved back across the beach. The water, flecked and layered with black and gold and yellow reminded him of some of the Impressionists.

Back at the hotel he went up to his room to unpack his things. His room had a small bay window with curtains hung across the spine of the D, a wardrobe, a dressing table with rosette handles, one of which came off in his hand when he pulled it. The drawer was floored with a page of *The Donegal Democrat*. Stooped over he read a report of a Gaelic match and laughed at the flowery parochial style. He'd had better compositions from his own lads. The carpet was threadbare and nosed its way into an old fireplace blocked by another page of newspaper. In one corner was a wash-hand basin which gulped and gurgled when anybody else in the house used theirs. High up on the wall was a black picture hook.

He packed what clothes he had neatly into the drawer. A fly bizzed at the bay window. He looked round for something to kill it with but could find nothing so he opened the window and shooed it out with his hand. If his mother had been there she'd have dealt with it in her own way. She hated flies. Her love of cleanliness was so surgical that she couldn't bear one in the room with her. One day when he was cleaning out the fire he went to the bin with ashes and found his only copy of *Death in Venice* lying on top of the potato peelings and bacon rinds. He picked it up and walked back into the house holding the book between his finger and thumb.

'Mother,' he yelled. 'Did you throw my *Death in Venice* in the bin?' He held up the book.

'I don't know. I might have.'

'In under God, *why?*'

'I killed a fly with it.'

James looked closely at the cover. There was a small red splash.

'Why do you kill flies with my books?'

'It must have been the nearest thing to hand at the time.' She shuddered. 'Horrible big buzzer.'

'Why don't you use the paper?' She didn't answer. 'Mother, sometimes you are incredible.'

'Such a fuss over an old paperback,' she muttered.

'It's *Death in Venice.*'

'It's all germs now.'

'I swear if you do it again, I'll leave. Get a flat of my own somewhere.' He walked out and wiped the cover with a damp cloth dipped in disinfectant. How many times had she done that? There were so many of his books missing even though he had made a firm rule never to lend them. Maybe that's where they were going. Into the bin. His mother had been hard to stick at times. He must stop thinking about her. Again he was feeling too hot. He filled the wash basin. The water was yellow-brown. It must be the turf. Small streams all over the bogs, 'glue-gold' was the colour of them. Invariably Hopkins found the right word. He splashed the cold water into his face.

There were other times when she was unforgettable, when he thought her the most beautiful woman in the world. He could sit and listen to her all night when she was entertaining guests. She talked to and questioned them with such quiet concern. She talked to them as if she loved them, as if she had singled them out from the common herd.

Many nights when they were on their own she would sit with one leg beneath her, always embroidering, and talk of her own girlhood. Of the big house in which she had lived, her mother's dress hissing on the hallway, the place full of Italians visiting from the Dublin Opera, of silver soup tureens, of nannies and cooks and servants. Late in life when, as she said herself, nobody else would take her, she fell for a whiskey traveller who was a Catholic. Her family disowned her. He was a handsome man and his oval photograph, with his Bismarck moustache and butterfly collar still hung on the wall beside her bed. Then, she said, he became his own best customer.

A thing that he could never understand about her was that she loved books but didn't respect them. She told him of an anthology of poetry she'd been given and of how each day she would go a long walk she would tear out several pages to take with her, being too lazy, she said, to cart the whole book about the countryside. He felt a lump in his throat and a hotness in his eyes as he thought of the neverness of her. He would *never* see her again. He must buy a hat tomorrow if it was warm and sunny. His bald spot became intolerably tender if he got it sunburned.

During tea he studied the faces around the dining room. He decided that he would have to make the effort to be sociable. On his way out he went to the table where the Brothers sat in the alcove.

'Excuse me, could I buy you a drink after your meal?' The biggest of the three raised his hands and laughed.

'Ah no thank you very much but we don't drink.' He had the flattest of Dublin accents. The others nodded in agreement. James bowed slightly and could think of nothing more to say. He went out into the bar himself. He was no good at this sort of thing. His mother had always made the approaches. She had an unerring instinct for choosing the right people. You could see them warming to her immediately as she began to talk. The Brothers would never have refused her if she had asked them. But would she have asked them? Probably not, with her instinct.

James ordered a beer. There was a man sitting reading a book at the far side of the bar. He had the book flat on his knees so that the cover was hidden. James took his drink and sat at the table next to him. He sipped his beer. The man read on, not looking up.

'Do you read much?' James asked.

'No. Not at all. Holidays mostly. Sometimes at night I'll read a bit if I can't get to sleep. It helps put me over.'

'Yes,' said James. 'What's the book?' The man showed him the cover. It was an American sex novel. A picture of a blonde in her slip with one foot on a chair so that you could see her stocking tops and the v of her lace panties.

'It was all I could get down here,' he said. 'Are you on holiday?'

James nodded and swallowed his beer.

'Will you have another?' said the man half rising out of his seat.

'No. No thanks, I must be off,' James answered quickly. 'How long are you staying?'

'Another week,' said the man.

'Then I'll see you around.'

As James moved past the bar, the manager put his head round the door and said in an undertone to the barman, 'John, you'll not forget the bottle of Powers for the Brothers' room.'

James walked out of town but the landscape was the same as far as the eye could see. A scatter of grey one-storey houses against the grey-green of the poor land. Networks of low stone walls fenced fields which were full of rocks themselves. He turned back seeing no variety and went back to his room to read Hemingway. At eleven he took his sleeping pill and fell asleep almost immediately. The last thing he saw was the picture hook above the mantelpiece, caught in a shaft of light from the street where the curtains did not quite meet.

'Cheapskates,' he thought, a favourite word of his mother's.

The next day he walked along the beach close to the water's edge. The tide was out and he discovered that he could walk past the rocks which had stopped him the previous night. After about a mile he came to another high projection of rock topped by tufted grass with a ravine at its centre. Round the corner of the rock he saw a girl. He ducked back then peeped out again to watch her. She was sitting on a rock drawing. Her long legs were bare and half folded under her. Her hair was yellow. He hesitated a moment then decided to walk past her to get a better look. He walked casually, his hands behind his back, looking out to sea and when he came level with her he glanced round. She smiled at him, guilty of her sketch book.

'Hello,' she greeted him. James stopped and went towards her. Close up he noticed that her midriff was bare, her blouse knotted beneath her breasts.

'Sketching?'

'Yes,' she said, throwing her arm over her drawing just as one of the boys in his class would do. 'Please don't look.'

'It's a lovely morning,' he said but felt it too banal a thing to say, so he added, '. . . for sketching. The light . . . it's just right.'

'Oh you know about things like that,' she said, starting up. 'Are you an artist?'

James smiled and edged his hip onto a rock. 'No . . . no I'm not.'

She was very beautiful, the more he looked at her. Pure skin, little or no make-up, blonde hair tied back, some strands of which had come loose and fallen down the side of her face. She wore a pink blouse and from where he sat above her he could see the slight curvature which began her breast. Her legs had the faintest trace of pale hair against the sunburned skin.

'May I see?' James asked. She laughed embarrassed, and said that it was absolutely useless. Her accent had class about it, not Northern, but definitely class.

'I'll show you because I've only started,' she said and opened the book. The page was dark grey for pastel and the line of the outcrop of rock had been sketched in, the line of sea and the far side of the lough.

'It's good,' said James looking at her. She bit her bottom lip.

'Then I'd better leave it like that,' she said laughing. 'I'd only ruin it.'

James handed the book back and asked, 'Are you on holiday?'

'Yes, we're staying at the hotel up there.' She pointed. 'Behind those trees.'

'It looks expensive.'

'Yes but it's gorgeous. An old Georgian mansion. Just the sort of place you'd like to own.'

'Are you staying long?'

She pulled a face. 'We'll be going on Sunday.'

'Who's "we"?'

'I'm here with my parents. That's why I go sketching. There's nothing else to do.'

'You like sketching then?'

'Yes, I love things,' she said. She waved her hand in the direction of the sea. '. . . Nature . . . I don't know how to put it. Drawing doesn't really help. If you could somehow get *into* it . . .'

'Have you read Hopkins?' James asked.

'No.' She shook her head from side to side, thinking.

'It's *all* there,' said James. '"There lives the dearest freshness deep down in things."'

'Oh *him*,' she interrupted. 'Yes I think I have. He's in *The Pageant*.'

'Yes,' said James, left with the rest of the poem inside him.

'Writing poems about it is just a different way of drawing it. It still doesn't help. I don't know. When you like things . . . you're taking in all the time, there's nothing going out. I suppose it has to get out somehow . . . or you'd burst.' She put her hand on her bare midriff as if she had indigestion.

'I don't think it's giving out,' said James. 'It's more a structuring of what we take in. Frost says that poetry is "a momentary stay against confusion".'

'Are you a teacher?'

'Yes. Does it show that much?'

'*No*. No it's just that you sound so like . . . so clever.'

They both laughed. 'What is there to do at nights here?' James asked.

'Nothing really – sometimes a sing-song in the bar.' She scraped a handful of sand and let it trickle from one hand to the other, then reversed her hands and poured it back again. A joke from an old Bob Hope film came to him.

'This must be where they empty all the old egg-timers.' She laughed appreciatively.

'What's your name?' he asked.

'Rosalind.'

'Mine's James – James Delargy.' He felt he should shake hands but didn't. 'Are there any nice walks about here?'

'Oh yes. The nicest walk is round the foreshore when the tide is out. You can walk for miles and miles.' She smiled up at him and with a finger hooked away a strand of hair which had fallen over her face. 'Would you like me to show you?'

'Yes,' said James. 'Can I see you tonight when the tide is full out again?'

She nodded, smiling happily.

James said, 'It won't be dark till about ten – and we could go for a drink.'

'I'm not . . . I don't drink,' said Rosalind.

'That's OK by me,' said James. 'You can take something.' Again she nodded and clutched her sketch pad to her chest.

'Shall I call up for you at your hotel?'

'No . . . no. I'll come down to you. Where are you staying?' He told her.

'At about eight?'

'Yes.' She put her sketch pad onto her knees. Some of the brown pastel had come off on her blouse. 'Oh look what I've done.' She made a face and tried to dust it off. Her breasts jigged to the touch of her own fingers but the stain remained.

There seemed nothing left to say so James took his leave of her. On his way back to the hotel he lifted a handful of gravelly sand and hurled it at the sea and saw the scatter of small splashes on the water beyond the first wave.

After tea James shaved meticulously and washed his feet in the wash-basin because it had been hot and he had neglected to bring sandals with him. He also looked with concern at his bald patch and saw that it was red. His mother had always said that she didn't know who would look after him when she was gone. He tried to think of Rosalind and how he was going to conduct the evening. She was young and didn't seem to have read very much. He could introduce her to lots of really good stuff. He pulled out the plug and the dirty water sucked away, echoing in all the other rooms of the hotel. He put on cream trousers, a polo necked sweater and slipped the Hemingway into the pocket of his linen jacket. He asked in the kitchen for brown polish and brushed his shoes. The white line of salt where the sea had washed over them disappeared, then he went into the bar to wait. It was a quarter to eight. He wondered if he should wait outside the hotel in case she would be embarrassed about coming into a bar on her own – but on holiday bars were not the same things. At the moment there were children playing around, crawling under tables, squealing and laughing. In a room off the bar a child monotonously played single notes on a piano, while others slid in sock-soles on the small maple dance floor. To pass the time James tried to read a few pages of Hemingway but found he couldn't concentrate.

At eight o'clock the girl from the reception desk came into the bar and looked around. She came over to James and said, 'Mr Delargy?'

'Yes.'

'There is a gentleman at reception to see you.' He followed the girl out. The man waiting there was tall and distinguished looking, grey hair with a small toothbrush moustache.

'Mr Delargy?' James nodded, half gestured to shake hands but seeing no response on the other's part, he stopped. 'May I buy you a drink?'

He was very abrupt. James was confused and followed him without a murmur. In the bar the elder man asked what he drank, then set up a beer and a small whiskey for himself.

'There seems to have been some misunderstanding,' he began. 'I don't want to be nasty about this but I want to be firm. My name is Somerville. I believe you met my daughter Rosalind on the beach this morning.' James nodded. 'I must inform you that my daughter is not yet fifteen and that I do not allow her to go out with boys whom I haven't vetted. I certainly do not permit her to go out unchaperoned with a man of your age. I apologise if I seem offensive but you must see my point of view.'

'I'm sorry, but I didn't realise she was so young,' James stammered.

'I admit she's a big girl for her age. Also it is mostly her fault for not telling you – but she's so naive. She let it slip at tea where she was going and I felt it my duty to come and see you. I hope you don't mind.'

'I . . . I . . . had no idea,' said James. 'She seemed so confident. I knew she was young but not *that* young. I can assure you anyway that she would have been in no danger with me.'

Somerville smiled and relaxed a bit. He drank off half his whiskey.

'She's a very beautiful girl,' said James.

Somerville accepted the remark as a compliment to himself. He drank off the rest of his glass and was about to rise to go saying, 'Thank you Mr Delargy for being so understanding . . .'

'Just a moment,' said James. He was at the bar before Somerville could refuse. He came back with the drinks and they both sat silent for a moment. They both raised their drinks at the same time for something to do.

'I see you're reading Hemingway,' said Somerville.

'Yes,' said James. 'I'd forgotten how good he was.'

'Like an ox talking,' said Somerville laughing.

'His characters may be but he has some very intelligent things to say about literature.'

'I'm joking really,' said Somerville but James went on.

'He says somewhere that what you read becomes part of your experience, if it is good, that is. Good writing must actually seemed to have happened to you. I think that is very perceptive.'

The other nodded. 'Hemingway is not my period. I read him when I was younger but remained unimpressed.'

'What do you do, Mr Somerville?'

'I teach English.'

'Oh so do I.'

'I lecture at Trinity.'

James edged forward on his seat. 'And what is your period?'

'Early seventeenth century.'

'Oh Donne and Herbert and Crawshaw? I love them,' said James excitedly.

'The prose is more my field. That's what I did my Doctorate in. Launcelot Andrewes, Bacon, Browne. Those chaps,' said Somerville. Gradually the parents came in and the children were rounded up from the bar room floor. The single notes on the piano stopped and the rest of the conversation proceeded in an air of good humoured and quiet concentration.

It was after twelve when Dr Somerville left to go back to his hotel. James had drunk much more than he had intended and, when he fell into bed, happy to have had such a good night, he did not need to take a sleeping pill. The picture hook seemed somehow bigger, repulsively static on the wall, triangular like a black fly. He closed his eyes and the bed seemed to race backwards. He opened them to stop the sensation. The picture hook throbbed in the shaft of light, annoying him intensely. James got up from bed and stood on the chair, nearly overbalancing, and pulled the curtains so that they met flush and the room was in complete darkness.

The next day he met Mrs Somerville with her husband for coffee, as arranged.

'My dear,' said Mrs Somerville. 'When he hadn't come home by twelve I could have sworn that you'd shot him,' and they all laughed. James thought how sad it was that his mother would never meet these lovely people. He was sure she would have approved.

THE DEEP END

On the way home in the empty bus the two boys were silent. They sat as usual in separate seats but made no attempt to avoid paying their fare. Paul sat, his damp towel clenched in the crook of his arm, looking down into the street at each stop. At Manor Street Olly knelt up and looked back at him.

'Say nothing to your Ma, for God's sake, Paul. We'd never get going again.'

'I'm not mad about going again – not for a while,' said Paul.

Olly unfurled his bundle and took out his togs and wrung them out, the droplets splashing onto the battened floor.

'Where are you for this afternoon?'

'Any dough?'

'Naw.' Olly got up and ran down the bus. 'See ya.' Halfway down the stairs he stopped and pulled a cigarette out of his top pocket.

'I'll smoke your half for you, Paul.'

'I hope it chokes you.'

Paul went home and couldn't eat his dinner. He went up to the bedroom and lay for a long time looking at the ceiling. His mother came up and put her head round the door.

'That's the last time you'll go to the baths – your guts full of oul' lime water – and God knows what else. I'm sure they do more than swim in the water.'

Paul suddenly felt his eyes fill with tears. Then he cried hard. His mother came over and put her arms round him, asking incredulously, 'What's wrong, what's wrong with my big man?'

They queued in the hallway and heard the distant echoing cease. Above them, on the wall, was an Artificial Respiration poster, its reds gone brown in the sun. Dotted lines and arrows showed the right motions. Somebody had drawn tits on the victim's back and added genitals to the man bending over him. Olly stood, one foot flat against the cream tiled wall, the other slanted like a prop.

'Away and ask her how long they'll be,' he said. Paul crushed his way up to the porthole and came back.

'Ten minutes.'

'Time for a feg.' With two fingers Olly dipped into his breast pocket and pulled out a cigarette. He straightened it out and tapped the loose tobacco into place on his thumb nail. 'Smoke one now and the other one after.'

Paul struck the match between the tiles. Olly cupped the flame in his hands, took two quick puffs then closed his fingers round the cigarette. He leaned back against the wall.

'Don't suck the guts out of it.' Olly turned his head away from Paul's reaching hand, taking the last ounce out of it.

'Come on, it'll be red hot,' said Paul grabbing the cigarette from him. He couldn't inhale as deeply as Olly so he blew the smoke down his nose and passed it back.

'What are they?'

'Parkies,' said Olly.

'They're OK.' Then after a moment Paul asked, 'Do you believe this cancer thing?'

'Naw, sure my Ma and Da both smoke like trains and look at the age they are.'

'Oul' Hennesy smoked and he's dead – fifty a day,' said Paul.

'You've gotta go sometime – where the hell did oul' Hennesy get the money. Fifty a day. Jesis.'

'All the doctors say it,' said Paul.

'Doctors are stupid. My Da was walking around for two weeks with a broken finger and they didn't even know. They had to send him to the hospital before they found out.' Olly tucked in the loose strands of tobacco at the soggy end with his finger.

'Does your Ma still not allow you?'

'Naw.'

'Mine gave me one yesterday – she said as long as nobody was in it was OK. She says it's better than smoking behind her back.'

'My Ma would do her nut if she knew.'

A small boy nudged Olly and, looking up at him, said, 'Give us your butt.'

'Fuck off, son,' said Olly dropping the remains of the cigarette on the ground and pressing it with a twist of his toe.

'What about clubbing up for currant squares when we get out?' Paul asked.

'From Lizzie's?'

'Yeah, they're dead on.'

'OK,' said Olly. 'How much have we?'

They took out their money and calculated. If bus fares weren't collected that was so much profit, but a keen conductor had to be allowed for. They had enough. Paul licked his lips and growled.

By now the first crowd had begun to come out in ones and twos. White faced, red eyed, some with their togs on their heads, others their hair wet and spiky, they tumbled out, shouting at each other at the tops of their voices. One boy in raggy jeans, both elbows out of his sweater climbed to the top of the turnstile gate, almost to the ceiling and slopped his wet togs down onto the back of his friend's neck.

'Get to hell out of it,' roared the attendant who had just come out. He stood threatening, his fingers hooked in the loops of his belt, brown muscled in a singlet and jeans. He wore black wellingtons with the white canvas rims turned down. He had a tattoo, blue and red on each arm. The boy scuttled down off the gate and crashed out the door. The attendant said something to the girl behind the pay box and the line began to jostle and fight to get through.

Paul shoved his way up to the arched hole in the perspex and pushed his money to the girl. She gave him a ticket, a towel and a pair of trunks. The towel was a freshly laundered dishcloth, still warm with a clean smell, the trunks a double red triangle held together with string. Paul used the Corporation towel for standing on and dried himself with his own soft towel. The gym teacher had told them the worst thing you could get out of the baths was athlete's foot and he himself stood on a towel. Paul's mother always harped on about polio.

'If you had to spend the rest of your days in a wheel-chair it would be a dear swim. The ones that swim over there, you never know what homes they've come out of. It's a bad area.'

'But the water's full of chlorine, Ma.'

'Chlorine, chlorine – what's the use of chlorine if you're going to get polio. Eh? Tell me that. Your father's too soft, allowing you. He says the swimming'll make a man out of you but he'll change his tune if it makes a polio victim out of you.'

Both boys ran down the corridor, their heels hollow yet pinging from the ceiling. They raced through the swing doors looking beneath each half door for a box without a pair of feet. They each got a box to themselves at the deep end. Paul climbed up onto the seat so that he could see out as he got stripped. The pool still moved from the previous session. It looked still enough on the surface but the black lane lines snaked too and fro continuously. He hauled off his pullover, shirt and vest as one unit and hung them on the peg. The same with his trousers and drawers. The whole lot hung like somebody deformed, humped with dangling arms.

Suddenly there was a cry smothered by a dull explosion. Paul looked out over the partition and saw a boy at the bottom of his dive, alone in the pool. He looked flat, spread-eagled, his hair middle shaded and smoothed by the water. He breast-stroked to the surface and blew out a farting noise.

'First in.' It was Olly. 'Get a move on, Paul,' he screamed.

Paul hopped about on one leg putting on his black trunks. Then he put the Corporation ones over them, tying the string at the sides. The red and black looked nice. If you *only* wore the Corporation ones your thing kept showing.

He blessed himself, said the first line of an Act of Contrition and went out of the box. He walked jerkily down to the three foot end, holding his elbows. The water splashed out on the sides and was cold underfoot. By now the pool was threshing with swimmers and the noise was deafening.

'Look at the ribs,' screamed Olly's head.

Paul moved down the steps at the three foot mark and stood on the last step, knee deep.

He splashed some water over his shoulders and face. Then he pushed himself off from the side screaming with cold. Paul had just learned to swim. He could breaststroke a breadth at the shallow end but above four feet he kept close to the bar. Somebody had once told him, 'If you can swim a breadth you can swim a mile,' but he didn't believe it. He stood for a while jumping up and down stirring the water with his hands. Olly swam down to him and they played diving between each other's legs for a while. Then Olly headed off for the high board. Paul half swam, half pulled himself along the bar to the deep end. Olly climbed the steps to the top board, swiping the wet hair from his eyes. Paul treaded water waiting and watching him. When he reached the top he held onto the railing, a boxer in his corner, then ran and launched himself into the air, his heels cocked and fifteen foot down, exploded into the water. He came up beside Paul.

'Come on and try,' he said. 'It's great.'

'Are you mad?'

'You're yella. Once you've done it once, it's dead easy. Come on.' He swam to the steps and Paul followed. They sloshed out of the water and began climbing the ladder. At the top Paul looked down at the squat, upturned faces and held tight to the rail.

'Ready?' Olly asked.

'You go first.'

'Go on, I want to watch you.'

'You go first or I won't go,' said Paul.

Olly ran and disappeared at the end of the wet matting on the board, plummeting out of sight. Paul blessed himself and waited until Olly came up again.

'Are you yella?' He laughed appearing up the ladder. He ran past Paul and jumped again holding his nose. Paul let go the bar and scrambled quickly down the ladder and jumped as high as he could off the side of the pool. The bubbles seethed up his nose and his ears pounded and rumbled. He came up near Olly.

'I did it.'

Olly swam over to him and said, 'Good for you. I thought you were chicken. Come on again.'

'Naw,' said Paul. 'Once is enough. What about playing tig?'

But the tig was no use because Olly would dive into the middle of the six foot end and couldn't be caught.

Afterwards Paul stood out on the side to get his breath back. The sour taste of the lime made him wish for his currant square now. It was colder out of the water than in. Goose pimples came out all over his body and the light hairs on his arms stood up. 'You could strike matches on ye,' his father had once said to him at the sea-side. 'It couldn't be good for him,' his mother added, huddled in the depths of her deck chair. Paul stood shivering and listening to the din. Splashing and slamming of dressing box doors mixed with a continuous jagged scream, which echoed and multiplied when flung back from the high glass roof. It started at the beginning of the session and stayed at the same sawing pitch throughout. The long whistle to end the session shrilled and the noise reached a crescendo as everybody plunged in for the last time.

Paul was near his box and felt too cold for a last fling. He pushed the half door shut and spread the cotton towel on the duck-boarding. He began to dry himself slowly. He peeled off his trunks and left them, a wet figure eight, at his feet. He felt alone in the box. The noise was outside, people whistling, shouting jokes, but inside he was safe and insulated. Private. He looked down at himself, at his wisps of hair. He wondered if he would ever have a bush like the gym teachers. 'You're on the verge of life now my dear boys – soon you will become men,' the Redemptorist, his black and white heart pinned to his chest, smiled. 'And I know you will all make very good men – every last one of you.' Paul dried himself and pulled on his drawers trying not to think about it any more. Then suddenly from outside there was a scream, totally different in tone from any of the shouting and larking that was going on.

'*Hey mister, mister.*'

Paul stood up on the seat and looked out. A boy, half-dressed, was running up and down the side of the pool pointing into it and screaming all the time, '*mister, mister.*' Paul looked and saw a still figure lying on the bottom at the deep end. The attendant raced past his box and plunged in. He scooped the body up off the bottom and

swam with it to the side. Another man took it from him, by an arm
and a leg. The boy's mouth was black and open. Paul sat down on
the seat so he couldn't see. Everything was completely silent now
except for one of the boys who was snivelling and crying. Paul dried
his feet and put on his socks. He pulled on his trousers and stood
up to look out again. In the middle of a quiet crowd of boys the
attendant was kneeling, his clothes darkened with the wet. The
boy's body was blue-grey and when the attendant did anything with
its arms, they flopped. Paul stood down and finished dressing. He
whispered over to Olly, 'Will we go?'

'Wait t'see what happens.' Olly, in his vest, hung over the half
door.

'Is he dead?' Paul hissed.

'Looks like it,' said Olly.

Paul sat down again. The box was painted dark green. Initials
and dates, crude guitar shapes of women with split and tits were
carved or drawn on every square inch of space. He began to read
them – 'G.B. WUZ HERE' – 'TONY IS A WANKER' – 'BMcK
1955.' He read these things over and over again until in the distance
he heard the bray of an ambulance. It drew close and stopped.
There were some sweet papers and a few dead matches lodged
beneath the struts of the duck-boards at his feet. He picked up his
togs and very slowly disentangled them from the red ones. Olly
came in dressed.

'What's happening?' Paul asked.

'They're away.'

Paul looked out. The crowd had gone and everyone was back in
their boxes getting dressed. Someone started to whistle but stopped.
The pool was absolutely still now, the black lines at the bottom ruled
rigid, perspective straight, the surface a turquoise pane.

They walked straddle-legged down the slippery edge of the pool
and threw their borrowed togs and towels into the bin. Outside at
the turnstile the girl had put a piece of cardboard over the porthole
and there was a queue, quieter than usual, waiting to see if they were
going to get in or not.

The boys walked down the steps and crossed the road to the bus stop at Lizzie's bakery. Olly looked at the currant squares in the window. About a quarter of a trayful had been sold. Then he too leaned his back against the window and the two of them stood, their heads turned, waiting for a bus.

II

A TIME TO DANCE
1982

FATHER AND SON

Because I do not sleep well I hear my father rising to go to work. I know that in a few minutes he will come in to look at me sleeping. He will want to check that I came home last night. He will stand in his bare feet, his shoes and socks in his hand, looking at me. I will sleep for him. Downstairs I hear the snap of the switch on the kettle. I hear him not eating anything, going about the kitchen with a stomach full of wind. He will come again to look at me before he goes out to his work. He will want a conversation. He climbs the stairs and stands breathing through his nose with an empty lunch box in the crook of his arm, looking at me.

This is my son who let me down. I love him so much it hurts but he won't talk to me. He tells me nothing. I hear him groan and see his eyes flicker open. When he sees me he turns away, a heave of bedclothes in his wake.

'Wake up, son. I'm away to my work. Where are you going today?'
  'What's it to you?'
  'If I know what you're doing I don't worry as much.'
  'Shit.'

I do not sleep. My father does not sleep. The sound of ambulances criss-crosses the dark. I sleep with the daylight. It is safe. At night I hear his bare feet click as he lifts them, walking the lino. The front door shudders as he leaves.

My son is breaking my heart. It is already broken. Is it my fault there is no woman in the house? Is it my fault a good woman should die? His face was never softer than when after I had shaved. A baby pressed to my shaved cheek. Now his chin is sandpaper. He is a man. When he was a boy I took him fishing. I taught him how to tie a blood-knot, how to cast a fly, how to strike so the fish would not escape. How to play a fish. The green bus to quiet days in Toome. Him pestering me with questions. If I leave him alone he will break my heart anyway. I must speak to him. Tonight at tea. If he is in.

'You should be in your bed. A man of your age. It's past one.'

'Let me make you some tea.'

The boy shrugs and sits down. He takes up the paper between him and his father.

'What do you be doing out to this time?'

'Not again.'

'Answer me.'

'Talking.'

'Who with?'

'Friends. Just go to bed, Da, will you?'

'What do you talk about?'

'Nothing much.'

'Talk to me, son.'

'What about?'

My son, he looks confused. I want you to talk to me the way I hear you talk to people at the door. I want to hear you laugh with me like you used to. I want to know what you think. I want to know why you do not eat more. No more than pickings for four weeks. Your face is thin. Your fingers, orange with nicotine. I pulled you away from death once and now you will not talk to me. I want to know if you are in danger again.

'About . . .'

'You haven't shaved yet.'

'I'm just going to. The water in the kettle is hot.'

'Why do you shave at night?'

'Because in the morning my hand shakes.'

*

Your hand shakes in the morning, Da, because you're a coward. You think the world is waiting round the corner to blow your head off. A breakfast of two Valium and the rest of them rattling in your pocket, walking down the street to your work. Won't answer the door without looking out the bedroom window first. He's scared of his own shadow.

Son, you are living on borrowed time. Your hand shook when you got home. I have given you the life you now have. I fed you soup from a spoon when your own hand would have spilled it. Let me put my arm around your shoulders and let me listen to what is making you thin. At the weekend I will talk to him.

It is hard to tell if his bed has been slept in. It is always rumpled. I have not seen my son for two days. Then, on the radio, I hear he is dead. They give out his description. I drink milk. I cry.

But he comes in for his tea.

'Why don't you tell me where you are?'
'Because I never know where I am.'

My mother is dead but I have another one in her place. He is an old woman. He has been crying. I know he prays for me all the time. He used to dig the garden, grow vegetables and flowers for half the street. He used to fish. To take me fishing. Now he just waits. He sits and waits for me and the weeds have taken over. I would like to slap his face and make a man out of him.

'I let you go once – and look what happened.'
'Not this again.'
The boy curls his lip as if snagged on a fish-hook.

For two years I never heard a scrape from you. I read of London in the papers. Watched scenes from London on the news, looking over the reporter's shoulder at people walking in the street. I know you, son, you are easily led. Then a doctor phoned for me at work. The poshest man I ever spoke to.

'I had to go and collect you. Like a dog.'

The boy has taken up a paper. He turns the pages noisily, crackling like fire.

'A new rig-out from Littlewoods.'

Socks, drawers, shirt, the lot. In a carrier bag. The doctor said he had to burn what was on you. I made you have your girl's hair cut. It was Belfast before we spoke. You had the taint of England in your voice.

'Today I thought you were dead.'

Every day you think I am dead. You live in fear. Of your own death. Peeping behind curtains, the radio always loud enough to drown any noise that might frighten you, double locking doors. When you think I am not looking you hold your stomach. You undress in the dark for fear of your shadow falling on the window-blind. At night you lie with the pillow over your head. By your bed a hatchet which you pretend to have forgotten to tidy away. Mice have more courage.

'Well I'm not dead.'

'Why don't you tell me where you go?'

'Look, Da, I have not touched the stuff since I came back. Right?'

'Why don't you have a girl like everybody else?'

'Oh fuck.'

He bundles the paper and hurls it in the corner and stamps up the stairs to his room. The old man shouts at the closed door.

'Go and wash your mouth out.'

He cries again, staring at the ceiling so that the tears run down to his ears.

My son, he is full of hatred. For me, for everything. He spits when he speaks. When he shouts his voice breaks high and he is like a woman. He grinds his teeth and his skin goes white about his mouth. His hands shake. All because I ask him where he goes. Perhaps I need to show him more love. Care for him more than I do.

I mount the stairs quietly to apologise. My son, I am sorry. I do it because I love you. Let me put my arm around you and talk like we used to on the bus from Toome. Why do you fight away from me?

The door swings open and he pushes a hand-gun beneath the pillow. Seen long enough, black and squat, dull like a garden slug. He sits, my son, his hands idling empty, staring hatred.

'Why do you always spy on me, you nosey old bastard?' His voice breaks, his eyes bulge.

'What's that? Under your pillow?'

'It's none of your fucking business.'

He kicks the door closed in my face with his bare foot.

I am in the dark of the landing. I must pray for him. On my bended knees I will pray for him to be safe. Perhaps I did not see what I saw. Maybe I am mistaken. My son rides pillion on a motor-bike. Tonight I will not sleep. I do not think I will sleep again.

It is ten o'clock. The news begins. Like a woman I stand drying a plate, watching the headlines. There is a ring at the door. The boy answers it, his shirt-tail out. Voices in the hallway.

My son with friends. Talking. What he does not do with me.

There is a bang. The dish-cloth drops from my hand and I run to the kitchen door. Not believing, I look into the hallway. There is a strange smell. My son is lying on the floor, his head on the bottom stair, his feet on the threshold. The news has come to my door. The house is open to the night. There is no one else. I go to him with damp hands.

'Are you hurt?'

Blood is spilling from his nose.

They have punched you and you are not badly hurt. Your nose is bleeding. Something cold at the back of your neck.

I take my son's limp head in my hands and see a hole in his nose that should not be there. At the base of his nostril.

My son, let me put my arms around you.

A TIME TO DANCE

Nelson, with a patch over one eye, stood looking idly into Mothercare's window. The sun was bright behind him and made a mirror out of the glass. He looked at his patch with distaste and felt it with his finger. The Elastoplast was rough and dry and he disliked the feel of it. Bracing himself for the pain, he ripped it off and let a yell out of him. A woman looked down at him curiously to see why he had made the noise, but by that time he had the patch in his pocket. He knew without looking that some of his eyebrow would be on it.

He had spent most of the morning in the Gardens avoiding distant uniforms, but now that it was coming up to lunch-time he braved it on to the street. He had kept his patch on longer than usual because his mother had told him the night before that if he didn't wear it he would go 'stark, staring blind'.

Nelson was worried because he knew what it was like to be blind. The doctor at the eye clinic had given him a box of patches that would last for most of his lifetime. Opticludes. One day Nelson had worn two and tried to get to the end of the street and back. It was a terrible feeling. He had to hold his head back in case it bumped into anything and keep waving his hands in front of him backwards and forwards like windscreen wipers. He kept tramping on tin cans and heard them trundle emptily away. Broken glass crackled under his feet and he could not figure out how close to the wall he was. Several times he heard footsteps approaching, slowing down as if they were going to attack him in his helplessness, then walking away. One of the footsteps even laughed. Then he heard a voice he knew only too well.

'Jesus, Nelson, what are you up to this time?' It was his mother. She led him back to the house with her voice blaring in his ear.

She was always shouting. Last night, for instance, she had started into him for watching T.V. from the side. She had dragged him round to the chair in front of it.

'That's the way the manufacturers make the sets. They put the picture on the front. But oh no, that's not good enough for our Nelson. He has to watch it from the side. Squint, my arse, you'll just go blind – stark, staring blind.'

Nelson had then turned his head and watched it from the front. She had never mentioned the blindness before. Up until now all she had said was, 'If you don't wear them patches that eye of yours will turn in till it's looking at your brains. God knows, not that it'll have much to look at.'

His mother was Irish. That was why she had a name like Skelly. That was why she talked funny. But she was proud of the way she talked and nothing angered her more than to hear Nelson saying 'Ah ken' and 'What like is it?' She kept telling him that someday they were going back, when she had enough ha'pence scraped together. 'Until then I'll not let them make a Scotchman out of you.' But Nelson talked the way he talked.

His mother had called him Nelson because she said she thought that his father had been a seafaring man. The day the boy was born she had read an article in the *Reader's Digest* about Nelson Rockefeller, one of the richest men in the world. It seemed only right to give the boy a good start. She thought it also had the advantage that it couldn't be shortened, but she was wrong. Most of the boys in the scheme called him Nelly Skelly.

He wondered if he should sneak back to school for dinner then skive off again in the afternoon. They had good dinners at school – like a hotel, with choices. Chips and magic things like rhubarb crumble. There was one big dinner-woman who gave him extra every time she saw him. She told him he needed fattening. The only draw-back to the whole system was that he was on free dinners. Other people in his class were given their dinner money and it was up to them whether they went without a dinner and bought Coke and sweets and stuff with the money. It was a choice Nelson didn't have, so he had to invent other things to get the money out of his mother. In Lent there were the Black Babies; library fines were worth the odd

10p, although, as yet, he had not taken a book from the school library – and anyway they didn't have to pay fines, even if they were late; the Home Economics Department asked them to bring in money to buy their ingredients and Nelson would always add 20p to it.

'What the hell are they teaching you to cook – sides of beef?' his mother would yell. Outdoor pursuits required extra money. But even though they had ended after the second term, Nelson went on asking for the 50p on a Friday – 'to go horse riding'. His mother would never part with money without a speech of some sort.

'Horse riding? Horse riding! Jesus, I don't know what sort of a school I've sent you to. Is Princess Anne in your class or something? Holy God, horse riding.'

Outdoor pursuits was mostly walking round museums on wet days and, when it was dry, the occasional trip to Portobello beach to write on a flapping piece of foolscap the signs of pollution you could see. Nelson felt that the best outdoor pursuit of the lot was what he was doing now. Skiving. At least that way you could do what you liked.

He groped in his pocket for the change out of his 50p and went into a shop. He bought a giant thing of bubble-gum and crammed it into his mouth. It was hard and dry at first and he couldn't answer the woman when she spoke to him.

'Whaaungh?'

'Pick the paper off the floor, son! Use the basket.'

He picked the paper up and screwed it into a ball. He aimed to miss the basket, just to spite her, but it went in. By the time he reached the bottom of the street the gum was chewy. He thrust his tongue into the middle of it and blew. A small disappointing bubble burst with a plip. It was not until the far end of Princes Street that he managed to blow big ones, pink and wobbling, that he could see at the end of his nose, which burst well and had to be gathered in shreds from his chin.

Then suddenly the crowds of shoppers parted and he saw his mother. In the same instant she saw him. She was on him before he could even think of running. She grabbed him by the fur of his parka and began screaming into his face.

'In the name of God, Nelson, what are you doing here? Why aren't you at school?' She began shaking him. 'Do you realise what this means? They'll put me in bloody jail. It'll be bloody Saughton for me, and no mistake.' She had her teeth gritted together and her mouth was slanting in her face. Then Nelson started to shout.

'Help! Help!' he yelled.

A woman with an enormous chest like a pigeon stopped. 'What's happening?' she said.

Nelson's mother turned on her. 'It's none of your bloody business.'

'I'm being kidnapped,' yelled Nelson.

'Young woman. Young woman . . .' said the lady with the large chest, trying to tap Nelson's mother on the shoulder with her umbrella, but Mrs Skelly turned with such a snarl that the woman edged away hesitatingly and looked over her shoulder and tut-tutted just loudly enough for the passing crowd to hear her.

'Help! I'm being kidnapped,' screamed Nelson, but everybody walked past looking the other way. His mother squatted down in front of him, still holding on to his jacket. She lowered her voice and tried to make it sound reasonable.

'Look Nelson, love. Listen. If you're skiving school, do you realise what'll happen to me? In Primary the Children's Panel threatened to send me to court. You're only at that Secondary and already that Sub-Attendance Committee thing wanted to fine me. Jesus, if you're caught again . . .'

Nelson stopped struggling. The change in her tone had quietened him down. She straightened up and looked wildly about her, wondering what to do.

'You've got to go straight back to school, do you hear me?'

'Yes.'

'Promise me you'll go.' The boy looked down at the ground. 'Promise?' The boy made no answer.

'I'll kill you if you don't go back. I'd take you myself only I've my work to go to. I'm late as it is.'

Again she looked around as if she would see someone who would suddenly help her. Still she held on to his jacket. She was biting her lip.

'Oh God, Nelson.'

The boy blew a flesh-pink bubble and snapped it between his teeth. She shook him.

'That bloody bubble-gum.'

There was a loud explosion as the one o'clock gun went off. They both leapt.

'Oh Jesus, that gun puts the heart sideways in me every time it goes off. Come on, son, you'll have to come with me. I'm late. I don't know what they'll say when they see you but I'm bloody taking you to school by the ear. You hear me?'

She began rushing along the street, Nelson's sleeve in one hand, her carrier bag in the other. The boy had to run to keep from being dragged.

'Don't you dare try a trick like that again. Kidnapped, my arse. Nelson, if I knew somebody who would kidnap you – I'd pay *him* the money. Embarrassing me on the street like that.'

They turned off the main road and went into a hallway and up carpeted stairs which had full-length mirrors along one side. Nelson stopped to make faces at himself but his mother chugged at his arm. At the head of the stairs stood a fat man in his shirtsleeves.

'What the hell is this?' he said. 'You're late, and what the hell is that?' He looked down from over his stomach at Nelson.

'I'll explain later,' she said. 'I'll make sure he stays in the room.'

'You should be on *now*,' said the fat man and turned and walked away through the swing doors. They followed him and Nelson saw, before his mother pushed him into the room, that it was a bar, plush and carpeted with crowds of men standing drinking.

'You sit here, Nelson, until I'm finished and then I'm taking you back to that school. You'll get nowhere if you don't do your lessons. I have to get changed now.'

She set her carrier bag on the floor and kicked off her shoes. Nelson sat down, watching her. She stopped and looked over her shoulder at him, biting her lip.

'Where's that bloody eyepatch you should be wearing?' Nelson indicated his pocket.

'Well, wear it then.' Nelson took the crumpled patch from his pocket, tugging bits of it unstuck to get it flat before he stuck it over his bad eye. His mother took out her handbag and began rooting about at the bottom of it. Nelson heard the rattle of her bottles of scent and tubes of lipstick.

'Ah,' she said and produced another eyepatch, flicking it clean. 'Put another one on till I get changed. I don't want you noseying at me.' She came to him, pulling away the white backing to the patch, and stuck it over his remaining eye. He imagined her concentrating, the tip of her tongue stuck out. She pressed his eyebrows with her thumbs, making sure that the patches were stuck.

'Now don't move, or you'll bump into something.'

Nelson heard the slither of her clothes and her small grunts as she hurriedly got changed. Then he heard her rustle in her bag, the soft pop and rattle as she opened her capsules. Her 'tantalisers' she called them, small black and red torpedoes. Then he heard her voice.

'Just you stay like that till I come back. That way you'll come to no harm. You hear me, Nelson? If I come back in here and you have those things off, I'll *kill* you. I'll not be long.'

Nelson nodded from his darkness.

'The door will be locked, so there's no running away.'

'Ah ken.'

Suddenly his darkness exploded with lights as he felt her bony hand strike his ear.

'You don't ken things, Nelson. You *know* them.'

He heard her go out and the key turn in the lock. His ear sang and he felt it was hot. He turned his face up to the ceiling. She had left the light on because he could see pinkish through the patches. He smelt the beer and stale smoke. Outside the room pop music had started up, very loudly. He heard the deep notes pound through to where he sat. He felt his ear with his hand and it *was* hot.

Making small *aww* sounds of excruciating pain, he slowly detached both eyepatches from the bridge of the nose outwards. In case his mother should come back he did not take them off completely, but left them hinged to the sides of his eyes. When he turned to look around him they flapped like blinkers.

It wasn't really a room, more a broom cupboard. Crates were

stacked against one wall; brushes and mops and buckets stood near a very low sink; on a row of coat-hooks hung some limp raincoats and stained white jackets; his mother's stuff hung on the last hook. The floor was covered with tramped-flat cork tips. Nelson got up to look at what he was sitting on. It was a crate of empties. He went to the keyhole and looked out, but all he could see was a patch of wallpaper opposite. Above the door was a narrow window. He looked up at it, his eyepatches falling back to touch his ears. He went over to the sink and had a drink of water from the low tap, sucking noisily at the column of water as it splashed into the sink. He stopped and wiped his mouth. The water felt cold after the mint of the bubble-gum. He looked up at his mother's things, hanging on the hook; her tights and drawers were as she wore them, but inside out and hanging knock-kneed on top of everything. In her bag he found her blonde wig and tried it on, smelling the perfume of it as he did so. At home he liked noseying in his mother's room; smelling all her bottles of make-up; seeing her spangled things. He had to stand on the crate to see himself but the mirror was all brown measles under its surface and the eyepatches ruined the effect. He sat down again and began pulling at the bubble-gum, seeing how long he could make it stretch before it broke. Still the music pounded outside. It was so loud the vibrations tickled his feet. He sighed and looked up at the window again.

If his mother took him back to school, he could see problems. For starting St John the Baptist's she had bought him a brand new Adidas bag for his books. Over five pounds it had cost her, she said. On his first real skive he had dumped the bag in the bin at the bottom of his stair, every morning for a week, and travelled light into town. On the Friday he came home just in time to see the bin lorry driving away in a cloud of bluish smoke. He had told his mother that the bag had been stolen from the playground during break. She had threatened to phone the school about it but Nelson had hastily assured her that the whole matter was being investigated by none other than the Headmaster himself. This threat put the notion out of his head of asking her for the money to replace the books. At that point he had not decided on a figure. He could maybe try it again some time when all the fuss had died down. But now it was all going to be stirred if his mother took him to school.

He pulled two crates to the door and climbed up but they were not high enough. He put a third one on top, climbed on again, and gingerly straightened, balancing on its rim. On tip-toe he could see out. He couldn't see his mother anywhere. He saw a crowd of men standing in a semicircle. Behind them were some very bright lights, red, yellow and blue. They all had pints in their hands which they didn't seem to be drinking. They were all watching something which Nelson couldn't see. Suddenly the music stopped and the men all began drinking and talking. Standing on tip-toe for so long, Nelson's legs began to shake and he heard the bottles in the crate rattle. He rested for a moment. Then the music started again. He looked to see. The men now just stood looking. It was as if they were seeing a ghost. Then they all cheered louder than the music.

Nelson climbed down and put the crates away from the door so that his mother could get in. He closed his eyepatches over for a while, but still she didn't come. He listened to another record, this time a slow one. He decided to travel blind to get another drink of water. As he did so the music changed to fast. He heard the men cheering again, then the rattle of the key in the lock. Nelson, his arms rotating in front of him, tried to make his way back to the crate. His mother's voice said,

'Don't you dare take those eyepatches off.' Her voice was panting. Then his hand hit up against her. It was her bare stomach, hot and damp with sweat. She guided him to sit down, breathing heavily through her nose.

'I'll just get changed and then you're for school right away, boy.' Nelson nodded. He heard her light a cigarette as she dressed. When she had finished she ripped off his right eyepatch.

'There now, we're ready to go,' she said, ignoring Nelson's anguished yells.

'That's the wrong eye,' he said.

'Oh shit,' said his mother and ripped off the other one, turned it upside down and stuck it over his right eye. The smoke from the cigarette in her mouth trickled up into her eye and she held it half shut. Nelson could see the bright points of sweat shining through her make-up. She still hadn't got her breath back fully yet. She smelt of drink.

On the way out, the fat man with the rolled-up sleeves held out two fivers and Nelson's mother put them into her purse.

'The boy – never again,' he said, looking down at Nelson.

They took the Number Twelve to St John the Baptist's. It was the worst possible time because, just as they were going in, the bell rang for the end of a period and suddenly the quad was full of pupils, all looking at Nelson and his mother. Some sixth-year boys wolf-whistled after her and others stopped to stare. Nelson felt a flush of pride that she was causing a stir. She was dressed in black satiny jeans, very tight, and her pink blouse was knotted, leaving her tanned midriff bare. They went into the office and a secretary came to the window.

'Yes?' she said, looking Mrs Skelly up and down.

'I'd like to see the Head,' she said.

'I'm afraid he's at a meeting. What is it about?'

'About him.' She waved her thumb over her shoulder at Nelson.

'What year is he?'

'What year are you, son?' His mother turned to him.

'First.'

'First Year. Oh, then you'd best see Mr MacDermot, the First Year Housemaster.' The secretary directed them to Mr MacDermot's office. It was at the other side of the school and they had to walk what seemed miles of corridors before they found it. Mrs Skelly's stiletto heels clicked along the tiles.

'It's a wonder you don't get lost in here, son,' she said as she knocked on the Housemaster's door. Mr MacDermot opened it and invited them in. Nelson could see that he too was looking at her, his eyes wide and his face smiley.

'What can I do for you?' he said when they were seated.

'It's him,' said Mrs Skelly. 'He's been skiving again. I caught him this morning.'

'I see,' said Mr MacDermot. He was very young to be a Housemaster. He had a black moustache which he began to stroke with the back of his hand. He paused for a long time. Then he said,

'Remind me of your name, son.'

'– Oh, I'm sorry,' said Mrs Skelly. 'My name is Skelly and this is my boy Nelson.'

'Ah, yes, Skelly.' The Housemaster got up and produced a yellow file from the filing cabinet. 'You must forgive me, but we haven't seen a great deal of Nelson lately.'

'Do you mind if I smoke?' asked Mrs Skelly.

'Not at all,' said the Housemaster, getting up to open the window.

'The trouble is, that the last time we were at that Sub-Attendance Committee thing they said they would take court action if it happened again. And it has.'

'Well, it may not come to that with the Attendance Sub-Committee. If we nip it in the bud. If Nelson makes an effort, isn't that right, Nelson?' Nelson sat silent.

'Speak when the master's speaking to you,' yelled Mrs Skelly.

'Yes,' said Nelson, making it barely audible.

'You're Irish too,' said Mrs Skelly to the Housemaster, smiling.

'That's right,' said Mr MacDermot. 'I thought your accent was familiar. Where do you come from?'

'My family come from just outside Derry. And you?'

'Oh, that's funny. I'm just across the border from you. Donegal.' As they talked, Nelson stared out the window. He had never heard his mother so polite. He could just see a corner of the playing fields and a class coming out with the Gym teacher. Nelson hated Gym more than anything. It was crap. He loathed the changing rooms, the getting stripped in front of others, the stupidity he felt when he missed the ball. The smoke from his mother's cigarette went in an arc towards the open window. Distantly he could hear the class shouting as they started a game of football.

'Nelson! Isn't that right?' said Mr MacDermot loudly.

'What?'

'That even when you are here you don't work hard enough.'

'Hmmm,' said Nelson.

'You don't have to tell me,' said his mother. 'It's not just his eye that's lazy. If you ask me the whole bloody lot of him is. I've never seen him washing a dish in his life and he leaves everything at his backside.'

'Yes,' said the Housemaster. Again he stroked his moustache. 'What is required from Nelson is a change of attitude. Attitude, Nelson. You understand a word like attitude?'

'Yes.'

'He's just not interested in school, Mrs Skelly.'

'I've no room to talk, of course. I had to leave at fifteen,' she said, rolling her eyes in Nelson's direction. 'You know what I mean? Otherwise I might have stayed on and got my exams.'

'I see,' said Mr MacDermot. 'Can we look forward to a change in attitude, Nelson?'

'Hm-hm.'

'Have you no friends in school?' asked the Housemaster.

'Naw.'

'And no interest. You see, you can't be interested in any subject unless you do some work at it. Work pays dividends with interest . . .' he paused and looked at Mrs Skelly. She was inhaling her cigarette. He went on, 'Have you considered the possibility that Nelson may be suffering from school phobia?'

Mrs Skelly looked at him. 'Phobia, my arse,' she said. 'He just doesn't like school.'

'I see. Does he do any work at home then?'

'Not since he had his bag with all his books in it stolen.'

'Stolen?'

Nelson leaned forward in his chair and said loudly and clearly, 'I'm going to try to be better from now on. I am. I am going to try, sir.'

'That's more like it,' said the Housemaster, also edging forward.

'I am not going to skive. I am going to try. Sir, I'm going to do my best.'

'Good boy. I think, Mrs Skelly, if I have a word with the right people and convey to them what we have spoken about, I think there will be no court action. Leave it with me, will you? And I'll see what I can do. Of course it all depends on Nelson. If he is as good as his word. One more truancy and I'll be forced to report it. And he must realise that he has three full years of school to do before he leaves us. You must be aware of my position in this matter. You understand what I'm saying, Nelson?'

'Ah ken,' he said. 'I know.'

'You go off to your class now. I have some more things to say to your mother.'

Nelson rose to his feet and shuffled towards the door. He stopped. 'Where do I go, sir?'

'Have you not got your timetable?'

'No sir. Lost it.'

The Housemaster, tut-tutting, dipped into another file, read a card and told him that he should be at R. K. in Room 72. As he left, Nelson noticed that his mother had put her knee up against the Housemaster's desk and was swaying back in her chair, as she took out another cigarette.

'Bye, love,' she said.

When he went into Room 72 there was a noise of oos and ahhs from the others in the class. He said to the teacher that he had been seeing Mr MacDermot. She gave him a Bible and told him to sit down. He didn't know her name. He had her for English as well as R. K. She was always rabbiting on about poetry.

'You, boy, that just came in. For your benefit, we are talking and reading about organisation. Page 667. About how we should divide our lives up with work and prayer. How we should put each part of the day to use, and each part of the year. This is one of the most beautiful passages in the whole of the Bible. Listen to its rhythms as I read.' She lightly drummed her closed fist on the desk in front of her.

'"There is an appointed time for everything, and a time for every affair under the heavens. A time to be born and a time to die; a time to plant and a time to uproot . . ."'

'What page did you say, Miss?' asked Nelson.

'Six-six-seven,' she snapped and read on, her voice trembling, '"A time to kill and a time to heal; a time to wear down and a time to build. A time to weep and a time to laugh; a time to mourn and a time to dance . . ."'

Nelson looked out of the window, at the tiny white H of the goal posts in the distance. He took his bubble-gum out and stuck it under the desk. The muscles of his jaw ached from chewing the now flavourless mass. He looked down at page 667 with its microscopic print, then put his face close to it. He tore off his eyepatch, thinking that if he was going to become blind then the sooner it happened the better.

MY DEAR PALESTRINA

'Come on, love, it's for your own good,' she said. Rooks from the trees above set up a slow, raucous cawing. Cinders had spilled on the footpath and they cracked and spat beneath their shoes, echoing in the arch of the trees overhead, as they walked the mile from the town to Miss Schwartz's place. The boy stayed one pace behind and slightly to the left of his mother. To show her determination, she had begun by taking his hand but it seemed foolish to be seen dragging a boy of his age. Although now they were separate they were so far gone along the road that she knew she had won. The boy stopped at the old forge and stared at the door into the dark, listening to the high pinging of the blacksmith's hammer.

'Don't have me to go back, Danny, or I'll make an example of you.' She waited, looking over her shoulder at him. His eyes were still red from crying.

Miss Schwartz had a beautifully polished brass knocker on her black front door. It resounded deep within the house. It seemed a long time before she answered. When she did, it was with politeness.

'Yes, can I help you?'

The boy's mother smiled back and nodded down the path to where the boy was standing.

'I want him to have piana lessons,' she said.

Mrs McErlane, panting after the walk, fell into an armchair, propped her bag on her knee and listened as Miss Schwartz struck single notes for her Danny to sing. His voice was clear but not rich and still had reverberations of the long afternoon's crying in it. Her long pale finger poked about the piano and no matter where it went Danny's voice followed it. Then she played clusters of notes and Danny repeated them. She asked the boy to turn away and struck a note.

'Can you find that note?' and Danny played it. She did this again and again and each time the boy found it. At the doorstep on the way out Miss Schwartz said that the pleasure in teaching would be hers. *Auf wiedersehen.*

'Did you hear that?' said Mrs McErlane on the way home. 'Anyway it will be good for you. It's a lovely thing to have. The others is too old to learn now.'

Danny said nothing but hunched his shoulders against the darkness and the cold of the night that was coming on.

'I hated to think of that piana going to waste,' she said.

Because the McErlanes had a boy young enough to learn, it was they who got the piano when Uncle George died. They also got a lawn mower and a vacuum cleaner, even though they had no carpet in the house.

The piano came in the night when Danny was in bed. When he had visited Uncle George, Danny would slip into the front room on his own and climb up on the piano stool and single-finger notes. He liked to play the white ones because afterwards, when he struck a black note it was so sad that it gave him a funny feeling in his tummy. The piano stool had a padded seat which opened. Inside were wads of old sheet music with film stars' pictures on the front.

Bing Crosby, Johnny Ray, Rosemary Clooney. He had heard her singing on the radio.

> A cannon-ball don't pay no mind
> Whether you're gentle or you're kind.

It was about a civil war. He liked the way she twirled her voice. When he tried to sing that song he always put on an American accent.

> Two brothers on their way
> One wore blue and one wore grey.

After school he walked to his first lesson on a road that fumed with dry snow and wind. The door of the forge was closed and the place silent. On the way out a car passed him, returning to town. A white face pressed itself up against the back window. White hair, blue glasses and a red tongue sticking out at him. Mingo. Danny hated Mingo, with his strange eyes and white fleshy skin. Some of the boys in school had told him that Mingo was from Albania and they were all like that there.

Miss Schwartz had a warm fire blazing in her front room.

'You must be cold,' she said. 'Come, warm your hands.'

Danny held out his chapped hands and felt the heat on them. He rubbed the warmed palms on his bare knees, trying to thaw them out. Miss Schwartz smiled.

'You are such a good-looking boy,' she said. Danny stood embarrassed, his brown eyes averted, looking down at the fire. His blond hair had been cuffed and ruffled by the wind and gave him a wild look.

'You look like the Angel Gabriel,' she said and pulled her mouth into a wide smile. 'Sit down – near the fire – and let me tell you about music.' She spoke with a strange accent, as if some of her words were squeezed into the wrong shape. Her mouth was elastic. Danny knew every word she said but it was not the way he had heard anybody talk before.

'What kind of music do you like?'

'I dunno,' said Danny after a moment's thought.

'Do you have a favourite singer?'

'I like Elvis.'

'Rubbish,' she said, still smiling. 'What I am going to tell you now you will not believe. You will not understand it, but I have to tell you all the same. I will teach you about things. I hope I will nurture in you a love you will never forget.' The smile had disappeared from her face and her eyes widened and drilled into Danny's. 'Music is the most beautiful thing in the world. Today beautiful is a word that has been dirtied, but I mean it truly. Beautiful.' She let the word hang in the air between them.

'Music is why I do not die. Other people – they have blood put in their arms,' she stabbed a fingernail at the inside of her elbow, 'I am kept alive by music. It is the food of love, as you say. I stress that you will not believe me, but what you *must* do is *trust* me. I will show it to you if you will let me. Rilke says that music begins where speech ends – and he should know.'

Danny looked at her and the two pin-head reflections of the fire in her eyes. She was good-looking, with a long thin face and a broad mouth which she was constantly contorting as she wrestled to make the strange words clear. She did not wear lipstick like his mother. Her jet black hair was pulled back into a knot at the back of her neck and her parting was straight, as if ruled. Danny had seen her from the back when she played the organ in church and occasionally when she had come into the town shops, a dark figure hardly worth notice, her basket on her stiff forearm, her wrist to the sky. But here she seemed to fill the room with her talk and her flashing hands. All the time she sat on the edge of her chair, leaning towards him, talking into him. He swayed back as far as his stool would let him.

'Wait,' she said. She got up and went over to a bureau and took out a sheet of paper from a typewriter. She held it up.

'Look. Look hard at this.'

Danny looked but could see nothing, only the slight curl at the bottom of the page where it had lain in the machine.

'I give you a white sheet of paper. It is nothing. But the black marks . . . The black marks, Danny. That is what makes it important. The music, the words. They are the black marks,' she said, and her whole face blazed with passion. 'I am going to teach you those marks. Then I am going to teach you to make the most wonderful music from them. Come, let us begin.' As she sat down at the piano she snorted, 'Elvis Presley!'

When the lesson was over Miss Schwartz got up and went out, saying that they both deserved a cup of tea. Danny sat on the piano stool and looked at the room. It was a strange place, covered in pictures. Behind the pictures the wallpaper was dark brown, or else so old that it looked dark brown. There were plants in pots standing in saucers all over the place. Large dark green spikes with leathery leaves, small hanging plants, one with a pale flower on it. The wind pressured round the house and buffeted in the chimney. He could hear the ticking of fresh snow on the windows and the drone of a lorry taking the hill.

'I hope it lies,' he said to himself. The fire hissed and blew out a small feather of flame.

Miss Schwartz, carrying a tray, closed the door with her toe, which peeped out from her dressing-gown. It was of black silk, long to the floor and hanging loosely about her body. On the back it had a strange Chinese pattern in scarlet and green and silver threads. It reminded Danny of the one the magician wore in the Rupert Bear strip in the *Daily Express*.

'Now, while we drink our tea I will have to play you some music,' she said. She lifted the lid of one of the pieces of furniture and put on a record. She turned it up so loud that the music bulged in the room. Danny had never heard anything like it and he hated it. It had no tune and he kept waiting for somebody to sing but nobody did. He ate two biscuits and drank his tea as quickly as he could. Then she let him go.

On his way home the January wind cut his face and riffled the practice music he carried clenched under his arm. In the telephone wires above he heard the sounds of a peeled privet switch being whipped through the air again and again and again. At the forge he crossed the road to have a closer look. It was more of a shack than a building, with walls made of corrugated iron and hardboard of different faded and peeling colours. Someone had cleaned a paintbrush by the door or had tried out various colours on the wall. The place was surrounded by bits of broken and rusting machinery from farms. From the dark came the rhythmic sound of hammering. Danny edged into the open doorway and it stopped. A man's voice came out of the blackness.

'What do you want, lad?'

Danny jumped.

'C'mere,' said the voice. Danny moved to the threshold, trying to see into the gloom. 'What can I do for you?'

'Just looking.'

'Well, you'll never see from out there. Come in.'

The place smelt of metal and coke fumes and oil. Danny could make out a man in a leather apron. He looked too young to be a blacksmith, with his tight black curly hair.

'What's your name?' he asked. When Danny told him he thought for a moment. 'Your Da's a bus driver? Am I right or am I wrong?'

The man talked as he worked, heating a strip of metal in the coke of his fire and hammering it while it was red. Each hammer blow pulsed through Danny's head like the record at Miss Schwartz's.

'And what has you up this end of town?' Danny told him he was going to music.

'To Miss Warts and all?' he shouted. 'I wonder would she like this song?' He began to sing loudly, and bang his hammer to the rhythm, 'If I was a blackbird'. When he came to the line 'And I'd bury my head on her lily white breast', he winked at Danny. He had a good voice and could get twirls into it – like Rosemary Clooney. When he had finished the song, he asked Danny about school. He didn't seem to think much of it because he said it was the worst place to learn anything. He talked a lot and Danny helped him to work the bellows for his fire. When he took the red hot metal out of the fire, it had tiny lights that flashed and disappeared. The man said that that was the dust touching it and burning up. As the smith worked, Danny looked at his arms, not muscled, but tight with sinews and strings, pounding at the metal. He shouted to make himself heard over his work.

'The schools make the people they want. They get rid of their cutting edge. That's how they keep us quiet.' He nodded that he wanted Danny to pump harder. 'It'll not always be like that. Our time will come, boy, and it'll not be horseshoes we'll be beating out. No, sir.'

Danny was breathless with the pumping. The blacksmith looked at him, raising one eyebrow.

'Are you the lad that was very ill not so long ago?'

Danny breathed and nodded.

'Then maybe you better quit and be off home.'

Danny picked up his music from the cluttered bench and blew the brown rust from it. As he left the man shouted after him,

'Just give us a call any time you're passing, son.'

Danny tried to walk the road in step to the fading ring of his hammer.

*

When he came through the back door his mother yelled at him,
  'Where's the good cap I knitted for you?'
  'Oh, sorry, I left it behind.'
  She began to help him unbutton his coat, scolding with concern.
  'You are not strong yet, you know. I don't know what that woman was thinking of, letting you out without it. Are your ears not freezing?'
  'I'm O.K.'
  'You are not indeed. I never met your equal for catching things. There's not much the doctors don't know about that you haven't had. Twice over maybe. You must look after yourself, Danny.'
  The boy went up to his room and lay on the bed. His mother was right. He seemed to be constantly ill. The last time had been the worst. The one nice thing he could remember about it was having the bed made while he was in it. He would lie there while his mother pulled all the bed-clothes off, then she would straighten the sheet beneath him, tugging it with exaggerated grunts. 'The weight of you!' she would say. He would run his fingers fan-like across the smoothness under him. His mother, separating out the clothes and standing at the end of the bed, would flap the upper sheet to make it fall soothingly on top of him. It came slow and cool and milky down over him with a breath of cotton-smelling air. It was almost transparent and he could look down at his feet and see himself in a white world – his tent, his isolation. The light came through, but he was cut off. He made no attempt to take the sheet down from his face. He heard her voice, then felt the heavier blankets fall across his body, the light disappearing. Only then would he turn back the sheet and look at her. He had wanted to remain suspended in the moment of the sheet, in its relaxation and whiteness, but it always came to an end. He knew that he made peaks at his head and at his toes. He had seen furniture covered this way, and his grandfather in the hospital morgue.
  'Now sit up for your medicine.' It had been white too. Cloying sweetness trying to disguise a revolting base flavour. His father gave him sixpence if he could keep it down. After a week he had a shilling on his bedside table. His mother opened *her* mouth when she gave him the stuff. She set the spoon down and lifted the bowl in

readiness. His tongue furred with the mixture. Little squirts of warm saliva came into his mouth and he gagged but it stayed down. 'Good boy. Another sixpence. Sure, you'll be rich by the end of the bottle.'

Now he rolled off the bed and decided to go downstairs and let his mother hear what he had learned that day.

'First, empty that,' she said. Danny went to the compost heap at the bottom of the garden with the scraps. On the way back he swung the empty colander and listened to the quiet hoot and whine of the wind through its holes. He liked listening to things. In the room with the two clocks he liked to hear how the ticks would catch up with one another, have the same double tick for a moment and then whisper off into two separate ticks again. The hiss of Miss Schwartz's dressing-gown as she moved. The thin squeak of his compass as he opened its legs. The pop his father's lips made when he was lighting his pipe. He left the empty colander on the draining board.

'Are you ready?' he asked her. His mother listened to his scales, her head cocked to one side, drying her hands on her apron. He played them haltingly.

'There's not much of a tune to that,' she said. 'How much do you have to practise?'

'Until I get it right, she says.'

'Who's "she", something the cat brought in?'

'Miss Schwartz.'

'Have a bit of respect, Danny.'

Danny seemed to get it right with little effort, but what little he did he had to be goaded into by his mother. There was nothing Miss Schwartz taught him that he couldn't do after several attempts. So, in the first months, Miss Schwartz increased the level of difficulty and the duration of his practice pieces. And he was always able for them.

Along the sides of the lane that led to her house Danny saw the yellow celandine and the white ones with the strange smell. Wild garlic, she had called them. He met Mingo coming down the lane to where his father had parked the car. Mingo made a vulgar noise with his mouth as they passed but Danny ignored him. Miss Schwartz held the door open and he gave her the envelope with the clinking money in it.

Seated at the piano, he asked,

'Is Mingo any good?'

'Mingo?'

'The boy with the white hair that's just left.'

'Is that what you call him? That boy . . .' she paused, 'is average.'

'Is he as good as me?'

'Do not worry about other people. You will go forward as fast as you are able.' She smiled at him the way he looked at her, then added, 'You knew more on your first day than Mingo, as you call him, will in all his life. Now let me hear you play.'

Danny played his piece and when he had finished she shrugged and smiled.

'It is perfect,' she said, 'but still it is mechanical. Danny, you are a little machine. A pianola. Listen.' She sat on the stool and began to play. Danny listened, watching her closed eyes, the almost impercep-tible sway of her body as she stroked music from the notes. 'At this point it must sing. *Cantabile.*' She talked over her playing, pointing out to him where he had gone wrong. 'Now try it again.'

Danny played the piece again and when it was over Miss Schwartz's eyes sparkled.

'That was much better,' she said. 'Beautiful. You learn so quickly.'

'I can't play like that at home,' he said, 'but here it's different.'

'I think,' said Miss Schwartz, 'it is time for an examination. It will please your mother. And I think it will please you because we will get a trip to the city. And . . .' she added after more thought, 'it will please me. I will write a note to your mother. Although I will not say this in the letter, if you have any difficulties with the bus fare I will pay it myself. Do not say it, of course, if there are no difficulties.'

They began to work on a new piece by her darling Schubert and when she felt they had accomplished enough she got up and made tea.

Alone in the room, Danny stared at the pictures. Silhouettes, she called them. Jet black outlines of composers she had named. Beethoven,

Mahler on the tips of his toes, Schubert. He liked Beethoven the best, the way his hair sprouted in all directions.

As they drank their tea she played again the record that she had played at their first lesson. Now Danny knew it and could hum the melody as it played.

Some weeks ago, when she had come back in with the tea, she had found Danny in the corner, crouched looking at her records. She kept them in a huge set of books, each page with a circular hole in it so that you could see the label of the record. Danny turned the stiff pages of the records, carefully looking at the labels, scarlet ones with a dog barking into a horn, green ones with the title in tilted writing. He took out a record and looked closely at its surface, angling it to the light. Intense black with light shining in the grooves. She handled them like eggs. When she came in all she said was, 'Be careful, Danny.' She poured the tea and then continued her sentence, 'or they will end up like this.' She leaned over and lifted a record which had a large bite out of its side.

'Some boys who come here are not as careful as you. Goodbye, Dinu Lipatti. I think I will have to make a flower-pot out of you. You see?' She pointed to one of her plants. A record had been folded up in some way to make a container. 'You heat it and you mould it until it is the shape you want. I hate to waste anything. That's what comes of the war.' She bit into her gingersnap and said through her chewing,

'I would like to stand on his glasses.'

Danny liked to dip his into his tea and bite the warm, mushy sweetness.

When he handed Miss Schwartz's note to his mother, she ruffled his hair with her hand.

'You're losing your blondness,' she said, 'but the sun in the summer should bring it back again.' When she had finished the letter, the boy looked at her for a decision.

'Yes, you can go,' she said. 'But you'll have to stay the night. I'll not have you travelling that much in one day. Maybe your Aunt Letty would keep you.'

*

In the city they went to the Assembly Rooms and Danny passed his examination with the highest commendation. On the way down the steps, Miss Schwartz took his hand and although he made a slight attempt to take it away, she held tightly on to it. Then without looking at him, staring straight ahead into the rush hour traffic, she said,

'It's *not* too late. You can be great. If you try you can be really great.' She squeezed his hand so hard it hurt. Then she let it go.

'Did you say that to me?' asked Danny.

'Yes, Danny. To you.'

Afterwards they met a friend of Miss Schwartz's and went for tea in The Cottar's Kitchen. Danny had never seen her in such a joyful mood. She laughed and talked and praised him so much that he became embarrassed. She called him '*mein Lieber*' and introduced him to her friend as her star pupil, her *Wunderkind*.

'. . . and this is Mr Wyroslaski. He plays the cello in a symphony orchestra.'

He was a tall man with a very thin face. He had dark brown eyes, deep eyes, not unlike Miss Schwartz's own. His hair was very long, almost like a woman's.

'Why do all music people have funny names?' Danny asked.

'Like what?' asked Miss Schwartz.

'Like Schwartz and Wyro . . . Wyro – your name,' he said, nodding at her friend, 'and all those composers.'

'Names do not matter; you, *mein Lieber*, will be a great musician one day.'

'My name is Danny McErlane,' and the way he said it made them all laugh. Miss Schwartz leaned across the table and smacked a kiss off Danny's forehead. He blushed and looked down at his plate.

'Besides,' said Mr Wyroslaski, 'there is John Field. He is an Irish composer. Names do not matter. What matters is the heart, the mind. Did you ever hear of a composer called Joe Green?'

Danny nodded that he hadn't.

'That is English for Giuseppe Verdi.'

'Who's he?' asked Danny. He joined uncertainly in the laughter his question had started. Mr Wyroslaski looked at him and produced a

large handkerchief from his pocket. He slowly folded it into a pad
which he licked and leaned over to Danny.

'Marysia, you leave your mark on everyone.' He rubbed Danny's
forehead hard. It surprised Danny that Miss Schwartz had a first
name. He sounded it over in his mind, Maur-ish-a, Maur-ish-a. He
never imagined himself calling her anything but Miss Schwartz.

Today she looked different. When she had come out of the Ladies'
Room her black hair was down, falling over her shoulders. Her
normally sallow cheekbones were pink and her eyes seemed to sparkle
and flash more than they did in the darkness of her sitting room at
home. She wore a brown suit and a blouse of creamy lace. At her
throat was a cameo brooch which matched the brown of her suit. It
was the first time Danny had seen her legs, the first time he had seen
her out of her dressing-gown.

Danny had begun to dislike Mr Wyroslaski. He had pulled away
from the handkerchief but the man's bony hand had held the back of
his neck so that he couldn't. Now as Wyroslaski listened to Miss
Schwartz his mouth hung open and his eyebrows were raised like pause
markings, as if he did not believe what she was saying. His face was
prepared for laughter even though nothing funny was being said. They
were talking too much. Danny began reading the stained menu. Then
Wyroslaski lowered one eyebrow and said something in a foreign
language at which Miss Schwartz laughed, covering her lower face
with both hands. She replied to him in the same sort of language.
Danny turned the menu over but there was nothing on the back of it.

Eventually she turned to Danny and said,

'He is such a handsome boy, my archangel, isn't he? *Mein Lieber*,
we all must go. Your Aunt Letty will be worried about you. Mr
Wyroslaski has kindly said that he will drive you there in his car.
What do you say?'

'Thank you,' said Danny.

'We'll drop you off and I'll see you in good time for the bus in
the morning.'

As they rose from the table, Mr Wyroslaski flicked his hair out
from his collar with his knuckled cellist's hand.

*

The next day on the long bus journey home, Miss Schwartz was quiet and often seemed not to be interested in or understand what Danny said to her. She did point out the freshness and greenness of everything. Hedges flashed by, fields moved, mountains turned in the distance.

'It is spring. The sap is rising, quickening in all things. Do you not feel it?'

'No,' said Danny. And they lapsed into silence again.

At the next lesson, Miss Schwartz opened the door in her familiar black dressing-gown.

'Well, Danny, have you forgiven me?'

'What for?'

'I thought you had fallen out with me. Is that not so?'

'No.'

'You did not feel neglected?'

Danny began searching through his pages for his piece. He shrugged.

'It was *your* day, Danny. It was wrong of me to enjoy it.' He set his music on the piano.

'What did you think of Mr Wyroslaski? Wasn't he . . .'

'He smiled too much,' Danny interrupted her.

'You *are* annoyed, aren't you, Danny?'

'No.'

And she touched his hair with her extended hand and her face opened in a warm smile of disbelief and delight.

After he played for her she asked,

'How did your mother like your certificate?'

'She says she's going to get Dad to frame it.'

'Tell her not to bother. There will be more. Bigger and better ones. And what's more, you can tell her I will give you extra lessons and it doesn't matter whether she can pay or not. Two a week for the price of one. How would you like that?'

Danny was not so sure, but he said yes to please her.

In July Danny's sister married. The remainder of the guests from the hotel all crowded into the McErlanes' front room after the reception.

Danny's mother sat stunned and a little drunk. Her husband, Harry, was even more drunk, but had through practice learned to keep going. He was asking everybody what they would have to drink. Aunt Letty, who didn't drink, was helping him pour the whiskeys and uncork the stout. Danny sat in the corner with an orange juice in his hand which he dared not drink. Everybody that day had bought him an orange juice.

'Well, that's that,' said Harry, falling back into an armchair, his knees still bent. He waved his thumb in the direction of the corner. 'There's only one left. The shakings of the bag has yet to go.'

'It'll be a while yet, Harry,' said a neighbour, 'and he'll only go when the notion takes him. He'll not be forced.'

Harry blinked his eyes and focused on whoever had spoken. It was Red Tam.

'Tam, I hope you're not meaning anything by that remark.'

'What do you mean "meaning"?'

'About being forced. There was no forcing at today's match and well you know it.'

'The child, Harry,' warned Mrs McErlane.

'My girl is a good girl. She'd have none of that sort of filth.' Danny's father spat the last word out.

'Aye, I know. Time will tell,' said Red Tam.

'What the bloody hell do you mean, "time will tell"? If it's a fight you want, Red Tam, we'll settle it right now.' He struggled to escape from the armchair. Red Tam put up his hands and laughed.

'I'm saying, Harry, that time will prove you right. That's all. You're too jumpy, man.'

Harry was not so sure. Mrs McErlane interrupted.

'Danny is going to play the piano for us. Won't you, son? A bit of entertainment will settle us all.'

'The old Joanna,' someone shouted above the din.

'Good stuff.' A spatter of applause went round the room. Danny blushed.

'I'd wash my hands of any girl that would allow herself to be led into that sort of dirt before marriage.'

'It happens, Harry. It happens.'

'Not in my house it doesn't.'

'Look at big Maureen from Bank Street. Thirty-two years old, they say. At her age you'd think she'd have known better.'

'An animal,' said Harry, 'if ever there was one. There was that many of them she didn't know who to blame. The beasts of the field . . .'

'Stop it, Harry. The child,' hissed Mrs McErlane. 'Go and get your music, son.' She turned in explanation to her neighbour, saying, 'He's not allowed to play without it.'

Danny lurched shyly from the corner, saying that he wouldn't, but hands grabbed him and guided him through the crowded room to the piano. He took out the music for the piece he had just been practising.

'What are you going to give us?'

Danny propped the music up, opened the lid and the room became silent, except for the noise of somebody in the kitchen washing dishes. He began to play a movement from a Haydn sonata.

'That's grand stuff,' said his father proudly through the music.

'Very highfalutin' but good. It's well done,' said Red Tam.

'He has the touch,' said Mrs McErlane. 'So his music teacher tells me. Miss Schwartz, y'know. But you'd know to listen to him yourself.'

Danny played on, the glittering phrases mounting in elegance. Letty leaned in from the kitchen and, aware that she had to be quiet, hissed,

'Harry, will you have another stout?'

'I will, aye.'

'Whisht till we hear,' said Danny's mother. Red Tam rang notes on his empty whiskey glass with a horny fingernail and waved it at Letty. The piece came to an end and Danny's fingers had barely left the keys but they were folding away his music. Everyone applauded loudly.

'What was that?' asked Red Tam.

'Haydn,' said Danny his voice barely audible.

'Grand. Do you know any Winifred Atwell tunes? Now there *is* a pianist. How she does it I just do not know. The woman must have ten fingers on each hand. Do you know "The Black and White Rag" at all?' Red Tam took a gulp of his new whiskey. 'Did you ever hear any of her, Harry?'

'Aye, she's on the wireless, isn't she?'

'You can say that again. She's never off it. The money that woman must be making.' He shook his head in disbelief. 'And her coloured, too.'

'Do you like the rock and roll, Tam?' said Mrs McErlane, winking, 'I thought it would be right up your street.'

'Indeed I do not.'

'You're right there,' Danny's father joined in, 'I can't take this classic stuff the boy is at all the time but I know for sure the rock and roll is rubbish.'

'I like *some* classic stuff,' said Tam. 'Mantovani . . .'

'I like good music – something with a bit of a tune to it,' Harry went on, 'Bing's my man.' He stuck the pipe in the corner of his mouth, his eyes closed, and he began to croon, slurring the words in an American accent,

'A'm dream – ing of a wha – ite Christmas.'

'Aye,' said Tam, interrupting the song, 'that's where the money is at. This rock and roll will not last.'

'It'll not be heard of in another year's time,' agreed Harry. 'The boy there could be making money before long. There's many's the dance band would snap him up if he was older. The classical stuff is all right. It gets the hands going. Good practice, y'know. But the bands is the place where the money is.'

'Or on the wireless,' added Tam. Harry rose and stood expansive and swaying in front of the fire.

'You did well at the speaking, Harry, for one that's not used to it,' said his wife.

'Aye. At least I kept it clean. Which is more than I can say for some.'

'Uncle Bob. Wasn't that a disgrace.'

One of the others, drunker than the rest, overheard and mimicked,

'"The bride and groom have just gone upstairs to get their things together."' Half the people laughed again at the joke. Harry said,

'That man Bob has a mind like a sewer.'

Danny threaded his way to the door and once upstairs threw what was left of his orange down the lavatory.

They worked hard all though that summer, the boy in shirtsleeves at the piano, Miss Schwartz, despite the heat, still in her silk dressing-gown. One day Danny discovered that she wore nothing beneath it because when she bent over to point out some complexity in the score the overlap of her gown rumpled and he saw cradled there the white pear shape of one of her breasts. He pretended not to understand the notation but when she bent over again her dressing-gown was in order.

'The black marks, Danny. Pay attention to the black marks.'

He felt his knees shaky and could not concentrate to play any more.

After the lesson they would go out to the small garden and have tea beneath the apple tree, tea with no milk but a slice of lemon in it – a thing Danny had never heard of. Miss Schwartz had pointed out to him when the flowers had fallen off the tree and each week they inspected the swelling fruit. Lying back in striped deck chairs they both watched the flickering blue of the sky as it dodged between the leaves.

Miss Schwartz had resurrected from the attic an ancient wind-up gramophone on which she played records outdoors. Danny came to know many pieces. Sometimes if there was a concert on the wireless she would open the kitchen window, turn the volume up full and point the set towards the garden. One day, during a performance of Mahler's '*Kindertotenlieder*', she said,

'You know, Danny, the reason I bought this house was because of the garden. We had one just like it when I was a girl. I was about your age when we had to leave it.'

'Where was it?'

'In Poland. A place called Praszka. I remember it as beautiful.'

'Why don't you go back?'

She laughed. 'Because I am too long away. The longer you are away the more you want to go back. And yet you realise the longer you are away the more impossible it is to return. The early monks had a phrase for it – what you suffer. If you died for God, that was simple. That was red martyrdom. If you left your country for God and lived in isolation, that was white martyrdom. To be an exile, to be cut off from your country is a terrible thing.' She smiled. 'I left, not for God, but for convenience. It was a time of fear.' She shuddered and looked up into the apple tree.

Danny sat stripped except for his shorts. He glanced up to where the music was coming from and saw himself reflected brightly in the window. His hair had grown longer and darker. Light from a spoon on the tray lying on the grass reflected into his face.

'But it is not so bad. There are compensations,' she said, smiling at him.

Many times on his way home Danny would stop off at the forge, if it was open, and listen to the blacksmith. He loved the way the man did not shave often and had black bristles on his chin like the baddies in cowboy comics. He was always joking and talking. 'Am I right or am I wrong?' was his favourite phrase. One day, sitting astride his anvil, he talked about Miss Schwartz.

'She's a rum bird, isn't she?'

Danny nodded.

'Why do you agree with me? The nod of the head is the first sign of a yes-man. Well, are you just a yes-man?'

'No,' said Danny and laughed.

'This bloody country is full of yes-men and the most of them's working class.' He dismounted from the anvil and began to rake the fire to life. 'Yes, your honour, no, your honour. Dukes and bloody linen lords squeezing us for everything we've got, setting one side against the other. Divide and conquer. It's an old ploy and the Fenians and Orangemen of this godforsaken country have fallen for it again.' He began to work the bellows himself and the centre of the fire reddened. Danny loved the colour of blue that the small flames took on when the fire was heating up. He could feel the warmth of the fire on the side of his face and his bare arm. The smith was now talking into the fire.

'But a change is coming, Danny Boy. We must be positive. Prepare the ground. Educate the people. Look to the future the way Connolly and Larkin did in 1913.'

He threw the poker down among the fire-irons with a clang and turned to Danny. His face changed and he smiled.

'You haven't a baldy notion what I'm talking about, have you?'

'No.'

'But am I right or am I wrong?'

'You're right,' was always Danny's answer.

It was about this time that Danny began to notice a change in Miss Schwartz. She became moody and did not smile or laugh as much as she used to. One day when he arrived early for his lesson, panting from running most of the mile, it was a long time before she opened the door. When she did she was thrusting a handkerchief up her sleeve and she had obviously been crying. Her eyes were heavy-lidded and red.

When she went in, she said, 'Get your breath back,' and began to water her plants from a small Japanese tea-pot, turning her back on him. She talked to the plants the way other people would talk to a pet. She said it encouraged them to grow.

'Lavish love and attention on growing things and they will not let you down.'

'What about your apple tree? Do you talk to it?'

'It hears music from the house.' She smiled weakly at her own answer.

'But I know houses . . .'

'Your piece, Danny. I want to hear it.'

Danny gave a small, knowing smile. Miss Schwartz half reclined on the sofa at the bay window, her feet gathered beneath her. She turned to face the light and waited. Danny set his music on the chair and began to play. It was the opening movement of the Beethoven C sharp minor Sonata. She disliked calling it, 'The Moonlight'. Danny looked round to see if she had noticed, but her eyes were closed. He played on, trying to feel the music as she would have felt it. Sunlight slanted into the room and Danny thought her face looked haggard. Some of her tight hair had come adrift and hung down by her throat.

When he finished Miss Schwartz opened her eyes and they were glassy with tears.

'How beautiful, Danny,' she said in a whisper.

'You didn't notice,' he said, his feet swinging on the stool.

'What?'

'I played it without the music.'

Miss Schwartz came to him.

'How utterly superb,' she said, taking his face in her hands. She put her arms around his head and gave him a tight squeeze of joy. Danny sensed the huge softness of her breasts against his cheek, enveloping his face, the faded scent of her, the goosefleshy wedge at her throat.

'Oh Danny, how superb.' This time she held him at arm's length, watching his blushes rise. Danny tried to dismiss it.

'I practised it –

all week end,' he said.

'Oh Danny,' Miss Schwartz let a gasp out of her. 'Say that again.'

'I prac –

-tised it all week end.'

'Danny, your voice is breaking.' She put one hand over her mouth, a look of disbelief in her eyes. She sat down at the piano and asked him to sing some of the notes she played. His voice was accurate but kept flicking an octave down. She sat at the piano, her fingers poised above the keyboard, touching it but not heavily enough to depress the keys. Her head was bowed.

'The purest thing in the world is the voice of a boy before it breaks,' she said, 'before he gets hair. Before he begins to think things – like that.' Her face looked the same way as when he played badly.

'But I hardly even notice it, Miss.'

'I do and that is sufficient,' she said. 'Today in the garden I will play you purity.'

The kitchen was full of a mute bustling as she made the tea.

Danny carried the tray out, she the record. It was a boy soprano singing Latin. A blackbird from the ridge-tiles of the roof sang loud enough to drown certain passages. When the music was finished Danny said,

'My Mum says to tell you that I'm going to Grammar School.'

'You passed your Qualifying!' Danny nodded. 'Oh, I'm delighted. Which school?'

'Our Lady's High.'

'Hm.' She thought for a moment and then smiled. 'They don't have a music teacher as yet.'

Danny sat in the school yard eating his cheese piece, a bottle of milk in his hand. He saw Mingo coming across to him, his white hair weaving through the crowd. He had started the Grammar in September as well, but everybody knew that his father was paying for him.

'Hiya, piss face,' said Mingo. 'You still going out to that black bitch for music?' Danny looked at him but could not answer because the tacky cheese had stuck to the roof of his mouth.

'Sucker,' said Mingo. 'I don't have to go any more. Haw-haw-haw.' He spoke the laughter in words.

'Why not?'

'Because my old woman just stopped me. She was talking to Schwartzy in town and she came home and said, "That's it, no more music for you, my lad." Haw-haw-haw. McErlane the sucker still has to go.'

'It's O.K. She's not bad.'

'She has a good pair of tits on her,' said Mingo, groping the air before him. 'She likes you, McErlane. You're her pet. Does she ever let you feel her?' Danny looked at Mingo's flickering white eyelashes – he was constantly blinking behind his tinted glasses. He wanted to punch him in his foul mouth. Instead Danny said,

'I saw them one day.'

'Her tits?'

'Yeah.'

'What were they like?'

'Just ordinary.' Danny gestured with his hands.

'How did you see them?'

'She opened her dressing-gown one day and she wasn't wearing a
. . . thingy.'

'Liar. I don't believe you.'

Danny shrugged and threw his crusts into the wastebasket.

'Were they nice bloopy ones?'

'Yeah.'

Danny sucked the bluish watery milk through a straw until it was
finished. It made a hollow rattling sound at the bottom of the bottle.
He asked Mingo,

'Are you going to music to anybody else?'

'There isn't anybody for miles, thank God.'

'I don't think I'd want to go to anybody else.'

'Aye, not if she shows you her tits, I don't blame you.'

There was a pause. Danny laced the used straw into a knot of
angles.

'She shows them to more than you,' said Mingo.

'What do you mean?'

'She's a ride.'

'What's a ride?'

'Haw-haw-haw, he doesn't know.' Mingo folded up with mock
laughter. 'She's going to have a baby.'

'So what?'

'So she's a ride.'

'How do you know?'

'My Mum says.'

'Your Mum's . . . a ride,' said Danny.

Mingo suddenly reached out and grabbed Danny by the ear, digging
his nails into it shouting,

'Nobody says that about my Mum.'

Danny yelled out in pain and punched. He struck Mingo on the
nose and dislodged his glasses. Mingo let go of Danny's ear and
turned and ran, clutching his glasses to his chest, a trickle of blood
on his white upper lip. He stopped at the far side of the playground
and made a large 'up ya' sign with two fingers. It began at the ground
and ended above his head. He kept doing it, jumping up and down

to exaggerate the gesture. Danny turned away in disgust and slotted
the empty milk bottle into the crate.

The road to Miss Schwartz's place was ankle-deep in brown scuffling
leaves. The apples on the tree had become ripe and she had given
Danny one. He bit into it and a section of its white flesh came away
with a crack. Juice wet his chin.

'It must be the music,' he said crunching.

Now he practised with real determination, getting up with his
father and doing an hour before school. He had to wait until his
father went out because he said he couldn't stand the racket first
thing in the morning. He did another hour in the evening before his
father came in. His mother didn't seem to mind. She slept through
the morning session and she would be out in the kitchen making
Harry's dinner for most of the evening practice. She was glad to see
the piano used so much. One evening Danny's mother came in to lay
the table and stood watching him play.

'Your hair is getting darker. I thought the sun would have helped,'
she said. Danny stopped playing.

'Mum,' he said, 'Miss Schwartz wants to know if you could pay
her in advance for this term.'

'Oh, I don't think so. Look at the money I had to lay out for your
uniform for the High.' She went to the cupboard and looked in the
jar on the top shelf.

'No, tell her I'm sorry but I just can't do it.'

'A whole lot of her pupils are leaving.'

'Why's that?'

'I don't know,' said Danny, closing the lid of the piano.

It was shortly after this that the biscuits stopped. Miss Schwartz
apologised and said that she was getting too fat. However, they still
had tea together.

Danny's father, being a bus driver, got the pick of all the papers left
in his bus, but the only one he would bring home was the *Daily
Express*. He had a great admiration for it.

'First with everything,' he said, 'and no dirt.'

From his armchair he read a piece to Danny that said that the Russians had launched a satellite into space and that it would be possible to see it for the next few evenings if conditions were right.

'It's wonderful too,' he said nodding his head. 'At one end of the world the Russians is firing things into outer space and we still have a blacksmith in the town shoeing horses.'

'He says he knows you,' said Danny.

'Who?'

'The blacksmith.'

'When were you talking to him?' His father's voice had risen in pitch.

Danny shrugged.

'After music,' he said.

'Well, you'll just stop it. You hear me? If I catch you in that forge I'll take my belt off to you.'

The loud voice brought Danny's mother out from the kitchen. Her head was cocked to one side with curiosity and concern.

'Who's this?' she asked.

'You know who – the blacksmith. If he's pouring the same poison into your ear, son, as he's been spewing out in the pub, he's a bad influence. He'd have you into guns and God knows what. Denying religion at the top of his voice.'

'God forgive him,' said Mrs McErlane.

'Aye, and what's more he said they weren't serious in 1922 because they didn't shoot a single priest.'

'Did he say that?'

'Do you hear me, Danny, steer clear of vermin like that or you'll feel the weight of my hand.'

The next lesson Danny had he told Miss Schwartz of the satellite. She agreed that they should go out at six and try to see it.

The night was cold, black and clear as a diamond. A swirl of stars covered the sky so that it seemed impossible to put a finger between two of them. And they stood and waited, their necks craned.

'Isn't it marvellous,' Miss Schwartz said. Danny said nothing. His eye was searching for the satellite.

'Can you see it?' he asked.

When they stopped walking, the crackling underfoot ceased and the silence seemed enormous. In the frost nothing moved. Then Miss Schwartz whispered,

'Look. Look there.' It was as if she had seen an animal and to speak would frighten it.

'Where?'

'Follow my finger.'

In the darkness Danny had to get close to look along the line of her arm. He smelt her perfume and the slightest taint of her own smell, felt his face brush the texture of her clothing.

'There,' she said, 'can you see it? Like a moving star. A little brighter than the rest.'

'Oh yes. I can see it now.'

They stood in silence, close to each other, watching the pin-point of light threading its way up the sky from the horizon. To their left was the faint orange dome of light from the town. When the satellite was directly above them it paused, or seemed to pause, and they held their breath, their faces dished to the sky. Miss Schwartz put her hand round Danny's shoulder.

'How utterly lonely,' she said. 'The immensity of it frightens me.'

They were silent for a long time, watching its descent down the other side of the sky, moving yet hardly moving. Some miles away a dog barked. A car's headlights fanned into the sky and they heard its engine as soft as breathing. Miss Schwartz said in a whisper,

'The music of the spheres. Do you hear it, Danny?'

'No. What is it?'

'It's a sort of silence,' she said and in the darkness he knew that she was smiling. Suddenly she returned to her normal voice.

'What I don't understand, Danny,' her fingers began to knead his shoulder, 'is how it stays up there. I'm very silly about these things. Why does it not fall down?'

'It's kind of suspended. Outside earth's gravity. I think the moon pulls it one way and the earth pulls the other and nobody wins – so it just stays up there. Something like that anyway. The papers say it will fall back to earth after a few months.'

'Caught between the heavens and the earth. How knowledgeable you are, Danny.'

'The science teacher told us today at school.' He began to tremble with the cold.

'Oh, but you are shivering. We must go in or your mother will be angry with me. If you catch a chill she will have my life.'

Inside Miss Schwartz made tea while Danny waited, sitting on his stool by the fire, listening to a record he had chosen himself.

'I'm glad that you picked that one,' she said when she came into the room. 'On Sunday at church I will play you your favourite.'

'Which?'

'The Bach. "*Liebster Jesu, wir sind hier*".'

'What does that mean?'

'"Jesus we are here".'

'Seems a funny thing to say. You'd think he'd know that.'

'Sometimes I wonder,' she said, approaching her tea with her mouth because it was so hot without milk or a slice of lemon.

On his way home Danny followed the wobbling yellow disc his torch made on the ground. He was not afraid of the dark but felt protected by it in some way. He noticed from a distance that light was coming from the forge. The door was open and a slice of the roadway in front of it visible. The blacksmith must have heard him because when Danny stopped outside he began to sing 'Oh Danny Boy'.

'Come in,' he shouted. From the threshold Danny refused.

'Why not?'

'My Dad says I'm not allowed.'

The blacksmith laughed and said that he had a fair idea why.

'What would he do if he caught you here?'

'Take his belt off to me.'

The man snorted and came to Danny in the doorway. He rucked up his leather apron and thrust his hands into his pockets.

'Danny,' he said and there was a long pause. 'You're coming to an age now when you've got to think. Don't accept what people tell you – even your father. Especially your father. And that includes me.'

Danny eased his hip on to a large tractor tyre propped by the door.

'Your Dad and I have very different views of things. He accepts the mess the world is in whereas I don't. We've got to change it – by force if necessary.'

'Did you see the satellite?' asked Danny. The blacksmith nodded and laughed.

'It takes the Russians. I bet the Yanks feel sickened. That's an example of what I'm talking about. Equal shares and equal opportunity leads to progress, Danny. The classless society. It'll happen in Ireland before long. There's nothing surer. Am I right or am I wrong?'

Danny smiled and said that he would have to go. The blacksmith touched him on the shoulder.

'If you want to come back here, Danny, you come. The belt shouldn't stop you. You've got to be your own man, Danny Boy.'

'I'll maybe see you.'

On the road Danny waited for the hammer blows so that he could walk in step but none came and he had to choose his own rhythm.

On Sunday Danny waited to hear the familiar thumping sound of Miss Schwartz taking her place in the organ loft. She was not the same religion as the McErlanes but she had told Danny that she had needed the money and that it was a chance to play regularly on the best organ for a radius of twenty miles. After mass she had taken him up several times into the loft and he had been astonished by the sense of vibration, the wheezes and puffs and clanks of the machinery which he hadn't heard from the church. He loved the power of the instrument when she opened the stops fully to clear the church.

He heard the door of the organ loft close and was surprised when he looked round to see a man. He was bald with a horse-shoe of white hair and horn-rimmed spectacles. Throughout the distribution of communion he played traditional hymns with a thumping left hand and a scatter of wrong notes. Afterwards he drove away in a white Morris Minor.

Outside on the driveway Father O'Neill talked to Danny's mother. The boy was sent on ahead while they talked. All that Sunday the house was full of whispers. Danny would come into a room and the conversation would stop. He thought Miss Schwartz must be ill.

The next day, the Monday before Christmas, when he came home from school his mother was sitting at the table writing a letter. He gathered his music and was about to go out when she called him.

'Here's a note for your music teacher.' Then she added, 'Don't be too disappointed, son.'

'What do you mean?'

'Never mind. Just you take that to your teacher and maybe she'll explain.'

On the road the wind was cold. Some hailstones had fallen and gathered into seams along the side of the road. The wind hurt the lobes of his ears and the tip of his nose.

He gave Miss Schwartz the note and she opened it jaggedly with a finger. She chinked the money into her hand, then read the letter. She looked as if she was going to cry but she stopped herself by biting her lip. Her teeth were nice and straight and white.

'Play for me,' she said.

Danny began to play the Field Nocturne he had been practising. The dark descended slowly. When he had finished she said,

'Let us not have a lesson. Let us play all the best things.'

'You didn't play the organ on Sunday. Were you sick?'

'Yes. I was indisposed.' She thought for a while, then put her hand to the back of her head and untied her hair. With a shake she let it fall darkly forward.

'I'm pregnant,' she said. Danny nodded.

'That means I'm going to have a baby.'

'Yes, I know.'

'They don't want me any more.'

'Why not? You're the best organist I've ever heard.'

'You can't have heard many. No more talk, Danny. That's enough. What are you going to play?'

'Can I have the light on?'

'No,' she said. 'Play me the Schubert. You know it well enough to play in the dark. It makes the other senses better. In the dark we are

148

all ears, are we not?' Her voiced sounded wet, as if she had been crying.

'Which one?'

'The G flat.'

Danny began to play. Somehow he felt a sense of occasion, as if she was willing him to play better than he had ever played before. To feel, as she had so often urged him, the heart and soul of what Schubert had heard when he wrote down the music. In the dark he was aware of her slight swaying as he played. Now she sat forward on the sofa, her long hair hanging like curtains on each side of the pale patch of her face. She sat like a man, her knees wide apart, her elbows resting on them. The melody, more sombre than he had played it before, flowed out over the rippling left hand. Then came the heavy base like a dross, holding the piece to earth. The right hand moved easily into the melody again, the highest note seeming never to reach high enough, pinioned by a ceiling Schubert had set on it. Like the black notes he had struck in Uncle George's room by himself creating a disturbing ache. The piece reached its full development and swung into its lovely main melody for the last time. It ended quietly, dying into a hush. Both were silent, afraid to break the spell that had come with the music. Danny heard Miss Schwartz give a sigh, a long shuddering exhalation and he too sighed. She leaned forward and switched on a small orange lamp which stood on the side table.

'Danny, you are my last pupil. They have taken all the others away from me. But I do not care about them. They are money. But you are the best. You are more than that. You are the best thing I have ever had and when they try to take you away from me . . .' She stopped and dipped her face into the handkerchief she had rolled in her hand. She looked up at him and began again.

'This is your last lesson. Your mother does not allow you to come here again.'

'Why not?' Danny's voice was high and angry. Miss Schwartz raised her shoulders and splayed out her hands.

'I think in our time together we have accomplished much, Danny. There is so much more technique that you have to learn. But your heart must be right. Without it technique is useless. Sometimes I am ungenerous and doubt others' sensitivity. It is hard to believe that someone can feel as deeply as oneself. It is difficult not to think of oneself as the centre of the universe. But I believe in yours, Danny. I see it in your eyes, in your face. Do you know what a frisson is?'

'No.'

'It is a feeling that you get. Indescribable. A shivering. Your hair stands on end when you hear or read or know something that is exceptionally beautiful. Did you ever get that?'

'No.'

'Have you ever cried listening to a piece of music – not from sadness but from the sheer beauty of it? Have you ever *felt* like crying?'

'No. I don't think I have.' Danny wanted to please her but she asked the question with such a seriousness, beseeched him, that to tell a lie would have been wrong.

'I can only compare it to something which you have not yet experienced. Something you would not understand. But it will come. I'm sure it will come. That is what is wrong with this world. People are like the beasts of the field. They know nothing of music or tenderness. Anyone whom music has spoken to – really spoken to – must be gentle, must be kind – could not be guilty of a cruelty.'

She stood up and was walking back and forth with her fists tight.

'*Mein Lieber*, in the light the pale people see nothing. The glare blinds them. It is easy to hurt what you cannot see. To drop bombs a million miles away.' She stopped walking and pointed her finger straight at him. 'One of your Popes had a great thing to say once. He had been listening to some music by Palestrina with Palestrina himself. He said to him, "The law, my dear Palestrina, ought to employ your music to lead hardened criminals to repentance." Do you think this,' and she hissed out the s sound, 'this town would do this to me if they had truly heard one bar of Palestrina? Listen. Listen to this.'

She stamped across the room and took out one of the books

of records. She put one on and turned the volume up full and announced,

'Palestrina.'

She sat down on the sofa, rigid with anger, electricity almost sparking from her hair.

'Close your eyes,' she commanded.

Danny closed his eyes and let his hands rest on his bare knees. The unaccompanied singing seemed to infuse the room with sanctity. The clear male voices, intricate and contrapuntal, became an abstraction. Stairs of sound ascending and yet descending at the same instant. Danny thought of what she had said, her tirade. He thought of being taken away from this room, never to be allowed back again to talk and work with Miss Schwartz. Never to be allowed to call in on the blacksmith and be talked to as if he were a man. The garden, the sunlight, the tea. Her concern for everything he did and said. The pumping of the bellows and smell of coke. Her perfume and her laugh, her plants, her music. Her bare breast. Am I right or am I wrong, *mein Lieber*? He thought of being deprived of all this, never to be allowed back to it. And he began silently in his own dark to cry.

Miss Schwartz saw the tears squeeze from his eyes and she jumped from the sofa, all her anger gone, and rushed to him. In her haste the tail of her dressing-gown caught a pot-plant and it tumbled to the floor. Black loam spilled out and the dislodged plant fell from the pot, displaying its tangled skirt of white roots. She knelt before him, her arms about his waist. She too was crying. She kissed his knees and he felt her long hair tickle his legs as she swung her head back and forth.

'You are one of us, my love.'

She continued to weep, the tears streaming down her face, wetting her chin. It was only now that Danny felt her fatness through her gown, not soft fatness, but a hard pumped-up bigness pressing against him. She held him so tightly, so closely that after a time he was unsure whether the hardness belonged to him or to her. To stop himself falling off the stool he put his hands around her neck and as she pressed her cheek to his he felt the sliding wetness of it. She smelled beautiful in the darkness of her hair. She began to move in time to the music, crushing his face to hers. He heard and felt her mouth implode small kisses on the side of his face, moving towards his mouth, but he wrenched his head to the side, not knowing what to do. They stayed like that until the record ended with a hiss and the tick-tick-tick of the over-run.

Miss Schwartz got up from her knees and straightened her dressing-gown. She pushed back her hair and sniffed loudly.

'Go, Danny. Now. At once.'

He stopped at the door, his hand on the handle. She was kneeling again, sweeping the springy black loam with her hands into a pile on the mat. She knelt on her gown so that it pulled taut over the hump of her stomach and for the first time Danny saw how big it was. Her hands, dirtied with the soil, hung useless from her wrists.

'Promise me one thing before you go,' she said. 'Find a good teacher. *Bitte, mein Lieber*. You might yet be great. Please – for me?'

Danny, unable to find the right words, nodded and left. Running in the swirling snow, the only thing he could think of was that she had not given him tea.

When he got home there was the worst row ever. Danny screamed and shouted at his mother, hardly knowing what he was saying. The answers they gave him he could not understand. They called her a slut and spoke of marriage and sin and Our Blessed Lady. He asked to be allowed back, he cried and pleaded, but his father ended it by thrashing him with his belt and threatening to take an axe to the piano.

Danny ran out into the night, down the garden, where he had built himself a hut of black tarred boards.

'Let him go, let him go,' he heard his mother scream.

The snow had lain and was thick under foot. The fields stretched white away from the white garden. Danny crawled into the darkness of his hut and squatted on the floor. He put his arms around his ankles and rested his wet cheek on his knees. He did not know how many hours it was he stayed like that.

He heard his mother coming out, her feet crunching and squeaking on the frozen snow.

'Danny,' she called, 'Danny.' She bowed down into the hut and took him by the arm. He had lost his will and when she drew him out, he came. The boy walked as if palsied, stiff and angular with the cold, his mother supporting him beneath his arm. He was numb, past the shivering point.

'Come into the heat, love,' she said, 'come in from the night. Join us.'

LIFE DRAWING

After darkness fell and he could no longer watch the landscape from the train window, Liam Diamond began reading his book. He had to take his feet off the seat opposite and make do with a less comfortable position to let a woman sit down. She was equine and fifty and he didn't give her a second glance. To take his mind off what was to come, he tried to concentrate. The book was a study of the Viennese painter Egon Schiele who, it seemed, had become so involved with his thirteen-year-old girl models that he ended up in jail. Augustus John came to mind: 'To paint someone you must first sleep with them', and he smiled. Schiele's portraits – mostly of himself – exploded off the page beside the text, distracting him. All sinew and gristle and distortion. There was something decadent about them, like Soutine's pictures of hanging sides of beef.

Occasionally he would look up to see if he knew where he was but saw only the darkness and himself reflected from it. The streetlights of small towns showed more and more snow on the roads the farther north he got. To stretch, he went to the toilet and noticed the faces as he passed between the seats. Like animals being transported. On his way back he saw a completely different set of faces, but he knew they looked the same. He hated train journeys, seeing so many people, so many houses. It made him realise he was part of things whether he liked it or not. Seeing so many unknown people through their back windows, standing outside shops, walking the streets, moronically waving from level crossings, they grew amorphous and repulsive. They were going about their static lives while he had a sense of being on the move. And yet he knew he was not. At some stage any one of those people might travel past his flat on a train and see him in the act of pulling his curtains. The thought depressed him so much that he could no longer read. He leaned his head against the window and although he had his eyes closed he did not sleep.

The snow, thawed to slush and refrozen quickly, crackled under his feet and made walking difficult. For a moment he was not sure which was the house. In the dark he had to remember it by number and shade his eyes against the yellow glare of the sodium street lights to make out the figures on the small terrace doors. He saw fifty-six and walked three houses farther along. The heavy wrought-iron knocker echoed in the hallway as it had always done. He waited, looking up at the semicircular fan-light. Snow was beginning to fall, tiny flakes swirling in the corona of light. He was about to knock again or look to see if they had got a bell when he heard shuffling from the other side of the door. It opened a few inches and a white-haired old woman peered out. Her hair was held in place by a net a shade different from her own hair colour. It was one of the Miss Harts but for the life of him he couldn't remember which. She looked at him, not understanding.

'Yes?'

'I'm Liam,' he said.

'Oh, thanks be to goodness for that. We're glad you could come.' Then she shouted over her shoulder, 'It's Liam.'

She shuffled backwards, opening the door and admitting him. Inside she tremulously shook his hand, then took his bag and set it on the ground. Like a servant, she took his coat and hung it on the hall stand. It was still in the same place and the hallway was still a dark electric yellow.

'Bertha's up with him now. You'll forgive us sending the telegram to the College but we thought you would like to know,' said Miss Hart. If Bertha was up the stairs then she must be Maisie.

'Yes, yes, you did the right thing,' said Liam. 'How is he?'

'Poorly. The doctor has just left – he had another call. He says he'll not last the night.'

'That's too bad.'

By now they were standing in the kitchen. The fireplace was black and empty. One bar of the dished electric fire took the chill off the room and no more.

'You must be tired,' said Miss Hart, 'it's such a journey. Would you like a cup of tea? I tell you what, just you go up now and I'll bring you your tea when it's ready. All right?'

'Yes, thank you.'

When he reached the head of the stairs she called after him,

'And send Bertha down.'

Bertha met him on the landing. She was small and withered and her head reached to his chest. When she saw him she started to cry and reached out her arms to him saying,

'Liam, poor Liam.'

She nuzzled against him, weeping. 'The poor old soul,' she kept repeating. Liam was embarrassed feeling the thin arms of this old woman he hardly knew about his hips.

'Maisie says you have to go down now,' he said, separating himself from her and patting her crooked back. He watched her go down the stairs, one tottering step at a time, gripping the banister, her rheumatic knuckles standing out like limpets.

He paused at the bedroom door and for some reason flexed his hands before he went in. He was shocked to see the state his father was in. He was now almost completely bald except for some fluffy hair above his ears. His cheeks were sunken, his mouth hanging open. His head was back on the pillow so that the strings of his neck stood out.

'Hello, it's me, Liam,' he said when he was at the bed. The old man opened his eyes flickeringly. He tried to speak. Liam had to lean over but failed to decipher what was said. He reached out and lifted his father's hand in a kind of wrong handshake.

'Want anything?'

His father signalled by a slight movement of his thumb that he needed something. A drink? Liam poured some water and put the glass to the old man's lips. Arcs of scum had formed at the corners of his sagging mouth. Some of the water spilled on to the sheet. It remained for a while in droplets before sinking into dark circles.

'Was that what you wanted?' The old man shook his head. Liam looked around the room, trying to see what his father could want. It was exactly as he had remembered it. In twenty years he hadn't changed the wallpaper, yellow roses looping on an umber trellis. He lifted a straight-backed chair and drew it up close to the bed. He sat with his elbows on his knees, leaning forward.

'How do you feel?'

The old man made no response and the question echoed around and around the silence in Liam's head.

Maisie brought in tea on a tray, closing the door behind her with her elbow. Liam noticed that two red spots had come up on her cheeks. She spoke quickly in an embarrassed whisper, looking back and forth between the dying man and his son.

'We couldn't find where he kept the teapot so it's just a tea-bag in a cup. Is that all right? Will that be enough for you to eat? We sent out for a tin of ham, just in case. He had nothing in the house at all, God love him.'

'You've done very well,' said Liam. 'You shouldn't have gone to all this trouble.'

'If you couldn't do it for a neighbour like Mr Diamond – well? Forty-two years and there was never a cross word between us. A gentleman we always called him, Bertha and I. He kept himself to himself. Do you think can he hear us?' The old man did not move.

'How long has he been like this?' asked Liam.

'Just three days. He didn't bring in his milk one day and that's not like him, y'know. He'd left a key with Mrs Rankin, in case he'd ever lock himself out again – he did once, the wind blew the door shut – and she came in and found him like this in the chair downstairs. He was frozen, God love him. The doctor said it was a stroke.'

Liam nodded, looking at his father. He stood up and began edging the woman towards the bedroom door.

'I don't know how to thank you, Miss Hart. You've been more than good.'

'We got your address from your brother. Mrs Rankin phoned America on Tuesday.'

'Is he coming home?'

'He said he'd try. She said the line was as clear as a bell. It was like talking to next door. Yes, he said he'd try but he doubted it very much.' She had her hand on the door knob. 'Is that enough sandwiches?'

'Yes thanks, that's fine.' They stood looking at one another awkwardly. Liam fumbled in his pocket. 'Can I pay you for the ham . . . and the telegram?'

'I wouldn't dream of it,' she said. 'Don't insult me now, Liam.' He withdrew his hand from his pocket and smiled his thanks to her.

'It's late,' he said, 'perhaps you should go now and I'll sit up with him.'

'Very good. The priest was here earlier and gave him . . .' she groped for the word with her hands.

'Extreme Unction?'

'Yes. That's twice he has been in three days. Very attentive. Sometimes I think if our ministers were half as good . . .'

'Yes, but he wasn't what you could call gospel greedy.'

'He was lately,' she said.

'Changed times.'

She half turned to go and said, almost coyly,

'I'd hardly have known you with the beard.' She looked up at him, shaking her head in disbelief. He was trying to make her go, standing close to her but she skirted round him and went over to the bed. She touched the old man's shoulder.

'I'm away now, Mr Diamond. Liam is here. I'll see you in the morning,' she shouted into his ear. Then she was away.

Liam heard the old ladies' voices in the hallway below, then the slam of the front door. He heard the crackling of their feet over the frozen slush beneath the window. He lifted the tray off the chest of drawers and on to his knees. He hadn't realised it, but he was hungry. He ate the sandwiches and the piece of fruit cake, conscious of the chewing noise he was making with his mouth in the silence of the bedroom. There was little his father could do about it now. They used to have the most terrible rows about it. You'd have thought it was a matter of life and death. At table he had sometimes trembled with rage at the boys' eating habits, at their greed as he called it. At the noises they made, 'like cows getting out of muck'. After their mother had left them he took over the responsibility for everything.

One night, as he served sausages from the pan Liam, not realising the filthy mood he was in, made a grab. His father in a sudden downward thrust jabbed the fork he had been using to cook the sausages into the back of Liam's hand.

'Control yourself.'

Four bright beads of blood appeared as Liam stared at them in disbelief.

'They'll remind you to use your fork in future.'

He was sixteen at the time.

The bedroom was cold and when he finally got round to drinking his tea it was tepid. He was annoyed that he couldn't heat it by pouring more. His feet were numb and felt damp. He went downstairs and put on his overcoat and brought the electric fire up to the bedroom, switching on both bars. He sat huddled over it, his fingers fanned out, trying to get warm. When the second bar was switched on there was a clicking noise and the smell of burning dust. He looked over at the bed but there was no movement.

'How do you feel?' he said again, not expecting an answer. For a long time he sat staring at the old man, whose breathing was audible but quiet – a kind of soft whistling in his nose. The alarm clock, its face bisected with a crack, said twelve-thirty. Liam checked it against the red figures of his digital watch. He stood up and went to the window. Outside the roofs tilted at white snow-covered angles. A faulty gutter hung spikes of icicles. There was no sound in the street, but from the main road came the distant hum of a late car that faded into silence.

He went out on to the landing and into what was his own bedroom. There was no bulb when he switched the light on so he took one from the hall and screwed it into the shadeless socket. The bed was there in the corner with its mattress of blue stripes. The lino was the same, with its square pockmarks showing other places the bed had been. The cheap green curtains that never quite met on their cord still did not meet.

He moved to the wall cupboard by the small fireplace and had to tug at the handle to get it open. Inside, the surface of everything had gone opaque with dust. Two old radios, one with a fretwork face, the other more modern with a tuning dial showing such places as Hilversum, Luxembourg, Athlone; a Dansette record player with its lid missing and its arm bent back, showing wires like severed nerves and blood vessels; the empty frame of the smashed glass picture was still there; several umbrellas, all broken. And there was his box of poster paints. He lifted it out and blew off the dust.

It was a large Quality Street tin and he eased the lid off, bracing it against his stomach muscles. The colours in the jars had shrunk to hard discs. Viridian green, vermilion, jonquil yellow. At the bottom of the box he found several sticks of charcoal, light in his fingers when he lifted them, warped. He dropped them into his pocket and put the tin back into the cupboard. There was a pile of magazines and papers and beneath that again he saw his large Winsor and Newton sketchbook. He eased it out and began to look through the work in it. Embarrassment was what he felt most, turning the pages, looking at the work of this school-boy. He could see little talent in it, yet he realised he must have been good. There were several drawings of hands in red pastel which had promise. The rest of the pages were blank. He set the sketchbook aside to take with him and closed the cupboard.

Looking round the room, it had to him the appearance of naked-ness. He crouched and looked under the bed, but there was nothing there. His fingers coming in contact with the freezing lino made him aware how cold he was. His jaw was tight and he knew that if he relaxed he would shiver. He went back to his father's bedroom and sat down.

The old man had not changed his position. He had wanted him to be a lawyer or a doctor but Liam had insisted, although he had won a scholarship to the university, on going to art college. All that summer his father tried everything he knew to stop him. He tried to reason with him,

'*Be* something. And you can carry on doing your art. Art is O.K. as a sideline.'

But mostly he shouted at him. 'I've heard about these art students and what they get up to. Shameless bitches prancing about with nothing on. And what sort of a job are you going to get? Drawing on pavements?' He nagged him every moment they were together about other things. Lying late in bed, the length of his hair, his outrageous appearance. Why hadn't he been like the other lads and got himself a job for the summer? It wasn't too late because he would willingly pay him if he came in and helped out in the shop.

One night, just as he was going to bed, Liam found the old framed print of cattle drinking. He had taken out the glass and had begun to paint on the glass itself with small tins of Humbrol enamel paints left over from aeroplane kits he had never finished. They produced a strange and exciting texture which was even better when the paint was viewed from the other side of the pane of glass. He sat stripped to the waist in his pyjama trousers painting a self-portrait reflected from the mirror on the wardrobe door. The creamy opaque nature of the paint excited him. It slid on to the glass, it built up, in places it ran scalloping like cinema curtains, and yet he could control it. He lost all track of time as he sat with his eyes focused on the face staring back at him and the painting he was trying to make of it. It became a face he had not known, the holes, the lines, the spots. He was in a new geography.

His brother and he used to play a game looking at each other's faces upside down. One lay on his back across the bed, his head flopped over the edge, reddening as the blood flooded into it. The other sat in a chair and stared at him. After a time the horror of seeing the eyes where the mouth should be, the inverted nose, the forehead gashed with red lips, would drive him to cover his eyes with his hands. 'It's your turn now,' he would say, and they would change places. It was like familiar words said over and over again until they became meaningless, and once he ceased to have purchase on the meaning of a word it became terrifying, an incantation. In adolescence he had come to hate his brother, could not stand the physical presence of him, just as when he was lying upside down on the bed. It was the same with his father. He could not bear to touch him and yet for one whole winter when he had a bad shoulder he had to stay up late to rub him with oil of wintergreen. The old boy would sit with one hip on the bed and Liam would stand behind him, massaging the stinking stuff into the white flesh of his back. The smell, the way the blubbery skin moved under his fingers, made him want to be sick. No matter how many times he washed his hands, at school the next day he would still reek of oil of wintergreen.

It might have been the smell of the Humbrol paints or the strip of light under Liam's door – whatever it was, his father came in and yelled that it was half-past three in the morning and what the hell did he think he was doing, sitting half-naked drawing at this hour of the morning? He had smacked him full force with the flat of his hand on his bare back and, stung by the pain of it, Liam had leapt to retaliate. Then his father had started to laugh, a cold snickering laugh. 'Would you? Would you? Would you indeed?' he kept repeating with a smile pulled on his mouth and his fists bunched to knuckles in front of him. Liam retreated to the bed and his father turned on his heel and left. Thinking the incident over, Liam knotted his fists and cursed his father. He looked over his shoulder into the mirror and saw the primitive daub of his father's hand, splayed fingers outlined across his back. He heard him on the stairs and when he came back into the bedroom with the poker in his hand he felt his insides turn to water. But his father looked away from him with a sneer and smashed the painting to shards with one stroke. As he went out of the door he said,

'Watch your feet in the morning.'

He had never really 'left home'. It was more a matter of going to art college in London and not bothering to come back. Almost as soon as he was away from the house his hatred for his father eased. He simply stopped thinking about him. Of late he had wondered if he was alive or dead – if he still had the shop. The only communication they had had over the years was when Liam sent him, not without a touch of vindictiveness, an invitation to some of the openings of his exhibitions.

Liam sat with his fingertips joined, staring at the old man. It was going to be a long night. He looked at his watch and it was only a little after two.

He paced up and down the room, listening to the tick of snow on the window-pane. When he stopped to look down, he saw it flurrying through the haloes of the street lamps. He went into his own bedroom and brought back the sketchbook. He moved his chair to the other side of the bed so that the light fell on his page. Balancing the book on his knee, he began to draw his father's head with the stick of charcoal. It made a light hiss each time a line appeared on the cartridge paper. When drawing he always thought of himself as a wary animal drinking, the way he looked up and down, up and down, at his subject. The old man had failed badly. His head scarcely dented the pillows, his cheeks were hollow and he had not been shaved for some days. Earlier, when he had held his hand it had been clean and dry and light like the hand of a girl. The bedside light deepened the shadows of his face and highlighted the rivulets of veins on his temple. It was a long time since he had used charcoal and he became engrossed in the way it had to be handled and the different subtleties of line he could get out of it. He loved to watch a drawing develop before his eyes.

His work had been well received and among the small Dublin art world he was much admired – justly he thought. But some critics had scorned his work as 'cold' and 'formalist' – one had written, 'Like Mondrian except that he can't draw a straight line' – and this annoyed him because it was precisely what he was trying to do. He felt it was unfair to be criticised for succeeding in his aims.

His father began to cough – a low wet bubbling sound. Liam leaned forward and touched the back of his hand gently. Was this man to blame in any way? Or had he only himself to blame for the shambles of his life? He had married once and lived with two other women. At present he was on his own. Each relationship had ended in hate and bitterness, not because of drink or lack of money or any of the usual reasons but because of a mutual nauseating dislike.

He turned the page and began to draw the old man again. The variations in tone from jet black to pale grey, depending on the pressure he used, fascinated him. The hooded lids of the old man's eyes, the fuzz of hair sprouting from the ear next the light, the darkness of the partially open mouth. Liam made several more drawings, absorbed, working slowly, refining the line of each until it was to his satisfaction. He was pleased with what he had done. At art school he had loved the life class better than any other. It never ceased to amaze him how sometimes it could come just right, better than he had hoped for; the feeling that something was working through him to produce a better work than at first envisaged.

Then outside he heard the sound of an engine followed by the clinking of milk bottles. When he looked at his watch he was amazed to see that it was five-thirty. He leaned over to speak to his father,

'Are you all right?'

His breathing was not audible and when Liam touched his arm it was cold. His face was cold as well. He felt for his heart, slipping his hand inside his pyjama jacket, but could feel nothing. He was dead. His father. He was dead and the slackness of his dropped jaw disturbed his son. In the light of the lamp his dead face looked like the open-mouthed moon. Liam wondered if he should tie it up before it set. In a Pasolini film he had seen Herod's jaw being trussed and he wondered if he was capable of doing it for his father.

Then he saw himself in his hesitation, saw the lack of any emotion in his approach to the problem. He was aware of the deadness inside himself and felt helpless to do anything about it. It was why all his women had left him. One of them accused him of making love the way other people rodded drains.

He knelt down beside the bed and tried to think of something good from the time he had spent with his father. Anger and sneers and nagging was all that he could picture. He knew he was grateful for his rearing but he could not *feel* it. If his father had not been there some- body else would have done it. And yet it could not have been easy – a man left with two boys and a business to run. He had worked himself to a sinew in his tobacconist's, opening at seven in the morning to catch the workers and closing at ten at night. Was it for his boys that he worked so hard? The man was in the habit of earning and yet he never spent. He had even opened for three hours on Christmas Day.

Liam stared at the dead drained face and suddenly the mouth held in that shape reminded him of something pleasant. It was the only joke his father had ever told and to make up for the smallness of his repertoire he had told it many times; of two ships passing in mid- Atlantic. He always megaphoned his hands to tell the story.

'Where are you bound for?' shouts one captain.

'Rio – de – Janeir – io. Where are you bound for?'

And the other captain, not to be outdone, yells back,

'Cork – a – lork – a – lor – io.'

When he had finished the joke he always repeated the punch-line, laughing and nodding in disbelief that something could be so funny.

'Cork a – lorka – lorio.'

Liam found that his eyes had filled with tears. He tried to keep them coming but they would not. In the end he had to close his eyes and a tear spilled from his left eye on to his cheek. It was small and he wiped it away with a crooked index finger.

He stood up from the kneeling position and closed the sketchbook lying on the bed. He might work on the drawings later. Or just fix them as they were. He walked to the window. Dawn would not be for hours yet. In America his brother would be getting ready for bed. Tomorrow would be time enough. He could phone from Mrs Rankin's this afternoon sometime – and a death certificate would be needed. There was nothing he could do at the moment, except perhaps tie up the jaw. The Miss Harts when they arrived would know everything that ought to be done.

PHONEFUN LIMITED

When she heard the whine of the last customer's fast spin – a bearded student with what seemed like a year's supply of Y-fronts – Sadie Thompson changed her blue nylon launderette coat for her outdoor one and stood jingling the keys by the door until he left. It was dark and wet and the streets reflected the lights from the shop windows. She had to rush to get to the Spar before it closed, and was out of breath – not that she had much to buy, potatoes, sugar and tea-bags. In the corner shop she got her cigarettes, the evening paper and a copy of *Men Only*, which she slipped inside the newspaper and put in her carrier bag. She slowly climbed the steep street in darkness because the Army had put out most of the street lights. She turned in at Number ninety-six. The door stuck momentarily on a large envelope lying on the mat.

She had the table set and the dinner ready for Agnes when she came in.

'Hello, Sadie, love,' she said and kissed her on the cheek. Beside Sadie, Agnes was huge. She wore an expensive silver-fox fur coat. Sadie did not like the coat and had said so. It was much too much for a woman whose only job was cleaning the local primary school.

'I'm knackered,' said Agnes, kicking off her shoes and falling into the armchair. There was a hole in the toe of her tights.

'Take off your coat, your dinner's ready,' said Sadie.

'Hang on. Let me have a fag first.'

She lit up a cigarette and put her head back in the chair. Sadie thought she looked a putty colour. She was grossly overweight but would do nothing about it, no matter what Sadie said.

'Are you all right?'

'I'll be all right in a minute. It's that bloody hill. It's like entering the Olympics.'

'If you ask me, you're carrying too much weight. When did you last weigh yourself?'

'This morning.'

'And what were you?'

'I don't know,' said Agnes laughing, 'I was afraid to look.'

With her head back like that her fat neck and chin were one. There were red arcs of lipstick on the cork-tip of her cigarette. Sadie served the mash and sausages.

'Sit over,' she said. Agnes stubbed her cigarette out and, groaning for effect, came to the table still wearing her coat.

'You'd think to hear you that you'd cleaned that school by yourself.'

'It feels like I did.' Agnes raised her fork listlessly to her mouth. 'Did the post come?'

'Yes.'

'Much?'

'It feels fat.'

'Aw God no.'

'You'll have to brighten up a bit. Don't be so glum.'

'God, that's a good one coming from you, Sadie. I don't think I've seen you smiling since Christmas.'

'I'm the brains. You're supposed to be the charm. I don't *have* to smile.' They ate in silence except for the sound of their forks making small screeches against the plate.

'I wish you'd take off your coat when you're eating. It looks that slovenly,' said Sadie. Agnes heaved herself to her feet, took off her coat and flung it on the sofa. She turned on the transistor. The news was on so she tuned it to some music.

'I need a wee doze before I brighten up. You know that, Sadie.'

'I suppose I'm not tired after a day in that bloody laundryette?'

Agnes nibbled her sausage at the front of her closed mouth, very quickly, like a rabbit. The music on the radio stopped and a foreign voice came on and babbled.

'That's a great programme you picked.'

'It's better than the Northern Ireland news.'

The foreign voice stopped and music came on again. Agnes finished what was on her plate.

'Is there anything for afters?'

'You can open some plums if you want.'

Agnes lurched out to the tiled kitchen and opened a tin of plums. She threw the circle of lid into the bucket and came back with the tin and a spoon.

'It's cold on your feet out there. There's a draught coming in under that door that would clean corn.' She ate the plums from the tin. Some juice trickled on to her chin.

'Want some?' She offered the half-finished tin to Sadie, but she refused.

'It's no wonder you're fat.'

'It oils my voice. Makes it nice for the phone.'

'I got you a *Men Only* if you run out of inspiration. It's there on the sideboard.'

'Thanks, love, but I don't think I'll need it.' Agnes drank off the last of the juice from the tin.

'You'll cut your lip one of these days,' said Sadie, 'don't say I didn't warn you.'

Agnes lit a cigarette and rolled one across the table to Sadie. She dropped the dead match into the tin.

'That was good,' she said. 'I'm full to the gunnels.' She slapped her large stomach with the flat of her hand in satisfaction. The foreigner began to speak gobbledegook again.

'Aw shut up,' said Sadie. 'Men are all the same no matter what they're speaking.' She twiddled the knob until she got another station with music. Almost immediately the music stopped and a man with a rich American drawl began to speak.

'Aw God, Sadie, do you remember the Yanks? He sounds just like one I had.'

'Will I ever forget them? They could spend money all right.'

'That's exactly like his voice. It's the spit of him.'

'Give us a light.' Agnes leaned over and touched Sadie's cigarette with her own. Sadie pulled hard until it was lit.

'I fancied him no end,' said Agnes. 'He was lovely. I think it was his first time but he pretended it wasn't.'

'I think you told me about him.'

'My Yankee Doodle Dandy, I called him. I can still feel the stubble of his haircut. It was like he had sandpapered up the back of his neck. Blondie. We sort of went together for a while.'

'You mean he didn't pay.'

'That kind of thing.'

'Better clear this table.' Sadie put the cigarette in her mouth, closing one eye against the trickle of blue smoke and began to remove the dirty plates. Ash toppled on to the cloth. She came back from the kitchen and gently brushed the grey roll into the palm of her other hand and dropped it into Agnes's tin. Agnes said,

'You wash and I'll dry.'

'What you mean is I'll wash and put them in the rack and then about ten o'clock you'll come out and put them in the cupboard.'

'Well, it's more hygienic that way. I saw in the paper that the tea-towel leaves germs all over them.'

'You only read what suits you.'

Sadie went out into the kitchen to wash up the dishes. She heard the programme on the radio finish and change to a service with an American preacher. It kept fading and going out of focus and was mixed up with pips of Morse Code. When she had finished she washed out the tea-towel in some Lux and hung it in the yard to dry. She could do her own washing at the launderette but she hated lugging the bagful of damp clothes home. There was such a weight in wet clothes. If she did that too often she would end up with arms like a chimpanzee. When she went back into the living room Agnes was asleep in her armchair beside the radio with a silly smile on her face.

Sadie picked up the large envelope off the sideboard and opened it with her thumb and spilled out the pile of envelopes on to the table. She began to open them and separate the cheques and money. On each letter she marked down the amount of money contained and then set it to one side. Agnes began to snore wetly, her head pitched forward on to her chest. When she had all the letters opened, Sadie got up and switched off the radio. In the silence Agnes woke with a start. Sadie said,

'So you're back with us again.'

'What do you mean?'

'You were sound asleep.'

'I was not. I was only closing my eyes. Just for a minute.'

'You were snoring like a drunk.'

'Indeed I was not. I was just resting my eyes.'

The ticking of the clock annoyed Agnes so she switched the radio on again just in time to hear 'The Lord is my Shepherd' being sung in a smooth American drawl. She tuned it to Radio One. Sadie said,

'Hymns give me the creeps. That Billy Graham one. Euchh!' She shuddered. 'You weren't in Belfast for the Blitz, were you?'

'No, I was still a nice country girl from Cookstown. My Americans all came from the camp out at Larrycormack. That's where my Yankee Doodle Dandy was stationed. You stuck it out here through the Blitz?'

'You can say that again. We all slept on the Cavehill for a couple of nights. Watched the whole thing. It was terrible – fires everywhere.'

'Sadie, will you do my hair?'

Sadie took the polythene bag bulging with rollers from under the table and began combing Agnes's hair.

'It needs to be dyed again. Your roots is beginning to show.'

'I think I'll maybe grow them out this time. Have it greying at the temples.'

Sadie damped each strand of hair and rolled it up tight into Agnes's head, then fixed it with a hairpin. With each tug of the brush Agnes let her head jerk with it.

'I love somebody working with my hair. It's so relaxing.' Sadie couldn't answer because her mouth was bristling with hairpins. Agnes said,

'How much was there in the envelopes?'

'Hengy-hee oung.'

'How much?'

Sadie took the hairpins from her mouth.

'Sixty-eight pounds.'

'That's not bad at all.'

'You're right there. It's better than walking the streets on a night like this.'

'If it goes on like this I'm going to give up my job in that bloody school.'

'I think you'd be foolish. Anything could happen. It could all fall through any day.'

'How could it?'

'I don't know. It all seems too good to be true. The Post Office could catch on. Even the Law. Or the tax man.'

'It's not against the law?'

'I wouldn't be too sure.'

'It's against the law the other way round but not the way we do it.'

'There. That's you finished,' said Sadie, giving the rollers a final pat in close to her head. She held the mirror up for Agnes to see but before she put it away she looked at herself. Her neck was a dead give away. That's where the age really showed. You could do what you liked with make-up on your face but there was no way of disguising those chicken sinews on your neck. And the back of the hands. They showed it too. She put the mirror on the mantelpiece and said,

'Are you ready, Agnes?'

'Let's have a wee gin first.'

'O.K.'

She poured two gins and filled them to the brim with tonic. Agnes sat over to the table. When she drank her gin she pinched in her mouth with the delightful bitterness.

'Too much gin,' she said.

'You say that every time.'

Agnes sipped some more out of her glass and then topped up with tonic. She began to sort through the letters. She laughed and nodded her head at some. At others she turned down the corners of her mouth.

'I suppose I better make a start.'

She lifted the telephone and set it beside her on the table. She burst out laughing.

'Have you read any of these, Sadie?'

'No.'

'Listen to this. "Dear Samantha, you really turn me on with that sexy voice of yours. Not only me but my wife as well. I get her to

listen on the extension. Sometimes it's too much for the both of us."
Good Gawd. I never thought there was any women listening to me.'
She picked up the phone and snuggled it between her ear and the fat
of her shoulder.

'Kick over that pouffe, Sadie.'

Sadie brought the pouffe to her feet. Agnes covered the hole in the
toe of her tights with the sole of her other foot. She sorted through
the letters and chose one.

'"Available at any time." He must be an oul' bachelor. O three one.
That's Edinburgh isn't it? Dirty oul' kilty.'

She dialled the number and while she listened to the dialling tone
she smiled at Sadie. She raised her eyebrows as if she thought she
was posh. A voice answered at the other end. Agnes's voice changed
into a soft purr which pronounced its -ings.

'Hello is Ian there? . . . Oh, I didn't recognise your voice. This is
Samantha . . . Yes, I can hold on, but not too long.' She covered the
mouthpiece with her hand and, exaggerating her lips, said to Sadie,

'The egg-timer.'

Sadie went out to the kitchen and came back with it. It was a
cheap plastic one with pink sand. She set it on the table with the full
side on top.

'Ah, there you are again, honey,' whispered Agnes into the mouthpiece,
'are you all ready now? Good. What would you like to talk about? . . .
Well, I'm lying here on my bed. It's a lovely bed with black silk sheets
. . . No, it has really. Does that do something for you? Mmm, it's warm.
I have the heating turned up full. It's so warm all I am wearing are my
undies . . . Lemon . . . Yes, and the panties are lemon too . . . All right,
if you insist . . .' Agnes put the phone down on the table and signalled
to Sadie to light her a fag. She made a rustling noise with her sleeve
close to the mouthpiece then picked up the phone again.

'There, I've done what you asked . . . You're not normally breathless, are you, Ian? Have you just run up the stairs? . . . No, I'm only
kidding . . . I know only too well what it's like to have asthma.'

She listened for a while, taking the lit cigarette from Sadie. She
rolled her eyes to heaven and smiled across the table at her. She covered
the mouthpiece with her hand.

'He's doing his nut.'

Sadie topped up her gin and tonic from the gin bottle.

'Do you really want me to do that? That might cost a little more money . . . All right, just for you love.' She laughed heartily and paused. 'Yes, I'm doing it now . . . Yes, it's fairly pleasant. A bit awkward . . . Actually I'm getting to like it. Ohhh, I love it now . . . Say what again? . . . Ohhh, I love it.'

She turned to Sadie.

'He's rung off. That didn't take long. He just came and went. Who's next?'

Sadie flicked another letter to her.

'London,' she said. 'Jerome. Only on Thursdays after eight.'

'That's today. Probably the wife's night out at the Bingo.'

She dialled the number and when a voice answered she said,

'Hello Jerome, this is Samantha.'

Sadie turned over the egg-timer.

'Oh, sorry love – say that again. Ger – o – mey. I thought it was Ger – ome. Like Ger-ome Cairns, the song writer. Would you like to talk or do you want me to . . . O.K., fire away . . . I'm twenty-four . . . Blonde . . . Lemon, mostly . . . Yes, as brief as possible. Sometimes they're so brief they cut into me.' She listened for a moment, then covering the mouthpiece said to Sadie,

'This one's disgusting. How much did he pay?'

Sadie looked at the letter.

'Ten pounds. Don't lose him. Do what he says.'

'Yes, this is still Samantha.' Her voice went babyish and her mouth pouted. 'How could a nice little girl like me do a thing like that? . . . Well, if it pleases you.' Agnes lifted her stubby finger and wobbled it wetly against her lips. 'Can you hear that? . . . Yes, I like it . . . Yes, I have *very* long legs.' She lifted her legs off the pouffe and looked at them disapprovingly. She had too many varicose veins. She'd had them out twice.

'You *are* a bold boy, but your time is nearly up.' The last of the pink sand was caving in and trickling through. Sadie raised a warning finger then signalled with all ten. She mouthed,

'Ten pounds. Don't lose him.'

'All right, just for you . . . Then I'll have to go,' said Agnes and she wobbled her finger against her lips again. 'Is that enough? . . . You just write us another letter. You know the box number? Good . . . I love you too, Ger – o – mey, Bye-eee.' She put the phone down.

'For God's sake give us another gin,' she said. 'What a creep!'

'It's better than walking the street,' said Sadie. 'What I like about it is that they can't get near you.'

'Catch yourself on, Sadie. If anyone got near us now they'd run a mile.'

'I used to be frightened of them. Not all the time. But there was one every so often that made your scalp crawl. Something not right about them. Those ones gave me the heemy-jeemies, I can tell you. You felt you were going to end up in an entry somewhere – strangled – with your clothes over your head.'

Agnes nodded in agreement. 'Or worse,' she said.

Sadie went on, 'When I think of the things I've had to endure. Do you remember that pig that gave me the kicking? I was in hospital for a fortnight. A broken arm and a ruptured spleen – the bastard.'

Agnes began to laugh. 'Do you remember the time I broke my ankle? Jumping out of a lavatory window. Gawd, I was sure and certain I was going to be murdered that night.'

'Was that the guy with the steel plate in his head?'

'The very one. He said he would go mad if I didn't stroke it for him.'

'What?'

'His steel plate.'

'I can still smell some of those rooms. It was no picnic, Agnes, I can tell you.'

'The only disease you can get at this game is an ear infection. Who's next?'

Sadie passed another letter to her.

'Bristol, I think.'

'This one wants *me* to breathe. Good God, what will they think of next?'

'I hate their guts, every last one of them.'

'Do you fancy doing this one?' asked Agnes.

'No. You know I'm no good at it.'

'Chrissake, Sadie, you can breathe. I never get a rest. Why's it always me?'

'Because I told you. You are the creative one. I just look after the books. The business end. Would you know how to go about putting an ad in? Or wording it properly? Or getting a box number? You stick to the bit you're good at. You're really great, you know. I don't know how you think the half of them up.'

Agnes smiled. She wiggled her stubby toes on the pouffe. She said, 'Do you know what I'd like? With the money.'

'What? Remember that we're still paying off that carpet in the bedroom – and the suite. Don't forget the phone bills either.'

'A jewelled cigarette holder. Like the one Audrey Hepburn had in that picture – what was it called?'

'The Nun's Story?'

'No.'

'Breakfast at Tiffany's?'

'Yes, one like that. I could use it on the phone. It'd make me feel good.'

As Agnes dialled another number Sadie said,

'You're mad in the skull.'

'We can afford it. Whisht now.'

When the phone was answered at the other end she said,

'Hello, Samantha here,' and began to breathe loudly into the receiver. She quickened her pace gradually until she was panting, then said,

'He's hung up. Must have been expecting me. We should get a pair of bellows for fellas like him. Save my puff.'

'I'll go up and turn the blanket on, then we'll have a cup of tea,' said Sadie. Agnes turned another letter towards herself and dialled a number.

Upstairs Sadie looked round the bedroom with admiration. She still hadn't got used to it. The plush almost ankle-deepness of the mushroom-coloured carpet and the brown flock wallpaper, the brown duvet with the matching brown sheets. The curtains were of heavy velvet and were the most luxurious stuff she had ever touched. She switched on the blanket and while on her hands and knees she allowed her fingers to sink into the pile of the carpet. All her life she had wanted a bedroom like this. Some of the places she had lain down, she wouldn't have kept chickens in. She heard Agnes's voice coming blurred from downstairs. She owed a lot to her. Everything, in fact. From the first time they met, the night they were both arrested and ended up in the back of the same paddy-wagon, she had thought there was something awful good about her, something awful kind. She had been so good-looking in her day too, tall and stately and well-built. They had stayed together after that night – all through the hard times. As Agnes said, once you quit the streets it didn't qualify you for much afterwards. Until lately, when she had shown this amazing talent for talking on the phone. It had all started one night when a man got the wrong number and Agnes had chatted him up until he was doing his nut at the other end. They had both crouched over the phone wheezing and laughing their heads off at the puffs and pants of him. Then it was Sadie's idea to put the whole thing on a commercial basis and form the Phonefun company. She dug her fingers into the carpet and brushed her cheek against the crisp sheet.

'Agnes,' she said and went downstairs to make the tea.

She stood waiting for the kettle to boil, then transferred the tea-bag from one cup of boiling water to the other. Agnes laughed loudly at something in the living room. Sadie heard her say,

'But if I put the phone there you'll not hear me.'

She put some custard creams on a plate and brought the tea in.

'Here you are, love,' she said, setting the plate beside the egg-timer. 'He's over his time.' Agnes covered the mouth-piece and said,

'I forgot to start it.' Then back to the phone. 'I can get some rubber ones if you want me to . . . But you'll have to pay for them. Will you send the money through? . . . Gooood boy. Now I really must go . . . Yes, I'm listening.' She made a face, half laughing, half in disgust, to Sadie. 'Well done, love . . . Bye-eee, sweetheart.' She puckered her mouth and did a kiss noise into the mouthpiece, then put the phone down.

'Have your tea now, Agnes, you can do the others later.'

'There's only two more I can do tonight. The rest have special dates.'

'You can do those. Then we'll go to bed. Eh?'

'O.K.,' said Agnes. 'Ahm plumb tuckered out.'

'You're what?'

'Plumb tuckered out. It's what my Yankee Doodle Dandy used to say afterwards.'

'What started you on *him* tonight?'

'I don't know. I just remembered, that's all. He used to bring me nylons and put them on for me.'

She fiddled with the egg-timer and allowed the pink sand to run through it. She raised her legs off the pouffe and turned her feet outwards, looking at them.

'I don't like tights,' she said, 'I read somewhere they're unhygienic.'

'Do you want to hear the news before we go up? Just in case?'

'Just in case what?'

'They could be rioting all over the city and we wouldn't know a thing.'

'You're better not to know, even if they are. That tea's cold.'

'That's because you didn't drink it. You talk far too much.'

Agnes drank her tea and snapped a custard cream in half with her front teeth.

'I don't think I'll bother with these next two.'

'That's the way you lose customers. If you phone them once they'll come back for more – and for a longer time. Give them a short time. Keep them interested.' She lifted the crumbed plate and the cups and took them out to the kitchen. Agnes lit another cigarette and sat staring vacantly at the egg-timer. She said without raising her eyes,

'Make someone happy with a phone call.'

'I'm away on up,' said Sadie. 'I'll keep a place warm for you.'

Sadie was in bed when Agnes came up.

'Take your rollers out,' she said.

Agnes undressed, grunting and tugging hard at her roll-on. When she got it off she gave a long sigh and rubbed the puckered flesh that had just been released.

'That's like taking three Valium, to get out of that,' she said. She sat down on the side of the bed and began taking her rollers out, clinking the hairpins into a saucer on the dressing table. Sadie spoke from the bed,

'Were you really in love with that Yank?'

'Yes, as near as possible.'

Agnes shook her hair loose and rolled back into bed. She turned out the light and Sadie notched into her back. She began to stroke Agnes's soft upper arm, then moved to her haunch.

'I've got a bit of a headache, love,' said Agnes.

Sadie turned to the wall and Agnes felt her harsh skin touch her own.

'My God, Sadie,' she said, 'you've got heels on you like pumice stones.'

THE DAILY WOMAN

She woke like a coiled spring, her head pressed on to the mattress, the knot of muscle at the side of her jaw taut, holding her teeth together. The texture of her cheeks felt tight and shiny from the tears she had cried as she had determined herself to sleep the night before. She lay for a moment trying to sense whether he was behind her or not, but knowing he wasn't. The baby was still asleep. She could tell by the slight squeaking movement of the pram springs from the foot of the bed whether it was asleep or not. The house was silent. She was a good baby. When she woke in the mornings she kicked her legs for hours. Only once in a while she cried.

Liz got up and went to the bathroom. In the mirror she saw where he had snapped the shoulder strap of her slip. It looked like a cheap off-the-shoulder evening dress. She examined her face, touching it with her fingertips. It had not bruised. He must be losing his touch. Her mouth still tasted of blood and she tested the looseness of her teeth with her index finger and thumb.

When she heard Paul thumping the sides of his cot she quickly finished her washing and went in to him. She tested if he was dry.

'Good for you,' she said. He was coming three and a half but she couldn't trust him a single night without a nappy. She gave him his handful of Ricicles on the pillow and he lay down beside them with a smile, looking at them, picking them up with concentration and eating them one by one like sweets. She went back to the kitchen and began heating the baby's bottle. The cold of the lino made her walk on tip-toe and she stood on the small mat, holding her bare elbows and shivering while the water came to the boil. She hated waiting – especially for a short time. Waiting a long time, you could be lazy or do something if you felt like it. She saw last night's dishes congealed in the sink, the fag-ends, but had no time or desire to do anything about it. In short waits she was aware of the rubbish of her life.

After the milk heated and while the bottle was cooling in a pot of cold water, she looked into the front room. Light came through the gap in the curtains. Eamonn lay on his back on the sofa, his shoes kicked off, breathing heavily through his slack open mouth. When she came back after feeding and changing the baby, he was still in the same position. She whacked the curtains open loudly. His eyes cringed and wavered and he turned his face into the sofa. He closed and opened his mouth and from where she stood she could hear the tacky dryness of it.

'Fuck you,' he said.

He lay there as she tidied around him. On the cream tiled hearth a complete cigarette had become a worm of white ash on brown sweat.

In the kitchen she began to wash up and make a cup of tea. They had run out of bread except for a heel of pan. She opened a packet of biscuits.

'Liz,' Eamonn called her. 'Liz.'

But she didn't feel like answering. She went and picked Paul out of his cot and let him run into the front room to annoy his Daddy. When she was sitting at her tea Eamonn came in, his shirt-tail out, and drank several cups of water. He looked wretched.

'There's a sliding brick in my head,' he said. 'Every time I move it wallops.'

Still she said nothing. He shuffled towards her and she looked out of the window at the corrugated-iron coal-house and the other pre-fabs stretching up the hill.

'Let me see,' he said and turned her face with the back of his hand. 'You're all right.'

'No thanks to you,' she said. The ridiculous thing was that *she* felt sorry for *him*. How could anyone do that to her? How could anyone knock her to the floor and kick her, then take off his shoes and fall asleep? Why did she feel pity for him and not for herself? He sat down on a stool and held on to his head.

'I suppose you don't remember anything,' she said.

'Enough.'

'I'll not stand much more of it, Eamonn.'

'Don't talk shit.' He wasn't angry. It was just his way. Sober she could handle him. The next day he never apologised – not once, and she had learned not to expect it. Last night he had got it into his head that the baby wasn't his. This was new and she had been frightened that in drink he might do something to it, so she had let him work out his anger on her.

Only she knew it was a possibility. Those nights had been long, sitting on her own minding her child, bored to tears with television, so that when Barney started to call – she had known him since her days in primary school – it had been a gradual and easy fall. He worked in a garage and was a folk singer of sorts. He made her feel relaxed in his company and she laughed, which was unusual for her. Even while they were at it behind the snibbed door of their small bathroom he could make her laugh – his head almost touching one wall while he got movement on her by levering his sock soles off the other.

Then he just stopped calling, saying that he was getting more and more engagements for his folk group. But that was nearly two years ago and she was disturbed that she should start being hit for it now. She wondered who had put it into his mind. Was it a rumour in that Provos club where he spent the most of his time drinking? God knows what else he got up to there. Once he had brought home an armful of something wrapped in sacking and hid it in the roof-space. When she pestered him as to what it was he refused to tell her.

'It's only for a couple of nights,' was all he would say. Those two days she fretted herself sick waiting for an Army-pig to pull up at the door.

Liz threw her tea down the sink.

'I suppose there's no money left,' she said, looking out the window. He made a kind of snort laugh. 'What am I going to use for the messages?'

'Henderson pays you today, doesn't he?'

'Jesus, you drink your dole money and I work to pay the messages. That's lovely. Smashin'.'

Paul had wandered in from the other room, shredding the cork tip of a cigarette butt, and Eamonn began to talk to him, ignoring her.

'Mucky pup,' he said taking it from between the child's fingers and roughly brushing them clean with his own hand.

'That's right, just throw it on the floor at your arse. I'm here to clean it up,' shouted Liz. She began thumpingly to wash the dishes. Eamonn went to the bathroom.

The hill to Ardview House was so steep that the pram handle pressed against the chest muscles just beneath her small breasts. Liz angled herself, pushing with her chest rather than her arms. It was a hot autumn day and the lack of wind made her feel breathless. Half way up she stopped and put the brake on with her foot.

'Paul,' she said, panting, 'get off, son, before I have a coronary.'

The child girned that he didn't want to but she was firm with him, lifting him under the armpits and setting him on the ground.

'You can hold on to the handle.'

In the pram, sheltered by its black hood, the baby was a pink knitted bonnet, its face almost obscured by a bobbing dummy. She continued up the hill.

She seemed to be doing this journey all the time, day in day out, up and down this hill. She knew where the puddles were in the worn tarmac of the footpath and could avoid them even though she was unsighted by the pram. A police car bounced over the crest of the hill, its lights flashing and its siren screaming. It passed her with a whumph of speed and gradually faded into the distance, spreading ripples of nervousness as far as the ear could hear.

When she turned off the road into the gravelled driveway she noticed that there was jam or marmalade on the black pram-hood. She wiped it with a tissue, but the smear still glistened. She wet her finger and rubbed it, but only succeeded in making her fingers tacky. The pram was impossible to push on the gravel and she pulled it the rest of the way to the house. Paul was running ahead, hurrying to get to the playroom. The Henderson children had left a legacy of broken but expensive toys and usually Paul disappeared and gave her little trouble until she had her work finished.

She wondered if Mr Henderson would be in. She was nervous of him, not just because he was her boss, but because of the way he looked at her. Of late he seemed to wait around in the mornings until she came. And then there was the money business.

Henderson was a big-wig who had made his money in paints, and on rare occasions when there were more than six guests his wife would invite Liz to dress up a bit and come and help serve dinner. Although a Unionist through and through, Henderson liked to be able to say that he employed Catholics.

'It's the only way forward. We must begin to build bridges. Isn't that right, Mrs O'Prey?' he'd say over his shoulder as she cleared the soup plates.

'Yes, sir,' said Liz.

In his house the other guests nodded.

'I make no secret of it. It's my ambition to become Lord Mayor of this town. Get others to put into practice what I preach.'

As she washed the dishes in her best dress she heard them laugh and guffaw in the other room.

The baby was sleeping, so Liz left her at the front door in the warm sunlight and went down to the pantry where she kept her cleaning things. She heard a door close upstairs and a moment later Mr Henderson came into the kitchen. He looked as if he had just had a shower and his hair, which was normally bushy, lay slick and black against the skin of his head. He wore a sage-green towelling dressing-gown knotted at the waist. His legs were pallid and hairy and he wore a pair of backless clog slippers. Standing with his back to her his heels were raw red.

'Good morning, Mrs O'Prey.'

She nodded at his back, Vim in one hand, J-cloths in the other, and excused herself. But he put himself between her and the door.

'That's a pleasant morning,' he said. 'Hot, even.'

She agreed. He bent to the refrigerator, blocking her way. He poured himself a glass of orange juice and leaned his back against the breakfast bar. He was tall and thin, in the region of fifty, but she found it hard to tell age. He wasn't ugly but she wouldn't have called him good-looking. His face had the grey colour of someone not long awake and his eyes behind dark-rimmed spectacles had the same look.

'How are things?'

'All right,' she said.

'Have you thought about my proposition?'

'Eh?'

'Did you think about my offer?'

'No,' she said and edged past him to the door to go upstairs. She began by cleaning the bathroom, hoping that Mr Henderson would leave for work before she would make the beds. She put his denture powder back in the cabinet and returned his toothbrush to the rack. She hosed round the shower with the sprinkler and with finger and thumb lifted a small scribbled clot of his black hairs which refused to go down the rose grating and dropped them into the toilet bowl. The noise of the flush must have camouflaged his footsteps on the stairs because Liz, squatting to clean some talc which had spilled down the outside of the bath, did not notice him standing in the doorway until he spoke.

'How remarkably thin you keep,' he said. She did not look round but was aware of a large gap between her jumper at the back and her jeans tight on her hips.

'It's hard work that does it.' She tried to tug her jumper down. He probably saw right into her pants. Let him. She turned round, her elbow resting on the lavatory seat. 'And not eating too much.'

'Oh, Mrs Henderson asked me to pay you this week.' He slippered off to his bedroom and came back a moment later with a wallet. He sat on the edge of the bath. If Liz was to sit the only place was the lavatory, so she stood while he drew clean notes from the wallet.

'She was in a rush this morning going out. How much is it?'

Liz told him and he counted out the twelve pounds. He set the money on the Vanitory unit, then went on taking out notes. Blue ones, slightly hinged from the bend of the wallet. Five – ten – fifteen she saw him mouth. He stopped at seventy-five. A strand of his damp hair detached itself from the rest and hung like a black sickle in his eye. He looked at her.

'I can afford it,' he said. 'It's yours if you want it.'

She could see herself reflected from neck to knees in a rectangular mirror that ran the length of the bath. Would he never give up? This was a rise of twenty-five from the last time. She remembered once up an entry doing a pee standing up for thruppence and the boys had whooped and jeered as she splashed her good shoes and had run off and never paid her. Afterwards she had cried.

'I can afford better but I want you,' he said. 'I'll leave it on the desk in my room.' His voice was hoarse and slightly trembling because she had not said no. He moved towards his room, saying over his shoulder, 'I'm not going in to the office this morning.'

Liz heard the one-stair-at-a-time stomp of Paul and went to the door to meet him.

'Muh,' he said.

'Yes, love.' She could feel the shake in her knees as she carried him down the stairs.

She began to scrape and put the accumulated dishes into the dishwasher. The bin yawned with bad breath when Paul pushed the foot-pedal with his hand so she emptied it and cleaned it with bleach. Her pelvis touched the stainless steel of the sink and she winced. She must have bruised. Eamonn would probably have gone back to bed now that he had it all to himself. He would get up about mid-day and go to either the pub or the bookies. Probably both. They were next door, the one feeding off the other. She had noticed a horseshoe of wear in the pavement from one door to the other. At night he would go to the Provos club. The drink was cheaper there because most of it was hi-jacked. He would not be home until midnight at the earliest and there was no guarantee they wouldn't have another boxing match. She breathed out and heard it as a shuddering sigh.

'Muh,' Paul said.

'Yes, love, whatever you say.'

What could she do with that kind of money? Eamonn would know immediately – he could smell pound notes – and want to know how she got it. If she got a new rig-out it would be the same. He would kill her. Before or after she had spent the money didn't matter. Her mother had always harped on that Liz had married beneath her.

She wiped down the white Formica and began to load the washing machine from the laundry basket. Or toys or kids. She could think of no way of spending where questions wouldn't be asked. At eleven she made a coffee. She opened a window and smoked a cigarette, sharpening its ash on a flowered saucer.

'Buh?' Paul asked, reaching her a pot lid.

'Thanks, son.' She took it off him and set it on the table.

When Liz reached three-quarters' way down her cigarette she stubbed it out with determination, bending it almost double. She got up and brought Paul with a biscuit and milk in his baby cup into the playroom.

'There's a good boy,' she said. 'Mammy will be cross if you come out.'

She had walloped him round the legs before for keeping her back with her work, so he knew what was in store for him if he wandered. She went outside and checked the baby in the pram. She was still asleep, so she closed the front door quietly and climbed the stairs.

In his room Mr Henderson sat at a small desk strewn with papers. At her knock he raised his glasses to his hairline and turned.

'Yes?'

'It's me.'

'Well?'

'All right,' she said. Her voice caught in her throat as if she had been crying for a long time. 'Just so long as you don't kiss me.'

'That will not be necessary.' His face broke into a frightened smile of disbelief. He was still in his dressing-gown, a furry thigh sticking out. He came to her, his arm extended – fatherly almost.

'You're sure? I would get very angry if you were to change your mind once we had started.'

She nodded. 'What do you want me to do?'

'I want you to lie down.' That was a favourite song of Barney's – 'Croppies Lie Down' – but now in her tension she couldn't remember the words.

'In fact I want you to do nothing. That's the way I like it.'

'Could I have the money?'

'Yes, yes.' He was impatient now and fumbled with the wallet, then saw the money on the desk. The roll of notes made a comfortable bulge in the hip pocket of her jeans. He locked the door as she lay on the bed. It was like being asked to lie on a doctor's couch. Mr Henderson knelt and patted and prodded her to his liking. No sooner was she settled than he said,

'Perhaps you'd better take your clothes off.'

She had to get up again. There was a hole in her pants stretched to an egg shape just below her navel. She turned her back on him then, when undressed, lay down, her body all knuckles.

His eyes widened and went heavy. He couldn't decide whether to take off his glasses or leave them on. He began to talk baby-talk, to speak to her as if she wasn't there. He told her how he had ached after her slim undernourished body for months, how he had watched her from between the banisters, how he loved to see her on her hands and knees and the triangle of light that he could always see between her thighs when she wore her jeans. He was fascinated by her bruises and kissed each one of them lightly. Spoke to her bruises. She was sweating a nervous sweat from her armpits. Praised her thinness, her each rib, the tent bones of her hips and her tuft of hair between. He smelt all over her as she had seen dogs do, but by now she had closed her eyes and could only feel the touch of his breath, his nosings. It went on for ages. Her fists were clenched. She tried to remember her shopping list. A pan loaf, maybe some small bread – sodas. Sugar – she needed sugar and potatoes and tea-bags and mince and corn-flakes. Mr Henderson climbed on to the bed, having opened her legs, but succeeded only in delivering himself somewhere in the coverlet with a groan. She looked down at him. His hair was still damp and moistening her belly. His face was hidden from her. The back of his neck was red and criss-crossed with wrinkles. Beneath the window she could hear her baby crying and farther away the sound of a blackbird.

When he got his breath back he went to the bathroom. Liz dressed in a hurry and went downstairs, trying to master the shudders that went through her like nausea. She inserted the dummy in the baby's mouth, grabbed Paul from the playroom and fled the house, drawing the pram after her against the gravel.

The kiosk outside the Co-op smelt of piss, would have smelt worse if it had not been for the ventilation of the broken panes. A taxi arrived within minutes and she coaxed the driver to collapse the pram and put it in the boot.

'In the name of God, Missus, how does this thing operate?'

In a traffic jam – there must have been a bomb scare somewhere – she fed the baby milk from a cold bottle.

Her mother lived at the other side of town and was surprised to see her drawing up in such style. Liz told the driver to wait and hurried her mother into accepting the story that a friend's husband had run off with another woman and the girl was in a terrible state and she, Liz, was going to spend the night with her, and Mammy would you mind the kids? Her mother was old but not yet helpless and had raised six of her own. At twenty-two Liz was the last and felt she could call on her for special favours. She gave her a fiver to get herself some wee thing. A tenner, she thought, would have brought questions in its wake.

'You're a pet,' she called to her, rushing from the door.

Coming from Marks and Spencer's, she walked past the Methodist Church in Donegal Place. An old man was changing the black notice-board which kept up with the death toll of the Troubles. She hesitated and watched him. He had removed a 5 from 1875 and was fumbling and clacking with the wooden squares which slotted in like a hymn board. He was exasperatingly slow and she walked on but could not resist looking back over her shoulder.

Going through security, the woman stirred her jeans and jumper tentatively at the bottom of her carrier bag. The hotel lobby was crowded with newsmen with bandoliers of cameras, talking in groups. She asked the price of bed and breakfast and found that she had more than enough. Would she be having dinner? Liz leaned forward to the clerk.

'How much?'

The clerk smiled and said anything from five to fifty pounds. Liz thought a moment and said yes. She wanted to pay there and then but the clerk insisted that she could settle her bill in the morning.

'Elizabeth O'Prey' she signed the register card, taking great care

to make it neat. At school she had never been much good but everybody praised her handwriting; teachers said she had a gift for it. She
had been Elizabeth Wilson and one of the few advantages of her
marriage, she thought, had been the opportunity of a flourishing Y
at the end of O'Prey. As she had signed for her family allowance and
sickness benefit she had perfected it.

She tried not to stare at the magnificence of the place, the plush
maroon carpet, the glittering lights, the immaculately uniformed staff.
She felt nervous about doing or saying the wrong thing. She didn't
have a posh accent like those around her and rather than put it on
she said as few words as possible. She was conscious of people looking
at her and was glad that she had changed in the shop. As the desk
clerk answered the phone she saw herself in a mirrored alcove, new
shoes, hair done, new peach-coloured summer dress, and was happily
surprised. For a second she didn't look like herself. Her Marks and
Spencer's polythene bag was the only thing that jarred. She should
have bought a real bag.

'Excuse me, madam,' said the clerk, clamping the ear-piece against
her shoulder, 'would you mind if security checked you out again?'

'They already searched me.'

'If you wouldn't mind.'

A woman in uniform came out and showed Liz to a small room.
She was stout with blonde curly hair bursting from beneath her
peaked cap, chewing-gum in a mouth heavy with lip-gloss. Her body
seemed pumped into the uniform. She searched Liz's carrier bag
thoroughly.

'Why are you searching me twice?'

'You have a Belfast address, you have no luggage.' She came towards
Liz, who raised her arms obediently. 'Why are you staying here?' Her
heavy hands moved over Liz's small breasts, beneath her arms to her
waist, down her buttocks and thighs. She had never been searched
as thoroughly as this before – a series of light touches was all she'd
had. This woman was groping her as if she expected to find something
beneath her skin.

'My husband put me out,' said Liz. A forefinger scored up the track
between her buttocks and she jumped.

'That's all right, love. We have to be sure.' She smiled, handing her back her carrier bag. 'I hope you and your man get it sorted out.'

A bell-boy who was twice her age turned his back to her in the quiet of the lift before he showed her to her room. He made no attempt to carry her polythene bag.

When she closed and locked the door she felt for the first time in years that she was alone. She could not believe it. She stood with her back to the door, her hands behind her resting on the handle. The room took her breath away. Matching curtains and bedspread of tangerine flowers with one corner of the sheets folded back to show that they too matched. She walked around the room touching things lightly. From her window she could see a wedge of red-brick Belfast vibrating in the heat. This height above the street she could hear no sound. She lay on the bed, trying it for size and comfort, and to her disappointment it creaked slightly. The bathroom was done in rust shades with carpet going up the outside of the bath.

The first thing she had decided to do was to have a shower. Her new dress did nothing to remove the crawling sensation on her skin when she thought of Mr Henderson. Before undressing she turned on the test card on the television just for a bit of sound. She had never had a shower before and it took her ages to get it to work, then even longer to get the temperature right, but when she did get in she felt like a film star. Her instinct was to save the hot water but she remembered where she was and how much she was paying. She must have stayed in the shower for twenty minutes soaping and resoaping herself, watching the drapes of suds sliding down her body and away. The bruises remained.

She put on the new underwear and felt luxuriant to be padding about free in her bra and pants. Although the shower was good she decided that before she went to bed she would have a bath so hot the steam would mist the mirrors. She would buy some magazines and smoke and read, propped up by all those pillows. Watch television *from* bed, maybe.

In the bar she felt good, for the first time in years felt herself. She sat at a stool at the counter and sipped a vodka and orange. The bar was loud with groups of people talking. She caught herself staring in the bar mirror as she looked around. A man came in and sat next to her on a free stool. She wondered if he was waiting for someone. He ordered a drink, asked her to pass the water jug for his whisky. She smiled. He slowly tilted the jug until it was upright and obviously empty and then they both laughed. He asked the barmaid for water.

'Are you American?' Liz asked. He nodded. He looked a good deal older than her, in his mid-thirties or forty, she guessed, with a plain face and a blond moustache. He had bad skin, pock-marked, but it gave him a rugged look. She imagined him on horseback.

'Yeah, and you?'

'Oh, I'm from here.'

'There's no need to apologise.' He laughed and poured water into his whisky slowly. She watched it mix in wreaths with the spirit. He tasted the drink and seemed satisfied. She became alone again as she bought herself cigarettes and matches. They drank separately in the noise. She crumpled the silver paper, dropped it in the ash-tray and offered him one. He refused with a spread hand. He asked the barmaid for a menu, which he studied.

'Are you gonna eat?' he asked. She nodded, with her mouth full of vodka and orange. 'It's quite good here. I can recommend their *coq au vin.*'

'Are you staying here?' He nodded. She asked him if he was on holiday and he said that he was working, a journalist of sorts.

'Oh, how interesting.' When she had said it she could have bitten her tongue out, it sounded so phoney. She heard Eamonn mimicking and repeating her tones, but this man did not seem to notice. She asked,

'What paper?'

The piece he would do would be syndicated. She nodded and took another sip of her drink. There was a pause as he studied the menu.

'Excuse my iggerence,' said Liz, 'but what does that mean – sin . . . sin . . .?'

'Sorry. It just means that the same story goes in lots of papers – and I get more money.'

Liz tap-tapped her cigarette with her index finger over the ash-tray but it was not smoked enough for any of it to fall.

'You say you're from here,' he said. 'If you don't mind me asking, which side are you on?'

'I'm sort of in the middle.'

'That can't help.'

'Well I was born nothing – but a Protestant nothing and I married a Catholic nothing and so I'm now a mixture of nothing. I hate the whole thing. I couldn't give a damn.'

'One of the silent minority.' He smiled. 'Boy, have you got problems.' Liz thought he was talking about her.

'Me?'

'Not you – the country.'

They talked for a while and went separately in to dinner. When he saw that she too was eating at a table on her own he came over and suggested that they eat together. She agreed, grateful for someone to help her with choosing from the menu. Rather than attempt to say the dishes, she pointed and he ordered. The array of knives and forks frightened her but she did what he did, American style, cutting up and eating with the fork alone. He told her that he had been a Catholic priest and that he had left when he had had a crisis of conscience, Vietnam, contraception, the nature of authority all contributing. As a priest he had written a weekly column for a Catholic paper in Boston, and when he left the Church to continue working in journalism was natural. He admitted to being married shortly after being laicised. She said she too was married.

He made her feel good, relaxed. In his company she felt she could say anything. After telling of himself he asked her questions about her life. The questions he asked no one had ever asked her before and she had to think hard to answer them. In her replies she got mixed up, found she was contradicting herself, but got out of it by laughing.

'This is like an interview on the T.V.,' she said and he apologised but went on asking her questions, about her life, about the way she felt and thought. His eyes were blue and gentle, widening at some of the things she said. Except for his pitted skin she found him attractive. He listened with the slightest inclination of the head, looking up at her almost. Being from America he probably didn't know about her accent. Maybe she looked high-class in her peach rig-out. Liz spoke until she realised she was speaking, then she became self-conscious.

'I hope you're not taking all this down,' she said laughing.

'No, but it sure helps to talk to someone like you – a nothing as you so nicely put it. It helps the balance.'

Hesitatingly she told him something of her relationship, or lack of it, with Eamonn. 'You have your troubles,' was all he would say.

When they had finished eating he suggested that they go through to the bar to have a liqueur. He was behind her, easing her seat away from the table before she realised it and he was equally attentive and concerned holding the bar door open for her.

'You're a gentleman,' she said.

'My old man used to say that a gentleman was someone who made a woman feel like a lady.'

He introduced her to Bailey's Irish Cream.

'It's gorgeous,' she said, 'like sweets. You could drink that all night.'

'You could not,' he said, smiling.

Liz settled back in the seat and lit a cigarette. She slapped her stomach lightly.

'God, I'm full,' she said, 'and I feel great. I haven't felt like this for ages.'

They had another Bailey's Irish Cream, which she insisted on buying. Then when he had finished it he said, slapping his knees,

'I must go. I have some work to finish for tomorrow. Will you excuse me?'

'Sure.' She tried to make it sound as if she was not disappointed at all but was conscious that some of his accent was invading her speech. She detained him a little longer, asking him to wait till she finished another cigarette but eventually he said he must go up to his room.

'I don't want to sit here on my owney-o,' said Liz. 'I think I'll just go up too.'

In the lift there was a silence between them. Liz felt she had to talk.

'What floor are you on?'

'I pressed number four and you're on six.'

'That's right.'

She told him her room number and then thought it too forward. She hadn't meant to tell him but the silence of the humming lift forced her to say it.

Getting out of the lift, he touched her arm with his hand, then shook hands.

'It's been a real pleasure meeting you,' he said. The lift doors nipped her view of his smile as he waved goodbye.

In her room the aloneness changed from what she had felt earlier. Now it seemed enforced. She wanted to go on talking. In the mirror she shrugged, made a face and laughed at herself. The only thing to read was a Bible on the bedside table and she was annoyed that she had forgotten to buy some magazines. She had the hot bath she had promised herself, but afterwards was too warm so she opened a window on to the distant sound of the street.

She prodded the buttons on the television set and for want of anything better settled on 'Call My Bluff' with that nice man with the pink bow tie and the moustache. In her new underwear she sat propped up on tangerine pillows, smoking – viewing in style. Where did they get the words from? Clinchpoop? Liz guessed it was the thing the man said about the plague but it turned out to be somebody who didn't know what to do – like eating peas with your knife or backslapping at a funeral. That was her, she thought. She never knew what to do at the time. Later on she knew what she should and could have done. And it was not just with manners. She had no control over the direction of her life. She was far too bloody soft. From now on she should lock Eamonn out and begin to fight her own corner – for the children's sake at least.

She jumped out of bed and pressed the channel buttons. After the ads it was part three of something so she switched off. The room was very quiet. She got back into bed again, hearing its annoying creak and the crispness of its sheets.

She should have told that Henderson to get knotted. It was the end of her job – there was no way she could go back there again. He would hang about like a dog every morning from now on pointing at her with his trousers. Resignation. That was all that was left to her. But then

Eamonn would want to know why she had quit. Tell him Henderson had made a pass at her – which was true. Maybe he'd want to know where she'd spent the night. She had run to her mother's before because of a fight. If he noticed she'd been away at all. The peach dress she would have to leave in the wardrobe. Or she could leave it at her mother's until she found an excuse to bring it home. Why hadn't she thought of it before? She could pass it off as good jumble sale stuff.

Pleased with herself, she lay down among the pillows and spread her feet warm and wide. With the lamp out, car headlights swung yellow wedges across the ceiling. The net curtains ballooned slowly and fell back again. She thought of her baby sleeping in the spare bed at her mother's, walled in by pillows, and Paul, open-mouthed in sleep, snuggling in to his Gran. 'That child has knees on him like knuckles,' the old woman had once complained. Liz spread her opened fingers across the sheets, trying to take up as much room as possible in the bed. She smelt the strange perfumed hotel soap off her own body, felt the summer night warmth on her face and tried, as she drifted off to sleep, to forget the fact that Eamonn, for the loss of her weekly wage, would kill her when he got her home – if not before.

THE BEGINNINGS OF A SIN

I believe he's late again thought Colum. He took a clean white surplice
from his bag and slipped it over his head, steadying his glasses as he
did so. It was five to eight. He sat on the bench and changed his
shoes for a black pair of gutties. Father Lynch said that all his
altar-boys must move as quietly as shadows. When he was late he
was usually in his worst mood. Sometimes he did not turn up at all
and Miss Grant, the housekeeper, would come over and announce
from the back of the church that Father Lynch was ill and that there
would be no Mass that day.

At two minutes to eight Colum heard his footstep at the vestry
door. Father Lynch came in and nodded to the boy. Colum had never
seen anyone with such a sleep-crumpled face in the mornings. It
reminded him of a bloodhound, there was such a floppiness about
his deeply wrinkled skin. His whole face sagged and sloped into lines
of sadness. His black hair was parted low to the side and combed
flat with Brylcreem. Colum thought his neat hair looked out of place
on top of the disorder of his features.

'Is everything ready?' Father Lynch asked him.

'Yes, Father.'

Colum watched him as he prepared to say Mass. He began by
putting on the amice, like a handkerchief with strings, at the back of
his neck. Next a white alb like a shroud, reaching to the floor. The
polished toe-caps of his everyday shoes peeped out from underneath.
He put the cincture about his waist and knotted it quickly. He kissed
the embroidered cross on his emerald stole and hung it round his
neck. Lastly he put on the chasuble, very carefully inserting his head
through the neck-hole. Colum couldn't make up his mind whether
he did not want to stain the vestments with hair-oil or wreck his hair.
The chasuble was emerald green with yellow lines. Colum liked the

feasts of the martyrs best, with their bright blood colour. Father Lynch turned to him.

'What are you staring at?'

'Nothing, Father.'

'You look like a wee owl.'

'Sorry.'

'Let's get this show on the road,' Father Lynch said, his face still like a sad bloodhound. 'We're late already.'

None of the other altar-boys liked Father Lynch. When they did something wrong, he never scolded them with words but instead would nip them on the upper arm. They said he was too quiet and you could never trust anybody like that. Colum found that he was not so quiet if you asked him questions. He seemed to like Colum better than the others, at least Colum thought so. One day he had asked him why a priest wore so much to say Mass and Father Lynch had spoken to him for about ten minutes, keeping him late for school.

'Normally when people wear beautiful things it is to make their personality stand out. With a priest it is the opposite. He wears so much to hide himself. And the higher up the Church you go, the more you have to wear. Think of the poor Pope with all that trumphery on him.'

After Mass Father Lynch asked him how the ballot tickets were going.

'Great. I've sold –'

'Don't tell me. Keep it as a surprise.'

In the darkness Colum stood at the door waiting. He had rolled up a white ballot ticket and was smoking it, watching his breath cloud the icy air. He pulled his socks up as high as he could to try and keep his legs warm. There was a funny smell from the house, like sour food. The woman came back out with her purse. She was still chewing something.

'What's it in aid of?'

'St Kieran's Church Building Fund.'

'How much are they?'

'Threepence each.'

The woman hesitated, poking about in her purse with her index finger. He told her that the big prize was a Christmas hamper. There was a second prize of whiskey and sherry. She took four tickets, finishing his last book.

'Father Lynch'll not be wanting to win it outright, then.'

He was writing her name on the stubs with his fountain pen.

'Pardon?'

'You're a neat wee writer,' she said. He tore the tickets down the perforations and gave them to her. She handed him a shilling, which he dropped into his jacket pocket. It was swinging heavy with coins.

'There's the snow coming on now,' said the woman, waiting to close the front door. He ran the whole way home holding on to the outside of his pocket. In the house he dried his hair and wiped the speckles of melted snow from his glasses. Two of his older brothers, Rory and Dermot, were sitting on the sofa doing homework balanced on their knees and when he told them it was snowing they ran out to see if it was lying.

He took down his tin and spilled it and the money from his pocket on to the table. He added it all together and counted the number of books of stubs. For each book sold the seller was allowed to keep sixpence for himself. Over the past weeks Colum had sold forty-two books around the doors. He took a pound note and a shilling and slipped them into his pocket. He had never had so much money in his life and there was still a full week to sell tickets before the ballot was drawn.

His mother stood at the range making soda farls on a griddle. When they were cooked they filled the house with their smell and made a dry scuffling noise as she handled them. He heard the front door close and Michael shout 'Hello'. At eighteen he was the eldest and the only wage earner in the house.

'Come on, Colum,' said his mother. 'Clear that table. The hungry working man is in.'

After tea they always said the Family Rosary. Colum would half kneel, half crouch at the armchair with his face almost touching the seat. The cushion smelt of cloth and human. He tried to say the Rosary as best he could, thinking of the Sacred Mysteries while his mouth said the words. He was disturbed one night to see Michael kneeling at the sofa saying the prayers with the Sunday paper between his elbows. Colum counted off the Hail Marys, feeding his shiny lilac rosary beads between his finger and thumb. They were really more suitable for a woman but they had come all the way from Lourdes. Where the loop of the beads joined was a little silver heart with a bubble of Lourdes water in it – like the spirit level in his brother's tool kit.

When it came to his turn to give out the prayer Colum always waited until the response was finished – not like his brothers who charged on, overlapping the prayer and the response, slurring their words to get it finished as quickly as possible. They became annoyed with him and afterwards, in whispers, accused him of being 'a creeping Jesus'.

At the end of each Rosary their mother said a special prayer 'for the Happy Repose of the Soul of Daddy'. Although he had been dead two years, it still brought a lump to Colum's throat. It wouldn't have been so bad if she had said father or something but the word Daddy made him want to cry. Sometimes he had to go on kneeling when the others had risen to their feet in case they should see his eyes.

It was Colum's turn to do the dishes. They had their turns written up on a piece of paper so that there would be no argument. He poured some hot water into the basin from the kettle on the range. It had gone slightly brown from heating. He didn't like the look of it as much as the cold water from the pump. In the white enamel bucket under the scullery bench it looked pure and cool and still. Where the enamel had chipped off, the bucket was blue-black. If you put your hand in the water the fingers seemed to go flat.

He dipped a cup into the basin, rinsed it out and set it on the table. Father Lynch had funny fingers. He had tiny tufts of black hair on the back of each of them. They made Colum feel strange as he poured water from a cruet on to them. The priest would join his trembling index fingers and thumbs and hold them over the glass bowl, then he would take the linen cloth ironed into its folds and wipe them dry. He would put it back in its creases and lay it on Colum's arm. He had some whispered prayers to say when he was doing that. Colum always wondered why Father Lynch was so nervous saying his morning Mass. He had served for others and they didn't tremble like that. Perhaps it was because he was holier than them, that they weren't as much in awe of the Blessed Sacrament as he was. What a frightening thing it must be, to hold Christ's actual flesh – to have the responsibility to change the bread and wine into the body and blood of Jesus.

He dried the dishes and set them in neat piles before putting them back on the shelf. Above the bench Michael had fixed a small mirror for shaving. Colum had to stand on tip-toe to see himself. He was the only one of the family who had to wear glasses. He took after his father. For a long time he had to wear National Health round ones with the springy legs that hooked behind his ears, but after months of pleading and crying his mother had given in and bought him a good pair with real frames.

He went to the back door and threw out a basinful of water with a slap on to the icy ground. It steamed in the light from the scullery window. It was a still night and he could hear the children's voices yelling from the next street.

The kitchen was warm when he came back in again. Radio Luxembourg was on the wireless. Colum took all his money in his pocket and put the stubs in a brown paper bag.

'I'm away, Mammy,' he said.

She was having a cigarette, sitting with her feet up on a stool.

'Don't be late,' was all she said.

He walked a lamp post, ran a lamp post through the town until he reached the hill which led to the Parochial House. It was a large building made of the same red brick as the church. He could see lights on in the house so he climbed the hill. It was still bitterly cold and he was aware of his jaw shivering. He kept both hands in his pockets, holding the brown bag in the crook of his arm. He knocked at the door of the house. It was the priest's housekeeper who opened it a fraction. When she saw Colum she opened it wide.

'Hello, Miss Grant. Is Father Lynch in?'

'He is busy, Colum. What was it you wanted?'

'Ballot tickets, Miss. And to give in money.'

She looked over her shoulder down the hallway, then turned and put out her hand for the money.

'It's all loose, Miss,' said Colum, digging into his pocket to let her hear it.

'Oh, you'd best come in then – for a moment.'

Miss Grant brought him down the carpeted hallway to her quarters – she had a flat of her own at the back of the house. She closed the door and smiled a jumpy kind of smile – a smile that stopped in the middle. Colum emptied the bag of stubs on the table.

'There's forty-two books . . .' he said.

'Goodness, someone has been busy.'

'. . . and here is five pounds, five shillings.' He set two pound notes and a ten shilling note on the table and hand-fulled the rest of the coins out of his pocket. They rang and clattered on the whitewood surface. She began to check it, scraping the coins towards her quickly and building them into piles.

'All present and correct,' she said.

Colum looked at the sideboard. There was a bottle of orange juice and a big box of biscuits which he knew was for the ticket sellers. She saw him looking.

'All right, all right,' she said.

She poured a glass of juice and allowed him to choose two biscuits. His fingers hovered over the selection.

'Oh come on, Colum, don't take all night.'

He took a chocolate one and a wafer and sat down. He had never seen Miss Grant so snappy before. Usually she was easygoing. She was very fat, with a chest like stuffed pillows under her apron. He had heard the grown-ups in the town say that if anybody had earned heaven it was her. They spoke of her goodness and kindness. 'There's one saint in that Parochial House,' they would say. For a long time Colum thought they were talking about Father Lynch.

In the silence he heard his teeth crunching the biscuit. Miss Grant did not sit down but stood by the table waiting for him to finish. He swallowed and said,

'Could I have ten more books, please?'

'Yes, dear.' She put her hands in her apron pocket and looked all around her, then left the room.

Colum had never been in this part of the house before. He had always gone into Father Lynch's room or waited in the hallway. Although it was a modern house, it was full of old things. A picture of the Assumption of Our Lady in a frame of gold leaves hung by the front door. The furniture in Father Lynch's room was black and heavy. The dining room chairs had twisted legs like barley sugar sticks. Everything had a rich feel to it, especially the thick patterned carpet. Miss Grant's quarters were not carpeted but had some rugs laid on the red tiled floor. It was the kind of floor they had at home, except that the corners of their tiles were chipped off and they had become uneven enough to trip people.

'Vera!' he heard a voice shout. It was Father Lynch.

Vera's voice answered from somewhere. Colum looked up and Father Lynch was standing in the doorway with his arm propped against the jamb.

'Hello, Father.'

'Well, if it isn't the owl,' said Father Lynch.

He wasn't dressed like a priest but was wearing an ordinary man's collarless shirt, open at the neck.

'What brings you up here, Colum?'

He moved from the door and reached out to put his hand on a chair back. Two strands of his oiled hair had come loose and fallen over his forehead. He sat down very slowly on the chair.

'Ballot tickets, Father. I've sold all you gave me.'

Father Lynch gave a loud whoop and slapped the table loudly with the flat of his hand. His eyes looked very heavy and he was blinking a lot.

'That's the way to do it. Lord, how the money rolls in.'

He was slurring his words as if he was saying the Rosary. Miss Grant came into the room holding a wad of white ballot tickets.

'Here you are now, Colum. You'd best be off.'

Colum finished his juice and stood up.

'Is that the strongest you can find for the boy to drink, Vera?' He laughed loudly. Colum had never heard him laugh before. He slapped the table again.

'Father – if you'll excuse us, I'll just show Colum out now.'

'No. No. He came to see me – didn't you?'

Colum nodded.

'He's the only one that would. Let him stay for a bit.'

'His mother will worry about him.'

'No she won't,' said Colum.

'Of course she won't,' said Father Lynch. He ignored Miss Grant. 'How many books did you sell?'

'Forty-two, Father.'

The priest raised his eyes to heaven and blew out his cheeks. Colum smelt a smell like altar wine.

'Holy Saint Christopher. Forty-two?'

'Yes.'

Miss Grant moved behind Colum and began to guide him with pressure away from the table.

'That calls for a celebration.' Father Lynch stood up unsteadily. 'Forty-two!'

He reached out to give Colum a friendly cuff on the back of the head but he missed and instead his hand struck the side of the boy's face scattering his glasses on the tiled floor.

'Aw Jesus,' said the priest. 'I'm sorry.' Father Lynch hunkered down to pick them up but lurched forward on to his knees. One lens was starred with white and the arc of the frame was broken. He hoisted himself to his feet and held the glasses close to his sagging face, looking at them.

'Jesus, I'm so sorry,' he said again. He bent down, looking for the missing piece of frame, and the weight of his head seemed to topple him. He cracked his skull with a sickening thump off the sharp edge of a radiator. One of his legs was still up in the air trying to right his balance. He put his hand to the top of his head and Colum saw that the hand was slippery with blood. Red blood was smeared from his Brylcreemed hair on to the radiator panel as the priest slid lower. His eyes were open but not seeing.

'Are you all right, Father?' Miss Grant's voice was shaking. She produced a white handkerchief from her apron pocket. The priest

shouted, his voice suppressed and hissing and angry. He cursed his
housekeeper and the polish on her floor. Then he raised his eyes to
her without moving his head and said in an ordinary voice,

'What a mess for the boy.'

Miss Grant took the glasses which he was still clutching and put
them in Colum's hand. Father Lynch began to cry with his mouth
half open. Miss Grant turned the boy away and pushed him towards
the door. Both she and Colum had to step over the priest to get out.
She led him by the elbow down the hallway.

'That's the boy. Here's your ballot tickets.'

She opened the front door.

'Say a wee prayer for him, Colum. He's in bad need of it.'

'All right, but –'

'I'd better go back to him now.'

The door closed with a slam. Colum put his glasses on but could
only see through his left eye. His knees were like water and his
stomach was full of wind. He tried to get some of it up but he
couldn't. He started to run. He ran all the way home. He sat panting
on the cold doorstep and only went in when he got his breath back.
His mother was alone.

'What happened to you? You're as white as a sheet,' she said,
looking up at him. She was knitting a grey sock on three needles
shaped into a triangle. Colum produced his glasses from his pocket.
Within the safety of the house he began to cry.

'I bust them.'

'How, might I ask?' His mother's voice was angry.

'I was running and they just fell off. I slipped on the ice.'

'Good God, Colum, do you know how much those things cost? You'll
have to get a new pair for school. Where do you think the money is
going to come from? Who do you think I am, Carnegie? Eh?'

Her knitting needles were flashing and clacking. Colum continued
to cry, tears rather than noise.

'Sheer carelessness. I've a good mind to give you a thumping.'

Colum, keeping out of range of her hand, sat at the table and put
the glasses on. He could only half see. He put his hand in his pocket
and took out his pound note.

'Here,' he said offering it to his mother. She took it and put it beneath the jug on the shelf.

'That'll not be enough,' she said, then after a while, 'Will you stop that sobbing? It's not the end of the world.'

The next morning Colum was surprised to see Father Lynch in the vestry before him. He was robed and reading his breviary, pacing the strip of carpet in the centre of the room. They said nothing to each other.

At the Consecration Colum looked up and saw the black congealed wound on the thinning crown of Father Lynch's head, as he lifted the tail of the chasuble. He saw him elevate the white disc of the host and heard him mutter the words,

'*Hoc est enim corpus meum.*'

Colum jangled the cluster of bells with angry twists of his wrist. A moment later when the priest raised the chalice full of wine he rang the bell again, louder if possible.

In the vestry afterwards he changed as quickly as he could and was about to dash out when Father Lynch called him. He had taken off his chasuble and was folding it away.

'Colum.'

'What?'

'Sit down a moment.'

He removed the cincture and put it like a coiled snake in the drawer. The boy remained standing. The priest sat down in his alb and beckoned him over.

'I'm sorry about your glasses.'

Colum stayed at the door and Father Lynch went over to him. Colum thought his face no longer sad, simply ugly.

'Your lace is loosed.' He was about to genuflect to tie it for him but Colum crouched and tied it himself. Their heads almost collided.

'It's hard for me to explain,' said Father Lynch, 'but . . . to a boy of your age sin is a very simple thing. It's not.'

Colum smelt the priest's breath sour and sick.

'Yes, Father.'

'That's because you have never committed a sin. You don't know about it.'

He removed his alb and hung it in the wardrobe.

'Trying to find the beginnings of a sin is like . . .' He looked at the boy's face and stopped. 'Sin is a deliberate turning away from God. That is an extremely difficult thing to do. To close Him out from your love . . .'

'I'll be late for school, Father.'

'I suppose you need new glasses?'

'Yes.'

Father Lynch put his hand in his pocket and gave him some folded pound notes.

'Did you mention it to your mother?'

'What?'

'How they were broken?'

'No.'

'Are you sure? To anyone?'

Colum nodded that he hadn't. He was turning to get out the door. The priest raised his voice, trying to keep him there.

'I knew your father well, Colum,' he shouted. 'You remind me of him a lot.'

The altar-boy ran, slamming the door after him. He heard an empty wooden coat-hanger rattle on the hardboard panel of the door and it rattled in his mind until he reached the bottom of the hill. There he stopped running. He unfolded the wad of pound notes still in his hand and counted them with growing disbelief.

EELS

The old woman sat playing solitaire, hearing the quiet click of her wedding-ring on the polished table top each time she laid her hand flat to study the ranks of cards. They were never right. Never worked out. A crucial king face down, buried – and the game was lost. She realised how futile it was – not only this particular game but the activity of playing solitaire, and yet she could not stop herself, so she dealt the cards again. They flipped down silently, cushioned as they slid on the shine of the wood. She was reluctant to cheat. She played maybe six times before she gave up, put the cards away and sat gnawing her thumbnail. Perhaps later, left alone, it would come out.

She moved to the kitchen and took her magnesia, not bothering with the spoon but slugging the blue bottle back, hearing the white liquid tilt thickly. She swallowed hard, holding her thrapple. She stopped breathing through her nose so as not to taste, and held her mouth open. She walked to the bedroom, still breathing through her mouth until she saw herself in the mirror with crescents of white at the sides of her open lips. When she closed her teeth she heard and felt the sand of the magnesia grate between them. Her skin was loose and wrinkled, hanging about the bones she knew to be beneath her face. There were crows' feet at the corners of her eyes. With one finger she pressed down beneath her eye, baring its red sickle. They watered too much when the weather was cold. She wiped the white from the sides of her mouth with a tissue and began dressing, putting on several layers against the cold, with her old cardigan on top. She combed her white hair back from her forehead and looked at the number of hairs snagged on the comb. She removed them and with a fidget of her fingers dropped them into the waste-paper basket.

She remembered as a girl at the cottage combing her hair in spring sunshine and each day taking the dark hairs from the comb and dropping them out of the window with the same fidget of her fingers. A winter gale blew down a thrushes' nest into the garden and it was lined and snug with the black sheen of her own hair. For ages she kept it but it fell apart eventually, what with drying out and all the handling it got as she showed it to the children in class.

She lifted her raffia basket and put into it the magnesia, the pack of cards and a handful of tea-bags. In the hall she put on her heavy overcoat. The driveway to the house had not been made up, even though the house had been occupied for more than three years. It was rutted with tracks which had frozen over. She stopped to try one with the pressure of her toe, to see how heavy the frost had been. The slow ovals of bubbles separated and moved away from her toe. They returned again when she removed her weight but the ice did not break. She shuffled, afraid of falling, the ice crisping beneath her feet. Above her she saw the moon in its last phase shining at midday.

The air was bitterly cold. She had a pain in her throat which she experienced as a lump every time she swallowed. She had to chew what little she ate thoroughly or she felt it would not go past the lump. Everyone accused her of eating like a bird. Everyone said that she must see a doctor. But she knew without a doctor telling her that she would not see another winter. In September her son Brian had offered to buy her a heavy coat but she had refused, saying that she wouldn't get the wear out of it.

On the tarmac road she walked with a firmer step. There was no need to look up yet. She knew the bend, the precise gap in the hedge where she could see the lough. First she had to pass the school. The old school had been different, shaped like a church, built of white stone. But still, the new one had good toilets – better than the ones that she as a monitress had had to share with the whole school. It had got so bad that she eventually learned to hold on for the whole of the day.

The sound of the master's voice rang out impatiently as she passed, shouting a page number again and again. She smiled and anticipated the gap in the hedge. The shoulder of the hill sloped down and she raised her eyes to look at the lough. It was there, a flat bar almost to the horizon, the colour of aluminium. She stopped and stared.

Round the next turn was the cottage, set by itself with its back to the lough. No one saw her. Not that it would really matter. She let herself in the front door with her own key and hung her coat on the hall-stand beside a coat of her son's. He never wore it because he went everywhere in the car. He had got fat with lack of exercise and the modern things that Bernadette fed him. Spaghettis and curries that made the old woman's gorge rise to smell them.

In the kitchen she felt the heat on her face. She opened the door of the Rayburn so that she could see the fire and its red glow. She sank into the armchair and extended her feet to warm her shins before putting the kettle on.

From where she sat she could see the lough framed between the net curtains of the back window. When she had moved house it hadn't really occurred to her that she would miss it but the first morning when she woke she had glanced towards the window and been aware of the difference – like passing a mirror when she had had her hair cut. Then with each waking morning the loss grew. She did not become used to the field at the back. It had a drab sameness. The lough was never the same, changing from minute to minute. Now it was the colour of pewter. Through all the years she had spent in this cottage the lough was a presence. She would stand drying dishes, her eyes fixed on it but not seeing it. Making the beds, she knew it was there behind her.

Suddenly the phone rang, startling her. She looked at it, willing it to stop. She began to count the rings. At ten they should have stopped but they went on. Insistently. When they did stop they left a faint trembling echo in the silence.

She moved to fill the kettle. What if it had been an accident? At Brian's place anything could happen to him. She remembered a Saturday in Cookstown when she missed the bus and had to go round to the garage to get a lift. Brian lay in dungarees beneath a jacked-up car, speaking out to her. She hated the whole place. It was like a dark hangar, full of the smell of diesel and the echoes of dropped spanners. Rain came in through a broken sky-light and stayed in round droplets on the oily concrete. A mechanic, whistling tunelessly, started a car and revved it until she thought her head would burst. She hated the fact that Brian owned this place, but what was worse was the fact that he had bought it with money earned from fishing. Always the men of her family had fished for eels.

The kettle began a tiny rattle on the range and she took a tea-bag from her basket and put it in a cup. When the water boiled she poured it, watching it colour from yellow to mahogany. She removed the plump tea-bag with a spoon and dropped it hissing into the range. The tea clouded with the little milk she added to it.

The eels had become profitable a couple of years before her husband Hugh had died. A co-op had been formed and the prices soared. Within the space of a couple of months cracked lino was thrown out and carpet appeared in its place. They changed their van for a new car – not second-hand new. But they had worked hard for it, snatching sleep at all hours of the day and night. Often she had seen Hugh making up the lines by the light of the head-lamps – four hundred droppers with hooks off each section of line, four lines in all, while she, with her back breaking, stooped, a torch in one hand, pulling the small slippery hawsers of worms from the night ground to bait every one of them.

One night she had taken a step to the side and stood on something that made her whole head reel, something taut and soft at the same time – something living. An eel. Eels. An *ahh* of revulsion followed by 'Mother of God'. She remembered the words exactly and remembered the hair of her head being alive and rising from her scalp. She had stepped back but another squirmed under her heel. Her torch picked out the silent writhing procession, crossing the land from one water to another. Out of the depths, into the depths. Glistening like a snail's trail. Shuddering at the memory, she almost spilled her tea.

She turned on the transistor and changed the wavelength from Radio One to the local station for the news. She heard without listening, staring at the lough. Accidents, killings. The lough will claim a victim every year, was what they said. It was strange that, because on the lough there were no real storms. The water became brown and fretted when the wind got up. Even so, there were windy nights when the men were out fishing that she worried, seeing the water see-saw in the toilet bowl. Last year Hugh had died in his bed, thank God. The cat died about the same time. Both were ill for long enough.

Only once in her life had she gone out with them in the boat. When she had asked, Hugh had laughed and scorned the idea but she had said that all her life she had been cooking for them and she was curious to know what they did. Besides, now that they had a cooker that could switch *itself* on there was no reason why she shouldn't. Every time Hugh looked at her – a spectator sitting in the prow of the boat with her arms folded – he shook his head in disbelief saying to Brian, 'As odd as two left feet.' And she knew it was a compliment. It was an open boat with an outboard and in the middle sat an oil-drum with a kitchen knife blade sharpened to a razor's edge protruding above the rim, like an Indian's feather. As the men lifted the lines, if there was an eel on, they walloped it into the drum, the blade slicing the line as they did so. She had felt a strange admiration for her husband and her son as they became involved in their work. They were so deft yet so unaware of her watching their deftness. She wanted to reach out and touch them but she knew she could not touch the thing that awed her, knew they would mock her if she tried to put it into words. She watched the writhe of brown and yellow eels build up inside the drum, intricate, ceaselessly moving, aware that each one had swallowed a hook. She was too soft, they all said. They had ridiculed her when, drowning a bagful of kittens, they caught her warming the water in the bucket to take the chill off it.

She finished her tea, swallowing hard, and while she remembered she returned the pointer on the transistor to Radio One and switched it off. It would be the kind of thing that Bernadette would notice. Always she had to leave the place exactly as she found it. One day when she had been on one of her 'visits' she had seen a young man crouching outside the garden gate at the back. She was not afraid but curious. As an excuse she had hung out a dish-towel and asked him what he was doing.

'I'm a student – of a sort. I'm looking at rocks.'

He had a bag over his shoulder and a hammer in his hand. She offered him a cup of tea and he accepted. He was young and full of an enthusiasm for learning that her own son lacked. But he had tried to talk down to her, using simple words to explain the geological research he was engaged in. She told him curtly that she had been a teacher.

'The latest theory,' he said, 'is that the continents are moving. These vast countries can move vast distances. But it takes a vast time.'

'I'm vastly impressed,' she said. 'More tea?'

He held out his cup by the handle and she filled it. His skin was pale and he had not shaved for several days, but his eyes were keen.

'Can you imagine it,' he said, 'that South America and Africa were once joined together? And now they are thousands of miles apart? The evidence is in the rocks. Think of the power.'

He set down his cup and slid one hand heavily over the other.

'Yes,' she said.

As they talked the boy smoked a lot of cigarettes, each time offering her one, which she refused. She asked him if he was married and he told her that he was engaged to a girl from Cookstown. After he graduated they would get married. To her surprise the old woman did not know her name or any of her connection when he said it. It was a changed place, Cookstown.

After he had gone she brought in the dish-towel and flapped it in front of the open window to clear the house of smoke. Bernadette had a sharp nose, which she wrinkled at any smell. She also detested the way her daughter-in-law held her shoulders high as she worked about the house – the clipped way she spoke, as if to say, 'I'll talk to you but I have my work to get on with.' Old before her years, that one. The house was perfect anyway, without chick nor child to untidy it. One of the things that had annoyed her most was the speed with which Bernadette had redecorated the cottage when they had moved out to the new bungalow. She couldn't have lived with the walls as they were, she said, giving that little shrug of her spiky shoulders.

The old woman moved to the table at the window and began a game of solitaire. The lough had become the colour of lead. She looked at the sky, now overcast. The snap-up roller blind was stuck all over with long-legged midges. They came in clouds in the summer and, like a smell, couldn't be kept out by shutting doors or windows.

She dealt quickly, the cards making a flacking noise as they came off the deck. Solitaire annoyed Bernadette. She thought it a waste of time. The old woman *knew* it was. All her life she had wanted to halt the time passing but she never felt like that until *afterwards*. She was either too busy or too tired to capture and hold the moment. Brian was now married and loosened his trousers after a meal. How long ago was it that she had taken his two ankles between the trident of her fingers to position him on his nappy? Or used egg-white to stiffen and hold in place the flap of hair that fell over his eyes before he had his first communion photograph taken? Or nudged him in his stained suit to the bedroom and let him lean his head on her shoulder while she fumbled at the laces of his shoes and became white with anger and fear that he had driven the van home in such a condition? Like everyone else, she had applauded at his wedding.

Jack on queen and she was stuck. There was nothing else to move and she pulled the cards towards her with a sigh of exasperation. She rose to go to the bathroom. As she climbed the stairs she put a hand on each thigh and pushed. There was a time when she could have bounded up them two at a time. In the bathroom the toilet-roll was olive green and went almost black in the bowl. She wandered the bedrooms, not recognising them as her own. The neatness, the colours. The view from the window had not changed. This was the room where she had given birth to Brian. The only detail she remembered from that night was the crackling of newspaper beneath her. To this day she couldn't bear to sit on a newspaper, even if it was beneath the cushion.

Downstairs she made another cup of tea and ate a dry biscuit, massaging it past her thrapple the way she had seen the vet help pills down the cat's throat. She found that it went down easier if she put her head back in the chair . . .

She woke in panic. It was dark and the rain was rattling against the window. For a moment she did not know where she was, thought the cottage was her own again. She switched on the table lamp and looked at the clock – a quarter past five. She began to gather her stuff. She washed the cup and returned it to its hook. She hadn't realised that it had been so late. As quickly as she was able she damped down the fire with slack and closed it up. Some spilled from the shovel on to the lino with a rattle and she cursed herself for her carelessness. She swept it in beneath the range.

Outside it was moonless dark and still raining but the cold of the morning had disappeared. The cottage was silent after the echoing slam of the door except for the gurgling of water in the gratings.

Behind the hill she saw the white fan of a car's headlights, then the electric glare as it broke the horizon. She watched it come towards the cottage. It slowed down and indicated before the lane end. Quickly she slipped through the gap in the hedge into the field. The car splashed and bounced through the pot-holes up the track. Unable to crouch much, the old woman put her neck forward and lowered her head. They must have left early. The cottage flooded with light. She heard Bernadette's voice, complaining as usual, say,

'You don't expect me to carry this weight, do you?'

The front door banged shut. The old woman stood in the field trembling.

'And what makes you so different?' she said. They were the first words she had spoken since Tuesday and they made the bones of her head vibrate. The moon was in its last phase and she felt the rain on the backs of her hands. Her tremble turned to nausea and panic and she shuddered. On such a night the eels would be moving through the grass. Her hair became live. She had seen Hugh's finger once when bitten by an eel, the bone like mother-of-pearl through the wound. Tensing the arches of her feet, she stepped awkwardly through the gap in the hedge. In the lane she kept to the side, avoiding the pot-holes. Somewhere a procession of eels would be writhing towards the lough. Out of the depths, into the depths. She turned her head and looked to see the water. She saw nothing but blackness, an infinity rising unbroken in an arch above her head.

Now as she looked at the cottage backed by darkness with its yellow windows reflected in the puddles, and in the knowledge that somewhere not too far away the earth was alive with eels – at that moment she knew her life was over. It hadn't come out. Not the way she wanted. She was aware of the lump in her throat and knew that her eyes were full of water. Beneath her feet continents were moving. She put her head down into the slanting rain and began the slow walk to the bungalow, her coat unbuttoned.

LANGUAGE, TRUTH AND LOCKJAW

Norman sat in the dentist's waiting room. Outside, the rain needled down from a grey sky. The wet shining roofs descended like steps to the sea. Because he was an emergency he had to wait for over an hour while people with appointments filed past him.

Then the dentist's bespectacled head appeared round the door and said,

'Mr Noyes?'

There were two dentists on the island and it was immediately obvious to Norman that he had picked the wrong one. As he called out his secret codes to his assistant he breathed halitosis. He dug into the molar that was causing the trouble and Norman yelled, his voice breaking embarrassingly.

'That seems to be the one,' said the dentist. 'I don't think we can save it. It's a whited sepulchre.'

He went to the window and filled a large syringe. Before he approached the chair he considerately hid it behind his back.

'Open up,' he said. 'That should go dead in a minute. On holiday?'

'Yes.'

'The weather has been poor.'

'You can say that again.'

He had known from the minute the trip had been proposed that everything would go wrong. Patricia said that he had helped in no small measure to *make* it go wrong by his bloody-minded attitude. When *she* was a child on holiday her father, when it rained, had dressed them up in bathing suits and wellies and Pakamacs and taken them for riotous walks along the beach. He had litten – her own word – blue smoke fires with damp driftwood. But now when it rained he, Norman, retreated to the bedroom with his books. His defence was that he had work to do and that he had agreed to the trip only on condition that he could finish his paper on Ryle.

'What do you do?' asked the dentist.

'I teach. Lecturing at the University.'

'Oh. What in?'

'Philosophy.'

'That's nice.'

Things were beginning to happen in his jaw like pins and needles.

'Where are you staying?'

'We have a bungalow up at Ard-na-something.'

'Oh yes. Beside the old Mansion House. Interesting neighbours this week.'

Norman supposed he was referring to the men he had seen staring at him over the wall. They stood for hours in the rain, immobile as sentries, watching the house. At night he heard hooting laughter and yelps and howls which previously he had only associated with a zoo.

'Open wide.' He hung a suction device like a walking stick in Norman's mouth. 'Relax now. Sometimes I think it would be better to hook that thing down the front of your trousers. Some patients sweat more than they salivate.'

The assistant smiled. From where he lay Norman could see that the middle button of her white coat was undone and he could just see the underslope of her breast in a lacy bra.

The dentist leaned on Norman's bottom jaw and began working inside his mouth. There was a cracking sound and the dentist tut-tutted and went to a cupboard behind the chair. He's broken it, thought Norman.

'How long are you here for?' asked the dentist.

'A ort igh.'

'That's nice.'

'I cank cose i jaw.'

'What?'

Norman pointed to his lower jaw making foolish noises.

'Oh,' said the dentist. He manipulated the jaw and clicked it back into place. 'The muscle must be weak.'

'Is it broken – the tooth?'

'No, it's out.'

Norman was astonished. He had felt nothing.

Patricia shouted out from the kitchen.

'Well, love, how did it go?'

Norman had to step over the children, who were playing with a brightly coloured beach-ball on the carpet of the hallway. Although it was five o'clock on a summer's afternoon the light had to be switched on.

'O.K. He pulled it.' Norman produced a Kleenex with its soggy red spot and offered it to his wife. She refused to look at it, telling him to throw it in the bin. She asked,

'Did you expect something from the fairies for it?'

'I just thought you might be interested, that's all.'

'Aww you poor thing,' she said, kissing him lightly on the cheek. 'Did you feel that? Perhaps I should kiss you on the side that's not numb.' She had a levity and a patronising approach to him in sickness which he did not like.

'I think I'll lie down for a while. One *ought* to after an extraction.'

'Whatever you say. Will you want something to eat?'

'What are you making?'

'Spaghetti.'

'We'll see.'

In the bedroom he kicked off his shoes and stood at the rain-spotted window. They were there again, standing amongst the trees at the wall. Their heads were just visible, hair plastered wet and flat. After enquiring at the shop they had found out that the Mansion House was a holiday home for the region and that a party of institutionalised men was staying there. When they saw Norman appear at the window they faded back into the trees.

He lay down on the bed and got beneath the coverlet. The room smelled damp. It had probably been empty over the summer months as well as the winter. Who in their right mind would want to stay beside such a place? He closed his eyes and his left ear began to whine like a high-pitched siren in the distance. He wondered if this was normal. With relief he heard the noise fade as his ear tingled back to ordinary sensation. He knew he was a hypochondriac. At night when he couldn't sleep, usually after working on a lecture or a paper, he would become aware of his heart-thud and lie awake waiting for it to miss. A discomfort in his arm, in time, would become a definite pain and a symptom of an impending heart attack. A discomfort anywhere else in his body would lead to thoughts of cancer. Laziness could be mistaken for debility, which would become a sure sign of leukaemia. This laziness could last for days and gave him much to worry about.

Although he did not say these things out loud somehow Patricia knew his nature and treated him in an off-hand way like a child. Before he married her she had been a primary school teacher and there was always a hint of it in the way she talked to him when he was ill or said he was feeling unwell. She had spotted the medical dictionary he had slipped in among his other books to be taken on holiday but he had made an excuse, saying that in remote places, like an island off the Scottish coast, anything could happen to her or the kids. She had pointed out to him that there was an air-ambulance service straight to the nearest fully equipped hospital on the mainland at any time of the day or night. At his insistence she had checked with the tourist board by phone that this was so.

Without articulating it they both knew that they had reached a stale point in their nine-year-old marriage. They no longer talked or argued as they once did and sarcasm coloured most of the things they said to one another.

Each year they went to the same place for a month's holiday along with other families they knew. In March Norman had been sitting reading the paper when Patricia said,

'I think we should go away for a holiday just by ourselves.'

'What about the children?'

'Oh, we would take *them*.'

'How can we be by ourselves if the children are there?'

'It would get us away from the same old faces. The same old interminable conversations. Get away somewhere isolated. We would be by ourselves at night.'

'But I have this paper to finish . . .'

'You're at the sports page already,' she squawked and fell about laughing. It was something which had endeared her to him when they first met, but now after ten years of knowing her it was something he couldn't understand – how something she considered funny seemed to take over her whole body and flop it about. One night at a party someone had told her a joke and she had slid down the wall, convulsing and spilling her drink in jerking slops on the floor. In the morning when he asked her she couldn't remember what the joke was about.

His tendency was to smile, a humour of the mind, something witty rather than funny affected him. There were times when the company about him were in fits of laughter and he couldn't see the joke.

The children in the hallway began to fight, then one of them broke into a howl of tears. Norman turned his good ear to the pillow. Children, especially of their age, were totally irrational. The younger was Becky, a gap-toothed six-year-old who refused to eat anything which was good for her and insisted on everything which was sweet and bad. John was two years older and had his mother's loud sense of humour. At least he ate cauliflower. He must have fallen asleep because the children wakened him with whispers, creeping round the bed.

'Mum says tea,' they shouted, seeing him awake.

Norman got up. His mouth tasted awful and he washed what remained of his teeth ruefully with peppermint toothpaste, thinking about old age. He sucked some spaghetti into the unaffected side of his mouth and crushed it carefully with his tongue against the roof of his mouth.

'How do you feel now, dear?' asked Patricia.

'So-so,' he said, 'I think the dentist must have served his time in an abattoir. My jaw is sore.'

'Look, Mum, there they are again,' said Becky.

'Who, dear?'

'The loonies.'

'So they are, God love them,' said Patricia.

Norman looked over his shoulder out of the dining room window. They were standing at the wall again, six of them. They had moved from outside the bedroom to outside the dining room. When they saw Norman turn his head they ducked down, then slowly came up again. The one who stood with his mouth hanging open shouted something unintelligible and the others laughed.

'You shouldn't call them loonies,' said Norman.

'Spacers, then,' said John.

'You shouldn't call them that either.'

'That's what they are, isn't it?'

Norman looked at his wife.

'I suppose it didn't mention this fact in the brochure for the house?'

'No, dear, it didn't. Four minutes from the beach was enough for me. Shall I pull the blind for you?'

'No, but it's something animal in me. I don't like to be watched while I'm eating.'

'It's good to know there's some animal in you.'

Norman gave her a look then switched his gaze to his son.

'John, is that the way to hold your fork?'

The rest of the evening the children spent watching the black and white television set which they had scorned when they first arrived. Norman went to the bedroom to do some work. He was writing a paper sparked off by Ryle's distinction between pleasure and pain – that they were not elements on the same spectrum, that positive quantities of one did not lead to minus quantities of the other. He had become involved in tortuous arguments about sadism and masochism. He had shown his draughts to the Prof who had said, after some consideration, that the paper was tending more to the physiological than the philosophic. He had added, looking over his glasses, that he much preferred a wank. 'Marriage is all right,' he had said, 'but there's nothing like the real thing.'

Norman never knew how to take him, never knew when he was serious. The man could be guilty of the most infantile jokes. He repeatedly accused Norman of talking a lot of hot Ayer and of being easily Ryled. What could you say to a man like that? He was always goosing and patting his young secretary – and she didn't seem to mind. He was a woolly existentialist who spoke about metaphysical concepts that could not be defined. He said that, with its pernickety approach to language, British philosophy was disappearing up its own arse while the world around it was in chaos. Also that British philosophy – including Norman – was like a butcher sharpening his knives. Eventually the knives would wear away but the meat would still be there to be cut. Norman thought, what more could you expect from the son of a County Derry farmer?

Norman had just written the first sentence of the severe rewriting the Prof had suggested when Patricia came into the room.

'Norman, the rain's gone off. Let's go for a walk.'

'But the writing is just beginning to go well.'

She put her arms around his neck.

'Don't be so solemn. It has stopped piddling for the first time since we arrived. There is even some blue in the sky. Come for a walk to the pier with us.'

Outside, the light had an eerie translucent quality. It was about ten o'clock and the low white sun had come through the cloud out over the Atlantic and was highlighting the gable ends of houses. The road was still wet and shining. The children in anoraks ran on ahead, leaving Norman and Patricia walking together.

'How's the toofy-peg?' Patricia asked.

'How is its absence, you mean.'

'Well, if you insist.'

'Not too bad now.'

'As night approaches.'

'You could put it that way.' He smiled. 'What do you think?'

'Yes. Holidays I feel like it more often.'

'Tomorrow this socket will begin to heal – usually that's bad news. Isn't it funny how you can never smell your own breath?'

He reached out and took her by the hand. Her face showed mock surprise but she responded by squeezing his fingers.

'Of course we don't have to kiss,' he said, smiling.

'Like an egg without salt. A total perversion.'

She leaned over and kissed him as they walked. They stopped in the middle of the road and kissed mouth to mouth lightly, friendly.

John whistled *wheet-weeo* at them from a distance and they laughed. Norman was much taller than she and it was easy for him to put his arm around her shoulder as they walked.

At eleven Patricia turned on the ancient electric blanket at its highest – it had gears, almost, instead of settings – to try to get rid of the damp smell. Norman was reading a journal by the fire. She sat opposite him, her hands empty. A grandfather clock ticked loudly in the corner.

'One of the ideas of this holiday was that we should talk,' she said.

'Uh-huh.' He turned the page.

'You don't talk to me any more.'

'I'm sorry, what's that?'

'We don't talk any more.'

He closed the journal with a smile but kept his place with a finger.

'O.K. What would you like to talk about?'

'Anything.'

The grandfather clock worked itself up to a long whirr before striking a quarter past.

'The more I think of it,' began Norman, 'the more I am convinced that there might be something in what the Prof says – that British philosophy is trying to commit hara-kiri. And I'm not sure that that is such a good thing. I would hate to end up believing the same things as that man.'

'I would like to talk about us. What we think, what we feel.'

'Hard words, Trish. "Think" and "feel". It's difficult to know what we mean by them. It's essential that we get our concepts straight.'

'Bollocks, Norman. Let's talk about something else.'

'Why? You said we could talk about anything.'

'O.K.' She thought for a moment, then said. 'Those people who stare over the wall. Do you think because they are less intelligent they have less vivid emotions?'

'What are "vivid" emotions?'

'You know what I mean.'

'Seriously I don't.'

'The kind of thing you find in Lawrence.'

'That man is a fog of urges. He's groping all the time – making up words. Blood consciousness; the dark forest of the human soul. Patricia, if you can't put a thing into language, it doesn't exist.'

'Norman, what utter . . .'

'To answer your question. It's a problem for physiologists or neurologists or somebody like that. I don't know what loonies feel.'

'It's no wonder we don't talk any more.'

'Why's that?'

'Because you talk such utter balls. That someone should dismiss Lawrence with a wave of . . .'

'Trish.'

'What?'

'Trish. Let's have a cup of tea and go to bed. Arguing will put us off. You can't make love when you're seething. Besides this tooth of mine is beginning to hurt.'

'Absence of tooth.'

'O.K. If we sit up much longer you'll go sleepy on me.'

Patricia sighed and made a cup of tea while Norman finished reading the article in his journal.

'It's a good question,' he said, softening his biscuit in his tea and sucking it into the good side of his mouth, 'but I honestly don't know the answer to it. Taken logically it would mean that the most intelligent men have the – as you call them – the most vivid emotional responses. That is obviously not true.'

'Not in your case anyway.' She smiled or sneered at him, he couldn't tell which because he only caught the end of it.

'But I thought we weren't going to argue.'

On holidays they had agreed to do equal shares of the housework. It was Norman's turn to wash the cups, which he did even though he had had a tooth out. While he was in the kitchen Patricia took a burning peat from the fire with a pair of tongs and incensed the bedroom.

'I love that smell,' she said. 'Do you want to come to bed now?'

'I'll just wait till the smoke clears.'

As he slowly dried the cups and tidied up, his tongue sought out the jellied cavity and he touched and tasted its coppery acidity. There was no pain in it now. Perhaps he was a better dentist than he gave him credit for. Just in case he took three Disprin dissolved in water before he locked up and turned out the lights.

In the bedroom Patricia lay reading with her bare arms outside the counterpane. Her hair was undone. A strange ululating cry came from the direction of the Mansion House. Norman looked out between the drawn curtains, half expecting to see six heads lined up at the windowsill to watch, but the Mansion House was in darkness. The sound, like a child's version of a long Red Indian war cry, came again, chilling him.

'God, what a place.'

He undressed and slipped in naked beside her nakedness. She was still a beautiful woman and, although he had come to know her body, he never ceased to be awed by it in total nakedness. She told him how aroused she was. A simple thing like holding hands earlier in the evening had been the start of it. Her voice was hushed. Her arousal touched him and they made love. Because of his condition he suggested that she did not put her tongue in his mouth. Nevertheless, Norman got the feeling that this was good sex in this strange, lightly creaking bed. When they came together he made an involuntary animal noise far back in his throat and his mouth fell wide open.

'Agggghrrrrr,' he said.

The noise he made was followed by an audible click. Patricia, with her eyes closed, was listening to her own breathing subside and touching his shoulders with her fingertips. She opened her eyes and looked at him. His mouth was open and his eyes were staring wide in fright.

'i aws gust,' said Norman.

'What?'

'i aw. It's gust.'

Patricia began to laugh, shaking and cupping her ear to him as if she couldn't hear properly.

'What are you saying?'

Norman pointed to his yawning mouth and said as clearly as he was able,

'ock jaw.'

'I thought you were having a heart attack.'

Now that she understood she advised him with amused concern that the best thing he could do in the circumstances would be to get off her. Norman struggled into a pair of pyjama bottoms and regarded himself in the mirror. He kept trying to close his mouth but nothing happened. Somewhere in his jaw the circuits had fused again. Over his shoulder he saw his wife's reflection sitting up in bed heaving in suppressed bare-breasted laughter. When he turned to face her with his mouth agape her laughter became sound. Loud, whinnying and vulgar.

'Oh Norman, you look so *stupid*. You're like one of the loonies,' she managed to say between wheezes. 'Are you kidding me?'

He turned away from her and tried to remember what the dentist had done. He took his lower jaw in his left hand and pushed. Nothing happened. He tried to push upwards and sideways and sideways and downwards but with no effect.

Patricia had put on her nightdress and was now standing looking at him in the mirror. She turned him and looked into his mouth.

'You look like the man in the moon,' she said, giggling. She tried to put it back into place. He had to bend his knees to let her reach up and he had his arms hanging loose by his sides. Patricia stepped back and looked at him, then subsided into peals of laughter again. 'Better still. One of those monkey moneyboxes.' She clapped her hands. 'You put a penny in his hand and he went – gulp.' She demonstrated. 'We had one with its jaw broken.' Norman turned away from her and scrabbled about in the cardboard box of his philosophy books until he found his medical dictionary. He wondered what heading would be the most helpful to read. With his jaw locked open he couldn't swallow his saliva and it drooled over his bottom lip on to the page. He pored over the book.

'anky.'

Patricia gave him a handkerchief from the open case on the dresser and he staunched his dribbles.

'I'm getting to interpret your grunts quite well,' she said. Norman could find nothing which related to his case except under tetanus which he was fairly sure he didn't have. He thought of going to the square and phoning from a callbox for the ambulance plane, until he remembered that he couldn't even speak and they would think he was drunk. Patricia would have to do it. He imagined arriving alone in the infirmary at Glasgow or somewhere in his pyjama bottoms and trying with gestures and groans to explain the complexities of what had happened. With great difficulty he told his wife the thought.

'If you're going out,' she said wiping the tears from her cheeks, 'we'll have to put a coffee-tin lid in your mouth to keep the draught out.' She fell on the bed and rolled about. 'You're agog,' she shrieked. 'Agog describes you perfectly. Norman, you're the perfection of agogness.'

'or ucks ake Trish,' he said, 'ee serious.'

The ululating noise from the Mansion House came again, ridiculing him.

Patricia was by now as inarticulate as he was. She was becoming almost hysterical and Norman, even in the midst of his trouble, wondered if he should slap her face to bring her out of it. It was obviously a nervous reaction to what had happened. As if he didn't have enough to cope with.

He went to the bathroom to see if a change of mirror would help. Sexual pleasure had reduced him to a slavering moron. He thought of D. H. Lawrence and Patricia's admiration for him. He pulled and pushed and wiggled at his bottom jaw. He looked and felt like one of the men who had peered at him over the wall. To be like this for ever. In the distance the grandfather clock tolled midnight. He had been like this for the best part of half an hour. He would *have* to go to hospital. There was the dentist but he didn't know where he lived. He didn't even know his name. Then suddenly he remembered that the Prof's wife had been a practising dentist at one time. He could phone him long distance and ask her advice. Again he remembered that he couldn't speak. It would only give the Prof another chance to say, 'Noyes, you're full of sound and fury signifying nothing.' The bastard.

All Patricia's squawking and hooting had wakened John and he came, puffy-faced with sleep, to the bathroom. He peed, forgot to flush it and walked past his father as he stared in the mirror.

'Hunggh,' said Norman. The boy turned. Norman pointed to the lavatory.

'What?'

'uh it.'

The child stood not understanding, holding up his pyjama trousers by the loose waist. Norman took him by the shoulders and led him back to the lavatory. A little saliva spilled on to John's head and Norman rubbed it.

'uh it.'

'Daddy, what's wrong?'

Norman lifted the child's hand and rested it on the handle – then pressed both hand and handle. The lavatory flushed noisily and the child staggered sleepily back to his bedroom.

'What's wrong with Daddy?' Norman heard him ask in the hallway.

'He's having a long yawn, dear. Now go back to bed.'

Patricia came in with the medical dictionary opened at a page.

'Look, this is it,' she said pointing to a diagram, 'down and out and *then* up. Here, let me try.'

She set the book on the Vanitory unit, stood on tip-toe, still consulting it over her shoulder, and took his jaw firmly in her hands. She pulled downwards and towards herself. Norman agghed and she pushed hard. There was a gristle-snapping sound and his mouth closed. He tried it tentatively, partially opening and closing it, like a goldfish.

'You've done it,' he said. He wiggled it laterally just to make sure. 'I was imagining all kinds of terrible things.' He laughed nervously.

'But you looked *so* funny, Norman. I'm sorry for laughing.' Her shoulders were still shaking.

'You have a strange sense of humour.' He wiped the shine off his chin with the handkerchief. 'The next time I get my foreskin caught in my zip I'll let you know and we can have a night's entertainment.'

Back in the bedroom Patricia imitated a chimpanzee with her mouth open and arms dangling and said,

'Poor Norm.'

When they were settled in bed he sighed.

'I thought I was a goner. The dentist says I must have a weak muscle.'

'There's nothing wrong with your muscle, darling,' she said and snuggled in to his side. The fine rain had begun again and he heard it hiss off the roof and the surrounding trees. He would never understand this crazy woman he was married to. It was hurtful to be laughed *at*. But he was grateful to her for putting his jaw back and, in a kind of thanksgiving, he resolved to take the whole family for a walk along the beach the next day to light bonfires, whether it rained or not.

He turned out the light. The yelling from the Mansion House seemed to have stopped but he couldn't be sure it would not begin again. In the dark, as they were drifting off to sleep, Patricia shook the bed with giggles in the same way as shudders remain after a long bout of crying.

III

THE GREAT PROFUNDO
1987

WORDS THE HAPPY SAY

After he had cleared the breakfast things he guided the crumbs to the edge of the table with a damp cloth and wiped them into his cupped and withered hand. He took out his board and laid it on the cleaned surface. Some people liked to work at a tilt but he had always preferred it flat in front of him. From his back window on the third floor he could hear the children moving along the driveway into the primary school. Because it was summer and the large lime tree, sandwiched between the blackened gable ends, was in full leaf, he could see them only from the waist down. He noticed the boys with rumpled socks and dirty shoes always walked together. Girls, neat in white ankle-socks, would hop-scotch and skip past in a different group. If he stood on tiptoe at the window he could see down into the small backyard but he no longer bothered to get up from his work for the diversion of seeing the new girl downstairs getting a shovel of coal.

He arranged his inks and distilled water and set his porcelain mixing-dish in the middle. Each shallow oval indentation shone with a miniature reflection of the window. He looked at the page he had been working on the previous day and his mouth puckered in distaste. He was unhappy that he had started the thing in English Roundhand and thought of going back again and beginning in Chancery.

> 'We, the Management and Staff of V.R. Wilson & Sons Bakery Ltd, wish to offer our heartfelt thanks and sincere gratitude to MR VERNON WILSON for all he has done in the forty-two years he has been head of V.R. WILSON & SONS BAKERY LTD . . .'

He worked quietly for an hour getting the Indian ink part finished, listening to the soft, pulled scratch of the pen, forming each letter in a perfect flow of black and at the perfect angle. He was always impatient to rub out the horizontal pencil guide-lines but took the precaution of making and drinking a cup of coffee before he did so. A page could be ruined that way. The rubber across damp ink could make a crow's wing of a down-stroke. He settled to drawing in pencil the embellishments to the opening W, then painted a lemon surround with tendrils of vermilion. He had to paint quickly and surely to avoid patchiness – a double layer of colour.

Suddenly he lifted his head and listened. There was a hesitant knock on the lower door. He rinsed his brush in the jam jar with a ringing sound and went down the short flight of stairs. He opened the door and saw a woman standing there.

'Are you the man that writes the things?' she asked. He nodded. 'I hope I'm not disturbing you.'

'No.' He felt he had to invite her in. He went up the stairs behind her and when they came to the landing she was unsure of where to go. To show her the way he went into his kitchen in front of her but realised that he should have let her go first for the sake of manners. She stood holding her basket not knowing what to do.

'Sit down,' he said and sat with his back to the table and waited.

'You do that lovely writing?' she said again. He smiled and agreed. 'I saw it in the church. That thing you did – for the people who gave money for the stained glass window.'

'The list of subscribers?'

'Do you do anything? I mean, not just religious things?'

'Yes.'

She was a woman about the same age as himself, maybe younger. Her whole appearance was tired – drab grey rain-coat, a pale oval showing just inside her knee where she had a hole in her tights, her shoes scuffed and unpolished. She looked down into her basket.

'How much would . . .?' She seemed nervous. 'Would you do a poem?'

'Yes.'

'How much?'

'It depends on how long it is. Whether you want it framed or not. What kind of paper.'

'It's very short.' She took a woman's magazine from her basket and flicked through it looking for the page. She leafed backwards and forwards unable to find it.

'Ah, here it's.' She folded the magazine at the right page and gave it to him. 'It's only four lines.' He glanced at the page and saw the poem framed in a black box.

'I could do that very reasonable,' he said. The corners of her mouth twitched into a relieved smile. 'Five pounds.' It was obviously too much for her because the smile disappeared and she set her hand on the arm of the chair as if she was about to stand up.

'That would be framed and all,' he added.

'Maybe some time again.' She kept looking into her basket.

'On the best paper.'

'What about cheaper paper?'

'Four pounds?'

Still the woman hesitated.

'That's still a pound a line. I didn't think it would be as much as that.'

'Any less and it'd be a favour,' he said. Already he was out of pocket. He stood up to end the bargaining. Again she looked down into her raffia basket. He saw two tins of cat food at the bottom.

'All right,' she said. 'Four pounds. How soon will it be done?'

'The end of the week. Call on Friday.'

She seemed pleased and nervous that she had made a decision.

After he had shown her out he read the poem.

> The words the happy say
> Are paltry melody
> But those the silent feel
> Are beautiful –

It was by E. Dickinson. He looked at the date on the magazine and saw that it was over three years old. He closed it and set it on the shelf. It was like the woman herself, dog-eared and a bit tatty. She'd had nice eyes but her skin had been slack and almost a grey colour as if she'd been ill. Yet there had been something about her which had made him lower his price. He was not used to bargaining – most of his jobs came in the post from a small advertising agency. What they couldn't be bothered to do in Letraset they passed on to him. But the work was not regular and he couldn't rely on it – unlike the diplomas he did each year for the teacher training college.

Two days later when he wrote out the poem he was dissatisfied with it and scrapped it. For the second attempt he wrote it on one of his most expensive papers and further surprised himself by using his precious gold leaf. He hated working with the stuff, held between its protective sheets, thin as grease on tea. It curled and twitched even when he brought the heat of his fingertips near it. Yet on the finished page it looked spectacular.

On the Friday he found that, instead of working in the morning, he was tidying the flat. It was not until late evening that he heard her at the door. He turned down the volume of the radio and went to answer it. She sat down when invited and placed her hands on her lap. Her appearance had improved. She wore a mauve print summer dress, a white Aran cardigan and carried a shoulder bag, which made her seem younger. The weak sun, squared by shadows from the crossbars of the window, lit the back wall of the room behind her.

'I'm sorry,' he said, 'it's not finished.' Her mouth opened slightly in disappointment. 'I didn't know whether you wanted the name on it or not.'

'What name?'

He held out the magazine and pointed to the name beneath the poem with his bad hand. It was as if he were pointing round a corner.

'E. Dickinson.'

The woman thought for a moment then nodded. 'Put it on.' She seemed quite definite. He folded the protective paper back from his work and reached for a pen.

'Can I see it?' she asked. He handed her the written poem and watched her face.

'Aw here,' she said. 'Aw here now.' Then she spoke the poem, more to herself than to him. As she read he watched her eyes switching back and forth across the lines.

'Lovely,' she said. 'Just lovely.' He was unsure whether she was praising his work or the poem. She handed it carefully back and he turned to the table to write the name.

'Can I watch?'

'Sure thing.'

She came, almost on tiptoe, to his shoulder and watched him dip the pen and angle the spade-like nib. As he wrote, his tongue peeped out from the corner of his mouth. When he had finished he blew on the page, tilting it to the light to see if it had dried.

'Where did you learn – all this?' she asked.

'I taught myself. Just picked it up.' He stood and went over to the shelf and took down a book. 'From things like . . . this 'Book of Hours.'

'Ours?'

He smiled and passed it to her. She smiled too, realizing her mistake when she read the title. She opened it gingerly. The pictures were interleaved with tissue paper which slithered in the draught she made turning the pages. Each tissue bore a faint mirror image of the drawing it protected. The book was an awkward size so she sat down and laid it across her knees. She looked at the pure colours, the intricacy of the work.

'This must have taken you years,' she said.

'I didn't do it.' He smiled. 'It's a printed book.'

'Oh.' She turned another page. He stood feeling idle in front of her.

'Would you like some tea?'

She looked up and hesitated.

'It's no bother,' he said. 'I've got milk.'

'All right. That would be nice.'

He put the kettle on and set out his mug and a cup and saucer for her. The crockery rattled loudly in the silence. The kettle seemed to take ages to boil. He asked her how she had known who he was and where he lived. She said that the priest had told her after she had admired the framed list of names in the church.

When he handed her the cup and saucer she set the book carefully to one side.

'It would be just like me to spill something on it.'

He sat down opposite her. The sound of the contact between her cup and saucer made him feel nervous.

'Do you like doing this work?'

'Yes, it suits me fine. I don't have to leave the house.'

'You're like myself,' she nodded in agreement. 'Once I've the one or two bits of shopping done, I stay put. I hate the city. Always have since the day and hour I moved here. And it's getting worse. You used to be able to have a chat in Dunlop's till they changed it into a supermarket. How can you talk to the check-out girl with a queue hopping behind you?'

'You haven't lost your accent.'

'And please God I never will.'

He finished his tea and stood up. He inserted the finished poem into its frame and began to tape up the back of it. He was conscious of her watching the awkward guiding movements of his bad hand.

'It's the quiet I miss the most,' she said. 'In the country you can hear small things.'

'Would you go back?'

'Like a shot.'

'Maybe some day you will.'

She smiled at this.

With an awl he made two holes in the wood frame and began to insert the screws. He said, 'You have a cat?'

'Yes. How did you know?'

He explained about seeing the cat food in her basket.

'It thinks it's a lion,' she said. 'We have a yard at the back with pot plants and it lies flat like it's in the jungle and his tail puffs up.' He laughed at her. She went on, 'What I like about cats is the way they ignore you. There's no telling what way they feel. If I want to be popular all I have to do is rattle the tin-opener and he's all over me, purring and sharpening his back on my shins.'

'What do you call it?'

'Monroe. My husband thought that one up – not my idea at all. At first we called it Marilyn until we found out it was a boy. Then we had it neutered because of the smell. We used to go a lot to the pictures.' After a pause she added, 'He's dead now God rest him.'

'Who?'

'My husband.' She set her saucer on the floor between her feet and held the cup in both hands. The sunlight on the wall behind her had changed from yellow to rose until it finally disappeared, yet the room seemed to hold on to some of the light. 'Since I got the TV there's no need to go out. All the good movies come up there.' She looked around the darkening room.

'I prefer the radio,' he said. 'It means I can work at the same time. Or look at the fire.'

He got to his feet and asked her if she felt chilly. Even though she said no, he lit the fire. The firelighter blazed in a yellow flame a few inches above the coal until it caught. It made a pleasant whirring noise.

'I couldn't be without the TV,' she said. 'It's like having another person in the house.' He smiled at her and began sweeping the hearth.

'Am I keeping you back?' she said suddenly.

'No. No. Not at all,' he said. 'It's not often anybody comes in.'

'Especially me,' she said. As the coals of the fire began to redden and burn without the help of the firelighter she talked about her childhood in the country: of making shadow pictures of monsters on the wall with a candle; of her elder sister scaring the wits out of her with stories of the devil at dances. She told of ringworm and of the woolly balaclava she had to wear to cover her bald patches; of sheep ticks and how the only way you could get them out of your skin was to burn their backsides with a hot spent match and then pluck them out while their minds were on other things. He listened to her shudder at the memory, but it was obvious from her voice that she loved it all.

When she waited for him to tell something of himself he shied away and asked her if she would like some more tea. He did tell her that he had never known his father and that his mother had died asking what time it was. Famous last words. What time is it? When he said this she held back her laughter until he laughed.

'What time *is* it?' she asked. He squinted through the gloom in the direction of the clock on the shelf and told her.

'What? I must go,' she said. But she did not get up.

'I've given you a bit of picture cord.' He hung the framed text on his finger for her to see. 'Although it's very light.'

'Light verse,' she said and laughed. He handed her his work and she held it at arm's length to admire it. He switched on the Anglepoise for her and it seemed very bright after the slow increase of dusk.

'It must be great to be an artist,' she said.

He pooh-poohed the idea saying that he couldn't draw to save his life. He said he was an artisan and added, seeing her blank look, 'A man with one skill.'

She set the picture down and opened her shoulder bag.

'Four pounds you said?' She took her purse from the bag and looked up at him, waiting for confirmation of the price.

'It doesn't matter,' he said. 'This one is free.'

'What?'

'I enjoyed doing it.'

'I wouldn't dream of it. Here,' she said and set the four pound notes on the table. He picked them up and offered them back to her. She took them and set them on the mantelpiece out of his reach.

'It's a lovely job of work. You must be paid.' She was now bustling, returning her purse to her bag, straightening her cardigan. She seemed embarrassed and he wished he had just taken the money without any fuss.

'I am very pleased with it,' she said. 'It was kind of you to offer. But no, thank you. And now I'll be off.'

He hesitated for a moment, then said, 'Let me wrap it for you.' He looked in a cupboard and found some brown paper he had saved. She sat down again to wait. He wrapped her magazine and the picture together, sellotaping down the triangular folds he had made.

A summer insect flew into the metal dome of the Anglepoise and knocked around like a tiny knuckle. She said in admiration that he was very good with his hands. He was aware of her embarrassment in the silence which followed. He held on to the parcel when he was finished and tried to think of something to say. He asked her if she had ever worked at anything. She said that for some years before she had married she had worked in a sewing-machine factory – years which had bored her stiff. He asked her if she had any children but she replied that they had not been blessed in that way. Her husband had worked with an X-ray machine before they knew the damage it could do. She averted her eyes and he did not know what to say. Eventually she stood up.

'You have more than one skill,' she said, looking at the neatness of the finished parcel. 'Thank you very much for the tea – and everything.' She stretched out to shake hands but it was an awkward clasping rather than a handshake, with his left hand in her right.

'I'll show you out,' he said, turning on the landing light. They went down the lino-covered stairs.

'Maybe I'll see you again – some time in church,' she said, looking up over her shoulder at him.

He nodded. 'Maybe. I eh . . .'

She waited for what he was going to say but he reached past her and opened the Yale lock. Sounds of children playing below echoed up the stair-well. She left smiling, clutching beneath her arm the parcel of her poem.

Upstairs again he sat down in front of the illuminated address for the bakery firm but did not begin to work. He stayed like that for a long time then punched the table hard with the knuckles of his fist so that the radio at his elbow bounced and gave a static crackle. It had been on all this time. He turned up the volume and filled the flat with the noise of voices he could not put a face to.

THE BREAK

The cardinal sat at his large walnut desk speaking slowly and distinctly. When he came to the end of a phrase he pressed the off-switch on the microphone and thought about what to say next as he stared in front of him. On the wall above the desk was an ikon he had bought in Thessaloníki – he afterwards discovered that he had paid too much for it. It had been hanging for some months before he noticed, his attention focused by a moment of rare idleness, that Christ had a woodworm hole in the pupil of his left eye. It was inconspicuous by its position, and rather than detracting from the impact, he felt the ikon was enhanced by the authenticity of this small defect. He set the microphone on the desk, pushed his fingers up into his white hair and remained like that for some time.

'New paragraph,' he said, picking up the microphone and switching it on with his thumb. 'Christians are sometimes accused of not being people of compassion – that the Rule is more important than the good which results from it.'

The phone rang on the desk making him jump. He switched off the recorder.

'Yes?'

'Eminence, your father's just arrived. Can you see him?'

'Well, can I?'

'You're free until the Ecumenical delegation at half four.'

'I think I need a break. Will you show him up to my sitting-room?' He made the sign of the cross and prayed, his hands joined, his index fingers pressed to his lips. At the end of his prayer he blessed himself again and stood up, stretching and flexing his aching back. He straightened his tossed hair in the mirror, flattening it with his hands, and went into the adjoining room to see if his father had managed the stairs.

The room was empty. He walked to the large bay window and looked down at the film of snow which had fallen the previous night. A black irregular track had been melted up to the front door by people coming and going but the grass of the lawns was uniformly white. The tree trunks at the far side of the garden were half black, half white where the snow had shadowed them. The wind, he noticed, had been from the north. He shuddered at the scene, felt the cold radiate from the window panes and moved back into the room to brighten up the fire. With a smile he thought it would be nice to have the old man's stout ready for him. It poured well, almost too well, with a high mushroom-coloured head. He left the bottle with some still in it, beside the glass on the mantelpiece, and stood with his back to the fire, his hands extended behind him.

When he heard a one-knuckle knock he knew it was him.

'Come in,' he called. His father pushed the door open and peered round it. Seeing the cardinal alone he smiled.

'And how's his Eminence today?'

'Daddy, it's good to see you.'

The old man joined him at the fireplace and stood in the same position. He was much smaller than his son, reaching only to his shoulder. His clothes hung on him, most obviously at the neck where his buttoned shirt and knotted tie were loose as a horse-collar. The waistband of his trousers reached almost to his chest.

The old man said, 'That north wind is cold no matter what direction it's blowing from.' The cardinal smiled. That joke was no longer funny but the old man's persistence in using it was.

'Look, I have your stout already poured for you.'

'Oh that's powerful, powerful altogether.'

The old man sat down in the armchair rubbing his hands to warm them and the cardinal passed him the stout.

'Those stairs get worse every time I climb them. Why don't you top-brass clergy live in ordinary houses?'

'It's one of the drawbacks of the job. Have you put on a little weight since the last time?'

'No, no. I'll soon not be able to sink in the bath.'

'Are you taking the stout every day?'

'Just let anyone try and stop me.'

'What about food?'

'As much as ever. But still the weight drops off. I tell you, Frank, I'll not be around for too long.'

'Nonsense. You've another ten or twenty years in you.'

The old man looked at him without smiling. There was a considerable pause.

'You know and I know that that's not true. I feel it in my bones. Sit down, son, don't loom.'

'Have you been to see the doctor again?' The cardinal sat opposite him, plucking up the front of his soutane.

'No.' The old man took a drink from his glass and wiped away the slight moustache it left with the back of his hand. 'That's in good order, that stout.'

The cardinal smiled. 'One of the advantages of the job. When I order something from the town, people tend to send me the best.'

He thought his father seemed jumpy. The old man searched for things in his pockets but brought out nothing. He fidgeted in the chair, crossing and recrossing his legs.

'How did you get in today?' asked the cardinal.

'John dropped me off. He had to get some phosphate.'

'What's it like in the hills?'

'Deeper than here, I can tell you that.'

'Did you lose any?'

'It's too soon to tell, but I don't think so. They're hardy boyos, the blackface. I've seen them carrying six inches of snow on their backs all day. It's powerful the way they keep the heat in.' The old man fidgeted in his pockets again.

'Why will you not go back to the doctor?'

The old man snorted. 'He'd probably put me off the drink as well.'

'Cigarettes are bad for you, everybody knows that. It's been proved beyond any doubt.'

'I'm off them nearly six months now and I've my nails ate to the elbow. Especially with a bottle of stout. I don't know what to do with my hands.'

'Do you not feel any better for it.'

'Damn the bit. I still cough.' The old man sipped his Guinness and topped up his glass from the remainder in the bottle. The cardinal stared over his head at the fading light of the grey sky. He could well do without this Ecumenical delegation. Of late he was not sleeping well, with the result that he tended to feel tired during the day. At meetings his eyelids were like lead and he daren't close them because if he did the quiet rise and fall of voices and the unreasonable temperature at which they kept the rooms would lull him to sleep. It had happened twice, only for seconds, when he found himself jerking awake with a kind of snort and looking around to see if anyone had noticed. This afternoon he would much prefer to take to his bed and that was not like him. He should go and see a doctor himself, even though he knew no one could prescribe for weariness. He looked at his father's yellowed face. Several times the old man opened his mouth to speak but said nothing. He was sitting with his fingers threaded through each other, the backs of his hands resting on his thighs. The cardinal was aware that it was exactly how he himself sometimes sat. People said they were the spit of each other. He remembered as a small child the clenched hands of his father as he played a game with him. 'Here is the church, here is the steeple.' The thumbs parted, the hands turned over and the interlaced fingers waggled up at him. 'Open the doors and here are the people.' Now his father's hands lay as if the game was finished but they had not the energy to separate from each other. At last the old man broke the silence.

'I'm trying to put everything in order at home. You know – for the big day.' He smiled. 'I was going through all the papers and stuff I'd gathered over the years.' He pulled out a pair of glasses from his top pocket with pale flesh-coloured frames. The cardinal knew they were his mother's, plundered from her bits and pieces after she died.

'Why don't you get yourself a proper pair of glasses?'

'My sight is perfectly good – it's just that there's not much of it. I found this.' His father fumbled into his inside pocket and pulled out two sheets of paper. He hooked the legs of the spectacles behind his ears, briefly inspected the sheets and handed one to his son.

'Do you remember that?'

The cardinal saw his own neat handwriting from some thirty years ago. The letter was addressed to his mother and father from Rome. It was an ordinary enough letter which tried to describe his new study-bedroom – the dark-brightness of the room in the midday sun when the green shutters were closed. The letter turned to nostalgia and expressed a longing to be back on the farm in the hills. The cardinal looked up at his father.

'I don't recall writing this. I remember the room but not the letter.' His father stretched and handed him the second sheet.

'It was in the same envelope as this one.'

The cardinal unfolded the page from its creases.

Dear Daddy,

Don't read this letter out. It is for you alone. I enclose another 'ordinary letter' for you to show Mammy because she will expect to see what I have said.

I write to you because I want you to break it gradually to her that I am not for the priesthood. It would be awful for her if I just arrived through the door and said that I wasn't up to it. But that's the truth of it.

These past two months I have prayed my knees numb asking for guidance. I have black rings under my eyes from lack of sleep. To have gone so far – five years of study and prayer – and still to be unsure. I believe now that I can serve God in a better way, a different way from the priesthood.

I know how much it means to her. Please be gentle in preparing her.

'Yes, I remember this one.'

'I thought you might like to have it.'

'Yes thank you, I would.' The cardinal let the letter fall back into its original folds and set it on the occasional table beside him.

'And did you prepare her?'

'Yes. Until I got your next letter.'

'What did she say?'

'She thought it was just me – doubting Thomas she called me.'

'It was a bad time. Every time I smell garlic I remember it.' He knelt to poke the fire. 'Another bottle of stout?'

'It's so good I won't refuse you.' His father finished what was left in the glass. The cardinal poured a new one and set it by the chair. The old man stared vacantly at the far wall and the cardinal looked out of the bay window. The sky was dark and heavy with snow. It was just starting to fall again, large flakes floating down and curving up when they came near to the window.

'You'd better not leave it too late going home,' he said. The old man opened his mouth to speak but stopped.

'What's wrong?'

'Nothing.' His father knuckled his left eye. 'Except . . .'

'Except what?'

'I suppose I showed that letter to you . . . for a purpose.'

'As if I didn't know.'

'I want to make a confession.' Seeing his son raise an eyebrow the old man smiled. 'Not that kind of confession. A real one. And it's very hard to say it.' The cardinal sat down.

'Well?'

The old man smiled a smile that stopped in the middle. Then he put his head back to rest it on the white linen chair-back.

'I've lost the faith,' he said. The cardinal was silent. The snow kept up an irregular ticking at the window pane. 'I don't believe that there is a God.'

'Sorry I'm not with you. Is it that . . .?'

'Don't stop me. I've gone over this in my head for months now.' The cardinal nodded silently. 'I want to say it once and for all – and only to you. I have not believed for twenty-five years. But what could I do? A son who was looked up to by everyone around him – climbing through the ranks of the Church like nobody's business – the youngest-ever cardinal. How could I stop going to Mass, to the sacraments? How could I? I never told your mother because it would have killed her long before her time.'

'God rest her.'

'Frank, there is no God. Religion is a marvellous institution, full of great, good people – but it's founded on a lie. Not a deliberate lie – a mistake.'

'You're wrong. I *know* that God exists. Apart from what I feel in here,' the cardinal pointed to his chest, 'there are convincing proofs.'

'Proofs are no good for God. That's Euclid.' The old man was no longer looking at his son but staring obliquely down at the fire. 'I know in my bones that I'll not be around too long, Frank. I had to tell somebody because I would be a hypocrite if I took it to the grave with me. I am telling you because we're . . . because I . . . admire you.' The cardinal shook his head and looked down at his knees.

'Do you know what the amazing thing is?' said his father. 'I don't miss Him. You'd think that somebody who'd been reared like me would be lost. You know – the way they taught you to talk to Jesus as a friend – the way you felt you were being looked after – the way you were told it was the be-all and the end-all, and for that suddenly to stop and me not even miss it. That was a shock. I'll tell you this, Frank, when your mother died I missed her a thousand times more.'

'Yes, I'm sure you did.'

'To tell the God's honest truth I miss the cigarettes more.'

The cardinal smiled weakly. 'If this was a public debate . . .' He seemed to sag in his chair. His shoulders went down and his hands lay in his lap, palm upwards. The snow was getting heavier and finer and was hissing at the window. The old man looked over his shoulder at the fading light.

'I'd better think of going. I wonder where John's got to?'

'Did he say he'd pick you up here?'

'Yes.' The old man looked his son straight in the eye. 'I'm sorry,' he said, 'but I wanted to be honest with you because . . .' he looked into his empty glass, 'because I . . .'

'You can stay the night and we can talk.'

'There's not much more to be said.' The old man got up and stood at the window looking down. He looked so frail that his son imagined he could see through him. He remembered him at the celebration after his ordination in a hotel in Rome banging the table with a soup-spoon for order and then making a speech about having two sons, one who looked after the body's needs and the other who looked after the soul's. When he had finished, as always at functions, he sang 'She Moved thro' the Fair'. The old man looked at his watch.

'Where is he?' He put his hands in his jacket pockets, leaving his thumbs outside, and paced the alcove of the bay window.

'If I may stand Pascal's Wager on its head,' said the cardinal, 'if you do not believe and are as genuinely good a man as you are, then God will accept you. You will have won through even though you bet wrongly.'

The old man shrugged his shoulders without turning. 'The way I feel that's neither here nor there. But this talk has done me good. I hope it hasn't hurt you too much.'

'It must have been a great burden for you. Now you have just given it to me.' Seeing the concern in his father's face he added, 'But at least I have God to help me bear it. I will pray for you always.'

'It's not as black as I paint it. Over the years there was a kind of contentment. I had lost one thing but gained another. It concentrates the mind wonderfully knowing that this is all we can expect. A glass of stout tastes even better.' The old man took one hand out of his pocket and shaded his eyes, peering out into the snow. 'Ah there he is now. It must be bad, he has the headlights on.'

'Does John know all this?'

'No. You are the only one. But please don't worry. I'll continue as I've done up till now. I'll go to mass, receive the sacraments. It's hard to teach an old dog new tricks.'

'That's the farthest thing from my mind.'

The old man turned and came across the room. The cardinal still sat, his hands open. His father took him by the right hand and leaned down and kissed him with his lips on the cheekbone. The hand was light and dry as polystyrene, the lips like paper.

The cardinal had not cried since the death of his mother and even then he had waited until he was alone but now he could not stop the tears rising.

'I will see you again soon,' said his father. Then, noticing his son's brimming eyes, he said, 'Frank, if I'd known that I wouldn't have told you.'

'It's not because of that,' said the cardinal. 'Not that at all.'

After he had seen his father to the door and had a few words with his brother – mostly about the need for them to get home quickly before the roads became impassable – the cardinal went back to his office. He sat for a long time with his elbows on the desk and his head in his hands. He blessed himself slowly as if his right arm was weighted and said his prayer-before-work. He picked up the microphone and spoke.

'The Church has a public and a private face. The Church of Authority and the Church of Compassion, the Church of Rules and the Church of Forgiveness. What the public face lacks is empathy. This was not so with Jesus. We who are within the Church must strive to narrow the gap that exists between . . . them. We know that . . .' His voice trailed away and he switched off the microphone. Then, with an effort that made him groan, he slid from the chair to kneel on the floor. The cushioned Rexine of the chair-seat hissed slowly back to its original shape. He joined his hands in prayer so that the knuckles formed a platform for his chin. When the words would not come he lowered his hands, and his interlocked fingers were ready to waggle up at him as in the childish game. He parted his hands and laid them flat on the chair.

In the car with John the old man sat forward in his seat watching the brightness of the snow slanting in the headlights.

'Did you do what you had to do?' he asked.

'Aye – it's all in the back,' said John. 'What do I smell?'

'Stout.'

'The odour of sanctity.'

The windscreen wipers, on intermittent, purred and slapped. In front of them the road was white except for two yellow-dark ruts.

'That snow's thick.'

'It'll get worse as we climb,' said John.

'Just follow the tracks of the boyo that's gone before and we'll be all right.'

From then on there was silence as John drove slowly and with great care up into the mountains.

THE DRAPERY MAN

I rise every day and walk the half mile up the hill to Jordan's place with his dog at my heels. I have to take it slowly, for the sake of the dog. It is a small brown and white short-haired terrier which he christened Pangur-Ban. Each evening I take her home with me to prevent Jordan, as he says, 'taking the air on the patio and tramping in shite, then walking it throughout the house.' She waddles and her tongue hangs out. Her paws slip on the stone mosaic footpath. The dog is as old in dog years as Jordan.

Today he has asked me to bring tennis balls. I have bought half a dozen packed like eggs in a plastic container which crackles as I walk up the hill.

I used to live with Jordan until things became intolerable. Then he rented a place for me, small but with a good view over the Atlantic. I am on my own when I want to be, which suits me. It suits him as well because a blind man needs to live on his own. He can remember where the furniture is, where he last set something down. The only drawback, Jordan tells me, is that he will probably die on his own, and that frightens him. He is in his seventies, has a bad heart and is expecting the worst.

He is sitting in a director's canvas chair in the middle of the converted barn tilting his head back to the light waiting for me. As soon as he hears the door he shouts, 'Here, girl.' Pangur-Ban barks twice and runs to him. Even if she doesn't bark he can hear her pads and claws on the stone floor. She wags her tail so much that her whole body seems to move. He scratches her head.

'And my drapery man.' I kiss him like we were father and son and lift the dog up on his knee. He caresses the back of my thigh.

He laughs, 'This morning when I awoke I had a little stiffness in my joints. One in particular.' He laughs. 'Isn't that good at my age?'

'I bet it didn't last long,' I say, moving away from him.

He is on edge – he wants to start a new painting even though we haven't finished the previous three. I have spent the last few days making canvases to his specifications – one seven feet by fourteen and then a smaller one, six by three.

'Give the big one a wash of turps and burnt sienna – as dilute as possible.'

Before he went blind completely he would inspect my colour mixing. He would tell me equal parts viridian and cobalt with just a smear of black and I would mix it for him. He then would bend over the tray, like a jeweller, squinting with his one good eye at the colour. 'Yes it's right,' or, 'More black.' It was about this time that he began to wear the glasses with the mudguards at the sides.

Since he has totally lost his sight he uses other things to denote colour. 'The blue vase beside the window – the shadowed side of it,' or, 'The maroon cover of *Marius the Epicurean*.' I begin to search the bookshelves.

'Who's it by?'

'Pater.' He gives a little sigh. 'Walter Pater – an English fuckin hooligan, if ever there was one.'

I find it and hold it up to the light. Jordan says, 'As a book it's rubbish – but it's the right colour.'

Occasionally he uses previous pictures of his own as a reference.

'I want the umber to be exactly what I used in "Harbinger Three".' And I have to try and remember! Reproductions are only the merest approximation. Colour slides are better but still their colour values are not accurate. Sometimes, when he is being particularly difficult or pernickety, I have to admit to cheating. I will tell him I remember the colour and have got it exactly. He has no way of knowing.

I change into what was a navy blue boiler suit. It is japped and stippled with every colour he has made me use. Because of the heat the only other thing I wear is my underpants. In the old days this used to drive him wild. I squeeze a fat worm of burnt sienna into a roller tray and drown it in turps.

He uses masking tape a lot. That way he can feel with his fingers what he can see in his mind.

'Three verticals of white, the three-quarter inch, spaced like cricket stumps.' I peel off the tape when the paint has dried, leaving livid white.

Sometimes he will say, 'Let me make a shape,' and approach the canvas with a stick of charcoal. He will draw big and simple out of the darkness of his head.

He has an amazing visual memory. To divide up his canvases he will refer me to a book of Flags of the World.

'The three bands should be like the South Vietnamese flag stood on its end,' or, 'The band at the bottom should be as broad as the blue stripe in the Israeli flag.'

The work is as hard as painting a room. He sits listening to the click of the roller and my breathing, fondling the bones of the dog's head. Sometimes her upright ears flick like a cat's when touched.

When the canvas is covered I sit down for a break but he becomes impatient with me.

'Get out what we did yesterday,' he says. I turn the outermost canvas from the wall to face him. He drops the dog on the floor and comes over to me, his arms out in front of him. His hands touch the surface and skim lightly over it feeling the layers of paint with the tips of his fingers, the direction of the brush strokes.

'That's the magenta?'

'Yes.'

'It's too loosely brushed. I wish you'd sprayed it.'

'Why didn't you say?'

'Could you bear to do it again?'

'I suppose so. Jordan, you're a perfectionist.'

'Oh fuck.' He cups one hand over his eyes. 'This is like trying to thread a needle with gloves on.'

I begin squeezing out some magenta.

'Why do you go on doing this?'

'Somebody's got to pay the rent – the rents. Two places.'

'Jordan – come on. You get the price of a house for one of these things.'

'Things! You philistine gobshite.'

'I didn't mean it that way.'

'It's the way it came out – it was your tone. A middle-class English whine.'

'The Irish are racists,' I say and storm out of the barn.

He shouts after me, 'It wasn't us who fucked up half the world.'

It takes me until midday to calm down.

'Jordan! Lunch!' He comes out on to the shaded side of the patio to join me. It is easy to prepare. A bottle of chilled Verde, some bread and pâté. He likes the local pâté and I spread each circle of crusty bread with a thick roof of the stuff. Three small pieces on a plate, easily located, easily eaten. The bread crackles as he bites into it.

'Oh for a piece of bread that doesn't bleed your gums,' he says, chewing. 'Right now I'd pay a fiver for a slice of Pan loaf. Something soft that'll stick to the roof of your mouth.'

I don't answer him and there is a long silence. He feels this for a while, then says, 'With regard to this morning. I still have pictures in my head which have to come out but they are limited by the clumsy technique I have to use. Imagine having to paint – not with a brush – but with an English gobshite.' This time it sounds funny and he senses my reaction. 'In the 'fifties I was attracted to Hard Edge. Now it is all that is left to me. I see the way Beethoven heard. For that reason alone we must continue.'

I am his eyes and his right hand. He will occasionally ask me to describe things. If it becomes a chore he will know from the tone of my voice and stop me.

'The Atlantic today is Mediterranean blue.' He laughs obediently. 'And at this moment I can see two yachts, one a mere arrowhead with a white sail, the other much closer, running behind a blue and white spinnaker.' That kind of thing.

He will always have a cutting remark to end with, like, 'It pays to increase your word power.'

*

I also read to him. He has become blind so late in life that he is unwilling to learn the new skill of Braille. He likes Beckett – even laughs at him – but I find his prose almost impossible to read aloud and quite, quite meaningless. I come from the kind of house where if my father saw me with a book in my hand he'd say, 'Can you not find something better to do?'

Flann O'Brien is also a favourite – especially the pieces from the *Irish Times* – but my English accent is intrusive and my attempts at an Irish one, so Jordan tells me, disastrous. He appreciates my version of a Home Counties voice reading the test match reports which arrive a day late from England. But because they are always a day late his excitement and anticipation is still the same.

'One of my great regrets is that I'll never see this fella Botham play.' This from a man who hasn't left Portugal for twenty-five years.

In the winter when cricket reports are scarce occasionally he asks me to read to him from Wisden's Cricketers' Almanack.

'A lizard has just appeared on the wall of your bedroom and is soaking up the sun. Its spine is an S. Why do they never end up straight?'

'We're all bent,' says Jordan and gropes for his wine glass. He drains what's left and stands. I lead him back to the barn and he lies down on the divan for a nap. He claims that he can sleep better during the day than at night. I go into the house to wash up the dishes, tidy and make his bed.

I first met him while on holiday in the Algarve about twenty years ago. My mother had been recently widowed and dreaded the thought of spending Christmas in the house. She also dreaded being alone and asked me to accompany her. At the time I was a student of Engineering Drawing and the holidays were sufficiently long to allow me to do this without missing anything. Mother and I had been there about a fortnight and were becoming bored with each other. Both of us admitted to a longing to hear English spoken again. We met Jordan coming out of a bistro. Because he was drunk he was speaking in English, shouting it over his shoulder at those who had annoyed him. Despite the fact that his accent was Irish and that he was well on in drink Mother pounced on him, so avid was she for conversation with someone other than me. She brought him back to our hotel for coffee.

Jordan Fitzgerald was his name. He was then a splendid-looking man in his early fifties, lean and tanned with a beard which was whitening in streaks. Mother simpered before him and asked him what he did.

'I'm a cricketer who paints.'

She became, if it was possible, more obsequious when she discovered just how famous an artist he was. She knew nothing of painting – for her, degrees of realism were degrees of excellence and all our house in London could boast of was a number of Victorian prints my father had looted from his own mother's house. Another factor which impressed her was the price his pictures could command. When she eventually got to see some of his work her comment to me afterwards was, 'I wouldn't give you tuppence for it.'

'Mother, he is one of Ireland's greatest artists and has the accolade of having work in the Tate.'

'I don't care where he's worked. I wouldn't hang one of those things on my wall. If your father was alive he could tell him what he was doing wrong.'

She thought his interest was in her, handsome in her mid-forties, but I knew by his eyes that I was the focus of his attention.

On the second last night of our holiday we had all been drinking heavily in our hotel and Mother went off to powder her nose.

Jordan leaned forward and said to me in a voice that was hushed and serious, 'You are beautiful. Why don't you walk up the hill later?'

I nodded and cautioned him with a look, seeing Mother coming back. He added, 'And I'll show you my retchings.' We both laughed uncontrollably at this.

'Have I missed a joke?' said Mother.

'I was just telling your handsome boy a story which would offend the ears of a lovely English lady like yourself. I hope you'll forgive me.'

She smiled coyly – a smile which said they are just men together.

But I did go to his house later that night. We had sex and I stayed with him the next night as well – or at least slipped back into the hotel at five in the morning. Mother remarked on how tired I looked and I proved it by sleeping on the train until Paris.

In the spring Jordan wrote to me one of the shortest letters I have ever received inviting me in almost gruff terms to spend the summer with him. In a PS he said that Mother would also be welcome – in September. I had just finished my course with the highest commendation and felt I deserved the summer off before looking for work. Mother agreed both to my going and to her visit later.

Once I asked him why he had left Ireland.

'It's no place for a homosexual painter who doesn't believe in God,' he said, then added after a moment's thought, 'Indeed it's no place for a heterosexual painter who's a Catholic.' But he cherished aspects of his country. He claimed to be able to quote the label on any bottle of Irish whiskey word for word. I tested him when I arrived back from London after Mother's funeral. I had brought him a bottle of Bushmills and challenged him to make good his boast.

'The label is black like a church window, with a gold rim. It has a vermilion band like a cummerbund across its middle and beneath that is a scatter of gold coins.'

'Correct. And the words? You have to quote the words before you can sample it.' He held his head in his hands and screwed up his eyes, smiling.

'Special old Irish whiskey. Black Bush. Original grant to distil – sixteen-', he paused slapping the top of his head, 'oh-eight. Blended and bottled by the inverted commas Old Bushmills, close inverted commas, Distillery Company Limited, Bushmills, County Antrim. Product of Ireland.'

'Correct – you're a genius.'

'There's more. At the bottom it says "registered label".'

He stood and we kissed. He told me how he'd missed me and asked with concern about Mother's cremation.

The nearest I could come to that party trick was to recite the French side of the HP Sauce bottle. '*Cette Sauce de haute qualité* . . . etc.' Jordan made me do it for his friends.

Afterwards he would always announce, 'He passed his exams with the highest condemnation.'

Sometimes I lie awake at night wondering what I will do when Jordan dies. I have given up my career and my life for him. I remember once reading about Eric Fenby, Delius's amanuensis, and feeling sorry for him. An intelligent man in touch with such talent but devoid of actual genius himself. I have become involved in painting but am useless at it – as useless as Beckett's secretary is at writing, if he has one – as useless as Beckett is, come to think of it.

It has occurred to me that I could, with the right amount of secrecy, continue to produce Jordan Fitzgeralds for a number of years to come, and say to the dealer that they came from stock. But that would necessitate getting him to sign blank canvases. I have never plucked up enough courage to ask him to do such a thing.

I think that Jordan took me on because I would do what I was told – to the letter – exactly. Engineering Drawing is that kind of science. Even then Jordan must have had intimations of his coming blindness. He said a philistine was what he wanted. If I was artistic it would interfere with the translation of his vision on to canvas.

After I had finished my first painting under his direction he went up to it and looked all over its surface from six inches. He nodded with approval.

'I'll call you my drapery man.'

'What?'

'An eighteenth-century caper. Portrait painters got a man in to do the time-consuming bits – the lace and the satin stuff. The best of them was Vanaken. Hogarth drew this man's funeral with all the best painters in London behind the coffin weeping and gnashing their teeth.'

The sound of the Hoover, even from the distance of the house, wakens him because when I switch it off I hear him calling me. I go across to the barn.

'Are we ready to start again?' he says.

'Okay.'

'If you have fully recovered from your high dudgeon.'

'I have.'

He puts on a querulous voice and says, 'Question. What particular altitude is dudgeon inevitably? Answer. High.' He laughs and slaps his knees.

'Did you take your pills?' He shakes his head and I have to go all the way back to the house and bring them to him.

When he has swallowed them he says, 'I want you to scumble the bottom third with sap green.'

'In a straight line?'

'No, tilt it slightly – like the top side of a T-square.'

When Mother came down that September I was still living with Jordan, but she thought nothing of it. I had my own room. He had his. Mother always thought sex was something which happened in a bedroom at night when everyone else had retired. I had warned Jordan to be discreet and he only approached me during the early evening when she went for her walk to the cliff top to feel the cool breeze come off the sea.

'It's my favourite time of day,' she said.

'Then why do you come here? In England it is that temperature all the time – and even cooler.' I was annoyed with her because she had made no mention of going home and it was the first of October. When I finally did broach the subject she said that she was waiting for me to go home with her.

'I am staying here.'

'But how will you live? You have to get a job.'

'Jordan is now my employer.'

'And what do you do, might I ask?'

'I help him. Make up canvases. Clean his brushes. Keep the place in order. Do the shopping. Allow him time to concentrate on painting.'

'A houseboy.'

'If you like. In pleasant surroundings at a temperature I enjoy. With one of the great artists of the twentieth century.'

Before I met Jordan I knew nothing of painting. But he got me interested – gave me books to read, pictures to look at. He would deride his renowned contemporaries – 'Patrick's a total wanker', 'McGill's line has all the subtlety of a car skid.'

All this bewildered me at the time, because I thought them all equally poor. I was more convinced of the worth of the Post-Impressionists. Jordan thought Picasso good enough to envy, and Bonnard. He thought Matisse uneven and as for Manet – he was a disgrace.

When I have finished scumbling with the sap green Jordan says, 'Make up a bowl of black and one of turquoise – straight from the tube. A third turps.' He takes the container of tennis balls and cracks it open. His fingers hesitate on their furry yellow surface. He removes one and lays his index finger diagonally across it. 'Watch the spin,' he says and flicks the ball across the barn. It bounces once, breaking back on itself about six inches. Pangur-Ban lurches forward as if to chase it, then decides not to and wags her tail.

'My brother and I used to play cricket, at a time when it was neither profitable nor popular. We had a backyard at home about ten by twelve and we had stumps chalked on one wall. The fielders were buckets – they could catch you out if the ball went in without bouncing. But there were always arguments about when the stumps were hit. We bowled underarm with a tennis ball and solved the arguments by soaking it. Then it left a wet mark on the stumps which could not be denied.'

Once a year a furniture van, hired by Jordan's London dealer, arrives and the driver and myself load the paintings on to it. For the last five years it has been the same man. He has no interest in art what-soever: 'They're big this year,' he says, or, 'He's using a lot of green.'

'He's Irish,' I say.

'Careful. Easy. He'll go mad if you scrape one of these things.' The van-driver speaks to me in whispers, which I find insulting. Somehow his conspiracy makes me no more than a houseboy. I resent this but do not know how to reprimand him. It's not worth it for once a year.

*

Jordan rarely, if ever, goes out.

'There's no point,' he says. 'One darkness is the same as another. The only way you can change the landscape for me is to bring in flowers – or pine cones – or fart, for that matter.'

The only place he goes is the bank in Albufeira. Once every three months I phone a taxi and take him there. I lead him into the bank by the arm and the manager is waiting to take his other arm.

'*Bom dia*, Jordan.' They go into an office while I wait at the counter. He has *never* told me how much he is worth – I suppose he has no idea himself.

When I have made up the bowls of colour he asks me to float a tennis ball in each.

'You would be as well to wear rubber gloves,' he says. 'Now I want you to press the black ball on that mimosa area to the left of the three masking strips – about an inch out. The outline should be fuzzy. Then I want a pyramid of them – just like the medals on the Black Bush bottle.'

We ceased to be lovers many years ago but I still feel a sense of responsibility to him. I can't leave him, particularly now that he is blind. Nobody else would put up with him. I find my release and relaxation elsewhere. The beaches here teem with beautiful bodies – the roads are full of young bare-chested boys who drive about on motorbikes which sound like hornets. But it is becoming more difficult year by year. I am forty-three and beginning to thicken. I have breasts like a teenage girl. I'm sure Jordan knows of my affairs but I have never told him.

My annoyance with him reaches peaks and I have walked out on him many times. One of the worst was when I asked him – point-blank – if he had screwed my mother and he said in his own defence, 'Not often.'

After that I slept on the beach for a week. When I went back he was very kind to me – told me that artists were a race apart. They did things differently because of the albatross of their sensitivity. I think on this occasion he even apologised to me.

*

The normal and frequent rows we have end with him yelling at me, 'Go, go. And good riddance! I am as weak as any other man.' But I always come back. It is not for the money that I am staying on – if I know Jordan he will leave me a year's wages and the rest will go to a Cricketing Trust, or Pangur-Ban.

When I have finished dabbing the tennis balls on the surface of the canvas he asks, 'How does it look?'

'Fine. Actually it looks really good.'

'Ectually,' he spits the word out. 'I wouldn't have told you to do it if I hadn't *known* it would look good.'

'The rubber S shows up negatively in some of them.'

'I knew it would.'

I lead him to the canvas and kneel him down in front of it.

'I cannot see it but I'm sure it has all the sadness of a thing finished.' He feels for the right-angled sides of the corner then signs it with a charcoal stick in his highstepping signature.

He stands with an effort and says, 'I'd like you to do my beard.' He stretches and sits again in his canvas chair. I lift the sharpest scissors and begin to cut his beard close. He likes it to look like a week's growth.

'Pure white,' I say.

'What past tense as applied to the propulsion of motor vehicles is snow as white as?'

I think for a while then guess. 'Driven.'

He caresses my buttocks and says, 'You're coming on.'

'Don't do that or I'll cut your lip.' He takes his hand away from me.

'Wait,' says Jordan. 'Get a saucer. Keep the hairs for me.'

'What?'

'Let's keep the hairs – they're white. Save them and use them in a painting some time.'

'Are you serious, Jordan?'

'Yes I am.'

I go and wash a saucer and dry it, then continue clipping his beard on to it.

'I never know with you, whether you're sending me up or not.'

'It's a great idea. Hairy paintings. I've used sand in the past – but to . . . I'd like to put something of myself into just one of these images.'

'You *are* joking.'

'If I could find the right medium to float them in. Save them anyway – let me think about it.'

I put the clippings from the saucer into a polythene bag, tie the neck in a knot and put it on the shelf.

'I want you to read to me tonight. Also I want to get drunk.'

I know that this is a command for me to stay with him until whatever hour he chooses and put him safely into his bed. His capacity for drink is prodigious and his aggression proportional to the amount taken. The only thing in my favour is that he is now physically weak and I can master him. He used to throw things at me but that ceased when he finally became blind.

'Very well,' I say. It has the makings of a long and difficult night.

The last session – about three weeks ago – he said to me, 'I'm getting through it quite well.'

'What?'

'My life. There can't be long to go now. The thought of suicide is a great consolation. It has helped me through many's a bad night. Do you know who said that?'

'No.'

'I didn't think you would. You have a *Reader's Digest* grasp of the world. Just promise me one thing – don't slot me into one of those wall cupboards in the graveyard.'

'But I will. And I'll put one of those nice ceramic photos of you on the door with little roses all round it.'

'Burn me and fritter my ashes on the ocean.'

Inevitably halfway down the bottle he will begin to cry. The tears will fill his eyes and spill over on to his cheeks and wet his beard. When he stops and blows his nose thoroughly in that navy hanky of his, he will say, 'It's amazing that the eyes work so well in that function but in no other way.'

If he cries tonight I'll really put the knife in – get even with him for today's nastiness. I'll ask him if he wants his tears kept. If he wants a phial of them put in one of his paintings. If I do say this there will be a God-awful row. He'll wreck the place. The one thing he cannot stand is to have his work ridiculed – even by me.

But no matter how furious the fight, the bitching, the name-calling, I will be back in the morning with Pangur-Ban at my heels. There is now a kind of unspoken acceptance that I am here until he dies.

MORE THAN JUST THE DISEASE

As he unpacked his case Neil kept hearing his mother's voice. *Be tidy at all times, then no one can surprise you.* This was a strange house he'd come to, set in the middle of a steep terraced garden. Everything in it seemed of an unusual design; the wardrobe in which he hung his good jacket was of black lacquer with a yellow inlay of exotic birds. *A little too ornate for my taste – vulgar almost.* And pictures – there were pictures hanging everywhere, portraits, landscapes, sketches. *Dust gatherers.* The last things in his case were some comics and he laid them with his ironed and folded pyjamas on the pillow of the bottom bunk and went to join the others.

They were all sitting in the growing dark of the large front room, Michael drinking hot chocolate, Anne his sister with her legs flopped over the arm of the chair, Dr Middleton squeaking slowly back and forth in the rocking-chair while his wife moved around preparing to go out.

'Now, boys, you must be in bed by ten thirty at the latest. Anne can sit up until we come back if she wants. We'll not be far away and if anything does happen you can phone "The Seaview".' She spent some time looking in an ornamental jug for a pen to write down the number. 'I can find nothing in this house yet.'

'We don't need Anne to babysit,' said Michael. 'We're perfectly capable of looking after ourselves. Isn't that right Neil?' Neil nodded. He didn't like Michael involving him in an argument with the rest of the family. He had to have the tact of a guest; sit on the fence yet remain Michael's friend.

'Can we not stay up as late as Anne?' asked Michael.

'Anne is fifteen years of age. Please, Michael, it's been a long day. Off to bed.'

'But Mama, Neil and I . . .'

'Michael.' The voice came from the darkness of the rocking-chair

265

and had enough threat in it to stop Michael. The two boys got up and went to their bedroom.

Neil lifted his pyjamas and went to the bathroom. He dressed for bed buttoning the jacket right up to his neck and went back with his clothes draped over his arm. Michael was half-dressed.

'That was quick,' he said. He bent his thin arms, flexing his biceps. 'I only wear pyjama bottoms. Steve McQueen, he-man,' and he thumped his chest before climbing to the top bunk. They lay and talked and talked – about their first year at the school, how lucky they had been to have been put in the same form, who they hated most. The Crow with his black gown and beaky nose, the Moon with his pallid round face, wee Hamish with his almost mad preoccupation with ruling red lines. Once Neil had awkwardly ruled a line which showed the two bumps of his fingers protruding beyond the ruler and wee Hamish had pounced on it.

'What are these bumps? Is this a drawing of a camel, boy?' Everybody except Neil had laughed and if there was one thing he couldn't abide it was to be laughed at. A voice whispered that it was a drawing of his girlfriend's chest.

Neil talked about the Scholarship examination and the day he got his results. When he saw the fat envelope on the mat he knew his life would change – if you got the thin envelope you had failed, a fat one with coloured forms meant that you had passed. What Neil did not say was that his mother had cried, kneeling in the hallway hugging and kissing him. He had never seen anyone cry with happiness before and it worried him a bit. Nor did he repeat what she had said with her eyes shining. *Now you'll be at school with the sons of doctors and lawyers.*

Anne opened the door and hissed into the dark.

'You've got to stop talking right now. Get to sleep.' She was in a cotton nightdress which became almost transparent with the light of the hallway behind her. Neil saw her curved shape outlined to its margins. He wanted her to stay there but she slammed the door.

After that they whispered and had a farting competition. They heard Michael's father and mother come in, make tea and go to bed. It was ages before either of them slept. All the time Neil was in agonies with his itch but he did not want to scratch in case Michael should feel the shaking communicated to the top bunk.

In the morning Neil was first awake and tiptoed to the bathroom with all his clothes to get dressed. He took off his pyjama jacket and looked at himself in the mirror. Every morning he hoped that it would have miraculously disappeared overnight but it was still there crawling all over his chest and shoulders: his psoriasis – a redness with an edge as irregular as a map and the skin flaking and scumming off the top. Its pattern changed from week to week but only once had it appeared above his collar line. That week his mother had kept him off school. He turned his back on the mirror and put on a shirt, buttoning it up to the neck. He wondered if he should wear a tie to breakfast but his mother's voice had nothing to say on the subject.

Breakfast wasn't a meal like in his own house when he and his mother sat down at table and had cereal and tea and toast with sometimes a boiled egg. Here people just arrived and poured themselves cornflakes and went off to various parts of the room, or even the house, to eat them. The only still figure was the doctor himself. He sat at the corner of the table reading the *Scotsman* and drinking coffee. He wore blue running shoes and no socks and had a T-shirt on. Except for his receding M-shaped hairline he did not look at all like a doctor. In Edinburgh anytime Neil had seen him he wore a dark suit and a spotted bow-tie.

Anne came in. '*Guten Morgen, mein Papa.* Hello Neil.' She was bright and washed with her yellow hair in a knot on the top of her head. Neil thought she was the most beautiful girl he had ever seen up close. She wore a pair of denims cut down to shorts so that there were frayed fringes about her thighs. She also had what his mother called *a figure.* She ate her cornflakes noisily and the doctor did not even raise his eyes from the paper. *Close your mouth when you're eating, please. Others have to live with you.*

'Some performance last night, eh Neil?' she said.

'Pardon?'

'Daddy, they talked till all hours.'

Her father turned a page of the paper and his hand groped out like a blind man's to find his coffee.

'Sorry,' said Neil.

'I'm only joking,' said Anne and smiled at him. He blushed because she looked directly into his eyes and smiled at him as if she liked him. He stumbled to his feet.

'Thank you for the breakfast,' he said to the room in general and went outside to the garden where Michael was sitting on the steps.

'Where did you get to? You didn't even excuse yourself from the table,' said Neil.

'I wasn't at the table, small Fry,' said Michael. He was throwing pea-sized stones into an ornamental pond at a lower level.

'One minute you were there and the next you were gone.'

'I thought it was going to get heavy.'

'What?'

'I know the signs. The way the old man reads the paper. Coming in late last night.'

'Oh.'

Neil lifted a handful of multi-coloured gravel and fed the pieces singly into his other hand and lobbed them at the pool. They made a nice plip noise.

'Watch it,' said Michael. He stilled Neil's throwing arm with his hand. 'Here comes Mrs Wan.'

'Who's she?'

An old woman in a bottle-green cardigan and baggy mouse-coloured trousers came stepping one step at a time down towards them. She wore a puce-coloured hat like a turban and, although it was high summer, a pair of men's leather gloves.

'Good morning, boys,' she said. Her voice was the most superior thing Neil had ever heard, even more so than his elocution teacher's. 'And how are you this year, Benjamin?'

'Fine. This is my friend Neil Fry.' Neil stood up and nodded. She was holding secateurs and a flat wooden basket. He knew that she would find it awkward to shake hands so he did not offer his.

'How do you do? What do you think of my garden, young man?'

'It's very good. Tidy.'

'Let's hope it remains that way throughout your stay,' she said and continued her sideways stepping down until she reached the compost heap at the bottom beyond the ornamental pool.

'Who is she?' asked Neil.

'She owns the house. Lets it to us for the whole of the summer.'

'But where does she live when you're here?'

'Up the back in a caravan. She's got ninety million cats.' Mrs Wan's puce turban threaded in and out of the flowers as she weeded and pruned. It was a dull overcast day and the wind was moving the brightly-coloured rose blooms.

'Fancy a swim?' asked Michael.

'Too cold. Anyway I told you I can't swim.'

'You don't have to swim. Just horse around. It's great.'

'Naw.'

Michael threw his whole handful of gravel chirping into the pond and went up the steps to the house.

That afternoon the shelf of cloud moved inland and the sky over the Atlantic became blue. The wind dropped and Dr Middleton observed that the mare's-tails were a good sign. The whole family went down the hundred yards to the beach, each one carrying something – a basket, a deckchair, a lilo.

'Where else in the world but Scotland would we have the beach to ourselves on a day like this?' said Mrs Middleton. The doctor agreed with a grunt. Michael got stripped to his swimming trunks and they taught Neil to play boule in the hard sand near the water. The balls were of bright grooved steel and he enjoyed trying to lob them different ways until he finally copied the doctor who showed him how to put back-spin on them. Anne wore a turquoise bikini and kept hooking her fingers beneath the elastic of her pants and snapping them out to cover more of her bottom. She did this every time she bent to pick up her boule and Neil came to watch for it. When they stopped playing Michael and his sister ran off to leap about in the breakers – large curling walls, glass-green, which nearly knocked them off their feet. From where he stood Neil could only hear their cries faintly. He went and sat down with the doctor and his wife.

'Do you not like the water?' she asked. She was lying on a sunbed, gleaming with suntan oil. She had her dress rucked up beyond her knees and her shoulder straps loosened.

'No. It's too cold.'

'The only place *I'll* ever swim again is the Med,' said the doctor.

'Sissy,' said his wife, without opening her eyes. Neil lay down and tried to think of a better reason for not swimming. His mother had one friend who occasionally phoned for her to go to the Commonwealth Pool. When she really didn't feel like it there was only one excuse that seemed to work.

At tea Michael took a perverse pleasure out of telling him again and again how warm the water was and Anne innocently agreed with him.

The next day was scorching hot. Even at breakfast time they could see the heat corrugating the air above the slabbed part of the garden.

'You *must* come in for a swim today, Fry. I'm boiled already,' said Michael.

'The forecast is twenty-one degrees,' said the doctor from behind his paper. Anne whistled in appreciation.

Neil's thighs were sticking to the plastic of his chair. He said, 'My mother forgot to pack my swimming trunks. I looked yesterday.'

Mrs Middleton, in a flowing orange dressing-gown, spoke over her shoulder from the sink. 'Borrow a pair of Michael's.' Before he could stop her she had gone off with wet hands in search of extra swimming trunks.

'Couldn't be simpler,' she said, setting a navy blue pair with white side panels on the table in front of Neil.

'I'll get mine,' said Michael and dashed to his room. Anne sat opposite Neil on the Formica kitchen bench-top swinging her legs. She coaxed him to come swimming, again looking into his eyes. He looked down and away from them.

'Come on, Neil. Michael's not much fun in the water.'

'The fact is,' said Neil, 'I've got my period.'

There was a long silence and a slight rustle of the *Scotsman* as Dr Middleton looked over the top of it. Then Anne half-slid, half-vaulted off the bench and ran out. Neil heard her make funny snorts in her nose.

'That's too bad,' said the doctor and got up and went out of the room shutting the door behind him. Neil heard Anne's voice and her father's, then he heard the bedroom door shut. He folded his swimming trunks and set them on the sideboard. Mrs Middleton gave a series of little coughs and smiled at him.

'Can I help you with the dishes?' he asked. There was something not right.

'Are you sure you're well enough?' she said smiling. Neil nodded and began to lift the cups from various places in the room. She washed and he dried with a slow thoroughness.

'Neil, nobody is going to force you to swim. So you can feel quite safe.'

Michael came in with his swimming gear in a roll under his arm.

'Ready, small Fry?'

'Michael, could I have a word? Neil, could you leave those bathing trunks back in Michael's wardrobe?'

On the beach the boys lay down on the sand. Michael hadn't spoken since they left the house. He walked in front, he picked the spot, he lay down and Neil followed him. The sun was hot and again they had the beach to themselves. Neil picked up a handful of sand and examined it as he spilled it out slowly.

'I bet you there's at least one speck of gold on this beach,' he said.

'That's a bloody stupid thing to say.'

'I'll bet you there is.'

Michael rolled over turning his back. 'I can pick them.'

'What?'

'I can really pick them.'

'What do you mean?'

'I might as well have asked a girl to come away on holiday.'

Neil's fist bunched in the sand.

'What's the use of somebody who won't go in for a dip?'

'I can't, that's all.'

'My Mum says you must have a very special reason. What is it, Fry?'

Neil opened his hand and some of the damp, deeper sand remained in little segments where he had clenched it. He was almost sure Anne had laughed.

'I'm not telling you.'

'Useless bloody Mama's boy,' said Michael. He got up flinging a handful of sand at Neil and ran down to the water. Some of the sand went into Neil's eyes, making him cry. He knuckled them clear and blinked, watching Michael jump, his elbows up, as each glass wave rolled at him belly-high.

Neil shouted hopelessly towards the sea. 'That's the last time I'm getting you into the pictures.'

He walked back towards the house. He had been here a night, a day and a morning. It would be a whole week before he could get home. Right now he felt he *was* a Mama's boy. He just wanted to climb the stair and be with her behind the closed door of their house. This had been the first time in his life he had been away from her and, although he had been reluctant because of this very thing, she had insisted that he could not turn down an invitation from the doctor's family. *It will teach you how to conduct yourself in good society.*

At lunch time Michael did not speak to him but made up salad rolls and took them on to the patio. Anne and her father had gone into the village on bicycles. Neil sat at the table chewing his roll with difficulty and staring in front of him. *If there is one thing I cannot abide it's a milk bottle on the table.* Mrs Middleton was the only one left for him to talk to.

'We met Mrs Wan this morning,' he said.

'Oh did you? She's a rum bird – feeding all those cats.'

'How many has she?'

'I don't know. They're never all together at the same time. She's a Duchess, you know?'

'A real one?'

'Yes. I can't remember her title – from somewhere in England. She married some Oriental and lived in the Far East. Africa too for a time. When he died she came home. Look.' She waved her hand at all the bric-à-brac. 'Look at this.' She went to a glass-fronted cabinet and took out what looked like a lace ball. It was made of ivory and inside was another ball with just as intricately carved mandarins and elephants and palm leaves, with another one inside that again.

'The question is how did they carve the one inside. It's all one piece.'

Neil turned it over in his hands marvelling at the mystery. He handed it carefully back.

'You wouldn't want to play boule with that,' he said.

'Isn't it exquisitely delicate?'

He nodded and said, 'Thank you for the lunch. It was very nourishing.'

He wandered outside in the garden and sat for a while by the pool. It was hot and the air was full of the noise of insects and bees moving in and out the flowers. He went down to the beach and saw that his friend Michael had joined up with some other boys to play cricket. He sat down out of sight of them at the side of a sand-dune. He lay back and closed his eyes. They had laughed at him in school when he said he didn't know what l.b.w. meant. He had been given a free cricket bat but there was hardly a mark on it because he couldn't seem to hit the ball. It was so hard and came at him so fast that he was more interested in getting out of its way than playing any fancy strokes. Scholarship boys were officially known as foundationers but the boys called them 'fundies' or 'fundaments'. When he asked what it meant somebody told him to look it up in a dictionary. 'Part of body on which one sits; buttocks; anus.'

He lifted his head and listened. At first he thought it was the noise of a distant seagull but it came again and he knew it wasn't. He looked up to the top of the sand-dune and saw a kitten, its tiny black tail upright and quivering.

'Pshhh-wshhh.'

He climbed the sand and lifted it. It miaowed thinly. He stroked its head and back and felt the frail fish bones of its ribs. It purred and he carried it back to the house. He climbed the steps behind the kitchen and saw a caravan screened by a thick hedge. The door was open and he had to hold it steady with his knee before he could knock on it.

'Come in,' Mrs Wan's voice called. Neil stepped up into the van. After the bright sunlight it was gloomy inside. It smelt of old and cat. He saw Mrs Wan sitting along one wall with her feet up.

'I found this and thought maybe it was yours,' said Neil handing the cat over to her. She scolded it.

'You little monkey,' she said and smiled at Neil. 'This cat is a black sheep. He's always wandering off. Thank you, young man. It was very kind of you to take the trouble to return him.'

'It was no trouble.'

She was dressed as she had been the day before except for the gloves. Her hands were old and her fingers bristled with rings. She waved at him as he turned to go.

'Just a minute. Would you like something to drink – as a reward?' She stood up and rattled in a cupboard above the sink.

'I think some tonic water is all I can offer you. Will that do?' She didn't give him a clean glass but just rinsed one for a moment under the thin trickle from the swan-neck tap at the tiny sink. She chased three cats away from the covered bench seat and waved him to sit down. Because the glass was not very clean the bubbles adhered to its sides. He saw that nothing was clean as he looked about the place. There were several tins of Kit-e-Kat opened on the draining-board and a silver fork encrusted with the stuff lay beside them. There were saucers all over the floor with milk which had evaporated in the heat leaving yellow rings. Everything was untidy. He set his glass between a pile of magazines and a marmalade pot on the table. She asked him his name and about his school and where he lived and about his father. Neil knew that his mother would call her nosey but he thought that she seemed interested in all his answers. She listened intently, blinking and staring at him with her face slightly turned as if she had a deaf ear.

'My father died a long time ago,' he said.

'And your mother?'

'She's alive.'

'And what does she do for a living?'

'She works in the cinema.'

'Oh how interesting. Is she an actress?'

'No. She just works there. With a torch. She gets me in free – for films that are suitable for me. Sometimes I take my friend Michael with me.'

'Is that the boy below?'

'Yes.'

'I thought his name was Benjamin. But how marvellous that you can see all these films free.' She clapped her ringed hands together and seemed genuinely excited. 'I used to love the cinema. The cartoons were my favourite. And the newsreels. I'll bet you're very popular when a good picture comes to town.'

'Yes I am,' said Neil and smiled and sipped his tonic.

'Let's go outside and talk. It's a shame to waste such a day in here.' Neil offered his arm as she lowered herself from the step to the ground.

'What a polite young man.'

'That's my mother's fault.'

They sat on the deckchairs facing the sun and she lit a cigarette, holding it between her jewelled fingers. Her face was brown and criss-crossed with wrinkles.

'Why aren't you in swimming on such a day?' she asked.

Neil hesitated, then heard himself say, 'I can't. I've got a disease.'

'What is it?'

Again he paused but this old woman seemed to demand the truth. 'A thing – on my chest.'

'Let me see?' she said and leaned forward. He was amazed to find himself unbuttoning his shirt and showing her his mark. In the sunlight it didn't look so red. She scrutinised it and hummed, pursing her mouth and biting her lower lip.

'Why does it stop you bathing?'

Neil shrugged and began to button up when she stopped him.

'Let the sun at it. I'm sure it can do no harm.' He left his shirt lying open. 'When I was in Africa I worked with lepers.'

'Lepers?'

'Yes. So the sight of you doesn't worry me,' she said. 'Watch that you don't suffer from more than just the disease.'

'I don't understand.'

'It's bad enough having it without being shy about it as well.'

'Have you got leprosy now?'

'No. It's not as contagious as everybody says.'

Neil finished his tonic and lay back in the chair. The sun was bright and hot on his chest. He listened to Mrs Wan talking about leprosy, of how the lepers lost their fingers and toes, not because of the disease but because they had lost all feeling in them and they broke and damaged them without knowing. Eventually they got gangrene. Almost all the horrible things of leprosy, she said, were secondary. Suddenly he heard Michael's voice.

'Mrs Wan, Mum says could you tell her where . . .' his voice tailed off seeing Neil's chest, '. . . the cheese grater is?'

'Do you know, I think I brought it up here.' She got up and stepped slowly into the caravan. Neil closed over his shirt and began to button it. Neither boy said a word.

At tea Michael spoke to him as if they were friends again and in bed that night it was Neil's suggestion that they go for a swim.

'Now? Are you mad?'

'They say it's warmer at night.'

'Yeah and we could make dummies in the beds like Clint Eastwood.'

'They don't *have* to look like Clint Eastwood.' They both laughed quiet sneezing laughs.

After one o'clock they dropped out of the window and ran to the beach. For almost half an hour in the pale darkness Neil thrashed and shivered. Eventually he sat down to wait in the warmer shallows, feeling the withdrawing sea hollow the sand around him. Further out, Michael whooped and rode the breakers like a shadow against their whiteness.

IN THE HILLS ABOVE LUGANO

I had first met Brendan through the Debating Society when he was a mature student at University doing medicine. I liked his moroseness, his intelligence and his drinking habits – which were much the same as mine at the time. We had been, despite the ten-year age difference, reasonably friendly. But it was with some surprise that I read his invitation to spend a week of the summer holiday with him and his wife in a place he had acquired for a month near Lugano in Switzerland.

'It'll be a reunion in the sun,' he wrote.

I really didn't know him all that well – but money for a provincial publisher is scarce and I had not had a real holiday for several years.

He met me off the train and his first words were, 'On a point of information?'

'What?'

'How are you, young fella?' He shook my hand with both of his, then put his arm around my shoulder on the way to the car. It is disconcerting to find that an acquaintance considers you his best friend, his soul mate, but I could do nothing about it. He was in good form and as we drove up into the hills above Lugano he kept smiling and shaking his head in disbelief.

'How many years is it?' he said.

'Five – six?'

'It's ten.'

'I don't believe you.'

'And we all swore we'd meet up again every year. The best laid plans – blah-blah.'

'Hey, this is some place.' The scenery was magnificent – dry ochre hills covered with trees and dense foliage, lakes lying blue in the hazy distance.

*

'This is my wife, Linden,' he said. She was a tall girl, young for him – about the same age as myself – with a wisp-like quality of beauty about her. She wore a simple white dress and her skin was a golden brown from the first fortnight of the holiday.

'Hi,' she said and looked away from me shyly.

We ate on the patio and continued to sit at the table and drink the very excellent local wine until darkness fell. At one point, when Brendan went off to get another bottle from the fridge, Linden leaned over and said to me, 'I'm glad you're here. He's been so down of late. Utterly, utterly black moods. You're the only one he's ever talked to me about.'

The fireflies came out, icy points of blue light, and flitted in the hot darkness. They hovered in one place for a moment then skidded off to another. Crickets kept up a constant trilling noise.

'How's the publishing?' Brendan asked.

'We've a very good Autumn list coming.'

'The last novel got excellent reviews.'

'I thought the author and I were the only ones who read those.'

'We keep abreast. No philistines here.'

'No,' said Linden. 'I admire what you're doing – and having the courage to publish poetry.'

'It doesn't take courage – just money.'

Later Brendan became nostalgic, inevitably talking about people whom Linden didn't know. I was aware that she was withdrawing from the conversation, her eyes straying away to look into the night or follow the path of a firefly. Brendan recalled our sessions together with a clarity I did not think was possible.

'Do you remember that afternoon in Hannigan's?'

I nodded. I could recall the bar and having been in it once or twice but had no recollection of being there with Brendan.

'And you made the statement that there was no such thing as an unselfish act.'

'Did I?'

He went on to outline my arguments from the past, the amounts we drank, who was in the company. It had obviously meant a great deal more to him than to me. And as he talked occasionally Linden caught me looking at her and once she smiled.

The next morning I awoke with a sore head. I felt dishevelled and awful as I made my way down to breakfast in my dressing-gown. Linden was sunbathing on her stomach at the side of the small pool, writing in a loose-leaf folder. When she noticed me she put on her bikini top and got up to make me coffee.

'I can do it,' I said. But she insisted. I think she was conscious of me looking at her because when she brought a pot of coffee and some croissants to the table she had put on an orange towelling beach robe.

'Did we talk rubbish last night?'

She smiled but did not answer.

'Where's Brendan?'

'Still abed.'

She sat down at the table, the perfume of her suntan oil wafting towards me. Just then a small middle-aged man in a navy T-shirt came across the patio. Looking neither right nor left he went down the three steps to the pool. He walked slowly, dragging his heels.

'Who's that?'

'He owns the place. Lives in a hut at the back during the summer.'

The man took a long pole with a net on it and skimmed some flower petals and leaves from the surface of the pool. He clattered the pole back in its place and left the same way he had come, paying no attention whatsoever to us.

'What a gloomy wee man.'

'Money makes some people miserable. He doesn't look like he'd own a place like this.'

'But . . . we're on our holidays.' I poured myself another coffee. 'Where did you two meet?'

'In a hospital in Toronto.' She smiled. 'I was visiting and he ran after me – the whole way up the corridor – and said, "I'm looking for an excuse to talk to you but I can't think of one."'

'He was always a smooth talker.'

'No, he really meant it. But I agree, the way he spoke was really neat.'

'And what did you do . . . before Brendan?'

'Anything, everything. I'd been to college and graduated. Drama. I'd modelled a bit. I went to LA and tried to get into the movies. I was screen-tested for *Alien*.'

'Really?'

'Yes. But Sigourney Weaver got the part.'

'Did you try for others?'

'It was then I met Brendan. I had to make decisions.' She laughed. 'He won.'

'Speak of the devil.'

Brendan appeared in bathing trunks, muttered a good morning and plunged into the pool.

Later he and I walked down to the supermarket while Linden got on with her sunbathing. The villa was at the end of a leafy lane and Brendan pulled a switch from the hedge as he walked. He deleafed it and whipped it about.

He talked about his research – he was working on the effects of certain inhaled gases on brain tissue – and managed to explain, even to me, some of the complexities and problems.

'I work on rats, of course.'

'Are their brains the same?'

'Elements are.'

'Who'd be a rat? Made to sniff your gases – brain damage – then killed to be examined?'

'It's for our good eventually.'

'I suppose so.' The air was hot and I was conscious of moving through it. 'Ahhh – this heat is wonderful,' I said.

'Wait until midday. Linden and I have taken to the siesta habit. It's all you can do when it's that hot.'

I raised an eyebrow. He whipped the switch across my backside.

'I didn't mean that, you adolescent.'

*

Because of my good Italian Brendan let me do all the transactions in the supermarket. After we had loaded a bag with groceries he said, 'Is it too early for a cure?'

'Why not?'

We sat outside on the patio of a small restaurant and ordered a bottle of white. The glasses when they were filled turned opaque with the coldness of the wine.

'You're getting a gut, Doctor,' I said. He slapped his paunch loudly.

'I am the age to wear it.'

'Linden is very beautiful.'

'Yes, I know.' His voice was quiet. He reached out with his stick and drew the point of it down the side of the glass, making a clear track in the condensation. Then he said, 'We've been brought up wrongly to deal with sexuality. Dogs have it right. And doctors.'

I waited for him to elaborate.

'A doctor meets a beautiful woman in his surgery and before you can say knife he has her stripped and lying down. A minute later he's palpated her breasts and sunk his finger in every available orifice. After that he can get to know her. That kind of thing should be socially compulsory. Dogs have it right. "I'd like you to meet Miss O'Neill," and instead of shaking hands you have a good look and a rummage between her legs and a good sniff. Get the trivial things out of the way first.'

'That's a bitter Swiftian vision. Not one that appeals to me.'

Brendan shrugged and bent his switch in an arc until it broke. 'A green-stick fracture,' he said and dropped it on the floor.

'It's got to be more beautiful than that. More spiritual.'

He laughed.

'It always amuses me when people make spiritual claims for the most *physical* of all human acts.'

'I don't want to be personal but does Linden agree with you about this?'

'We don't talk about it. This is why I'm so glad to see you. We can say anything to each other. Between friends nothing is barred.'

Brendan slugged off what was left in his glass and refilled it. I did not know what to say to his assumption of our closeness.

'For Christsake, why should we associate physical beauty with sexuality – it's not even physical beauty but a perfection of averageness. None of your black women with broad noses or fat Renoir nudes nowadays. They have to conform to the soft porn magazine. Fuck me, what crassness! What a load of fuckin baloney!'

I felt uncomfortable and tried to change the subject. The thought of Brendan in one of his utterly black moods for the rest of the holiday scared me. I suggested another bottle.

'Why not,' he said.

'Linden tells me she nearly got into films.'

He looked at me askance. 'An extra. She tried to get taken on as an extra in *Alien*.'

'There were no extras in *Alien*. It was all set on a spaceship.'

'Maybe it was *Reds*, then. There were thousands of extras in that.'

'You don't encourage her much.'

'It all exists in here with Linden.' He tapped his temple. I didn't like to probe any further but smiled down at my white knees.

We finished the second bottle between us and returned to the villa. Linden put her arm round Brendan's thickening waist and they went off for a siesta. In my room I slept almost immediately after the wine. When I woke I heard a strange noise – it must have been Linden – a kind of suppressed whimpering. Hissing whispers. Afterwards when they came down to the poolside there seemed to be nothing amiss and he laughed at some joke she had made. But she would not repeat it for me.

In the evening when Brendan was preparing the meal Linden and I sat on the patio drinking Camparis. Brendan's voice floated out into the night imitating a French tenor, singing 'Pour un baiser'.

'Do you see how good you are for him,' said Linden.

I nodded, unable to think of anything to say. The ice clicked and cracked in my glass. Her initial shyness of me seemed to have gone. She looked at me and her eyes held for longer than they should. I was unable to return her gaze and bowed my head. When I raised it again her eyes were still there – dark and beautiful – fixed on me. I called in to Brendan in the kitchen, 'Anything I can do to help?'

*

The next morning was very much the same as the first two. I went down to the pool in my dressing-gown and Linden was stretched out on a sunbed with her ring binder open on the ground in front of her. But she was asleep. I went over to her and before I cleared my throat I could not resist looking at her. I could see the wonderful length of her brown back, the side of her breast where it pressed softly against the sunbed. Her black hair was up to let the sun at her shoulders. I tried to tiptoe away but suddenly she wakened.

'Hi,' she said and smiled. She put on her top and sat up, flicking her hair back.

'What's the file?'

'Something I'm working on.'

'Like?'

'A screenplay.'

'I've never seen one of those. May I?'

'You of all people. No. I'd be embarrassed. It has no shape to it yet. Let me get you some coffee.'

'No. Let *me* get *you* some – for a change.'

We sat and talked for about an hour, drinking our way down a whole pot of coffee. I discovered that she and Brendan weren't actually married.

'It seems the easiest thing to say. We've been together for about eighteen months now. I needed the protection of one person – a moat if you like.'

'From?'

'From being hounded. I was getting into a lot of bad emotional relationships.' She indicated her body with her spread hands as if to explain. 'Every man I met wanted me on my back.' I stared at my knees which had turned pink from yesterday. Somewhere in the house a door slammed.

'The top of the marning, to yis,' said Brendan and he strode between us to dive into the pool. When he surfaced, blowing like a whale, he shouted, 'That kitchen's beginning to stink.'

I offered to help Linden and she asked me to take the rubbish down to the bin. I tied two bulging black bags which, by the smell coming from them, were a risk to our health and took them down the steps to the side of the house. The man in the navy T-shirt came round the corner with a similar black bag tied at the neck. We were too close for him to have ignored me.

'*Buon giorno*,' I said. He nodded. I wondered if he had some disease or an eye infection because his face was streaming with tears.

'*Cosa di male?*' I asked him, when I realised he was simply crying. He sniffed and rubbed his forearm across his face, said it was nothing. I held the heavy lid of the drum open for him and he thanked me. When I let it slam into place he told me that it was an anniversary for him. He took out a handkerchief and wiped his mouth and eyes. This day twelve years ago, he said, a terrible thing had happened. His only daughter had been murdered. Just walking in the hills above Lugano. They never got the man who did it. She was just twenty years of age. Just beginning her life. I stood there, my hands empty, trying to make sense of his oddly-accented Italian. Why does that kind of thing happen? You sound like an intelligent man. Tell me.

'*Peccato . . . peccato . . .* I'm sorry,' was all I could think of. He turned muttering to himself and walked away from me. Had I made a mistake – taken him up wrongly? When I told Brendan and Linden about the conversation Brendan just shrugged.

'He might be telling the truth. Who knows? Anyway, we were all canning peas outside Spalding.' He laughed but Linden was obviously disturbed by the story because she barely spoke a word all afternoon.

In the early hours of the morning I awoke and, as sometimes happens when I have had too much to drink, could not get back to sleep again. Eventually I got up to go to the lavatory. The window, which overlooked the pool, was open and insects hummed and fluttered round the light bulb. I looked out and saw the pale figure of Brendan squatting beside the pool. He was totally naked. My eyes were attracted to the knot of gristle and hair between his thighs. He was hunkered down, staring at the lit glassy pane of turquoise water. Even from this distance I could see the blackness in his eyes which did not move but seemed hypnotically riveted on the surface or in the depths of the water. Occasionally he flicked his hanging penis with his fingers the way another man would touch his moustache or adjust his glasses on the bridge of his nose. For some reason I directed my stream quietly down the side of the bowl and did not flush the toilet after me.

I could not sleep and read a Moravia from my bedside shelf for an hour or so until dawn. I don't know whether it was curiosity or another call of nature made me go to the lavatory again but Brendan was still there in the milky morning light. He had changed his position and now sat on the side of the pool with his feet dangling in the water. But his eyes stared in the same fashion, looking at nothing and at everything.

The next night at dinner Brendan drank heavily and was argumentative and objectionable. Both Linden and I were constantly putting our hands over our glasses as he poured glass after glass of wine for himself. It was a very hot night and I could see the sweat standing out on his face the more he drank. At the coffee stage he produced my gift of duty-free Irish whiskey and poured himself a tumblerful. And another. The crickets kept up their calls like unanswered phones in the woods.

'Do you write a screenplay with a specific actress in mind?'

Brendan sniggered and I looked at him but he didn't say anything.

'No,' said Linden. 'You can think of the best actress. If you write the character well, the actress should be able to make it believable.'

'De Niro . . . Streep . . . Fonda . . . Jack Nicholson,' Brendan listed the names punctuated by snorts of laughter. Linden ignored him and because she was talking directly to me I had to do the same.

'How do you know how to set about it?'

'There was a section on my drama course. My course tutor said I handled it well.'

'I'll bet he did,' said Brendan. He laughed and slammed the table with his hand so that the spoons rang. Linden looked at me and began to bite her thumb-nail. Brendan poured himself another very large whiskey and sipped it noisily.

'Can I ask what is it about?'

Linden shrugged. She picked up a piece of card and began to fan herself. The motion wafted her perfume towards me.

'It's about a woman who's trying to come to terms with herself and her life. She started out as a beautician then got into the manufacturing side of make-up. It's the irony of the outside and the inside. And how she copes with success.'

'Sounds interesting.'

'Why . . . WHY', shouted Brendan, 'don't you write about something you KNOW about? Fuck success. Why don't you write about failure, Linden. Eh? Failure with a capital F?'

She did not turn her head to him but kept staring out into the darkness. Tears came into her eyes but she quickly blinked them away.

'You're drunk,' she said. 'Go to bed.'

'Ah-ha, you've rumbled me.' He began to sing, 'Noo-bod-ee loves like an Irishman.' He swung his arms wide and toppled an empty wine bottle. It smashed among our feet on the stone floor of the patio.

'GO TO BED.' Linden's voice was tight with anger. They got up simultaneously as if they were about to come to blows but Linden went to get a brush and Brendan bounced off the jamb of the door and staggered across the room to the stairs.

I sat on the chair and listened to the empty echoing sound of broken glass being thrown in the bucket. Linden came back and lowered herself into her chair.

'I'm sorry about this.'

'Not to worry.'

'It must be very embarrassing for you. To have to sit and talk to your friend's wife.'

'Actually I feel more relaxed now that he's gone.'

'I think I deserve a drink,' she said. In the American fashion she filled her glass with ice-cubes then poured herself a whiskey. She pointed the bottle at me and I nodded. When she sat again she put the cold glass to her forehead.

'It's so warm tonight.' The fireflies flicked out beyond the lights of the pool. 'I so hate him when he's like that.'

'Drink changes some people.'

'Please, don't talk about him.' She rearranged her long legs and tucked one heel up underneath her. 'Tell me about publishing.'

'What about it?'

'Finding someone new. That must be exciting.'

'Yes, it is. But if they're any good they move on to a big London house.'

'I've written a novel – a short one.'

'Really?'

'It's been rejected by lots of publishers back home in the States. One of them was kind enough to say it would make a good screenplay. That's what I'm working on at the moment.'

I began to wonder if, at last, I'd discovered why Brendan had invited me. Had she coaxed him? I wiped the perspiration from my forehead with the bottom of my shirt.

'Would you like me to read the novel?'

'It's very kind of you to offer but . . . no. I think I see its faults now.'

'What's it called?'

'I'm sorry I brought it up. Can we just leave it?'

She swirled her ice-cubes in her glass and drained off her drink.

'Too long for a title.' She smiled and stood.

'I think', she said, 'I'm going to swim. Do you want to join me?'

'Okay.' She stood up, her hands reached down to the hem of her dress and with one sweeping movement she pulled it off over her head, shaking her hair loose as she did so. She was wearing only the briefest of white underwear. She skipped away as if she was shy or modest and dived into the pool.

'I'll be down in a moment,' I said. Upstairs I had some difficulty in getting into my bathing trunks and it didn't help to hear Brendan's heavy snores from the bedroom. I had just come out on to the patio when I heard her scream. She threshed towards the edge of the pool making a kind of whinnying noise.

'What is it? What's wrong?' She pulled herself up on straightened arms, sat on the side and winced.

'Something . . . an insect . . . huge . . .' I looked and saw in the lights of the pool what looked like a grasshopper with whirring wings. But it was the size of a big, fat cigar.

'It's horrible. It hit me in the face.' She was still shuddering with nausea at the thought of it. I reached for the pole with the net and captured the thing and pulled it nearer to inspect it.

'It's a locust, by God.'

'Kill it. It's horrible.'

'If you think I'm putting my bare foot on that . . .'

I sank the net and held the insect under the water. Its elbows and knees made frantic rowing motions and its wings twitched. My dry shoulder was touching Linden's wet one as she tried to see into the net.

'It must have come millions of miles,' I said. 'Thought you only got them in Africa.'

'Hold it under for five minutes,' said Linden. She put her wet arm on my back and I flinched.

'You're wet.' Coming out of the water her underwear had become almost transparent and I kept looking away, or at least looking at her face. I toppled forward into the pool and began to swim up and down.

'This is lovely.'

'I'm not going in with that thing there,' she said. She went up the steps and poured two more drinks and brought them down to the poolside. She was drying her hair when I got out.

'Is this for me?' She nodded and drank a little of her own. I lifted the net and saw no movement from the creature. 'Stone dead.' I sat down beside her on the sun-bed.

'Be careful with the glass on the patio. In your bare feet,' she said. 'I'll do it properly tomorrow.'

I kissed her, lightly at first – in a friendly fashion almost. She responded and kissed me with passion. She was like a coiled spring, full of unexpected jumps and starts. When I touched her breasts she gritted her teeth and tensed.

'What's wrong?' I could barely speak.

'I keep expecting pain. Brendan likes to . . . he hurts me.'

At the mention of his name I drew away from her. She sat with her hands between her knees and her head bowed.

'I'm sorry,' she said. Suddenly there was a whirring, chattering noise at our feet as the locust lurched out of the net. Linden screamed again and it took to the air, throbbing like some machine, and disappeared into the dark.

'It's gone. It's okay now,' I said, putting my arms around her shoulders. I tried to kiss her again but she tucked her chin into her shoulder. I kissed her arms and shoulders. I was shaking now.

'I love you,' she said. 'Have done since the day you arrived.'

'You're one of the most beautiful women I've ever met. I cannot believe I am so close to you.' She allowed me to kiss her again. 'He's asleep. I heard him snoring.'

'We'll go to your room. There's a lock on the door.' Linden did not put on her dress again but tiptoed up the stairs in front of me with it draped over her shoulder. I was relieved to hear that Brendan had stopped his snoring.

Throughout our love-making she kept saying over and over again, 'You're so gentle.' When it was finished she said once more that she loved me.

'I want you to take me away from him.' There was a long silence between us.

'Is it that serious?'

'Your friend . . . is . . . My pain is the only thing that arouses him.'

'Brendan? That's hard to believe.'

'You haven't been to bed with him.'

'True.'

'In the beginning it was fine . . . but now he has to . . . he brings things home from the hospital . . .'

'Like what?'

She turned her face away from me. Her lips moved but no sound came out.

'I can't begin to understand that.' I was tracing out her body with my fingers. Soon the talk stopped and we made love again. I tried to persuade her that this was a night we could both cherish in our memories – a photograph – a searing flash – but again she said, 'I love you. I want to go away with you.'

It was four o'clock when she left my room, quietly unsnibbing the door. Almost immediately I heard voices in the corridor. Brendan must have seen her coming from my room in that half-clothed state. I lay there naked and nervous wondering what I could do. A toilet flushed and Brendan's heavier footsteps came to my door. He pushed it open and stood there, still fully-dressed.

'Hi,' I said. He looked at me and slowly tapped the side of his temple.

'It all happens in there with Linden. Remember that.' Then he was away.

I could not sleep, of course. I remembered people in Zurich whose address I could get from the telephone book. At five I began to pack and as the dawn came up I was going quietly down the stairs. I left them a brief thank you note on the kitchen table. Outside it was already warm and the birds were singing. I looked back at the villa and saw the owner in his navy T-shirt sitting at the window of his hut. I felt I had to wave to him and he answered by raising his hand in a kind of tired salute.

END OF SEASON

The elder Miss Bradley walked to the end of the small pier and stood listening to the sea thumping in from below. White horses flecked the bay and the wind was strong enough to make her avert her face from its direction. She was convinced that the summer was over. A week back at school and already the first gale of winter. On this exposed coast with no trees autumn did not exist.

She liked to come here on her way home, particularly on windy days. It rinsed the experience of school from her. She did not stand long – a minute, perhaps two, facing into the wind with her eyes closed. Then she turned on her heel and walked slowly, leaning back into the wind, trying not to let its strength fluster her or make her movements awkward.

The briefcase was heavy with jotters and she wished she had brought the car. The school was only three-quarters of a mile from the house but each day she debated whether or not she should walk the distance for the good of her health. It would not do to have two invalids in the one house.

The family home was one of a terrace of cream-painted houses, set back from the road behind long, well-kept gardens. Some of the houses still had little gibbets overhanging the pavement with 'Bed & Breakfast' signs swinging in the wind. As she walked up the path she faintly heard her sister, Kathleen, laughing and thought it odd – a feeling which increased when she opened the front door and smelt tobacco smoke. In the front room a man sat in her armchair beside the bookcase, with his back to the light, talking.

'Ah Mary, there you are,' said her sister. The man stood up politely. 'You remember Mr Maguire?'

'Eh . . . yes, indeed.'

In his hand Mr Maguire held their old guest book. He sat down again and opened it so quickly that he must have had his finger in the place. 'I was just looking at when we were here last.' He passed the book to Mary. She found Mr and Mrs Maguire whose stay was dated July 1958.

'We were on our honeymoon,' he said. 'We had only booked one night but we stayed a week.' The man had a distinct Belfast accent.

'Mr Maguire thought we were still a guest house,' said Kathleen.

'Oh no. We stopped that a long time ago.' Mary flicked to the last entry in the book. 'In 1971.' She set it on the sideboard and, rubbing her hands, moved closer to the fire.

'It's like January,' she said. 'Is the kettle on?'

Her sister asked Mr Maguire if he would have more tea.

'I wouldn't say no.' He handed over his empty cup and saucer and Kathleen rattled it on to the tray with her own. She elbowed her way out of the door to the kitchen, leaving Mary and the stranger in silence.

'Are you looking for a place to stay?' Mary asked.

'Yes. I decided to treat myself to a holiday. It's years since I've gone anywhere.'

'Have you tried any of the other guest houses?'

'No. This is where I wanted to come.'

'It was nice of you to remember us.'

'It's funny how well you remember good times, holidays,' he said. 'I'm sure you don't remember us. We would have been one couple in a crowded summer.'

'Yes, sometimes it's difficult. But I rarely forget a face. Names, yes.'

Mary sat down on the rug in a delicate side-saddle posture and shivered. From her low position she could see the man's immaculately polished shoes. Her mother had always told her a man's footwear was the key to his character. 'Beware of someone with dirty shoes,' she had said. 'Even worse is the man who has polished his shoes but neglected to do his heels. But worst of all is the man with black polish stains on his socks. It's the ultimate sloth.' Mary looked up at him but his face was in shadow because his back was to the grey light from the window. He wore an open-necked shirt, a pair of trousers too light for his age and a blue sweater with a small emblem of a red jaguar on it.

'And Mrs Maguire?'

'My wife died last December.'

'Oh I'm sorry.'

'She had been ill for a long time. It was a merciful release.'

'Oh I am sorry,' she said. 'What brings you back to this part of the world?' He hesitated before answering.

'I wanted to see Spanish Point. Where the galleon went down. *The Girona.*'

'Yes, I walk out there frequently myself. There's nothing much. Rocks, sea.'

'I was at an exhibition in the museum – of the stuff they brought up – and I thought I'd just like to look at the place. Imagine it a bit.'

Kathleen's voice called loudly from the kitchen. Mary excused herself and went out.

'He wants to stay for a couple of nights,' whispered Kathleen. 'I told him I'd have to ask you. What do you think?'

'How do you feel about it? Can you cope?'

'Yes, I don't mind. The money would come in handy.' Mary was about to go back to the other room when her sister held her by the arm.

'But listen to this,' Kathleen laughed and wheezed. 'We had been talking about books. He tells me he reads a lot – as a matter of fact he's book mad – and when I came in with the tea I said "Do you like Earl Grey?" and he says, "I don't know. What did he write?" Isn't that marvellous?' Mary smiled and nodded while Kathleen giggled uncontrollably, saying to herself, 'Stop it Kathleen,' and slapping the back of her wrist. She straightened her face and set out some more biscuits on a plate. Then she burst out laughing again.

'He kept talking about the eedgit, at one stage.'

'The what?'

'The book "The Eedgit". One of the big Russians. He meant *The Idiot.*'

'Oh,' said Mary.

'Really, Kathleen, control yourself.' Her sister again straightened her face and picked up the tray. Mary opened the door for her.

'It'll be something for me to do,' Kathleen whispered over her shoulder as she led the way into the other room.

'That'll be fine, Mr Maguire,' she said. 'If you'll give me a minute I'll fix up your room for you.' He edged forward in his seat and made a vague gesture as if to assist Kathleen with the tray.

'Thank you very much,' he said and smiled up at the two sisters. 'I'll try and cause as little disruption as possible.' Mary sat on the rug again to be near the fire. Mr Maguire sipped from his cup holding his saucer close to his chest.

'Why did you stop the bed and breakfast?' he asked.

'Several reasons,' said Kathleen. 'Me for one. My asthma was getting intolerable. It's really a nervous condition with me. The very thought of summer would bring on an attack. Then there was the Troubles, of course. After 'sixty-nine people just stopped coming. Now we call this place the last resort.'

'When we were here the place was full of Scotch.'

'Yes, and the same ones came back year after year. But after the Troubles started nobody would risk it. Then Mary got a job teaching when the new school was built.'

'And mother died,' said Mary.

'Oh did she? I never saw her. We just heard her – upstairs.'

'She was very demanding,' said Kathleen, 'and I was in no position to cope with her. It was she really who insisted that we keep the place open. All her life she had a great fear of ending up in the poor-house. She was the one who had the bright idea of extending out the back just before the slump. We're still paying the mortgage.'

Mr Maguire set his cup and saucer on the hearth. 'Do you mind if I smoke a pipe?' He addressed Mary who turned to her sister.

'Kathleen?'

'I like the smell of pipe-smoke. It's cigarettes I can't stand.'

Mr Maguire took out a small pipe and a yellow plastic pouch. He filled the pipe as he listened to Kathleen talk about the old days when the house was full of guests. Mary watched him press the tobacco into the bowl with his index finger. When he struck the match he whirled his hand in a little circle to attenuate the flare before holding the match to his pipe. The triangular flame gave little leaps as he held it over the bowl and drew air through it, his lips popping quietly.

Throughout the whole operation he continued to nod and say 'hm-hm' to Kathleen's talk.

'You'll just have to take us as we are,' she was saying, 'not being officially open and all that. I'll give you a key and you can come and go as you like.'

'Thank you,' said Mr Maguire, striking another match.

'And breakfast. Would you like a fry in the morning?'

'Yes, please. It's the only time I ever do have the big fry. I wouldn't think I was on holiday if I didn't. Do you still bake your own wheaten bread?'

'No. My asthma. The flour can sometimes go for it. Let me get you an ashtray,' said Kathleen, jumping up. Mr Maguire sat with a tiny bouquet of dead matches between his fingers.

'Did you ever think of selling?'

Kathleen laughed and Mary smiled down at the fire.

'We tried for three years,' said Kathleen. 'Would YOU want to buy it? The ads were costing us so much that we had to take it off the market.'

When the tea was finished Kathleen showed him up to his room, talking constantly, even over her shoulder on the stairs. Mary followed them, her hands tucked into opposite sleeves, like a nun. The bed was stripped to its mattress of blue and white stripes. Mr Maguire set his bag by the window.

'I'll put the electric blanket on to air the bed for you,' said Kathleen.

'Thank you,' he said. 'You get a great view from this window.' Mary stared over his shoulder at the metallic sea. His face in the light was sallow and worn, with vertical creases down each side of his mouth and his forehead corrugated into wrinkles as he spoke. He wouldn't win any prizes for his looks but somehow his face suited him. He gave the impression of being an ex-sportsman, wiry and tough, sufficiently tall to have developed a slight stoop of the shoulders. He had enough hair to make her wonder whether or not it was a toupee. If it was it was a very convincing one.

'Where's a good place to eat now?'

'The Royal do a nice meal,' said Kathleen.

'The Royal?'

'Is that too expensive?'

'It was in my day.'

Kathleen lifted the foot of the bed and eased it out from the wall.

'Try the Croft Kitchen,' she said. 'I think they're still open. What little season there is, is over.' Seeing him hesitate she added, 'It's on High Street opposite what used to be the Amusements.' She stepped out on to the landing. 'The bathroom is second on your right. The light switch is on the outside.'

'Yes, I remember.'

'I'll just get some bed-linen.' Kathleen hurried off.

'She's excited,' said Mary, her voice lowered. Mr Maguire smiled and nodded. His voice was as quiet as hers.

'On our honeymoon,' he said, 'my wife went to the bathroom . . .' Mary withdrew her hands from her sleeves and straightened a picture, '. . . and someone turned out the light on her. She was terrified. She heard a footstep, then the light went out, then breathing. The poor woman sat for half the night in the dark before she had the courage to come out. I was sound asleep, of course.'

'How awful,' said Mary.

Kathleen strode in, the fresh bed-linen pressed between her arms like a white accordion. 'Right, there's work to be done,' she said, dumping them on the bed.

That night even though she felt tired and had gone to bed early Mary could not sleep. She heard Mr Maguire come in at a reasonable hour. Apart from a little throat-clearing he himself was quiet but she heard everything he did – the popping of the wash-hand basin in her own room as he used his, the flush of the toilet from the end of the corridor, through the wall the creaking of his bed as he got into it. It seemed hours before she heard the snap of his bedside light being switched off and she wondered what book it was that kept him reading so late.

She woke several times and each time was wet with perspiration, so much so that she was afraid she had had an accident. She felt like the shamelessly vulgar girl on the calendar which hung above the cash desk in the garage, emerging from the waves in a dripping white chemise which concealed nothing. Her condition was becoming worse instead of better. At times in front of her classes she felt as if there was a hole in her head and she was being filled from top to toe, like a hot-water bottle. Some months ago Kathleen had become alarmed seeing her sister steady herself with her knuckles on the kitchen table, her face red and wet with perspiration.

'What's wrong?'

Mary had simply said that her ovaries were closing down. The inner woman was giving up the ghost, but not without a struggle. She showered twice a day now – when she got up in the morning and before her evening meal. She refused to go to the doctor because, she said, the condition was normal. The *Home Encyclopedia of Medicine* told her all she wanted to know. Letters in women's magazines frequently dealt with the subject, in some cases in embarrassing detail. It was a sign of the times when you bought a perfectly middle-of-the-road woman's magazine and were frightened to open the pages because of what you might read: sex mixed in with the knitting patterns; among the recipes, orgasms and homosexuality and God knows what. She was embarrassed, not on her own behalf but for the teenagers in her classes. Magazines like the ones she bought would inevitably be going into all their homes. Each time her eyes flinched away from reading such an article she blushed for the destruction of her pupils' innocence. As for some of the daily papers, she wouldn't give them house-room.

Mr Maguire cleared his throat and she heard the twang of him turning in his seldom-used bed.

During the last class of the day Mary stood staring, not out, but at the window. On this the leeward side of the school, the glass was covered with rain droplets which trembled at each gust of wind. Behind her a fourth-year class worked quietly at a translation exercise. She was proud of her reputation for having the most disciplined classes in the school. She knew the pupils disliked her for it but it was something they would thank her for in later life.

At ten to four she saw Mr Maguire walking out of town with his hands clasped behind his back and his head down into the wind. When she eventually got out of school he was standing smiling at the gate.

'I thought it must be that time,' he said, 'and I was just passing.' He offered to carry her bag but she said that it was light enough. They began walking into the fine drizzle.

'What a day that was. Do you have children, Mr Maguire?'

'No, my wife was never a well woman. It would have been too much to ask.' Again she was struck by the coarseness of his accent. His face relaxed and he smiled. 'Where did all the books come from in your house?' he asked.

'That was my father mostly. He was Headmaster of the local Primary. He was interested in all sorts of things. Nature study, science, history. We were always used to books in the house.'

'Lucky. I had to do all the work myself. At a very late stage. Imagine sitting your A-levels for the first time at fifty.'

'Is that what you did?'

'I'm afraid so.'

'I admire that.'

Mr Maguire shrugged shyly.

'Not everybody does. My wife used to make fun of me. But she had a very hard time. She was in a lot of pain and couldn't understand. I think she was jealous of the time I spent reading. She thought it was a hobby or a pastime or something like that. She couldn't have been further from the truth.' Seeing Mary change her briefcase from her right to her left hand Mr Maguire insisted that he carry it. She reluctantly let him take it.

He continued talking. 'When you find out about real education you can never leave it alone. I don't mean A-levels and things like that – you are just proving something to yourself with them – but books, ideas, feelings. Everything to do with up here.' He tapped his temple. 'And here.' He tapped the middle of his chest.

Mary asked, 'What do you like to read then?'

'The classics. Fiction. Good stuff.'

The wind tugged at his hair, blowing it into various partings. It was definitely not a toupee.

'I sometimes stop here and walk to the end.' She pointed to the pier, its back arched against the running sea. Occasionally a wave broke over it and spray slapped down on the concrete. Some boys with school-bags were running the gauntlet along the pier.

'They'll get soaked, or worse,' said Mr Maguire.

'That's nothing. This summer I saw them ride off the end on a bicycle. They had it tied to one of the bollards so's they could pull it up each time. I couldn't watch. It gave me the funniest feeling. I had to go away in the end.'

When they got back to the house Mr Maguire set her briefcase in the hall, nodded to her and climbed the stairs. Mary went to the kitchen and sat on a stool beside the Rayburn drying out as the kettle boiled.

'Where's our guest?' asked Kathleen.

'Upstairs.'

'He's a strange fish. But nice.'

'Yes, you and he certainly seem to get along,' said Mary. Kathleen rolled her eyes to heaven.

Mary laughed and said, 'He walks like the Duke of Edinburgh.' She stood up and did an imitation backwards and forwards across the kitchen, her hands joined behind her back, her head forward like a tortoise.

Kathleen giggled, saying, 'I was making his bed today and do you know what he's reading? Or at least has lying on his bedside table.'

'I've no idea.'

'A book of English verse.'

'Why not?'

'It doesn't tally somehow. Him and poetry. And do you know – he's brought a full shoe-polishing kit with him. Brushes, tins, cloths, the lot. Mother would have been so pleased.'

'You shouldn't nosey.'

'I couldn't help seeing them. I had to move them out of the way to make the bed.'

'What's wrong with being careful about your appearance?'

'Nothing. But it does seem a bit extravagant.'

Kathleen heard Mr Maguire's footsteps on the landing and bounded to the kitchen door.

'There's a cup of tea in the pot, Mr Maguire,' she called.

When he came in Mary smelt soap off his hands as he reached in front of her for his cup.

'Well, how was your day?' asked Kathleen.

'The rain drove me home,' he smiled. His hair was dark and neatly parted, as if he had used hair-oil. 'You see how I call it home already.' Kathleen offered him a biscuit but he refused.

'How was your meal in the Croft Kitchen last night?'

'It was closed.'

'Where did you eat then?'

'The café on the front. It was good. Reasonable too.'

'Eucch, what a place,' Kathleen shuddered. 'All those sauce bottles on the tables. They're encrusted.'

'No, it was fine, really.'

'Look, we don't eat extravagantly ourselves but you're welcome to join us this evening.'

'Ah now that wouldn't be fair.'

'We're just having mince and carrots. It's no bother to set a place for an extra one.' Mr Maguire hesitated. He looked at Mary who was staring into her cup. She raised her eyes to him.

'Why don't you stay?' she said.

'Only on one condition. You must charge me extra.'

'That's settled then,' said Kathleen. 'We can haggle about the price later.'

'It's very kind of you. Both of you.'

Mr Maguire appeared at dinner time wearing a tie but no jacket. Mary sat opposite him, the tails of hair at her neck still damp from the shower, while Kathleen served and talked.

'There's a whist drive tonight in the hall, Mr Maguire. Guests are very welcome.'

'I'm sorry,' said Mr Maguire, 'I was never any good at card games – especially whist. Partners depending on you to play the right card. I played once or twice and at the finish up my shins were black and blue.'

'I *have* to go,' said Kathleen. 'I'm organizing a table. Mary, will you run me up? I have all those cups and saucers and things.' Mary nodded.

'Can you not drive?'

'No, I'm too nervous. But Mary is very good, runs me everywhere.'

Kathleen took on the responsibility of the silences and when one occurred she talked, mostly to Mr Maguire.

'What do you do?'

'At the moment, nothing. I've just been made redundant. One of the three million.'

'Oh that's too bad.'

'Yes, when I got my redundancy money I said to heck, I'll treat myself to a holiday.'

'You were just right,' said Kathleen. 'You can't take it with you.'

'There'll be none of it left to take with me.'

Both sisters smiled. Mr Maguire looked at Mary and she felt obliged to speak.

'What did you work at?'

'In a big warehouse. Spare parts for cars.'

'Oh I see,' said Mary.

'I'd been there for most of my life.'

'Then you know a bit about cars?'

'A bit.'

'It's just that mine is not going properly.'

'What is it?'

'A Fiat.'

'No, I mean what is the problem?'

'It seems to have no power, sluggish.'

'I could have a look at it tomorrow.'

Kathleen interrupted. 'But I thought you were going tomorrow?'

'Would you mind if I stayed the weekend? I have no real reason to rush back.'

'Certainly,' said Kathleen. 'Especially if you can fix the car.'

'Thank you.' Mr Maguire had cleared his plate in a matter of minutes. Kathleen offered him second helpings.

'It's the sea air,' he said. 'Gives you an appetite. This is what I cook mostly for myself because it's easy.' Then he seemed embarrassed. 'I'm sorry. This tastes a hundred times better than my efforts. I just mean that it doesn't take much looking after on the stove.'

'I gather you don't like cooking?'

'No. At home I do a standard menu. The boiled egg. The mince. When you're on your own food doesn't seem as interesting. I find it hard enough to get through a whole loaf without it going blue mould.' He laughed. 'I eat watching the news with my plate on my knees. Rarely set a table.'

'Is there any chance you'll get another job?'

'I doubt it. The car trade is in a bad way and it's the only one I know. I'm fifty-six now. Prospects – poor.' He shrugged. Mary looked at his hands. They were big and red, making toys of his knife and fork. The nail of his thumb was opaque like a hazelnut.

'I don't really want a job,' he said. 'Now I'll have time to do what I want.'

'What's that?'

'Read. Dig my plot. I'm going to do this Open University thing. On television. I've just enrolled but it doesn't start until next January. I paid the fees out of my redundancy.'

'You make the dole sound like a good thing.'

'I've always been keen. If there's a WEA class on the go, I'm your man. History, English, Philosophy – there was a Botany year but I couldn't make head nor tail of it. Anything and everything, I'm a dabbler.'

Kathleen got out of the car at the church hall balancing a cardboard box full of trembling cups. She slammed the door with her heel.

'Hey, just you be careful with that Mr Maguire, Mary,' she said through the driver's window.

'He's a bit down-market for me, dear.' Mary laughed. 'Besides it's you he fancies.'

'Will you pick me up?'

Mary nodded.

On her way back she was irritated again by the lack of energy in the engine. On the hill of the High Street it seemed barely to have sufficient power to pull her up. She thought about Mr Maguire.

'Thank God it's Friday,' she said aloud.

She had kicked off her shoes and was just sitting down to look at the paper when there was a quiet rap on the door. Mr Maguire stood there with a light bulb in his hand.

'I'm sorry to trouble you,' he said, 'but my reading light has gone and I wondered if you had a spare one?' Mary, in stockinged feet, climbed on to a stool and produced a new sixty watt bulb from a high cupboard. She exchanged bulbs with him and for some reason felt foolish. He stood for a moment with the cardboard package in his hands.

'Is it raining?' he asked.

'No, not now.'

He moved the piece of card that held the bulb in place against the corrugations of the package, rippling it.

'Are you busy this evening?' he asked. Mary hesitated.

'No.'

'Would you like to go somewhere – for a drink perhaps?'

'I don't like going into pubs.'

'The hotel – we could go to the Royal, just for a while. An orange juice, if you like.'

Mary was now swinging the dead bulb by its tiny pins between her finger and thumb. 'It's Friday,' she said. 'Why not?'

Mr Maguire smiled. 'In about half an hour then?'

'Yes.'

He turned quickly, holding up the new light bulb in a gesture of thanks. For a ridiculous moment she expected it to light as if he was some kind of statue.

She closed the door and, out of habit, before she threw the used bulb in the waste-paper basket she shook it close to her ear. There was no tinkling sound. She switched off the standard lamp and removed the hot bulb with a serviette. Mr Maguire's bulb lit when she switched it on.

*

303

In the hotel lounge after the first sip of her sherry she took a tissue from her handbag and wiped the red crescent stain of her lower lip from the rim of the glass. Mr Maguire was drinking Guinness. She sat on the edge of her seat, her shoulders back. Her mother had always chivvied her about 'bearing'. One day as they walked to church she had prodded Mary between the shoulder-blades with the point of her umbrella.

'If you want to keep your bosoms separate – don't slouch.'

She could feel the ferrule to this very day. And yet now, without being told, she did everything her mother had asked of her.

'Relax,' said Mr Maguire. Muzak took away from the early evening hush.

'I'm not used to places like this. I've only been here at weddings.'

'It's a nice place.'

'The word'll be out on Monday that Miss Bradley was seen boozing with a man.'

Mr Maguire laughed.

'What do you teach?'

'German and a little French.'

'Have you been to Germany?'

'No, but I taught for a year in a German-speaking part of Switzerland. In a beautiful place called Kandersteg.'

'I've never been abroad. Never in anything bigger than a rowing-boat. And if you ever hear of me being killed in a plane crash you'll know it fell on me.'

'It was up in the mountains. A typical Swiss village with cuckoo-clock houses and snow when you looked up. The children were so well behaved it was a dream to teach there.'

Mr Maguire took out his pipe and lit it. By his face and the tilt of his head he was still listening to her.

'It was like a holiday really – it's funny how you remember the good things so vividly.'

'Maybe it's because there's so few of them,' he said. 'I remember my honeymoon as if it was yesterday. This town, your house. It was a cold summer. I sat with you by the Rayburn and we talked to the wee small hours.

'We did?'

'Well, once, maybe twice. And then one night I remember you were going to a dance. You were in your stockinged feet frantically looking for your shoes. You left a wake of scent behind you.' Mary laughed, covering her mouth with her hand. Mr Maguire drew large rings around himself with his arms. 'You were out to here with petticoats. The dress was white with green flecks in it.'

'That's right, that's right. I remember that one. Parsley Sauce we used to call it. Those were the days when you had so few dresses you gave them names.' She rolled her eyes to heaven. It was as if he had produced an old photograph of her. 'Isn't it awful that I remember the dress but I've no recollection whatsoever of you.' Suddenly her face straightened in mock disapproval. 'And you noticed all this on your honeymoon?'

'You have no control over what you notice.'

'And where was your wife when you were sitting talking to me – to the wee small hours?'

'She was ill even then. She always went to bed early. I'm a night-owl myself.'

'Oh dear me,' she said. 'What a thing to remember – old Parsley Sauce.' Mr Maguire bought more drinks and Mary began to feel relaxed and warm.

'I'm glad we're here,' she said. 'This is nice.'

Some ex-pupils of hers came in and sat at the bar. They nodded and smirked towards the corner where she sat.

Mr Maguire asked her about what books she read and she told him she was an escapist reader. Four or five library books a week she got through. Anything, just so long as it didn't make too many demands on her. And of course nothing which would disturb. None of that embarrassing nonsense. It was hard to avoid nowadays. Library books should have warnings on the covers – be graded like films. Kathleen was different – she went in for the more heavy-weight stuff.

Mr Maguire said that unless a book was making him puzzle and think he would throw it away. He had read more first chapters than anybody else in the world. With regard to the embarrassing stuff, if it was not written for pornographic reasons he could accept it. It was a part of life the same as any other.

Mary refused another sherry saying that her head was already light, but insisted on buying Mr Maguire another bottle of Guinness, provided he wanted a third. After all, he was on the dole and she was working. When she returned with the poured glass Mr Maguire said, 'Books should not be a means of escape.'

'Why not? We're surrounded by depressing things. Who wants to read about them? When I read I prefer to be transported.' Suddenly she put her hand over her mouth in horror. 'Kathleen!' she said. 'I promised to pick up Kathleen. What time is it?'

All the lights were out in the church hall and Kathleen was pacing up and down. Mr Maguire carried her box of cups for her as Mary apologised for being late. For once Kathleen was quiet. The only sound coming from the back seat was the whine of her inhaler. In the house she slammed doors.

'There are some left-over sandwiches there,' she said.

As Mary made the tea she dropped a spoon twice and giggled. She felt very silly and likable but was aware of herself hurrying to get back to the other room where Kathleen and Mr Maguire were alone.

The next morning she slept late and was wakened by the constant revving of an engine. She looked out and saw Mr Maguire in a navy boiler suit beneath the open bonnet of her car, tinkering. Before going downstairs in her dressing-gown she freshened up and made herself look presentable. Mr Maguire came in, his oily hands aloft, and washed at the kitchen sink. Kathleen, also in her dressing-gown, offered him a cup of tea from the pot.

'I think you should see a big improvement,' he said. 'When did you last have it serviced?'

'Goodness,' said Mary. 'I can't really remember.'

'I reset your points, put in three new plugs . . .'

'I know nothing about it. You might as well be talking double Dutch.' Mr Maguire shook his head in disbelief and sat down at the table.

'You look very smart,' said Kathleen, looking at his boiler suit.

'I always carry this in the boot. I've been caught before, changing a wheel on a wet night.'

'But it's so clean.'

Mr Maguire nodded and turned to Mary.

'Would you like to try her out?'

'Let me get dressed first. Kathleen, would you like to come for a run?'

'No, I've things to do.' She said it with an echo of the previous night's bitterness still in her voice.

'Very well, suit yourself.'

They drove towards Spanish Point. Mary was delighted with the change in the car – it even sounded different. She said so to Mr Maguire, now back in his casual wear. She herself wore trousers – a thing she never did on teaching days. Mr Maguire said, 'The thing that really fascinated me about this wreck was a ring they found. Gold, with an inscription round the inside. *No tengo mas que dar te.*' With his Belfast accent his attempt at pronunciation was comical.

Mary smiled. 'More double Dutch.'

'It's Spanish. It means, "I have nothing more to give thee".'

'That's nice.' She changed down through the gears as they came up behind a tractor.

'I thought it very moving – to see it after all those years. What I wondered was this. Was he taking it back as a present for a loved one in Spain or had somebody given it to *him* as he sailed away with the Armada? It makes a big difference.'

'Yes, I suppose it does.' Mary indicated and passed the tractor, giving a little wave over her shoulder.

'That's Jim McLelland,' she said.

They walked awkwardly on a beach of apple-sized stones, hearing them clunk hollowly beneath their feet. Mary had to extend her arms for balance and once or twice almost had to clutch at Mr Maguire.

'This is silly,' she said. They halted and looked across at Spanish Point. Now that the rumble of stones had stopped it was very quiet.

307

'Mary.' Hearing him use her name for the first time she looked up startled.

'Yes?'

'You're a remarkable woman,' he said. 'I told you that I came on holiday to see this place.' He nodded to the black rocks jutting out into the sea. 'That's not the whole truth.' Mary began to feel frightened, alone on a beach with this man she hardly knew. She picked up a stone and moved it from hand to hand. It was the tone of his voice that scared her. He was weighing his words, not looking at her.

'I had a memory of this town that was sacred in a way. And over the last couple of days I realise that it is partly your fault – I don't mean fault. I mean you're part of what's good about it.' Still he didn't look at her but continued to stare out to sea. Mary could think of nothing, afraid of what he would say next.

'I had forgotten about you, but not completely. Can you imagine how surprised I was when you were still here?'

'I've no idea.' She couldn't prevent the sarcasm in her voice. But he seemed not to notice. She threw the stone with a clatter at her feet and rubbed her hands together to clean them.

'I think we'd better be getting back,' she said. They turned and began to walk towards the car.

'I'm sorry. I hope I haven't overstepped the mark.'

'I'm not sure what you mean.'

'These past few days have been very real for me. You turn out to be . . .' he paused, 'better than I remembered. You have a kind of calm which I envy. A stillness inside.' Mary smiled at him and walked round to the driver's door.

'You don't know me at all', she said, 'if you think I'm calm and still. I'm shaking like a leaf with the kind of things you're saying.'

'I'll just say one more – and that'll be the end of it. I'd like you to think about the idea of marrying me.'

She turned to him, her eyes wide and her mouth dropping open. She laughed. 'Are you serious?'

Mr Maguire smiled slightly as he stared at her, his brow creased with wrinkles. 'Yes, I am.'

'I don't even know your first name.'

'Anthony.'

'You don't look like an Anthony, if you don't mind me saying so.'

'You don't have to say anything. All I want you to do is give it some thought.'

Mary turned on the engine, indicated left and did a U-turn to the right but stalled midway. She tried to switch on the engine again.

'What have you done to this machine?' she said.

'Would you like me to drive?'

Mary agreed and he drove her home in the most embarrassing silence she had ever known.

Mr Maguire climbed the stairs. Mary went straight to the kitchen where she heard Kathleen singing.

'Well?' said Kathleen. 'Big improvement?'

Mary sat down on the stool by the Rayburn. She said, 'Make me a cup of tea. I need it badly.'

'What's wrong? Did it break down?'

Mary began to laugh. 'You'll never believe this.' Her sister turned from filling the kettle. 'But I've just been proposed to.'

'What? Who?' Her voice was a screech. Mary hushed her and rolled her eyes to the ceiling as Mr Maguire closed a door. 'I don't believe you. You'll find out then if it's a real toupee.'

'It's not funny,' said Mary, still laughing. 'I was there.'

'What did you tell him?'

'I said I'd think about it.'

As Kathleen made the tea her shoulders shook.

'You'd end up keeping the shine on his wee shoes. And the crease in his boiler suit. Mother would be pleased.' She wiped her eyes and gave her sister a cup.

'You're not seriously thinking about it?'

'No, but . . .'

'But what?'

'It's just that I've never really been asked.'

'You have so. Twice. You told me.'

'But they were ludicrous.'

'And this one isn't?'

'There's something gentlemanly about him.'

'A gentleman of leisure. He's on the dole, Mary.' Kathleen grinned again. 'Did he go down on one knee?'

'Don't be silly.'

Later that afternoon when the laughter had worn off and Mr Maguire had gone for a walk Kathleen said, 'And what would become of me?'

'For goodness' sake Kathleen, I only said I would consider it.'

'I don't think I'll be able to manage on my own. Financially.'

'Kathleen! Will you excuse me. I'd like to make up my own mind on this one.'

Mary went to her bedroom and sat looking at herself in the dressing-table mirror. A hot flush came over her and she watched her face redden, like an adolescent blushing. She flinched at the thought of a kiss from Mr Maguire. And yet he would make a good companion. Eccentric, yes – but basically a good man. In so far as she knew him. Pinpoints of sweat gleamed on her forehead and upper lip. She pulled a tissue from the box on the dressing-table and dabbed herself dry, then she lay down on the bed. Perhaps she should stall him. Write letters for a period. That way things would not be complicated by his physical presence. By that time, with any luck, these fits would have passed and she would have returned to normality. Stall him. That was the answer. He would enjoy writing to her. It would give him a chance to quote poetry. For some reason Kandersteg came into her mind and with a little thrill she thought of going there on her honeymoon. In July just as soon as the school holidays had started. She would have to do all the translation for Mr Maguire. They could call and see if Herr Hauptmann was still alive and they could relive their days at the school while poor Mr Maguire would have to stare out the window at the beautiful view: the grey clouds of mist that moved against the almost black of the forest; the cleanness, the tidiness of their streets; the precision with which the trains came and went, not to the minute, but to the second; Herr Hauptmann's hazel-coloured eyes as he listened to her.

*

At dinner Kathleen, activated by nervousness, talked non-stop until she left the room to make the coffee. Mr Maguire nodded his head as if it had become a reflex to the torrent of words and one that he could not stop even when she had left the room. He whispered to Mary, 'Kathleen's problem is that she hasn't heard of the paragraph.' He said that he would like to settle his bill as he would be leaving first thing after Mass in the morning when the roads would be relatively traffic free.

Mary said, 'It might be nice if we walked up to the hotel later. I'd like to make my position clear.'

'Yes, that would help.'

'About eight?'

After Mr Maguire had excused himself Mary said to her sister, 'I'm going for a walk with him later.'

'It makes no difference to me. I have to go to the church to do the flowers.'

'Oh that's right. It's Saturday . . .' Kathleen began to stack the cups on to the tray with a snatching movement.

'Have you made up your mind how you're going to tell him?'

'I'm not sure,' said Mary. 'I'm not even sure *what* I'm going to tell him.'

'Don't allow me to influence you one way or the other. You can do whatever you like. All I hope is that you won't do something you'll regret for the rest of your life. And if you go traipsing off with him I'll need some help with the mortgage.'

'There's no question of that.' Mary was aware that her voice had risen. 'You can be sure that I'll be sensible about it. If I've waited this long . . .' Kathleen carried the tray out to the kitchen and set it on the draining-board with a crash.

At eight o'clock they both left their rooms. Mr Maguire, his shoes burnished, wearing a tie and jacket, walked like the Duke of Edinburgh, one hand holding the other by the wrist behind his back. The night was windless and at intervals between the glare of the street lights they could see stars. Mary was conscious of her heels clicking on the paving stones and was relieved when she came to the softer tarmac footpath where she could walk with more dignity.

Mr Maguire cleared his throat and asked, 'Well, did you think about what . . .?'

'Yes, but don't talk about it now. Talk about something else.' Mr Maguire nodded in agreement and looked up at the sky for inspiration.

'What is it that makes your life worthwhile?'

'I don't know.' She laughed nervously and tried to give an answer. 'What a strange question. I suppose I help children to learn something – the rudiments of another language. And I help Kathleen who cannot work . . .'

'I don't mean worthwhile to others. But to yourself.'

'Sometimes, Mr Maguire, you say the oddest things. I'm sorry, I don't see the difference.'

'Take it from another angle. What makes you really angry?'

She felt her shoulder brush against his as they walked. 'The kind of thing that's been going on in this country. Killings, bombings . . .'

'If you were to give one good reason to stop someone blowing your head off tonight, what would it be?'

'I've jotters to correct for Monday.' Mr Maguire laughed. 'Well there's that and children and love and Kathleen . . .'

'And?'

'And I've dresses I've only worn once or twice. And the sea. And the occasional laugh in the staffroom. Just everything.'

'You would be part of the reason I would give.'

There was a long pause and Mary said, 'Thank you. That's very nice of you. But as I say I'd prefer to wait until we were settled inside before we have our little talk.' Mr Maguire shrugged and smiled. Mary veered off to look in Madge's Fashions which was still lit up. There was a single old-fashioned window model with painted brown hair instead of a wig. White flakes showed where the paint had chipped, particularly at the red fingernails.

'They've changed this dress since yesterday,' said Mary. 'I like that one better.' She joined Mr Maguire in the middle of the pavement still looking back over her shoulder.

*

They sat at the same table as the prevous night and Mr Maguire bought the same drinks.

'They'll be calling me a regular next,' said Mary, as he slipped into the seat beside her. 'Well now. I think . . . First of all let me say that I find it extremely difficult to talk in a situation like this. I'm out of my depth.' She tried not to sound like she was introducing a lesson, but what she said was full of considered pauses. She spoke as quietly as she could, yet distinctly. 'You are an interesting man, good – as far as I know you – but these are not reasons', she paused yet again, 'for anybody to get married. It has happened so quickly that there is an element of foolishness in it. And that's not me.'

'It's me,' said Mr Maguire, laughing.

'There are so many things. I'm not a free agent. Kathleen has got to be considered.'

'She can fairly talk.'

'Yes, sometimes it's like living with the radio on. She never expects an answer.'

'Do you love her?'

'I suppose I must. When you live with someone day in, day out, the trivial things become the most important.' She sipped her sherry and felt the glass tremble between her fingertips. 'And there are other things which frighten me. I don't think I'm that sort of person.' Mr Maguire looked at her but she was unable to hold his eye and her gaze returned to her sherry glass.

'My wife was in poor health for many, many years – so that aspect of it should not worry you. I am in the habit of – not. I would respect your wishes. Although I miss someone at my back now when I fall asleep.' Mary thought of herself slippery with sweat lying awake making sure to keep space between herself and Mr Maguire's slow breathing body.

'I can't believe this is happening to me.' She laughed and turned to face him, her hands joined firmly in her lap. 'My answer is – in the kindest possible way – no. But why don't you write to me? Why don't you come and stay with us for longer next year? Writing would be a way of getting to know each other?'

'Your answer is no – for now?'

'Yes,' said Mary. 'I mean it's ridiculous at our age.'

'I don't see why. Could I come at Christmas?'

She thought of herself and Kathleen in new dresses, full of turkey and sprouts and mince pies, dozing in armchairs and watching television for most of the day. The Christmas programmes were always the best of the year.

'No. Not Christmas.'

'Easter then?'

'Write to me and we'll see.'

Mr Maguire smiled and shrugged as if he had lost a bet.

'You've kind of taken the wind out of my sails,' he said.

The next morning when she got up Mr Maguire had gone. Kathleen had called him early and given him his breakfast. When he had paid his bill she had deducted a fair amount for the servicing of the car.

After Mass, surrounded by the reality of the Sunday papers, Mary thought how silly the whole thing had been. The more she thought about the encounter the more distasteful it became. She resolved to answer his first letter out of politeness but, she said firmly to herself, that would be the finish of it.

On Monday she was feeling down and allowed herself the luxury of a lesson, taught to four different levels throughout the day, in which she talked about Kandersteg, its cuckoo-clock houses and the good Herr Hauptmann.

THE GREAT PROFUNDO

The river was so full after the recent rains that the uprights of the bridge became like prows and for a time I was under the impression that the bridge, with myself on it, was moving rapidly forward. So absorbed was I in this illusion that I accepted the sound as part of it. It was high pitched and sentimental, sometimes submerged beneath the noise of the traffic, sometimes rising above it, full of quaverings and glissandi. My curiosity was aroused to see what instrument could make such a noise. Others must have been similarly drawn because a crowd of about fifty or sixty people had gathered in a ring on the left bank of the river – women shoppers, men with children on their shoulders, young fellows elbowing each other for a better position. In the centre stood a tall man speaking loudly and waving his arms. I edged forward and was forced to stand on tiptoe. Still I could not trace the source of the music which at that moment suddenly stopped. Now everyone's attention was directed at the man in the centre whose eyes blazed as he shouted. He walked the cobblestones on bare feet, spinning on his heel now and again to take in the whole circle of the crowd. On the ground in front of him was a long, black case. With a flourish he undid the latches and flung open the lid. Inside was red plush but I could see little else from my position at the back.

'It is not for nothing that I am called the Great Profundo,' shouted the man. He wore a scarlet shirt, with the sleeves rolled up and the neck open, but his trousers looked shabby above his bare ankles. They bulged at the knees and were banded with permanent wrinkles at his groin. His hair was long and grey, shoulder length, but the front of his head was bald so that his face seemed elongated, the shape of an egg. He was not a well-looking man.

'What you will see here today may not amaze you, but I'll lay a

315

shilling to a pound that none of you will do it. All I ask is your undivided attention.'

I noticed a figure sitting by the balustrade of the river who seemed to be taking no interest in the proceedings. He must have been the source of the earlier music because in his hand he had a violinist's bow and, between his knees, a saw. The handle rested on the ground and the teeth of the saw pointed at his chest. He was muttering to himself as he began to pack these implements into a large holdall.

'I want you to look closely at what I am about to show you.' The Great Profundo stooped to his case and produced three swords. Épées. Rubbing together their metal cup handguards made a distinctive hollow shearing sound. He threw one to be passed around the crowd while he clashed and scissored the other two for everyone to hear.

'Test it, ladies and gentlemen. Check that it's not like one of these daggers they use on stage. The ones where the blade slips up into the handle. There are no tricks here, citizens; what you are about to see is genuine. Genuine bedouin.'

After much to-do he swallowed the three épées (they were thin with buttons at their ends no bigger than match-heads) and staggered around the ring, his arms akimbo, the three silvery cups protruding from his mouth. The audience was impressed. They applauded loudly and goaded him on to do something even more daring.

Next he produced what looked like a cheap imitation of a sword – the kind of thing a film extra, well away from the camera, would carry. It had a broad flat aluminium blade and a cruciform handle of some cheap brassy metal. He produced a twin for it and handed them both around the crowd while he cavorted on the cobblestones shouting interminably about his lack of trickery and the genuineness of what he was about to perform.

'While I want your undivided attention, I would like you all to keep an eye out for the Law. They do not approve. They'll turn a blind eye to trumpet players, tumblers and card-sharpers, but when it comes to the idea of a man putting himself into mortal danger on the public highway they have a very different attitude.'

The crowd immediately turned their heads and looked up and down the river-bank.

'You're okay,' shouted a woman.

'On you go.'

He took back both the swords from the crowd and held them to his chest. He straddled his legs, balancing himself, and put his egg-shaped head back, opening his mouth with an elaborate and painful slowness. I felt like saying, 'Get on with it. Skip the palaver.' The man swallowed both the swords, walked around the ring, staring skywards, then hand over hand extracted them to the applause of the crowd.

'And NOW, ladies and gentlemen,' the man shouted in a voice that heralded the finale of his act, glancing over his shoulder to check that the Law, as he called them, were not to be seen, 'I will perform something which will be beyond your imagination.'

He reached into his black case and produced a sword – a long and heavy Claymore. He tried to flex it, putting all his weight on it with the sole of his bare foot, but was unable to; then with a mighty two-handed sweep he swung it at the cobblestones. It rang and sparks flew. He balanced it on its point. The blade alone seemed to reach to his receding hairline. He stood there letting the crowd take in the length of the sword he was about to swallow. He spread his arms. The spectators became silent and the noise of the traffic on the bridge was audible. He lifted it with feigned effort, balanced the blade for a moment on his chin, then lowered it hand over hand down his throat. To the hilt. When it was fully inserted the crowd cheered. Planting his bare feet, like someone in a dream, his head at right-angles to his body, I could hear even from my position at the back the harsh rasps of the performer's breath escaping past the obstruction in his throat as he moved round the ring of people.

This time I was impressed. There was no physical way he could have swallowed that last sword – it would have had to come out of his toes. There was a trick somewhere but I joined in the applause as he withdrew the six-foot sword from his throat. At this point I felt someone push me, and the small man whom I had seen pack away his saw elbowed his way into the middle and extended his hat to begin collecting. My money was in one of my inner pockets and it would have meant unbuttoning my overcoat.

'No change,' I said.

'It's not change we want,' said the saw-player and forced his way past me. As the crowd dispersed I hung around. The Great Profundo was packing his equipment into his case. After each item he would sweep back his long hair and straighten up. The saw-player was raking through the hat, taking out the coins of the highest denomination and arranging them into columns on the balustrade. The Great Profundo sat down to put on his boots.

'Excuse me, gentlemen,' I said, dropping some coins into the hat. 'I am a student at the University and I couldn't help seeing your act. Very interesting indeed.'

'Thank you,' said Profundo. After all the shouting his voice sounded soft. 'It's nice to get praise from a man with certificates.'

'Not yet, not yet. I'm still an undergraduate. I tell you I'm a student, not for any particular reason, but because I want to make a proposition to you.' The Great Profundo looked up from his lace tying. I noticed he did not wear socks. 'I am the treasurer of a society in the University which, once or twice a year, uses live entertainment. Would either, or both, of you gentlemen be interested in performing for us?'

'How much?' asked the saw-player from the balustrade.

'We can afford only a small fee. But you may take up a collection at the actual function.'

'If they gave as much as you did just now, there'd be no point,' said the man counting the money.

'What would the University want to look at the likes of us for?' the Great Profundo said, smiling at the thought.

'Our society certainly would. It's called the "Eccentrics Genuine Club". We meet every month and have a few pints, sometimes entertainment.'

This was not the whole truth. We had met twice that year, and on both occasions the entertainment had been female strippers.

'Who?' asked the saw-player.

'Musicians. The occasional singer. That kind of thing.'

'We'll think about it,' said the Great Profundo. He wrote out his address and I said I would contact him after the next committee meeting.

As I walked away from them I heard the saw-player say, 'Eight pounds, some odds.'

'If my mother was alive, Jimmy, she'd be proud of me. Going to the University.' The Great Profundo laughed and stamped his boot on the ground.

The committee of the Eccentrics Genuine Club was delighted with the idea and even suggested a more generous sum of money than they had given to each of the strippers. However, divided between two entertainers, it still wasn't enough. I made a speech in which I said that if they valued their reputation for eccentricity – haw-haw – they would fork out a little more. A saw-player and a sword-swallower on University territory! What a coup! Who could refuse, no matter what the cost? The committee eventually approved, somewhat reluctantly, twice the sum given to the strippers. And they had no objection to a collection being taken on the night of the performance.

With this news and the idea of interviewing him for the University newspaper, I drove to the Great Profundo's. It was a part of the city where walls were daubed with slogans and topped with broken glass. I parked and locked the car. Then, seeing some children playing on a burst sofa on the pavement, I checked each door-handle and took my tape-recorder with me. It was an expensive one – the type professional broadcasters use – which my father had bought me when I'd expressed an interest in journalism.

There was a selection of names on bits of paper beneath the doorbells of the tenement. The name on the bell of 14c was Frankie Taylor. I rang it and waited. Papers and dust swirled in the corners. A window opened and the man himself leaned out.

'Remember me?' I shouted. The figure at the window nodded and waved me up. The stone stairway smelled badly of cooked food. The Great Profundo was on the landing, waiting barefoot, when I reached the fourth floor.

'Yes, I remember,' he said and shook hands. 'The student. Those stairs knacker the best of us.' He led me, breathing heavily, into the flat and offered me a chair which I declined. Would he be free – would he and the saw-player be free – on the evening of the thirteenth of next month? The sword-swallower shrugged and said that it was very likely. He sat down in his armchair and folded his knees up to his chest. Then he sprang up again and asked me if I would like a cup of coffee. I refused politely. I offered to write down the date and time of the meeting but Profundo assured me that they would be there. He sat down again and began to finger his toes.

'Would you like a beer?'

'What kind?'

He jumped off the chair and said, 'I'll see what I've left. I didn't know you'd be coming.' He opened a cupboard and closed it again, then left the room. I went over to the window to check that my car was still in one piece.

Profundo came back with three cans of lager held together by plastic loops.

'Tennent's. From Christmas,' he said. He jerked one free and handed it over and took another himself. 'Don't be worrying about the car. It's safe enough down there. The neighbours will keep an eye on it.'

I took the seat he had previously offered and said, 'There's another thing I'd wanted to ask you. I work for a student newspaper, *Rostrum*, and I was wondering how you would feel about giving an interview some time.'

'Me?' I applied pressure to the ring-pull and the can snapped open. From the triangular hole the lager was fizzy and tepid. 'Why me? What could I tell you?'

'Our readers are interested in a lot of things. I'm sure with the life you've led it couldn't fail.'

'Aww here now . . .' He laughed and looked down at his feet. Without Jimmy, the saw-player, he seemed defenceless. He was a shy man, unable to look me in the eye. His voice was quiet, conversational – not strident like he had been by the river-bank.

'If it's of any help to you . . . in your studies, like . . . Oh would you like a glass?'

'No thanks,' I said. 'Are you busy? Would you mind doing it now?'

'Do I look busy?' he said spreading his hands. I set up my machine, took a slug from the can and began my interview. (*See Appendix.*)

*

The bar in the students' Union was hired for the night of the thirteenth and a low platform stage erected against one wall. In my role as treasurer I was obliged to be around so another of the members of the Eccentrics Genuine was sent in his car to pick up the pair of performers. There was a splendid turn-out – everyone in formal evening wear – and I was pleased at the thought of covering expenses from the door money alone. After that, what we made on new membership and the bar was profit. I myself was responsible for about forty new members that night: part of the rugby club, friends from the Young Conservatives, Engineers, Medics and, most extraordinary of all, some people from a recently formed Society of Trainspotters.

The entertainment was due to begin at nine o'clock and for about an hour and a half before that the bar was pandemonium. I have never seen students drink so much – even the Eccentrics Genuine. As early as eight o'clock they all began clapping and singing 'Why are we waiting?' But it was all very good-humoured.

At a quarter to nine I was informed of the arrival of the artists and went to welcome them. They were both standing in the corridor outside. The Great Profundo shook hands warmly. Jimmy nodded and said to me, 'Is there anywhere we can change, get the gear sorted?'

'Pardon?'

'Like a dressing-room?'

'No. No I'm sorry. I hadn't thought you would need one – what with the street and all that.'

'Street is street and indoors is indoors.'

'It's okay, this'll do,' said Profundo. He began stripping off his checked shirt and getting into his scarlet one. He had a surprisingly hairy chest. 'You go ahead, Jimmy, warm them up.' Jimmy continued grumbling and got out his bow and saw. Profundo edged past him and took a look through the glass doors.

'A full house, by the look of it.' Then he stopped. 'Is there no women in there?'

'Not in the Eccentrics Genuine,' I said. 'It's one of the Club rules.'

'We're not *that* eccentric,' said another member of the Committee. 'We know how to enjoy ourselves.'

I slipped in at the back to listen to Jimmy's performance. The melody he played was the same one I had heard that day on the bridge but within the confines of the hall it sounded different, more sentimental. The notes soared and trembled and swooped. One member of the audience, just to my left, took out a white handkerchief and pretended to mop his eyes. In playing the saw there is a great deal of vibrato required to give the notes texture. The player's left hand quivers as the saw changes pitch.

'He's got Parkinson's disease,' shouted one of the new Medic members. But apart from that he was listened to attentively and applauded when he finished his selection.

Afterwards there was a great dash for the bar. Everyone considered it an interval and I had to hold back the Great Profundo until the crowd was settled again, which took some considerable time. While he waited patiently I pointed out to him that the floor was awash with beer, which might be awkward for him in his bare feet.

'And now, gentlemen of the Eccentrics Genuine Club, it is my great pleasure to introduce to you the one and only, the great, the profound, the Great Profundo . . .' I gave him such a buildup in the old music-hall manner that the audience were on their feet applauding as he made his entrance. He ran, carrying his black case on his shoulders, and took a jump up on to the stage. For a man of his age he was almost lithe. His movements as he opened his box of tricks were sweeping and athletic.

On my first encounter with him I had not noticed that his patter, which he began almost immediately he reached the stage, was so juvenile. He had not tailored his talk for such an audience as the Eccentrics Genuine. They laughed politely at some of his jokes. When he inserted the three épées and held his arms out wide for approval there was a kind of ironic cheer. His act lacked music and somebody began a drum-roll on one of the tables. This was taken up throughout the room until the bar throbbed with noise. Some others began to imitate a fanfare of trumpets. When he inserted the two aluminium film-extra swords someone said, not loudly, but loudly enough, 'He's naive. He'd swallow anything.' There was a great deal of laughter at this, suppressed at first in snorts and shoulder-shaking, but which finally burst out and echoed round the bar. He silenced them by taking out the Claymore. There was a small three-legged stool beside him, on which Jimmy had sat to play his saw, and the Great Profundo, with gritted teeth, swung the broadsword and imbedded the blade a full inch into it. He had to put his foot on the stool and tug with all his might to free it and this occasioned yet more laughter. He stood the point of the sword on the small stage to let them see the length of it in relation to his height. A voice said, 'If you stuck it up your arse we'd be impressed.'

And yet he went on. He did his hand over hand lowering of the blade into the depths of himself to the accompaniment of drumming on the tables. When it was fully inserted, he spread his arms, put his head back and paraded the stage. Some of the crowd were impressed because they cheered and clapped but others kept laughing, maybe because they were drunk, maybe at a previous joke. Then the tragedy happened.

The crowd could see it coming because they suddenly quietened. With his head back the Great Profundo took one or two paces forward and stepped off the edge of the platform. He came down heavily on his right foot which slipped on the wet floor. He managed to remain upright but uttered a kind of deep groan or retch which everyone in the audience heard. He stood there, not moving, for several seconds, then he withdrew the sword and made his exit. Some of the crowd stood and applauded, others made straight for the bar. Jimmy tussled among them with a yellow plastic bucket to take up a collection.

Afterwards in the corridor I apologised for the behaviour and handed over the cheque to the Great Profundo.

'It's both on the one. I didn't know Jimmy's second name so I made it all out to Frankie Taylor.'

'Thanks.' In the corridor lights Profundo's face looked grey.

'I'll take it,' said Jimmy. 'Your audience is a bunch of shit.'

'I think we may have opened the bar too early. I'm sorry.'

'You're right there. All the fuckin money's going over the counter. They gave three pounds. I haven't seen pennies in a bucket for twenty years.'

Before putting the Claymore back in its case Frankie wiped its blade with a small damp cloth. Against the whiteness I saw specks of red.

'Will you not have a drink?' I said. 'On the house.'

They refused. They were in a hurry to leave.

When I rang the bell of 14c it was Jimmy who put his head out of the window and called me up. The door was ajar when I reached the fourth floor. Jimmy was searching for something in a cupboard. He barely looked up at me.

'Where's the man himself?' I said.

'Did you not hear? He's in hospital.'

'What?'

'He was pishing black for a week before he went to see about it. Must have been bleeding inside.'

'Is it serious?'

'They don't know whether he'll do or not. If you saw the colour of him you wouldn't hold out much hope.'

Jimmy continued to rummage among the clothes and papers. He lifted a black brassière and looked at it.

'Where the hell did he get all the women's stuff?' he muttered, more to himself than to me. 'What did you want to see him about?'

'Just to say hello. And to tell him the article will be in the next issue.'

'A lot of good that'll do him.'

He held a pullover up to his chest, saw the holes in the sleeves and threw it back into the cupboard.

'I also wanted to return something I'd borrowed.'

'What?'

'To do with the article.'

'I'll give it to him.'

'I'd prefer to hold on to it, if you don't mind.'

'Suit yourself,' he said and closed the cupboard door. 'But the man'll be dead before the week's out.'

APPENDIX
THE GREAT PROFUNDO – SWORD-SWALLOWER
(*Rostrum* vol. 37, no. 18)

The interviewer deliberated long and hard about whether or not to include certain parts of the following material but felt justified in doing so because it is the truth. Once a writer, be he novelist, critic or journalist, fails to report the world AS HE SEES IT *then he has failed in his craft.*

The interviewer visited the subject at his home in Lower Coyle Street. The apartments were small and sparsely furnished with little regard for order or taste. It was a sparseness which derived not from asceticism but poverty. During the interview the subject was, at first, nervous – particularly about speaking in the presence of a tape-recorder – then, when he forgot about it, animated. Throughout the subject was barefoot and fiddled continually with his toes.

INTERVIEWER: Could you tell us something about how you became involved in such an odd profession?

PROFUNDO: Is it on now? Okay. Right. Oh God, I don't know. I was always interested in circuses and things. It was about the only entertainment we ever got where I was brought up.

INTERVIEWER: Where was that?

PROFUNDO: In the country – a village about thirty miles south of here. The circus would come through about twice a year. In the summer and maybe at Christmas. I just loved the whole thing. The smell of the animals – the laugh you had when they crapped in the ring. Some of those people! One minute you'd see them collecting money at the door, the next they'd be up on a trapeze. No safety-net, either. Anyway, I was about sixteen at the time and they'd organised a speed-drinking contest. I didn't want to win in case my mother found out – she was very wary of the drink – but I could pour a pint down like that. (*He mimics the action.*) Like down a funnel. I have no thrapple, y'see. It was a fire-eater who told me this – I thought I was just normal. He took me under his wing and got me at the sword-swallowing.

INTERVIEWER: Did you join the circus?

PROFUNDO: Not that year, but I did the next. That was the year they had the six-legged calf. It's a thing I don't like – the way they use freaks. I don't mean the wee midgets and all that – they earn good money and they can't work at much else. But I remember paying to go into a tent to see this beast. It was just deformed, that's all. Two half-bent extra legs sticking out its behind. I felt sorry for it – and a bit sick. But I said nothing. They took me on as a roustabout. I tried all kinds of things at the beginning. Acrobat – anything anybody would teach me.

(At this point the subject demonstrated a one-armed horizontal handstand on the edge of the table. The sight brought to mind the paintings of Chagall where peasants float above their world with no visible means of suspension. This physical activity seemed to banish his nervousness and he warmed to his theme.)

That's not good for me at my age. It's why I concentrate on swords now. Doesn't take as much out of you.

INTERVIEWER: Do you still enjoy it?

PROFUNDO: It's hard graft in all weathers and lately I've begun to have my doubts. But if I gave it up what could I do? How'd I pass the day? One of my main difficulties is that I'm not good with an audience. There's guys can come out and have a crowd eating out of their hand right away with a few jokes. That's hooring. All the time they're saying, 'Like me, like me for myself. It doesn't matter what my act is, I want you to like *me*.' If your act is no good, what's the point. It's the reason *you* are out there instead of one of them. People love to think they could do it – with a bit of practice. That's what's behind the oldest trick in the circus. Somebody asks for a volunteer and grabs a woman from the audience. He throws her around – on a horse or a trapeze or a trampoline – and we get flashes of her knickers, and all the time she's holding on to her handbag. You'd be amazed at how many people fall for it. But it's a plant. I loved playing that part – sitting up on the benches pretending you were the little old lady.

INTERVIEWER: And when did you begin to major in the sword-swallowing?

PROFUNDO: Oh that must have been thirty years ago. It was a good act – then. Not the way you saw it the other day. (*Laughs*) In those days I had STYLE. A rig-out like one of those bull-fighters, gold braid on scarlet, epaulettes, the long black hair and a voice that'd lift the tent. And the swords. D'you see those things I've got now? Rubbish – except for the Claymore.

INTERVIEWER: What happened to the good ones?

PROFUNDO: I'm sure they ended up in the pawn. But it wasn't me put them there. D'you know the way I hand them round for the people to test? Well there's some cities I've been in – I'll not mention their names – when I handed them round they never came back. Somebody buggered off with them. But times were very hard just after the war. I don't really blame people. You deserve all you get handing expensive items like that into a crowd. But some of them were real beauties. I collected them all over Europe.

INTERVIEWER: I didn't realise you'd been that far afield.

PROFUNDO: After the war in France was the best. People had seen such desperate things. They wanted to be amused, entertained.

INTERVIEWER: But there couldn't have been a lot of money about – just after the war.

PROFUNDO: Whose talking about money? I'm talking about when it was best to be in front of an audience. They appreciated me. I had fans. Artists came to draw me.

INTERVIEWER: Artists?

PROFUNDO: Well, one artist – but he came time and time again. I didn't know who he was at the time – a small man with a white beard and glasses. He didn't talk much – just drew all the time.

(At this point the subject sprang from his seat and rummaged beneath his bed and produced a dog-eared folder from a suitcase. It contained newspaper clippings and photographs of himself

and in a cellophane envelope a signed drawing by Matisse.)
(See Illustration.)

What do you think of that, eh?

INTERVIEWER: This must be worth thousands.

PROFUNDO: I know it's valuable but I wouldn't sell it. Not at all. I didn't much like it at the beginning – I mean it's just . . . But I got to like it the more I looked at it. He did about thirty of me. Somebody tells me there's one hanging in New York somewhere.

INTERVIEWER: Do you think I could borrow it to reproduce with the article?

PROFUNDO: Sure. But I'd like to have it back.

INTERVIEWER: Of course. Why don't you frame it and put it on the wall.

PROFUNDO: You'd just get used to it then. This way I see it once every couple of years – when somebody calls. Then it's fresh. Far better under the bed. The last time it was out was to show to Jimmy. He didn't think much of it.

INTERVIEWER: I was going to ask you about him. Where does he fit in?

PROFUNDO: I met Jimmy a couple of years ago when I came back to work this place. The hardest thing about street work is gathering a crowd. He does that for me. The sound of that bloody saw attracts them from miles away and they all stand about listening. Once they're all there I go straight into the routine. We split the proceeds. Jimmy has a good money head on him.

INTERVIEWER: I'd say so.

(The subject offered his last can of lager which was refused. He went to the kitchen to get two glasses in order to share it. In his absence the interviewer noticed that the subject had, in his rummagings in one of the cupboards, disturbed a box, which on closer inspection was seen to contain a variety of ladies' underwear. The interviewer in all innocence asked the following question when the subject returned.)

INTERVIEWER: Do you have family? Daughters?

PROFUNDO: No? I'm by myself here.

(The subject then realised that the question was brought about by the contents of the box. He seemed embarrassed.)

Oh that. You weren't meant to see those. Is that machine of yours still going?

INTERVIEWER: No. I've switched it off now. I hope you're not offended by this question, but are you homosexual?

PROFUNDO: No, I'm not offended and no, I'm not a homosexual. I've been in love with many women in my time. Sometimes I like to imagine myself as one. Wearing their clothes is a kind of tribute to them. It does no one any harm.

INTERVIEWER: *(After an awkward silence)* And how do you see the future?

PROFUNDO: I wait for it to come and then look at it *(laughs)*.

INTERVIEWER: And lastly what about trade secrets? Can you tell any?

PROFUNDO: There aren't any to tell. You'd better switch your machine on again. Okay? Trade secrets. I used to keep the blades very clean – wipe them down with spirit. But there's as many germs on the bread that goes into your stomach, so after a while I stopped that.

INTERVIEWER: But *how* on earth do you swallow that big one?

PROFUNDO: The Claymore? The same way as all the others. It's a craft. I can't explain it. I once worked with a man who could eat light bulbs, pins and needles, but I could never do that kind of thing. My talent is different.

INTERVIEWER: Thank you.

REMOTE

Around about the end of each month she would write a letter, but because it was December she used an old Christmas card, which she found at the bottom of the biscuit tin among her pension books. She stood dressed in her outdoor clothes on tiptoe at the bedroom window waiting for the bird-watcher's Land Rover to come over the top of the hill two miles away. When she saw it she dashed, slamming the door after her and running in her stiff-legged fashion down the lane on to the road. Her aim was to be walking, breathing normally, when the Land Rover would indicate and stop in the middle of the one-track road.

'Can I give you a lift?'

'Aye.'

She walked round the front of the shuddering engine and climbed up to sit on the split seat. Mushroom-coloured foam bulged from its crack. More often than not she had to kick things aside to make room for her feet. It was not the lift she would have chosen but it was all there was. He shoved the wobbling stick through the gears and she had to shout – each month the same thing.

'Where are you for?'

'The far side.'

'I'm always lucky just to catch you.'

He was dressed like one of those hitch-hikers, green khaki jacket, cord trousers and laced-up mountain boots. His hair was long and unwashed and his beard divided into points like the teats of a goat.

'Are you going as far as the town this time?'

'Yes.'

'Will you drop me off?'

'Sure. Christmas shopping?'

'Aye, that'll be right.'

*

The road spun past, humping and squirming over peat bogs, the single
track bulging at passing places – points which were marked by tall
black and white posts to make them stand out against the landscape.
Occasionally in the bog there were incisions, a black-brown colour,
herring-boned with scars where peat had been cut.

'How's the birds doing?' she shouted.

'Fine. I've never had so many as this year.'

His accent was English and it surprised her that he had blackheads
dotting his cheekbones and dirty hands.

'Twenty-two nesting pairs – so far.'

'That's nice.'

'Compared with sixteen last year.'

'What are they?'

He said what they were but she couldn't hear him properly. They
joined the main road and were silent for a while. Then rounding a
corner the bird-man suddenly applied the brakes. Two cars, facing in
opposite directions, sat in the middle of the road, their drivers having
a conversation. The bird-man muttered and steered round them, the
Land Rover tilting as it mounted the verge.

'I'd like to see them try that in Birmingham.'

'Is that where you're from?'

He nodded.

'Why did you come to the island?'

'The birds.'

'Aye, I suppose there's not too many down there.'

He smiled and pointed to an open packet of Polo mints on the
dashboard. She lifted them and saw that the top sweet was soiled,
the relief letters almost black. She prised it out and gave it to him.
The white one beneath she put in her mouth.

'Thanks,' she said.

'You born on the island?'

'City born and bred.' She snorted. 'I was lured here by a man
forty-two years ago.'

'I never see him around.'

'I'm not surprised. He's dead this long time.' She cracked the ring
of the mint between her teeth.

'I'm sorry.'

She chased the two crescents of mint around with her tongue.

'What did he do?'

'He drowned himself. In the loch.'

'I'm sorry, I didn't mean that.'

'On Christmas Day. He was mad in the skull – away with the fairies.'

There was a long pause in which he said again that he was sorry. Then he said, 'What I meant was – what did he do for a living?'

'What does it matter now?'

The bird-man shook his head and concentrated on the road ahead.

'He was a shepherd,' she said. Then a little later, 'He was the driver. There should always be one in the house who can drive.'

He let her off at the centre of the village and she had to walk the steep hill to the Post Office. She breathed through her mouth and took a rest halfway up, holding on to a small railing. Distances grew with age.

Inside she passed over her pension book, got her money and bought a first-class stamp. She waited until she was outside before she took the letter from her bag. She licked the stamp, stuck it on the envelope and dropped it in the letter box. Walking down the hill was easier.

She went to the Co-op to buy sugar and tea and porridge. The shop was strung with skimpy tinselled decorations and the music they were playing was Christmas hits – 'Rudolf' and 'I saw Mammy Kissing Santa Claus'. She only had a brief word with Elizabeth at the check-out because of the queue behind her. In the butcher's she bought herself a pork chop and some bacon. His bacon lasted longer than the packet stuff.

When she had her shopping finished she wondered what to do to pass the time. She could visit young Mary but if she did that she would have to talk. Not having enough things to say she felt awkward listening to the tick of the clock and the distant cries of sea birds. Chat was a thing you got out of the habit of when you were on your own all the time and, besides, Mary was shy. Instead she decided to buy a cup of tea in the café. And treat herself to an almond bun. She sat near the window where she could look out for the post van.

The café was warm and it, too, was decorated. Each time the door opened the hanging fronds of tinsel fluttered. On a tape somewhere carols were playing. Two children, sitting with their mother, were playing with a new toy car on the table-top. The cellophane wrapping had been discarded on the floor. They both imitated engine noises although only one of them was pushing it round the plates. The other sat waiting impatiently for his turn.

She looked away from them and stared into her tea. When they dredged him up on Boxing Day he had two car batteries tied to his wrists. He was nothing if not thorough. One of them had been taken from his own van parked by the loch shore and the thing had to be towed to the garage. If he had been a drinking man he could have been out getting drunk or fallen into bad company. But there was only the black depression. All that day the radio had been on to get rid of the dread.

When 'Silent Night' came on the tape and the children started to squabble over whose turn it was she did not wait to finish her tea but walked slowly to the edge of the village with her bag of shopping, now and again pausing to look over her shoulder. The scarlet of the post van caught her eye and she stood on the verge with her arm out. When she saw it was Stuart driving she smiled. He stopped the van and she ducked down to look in the window.

'Anything for me today?'

He leaned across to the basket of mail which occupied the passenger seat position and began to rummage through the bundles of letters and cards held together with elastic bands.

'This job would be all right if it wasn't for bloody Christmas.' He paused at her single letter. 'Aye, there's just one.'

'Oh good. You might as well run me up, seeing as you're going that way.'

He sighed and looked over his shoulder at a row of houses.

'Wait for me round the corner.'

She nodded and walked on ahead while he made some deliveries.

The lay-by was out of sight of the houses and she set her bag down to wait. Stuart seemed to take a long time. She looked down at the loch in the growing dark. The geese were returning for the night, filling the air with their squawking. They sounded like a dance-hall full of people laughing and enjoying themselves, heard from a distance on the night wind.

ACROSS THE STREET

On summer evenings she used to practise the flute in front of a music-stand with the window open. She played with verve, her elbows high, her body moving to the tempo of the music. Every time she stopped she flicked her shoulder-length hair with her hand and, with a little backward-shaking motion of her head to make sure it was out of her way, she would begin again. In the pauses of her playing Mr Keogh could hear the slow hooting of pigeons.

From his window on the opposite side of the street he would sit on his favourite chair, a round-backed carver which supported his aching back, and watch her. He fitted the chair the way an egg fits an egg-cup. His fat hand would rest on the top of his blackthorn stick and when she had finished a piece he would knock its ferrule on the floor between his splayed feet in appreciation.

'The girl done well – the girl done very well,' he would say. Once Mrs O'Hagan, the landlady, had come the whole way up the stairs to see what he wanted.

'Me? Nothing. I'm just at one of my concerts.'

'You might have been having a heart attack,' she said and slammed the door. 'You'll cry wolf once too often,' he heard her shout from the landing.

If the afternoon was sunny he would come down the stairs stepping carefully sideways one at a time and sit with Mrs O'Hagan at the front doorway. The houses were terraced and each was separated from the street by a tiny area of garden just wide enough for Mr Keogh to stretch out his legs. Most of the other houses had privet hedges and a patch of mud or weeds but Mrs O'Hagan's had white iron railings and was flagstoned. Window-boxes and a half barrel, painted white, bloomed with azaleas, nasturtiums and begonias. There was also a little windmill with a doll figure of a

man in a red waistcoat supposedly turning the handle every time
the wind blew.

'It's a bit like the tail wagging the dog,' Mr Keogh had said, pointing
his pipe at it. When he smoked in this garden Mrs O'Hagan insisted
that he bring out an ashtray for his spent matches. Once he had
struck a match on the cement between the bricks and she had looked
at him in such a way that he knew never to attempt it again.

She always sat on a canvas chair and knitted while he used the
more substantial wooden chair from the hallway. She knitted jumpers
and pullovers and cardigans for the church bazaars at great speed.
Mr Keogh noticed that she never looked at her hands while she was
working but could keep the street and everything that moved in it in
view. Sometimes he read the paper but in bright sunlight the tiny
newsprint and the whiteness of the paper created such a glare that
it hurt his eyes.

'There's your little concert artiste,' said Mrs O'Hagan. Mr Keogh
looked up and saw the girl coming from Mrs Payne's door on the
opposite side of the street. She wore a long kaftan and, putting her
head down, walked quickly along the street. Away from her music-stand
she seemed round-shouldered.

'She can fairly tootle,' said Mr Keogh.

'Aye, she's always in a hurry somewhere.'

After lunch, if it was not raining, Mr Keogh liked to walk the quarter
mile to Queen Alexandra Gardens. He would sit on the first vacant
bench inside the gate to recover his breath. One day he saw his
flautist. She lay back with her face tilted and the undersides of her
arms turned awkwardly out to catch the sun. Her eyes were closed.
The weight of Mr Keogh descending at the far end of the seat made
her look round.

'That's the weather, eh?' he said. She smiled a kind of wan grin
then went back to her sun-bathing. A little later when he was breathing
normally he said, 'You play the flute very well.'

'How do you know that?' The girl sat up and looked at him.

'I live opposite you.'

'I didn't know you could hear.'

'It's like everything else,' said Mr Keogh. 'There's not much you can do in this world without people getting to know.'

She shrugged and assumed her former position, feet thrust out, neck resting on the back of the bench. He noticed that when he moved she bounced slightly at the other end of the seat. He tried to keep still. He cleared his throat and asked, 'Are you working?'

'Does it look like it?'

In the silence that followed Mr Keogh took his pipe from his pocket and lit up. What little wind there was carried the smoke to the girl.

'What a good smell,' she said without opening her eyes. Mr Keogh smiled and puffed little clouds into the air. He closed down the silver lid and sat back. The girl jigged at the other end of the bench. She sat forward and scrabbled in her bag, produced a cigarette and lit it. She did this with the same urgency as she walked – as she played the flute.

'I used to play,' he said.

'The flute?'

'The cornet. In a band.'

'Oh.'

'A police band.'

One of the old march tunes went through his head and he began tapping his foot to it. He didn't whistle but clicked his tongue. The girl got up and walked away with short quick steps, her head down. She disappeared behind a clump of laurel bushes. Later, when he was leaving the park, he saw her sitting alone on a bench, her wrists still turned to the sun.

That evening in the twilight he watched her. She had switched on the light in her room with its massive white paper ball of a shade. She played a melody, some phrases of which reminded him of a tune he knew from County Roscommon. Often he had heard a flute played in the band hut and always was conscious of the spit and blow and breathiness of it. But now from across the street it was a pure sound, filtered by distance, melodic only. Her playing suddenly stopped and she made frantic flapping motions with her hands. She came forward, closed the window and pulled the curtains. Moths. Drawn by the light. Mr

Keogh did not like them himself. If there was a moth, or worse a daddy-longlegs, in the room he could not sleep until it was dispatched with a firm rap from a rolled newspaper.

Mr Keogh groped his way from the chair to the bed and turned on his light. He toed off his shoes and flexed his feet. Slip-on shoes were the boon of his old age. For years he had made do with the kind of police boots he had worn in the force. Morning and night he had nearly burst blood vessels trying to tie and untie them. Now in the mornings he just put his socks on while lying in bed, swung his feet out and, with a little wiggling pressure, would insert them into his shoes, while his eyes stared straight ahead crinkling in a smile at the ease of it all. At one time he had been glad of the big boots, had even added steel tips to them so that they would make more noise. The last thing in the world he wanted was to confront and grapple with a surprised burglar. Give them plenty of time to run. That way nobody got hurt, especially him.

It was funny how the size of the feet never changed after a certain age. For as long as he could remember he had taken size eleven while the waistband of his trousers had doubled. His mother had made him wear shoes to school but he had preferred to take them off and hide them in the ditch until he was coming home. He did not want to be any different from the rest of the boys. When he did get home the first thing he would do would be to take the shoes off. His mother praised him for not scuffing them until she found out his trick, then she beat him with a strap for letting the family down in front of the teacher.

A thing they'd learned in the Force for an emergency birth was to ask the woman what size of shoes she took. The bigger the feet the easier the birth.

In his pyjamas he rolled on to the bed and into the depression his body had made in the down mattress. He slept, when he ever did sleep, propped on pillows because of his hernia. The doctor had said there was a gap in him somewhere but Mr Keogh had refused to allow an exploratory operation to find out where. A lump you could find, a gap was a different kettle of fish. The nearer he slept to the upright position the less it bothered him.

He turned out the bedside lamp and watched the sliver of light coming through the girl's curtains which had not been drawn exactly. Occasionally he saw her shadow fall on them as she moved around but she passed the slit of light so quickly that he could get no sense of her. She could have been naked for all he knew.

'What's that you're up to?' said Mr Keogh.

'Doily mats.'

The little man in the red waistcoat did not move, the day was so still. Mr Keogh wore a floppy straw hat to protect his baldness from the burning sun. He had had it since the days he dug a vegetable plot by the Waterworks. The cat had settled herself in the small square of shadow beneath Mrs O'Hagan's chair.

'What about the knitting needles?'

'This is crochet.'

Mr Keogh nodded and tilted his hat farther over his face. Mrs O'Hagan looked up at him, her hands still whirling.

'It's just a different way of tying knots,' she said. 'That's all knitting is when you come to think of it.'

Mr Keogh wiped the sweat from his forehead where the rim of his hat made contact.

'You look like you're melting,' said Mrs O'Hagan. He looked across at the shadowed side of the street. Up at his flautist's window. She was there for a moment. Next thing he knew she was skipping across the road towards him. There was something very different about her. It was her hair. She stopped at the gate.

'Can I have a light?' She held up her cigarette.

'Sure thing.' Mr Keogh leaned his bulk in the chair to get at his pocket and took out a box of Swan matches. She came through the gate and nodded to Mrs O'Hagan. Mr Keogh's fat fingers probed the box and some of the matches fell to the ground. The girl stooped to lift them. She struck one on the tiled path, lit her cigarette and tossed the match away. Mrs O'Hagan followed its direction with her eyes. Mr Keogh offered her a little sprig of matches in case she should need them later but she refused them.

'You've had your hair done,' he said.

'Yes.' The girl reached up and touched it as if she couldn't believe. It was done in an Afro style, a halo frizzed out round her face. 'I need something to keep me going.' She laughed and it was the first time Mr Keogh had seen her do so. He saw too much of her gums.

'Have a seat,' said Mr Keogh. He was struggling to rise from his chair but the girl put out a hand and touched him lightly.

'I'll sit on the step.' She sat down and drew her knees up to her chin. She was wearing a loose white summer skirt which she held behind her knees to keep herself decent. She was in her bare feet and Mr Keogh noticed that they were big and tendony. It was as if they were painted brown. Her arms were also deeply tanned.

'Do you like it?'

'Yes.' Mr Keogh put his head to one side. 'It makes you look like a dandelion clock.' He inhaled and blew out in her direction saying, 'One o'clock, two o'clock.' She held her springy curled hair with both hands as if to keep it from blowing away and laughed again.

She tilted her face up to the sun and sighed, 'You certainly picked the right side of the street to live on.'

'I can never see', said Mrs O'Hagan 'why people want to smoke in heat like this. In the winter I can understand it.'

Mr Keogh took out his pipe and began to fill it from his pouch. Mrs O'Hagan looked away from him to the girl.

'What's your name, dear?'

'Una.'

Mrs O'Hagan repeated the name as if she had never heard it before. The girl raised the cigarette to her mouth and Mr Keogh noticed how closely bitten her nails were, little half moons embedded on the ends of her fingers, the skin bulbous around them.

'I'm Mrs O'Hagan and this is Mr Keogh from County Roscommon.'

'We've met.'

'So I gather.'

Mr Keogh lit his pipe with two matches held together. Just as he was about to set them on the arm of his chair Mrs O'Hagan got up and said, 'I'll get you both an ashtray.' She disappeared into the darkness of the hallway, stepping over the girl's feet.

Between puffs Mr Keogh said, 'Do you play the flute just for fun?'
She nodded.

'With anybody else?'
She shook her head.

'I used to play in a band,' he said. 'We had the best of crack. The paradiddles and the flam-paradiddles.'

'In the name of God what are they?' said Mrs O'Hagan, coming back with an ashtray, a Present from Bundoran. The girl immediately tapped the ash from her cigarette into it.

'They're part and parcel of the whole thing,' said Mr Keogh.

'I play music for the music,' Una said, 'but I can never play it well enough to please myself.' She spoke rapidly, her eyes staring, inhaling her cigarette deeply and taking little bites of the smoke as she let it out. A different girl entirely from the one he had met in the Gardens. 'If I could play as well as I want I would be overcome and then I couldn't go on.'

'We had to march *and* play at the same time. To get the notes right *and* the feet. No time for sentiment there, eh?'

'Maybe that's why I don't like brass bands,' said Una. There was a long silence. Mrs O'Hagan's hands still zigzagged around her half-made doily.

'Where are you from?'

'Tyrone-among-the-bushes. Near Omagh.' Una said it as if she was tired of answering the question.

'And what are you working at?'

'I'm not. I was slung out of University two years ago and I've applied for jobs until I'm sick.'

'Would you not be far better off at home if you have no job to go to?'

The girl gave a snort as if that was the stupidest thing imaginable. She stubbed out her cigarette and turned to Mr Keogh.

'You're the first policeman I've ever talked to. It gives me a funny feeling.'

'Why?'

'I don't know.'

'It was a long time ago.'

'I just don't like cops – usually.' She smiled at him and he adjusted his sunhat so as to see her better.

'Do you – did you not find that people were very wary of you?'

'No – and maybe, yes. Most of my friends tended to be in the Force.'

'That's what I mean.'

'We tended to be outside things.'

'Like football grounds.' They both laughed.

Mrs O'Hagan rose from her chair and said, 'Cup of tea Mr Keogh?' He nodded. 'And you?'

'Yes, please.'

When Mrs O'Hagan had passed, the girl propped her bare feet high on the jamb of the door and clutched her dress to the undersides of her thighs.

'Mr Keogh from County Roscommon,' she said quietly and began to gnaw the side of her thumb-nail.

'I hated it. But then what else could I do?'

The girl shrugged and switched to gnawing her index finger.

'It's a pity you didn't come from County Mayo.'

'Why?'

'Mr Keogh from the County Mayo sounds better.'

'I wouldn't be seen dead coming from there.' He adjusted his hat to let some air in underneath, then he sighed, 'Una from Omagh.'

Mrs O'Hagan came out with a tray, lifting it exaggeratedly high to clear the girl's head as she sat on the step. They had tea and talked and Una borrowed two more matches and smoked two more cigarettes one after the other. Then she was away as quickly as she had come, skipping on her big bare feet across the hot street.

The conversation with the girl that day had disturbed him. He rarely thought of his days in the police now. Before going to bed he opened his cupboard and had a cup from the brandy bottle left over from Christmas. As a policeman he had been timid and useless. The only way he had survived was to hide behind the formulae of words they had taught him. If he got the words right, that combined with his awesome size and weight – in those days he was sixteen stones of muscle – would generally be enough to make people come quietly. But every time he arrested someone his knees would shake.

In drinking to forget he constantly remembered. He knew there were more important and awful things which had happened to him but one in particular stuck out. It was in Belfast shortly after he'd arrived. He had been called to a house where a man was threatening to commit suicide and he'd been met by a trembling neighbour.

'He's up in his room,' she said.

When he'd gone up and opened the bedroom door there was an old man, the sinews standing out on his neck, sitting naked on the bed with a cut-throat razor in one hand and his balls clutched in the other. There were pigeons perched along the iron bedstead, cooing and burbling. The place was white with birdshit, dressing-table, drawers, wardrobe.

'I'm gonna cut them off,' the old man had screamed. The window was wide open and the pigeons came and went with a clattering of wings.

'Suit yourself,' Keogh had said and had begun to move gently towards him. He had taken the razor from him and had intended to wrap him in the quilt but it was so congealed it had come off the bed stiff in the shape of a rectangle. He had taken a coat from the wardrobe, the shoulders of which were streaked with white.

Mr Keogh poured himself another cupful of brandy and wondered why that memory, more than all the others, frightened him so much.

He saw the girl Una several more times and each time she had changed. Once she was so excited and in such a hurry going to an interview for a job that she rushed past him giving the last part of the information walking backwards. The next time, in the supermarket, when he asked her about the job she barely acknowledged his presence and walked past him with a single item elongating her string bag. Her hair had lost some of its bushiness and had begun to lie on each side of a middle parting. She had cold sores on her upper lip which made her mouth look swollen and ugly. But from a distance it was not noticeable – like the spit and breathy sounds. Perhaps this was the reason she stopped playing the flute. Nevertheless Mr Keogh continued to watch her moving about her room. As winter approached it got dark earlier and she would turn on her light at about six. She did not bother to pull the curtains and Mr Keogh would sit in his chair and look across the street at her as she did her ironing or sat reading a magazine. Once she dodged into the room wearing only her underwear but by the time he had straightened up in the seat she was away. It wasn't that he wanted a peepshow, to be part of her privacy was enough. It gave him as much pleasure to watch her ironing as it did to see her half-dressed.

Then one night she did what he was doing and he worried for her. He had come into his room and without turning on his light looked across at her window. The place was in darkness. He sat down in his chair and waited. Staring in the darkness he thought he saw her shape sitting in the window and he felt his eyes were playing tricks on him. It must have been half an hour later when the shape moved away and it was her. After a minute she came back and sat again for the rest of the evening, just a pale smudge of a face staring down into the street. How many girls of nineteen years of age pass a Saturday night like this?

He drew his curtains and went to bed feeling heavier than ever before. He was wakened by what sounded like the slamming of a car door in the street. The luminous hands of his alarm clock said half past one. A blue light flashed a wedge on and off against the ceiling. He pulled himself from the hollow of his bed and bunching the waist of his pyjama trousers with one hand parted the curtains a little more with the other. An ambulance sat outside, its rear doors open. Farther down the street, a police car. A neighbour had come into the street to see what was happening. The door of Una's house was open. Mr Keogh put on his shoes and overcoat, took his stick and went down the stairs sideways one at a time as quickly as he dared. In the street he talked to the neighbour but he knew as little as himself. Their breath hung in the air like steam. Mr Keogh ventured up the pathway then into the lighted hall.

'Hello?'

'Hello?' The landlady's weak voice answered back.

'What's wrong?' Mrs Payne came into the hallway. She was in her dressing-gown holding tightly on to her elbows. Her face was white. A police officer stood by the kitchen door writing something down on his pad. She rolled her eyes up at the ceiling. Heavy footsteps thumped about making the pendant light tremble.

'The wee girl. She took a bath and . . .' She drew her finger across one of her wrists. 'If I hadn't needed the toilet she'd have been there till the morning.' Her mouth wobbled, about to cry. She leaned against the wall for support.

'Is she dead?'

'I don't know. I'm not sure.'

The thumping from up the stairs increased and an ambulance man appeared carrying one end of a stretcher. Mr Keogh and Mrs Payne had to back out of the hallway to let them pass. Through the fanlight Mr Keogh saw the struggle the men had to get down the narrow stairs. On the stretcher between them was a roll of silver paper with Una's blonde hair frizzed out of it at the top. What they were carrying looked like some awful wedding buttonhole. The silver paper glittered in the street lights as the men angled the stretcher into the ambulance. Her face was as white as a candle. A voice crackled from a radio in the police car. Mrs Payne stood with both hands over her mouth. The doors slammed shut and the ambulance took off in silence and at speed with its blue light flashing. The police officer came out of the house and they drove off after the ambulance.

He went in to see if Mrs Payne was all right. She was trembling and crying.

'Sit down, sit down.' She sat and rubbed her eyes and nose with the sleeve of her dressing-gown. 'Is there anything I can do?'

'Mr Keogh,' she said, her voice still not steady. 'You'll have seen things like this before. Would you check the bathroom for me? I couldn't. I just couldn't face it.' And she began to cry again.

Mr Keogh climbed the stairs as if his whole body was made of lead. Back in his room Mr Keogh sat down on the bed until his breathing returned to normal. He listened and could faintly hear Mrs O'Hagan's rhythmic snoring. He tried to toe off his shoes but without socks the soles of his feet had stuck. Grunting with effort he reached

down and pushed them off. The alarm clock said ten past three. He
got to his feet and poured himself a half cup of brandy and drank
it quickly. He poured himself another and sat down. The ambulance
men had let the bath out. He knew that the water would have looked
like wine. But they hadn't taken time to clean up. Liver-coloured clots
had smeared the white enamel and these Mr Keogh had hosed away
with the shower attachment. The razor-blade he threw in the waste
basket. Her clothes, the kaftan and blouse, had been neatly folded
on the bathroom chair. Her Dr Scholls stood hen-toed beneath it.
The brandy warmed him and fumed in his chest. He held his head
between his hands and prayed to God that she wasn't dead. If he
had ever married and had children she would have been the age of
his grandchild. He drank off the second cup, closing his eyes. Whether
she was dead or not, the fact remained that she didn't want to live.
If it had been him, he could have understood it. Except that they
would never have been able to lift him out of the bath. He snorted
a kind of laugh and got off the bed to pour himself another drink.
He took off his overcoat and hung it on the hook behind the door.
She must have been suffering in her mind. He wondered why it had
so affected him – he had seen much worse things. A mush of head
after a shotgun suicide, parts of a child under a tram. He couldn't
say it was because he knew her, because he didn't really. Was it guilt
because he had intruded on her privacy by watching her? The brandy
was beginning to make his lips numb. He rolled into his bed, propped
himself up on his pillows and took the brandy in sips. It was not
having the effect he wanted. Instead of consoling him he was becoming
more and more depressed. He remembered her at the window with
her elbows high and the mellow flute sounds coming across to his
room.

'It's like everything else,' he said aloud. He turned to the clock and
asked, 'What time is it?' A quarter to four. Fuck it anyway. What's
the difference between a paradiddle and a flam-paradiddle? A flam?
Very few of the drummers he had actually liked. They were a breed
apart. Why? Why? Why did she do it? She had so much going for
her.

'Jesus Christ the night,' he said and rolled out of bed. The floor seesawed beneath him and he had to hold on to the armchair. He established where the wall cupboard was, reached out and grasped the handles. He opened both doors and began to look through the contents stacked inside. He knelt down in case he fell down and allowed his eyes to explore the contents. A tea-tray and Phillips Stik-a-Sole advertisement were in the way and he threw them out. But when he pulled them some other stuff fell down with a crash.

Behind a wireless with a cloth and fretwork front he found the small black case. He took it out and skimmed a beard of dust from the top of it with his hand. He blew on it as well but the dust was stuck. He stood up and fell back on the bed. He opened the catches and lifted the lid. It was so long since he had seen it. The silver shine of it had gone – it looked dull like pot aluminium.

'Stop. Stop everything.' He lay across the bed and had another drink from the cup on his bedside table. He turned back to the cornet and picked it out of its purple plush. He hawed on it and tried to rub it with the sleeve of his pyjamas. The valves were a bit stiff, but what comfort to get his little finger into that hook. It felt right. It balanced. He raised it to his lips and only then realised that the mouthpiece wasn't fitted. Fuck it. In the purple plush there were three. He selected his favourite and slotted it into the tube. He wiggled the valves up and down with his fingers trying to free them. A march came into his head and his foot began tapping to it. He cleared his throat, thought better of it and had another drink of brandy, then raised the cornet to his lips. What came out sounded like a fart.

'Who did that?' he said and laughed. He raised the instrument again and this time it was better. He got the tune and it was loud and clear. He knew it so well he couldn't remember the name of it. He didn't tap his bare foot but stamped it up and down to the rhythm of the march. He found he was short of puff very quickly.

'What else?' he said. Occasionally they used to have jazz sessions after band practice and Brian Goodall would sing. He began to play, hearing the voice, knowing the words. His foot stamped to the slow beat and his heel hurt and the notes, now harsh, rang out.

With a crash his bedroom door burst open and Mrs O'Hagan stood there in her nightdress.

'In the name of God Mr Keogh what are you up to?' He smiled and turned slowly to face her.

'A late hour,' he said and laughed.

'Do you know what time it is? Some of us have to be up for Mass in the morning.'

'Sorry. But that wee girl across the street . . .' It came out slurred. Mrs O'Hagan sniffed the air and looked at the almost empty brandy bottle.

'If this ever happens again, Mr Keogh, you can find yourself another place to live.' She slammed the door as hard as she could.

'The boy done bad – the boy done very bad,' he said and rolled over on to the bed. He fell asleep almost immediately.

At midday he woke up with his head pounding and the track of the cornet imprinted in his side where he had slept on it.

IV

WALKING THE DOG
1994

WALKING THE DOG

As he left the house he heard the music for the start of the Nine O'Clock news. At the top of the cul-de-sac was a paved path which sloped steeply and could be dangerous in icy weather like this. The snow had melted a little during the day but frozen over again at night. It had done this for several days now – snowing a bit, melting a bit, freezing a bit. The walked-over ice crackled as he put his weight on it and he knew he wouldn't go far. He was exercising the dog – not himself.

The animal's breath was visible on the cold air as it panted up the short slope onto the main road, straining against the leash. The dog stopped and lifted his leg against the cement post.

'Here boy, come on.'

He let him off the leash and wrapped the leather round his hand. The dog galloped away then stopped and turned, not used with the icy surface. He came back wagging his tail, his big paws slithering.

'Daft bugger.'

It was a country road lined by hedges and ditches. Beyond the housing estate were green fields as far as Lisburn. The city had grown out to here within the last couple of years. As yet there was no footpath. Which meant he had to be extra careful in keeping the dog under control. Car headlights bobbed over the hill and approached.

'C'mere!'

He patted his thigh and the dog stood close. Face the oncoming traffic. As the car passed, the undipped headlights turned the dog's eyes swimming-pool green. Dark filled in again between the hedges. The noise of the car took a long time to disappear completely. The dog was now snuffling and sniffing at everything in the undergrowth – being the hunter.

The man's eyes were dazzled as another car came over the hill.

'C'mere you.' The dog came to him and he rumpled and patted the loose folds of skin around its neck. He stepped into the ditch and held the dog close by its collar. This time the car indicated and slowed and stopped just in front of him. The passenger door opened and a man got out and swung the back door wide so that nobody could pass on the inside. One end of a red scarf hung down the guy's chest, the other had been flicked up around his mouth and nose.

'Get in,' the guy said.

'What?'

'Get in the fuckin car.' He was beckoning with one hand and the other was pointing. Not pointing but aiming a gun at him. Was this a joke? Maybe a starting pistol.

'Move or I'll blow your fuckin head off.' The dog saw the open door and leapt up into the back seat of the car. A voice shouted from inside,

'Get that hound outa here.'

'Come on. Get in,' said the guy with the gun. 'Nice and slow or I'll blow your fuckin head off.'

Car headlights were coming from the opposite direction. The driver shouted to hurry up. The guy with the gun grabbed him by the back of the neck and pushed – pushed his head down and shoved him into the car. And he was in the back seat beside his dog with the gunman crowding in beside him.

'Get your head down.' He felt a hand at the back of his neck forcing his head down to his knees. The headlights of the approaching car lit the interior for a moment – enough to see that the upholstery in front of him was blue – then everything went dark as the car passed. He could hear his dog panting. He felt a distinct metal hardness – a point – cold in the nape hair of his neck.

'If you so much as move a muscle I'll kill you. I will,' said the gunman. His voice sounded as if it was shaking with nerves. 'Right-oh driver.'

'What about the dog?' said the driver.

'What about it? It'd run home. Start yapping, maybe. People'd start looking.'

'Aye, mebby.'

'On you go.'

'There's something not right about it. Bringing a dog.'

'On you fuckin go.'

The car took off, changed gear and cruised – there seemed to be no hurry about it.

'We're from the IRA,' said the gunman. 'Who are you?'

There was a silence. He was incapable of answering.

'What's your name?'

He cleared his throat and made a noise. Then said, 'John.'

'John who?'

'John Shields.'

'What sort of a name is that?'

It was hard to shrug in the position he was in. He had one foot on either side of the ridge covering the main drive shaft. They were now in an area of street lighting and he saw a Juicy Fruit chewing-gum paper under the driver's seat. What was he playing the detective for? The car would be stolen anyway. His hands could touch the floor but were around his knees. He still had the dog's lead wrapped round his fist.

'Any other names?'

'What like?'

'A middle name.'

The dog had settled and curled up on the seat beside him. There was an occasional bumping sound as his tail wagged. The gunman wore Doc Martens and stone-washed denims.

'I said, any other names?'

'No.'

'You're lying in your teeth. Not even a Confirmation name?'

'No.'

'What school did you go to?'

There was a long pause.

'It's none of your business.' There was a sudden staggering pain in the back of his head and he thought he'd been shot. 'Aww – for fuck's sake.' The words had come from him so he couldn't be dead. The bastard must have hit him with the butt of the gun.

'No cheek,' said the gunman. 'This is serious.'

'For fuck's sake, mate – take it easy.' He was shouting and groaning and rubbing the back of his head. The anger in his voice raised the dog and it began to growl. His fingers were slippery. The blow must have broken the skin.

'Let me make myself clear,' said the gunman. 'I'll come to it in one. Are you a Protestant or a Roman Catholic?'

There was a long pause. John pretended to concentrate on the back of his neck.

'That really fuckin hurt,' he said.

'I'll ask you again. Are you a Protestant or a Roman Catholic?'

'I'm . . . I don't believe in any of that crap. I suppose I'm nothing.'

'You're a fuckin wanker – if you ask me.'

John protected his neck with his hands thinking he was going to be hit again. But nothing happened.

'What was your parents?'

'The same. In our house nobody believed in anything.'

The car slowed and went down the gears. The driver indicated and John heard the rhythmic clinking as it flashed. This must be the Lisburn Road. A main road. This was happening on a main road in Belfast. They'd be heading for the Falls. Some Republican safe house. The driver spoke over his shoulder.

'Let's hear you saying the alphabet.'

'Are you serious?'

'Yeah – say your abc's for us,' said the gunman.

'This is so fuckin ridiculous,' said John. He steeled himself for another blow.

'Say it – or I'll kill you.' The gunman's voice was very matter-of-fact now. John knew the myth that Protestants and Roman Catholics, because of separate schooling, pronounced the eighth letter of the alphabet differently. But he couldn't remember who said which.

'Eh . . . bee . . . cee, dee, ee . . . eff.' He said it very slowly, hoping the right pronunciation would come to him. He stopped.

'Keep going.'

'Gee . . .' John dropped his voice, '. . . aitch, haitch . . . aye jay kay.'

'We have a real smart Alec here,' said the gunman. The driver spoke again.

'Stop fuckin about and ask him if he knows anybody in the IRA who can vouch for him.'

'Well?' said the gunman. 'Do you?'

There was another long pause. The muzzle of the gun touched his neck. Pressure was applied to the top bone of his vertebrae.

'Do you?'

'I'm thinking.'

'It's not fuckin Mastermind. Do you know anybody in the Provos? Answer me now or I'll blow the fuckin head off you.'

'No,' John shouted. 'There's a couple of guys in work who are Roman Catholics – but there's no way they're Provos.'

'Where do you work?'

'The Gas Board.'

'A meter man?'

'No. I'm an E.O.'

'Did you hear that?' said the gunman to the driver.

'Aye.'

'There's not too many Fenians in the Gas Board.'

'Naw,' said the driver. 'If there are any they're not E.O. class. I think this is a dud.'

'John Shields,' said the gunman. 'Tell us this. What do you think of us?'

'What do you mean?'

'What do you think of the IRA? The Provos?'

'Catch yourselves on. You have a gun stuck in my neck and you want me to . . .'

'Naw – it'd be interesting. Nothing'll happen – no matter what you say. Tell us what you think.'

There was silence as the car slowed down and came to a stop. The reflections from the chrome inside the car became red. Traffic lights. John heard the beeping of a 'cross now' signal. For the benefit of the blind. Like the pimples on the pavement. To let them know where they were.

'Can you say the Hail Mary? To save your bacon?'

'No – I told you I'm not interested in that kind of thing.'

The driver said,

'I think he's okay.'

'Sure,' said the gunman. 'But he still hasn't told us what he thinks of us.'

John cleared his throat – his voice was trembling.

'I hate the Provos. I hate everything you stand for.' There was a pause. 'And I hate you for doing this to me.'

'Spoken like a man.'

The driver said,

'He's no more a Fenian than I am.'

'Another one of our persuasion.' The gunman sighed with a kind of irritation. The lights changed from orange to green. The car began to move. John heard the indicator clinking again and the driver turned off the main road into darkness. The car stopped and the hand brake was racked on. The gunman said,

'Listen to me. Careful. It's like in the fairy tale. If you look at us you're dead.'

'You never met us,' said the driver.

'And if you look at the car we'll come back and kill you – no matter what side you're from. Is that clear? Get out.'

John heard the door opening at the gunman's side. The gunman's legs disappeared.

'Come on. Keep the head down.' John looked at his feet and edged his way across the back seat. He bent his head to get out and kept it at that angle. The gunman put his hands on John's shoulders and turned him away from the car. There was a tree in front of him.

'Assume the position,' said the gunman. John placed his hands on the tree and spread his feet. His knees were shaking so much now that he was afraid of collapsing. 'And keep your head down.' The tarmac pavement was uneven where it had been ruptured by the tree's roots. John found a place for his feet.

The dog's claws scrabbled on the metal sill of the car as it followed him out. It nudged against his leg and he saw the big eyes looking up at him. The gunman said,

'Sorry about this, mate.' John saw the gunman's hand reach down and scratch the dog's head. 'Sorry about the thump. But we're not playing games. She's a nice dog.'

'It's not a she.'

'Okay, okay. Whatever you say.'

The car door closed and the car began reversing – crackling away over the refrozen slush. In the headlights his shadow was very black and sharp against the tree. There was a double shadow, one from each headlight. From the high-pitched whine of its engine he knew the car was still reversing. It occurred to him that they would not shoot him from that distance. For what seemed a long time he watched his shadow moving on the tree even though he kept as still as possible. It was a game he'd played as a child, hiding his eyes and counting to a hundred. Here I come, away or not. The headlights swung to the trees lining the other side of the road. His dog was whimpering a bit, wanting to get on. John risked a glance – moving just his eyes – and saw the red glow of the car's tail lights disappearing onto the main road. He recognised where he was. It was the Malone Road. He leaned his head against the back of his hands. Even his arms were trembling now. He took deep breaths and put his head back to look up into the branches of the tree.

'Fuck me,' he said out loud. The sleeve of his anorak had slipped to reveal his watch. It was ten past nine. He began to unwind the leash from his hand. It left white scars where it had bitten into his skin. He put his hand to the back of his head. His hair was sticky with drying blood.

'Come on boy.' He began to walk towards the lights of the main road where he knew there was a phone box. But what was the point? He wouldn't even have been missed yet.

The street was so quiet he could hear the clinking of the dog's identity disk as it padded along beside him.

THE GRANDMASTER

The lights beside the hotel swimming-pool were turned out at midnight. One moment Isobel was staring down from the ninth floor and the next there was nothing but darkness and the sound of crickets. She pulled the curtains and undressed for bed.

The knickers she was wearing were smaller than her bikini bottoms so she could see in the full-length mirror a margin of Scottish pale around her waist and groin. Everything else was red. Including her breasts.

'Jesus – how utterly . . .'

Her blood throbbed. She slipped a cotton nightdress over her head and gently lowered herself onto the bed nearest the window. For a while she attempted to read but could not concentrate. Then she switched out the light and tried to sleep. In the dark she felt she could take her pulse on any part of her exposed skin. The hotel radio had a digital clock which now showed one sixteen and still there was no sign of her daughter. She blew on her arms and it soothed them momentarily.

She began to shiver. It came in waves. When she tensed it was difficult to control. If she relaxed the teeth-chattering stopped briefly. She switched on the light, got up and found a strip of paracetamol in her wash-bag and punched out two from the foil, swallowing them with a swig of bottled water.

Within a few moments she was too hot again. She soaked a towel and took it to bed with her. She dabbed her face and shoulders and down the front of her nightdress between her breasts. Her watch on the bedside table agreed with the radio clock.

'Damn and blast her.'

Isobel was lying on her bed, trying not to make contact with any of it, when Gillian came in. The girl didn't even look at her.

'Where on earth have you been?'

'The disco.'

'Oh – I'm glad you were somewhere safe. An English lager lout or two . . . Do you know what time it is?'

The girl shook her head, went into the bathroom and closed the door. Isobel heard the taps running and the flushing and the teeth-brushing. When Gillian came out she was in her pyjamas.

'For your information it's two o'clock, girl.'

Gillian looked over at the digital clock.

'It's one fifty-two,' she said and got into her bed. She pulled the sheet up over her shoulder and turned her face to the wall.

'Who with?'

'Who with what?'

'Captain Plum . . . in the Library . . . with a bloody spanner. I mean who did you go to the disco with?'

'Everybody.'

'Oh I'm glad everybody was there – everybody who?'

'Everybody from here. Give over, Mum. We're on our holidays.'

'Don't you talk to me like that, Gillian. There's not too many thirteen-year-olds who'd be allowed out to this time of the morning.'

'I came home *early*, for God's sake. Everybody's away on somewhere else. I feel such a baby.' Gillian put on a childish voice. '"I have to go home. My mammy says."'

Isobel gave a sigh and said,

'You were okay the day you were born but it's been downhill ever since.' Gillian pulled the sheet up over her head. 'I'll come with you next night.'

'No way.'

'D'you think I'd cramp your style?' The girl didn't answer. 'Did it ever occur to you that *you* might be cramping *my* style?'

Gillian shrugged beneath her sheet. 'What are you on about?'

'Gillian – just promise me one thing – never marry a physics teacher.' Isobel began to make small sniffing noises. Her daughter hesitated, wondering if this was tears. Isobel said,

'You've been smoking again.'

'Honest no.'

'I can smell it, Gillian.'

'Piss off, Mum.'

'That kind of language may make your father laugh – but not me.'

'Everybody else smokes. It just gets in your clothes from the bar.'

'Gillian?'

'What?'

'Look at me and tell me you haven't been smoking.'

With a sigh of irritation the girl turned in her bed to face the room. 'Jesus – Mum.' Gillian was aghast, laughing. She sat up, her elbow on her pillow. 'What a face! You're puce – positively puce.'

'That is not the issue at the moment. We're talking death by smoking – not skin cancer.' Isobel's voice had dropped, her daughter's rose with incredulity.

'Everyday this week you've been moaning on and on and on at *me* not to get too much sun . . .'

'One time I got really badly burnt . . .'

'But you've been wearing factor a zillion.'

'Not today I wasn't. I want a tan too.'

'You've really overdone it.'

'Just a tad, dear. Just a tad.'

'Is it sore?'

'Hot.' Her chin began to shiver.

'Are you all right?'

'Yeah,' said Isobel. She slid down in the bed and pulled the sheet up to her neck. 'A bit feverish. But I'll be okay in the morning.'

'Turn out the light?'

'Yeah – I'll look better that way.'

It had been five years since Isobel had shared a bedroom and now, even after a week, she was not used to it – sounds of breathing, of springs twanging at each turn, the slither of sheets being pulled up or kicked away. Later her daughter's heavy breathing or snoring would keep her awake. All she could do then was lie and stare at the bedroom wall in the light from the digital clock. At home she could have gone down and made hot milk or something. When neither of them could sleep, both were aware of it. The sound of steady breathing was absent, twisting and turning became more frequent the longer they did not sleep, there was a sound of yawning.

'Mum?'

'What?'

'Are you asleep?'

'Yes – I'm absolutely sound.'

'You know that hotel at the far end of the beach?'

'The maroon one?'

'Naw – next to it – The Corvo or something.'

'Mm-mm.'

'They have chess in there.'

'I suppose it makes a change from playing pool.'

'There's a guy plays twelve people at once. He's great.'

'How many hands has he got?'

'I was going really well too. Until he took one of my rooks. I was just so *stupid* not to see it coming.'

'I didn't know you could play.'

'I can't wait to get back at him. He just shrugged and took the rook. I couldn't *believe* I'd made a move like that.'

'I presume this was before the disco.'

'Thursday night – I'm going back. It'll be my last chance before we go home.'

Isobel eased herself off the bed and went to the bathroom to cool her face again. A square of light fell on the wall opposite the bathroom. 'I can't go to the beach tomorrow – looking like this.' Isobel turned out the light and groped her way to her bed. She lay down and started blowing on her skin.

'I wish I'd some calamine.'

'I've got some.'

'I don't believe it. You angel.' Gillian got out of bed and went to the bathroom. 'Why didn't you bloody tell me sooner?' Isobel switched on the bedside light. Her daughter came from the bathroom with cotton wool and a bottle of pink calamine lotion.

'Thanks,' said Isobel, holding out her hands.

'It's okay. I'll do it for you. Close your eyes.' Isobel lay back on the pillow and heard the thick liquid glug as Gillian upended the bottle onto the cotton wool pad.

'This is not like you, Gillian – to have foresight.' She felt the coolness on her forehead and her eyelids and her cheeks. 'Oh that's lovely.'

'Dad bought it for me last year in Majorca. I just never took it out of my wash-bag.'

'Oh – well despite that – it's working. It's so soothing.'

Gillian changed the cotton wool pad for a fresh one and began again.

'I'd like to work in a beauty parlour or somewhere.'

'I don't think you have the intellectual mettle for it.'

'It's so relaxing.'

'It's me that's supposed to relax – not the therapist.' But Isobel ummed and sighed as the treatment continued.

'What did *you* do tonight?' asked her daughter.

'I hung out with some people in the bar. We chilled out together.'

Gillian snorted and did her mother's arms and the scarlet tip of each shoulder. Isobel started to laugh silently.

'What? Mum, what is it?'

'A terrible rhyme. A little pal o' mine soothed me with calamine.'

'That's the pits. It's awful.'

Isobel felt the bottle being pushed into her hands.

'You can do your boobies yourself,' said Gillian.

Isobel and her daughter sat on the patio of the Hotel Condor, waiting. In the flashing darkness there was a disco on for the very young ones.

'You look a mess.' Isobel had to shout above the noise. 'It's no wonder people think you're a boy.' The girl's hair was cut short and she wore a white T-shirt hanging out over her khaki shorts. Her chest was still very flat. Between records the sound of crickets was incessant.

'And stop that with your nails.' Gillian was gnawing, not her nails, but the skin around her nails. 'Gill – i – an.' The girl took her hand away from her mouth and said,

'What does a cricket look like?'

'It's a beetle kind of thing. I've never seen one.'

'They sound like a herd of telephones.' Gillian stood and went towards the nearest one. Immediately she approached the source of the sound, it stopped.

'They hear you coming.' She went towards another one in a flower-bed at the top of the steps and the same thing happened. The first one started up again. Gillian whirled round.

'Sneak – ee. Show yourself.' She gave up and came down the steps. 'He's late. It said ten o'clock.'

'Are you sure it's the right night?'

'Och Mum –'

'Check the notice.'

'The place is set up.'

Inside in the lounge a group of card tables covered with green baize had been formed into a square in the centre of the room. Other families sat about, drinking or playing cards, their children running in and out to the flashing coloured lights and music of the patio. They all seemed to be Spanish or French – not British, not English-speaking. Isobel stood up and walked into the hotel lobby where the notice board was.

Her daughter followed her. There was a photograph of the chess player beside printed information about him in three languages.

'He looks like a bit of all right.'

'Mum.'

'He's very intense.'

'He's very late,' said Gillian. The information said he was a Grandmaster and the Catalan champion. He would challenge twelve opponents simultaneously two evenings a week. Tuesdays and Thursdays.

They made their way into the lounge where the tables were set up. Gillian pulled a face and sat down in the deep leather armchair, folding her legs up beneath her.

'All the grace of an ironing board,' said Isobel.

The music they were playing at the disco was old-fashioned stuff – the Beatles, Nina Simone – 'My Baby Just Cares for Me', Glen Miller's version of 'Begin the Beguine'. It became louder each time one of the children ran out through the patio doors. When the auto-matic doors slid shut, it became distant again.

'Where did you learn to play chess?'

'Dad.'

'Oh – I thought maybe they'd taught it in school.' A waiter passed and she ordered a glass of white wine and a Coke for Gillian. 'When, might I ask?'

'I dunno. Over in his place. Days when there was nothing to do. Days when it was raining.'

'I'm surprised he was sober enough . . .'

'Don't say that.'

'It's true but.'

'He's better – a lot better.'

'No matter how hard he tried he could never teach me. I know the moves all right but the overall thing . . . It's the horse that does the L-shape . . .'

'The knight, Mum.'

'I hadn't the patience for it. We had rows, even about that.'

'When you talk about Dad why d'you always use a voice like that?'

'Like what?'

'You know – "We had rows, even about that."'

'I suppose it's a defence mechanism. When you're left like me, defence is the only method of attack.'

Gillian swung her feet onto the marble floor and stood up.

'Where is he?' She went over to the doorway and looked into the lobby. The waiter arrived and set the drinks on the low table. Isobel called her daughter. When Gillian came back she sipped her Coke standing.

'Your sunburn has cooled down a bit,' she said.

'So it should – after forty-eight hours.'

'It'll peel – when we get back home.'

Isobel crossed her legs and her sandal hung from her foot.

'Mum – for God's sake.'

'What have I done now?' Her daughter nodded to the sandalled foot moving in time to the disco music.

'Only old people do that.'

*

There was a flurry in the hallway and some boys came running with small wooden boxes. They ran up to the square of card tables and set them on the baize. One of the boys had a roll of plastic green-and-white chequered boards which he laid out like place mats, one beside each box. People's heads turned, waiting for the Grandmaster. He came, talking and gesticulating, in the midst of a crowd.

'About bloody time,' said Gillian. She got up and walked to the tables. The lid of each box had a small gouge shaped like a fingernail to help slide it open. Gillian struggled with hers and when it eventually came the plastic chess pieces spilled out all over the table. Isobel pretended to raise her eyebrows and Gillian blushed.

A member of the hotel staff moved one card table aside so that the Grandmaster could get into the middle. The challengers took their seats and began setting up the boards with the white pieces to the inside. The Grandmaster stood in the middle, his hands loosely clasped behind his back. He recognised some of the players from previous nights and smiled at them. His opponents varied greatly in age. One man, smoking a Gauloise, looked like he was in his eighties. Younger family-men joked over their shoulders to their wives and children, their Spanish voices louder than usual with prematch nerves. Two boys, about ten years of age, had agreed to play as one.

Isobel came to the tables and stood behind her daughter as she set up the pieces.

'He has nice eyes,' she said. 'His eyes make you like him immediately.'

'Mum, don't loom. Sit down somewhere.' Gillian elbowed her haunch but her mother paid no attention – she was staring at the Grandmaster.

He was in his late forties but boyish-looking and very thin. His beard was beginning to grey. He wore a shirt with a Mondrian-like pattern and Levi's held up by a belt with a slightly too ornate buckle. A showman of sorts, an artist, thought Isobel as she smiled and caught his eye.

'This is my daughter in whom I am well pleased.'

'Oh Mum please – please don't,' said Gillian.

But although he didn't understand, the Grandmaster returned

Isobel's smile and inclined his head in a kind of salute to Gillian. He checked around to see that all the boards were set up and then went to the first challenger and shook hands. He gave a little smile then made his first move. He did this with all twelve challengers.

Isobel sat down at a little distance to watch. Gillian waited until the Grandmaster came around again to reply with her move. Isobel could not take her eyes off him. His concentration was immense. It would have taken an earthquake to make him look up. When he moved one of his pieces there was an uncertain hovering of his fingers over the pawn or the queen or whatever, a hesitation – then a definite snatching movement, as if to say – how could I have hesitated for so long? There cannot be any other move.

He wore an expensive watch and two gold rings on the same finger – a thin one and a fat one. Sometimes when his hands rested on the table his shoulders were high, almost above his head, his face staring down in concentration at the board. When he captured a man there was a plastic 'tink' as his piece dislodged the one it was taking. Almost a violence – a return to what the game represented – a formalised battle. This happened especially when it came to an exchange with the old man who smoked the Gauloises.

Any time he made a move to put his opponent in check he did not say the word *check* but tapped the black king with a quick movement.

Isobel got herself a glass of white wine. She was getting bored with the chess with its absence of words. The only thing of interest was the Grandmaster.

It amazed her that it was all inside his head, the drama. There was nothing to see. Little or no outward sign. Sometimes his head moved almost imperceptibly, miming the course of an exchange. 'I take you, you take me back.' He was like an anchorite, a holy man. She felt that if he wanted to he could lower his heart-beat despite the noise of the disco, the bustle of the hotel. She drained her wine glass and ordered another.

There was a ripple of applause as the two boys playing as one were checkmated. They knocked down their king and giggled. The Grandmaster smiled and ruffled their heads. They came running to their parents who made much of them. Isobel smiled and made a gesture of silent applause, indicating the boys. The mother leaned forward and said something in Spanish. Isobel shook her head.

'English,' she said. 'I mean Scottish – I just speak English.'

'My English not good,' said the woman. 'A little.' Having said this both women sat forward in their chairs. Then gradually, having nothing more to say, they leaned back and turned again to watch the game. The next time Isobel caught her eye the Spanish woman pointed towards the square of tables.

'¿Your child?'

'Yes.' Isobel nodded vigorously. Gillian had blinkered herself by pressing both hands to the sides of her head and was staring down at the board between her elbows.

'That is my daughter.' As she said it she blushed and smiled.

'¿Daughter?' They seemed surprised. '¿Did you teach her?' The Spanish woman mimed the moving of chessmen.

'No – in school. She learned in school.' Again they remained poised on the edge of their seats but the communication seemed too difficult and gradually they both sagged back to their original positions.

Over the next hour or so several more opponents resigned or were checkmated and the Grandmaster stopped to explain where they had gone wrong or how he had outmanoeuvred them. After the remorselessness of his play he became a teacher – leaning down confidentially, pointing out the sins, advising for the future.

Isobel got up to stretch her legs and walked out onto the patio. It was still warm. There were only about half a dozen children left at the disco, chasing one another rather than dancing. Their parents sat drinking with their backs to the pool, keeping an eye. This crowd was English – words she recognised floated towards her when the music stopped. She gave them a wide berth, walking round the paths on the terracing. The DJ must have run out of records because he began to play the same ones again. The Nina Simone, the Glen Miller.

By the time she went back into the lounge there were only two challengers left. Her daughter and the old man who smoked the Gauloises. The defeated players and their families were gathered round to watch the final stages. The crowd had swelled to fifty or sixty with guests coming back into the hotel at bedtime. Isobel edged her way to a position where she could see her daughter's face.

The Grandmaster made his move against the old man, whose response was to pull another cigarette from the packet lying by his hand on the table. He could see what was unfolding. He tugged a match free from the booklet and lit up. He coughed and his face went bright red. He was shaking his head in disbelief that he should have walked into such a trap. He cursed and surrendered by turning over his king.

Gillian waited for the Grandmaster to turn and face her before making her move. She looked up at him defiantly. He registered no surprise but took a long time before he made his reply. As far as Isobel could see they had equal numbers of pieces left but she could not tell who had the advantage. She watched the spectators' faces, trying to gauge who was winning and, more importantly, when the game would be over. She yawned and looked at her watch.

The disco music stopped and Isobel became aware of smaller sounds – distant coughing, glasses clinking behind the bar, the sneeze as the automatic doors opened and closed. It was now after midnight. The DJ wheeled a trolley containing his turntables and speakers into the lounge to store them for the night. One of the wheels needed oil. It screeched every time it turned.

'Por favor . . . por favor,' whispered the disc jockey. People in the crowd stepped aside to let him through. But neither Gillian nor the Grandmaster looked up from the board.

Some people in the crowd – certainly the parents of the two youngest boys and others they had told – realised that Isobel was the mother of the child player. She yawned again but this time tried not to open her mouth. Gillian made a move. The Grandmaster's fingers went up to his beard as he considered. Isobel felt another yawn rising and proceeded to yawn with her teeth clenched.

After what seemed an endless pause the Grandmaster moved a pawn. Gillian was now taking almost as long to reply. At half past twelve the Grandmaster smiled and raised his eyebrows at Gillian. He said something in Spanish. Gillian looked blankly at him. The

Grandmaster turned and looked around the crowd. He called a girl – Spanish-looking, about twenty years of age, and they spoke in Spanish. The girl turned to Gillian.

'This is my father.' She put her hand out to indicate the Grandmaster. 'And I translate for him. My father would like to offer you a draw.'

Gillian was unsure.

'¡Tablas!' said the Grandmaster to the crowd. They burst into applause. They smiled and the clapping went on and on. Isobel joined in. Gillian began to blush – it was as if she had only realised now that people had been watching. The Grandmaster offered his hand and Gillian, still not sure, shook it. The old man who smoked the Gauloises struggled forward and slapped her on the back. He said something in Spanish to the Grandmaster who laughed. Gillian got to her feet. Isobel edged forward and said,

'I suppose congratulations are in order?'

Gillian's face was sullen – she always hated being the centre of attention. The Grandmaster put his arm around his daughter's shoulder. His eyes met Isobel's and he leaned forward to speak. His daughter translated.

'My father says he is very good.'

'Who?'

'Your son. He is very good.'

'It's my daughter.' The Spanish girl turned to her father and explained. He seemed embarrassed and apologetic.

'He says he is very sorry – *she* is very good. Your daughter is very good.'

'Oh, thank you.' Isobel turned to Gillian who was tugging at her elbow.

'Come on, Mum.'

'How good is that?' His daughter, her hand resting on her father's, relayed the question. The Grandmaster shrugged and pushed out his lip.

'Excellent,' he said in English. His daughter listened to what he had to say then translated,

'He means she is *very, very* good. In the world. By any standard.'

'Her father was very good at it. He taught her.' Both the Grandmaster and his daughter looked around, possibly expecting to see the person in question but there was only the eighty-year-old man fussing around the tables.

'But he's not with us here. Fortunately.' Isobel smiled. 'Where can a game like this lead?' He listened to the question and smiled.

'Nowhere,' translated his daughter, 'but she may enjoy it.'

The crowd had now completely dispersed.

On the way back to their own hotel Isobel sensed her daughter's anger. They walked, as always, a little apart – as if they were not with each other. There was something about the way her sandals were slapping the ground.

'And what's wrong with you?'

'I could've won. He's a cheat.'

'What do you mean?'

'He was cheating. I was going to win. I could see a way to win. And I think he saw it too – that's when he offered me a draw.' Gillian was close to tears. 'And that was my last chance. Men cheat. Everybody cheats.'

'I doubt very much if that's true. Besides it's no big deal.'

'It's no big deal? It's no big deal. I'm . . . I . . . oh fucking hell . . .'

'Forgive me not getting worked up about something your father is entirely responsible for.'

'I might have known that was at the back of it.'

'Gillian, he's a Grandmaster. He could see better than *you* that it was going to be a draw.'

'Don't *say* that – I *hate* when you do that. As if I knew nothing. As if I was too young to know *anything*. You don't even know the fucking moves and you're siding with him.'

'Gillian – please. Your language is deteriorating.'

'You do it with everything – teacher knows best – the doctor knows best – Mum knows best.'

'Not another street scene, please.'

'I *hate* people talking down to me.'

'And how many degrees have you got? Maybe you could remove my appendix later on tonight?'

'According to you even Dad knows nothing.'

'Brain cells aren't destroyed overnight, you know. But he's certainly working hard at it.'

'Oh you – you fucking cow. Why'd you . . .'

'How dare you – how dare you call me that.' Isobel swung her open hand at the girl's face. There was the crack of skin to skin. Gillian screamed and ran off into the dark, her sandals slapping the metalled surface of the road.

'Gillian!' Isobel watched her run from the light of one street lamp through shadow to the next. She followed the white T-shirt and saw her daughter turn down the steps to the beach.

'Bloody bloody bloody bloody hell.'

The beach café was closed and the beach was in darkness. There was sufficient moonlight to outline the boats and pedalos and stacked sunbeds. Isobel threaded her way through them to the water's edge. She could see no sign of Gillian. She knew not to shout her name. To the left-hand side of the beach was a jumble of rocks and boulders. She was not sure but she thought she saw a pale patch which could be her daughter. She walked towards the rocks. A cigarette – small as a pinhead from this distance – glowed and went out again. The nearer she got the surer she was it was Gillian. She was squatting on a rock at the height of her mother's head. She inhaled her cigarette and her cupped hand glowed in the dark. The sea slapped in, in small Mediterranean waves.

'I'm sorry.'

'Fuck away off.'

'I lost my temper. I shouldn't have hit you. You are old enough and ugly enough not to be hit.' Isobel turned her back to the rock and leaned her head against it. 'That was my own mother's doing. I swore it would never happen again. I don't know which was worse – being hit or – having to listen. My mother had the most sarcastic tongue I ever heard. I swore it would never happen to me. But being a teacher doesn't help.' She looked up at her daughter. The cigarette glowed again, then came sailing down past her head to hiss out in the sea at her feet.

'Sometimes I say things. Things I don't mean. Things I'm sorry for afterwards. And I don't have the courage to take them back. That's the times I'm most like her. Dearest mother. And I hate myself.' The cigarette butt was white bobbing against the dark water. 'If there is somewhere still open why don't we go and have a drink – talk about this?'

'I said fuck away off.'

'You're becoming a tad repetitive.'

'You just want to suck in with me.'

'Gillian, please. Do me a favour.' Her mother gave a sigh and said, 'You were okay the day you were born but it's been downhill ever since.'

At the square a small bar was open. Several tables were still out on the pavement and there was a light on inside. Isobel went in and ordered a glass of wine and an orange juice. An old man with spectacles stood at the counter eating *tapas*. He stared at her, his jaws revolving. The boy who served her was good-looking but young. A son more than a lover. Outside she set the drinks on the table and sat down. In the light from the open doorway she could see that Gillian had been crying for a long time – her face looked puffy and sullen. The girl put her feet on a chair, and turned her body away. Isobel offered her a sip of wine but she refused.

'Each generation tries to make a change for the better – however small. To put one particular piece of debris in the bin.'

'Huh – what was yours?'

'My mother and I never talked. Like now.'

'Great. This is just great. What I really wanted. All my dreams fulfilled. Talking to my mother.'

'Believe me, it's better than taking the huff. We were a family of huffers – for days, weeks on end.'

'I would prefer that.'

'Gillian – I know – I think I know your pain – about how difficult things have been.'

'Like fuck, you do.' Isobel put her hand out to touch the girl's arm but Gillian pulled away and began to search in the pocket of her shorts. She took out a packet of Gauloises and a book of Hotel Condor matches. She tapped a cigarette on the table and lit up.

'That's another thing we should talk about.'

'What?'

'Smoking.'

'Why?'

'Because it kills people.'

'Good.' She inhaled deeply and blew two streams of smoke down her nose. 'That's what it's for.'

'Remember the sticker on the front door – My Mum's a smoker buster. It was the hardest thing I ever did – giving it up. To please you.'

'Gee – thanks.'

'We can get around to talking about stealing from old men some other time.'

'I didn't steal them. He just left them on the table.'

The man who'd been eating the *tapas* came out of the doorway and wandered up the cobbled street a little unsteadily. There was a cricket nearby ringing at great volume.

'That's your story.'

'Shut the fuck up,' Gillian yelled. Then she started laughing. 'I mean the insect – not you, Mum.' Her mother smiled.

'My own mother used to say that it gave her great pleasure to say to people "This is my daughter". Well tonight I understood that. I think I even blushed at one point.'

'Are you taking the piss? Is that sarcastic?'

'No. I felt proud of you. Maybe for the first time.'

'But it was Dad taught me. Nothing to do with you.'

'I felt proud of you despite the fact that the chess was *his* doing. The Glasgow grandmaster. I suppose you can't wait to tell him.'

'What?'

'About the draw.'

'It's none of your business.'

'Gillian – help me to like you.'

'But I don't *want* you to like me. I hate myself – how can anybody else like me.' Her chin began to flex and the girl cried again. 'The whole thing is so fucking stupid. Five years of fucking stupidness.'

Isobel put her arm around her shoulder expecting her to flinch away but she did not. She felt the shakes of her crying and patted her shoulder.

'Where's the calamine?' she said and smiled. They both sat for a long time not saying anything – the night filled with the sound of crickets.

A SILENT RETREAT

The game was almost over. A boy coming in from the wing chipped the ball over the goalkeeper's head and it bounced between the posts.

'For Godsake Declan. What are you playing at?'

'Me? Where's the full backs. I'm out narrowing the angle.'

'Godsake.'

At the back of the school playing-fields the jail wall was so high it created echoes. In the trees around the pitch starlings were making metallic noises with occasional swooping notes. It was getting dark. Because it wasn't a real match the boys wore their own kit – and just knew who was on which side.

'Next goal's the winner.'

The ball had bounced across the track and Declan hopped the fence and kicked it out from there. A voice said,

'Bloody eejit.' Declan looked round startled. There was nobody there. Only the B-Special on guard duty at the foot of the jail wall. 'You were too far out. You should never let anybody chip you like that.' It *was* the B-Special. In all his years at the school Declan had never heard one of these guys speaking. Yet they were always there, day and night, at the base of the thirty-foot grey brick wall. They'd worn a track in the grass pacing up and down. Declan looked over his shoulder.

'D'you say something?'

'Yeah. I said you were too far out.'

'Says who?'

'Says me.'

'And what would you know about it?'

'More than you think, sonny boy.'

They were separated by a distance of twenty or thirty feet. The B-Special was up on a low terracing of grass. It seemed a stupid

375

distance to continue talking. Declan looked over his shoulder to check which end of the field the ball was.

'I used to be a talent scout,' said the B-Special.

'Aye, that'll be right.'

'Naw, seriously.'

'Who for?'

'A club across the water.'

'Bollicks.' Declan vaulted the two-stranded wire fence and ran into his goal. The cold was really getting to him now. He wanted to jump up and down, to slap his arms, but he was conscious of being watched. He didn't want to look foolish, jumping about like a kid for no reason. Lights came on in the top row of windows in the jail – the Republican wing.

One night they had heard the prisoners from there shouting and rattling metal things against their windows. Tin mugs, it had sounded like. That was bad. Thinking about them in there. But what was worse was knowing the prisoners could hear *them* – playing football – shouting when they scored – arguing about whose throw-in it was. People were really annoying about these things – throw-ins and corner kicks. This was what carried into the jail. Bickering. People who could go home for their tea or walk down the street or do anything they liked – people who were free – arguing and bickering.

A guy in a Celtic shirt led a charge out of the gloom and connected with a shot. Declan leapt and got his fingertips to it, deflecting it for a corner. Somebody slapped him on the back as he lay in the mud.

'Saved, wee man.'

What if the guy *was* a talent scout? Had he seen that? The corner was taken and the ball cleared.

After a while there was a bit of shouting and a ragged cheer at the other end.

'Is that it?' Declan called but nobody paid any attention to him. The boys began to move away. He could hear the twang of wire and the scuffling of boots on the cinder track as they made their way down to the classroom where they changed.

'Thanks for telling me,' he shouted at them. Still they ignored him.

He ran back to the goalposts to collect his cap with his money rolled in it.

'Hey, c'mere.' Declan looked up. It was the B-Special again.

'What?'

'I said c'mere.'

Declan scissor-stepped over the wire fence and paused at the foot of the embankment. The B-Special said,

'I wanna ask you something.'

Declan waited.

'Come up here.'

Declan looked round. The others had disappeared. Away in the distance a light came on in the Nissan hut classroom. He dug his studs into the grassy slope and moved up a bit.

'I'm not gonna bite you.'

Declan shrugged in the darkness.

'The thing I wanna ask you is – that's a Roman Catholic school, right? Well answer me this. There's Roman Catholic priests in there, right? I see them walking round the track.'

Declan nodded, still waiting for the question.

'D'you smoke?'

'Yeah.'

The B-Special reached into his pocket. The material of his raincoat sleeve made a kind of whistling noise as it slid against itself. Declan could see the pale cigarettes sticking out of the packet offered to him in the darkness. His hands were dirty but the mud had almost dried. He reached over and took one. There was a metallic clunk and a Zippo lighter flamed.

'Maybe I'll keep it for later,' Declan said.

'You'll fuckin smoke it now.' Declan didn't know whether the man was joking or not. He lit Declan's cigarette and one for himself. In the light from the Zippo Declan saw that the man had a thin black moustache. He looked far too young.

'My question is this – these Roman Catholic priests – what do they do for sex?'

'They don't do anything. They're celibate.'

'What age are you, son?'

'Sixteen.'

'If you believe that you'll believe anything.'

'I am. I'll be seventeen in March.'

'Naw – I mean the celibate item.'

'They don't get married or anything.'

'It's the anything part I wanna hear about.'

'They give themselves to God. To being good.'

'And those black dresses they wear –'

'Soutanes.'

'Whatever you call them . . . All them buttons – walking round the track with their hands behind their backs. Or in their pockets, more like. Are you trying to tell me those guys do nothing. And they have equipment the same as the rest of us.'

'Yeah – as far as I know.'

'You're gullible, son. Dead gullible. They're a crowd of fuckin hypocrites. Liars.'

There was a long silence. Declan inhaled the smoke and put his head back and blew it out as if he was in the confined space of a toilet cubicle. He would have to stay here and finish the cigarette. The Dean or somebody might be hanging around the changing rooms. He had been caught twice – in the Dean's words – 'engaging in his habit'. And caned both times. 'You, of all people, should know that it stunts your growth.'

'Liars and hypocrites,' said the B-Special again.

'They are not.'

'How do you know?'

'I know some priests and maybe . . .'

'Maybe what?'

'I'm maybe going to . . . be one.'

'What – a priest?' The B-Special laughed, a low kind of chuckle. 'Fuck me.' He shook his head from side to side. 'I'm always putting my foot right in it.' He cleared his throat. 'I find that very sad. A waste – because you were shaping up as all right of a lad to me. What's your name?'

'Declan.'

'Declan what?'

'Declan MacEntaggart.'

The B-Special laughed, this time out loud, and said,

'You'd better be a priest because you'll not get too many jobs with a name like that. Are you a boarder or a day-boy?'

'A boarder.'

'From where?'

'Ardboe.'

'Fucksake. Where's that?'

'Lough Neagh – near Cookstown.'

'That's Republican territory up there. Crowd of rough men, by all accounts.'

'Where are you from?'

'Glengormley.' The B-Special unslung his gun and set it barrel up against the foot of the wall. He then hunkered down to smoke his cigarette. His head was now almost on a level with Declan's. 'See this,' he said, nodding at the wall. 'You get bored out of your fuckin mind at this.'

'You weren't scouting for any team.'

'Only taking the piss. I wanted you to make a couple of good saves. I was bored outa my mind up here.'

Declan felt spits of rain on his bare legs. The few saves he had made earlier had covered his haunch and side in black wet muck. Goalmouth cinders left fine scores of blood on his knees. He tried to get to the end of his cigarette. He took several quick puffs at it so that it became hot and soft.

'You're rushing that,' said the B-Special. He straightened up from his crouched position.

'It's freezin. I gotta go. The rain's starting.' Declan tossed the lit cigarette on the grass and squashed it with the studs of his boot.

'When are you going to give me that back?'

'What?'

'The fag.'

'You're taking the piss again.'

'I'm not fuckin made of money. You owe me one, kid. I'll be here tomorrow afternoon again. Same time.' The B-Special finished his cigarette and spun it away into darkness.

'I can't.'

'Why not?'

'The whole school is on silent retreat tomorrow.'

'Silent retreat? What in the name of God's that?'

'A day when people don't talk. They pray.'

'Sounds like an army. Tip-toeing. Backwards.' He laughed and so did Declan.

'How can I give you back your fag – if I don't even know who you are – or what you look like?'

The B-Special changed his position and suddenly a bright torch shone in Declan's eyes. The B-Special turned it on himself, lighting up his face from below. Declan could barely see because his eyes were recovering from the sudden glare. Bright spits of rain crossed its beam.

'That's me,' said the B-Special. 'Special Constable Irvine Todd.' He looked about nineteen but was probably older. He had one of those young faces – so young that he tried to age it with a moustache.

'Maybe see you,' said Declan and danced down the slope sideways. He shook some coins from his cap and pulled it tightly on his head. The B-Special shouted after him.

'Hey!' Declan turned. The torch beam wobbled across the high wall. 'This never happened.'

'What?'

'You and me – talking. It's against the rules, fuck them. Okay?'

'Fair enough,' said Declan. Constable Irvine Todd was shining his torch at the wall, wiggling it, gliding the bright circle away from him until it became a bright ellipse then plucking it back again.

'Bloody eejit,' said Declan. He was now over the wire and running towards the light of the changing rooms.

When it began to get dark Declan headed for the track. A flock of starlings swooped over the jail wall and condensed as it changed direction. There were only one or two boys walking round – on their own because of the silence. A uniformed guard was standing at the foot of the jail wall, partly hidden by bushes. Declan walked past him once, trying to see if it was Special Constable Irvine Todd. This guy wore the peak of his hat pulled down low on his face and was at such a distance he could have been anybody. If Declan climbed the fence and sneaked up and it wasn't the one he knew the guy might shoot him. B-men had a reputation for being trigger-happy. The starlings settled in the trees at the far side of the track and began chattering. Declan waited and stared up at the B-Special.

'Hey!' It felt ridiculous because Declan spoke the word instead of shouting it. The B-Special turned his head.

'It's you again.'

'Yeah.'

'I'm dying for a smoke, son.'

Declan looked all round then stepped over the wire. He was screened from the track now by the bushes.

'The excitement up here's been fierce. My nerves is jangling. Three murders and a rape and ten breakouts.' Declan put his hand in his pocket and produced the cigarettes. A white packet of Senior Service. 'Jesus, where do you get the packets of five?'

'The day-boys go down for us. I told him ten but he musta been deaf.' Todd produced his Zippo lighter and took a cigarette from the packet.

'Whatcha mean the dayboys go down for you?'

'We can't. We're not allowed out.' Declan slid the flap closed.

'Why not?'

Declan shrugged. 'School rules – boarders' rules.'

'They don't trust apprentice priests?'

'Not all of us are going on for the priesthood.'

'Fuck that for a lark.' Declan was putting the thin packet back in his pocket. 'Are you not having one yourself?'

'Naw –' Declan looked over his shoulder. 'I've gotta go.'

'For fucksake. I'll look a right prick standing here smoking on my own.'

'It's a bit risky.'

'Have a cigarette, big lad. If anybody objects I'll blow their legs off.' He slapped his gun with the flat of his hand. 'Come on.' He flicked the lighter and held it out to Declan. In the wind the flame fluttered blue within the metal guard. Declan took out the packet again and got a cigarette. He hurried to light it.

'Thanks.' He cupped the cigarette in the palm of his hand and nodded at the gun. 'What is it, anyway?'

'A gun.' Declan smiled. The B-Special said, 'A nine millimetre Sten. They make the handles outa paper clips.'

'It's like your lighter. All those holes in the barrel.'

'You might as well have a fucking spear. No accuracy. You just can't keep it down.' He imitated firing the gun from his waist. 'Dju-dju-dju-dju – a figure of eight pattern. No matter how hard you try you can't keep it down – it goes all over the fuckin place.'

'I know nothing about guns,' said Declan. He felt safer crouching down. The B-Special leaned against the jail wall.

'What did you say you were doing today?'

'A silent retreat.'

'That's it.' The B-Special snapped his fingers. 'I was trying to remember the name for my Ma. A silent retreat. I couldn't remember.'

'Were you talking to your . . . mother about . . .?'

'Aye, last night. I says "Ma, you'll never believe it but I was talking to somebody who's going to be a Roman Catholic priest." I like to tease her. It drives her round the bend. She's a fierce oul bigot.' He shook his head and laughed. 'Tell me this – what's the point? What good's it going to do anybody?'

'What?'

'Silence. Not speaking?'

There was a pause.

'It allows you to listen to what God is saying to you.'

'You didn't think *that* one up yourself.' Todd stared at him. 'That's Roman Catholic priest talk, if ever I heard it.' Declan didn't answer. 'And what did he – with a capital aitch – say to you today?'

'This is not a subject to joke about. It's private.'

'Point taken – it's like sex. What's your name again?'

'Declan.'

'Tell me this, Declan, do you intend to get your hole, before you become a priest?'

'Don't be so bloody filthy.' Declan straightened up from his crouching position with the intention of going. The cigarette was too big to throw away and he couldn't walk down onto the track with it. He looked at it between his fingers.

'Okay, okay. Stay where you are. I like to take the piss now and again. But you're beginning to sound a bit like my Ma.'

'Naw, really. I better be going.'

'Getting on your high horse, eh? Grammar School boy tells one of Her Majesty's Special Constables to get stuffed.'

'It's not that. I don't like filth.'

'Like what?'

Declan shrugged.

'Sex things . . . things like that are just . . .'

'It's the world, son. You'd better get to know it if you're gonna spend the rest of your life tidying it up. You better know what happens beneath the blankets – every fuckin push and pull of it – before you go telling people what they're not allowed to do.'

'Shakespeare didn't have to murder somebody before he wrote "Macbeth".'

'You're trying to blind me with science now.' Declan looked down at his feet, trying not to laugh. The worn patches of his black leather shoes had gone pale with walking through the wet grass. 'You've got to know the ins and outs of everything.' The B-Special paused. 'Do you know there's a brave bit of rummaging goes on down by the handball alleys.'

'Rummaging?'

'Boys rummaging in each other's trousers.'

'You're making that up.'

'Swear to God. I can see it all from up here. Queer as fuck – these boarding schools.'

'Look, I shouldn't be here.'

'And I shouldn't be talking to you. But I am, ampta?'

The lights came on in the Republican wing of the jail. Declan threw his cigarette into the grass.

'I'd better go.'

'Do you have any friends in there?'

'Where?'

The B-Special nodded to the lit windows.

'No.'

'Are you a Republican?'

'I'd like to see a United Ireland, if that's . . .'

'How could you have a United Ireland with you and me in it?' He laughed out loud and punched the air. 'Fuck the Pope and No Surrender.' Declan smiled at the slogans. 'Nahhh – you're too nice a young lad to be friends with that scum. Sometimes I think this wall's here to stop people breaking in and lynching the bastards. Here – have another.' The B-Special held out a packet of ten Gallagher's Blues. Declan refused.

'Two in a row makes me dizzy.'

'You're the first Roman Catholic I've ever talked to – apart from one guy in work.'

'Work?'

'Aye, this caper is only part-time. In the mornings I do a milk round – white coat in the mornings, black at night. The money's no great shakes but it's better than nothing. If the milk round paid more I wouldn't have to be standing here like some kind of a fuckin doo-lally talking to you.'

'Thanks a lot.'

'But there's advantages – barmen are shit scared of us. A couple of us go into a pub in uniform and the drink's all free – and as much as you can smoke. Here.' He held out his packet of cigarettes again. Declan hesitated. 'Are you too good for my brand? I suppose you'd smoke them if they were Gallagher's Greens.'

'Naw – naw it's not that.'

'At least it's a packet of ten.'

Declan took a cigarette and was about to light it when he heard something down on the track. He paused and stared into the darkness.

'Wait.' The B-Special clunked the lid of the Zippo back into place putting out the flame. He said,

'Who is it?'

'I dunno.'

The figures came closer, their feet impacting on the cinder track. Declan could now hear their voices, then he recognised the deep laugh.

'It's the Dean,' he said, crouching down. He heard the other voice indistinctly, but enough to know who it was.

'So what?'

'Shh . . .'

'What's wrong?' said the B-Special. Declan shushed him again. The B-Special's voice changed to a whisper. 'Christ boy, you're really afraid of these guys.' He hunkered down beside where Declan was crouching and slapped the metal of the Sten with his open hand. 'Do you want me to cut them in half with this?' Declan shook his head and put a warning finger to his lips. The walking priests were right below them now. Declan imagined he could see their white collars at the same height in the dark. Their voices were low and he could not make out what they were saying. They passed and Declan stood up again. The B-Special whispered,

'Which one's the Dean?'

'The nearest.'

'And the other one?'

'Father Cairns – teaches Latin. He's okay.'

'No Jesuit's okay.'

'They're not Jesuits.'

'They're all fuckin Jesuits as far as I'm concerned.'

'You don't listen.'

The B-Special leaned forward and spun a spark from the Zippo wheel with his thumb.

'You don't really believe in God, do you?'

Declan lit his cigarette and breathed out the smoke. 'I do. Very much so.' He looked after the priests on the track. He could hear them faintly but he could no longer see them. He cleared his throat and said, 'The world is a very complex place. Right?'

'Aye, one-way streets . . . singing . . .' The B-Special paused and thought. 'And fuckin glass lampshades with dead flies in them. My Ma hates that.'

'Well, something as complex as the world just couldn't happen. There must be a supreme intelligence behind it. Right?' The B-Special nodded in an exaggerated fashion, mocking Declan's seriousness. Declan ignored him.

'How many times would you have to take all the bits of a watch and throw them up in the air before they'd land and start telling the time?'

'A hell of a lot. One hell of a lot.'

'So . . .'

'So what?'

The argument as he remembered it being outlined in Canon Sheehan's *Apologetics* had seemed simple. He hesitated.

'I mean if the world is as complex as a watch – which you have just agreed – then a watchmaker – aye ee – God, or some intelligence called God, had to put it together.'

'That is SO FUCKIN STUPID I can hardly believe you said it, Declan. The most complicated thing I know is my fuckin milk round. Who made that up? God? It just happened. People who drink milk live in different places. It's as simple as that.'

'I think you're being purposefully stupid.'

'Oh you do, do you?'

'Yes.'

'The world is not complex. It's dead fuckin simple. A stone is a stone. And a wall is a wall.' He slapped the wall with the flat of his hand. 'And this wall is full of fuckin stones. Am I right? Is that complex or simple?'

'There's no point,' said Declan. He began backing down the slope.

'You're so like a Roman Catholic priest, Declan – I think you'll be one.'

'I hope so.'

'I think you'll go the whole hog and become a Jesuit.'

'I'm away back now.'

'Why would anyone want to be a Roman Catholic priest? It's SO totally fuckin perverse – God gave you a dick TO USE.'

'You're being filthy again.'

'No – I'm serious.'

'You don't understand.'

'I certainly do not. I need to have certain items explained to me.'

'God gave us appetites. By abstaining – by denying ourselves things we become stronger people. Going off sweets in Lent, kinda thing. Discipline. It doesn't mean to say there's anything wrong with sweets.'

'Why don't you abstain from learning then, from studying. Why don't you stay stupid – like me? That'd be a great sacrifice. For fucksake, who do you think you're kidding? I left school at fourteen and it was the wisest move I ever made.'

'I think you've an inferiority complex.'

'Huh! Listen to him. Listen to the second-class citizen,' said the B-Special. 'I suppose you want me to be an A-Special.'

'There's no such thing,' said Declan.

'There fuckin IS. Was. In the twenties. They were needed to keep you bastards getting too big for your boots.' He stabbed his forefinger at Declan's face. 'What age did you tell me you were, son?'

'Seventeen next month.'

'Well, stop fuckin patting me on the head. You have that Papish tone in your voice.'

'You're far too touchy. I wasn't meaning any of that.'

'So – I'm far too touchy – eh?' He thought for a moment then raised the Sten gun and swung it slowly round until the muzzle pointed at the boy. 'I'm a man with an inferiority complex?' The bones of Declan's chest felt as if they were about to cave in. He said,

'I don't know much about guns but I know that's definitely not allowed.'

'I never was one for the rules, was I, Declan?' He was using the gun like a rifle, sighting along the barrel at Declan's heart. They stood like that for what seemed a long time. Declan was afraid that he was going to faint. He kept swallowing.

'You're being really stupid . . .' Declan heard his own voice shaking.

'That's because I haven't had a great education . . .' Declan found the power to move and began to edge down the slope. 'Stay where you are and finish your cigarette.' The boy hesitated.

'Stop pointing that thing at me.'

'I'm giving the orders. Say your prayers. Yes – yes what a good idea. Say after me – Our father WHICH art in heaven . . .'

Declan backed down the slope staring at the gun. It was almost pitch dark now. He flung what remained of the cigarette away and stepped over the wire onto the track. He wanted to run but he walked as casually as he could. The B-Special shouted after him,

'Education nowadays isn't worth a tup-ney fuck. I'm glad I left when I did.'

Declan didn't look over his shoulder but he felt the gun pointing at the middle of his back and the sensation burned there all the time he was walking towards the lights of the school. It seemed to take ages before he had the courage to turn.

Even in the dark, the whiteness of his face must have been visible at a distance. From the base of the wall the B-Special shouted at the top of his echoing voice,

'Fuck the future.'

AT THE BEACH

They sat opposite each other across the table in the small apartment. He was just out of bed. The first thing he had done was to peer through the slats of the shutters at the view – white apartments, two cranes and, beyond, the blue of the Mediterranean. He wore under-pants and a shirt to cover his stomach. She had risen earlier to go to the Supermercado for some essentials. The *Welcome-pack* was only meant to get them through the night – tea-bags, some sachets of coffee, a packet of plain biscuits.

'The price of cereal would frighten you,' she said. He nodded, trying to open the cardboard milk carton. 'I'm not exactly sure what it is in pounds or pesetas but that packet of All-Bran costs the same as a bottle of brandy.'

'It's worth it for the bowels. The bowels will thank me before the week's out.' He tried to press back the winged flaps of the waxed carton but they bent and he couldn't get it open. 'Fuck this.' He stood up and raked noisily through the drawer of provided cutlery for a pair of scissors. She was looking in the cupboards under the sink.

'Hey – a toaster.' She held it up. He smiled at its strange design – it was as if someone had removed the internal workings of an ordinary toaster. She plugged it in to see if it would work and the wires glowed red almost immediately. The socket was beneath the sink so the toaster could only sit on the floor. 'Stamped with the skull and cross-bones of the Spanish Safety Mark.' She put on two slices of bread.

'Is this goats' milk?' He made a face but persevered spooning the All-Bran into his mouth.

'I didn't get you a paper – they only had yesterday's. And we read yesterday's on the plane.'

'We want a holiday from all that.' He reached down and brushed an ant off his bare foot. 'Did you sleep?'

'It was getting light through the shutters,' she said. 'The crickets went on all night. They're so bloody loud.'

'What's it like outside?'

'Hot – and it'll get worse as the day goes on. The Supermarket has . . .' She laughed. 'I was going to say central heating but I mean . . .' She wobbled her hand above her head.

'Air conditioning.'

'Yeah – you come out onto the street and feel that hot wind – like somebody left a hair-dryer on. The Supermarket's a Spar, would you believe. I thought they only existed in Ireland. And I got Irish butter – here in Spain.'

He killed an ant on the table with his thumb.

'These wee bastards are everywhere.' He bent forward and stared down at the maroon tiled floor. 'Look – Maureen.'

'The toast.' She hunkered down and turned the bread just as it was beginning to smoke.

When they had eaten breakfast they made love and after a while he said, 'I love you,' and when her breath had come back she said,

'Snap.' She reached out and touched the side of his face. 'I mean it, Jimmy,' she said and smiled, hugging him to herself. Their faces were close enough to know they were both smiling.

In the plane Maureen had bought a long-distance Fly-Travel kit which contained light slippers and a neck pillow. It also included some stickers which said *Wake for Meals*. Jimmy stuck one on his forehead and pretended to be asleep. Maureen laughed when she saw it.

'It's what life's all about,' he said. He put on his salesman's voice. 'Have you seen our other bestselling sticker, sir? *We give birth astride the grave.*'

'Wake for meals.' Maureen said it aloud again and laughed. 'Let me have a shower – then we'll find out where this pleasure beach is.'

He laughed and said, 'We *know* where it is.'

They followed the signs which said *Playa*. His hands were joined behind his back, she carried a bag with the camera and the towels and stuff. They stopped on the hill overlooking the beach to study which part of it would suit them best. The place was crowded and colourful.

Sun-beds were stacked at intervals. When they got down they took one each and camped near the beach bar. Jimmy sat on his like a sofa while Maureen stepped out of her dress. She had her bathing suit on. She stood putting sun cream on her shoulders and legs.

'Do my back,' she said, handing him the bottle. She lay on her front on the sun-bed. He squeezed some cream into the palm of his hand and began to rub it into her skin. He looked around him. Most of the women were bare-breasted. Everyone seemed to be tanned. Mediterranean people with jet-black hair and dark olive eyes.

'We're pale as lard,' Jimmy said.

'Only for a day or two. Who cares anyway – nobody knows us here.'

'I care,' he said – then after a pause, 'Nipples the colour of mahogany.'

'What?'

'Never mind.'

'Act your age, Jimmy. They're young enough to be your daughters.'

'I can look, can't I? Anyway, who's talking about girls – the boys have nipples, too.'

When he finished doing her back he did his own arms and legs. He opened his shirt and saw the pallidness of his own skin. If anything, it was whiter than Maureen's.

'Don't forget the top of your feet and . . . your bald spot.'

'I meant to buy a fucking hat.' When he had his body covered with cream he joined his hands and rubbed the top of his head with his moist palms as if he was stretching. Then he lay down on his back. That way his gut was less noticeable.

'Do you miss the girls?' Maureen said.

'Like hell. It's about bloody time we got away by ourselves.' He laughed and said, 'It's like it used to be. Just you and me, baby.'

'It's different now.' Even though her eyes were closed she made an eye-shade cupping her hand over her brow. 'Maybe better.'

'God it's hot.'

'That's what we paid all the money for.'

'Did you remember to put the butter back in the fridge?' Maureen nodded.

'I hate butter when it's slime.'

'I hate *anything* when it's slime.'

'This place makes me so . . .' Jimmy looked around at the people sprawled near him. If they were reading books he could tell by the authors whether or not they were English-speaking. Jilly Cooper, Catherine Cookson, Elizabeth Jane Howard. Others who just lay there sunbathing gave no clue. So he lowered his voice. 'It makes me so fucking randy.'

A couple in their early twenties came up and kicked off their sandals. They dropped all their paraphernalia on the sand and began to undress. Jimmy watched the girl, who was wearing a flimsy beach dress of bright material like a sarong. Beneath she wore a one-piece black swimsuit. The lad pulled off his T-shirt. He was brown with a stomach as lean as a washboard. He said something to his girlfriend and she replied, laughing. They sounded German or Austrian. The girl elbowed her way out of the shoulder straps of her bathing suit and rolled it down, baring her breasts. She continued rolling until the one-piece was like the bottom half of a bikini. They both sat down and the girl took a tube from her basket. She squirted a teaspoonful of white cream onto her midriff and began rubbing it up and over her breasts. They lifted and fell as her hand moved over them. She looked up in Jimmy's direction and he quickly turned his head towards Maureen.

'What?' said Maureen, sensing his movement.

'Nothing.' He shook his head.

About mid-day Jimmy put his shirt on and they went up to the patio of the beach bar for a drink and something to eat. They sat in the shelter of a sun umbrella looking over the beach. The luminous shadow cast by the red material of the umbrella made them look a slightly better colour. Maureen leaned towards him and said,

'Don't look now but I hear Irish voices.'

'Jesus – where?' Jimmy, with his elbows on the table, arched both hands over his brows and pretended to hide.

'Behind me and to the left.'

Jimmy looked over her shoulder. There were three men around a table smoking. They all were wearing shirts and shorts. One of them had a heavy black moustache. Maureen was about to say something when Jimmy shushed her. He listened hard through the foreign talk and rattle of dishes. He heard some flat vowels – but they could have been Dutch or Scottish. American even.

'I'm not sure,' said Jimmy.

'Well, I am.'

'Let's steer well clear.'

A waiter approached their table.

'Try your Spanish,' said Maureen.

'Naw – it's embarrassing.' But when the waiter opened his pad Jimmy said, 'Dos cervezas, por favor.'

'Grande o pequeño?'

Jimmy cleared his throat.

'Uno grande y uno pequeño,' he said.

'That's one large and one small, sir.'

Jimmy nodded. 'Gracias.'

'De nada.' The waiter disappeared indoors to the restaurant. Jimmy raised his eyebrows in a show-off manner.

'Not bad at all,' said Maureen. 'I hate all the th's – like everybody's got a lisp.'

When the beers came they toasted each other. Every time he raised his glass an ice-cold drip would fall down the open front of his shirt onto his belly and startle him. He cursed – thought there was a crack in the glass or the beer mat was wet.

'They put the stupid fuckin beer mat round the stem instead of underneath.' Maureen pointed out to him it was condensation. The beer was cold – the air was hot – condensation formed on the outside of the glass – each time he picked it up it would drip on him. The beer mat round the stem was a none too successful attempt to prevent this.

'You're too smart for your own good,' he said.

393

Maureen looked up at the menu displayed on the wall.

'We'll have to eat a paella some night.'

'Yeah – seafood.'

'It's a kind of enforced intimacy. They only do it for two people.'

'No paella for spinsters.'

'Or priests.'

'If it was in Ireland they'd make it for *his Riverence* and throw the half of it out.'

They both smiled at the thought. There was a long silence between them. Jimmy shifted his white plastic chair closer to hers. His voice dropped to a whisper.

'Who – I don't know whether I should ask this or not . . .'

'What?'

'Naw . . .'

'Go on.'

'Who was the first man you ever did it with?' She stared at him. 'You don't have to tell me – if you don't want to.'

'I don't want to and it's none of your business.' She spoke quietly and without anger.

'Can you remember the first time you had an orgasm? I mean – not even with somebody. By yourself, even.'

'Not really. All that early stuff is smudged together.'

'Come on,' he whispered. 'That's one of those questions like where were you when they shot Kennedy. Everybody knows. The first time that happens to you it's like being in an earthquake or something. You *remember*. It's like your first kiss . . .'

She hesitated and screwed her face up. 'It might have been the back of a car . . .' He leaned forward to hear her better. 'This is nonsense. Why do you want to know?'

'We've been married twenty-five years. We should have no privacy – no secrets from one another.'

'This is just stirring up poison.' She looked away from him at the sea. There were pedalos and wind surfers criss-crossing the bay.

'I just want to know.'

'It's like picking scabs on your knee. No good'll come of it.' She finished her beer and stood up. 'I'm going for a swim.'

When she had gone Jimmy sat staring at the white table top. He raised one finger at the waiter and said,

'La cuenta, por favor.'

They swam and dried off, then reapplied the sun cream. They did each other's back.

'It was a bit nippy getting in at first,' said Maureen. 'I didn't expect that. But it was lovely when you got down.'

The German or Austrian couple had gone off. Jimmy picked them out from the other bathers. They were playing knee-deep in the waves with a velcro ball and bats which fitted onto the hand. If the ball touched the glove even lightly it stuck fast.

Maureen settled down on her front, crossing her arms as a pillow for her cheek. She sighed.

'This is *so* nice. I deserve it.'

'I'm sorry about that – that before the swim – up at the bar. But sometimes – there's a thing in me that . . . wants to *know* about you before I met you. There's a part of me that's jealous of the time when I didn't know you.'

'Jimmy . . .'

'What?'

'You're starting again.'

'Sorry.'

'Where do you think the girls are? Right now,' said Maureen.

'God knows. Half way across the Nevada desert. New Orleans? L.A.? I just hope they don't hitch. Them hitching makes me nervous. Bloody lorry-drivers.'

'They'll be fine.'

The German couple came up the beach, laughing, their hair sleeked and wet. The boy dropped the bat and ball game beside Maureen. The girl rolled down her bathing suit again and lay down on her back just a few feet from Jimmy. She was breathless. Her wet stomach rose and fell as she gasped for breath. Jimmy stared at her. Gradually over a minute or so her breathing became normal. She turned to get the sun on her back and her breasts appeared columnar before she eased herself down.

'How does that work?' Maureen asked.

'What?'

'That bat and ball game.'

'Velcro.'

'Oh . . .'

'Two materials – one has hooks, the other loops. When they hit they stick.'

'I've only seen it used as a zip.'

'It was one of those ideas that came from nature. The burr sticking to the animal hair.'

'Clever balls.'

'I've just expanded your world for you, Maureen. You should be grateful.'

To avoid the risk of sunburn they went back to the apartment at three o'clock. They walked slowly through the heat.

'I feel utterly drained,' said Maureen. There was a flight of steps to where their apartment was and they both paused half way up.

'It's the heat,' said Jimmy and they both smiled at each other. He leaned against the wall which was in shadow. The stones forming the wall were round and porous.

'They build everything here out of Rice Crispies.'

A lizard suddenly appeared on the sunlit side of the wall. 'Behind you Maureen.' She looked and stood still. It had come to a halt in an S-shape. It was bright green. With a flicker of movement it was gone as suddenly as it had appeared.

'Wasn't it lovely to see that?' said Maureen. 'I've never seen one before. They move so fast.'

'They're cold-blooded, that's why they seem so energetic in this heat. It's like us going for a run on a frosty morning.'

'I feel my world expanding all the time.'

The shutters were closed and the place was dark. They had a shower together and Maureen got to choose the luke-warm temperature of the water. Then they made love again.

'We'll not be able to stick the pace', said Jimmy, '– without the kids.'

'Today is lovely but I don't want you – y'know – every time we close that door. We need our own space.' She was boiling the kettle for a coffee and it seemed to take ages. The room was still dark but slivers of the harsh hot light and white buildings could be seen through the top slats of the shutters. Jimmy sat in his white towelling dressing-gown looking down at the table. The ant population had increased since the morning.

'They're after our toast crumbs,' he said. They seemed to be forming a line to and from the table, clustering round a crumb or an almond flake from a biscuit. There were too many now to start killing them.

'Just let them be,' said Maureen. 'It's not as if they bite.'

Jimmy was following the line to its source. Down the table leg and across the kitchen floor to the jamb of the bathroom door. There was a millimetre gap between the wood and the tiles and ants were disappearing into it. Others were coming out.

'There must be a nest somewhere.'

'Or a hill,' said Maureen.

'Maybe they've been on this route for ten million years,' he said. 'Somebody just built this place in their way fifty years ago. This is their track – why should they change just because some bastard of a developer puts a house in their way.'

She poured two coffees and set one on the table for him. She side-stepped the shifting black line of ants and said,

'They do no harm to anybody.'

He decided to watch one – it seemed sure of itself heading away from the table with news of food. It came face to face with others and seemed to kiss, swerve, carry on. Away from the main line there were outriders exploring – wandering aimlessly while in the main line the ants moved like blood cells in a vein.

'There's no point in killing one or two. The whole thing is the organism. It would be like trying to murder somebody cell by cell.'

'Just let them be.'

'The almond crumbs are yours,' he said but still he flicked ants from his bare feet whenever he felt them there.

*

397

The next day they went to the beach and sat in the same place. Jimmy looked around and saw that Jilly Cooper, Catherine Cookson and Elizabeth Jane Howard were just behind him.

'We're all creatures of habit,' he said. 'It's as bad as the fucking staff room.' The mid-day sun made the sand hot to the touch. Maureen had moved from Factor Fifteen and was putting on Factor Six. He did her back for her and she lay down.

'We agreed not to talk about things like that.'

'Okay – okay.'

'Until we get back.'

They lay there roasting for about thirty minutes, Maureen flat out, Jimmy resting on his elbows taking in the view. He had bought a white floppy hat with little or no brim and a pair of sun-glasses in the Supermercado. The glasses gave him greater freedom to look around without noticeably moving his head.

'The Germans are absent,' he said, 'and no note.'

'Which Germans?'

'The Velcro Germans.'

'I didn't realise they were Germans. What is the Assistant Head's particular interest there?'

'Nothing. They just haven't turned up.'

'Liar.'

'The girl is a class act – a bit magnificent.'

Maureen laughed and rubbed a little cream onto her nose with her little finger.

'Do you fancy a walk?' she said.

'Yeah sure.' He put on his shirt and let it hang out over his shorts and they walked to the rocky cliff at the far end of the beach. People here were brown and mostly Spanish-speaking. There was a lot of laughing and shouting.

'It seems to be compulsory not to listen. People all speak at the same time.'

'That's because you don't have the faintest idea what they're saying. Two people from Derry would sound just the same – if you didn't know – if your English . . .'

'They just seem to interrupt each other all the time.'

They swam off the rocks and the water seemed warmer than the previous day. As they walked back across the beach Jimmy took Maureen's hand. They nudged up against each other and fleetingly she put her head against his shoulder.

'This is *so* good,' she said. 'I like Public Displays of Affection – no matter what you say.'

'Why does it matter when nobody knows us?'

'I know us,' she said. 'Sometimes you can be so bloody parochial.'

In the middle of the afternoon the German couple arrived and sat down about three feet to the left of the spot where they had been the day before. From behind his sunglasses Jimmy watched the girl undress. Today she wore the bottom half of a white bikini. He heard the boy use her name. *Heidrun*, he called her. Jimmy tried to nod hello to her but she didn't notice. She shook out, then spread a large towel, adjusting and flattening the corners. All her attention was taken up with her friend.

'They might as well be on a deserted beach in Donegal,' said Jimmy, nodding at the couple. Heidrun knelt down on the spread towel and her boyfriend leaned over and nuzzled into her neck. They both lay down face to face, their feet pointing in Jimmy's direction.

'They'd be covered in goose-pimples,' said Maureen. Jimmy stared at the gusset of the white bikini facing him. It was as if the closeness of the German couple had some influence on them and Jimmy and Maureen moved closer together. He whispered in her ear.

'Why is it that the only woman on the beach who seems to have any pubic hair is you?'

'You mean you go around looking?'

'A man cannot help but notice these things.'

'You mean a Catholic repressed man. A lecher. A man with a problem.'

'You lie there like some kind of a farmer's wife from the backabeyond or . . . or somebody from Moscow.'

'I meant to do it before I came away – but with the rush and all . . . It's not that obvious – is it?' She looked down at herself.

'Not really but . . .'

'Anyway, who's looking at me in that tone of voice – at my age. Catch yourself on, Jimmy. Go and buy me an ice cream.'

He got to his feet and put on his shirt. 'What flavour?'

'The green one with the bits of chocolate in it.'

'What's it called?'

'Jesus, you can point, can't you?'

He fiddled in her purse for pesetas, then went off towards the bar.

At the bar he noticed again the three suspected Irishmen from the first day. They sat beside the counter. Jimmy listened as he pointed out and bought the ice-cream. Maureen was right again. They were definitely from the North of Ireland. They were talking about football. Something about Manchester United and the English league. Two of them wore tartan shirts, the third a T-shirt with Guinness advertising on it.

When he got back to Maureen he gave her the ice-cream.

'I saw your friends up there. I think they're RUC men.'

She licked the peppermint green and crunched a bit of the chocolate.

'What makes you think that?'

'I dunno. They look like Chief Constables or Inspectors. I feel sorry for them. If you were a policeman in the North where would *you* go for your holidays?'

She didn't answer. She nodded towards the German couple.

'There's been plenty of PDA since you left.' She smiled and winked at Jimmy. The couple were lying with their faces an inch apart staring into each other's eyes. Occasionally the boy would trail the back of his knuckles down her naked side. Maureen beckoned Jimmy's ear to her mouth.

'Meine Liebe,' she whispered.

That evening on the patio of *Nino's* they decided to have the seafood paella for two. They had been given complimentary glasses of a local sherry and Jimmy asked to have the order repeated. He would pay for them. As he suspected, when the waitress brought the drinks she said, 'On the house.'

Jimmy drank Maureen's second drink as well as his own two.

When the waiter brought the double paella he showed it to them. They both nodded in appreciation at its presentation. It was served from a much-used, blackened pan and the waiter made sure to divide everything equally. Three open navy blue mussel shells to one plate, three to the other. One red langoustine to you and one to you.

Maureen hated it – wet sloppy rice with too much salt and the most inaccessible parts of shellfish. Things that had to be broken open and scraped, recognisable creatures which had to have their backs snapped and their contents sucked. At one point Maureen raised her eyes and gave a warning to Jimmy. The three Northern Ireland men were sitting down at the next but one table from them. She scrutinised them.

'I'm sure they're not policemen.' They were directly behind Jimmy and he had to twist in his chair to see them. One of them caught his eye and recognised him from the beach. They nodded politely to each other.

'They're like people out of a uniform of some kind,' said Jimmy. 'Maybe they're screws – from Long Kesh.'

'Or security men.'

Maureen gave up on the paella.

'How do you tell a lie in Spanish – it was lovely but there was too much of it?' There was a lull in the noise of conversation and dish-rattling and Maureen heard a name float across from the next but one table. Jimmy said,

'If you are not willing to talk about your early sexual experiences – I am.'

'Not again.'

'In those days I was a vicious bastard – every time I went out with a woman I went straight for the conjugular.'

She laughed and said, 'You think I didn't notice.' She paused and looked at him. 'You made that up.'

'Of course I did. I just said it, didn't I?'

'No I mean you thought it up one day and then waited for a time when you could use it. Tonight's the night.'

He nodded vigorously, pouring himself another glass of wine. Maureen put her hand over the top of her own glass.

Another, different name came floating across from the Northern Ireland table. Maureen made a face as if something was just dawning on her.

'I know,' she said when she had swallowed the food in her mouth. 'They're priests. The first name I heard was Conor and now there's Malachy.'

'Catholic names don't make them priests.'

'But black socks do.'

'Keep your voice down. If we can hear them they can hear us.'

'Two of them's wearing black socks,' whispered Maureen. 'It all fits now. Why would three aging men go away on holiday together?'

'A homosexual ring?'

'They never go *on* the beach. They never take their clothes off. They are keeping an eye on each other. Since the Bishop of Galway nobody trusts anybody else.'

'One of them has a moustache.'

Maureen looked over his shoulder and checked.

'So?'

'I've never seen a priest with a moustache.'

'Maybe there's two of them priests and the one with the moustache is the priest's brother. You're right – the one with the moustache is wearing white towelling socks.' Jimmy checked under the table. Maureen smiled and said, 'There's nothing worse than a priest's brother. All the hang-ups and none of the courage.'

'Are they drinking?'

'Yes.'

'They probably *are* priests then.' They laughed at each other. Jimmy reached out and covered her hand with his. 'Would you like coffee or will we get another bottle?'

'Coffee is fine for me.'

'I'm sorry to go on about this – but there must have been no shortage of men *trying it on* before me.'

Maureen stared at him. 'What is this – where did all this shite suddenly come from, Jimmy?'

'I've just been thinking. Seeing things that remind me. You were a very attractive woman when we first met . . .'

'Gee thanks . . .'

'No I don't mean that. You still are. I'm saying – in comparison to others in the field.'

'In the field – you're making it sound like a cattle fair – have a good look at her teeth.'

'That's a horse fair you're thinking of.'

'Jimmy.' She stared hard at him. 'Teach me how to be right all the time?'

'It wouldn't work – two in the one family.'

'Then one of us would have to leave,' said Maureen. 'It's that time of life. Everybody is leaving everybody else. They stayed together for the kids. Now that's over.'

'You don't feel like that, do you?'

Maureen looked at him and smiled. She shook her head.

'Not yet.'

They walked back to the apartment across the dark beach. They both took off their shoes and walked ankle deep at the water's edge. It was warmer than during the day. There was a white moon reflected on the water. They held hands again until Jimmy stopped for a piss in the sea. Maureen walked on.

In the apartment Jimmy fell down onto the sofa.

'I'm going to have a drink of that duty-free whiskey before it's all drunk.'

'And who's liable to drink it?'

'Me.' He grinned and rose to pour himself one. She laughed at him.

'Have you drunk all *that* since we came here?'

'Lay off. I'm on my holidays too.'

'But we drink a bottle of wine – minus one glass for me – every night as well.'

'Over dinner.'

'That makes no difference.'

'Plus a few beers. Maureen, will you stop counting. And some of that Spanish fucking gin.'

'With no ice.'

'Ice is where the bugs get in.' He diluted his whiskey with bottled water *sin gas* he had bought for the purpose. 'Speaking of which . . .'

He moved to the bathroom and looked down at the tiled floor.

'Holy shit! Maureen will you take a look at this.' He hunkered down and sipped his whiskey.

'Oh my God,' said Maureen. What had been a trickle of ants was now a torrent – a stream that was moving both ways. From the chink in the bathroom tile they moved across the floor in a bristling stream to the table leg, up the table leg onto the table – into the cereal packets. The stream divided and part of it went to the rubbish bin where they had thrown their leftovers – melon rinds, tea-bags, stale bread.

'It's fizzin with them,' said Maureen, lifting a bread wrapper from the bin between her finger and thumb. 'Are they just a fact of life. Will we have to put up with them all the time we're here?'

'As long as they're not in the bed,' said Jimmy. As he stood up some of his whiskey slopped over. The ants panicked, began moving faster. The stream parted and moved around the droplets of whiskey, ignoring it. 'Why don't they get pissed?'

'Maybe they will do – after work,' said Maureen.

'They're really prehistoric, aren't they. And so *silent*. In the movies there would be a soundtrack.'

Maureen made tea with a tea-bag in a mug and they went out onto the small balcony. There was a candle in a bottle left by a previous tenant and Maureen lit it and set it on the white plastic table. Jimmy sipped his whiskey and put his feet up on the balcony rail.

'I just love being in my shirt-sleeves at this time of night. Can you imagine what it's like at home?' Maureen sighed a kind of agreement. The moon was low in the sky and criss-crossed by the struts of two cranes. Had the moon not been there the cranes would have been invisible. Jimmy nodded towards the candle.

'Somebody from the north. Remember that holiday in Norway?' Maureen nodded. 'Candles everywhere. The kids loved it. Flames burning *outside* restaurants. Never pulling their curtains – you could follow people moving from room to room.'

'You certainly did.'

'The electric bills – light shining out of everywhere. Here it's the opposite. Shutters – keep the light out. It's impossible to get the slightest glimpse inside a Spanish or an Italian house.' Jimmy sipped his whiskey and held it in his mouth for a while, savouring it. It was a thing he knew annoyed her. They didn't speak again for some time.

'You *really* don't like to talk about this stuff, do you?'

'No,' she said.

'I just want to know what happened to you before I met you.'

'I've told you everything there is to know – chapter and verse. Everything about my home and school . . .'

'But not sexually. You never mention anything about that.' She sipped her mug of tea holding it with both hands – the way she would sip tea in the winter. 'I'm jealous of not knowing you then. Your school uniform. Your First Communion. I am jealous of all the time I was not with you.'

'That's a kind of adolescent – James Dean – kind of thing to say.'

'I am jealous of every single sexual act *in which I was not involved.*'

She looked at his face in the candle light and realised he was serious.

'Jimmy, why are you torturing yourself about this? Leave it alone. Why should all this come up now – after twenty-five years? Maybe you feel threatened. Now that you're out of shape and balding you feel threatened.'

'Fuck off.'

'I'm going to bed.' She got up and went the long way round the table so he wouldn't have to take his feet down off the balcony rail.

He heard her shut the latch on the bedroom door and the creak of the bed as she got into it. He poured himself another whiskey larger than the last because she was not there to see the size of it. He drank several more glasses equally large and listened to the crickets and the English voices that were continually passing in the street below.

When Maureen woke at 4 am he still had not come to bed. She found him in the chair, his head tilted back, his mouth open and slanting in his face.

'Are you okay, Jimmy?' She put her arm beneath his and got him to his feet. He was mumbling something about 'those fucking priests' as she eased him down onto the bed and started to take his shoes off.

He was sick the next day and, although he tried to hide the fact by going out of the room, Maureen could hear the crinkling of him in the bathroom pressing indigestion tablets out of their tinfoil pack. When she accused him of drinking foolishly he blamed the paella.

'You've never done that in your life before, Jimmy. Not to my knowledge.'

'Got a bit pissed?'

'No – passed out – sitting in your seat.'

'I fell asleep, for fucksake.'

'I'm going to get you one of those wee stickers printed which says *Wake for Drinks*.' Maureen went to the fridge to put away the butter.

'Oh my God,' she said, 'would you look at this?'

'What?'

'There's ants crawling up the rubber seal of the fridge door.'

'We'll have to do something.'

In the coolness of the Supermercado Maureen, with the help of a small Spanish dictionary, made herself understood to the man she liked at the checkout. She wanted to kill ants. The man nodded, went off down between the aisles and came back with an orange-coloured tube.

'You have children?' he asked.

'Yes – two girls.'

He made a face which said – oh well, I don't think this is a good idea. He pointed at the black skull and crossbones on the side of the tube. Maureen realised what he meant and laughed at herself.

'My children are not here. They are big. Away.' He smiled and raised an eyebrow which Maureen interpreted as – you don't look old enough to have grown-up children. It was soft soap but she still liked him.

'Where ants come in.' He directed the nozzle downwards. Maureen nodded that she understood.

When she got back Jimmy was lying on the sofa still looking hung-over. She handed the tube to him and he insisted on looking up the instructions and ingredients in the dictionary.

'Jesus – it seems to be honey and arsenic.'

'The guy says you have to put it down where they're coming in.'

Jimmy heaved himself off the sofa and squatted down by the bathroom door. The stream of ants was now so dense that they blackened the floor in an inch-wide band. Millions coming, millions going. He unscrewed the lid and aimed the oily liquid into the crack they were pouring in and out of.

'Try this for size, my little ones.' Several drops fell on the tiles of the bathroom floor. Jimmy stood up and washed his hands thoroughly. Maureen came to see the effect the stuff was having.

'They are going daft, Jimmy. They're all lining up to drink it. Look at them.' The ants were now streaming in all directions but the main movement was to line up along the edge of the liquid. 'They can't leave it alone. Look they're dying.' The ones on the margin of the poison had ceased to move. Others nudged them aside to get at it. Maureen looked at the tile where the single drops had fallen. Ants had gathered round the edge of the drop and ceased to move.

'They're like eyelashes round an eye,' said Maureen.

'Christ – it's very dramatic stuff.' Jimmy looked down at the floor still drying his hands. 'Goodnight Vienna.'

Maureen went out to go to the beach. If Jimmy felt better he would join her later. She had to pass the Supermercado so she stepped inside and gave the thumbs up to the guy at the checkout about the efficiency of the ant stuff. He nodded his head and smiled.

It was on the way down the hill that it occurred to her that maybe he didn't know what she'd been referring to. She became embarrassed at the thought. Maybe he didn't even know who she was – a man like him would smile at all his customers.

*

It was nice to be on her own. She felt good about herself. Her tan was beginning to be evident without being red. The pale stripe beneath her watch-strap acted as a kind of indicator. She was in no hurry to get to the beach and walked towards the old town looking in shop windows. She did not want to buy anything – just to look. Most of the shops were closed and she realised that it was *siesta*. The streets were empty. It was eerie – like in a movie after the bomb had been dropped. The flat stones of the pavement were hot and shining and she got the notion that she would slip on them if she was not careful. Pasted to a wall were posters for a fiesta which coincided with their last night. There were to be fireworks starting at 11 pm in the square at the harbour front.

She was now moving through an area of the town where she hadn't been before. The façade of a church appeared as she came round a corner. It seemed to grow out of a terrace of houses and looked very old and very Spanish. She walked along the street towards it. She was not knowledgeable about these things but she guessed it was mediaeval. In the curved arch above the door white doves blew out their chests and made cooing, bubbling noises. The main door was huge and ancient – studded with iron nails, each shaped like a pyramid. There was a smaller door cut into it. She tried the handle but found it locked. Now that she was excluded she wanted to see the inside more than ever. Several yards to the left of the main door was another side door. She was unsure whether it belonged to the next house or the church. She tried the handle and it swung open.

'Ah . . .' She stepped in. It wasn't really inside the church but in a colonnade alongside. At this end it was dark and cool but the far end was brilliant with sunshine. In between the colonnade of columns, arches of shadow sliced onto the walkway. She had a memory of looking out from a dark wood into sunlight. The door closed behind her with a rattle as the catch clicked. There appeared to be no way into the church from here. She walked down the colonnade towards the sunshine, listening to the slight itching sound the soles of her shoes made with the sandstone floor. The arches were curved, held up by pillars of blond stone which got lighter

and lighter as they neared the source of the sunlight. Was she
sufficiently dressed to go into the church? Her white T-shirt left
her arms bare, but nobody could object to her Bermuda-length
shorts. She felt slightly nervous – like a child expecting to be scolded
for trespassing or intruding where she had no right to be. What if
some *Monsignor* were to turn the corner and begin shouting at her
in Spanish, yelling at her that this was the Holy of Holies. She
paused and thought of going back. But she was so curious to see
what lay beyond the source of the light. She walked hesitantly
down the arcade and came upon a small square. It took her breath.
There was something about it which made her love it with an
intensity she had rarely experienced. There was no fear now of
being caught. In some way she felt she had the right to be here. It
was a square or atrium made of the same blond stone as the columns
which formed the cloisters around its perimeter. In the centre was
what looked like a font set up on a dais of steps. It had a spindly
canopy of wrought iron. Maureen moved near the font and turned
slowly to look around her with her head tilted back, looking up.
Windows, three sets in each wall, overlooked the small courtyard
but there appeared to be no one living behind them. There were
no shutters, no curtains. Empty rooms. The sun was almost directly
overhead. When she sat down on the steps the stone was warm.
She was aware of the absolute silence – aware that outside this
cloister was the quietness of a town in *siesta*. Inside, everything
was intensified. Suddenly the silence was broken by the clattering
of wings as several white doves flew onto the tiled roof. Maureen
stood up and climbed the steps to the font. She leaned her elbows
on the rim and looked at the round hole or shaft in the middle of
it. She gave a little jump and leaned on her forearms, her feet off
the ground, and looked down into the shaft. There was a white
disc at the bottom.

'It's a well.' She unslung her bag from her shoulder and found a
25 peseta coin – the one with a hole in it – and dropped it down.
Nothing happened and she was amazed at the silence. How could
there be nothing? Where was the sound of the coin dropping into
the water below –

spluck!

She couldn't believe the depth. She took another coin and dropped it and counted as if making an exposure. A thousand and one – silence – a thousand and two – silence – a thousand and three – still silence – a thou –

spluck!

She heaved herself up again and looked into the well. The disc of light at the bottom rippled. There was something so *right* about this place. It was affecting her body. Her knees began to tremble. She held tight to the well head. She had to sit down on the steps and lean her back against the font.

She sat for the best part of an hour, sunbathing and absorbing the place. Occasionally she changed her position on the steps or walked in and out of the shadow of the cloisters. The place emphasised her aloneness. It felt as if it had been made for her and she should share it with no one. The cloister was a well for light – the cloister was a well for water. The word *Omphalos* came into her head. She connected the word to a poem of Heaney's she'd read somewhere. The stone that marked the centre of the world. The navel.

The sunlight and the clarity of the air squeezed into such a small space by the surrounding roofs became a lens which made her see herself with more precision. She did not think of herself as a middle-aged woman – she was still the same person she had been all her life – a child being bathed by her own mother – a teenager kissing. She was the same bride, the same mother-to-be in white socks and stirrups on the delivery table. Her soul was the same as that younger girl. She *felt* the same.

Soul was a word. What did it mean? People talked of stripping away layers to reveal the soul. It was not buried deep within her. It wasn't like that at all. Her soul was herself – it was the way she treated other people, it was the love for her children, for the people around her and for people she had never seen but felt responsible for. Her soul was the way she treated the world – ants and all.

She smiled at herself. In this place she knew who she was. In the hour she'd been here it had become sacred. She would remember this haven – this cloister – for the rest of her life.

By the time she got to the beach Jimmy was already there. He was lying flat out on a sun-bed with his back to the sun. Maureen went up and nudged his elbow with her shin.

'Hi.'

'Buenos días,' he said. He looked up sideways at her. 'Where have you been?'

'Around. I went up into the old town.'

'See anything?'

'The shops were closed. So was the church. Siesta.'

'What kept you?'

'Exploring. I had a coffee. Sat in an old courtyard for a while.' It was too late in the day to get the value out of lying on a sunbed so she began spreading a towel, having flapped it free of sand. 'Oh there's a fiesta tomorrow night – fireworks, specially for us leaving.'

'That's nice of them.'

'How are you feeling now?'

'Hunky dory.' But he groaned all the same when he was turning over to get the sun on his chest. He cradled the back of his head in his hands and from between his feet watched the German girl and her boyfriend. 'You missed it earlier on,' he said. 'I'm sure she was lying on his hand.'

'Jimmy – leave them alone. Don't be such a . . .'

'Remember that?'

'Sometimes I don't know what goes on in men's minds.' She took off her shorts and T-shirt and lay down on the carefully spread towel. The beach was noisy – an English crowd were shouting their heads off at the water's edge – there was a baby crying having its nappy changed – euro-pop played and dishes rattled constantly in the beach café. 'Or whether they've got minds at all.'

The next evening before they went out to eat they decided to try and get the whiskey 'used up' before going home. Because it was their last night they decided to dress up a bit. They sat on the balcony while it was still light. Maureen had a small whiskey and he a much bigger one.

'I better leave enough for a nightcap,' said Jimmy.

'But you'll be drinking all evening.'

'A nightcap's a nightcap. We judged the bottle well.'

'We?'

'Almost as well as the All-Bran. If we were to stay here a day longer the bowels would grind to a halt.'

They sat staring at the view – the sea straight at the horizon – the white buildings, the palm trees, the cranes.

'I'm going to miss this,' said Maureen. All that week they had seen no-one working on the unfinished apartments. The cranes were unmanned but they moved imperceptibly – at no time did they respond like a weather vane to the wind but whenever Maureen or Jimmy had occasion to look up the cranes would be in different positions and at different angles to each other.

'The recession must be hitting here too,' said Jimmy.

'It's back to normal next week.'

'Don't mention it – don't ruin our last night.'

'I think – I've been thinking . . . now that the kids are practically gone I might try and get a job.'

'Doing what?'

She shrugged.

'I might train for something.'

'At your age?' said Jimmy. 'No chance.'

'Why do you always put me down?'

'I'm just being *realistic*, Maureen.'

'I got three distinctions in A levels. I held a good job in the photo works up until you came along.'

'They were the days of black and white.' He laughed.

'They were the days when they sacked you for being pregnant.'

He finished his whiskey and stood.

'We'd better go if we want to eat *and* firework. Do I look okay?'

'Yeah, fine.' She picked a few grey hairs off the collar of his navy blazer and dusted away some dandruff.

'You look good,' he said and kissed her.

During the meal in the restaurant Jimmy drank three-quarters of the bottle of wine. He dismissed white wine as not drinking at all – 'imbibing for young girls', he called it. By the time they'd had their coffee Jimmy had finished the bottle. Maureen noticed that he was looking over her shoulder more than usual during the meal. She glanced round and saw an attractive, tanned girl in a white dress sitting by herself.

'She's lovely, isn't she?' said Jimmy.

Maureen nodded. 'Why's she by herself?'

'Because her lover has just gone to the crapper.'

'And there was me building a romantic story . . .'

'Do you want the rest of your wine?'

Maureen shook her head. He poured what was left of her glass into his.

'Get the bill, Jimmy.' He put his arm in the air and attracted the attention of the waiter. Left alone again he said,

'A woman by herself is the most erotic thought a man can have.'

'What d'you mean?'

'By herself she is the complete item. The brain, the body, the emotions. In the shower, in bed. Uninterfered with. Herself.'

'I still don't understand.'

'Sexy. Absorbed. Unreachable. Aloof. Detached.'

'I thought sexy was the opposite of detached.'

'A woman in a shop', said Jimmy, 'by herself is absorbed – choosing something to wear – looking through a rack of dresses.'

'Or even studying a book – or even *writing* a book.'

'You're really fucking bolshie this evening.'

The partner of the woman in white returned to the table.

'He's back,' said Jimmy. Maureen twisted in her seat to see.

'They can't be married,' she said. 'She smiled at him. That's very early days. Second or third date.'

'Remember that?'

She smiled and put her hand on his.

'I do,' said Maureen. 'Vividly.'

'That was a time of finding out . . . of knowing everything there is to know . . . There must be no privacy between people in love.'

'Crap Jimmy. You're talking the impossible. Anyway, there can never be a situation where you know *everything* about another person. It's harder to know one thing *for sure*.'

'Maybe.'

'When there's nothing left to know there's no mystery. We would all be so utterly predictable.'

The waiter brought the bill and they paid and left. Maureen checked her watch and saw there were only a couple of minutes before the fireworks were due to start. They walked quickly towards the main square.

It was a large open area overlooking the harbour. At the back of the square were the dark shapes of civic buildings. Gardens and pavements and steps descended to the sea. There were trees of different varieties symmetrically spaced. Looped between the trees were what looked like fairy lights but they were not working. Jimmy pointed them out to Maureen and laughed.

'They're about as organised as the Irish,' he said. 'If they had a microphone it'd whine.'

The square was filled with local people waiting for the fireworks. Amongst them, holidaymakers like Jimmy and Maureen were obvious.

Suddenly there was a whoosh of a rocket followed by an ear-shattering bang. Both Maureen and Jimmy jumped visibly. There was a sound of drums and the raucous piping noise of a shawm and ten or so figures pranced into the middle of the square.

'It's the fucking Ku-Klax-Klan,' said Jimmy.

They were dressed in white overalls, some like sheets, some like rough suits. Their heads were hidden in triangular hoods with eye-slits. Two or three of them were whacking drums, all of them were dancing – leaping and cart-wheeling.

'I don't like the look of these guys.'

'They're really spooky.'

'Like drunk ghosts.'

'They're more like your man – Miro,' said Maureen. The figures danced and dervished around, whirling hand-held fireworks and scattering fire crackers amongst the crowd who screamed and jostled out of their way.

'Jumpin jinnies, we used to call those,' shouted Maureen. The troupe of dancers pushed sculptures on wheels with fireworks attached – shapes of crescent moons, of angular trees, of whirling globes – from which rockets and Roman candles burst red and green and yellow over the heads of the public. Between the feet of the bystanders crackers exploded. The air was filled with screams of both adults and children as they leapt away from them.

'Jesus – this is so dangerous,' said Jimmy. 'They're breaking every regulation in the book.' The drums pounded and the pipe screeched on. As the sculptures were swung round they gushed sparks – sometimes it looked as if the sculptures moved *because* of the sparks – jet-propelled.

'Those robes must be fire-proofed. This wouldn't be allowed at home. It scares the shit outa me – All-Bran or no All-Bran.'

'It's so utterly primitive – prehistoric,' said Maureen.

'How could it be prehistoric. Gunpowder was invented in the middle ages.'

'There would have been an equivalent – fire, torches, sparks.'

'Come on let's get outa here before somebody gets hurt.'

The troupe had split up and before Jimmy and Maureen could move three dancers had run up the steps and appeared behind them. Close up their robes were embroidered with Miro-like symbols. One of them held aloft a thing that looked like the spokes of an umbrella. Suddenly it burst into roaring fire – five Catherine wheels with whistles on them spraying sparks in every direction. They rained down on the crowd – white magnesium sparks – drenching them in light and danger and everyone screamed and covered their heads with their hands.

'Fucking hell,' shouted Jimmy. Maureen saw the white hot sparks bouncing off the cobblestones like dashing rain – white, intense, like welder's sparks. She tried to cover her head – she knew the skin of her shoulders was bare. But she felt nothing. Neither did Jimmy. They ran, Jimmy elbowing his way through the crowd away from the dancers, pulling Maureen after him by the hand. On the edge of the crowd they looked at each other and laughed.

'They're like kids' hand-held fireworks,' said Jimmy. 'They're harmless. Fuckin sparklers.'

'Are you sure?'

'I'm not going back to check, I'll tell you that.'

Again there was a series of enormous explosions just above their heads so that Maureen screamed out. What Jimmy had thought were broken fairy lights were fire crackers going off a few feet above their heads. They both ran holding hands.

They stopped at a small pavement area outside a bistro still in sight of the fireworks and they were both given a free sherry. The three supposed priests sat at a table near the door. They nodded recognition to each other. Jimmy ordered Menorcan gin and because he was going home the next evening allowed the barman to fill the glass with ice. They sat at the same side of the table, shoulder to shoulder, at a safe distance from the fireworks.

'It's pure street theatre,' said Maureen. 'The audience are involved because of their fear. The adrenalin flows. The costumes, the music, the fire –'

'It could never happen at home.'

'Yeah, we kill people outright.'

'The danger brings pleasure. It involves the audience totally.'

'Look,' said Jimmy. The young German couple were walking away from the fireworks. They had an arm around each other. They stopped to kiss and the boy slid both his hands down onto Heidrun's backside to hold her closer.

'They make a fine couple – even though we don't know their language.' When the kiss was finished the lovers walked past the bistro. The boy's hand was worming its way down the back of her shorts and Heidrun was leaning her blonde head against his shoulder.

Jimmy mimicked the gesture and laid his head on Maureen's bare shoulder.

'I'd still be interested to know how far you went with previous – the men before me? You knew some pretty good tricks.'

She looked at him tight-lipped then moved away from his head.

'I wouldn't like to see you with another man *now* – but I'd like to have seen you with one *then*.'

'This got us nowhere before,' she said quietly. 'Jimmy, give it a rest.'

'No, why should I? Tell me about the first time you came, then.'

'I would if I could – if it's SO important to you. But I can't so I won't. Would you like to ask your daughters this question the next time you see them?'

'Don't be stupid. That's a totally different thing.'

'I don't see why.'

'Why can't you tell me?' said Jimmy. 'You're repressed. Why can't we talk openly about this?'

'It's *you* that's repressed,' she almost shouted, 'wanting to know stuff like that. It's becoming a fixation.'

'It was a question I'd always wanted to ask. I thought – what better time. Holiday. Alone. No kids.'

'No time is a good time for questions like that.'

When she lifted her sherry her hand was shaking.

'Don't make such a big thing of it.'

'When you do those kind of things with people there's a pact – a kind of unspoken thing – that it's private – that it's just between the two of you. Secrecy is a matter of honour.'

'So you *have* done it.'

'No – *don't be so stupid* – it could be just kissing or affection or kidding on or flirting. Whatever it was it's none of your fucking business.'

She did not finish her sherry but got to her feet.

'I'm going home. You can stay here with your priests, if you like.'

At about three o'clock Jimmy crawled into bed beside her and wakened her from a deep sleep. He was drunk and crying and apologising and patting her shoulder and telling her how good she was and how much she meant to him and that he would never ever ever leave her.

He was a pest but that's the way he was and she could like it or lump it. But she was a wonderful woman.

'Jimmy, shut up – will you?' Now that he had disturbed her she got up and went to the bathroom. When she came back he was snoring loudly. She closed the latch of the bedroom door so that he wouldn't waken and tried to get some sleep on the sofa. She felt alone on the narrow rectangle of foam – lonely even – a very different feeling to the wonderful solitariness she had experienced in the cloisters. She couldn't sleep. The thought of leaving Jimmy came into her head but it seemed so impossibly difficult, not part of any reality. Nothing bad enough had happened – or good enough – to force her to examine the possibility seriously. Where would she live? How could she tell the girls? What would she tell her parents? Jimmy was right about getting a job. It seemed so much simpler to stay as they were. The status quo. People stayed together because it was the best arrangement. She slept eventually and in the morning she could not distinguish when her deliberations had tailed off and turned to dreaming.

'Jimmy, I think we should try and salvage something from the last day.' She spoke to wake him. Startled, he turned in the bed to face the room. Maureen had the large suitcase open on the floor. She was holding one of his jackets beneath her chin then folding the arms across the chest. She packed it into the case, then reached for another. Jimmy tried not to groan. He sat on the side of the bed and slowly realised he was still in his clothes. She must have taken his shoes off him. He put his bald head in his hands.

'Is the kettle boiled?'

'It was – a couple of hours ago.'

He got up and finished the packet of All-Bran – bran dust at this stage. He made tea and a piece of toast in the skeletal toaster. Maureen continued to pack.

'What time's the flight?' he asked.

'Eighteen hundred hours.'

'I hate those fucking times. What time is that?'

'Minus twelve. Six o'clock.'

Jimmy had a shower and changed his clothes. After he cleaned his teeth he packed everything in sight into his washbag. He came out of the bathroom with a towel round his middle. He was grinning. Maureen was kneeling on the floor packing dirty washing into a Spar plastic bag.

'I've got the hang-over horn.'

'Well, that's just too bad. There's things to be done.'

'Indeed there are.'

Maureen got a brush and a plastic dust-pan. The living room floor was scritchy with sand spilled from their shoes. Earlier in the week Jimmy had knocked over a tumbler and it had exploded on the tiled floor into a million tiny fragments. She thought she had swept them all up at the time but still she was finding dangerous shards in the dust.

Between the bathroom and the living room the dead ants still blackened the margins of the honey-poison. There was no mop and she had not wanted to sweep them up and make the floor sticky underfoot. Now it didn't seem to matter and she swept the whole mess onto the dust pan. Individual ants had lost their form and were now just black specks. She turned on the tap and washed them down the plug hole.

Jimmy was sent down the street to the waste-bins while she put any usable food in the fridge as a gift for whoever cleaned up. When he came back everything was done and the cases were sitting in the middle of the floor. Maureen was drinking a last coffee and there was one on the table for him.

He stood behind her chair and put his arms round her.

'I'm sorry,' he said. 'About last night. Going on and on about those . . .' He kissed the top of her hair.

'Jimmy – promise me. You mustn't annoy me about that again.'

'Okay – scout's honour.' He began massaging the muscles which joined her neck and shoulders.

'Oh – easy – that hurts.'

'What time do we have to vacate this place?'

'Mid-day.'

He bent over and whispered, 'That gives us twenty minutes.'

They left their luggage at the Tour company headquarters for the remaining hours and went down to the beach. They walked along to the rocky promontory at the far side.

'I've really enjoyed this,' said Jimmy. 'The whole thing.'

'Who did you meet up with last night?'

'They said they were social workers. Which means they admitted to being priests in mufti. They were okay.'

'What did you talk about?'

'I'm afraid eh . . . Large chunks of it are missing. We seemed to laugh a lot. I think they were every bit as pissed as I was.'

'I don't like the look of them. They're the kind of people who'd go out of their way to take a short cut.'

They sat on the rocks watching the sea swell in and out at their feet.

'It's very clear,' said Jimmy. The water was blue-green, transparent.

'You can be a real pest when you come in like that. You look so *stupid.*'

'Sorry.'

They became aware of an old couple in bathing suits paddling into the sea close by the rocks. They looked like they were in their eighties. The woman wore a pink bathing cap which was shaped like a conical shell. Her wrinkled back was covered in moles or age spots as if someone had thrown a handful of wet sand at her back. The old man had the stub of an unlit cigar clamped in the corner of his mouth. Their skin was sallow. Mediterranean but paler than those around them for not having been exposed to the sun – although their faces and arms were the nut-brown colour of people who had worked in the open. The old man was taking the woman by the elbow and speaking loudly to her in Spanish, scolding her almost. But maybe she was deaf or could not hear, her ears being covered by the puce conical cap. She was shaking her head, her features cross. They were thigh-deep and wading. When the water rose to her waist she began to make small stirring motions with her hands as if she were performing the breast stroke. She made the sign of the cross. The old man shouted at her again. She dismissed him with a wave of her hand, then submerged herself by crouching down. She kept her face out of the water. The old man reached out from where he stood and cupped his hand under her chin. She began to make the breast-stroke motions with her arms, this time *in* the water. The old man shouted encouragement to her. She swam about ten or twelve strokes unaided until she swallowed sea water, coughed and threshed to her feet. The old man yelled and flung his damp cigar stub out to sea.

'Jesus – he's teaching her to swim.' Jimmy turned and looked up at his wife. Maureen was somewhere between laughing and crying.

'That's magic,' she said. 'What a bloody magic thing to do.'

THE WAKE HOUSE

At three o'clock Mrs McQuillan raised a slat of the venetian blind and looked at the house across the street.

'Seems fairly quiet now,' she said. Dermot went on reading the paper. 'Get dressed son and come over with me.'

'Do I have to?'

'It's not much to ask.'

'If I was working I couldn't.'

'But you're not – more's the pity.'

She was rubbing foundation into her face, cocking her head this way and that at the mirror in the alcove. Then she brushed her white hair back from her ears.

'Dermot.'

Dermot threw the paper onto the sofa and went stamping upstairs.

'And shave,' his mother called after him.

He raked through his drawer and found a black tie someone had lent him to wear at his father's funeral. It had been washed and ironed so many times that it had lost its central axis. He tried to tie it but as always it ended up off-centre.

After he had changed into his good suit he remembered the shaving and went to the bathroom.

When he went downstairs she was sitting on the edge of the sofa wearing her Sunday coat and hat. She stood up and looked at him.

'It's getting very scruffy,' she said, 'like an accordion at the knees.' Standing on her tip-toes she picked a thread off his shoulder.

'Look, why are we doing this?' said Dermot. She didn't answer him but pointed to a dab of shaving cream on his earlobe. Dermot removed it with his finger and thumb.

'Respect. Respect for the dead,' she said.

'You'd no respect for him when he was alive.'

She went out to the kitchen and got the bag for the shoe things and set it in front of him. Dermot sighed and opened the drawstring mouth. Without taking his shoes off he put on polish using the small brush.

'Eff the Pope and No Surrender.'

'Don't use that word,' she said. 'Not even in fun.'

'I didn't use it. I said eff, didn't I?'

'I should hope so. Anyway it's not for him, it's for her. She came over here when your father died.'

'Aye, but he didn't. Bobby was probably in the pub preparing to come home and keep us awake half the night.'

'He wasn't that bad.'

'He wasn't that good either. Every Friday in life. Eff the Pope and NO Surrender.' Dermot grinned and his mother smiled.

'Come on,' she said. Dermot scrubbed hard at his shoes with the polishing-off brush then stuck it and the bristles of the smaller one face to face and dropped them in the bag. His mother took a pair of rosary beads out of her coat pocket and hung them on the Sacred Heart lamp beneath the picture.

'I'd hate to pull them out by mistake.'

Together they went across the street.

'I've never set foot in this house in my life before,' she whispered, 'so we'll not stay long.'

After years of watching through the window, Mrs McQuillan knew that the bell didn't work. She flapped the letter-box and it seemed too loud. Not respectful. Young Cecil Blair opened the door and invited them in. Dermot awkwardly shook his hand, not knowing what to say.

'Sorry eh . . .'

Cecil nodded his head in a tight-lipped way and led them into the crowded living-room. Mrs Blair in black sat puff-eyed by the fire. Dermot's mother went over to her and didn't exactly shake hands but held one hand for a moment.

'I'm very sorry to hear . . .' she said. Mrs Blair gave a tight-lipped nod very like her son's and said,

'Get Mrs McQuillan a cup of tea.'

Cecil went into the kitchen. A young man sitting beside the widow saw that Mrs McQuillan had no seat and made it his excuse to get up and leave. Mrs McQuillan sat down, thanking him. Cecil leaned out of the kitchen door and said to Dermot,

'What are you having?'

'A stout?'

Young Cecil disappeared.

'It's a sad, sad time for you,' said Mrs McQuillan to the widow. 'I've gone through it myself.' Mrs Blair sighed and looked down at the floor. Her face was pale and her forehead lined. It looked as if tears could spring to her eyes again at any minute.

The tea, when it came, was tepid and milky but Mrs McQuillan sipped it as if it was hot. She balanced the china cup and saucer on the upturned palm of her hand. Dermot leaned one shoulder against the wall and poured his bottle of stout badly, the creamy head welling up so quickly that he had to suck it to keep it from foaming onto the carpet.

On the wall beside him there was a small framed picture of the Queen when she was young. It had been there so long the sunlight had drained all the reds from the print and only the blues and yellows remained. The letter-box flapped on the front door and Cecil left Dermot standing on his own. There were loud voices in the hall – too loud for a wake house – then a new party came in – three of them, all middle-aged, wearing dark suits. In turn they shook hands with Mrs Blair and each said, 'Sorry for your trouble.' Their hands were red and chafed. Dermot knew them to be farmers from the next townland but not their names. Cecil asked them what they would like to drink. One of them said,

'We'll just stick with the whiskey.' The others agreed. Cecil poured them three tumblers.

'Water?'

'As it is. Our healths,' one of them said, half raising his glass. They all nodded and drank. Dermot heard one of them say,

'There'll be no drink where Bobby's gone.' The other two began to smile but stopped.

Dermot looked at his mother talking to the widow.

'It'll come to us all,' she said. 'This life's only a preparation.'

'Bobby wasn't much interested in preparing,' said the widow. 'But he was good at heart. You can't say better than that.' Everybody in the room nodded silently.

Someone offered Dermot another stout, which he took. He looked across at his mother but she didn't seem to notice. The two women had dropped their voices and were talking with their heads close together.

One of the farmers – a man with a porous nose who was standing in the kitchen doorway – spoke to Dermot.

'Did you know Bobby?'

Dermot shook his head. 'Not well. Just to see.' He had a vision of the same Bobby coming staggering up the street about a month ago and standing in front of his own gate searching each pocket in turn for a key. It was a July night and Dermot's bedroom window was open for air.

'I see your curtains moving, you bastards.' A step forward, a step back. A dismissive wave of the hand in the direction of the McQuillans'. Then very quietly,

'Fuck yis all.'

He stood for a long time, his legs agape. A step forward, a step back. Then he shouted at the top of his voice,

'Fuck the Pope and . . .'

Dermot let the curtains fall together again and lay down. But he couldn't sleep waiting for the No Surrender. After a while he had another look but the street was empty. No movement except for the slow flopping of the Union Jack in Bobby Blair's garden.

Cecil came across the room and set a soup-plate full of crisps on the hall table beside Dermot.

'Do you want to go up and see him?'

Dermot set his jaw and said,

'I'd prefer to remember him as he was.'

'Fair enough.'

The man with the porous nose shook his head in disbelief.

'He was a good friend to me. Got my son the job he's in at the minute.'

'Bully for him.'

A second farmer dipped his big fingers in the dish and crunched a mouthful of crisps. He swallowed and said to Dermot,

'How do you know the deceased?'

'I'm a neighbour. From across the street.'

'Is that so? He was one hell of a man. One hell of a man.' He leaned over to Dermot and whispered, 'C'mere. Have you any idea what he was like? ANY idea?'

Dermot shook his head. The farmer with the porous nose said,

'When Mandela got out he cried. Can you believe that? I was with him – I saw it. Big fuckin tears rolling down his cheeks. He was drunk, right enough, but the tears was real. I was in the pub with him all afternoon. It was on the TV and he shouts – what right have they, letting black bastards like that outa jail when this country's hoachin with fuckin IRA men?'

He laughed – a kind of cackle with phlegm – and Dermot smiled.

The signs that his mother wanted to go were becoming obvious. She sat upright on the chair, her voice became louder and she permitted herself a smile. She rebuttoned her coat and stood up. Dermot swilled off the rest of his stout and moved to join her on the way out. The widow Blair stood politely.

'Would you like to go up and see him, Mrs McQuillan?' she said.

'I'd be too upset,' she said. 'It'd bring it all back to me.' Mrs Blair nodded as if she understood. Cecil showed them out.

In their own hallway Mrs McQuillan hung up her coat and took an apron off a peg.

'Poor woman,' she said. 'Did they ask you to go up and see him?'

'Aye.'

'Did you go?' Her hands whirled behind her back tying the strings of the apron.

'Are you mad? Why would I want to see an oul drunk like Bobby Blair laid out?'

He went into the living room and began poking the fire. Their house and the Blairs' were exactly the same – mirror images of each other. His mother went into the kitchen and began peeling potatoes. By the speed at which she worked and the rattling noises she made

Dermot knew there was something wrong. She came to the kitchen doorway with a white potato in her wet hands.

'You should have.'

'Should have what?'

'Gone up to see him.'

'Bobby Blair!' Dermot dropped the poker on the hearth and began throwing coal on the fire with tongs.

'Your father would have.'

'They asked *you* and you didn't.'

'It's different for a woman.'

She turned back to the sink and dropped the potato in the pot and began scraping another. She spoke out to him.

'Besides I meant what I said – about bringing it all back.'

Dermot turned on the transistor and found some pop music. His mother came to the door again drying her hands on her apron.

'That poor woman,' she said. 'It was bad enough having to live with Bobby.' She leaned against the door jamb for a long time. Dermot said nothing, pretending to listen to the radio. She shook her head and clicked her tongue.

'The both of us refusing . . .'

As they ate their dinner, clacking and scraping forks, she said,

'It looks that bad.'

'What?'

'The both of us.'

Dermot shrugged.

'What can we do about it?'

She cleaned potato off her knife onto her fork and put it in her mouth.

'You could go over again. Say to her.'

'What?'

'Whatever you like.'

'I don't believe this.'

She cleared away the plates and put them in the basin. He washed and she dried.

'For your father's sake,' she said. Dermot flung the last spoon onto the stainless steel draining-board and dried his hands on the dish towel, a thing he knew she hated.

He slammed the front door and stood for a moment. Then he walked across the street, his teeth clenched together, and flapped the letter-box. This time the door was opened by a man he didn't know. Dermot cleared his throat.

'I'd like to see Bobby,' he said. The man looked at him.

'Bobby's dead.'

'I know.'

The man stepped back then led the way into the hallway. The farmers were now standing at the foot of the stairs. The one with the porous nose was sitting on the bottom step swirling whiskey in his glass.

'Ah – it's the boy again,' he said. The man led the way up the stairs. Dermot excused himself and tried to slip past the sitting farmer. He felt a hand grab his ankle and he nearly fell. The grip was tight and painful. The farmer laughed.

'I'm only pulling your leg,' he said. Then he let go. It was like being released from a manacle. Somebody shouted out from the kitchen.

'A bit of order out there.'

In the bedroom the coffin was laid on the bed, creating its own depression in the white candlewick coverlet. The man stood back with his hands not joined but one holding the other by the wrist. Dermot tried to think of the best thing to do. In a Catholic house he would have knelt, blessed himself and pretended to say a prayer. He could have hidden behind his joined hands. Now he just stared – conscious of the stranger's eyes on the back of his neck. The dead man's face was the colour of a mushroom, his nostrils wide black triangles of different sizes. Fuck the Pope and No Surrender. Dermot held his wrist with his other hand and bowed his head. Below the rim of the coffin there was white scalloped paper like inside an expensive box of biscuits. The paper hid almost everything except Bobby's dead face. Instead of candles the room was full of flowers. The only light came through the drawn paper blinds.

From downstairs came the rattle of the letter-box and the man murmured something and went out. Left alone Dermot inched nearer the coffin. His father was the only dead person he had ever seen. He pulled the scalloped paper back and looked beneath it. Bobby was wearing a dark suit, a white shirt and tie. Where his lapels should have been was his Orange sash – the whole regalia. All dressed up and nowhere to go. Dermot looked up and saw a reflection of himself prying in the dressing-table mirror. He let the scalloped paper drop back into place. Footsteps approached on the stairs.

Two oldish women were shown in by the stranger. One was Mavis Stewart, the other one worked in the papershop. Mavis looked at the corpse and her lower lip trembled and she began to weep. The women stood between Dermot and the door. Tears ran down the woman's face and she snuffled wetly. The woman from the papershop held onto her and Mavis nuzzled into her shoulder. She kept repeating, 'Bobby, Bobby – who'll make us laugh now?' Dermot edged his way around the bed and stood waiting. The women took no notice. Mavis began to dry her tears with a lavender tissue.

'I never met a man like him for dancing. He would have danced the legs off you. And he got worse when the rock and roll came in.' Dermot coughed, hoping they would move and let him pass.

'And the twist,' said the woman from the papershop. 'I think that boy wants out.'

Mavis Stewart said,

'Sorry love,' and squeezed close to the bed to let him pass. Dermot nodded to the stranger beside the wardrobe.

'I'm off.'

'I'll show you out.' The stranger went downstairs with him and went to open the front door. Dermot hesitated.

'Maybe I'd better say hello to Mrs Blair. Let her see I've been up. Seeing Bobby.'

He knocked on the living-room door.

'Yes? Come on in.'

He opened it. Mrs Blair was still sitting by the fire. She was surrounded by the three farmers. Dermot said,

'I was just up seeing Mr Blair.'

'Very good, son. That was nice of you.' Then her face crumpled and she began to cry. The farmer with the porous nose put a hand on her arm and patted it. Dermot was going to wave but checked his arm in time. He backed into the hallway just as young Cecil appeared out of the kitchen. It was young Cecil who showed Dermot out.

'Thanks for coming,' he said. 'Again.'

IN BED

The buzzer sounded long and hard – a rasp which startled her even though she knew to expect it – maybe *because* she knew to expect it. She splayed her book on the carpet so as not to lose her place and went across the hall to her daughter's bedroom – moving quickly because the long buzz created a sense of urgency. The girl was crouched on the bed, her face turned towards the door in panic.

'Mum, another one,' she said and pointed to her hand pressed down hard on the pillow.

'Take it easy. Relax.' Her mother hurried out of the bedroom and came back with an empty pint glass from the kitchen.

'How can I relax with a thing like that in bed? It might breed, might be laying eggs.'

'Wait.'

'Dad uses a bar of soap. Don't let it get away.' The girl's face was anxious and much whiter than usual. She was wearing pyjama bottoms and a football shirt of red and white hoops. 'I hate them – I hate them.' Her voice was shaking. Her mother approached the pillow with the pint glass inverted.

'Easy now – lift your hand.'

The girl plucked her hand away. The black speck vanished – it was there, then, suddenly, it wasn't – before the glass could be slammed down. The girl screamed.

'It's jumped.'

'Blast.'

The girl held her hair back from her face, peering down at the surface of the sheet.

'It's gone – it's got away.'

'Aw no . . .'

'Oh I hate them, I really hate them.' The girl's voice was on the edge of tears. She was shuddering. 'They make me feel so . . . dirty.' Her mother bent over and stared closely at the surface of the white sheet, pulling it towards her a little to flatten a wrinkle.

'Don't move,' she whispered. The girl gave a little gasp.

'Where? Where is it?'

Her mother raised the glass and quickly pressed it down onto the sheet.

'Gotcha.'

The girl bent over and looked inside. She pulled up her lip in distaste when she saw the black speck.

'Eucchh.' It jumped again and she squealed even though it was inside the glass. 'I'm never going to let that cat in here again. I hate it.'

'Take over,' said her mother. 'Press it down tight. Don't let it out.'

She went out of the bedroom and her daughter heard her filling a basin with water. She pressed the glass down until her arm ached. The rim of the glass dug into the sheet and made the centre swell like a pin-cushion. The flea disappeared.

'Oh no. Mum!' She put her face down close. The black speck reappeared. Her mother came back, forced to take short steps with the weight in the plastic basin. Some of the water slopped over the sides and formed droplets on the carpet.

'Here,' she said. 'Let me at it.' She set the basin on the floor and looked around. She took a Get Well card from the mantelpiece and turned it over to the plain white side. Her daughter let go of the glass and the mother began to slide the card beneath it while still pressing down.

'Don't let it get away,' said the girl. She was holding her hair back with a hand on either side of her face. The black speck was flinging itself into the roof of the pint glass.

'Easy does it.' Her mother completed sliding the card all the way across. She picked the whole lot up and showed it to the girl. The trapped speck did not move.

'They're so thin,' said the daughter. 'One-dimensional.'

'Two-dimensional – that's so's they can move through the animal's fur.' Her mother squatted down beside the basin and held the glass over the water. 'I feel like a priestess or a magician or something. A new rite. Releasing the flea. Dahdah.' She lowered the card partially into the water then withdrew it, leaving the flea floating. They both peered closely at it.

'Look at the legs – the length of them,' said the girl, leaning over the side of her bed. Her mother nodded.

'That's why they can jump over the Eiffel Tower.'

The flea was in a panic, cycling round the surface of the water, travelling backwards. The girl flopped back on her pillows, panting.

'Oh God,' she said.

'What?'

'That's really exhausted me.'

'Rest for a while.' The girl nodded. She was very white now.

'You've ruined my card,' she said. 'It looks all weepy.' The water had made the ink run. Her mother patted it dry against the carpet.

'It's an old one,' she said.

'I like to keep them all. Let me see it.' Her mother turned over the face of the card and handed it to her. It was a picture of a person in bed covered from head to foot in bandages. 'Oh, that's really ancient – two years ago, at least. From Johnny.' All the volume had drained out of her voice.

Her mother was bent over still staring at the flea.

'It's not floating,' she said. 'Surface tension. It's in a kind of dimple on the surface.' She looked up at her daughter but the girl didn't move. She just lay there with the card in her hand and her eyes closed. She could hear her breathing through her nose.

With her finger she sank the flea to the bottom of the basin and got up and tip-toed out.

About an hour later the buzzer rasped again and the mother went in.

'Could I have my tea now?'

'Anything to eat?'

'One bit of toast – no marmalade.'

When the supper was made she carried in the tray and set it on the chest of drawers. She pulled her daughter up into a sitting position, and propped her large sitting-up pillow behind her, then put the tray across her knees.

'Do you want me to stay?'

The girl shrugged. 'Whatever you like.' The wind rattled the windows and rain scudded against the panes. Her mother sat down on a bedside chair.

'It's a terrible night.'

The girl nodded and sipped her tea. The draught made her mobile rotate. A year ago, when she'd rallied slightly, she'd lain on her side in the darkened room and, with a little help from her father, had made a papier-mâché model of the sun. She was pleased with it. Then she made the earth and moon in the months that followed. When they were all finished she said, 'And on the seventh month she rested.' Now the heavenly bodies hung from the ceiling on threads above her bed. 'Give me something to stare at,' she'd said. 'Like a baby in her pram.' The earth was realistic, with blue oceans and brown-coloured land, but the sun and moon had faces. The yellow sun had spikes radiating from it and half the grey moon's face was covered in black shadow.

'How's our friend getting along?' said her mother. She looked towards the basin still on the floor.

'How does anything travel like that? It just hurls itself anywhere. Doesn't know if it's going to land in the fire – or my tea or anywhere.'

'A leap in the dark,' said her mother and smiled.

'What a life.' She bit at the edge of her piece of toast. 'Well, it's over now.'

'So . . .' Her mother leaned back in the chair and joined her hands behind her head. From the quiet tone of voice the girl knew immediately what was going to be said.

'This has been a better . . . It's been a less bad month.'

'I don't want to talk about it.'

The girl chewed her toast – then leaned forward to take a sip of the tea. She always drank it hot with very little milk in it.

'Compared to this time last year,' said the mother.

The girl's voice was on the edge of tears so the mother stopped talking. Her daughter rubbed her eyes, then stared straight in front of her, still chewing.

'Where's Dad?'

'He took your wee sister to the pictures. Just to get out.'

'What's the film?'

'Something in the Odeon. With Matt Dillon in it.'

'He's amazing.'

The sun swung almost imperceptibly from side to side. The earth turned slowly to face the moon.

'Any time we got a flea at home,' said her mother, 'it was blamed on the picture house. I used to come up in lumps and Mum'd say, "When were you last at the pictures?" There was never any possibility that you could've picked it up in church.'

'Or school.' She lifted her tray off her knees and offered it to her mother. 'I'm too tired. I'll have to lie down.' She toppled her sitting-up cushion onto the floor and keeled over flat on the bed. Her mother set the tray on the dressing-table and sat down on the chair again. She said,

'Take it easy.'

After a moment the girl leaned over and looked at the basin on the floor.

'Where is it?'

'It's still there. Don't panic.'

'Give me the backscratcher.'

Her mother handed it to her. It was a stick with a small fake hand at the end of it, the fingers curled up. The girl dipped it into the water and tried to squash the flea between the plastic knuckles and the bottom of the basin.

'Love . . .' Again the quiet tone.

'Talking about it doesn't change anything.'

'It gives a purpose. Goals. Something to aim at.'

The girl had turned the plastic hand round and was now trying to cradle the flea in its palm. Every time she brought it to the surface the flea slipped sideways off into the water.

'What's the point?' she said.

'You're sick. You're twenty-one years of age. You've improved. Someday you'll be better. We have to prepare for that. Aim at it.'

'Huh.' She rolled her eyes away from her mother and looked up at the papier-mâché globes above her. 'Improved.' Her eyes filled with tears. Then she whipped the backscratcher down onto the surface of the water with a slap, splashing it over the carpet. She buried her face in her arm. She was half shouting words, half crying them – this is what talking about it does, she was trying to say. Her mother went to sit on the bed beside her and put an arm around her shoulder. The girl was shuddering and shouting into her hair and the crook of her arm and the tumbled sheets. Her words were wet and distorted.

'I'm not, I'm not,' said her mother. 'Not for one minute am I blaming you. All I'm saying is that this time last year – no, two years ago – you couldn't get to the bathroom on your own . . .' The mother held tightly onto her daughter's shoulder. It was sharp with thinness under the material of the football shirt. Eventually the girl stopped crying. Her mother went to the bathroom and damped a face-cloth with hot water and brought it to her.

'Crying doesn't help,' said the girl. 'Nothing helps.' The cloth steamed as it was opened. Her mother massaged her daughter's face. 'What time will Dad be back?'

'Ten? Half ten?'

The girl leaned out of bed, picked up the backscratcher again and began to stir the basin with it.

'Maybe don't tell him I was crying.'

'Okay.'

She withdrew the plastic hand and this time the flea was stuck to the back of it. She brought it up close to her face to inspect it, curling up her lip as she did so. Suddenly it jumped.

'It's alive,' she screamed.

'I don't believe it. It can't be.'

'It is.'

'God Almighty.'

Both women squealed and laughed with the shock it had given them.

'The flea jumped over the moon,' said the girl and continued to laugh. She lay back on her pillows, her shoulders shaking, her hand over her mouth. Her mother smiled and straightened out the coverlet. She bent over, her eyes only inches above it, staring.

'Right,' she said, '– let's take it from the very beginning.' Her mother searched every visible inch of the coverlet but could see nothing. 'Don't worry – we'll find it before it finds you. It's only a matter of time.' She reached out and with a licked finger touched every speck.

'No.'

Every black particle.

'No.'

Any crumb.

'Definitely not.'

The girl listened to her mother's voice with closed eyes.

COMPENSATIONS

Ben, the younger boy, was copying down the football scores into the sports-page as a voice on the wireless called them out. His brother, Tony, sat with his ear almost against the loudspeaker. The boys' grandfather was reading the other pages of the paper. Ben felt he could guess the score from the high or low way the announcer said the team's name. When the results were finished the boys' grandmother spoke out from the kitchen.

'Well, Ben?'

'Where's the coupon?'

'It should be behind the clock.'

'It's not.'

'Wait now.' Grandma, drying her hands, came in and looked in the flap beneath the calendar. 'Do you think we've won?'

'No chance.'

'You never know. Somebody has to win them.'

'It'll never be us. We never have any luck,' said Tony and went upstairs.

She found the pools coupon beneath the bowl on the sideboard along with other bits of papers – printed prayers for a speedy recovery, novenas, the bread card – and handed it to Ben. The pools sheet was like the bread card – boxes of ruled blue lines.

She said,

'Wouldn't that be the quare surprise for them coming back?'

'No chance.'

'They could do with the money after paying for a jaunt like this.'

Ben looked at the grid of eight draws his grandfather had chosen and compared them to the actual results. The old man said it didn't matter about the teams – he just plumped for the same eight draws every week. Football know-alls never won.

438

'The first one's wrong.' He handed the results to Granda Coyle with a shrug and a shake of the head. The old man peered down at the sports-page through his glasses. He hadn't shaved well and had missed sandy white hairs at the corners of his mouth. Ben put the coupon behind the clock and asked,

'When's the tea?'

'Just as soon as I choose to make it.'

Grandma moved back out to the kitchen. She fried three eggs, scrambling them on the pan with a fork, and divided them into four. A slice of bacon each and soda bread which she'd baked earlier. The soda bread was always served dry side up hiding the bacon and egg. She set the four plates on the table.

'Sit over,' she said. 'And give your Granda a tap.'

Ben reached out and touched his grandfather's arm. The old man looked out from behind the newspaper and saw the tea ready.

'Thanks,' he said. He unhooked the wire legs of his glasses from behind his ears and heaved himself to his feet.

Grandma opened the door and shouted up the stairs,

'Tony – Tony your tea's ready.'

Nobody spoke as they ate. Ben listened to the noises they all made. His grandfather's mouth was shut as he chewed but he breathed heavily down his nose. Grandma had a knob of gristle at the hinge of her jaw which sometimes clicked – like somebody pulling their knuckles. Tony deliberately opened his mouth to annoy Ben, letting him see the half-chewed contents.

'Stop that,' said Grandma.

'How long to go now?' asked Ben.

'Three days – it's past the halfway mark.'

'What day do they come back?' asked Tony.

'If I told you once, I've told you a thousand times. Wednesday.'

'What time?'

'How would I know. I'm not flying the plane.'

'What are they saying?' asked the old man, cupping his ear towards Grandma. She leaned forward and shouted,

'Just – when are they coming back.'

The old man nodded and stared at Ben.

'Wednesday,' he said. 'They'll be back on Wednesday.'

'Why don't you wear that hearing-aid of yours?'

'What?'

'Never mind. It's not important.' Grandma dismissed the whole thing with a wave of her hand.

The boys had been told that their mother and father had gone to France. They didn't know much about France – the only thing Ben knew was that French films were dirty so when his grandmother said they were on a pilgrimage he felt better. People went on pilgrimages to places in Ireland – to Knock and Lough Derg. One of the teachers in the primary school, Mister Egan, went to Lourdes every summer to help with the sick and the dying. Working in the baths, lifting the afflicted out of their wheelchairs, lowering them into the holy waters. Everybody said he was a saint – and they always remarked how he never got anything himself – no matter what diseases had washed off into the water.

The door bell rang and Grandma stopped chewing.

'In the name of God . . .' she said. She closed her eyes. 'Nurse Foley.'

'Well I'm off,' said Tony, wiping his mouth with his hand. 'I couldn't stand the excitement.'

Both brothers got up from the table. Ben went to open the vestibule door and Tony ran upstairs.

Nurse Foley smiled and walked down the hall past Ben.

'Hello Tony,' she called up the stairs at Tony's heels.

'Hi.'

When Nurse Foley came into the kitchen she said in a kind of aghast voice – 'You're not at your tea, are you?' Grandma smiled. Granda didn't even look up. Nurse Foley went and sat by the fireside facing towards the table. Before she sat down she smoothed both hands down her coat at the back of her knees to make sure she wasn't going to crease it.

'Take off your coat,' said Grandma.

'I'm not staying,' said Nurse Foley.

Granda made an excuse that he was going to get his hearing-aid and left the room. Nurse Foley was about the same age as Grandma and dressed in much the same way, except in black. Ben had heard that one of Nurse Foley's jobs was washing the dead. How could anybody do that? How could a woman do that – especially if it was a dead man. He looked at her knuckly hands unbuttoning her coat. There was a blue apron hidden underneath.

'Would you look at me. I took a last-minute notion to go to confession and I just dashed. Sure nobody'd mind the apron, especially Himself.' She rolled her eyes up to heaven.

'Would you take a cup of tea – there's plenty in the pot.'

'If it's going spare – I wouldn't mind.'

Grandma got a cup and saucer from the cupboard.

'A snig of sugar?' she asked, smiling.

'And just the one milk,' said Nurse Foley and gave a sort of laugh. Grandma passed the tea over to her.

Granda came back with his hearing-aid clipped to the front of his cardigan. Ben thought it looked like a small bakelite wireless. Sometimes when Granda tried to turn the volume up, it gave a shrill whistle and annoyed everybody, including him. He sat down in the corner and looked from one woman to the other so that the wire which led up to the flesh-coloured thing in his ear became more obvious.

'Was there many at confession?' asked Grandma.

'A good few,' said Nurse Foley, 'but there was three priests hearing. They were getting through them rightly.' The empty saucer remained on her lap as she sipped her tea. Grandma said,

'I meant to go myself. But it'll keep till next Saturday.'

'Och Mrs Coyle – sure don't I see you at the altar rail every morning in life.'

Grandma nodded, tight-lipped.

'There's some hard praying to be done.'

Nurse Foley shook her head in agreement and sighed.

'Any word from them?'

'Not a thing – sure a postcard takes ages. The best part of a fortnight. So I'm told.'

'I suppose so.'

Nurse Foley's face was solemn but when she turned to the boy she smiled.

'Well, Benedict – any luck with the pools this week?'

Ben shook his head. Grandma said,

'Divil the bit.'

'Wouldn't it have been great to be able to hand them the seventy-five thousand as they stepped off the plane,' said Nurse Foley. Grandma nodded her head and smiled a bit.

'It'd be a little compensation.'

'Och I know that – Mrs Coyle. No question.'

'But isn't it typical of you, Nurse Foley – wanting to win so's you could give it away to somebody else.'

'Acchh – sure what would I want with all that money.'

When Ben looked up at her she winked and laughed. Grandma said,

'It was good of you to lend them the suitcase.'

'I'm just glad to see it used. And where would I be going at my age?' Nurse Foley shook her head again. 'They've had no luck whatsoever. But maybe that'll change, please God. Only time will tell.'

'The Lord works in mysterious ways,' said Grandma.

'His wonders to perform,' said Nurse Foley. 'I just hope he can keep his strength up. Although how anybody eats the slime and muck the French eat I have no idea. Did you ever taste garlic? It would turn your stomach. And they put it in *everything*. Like the way we use salt here.'

'And snails, I believe.'

'What are you talking about – horses, Mrs Coyle. They ate horses.'

'Away –'

And then after a pause in which Grandma shook her head Nurse Foley repeated,

'Horse meat – how-are-you.'

'Och away . . .'

The fire crumbled and sparks flew up the chimney.

'Ben, get a shovel of coal.' Ben did as he was told and went to the coal-hole in the back yard. The new coals were damp and hissed when they went on the fire. Ben set the shovel outside the back door and came into the room again.

'And what about her?' said Nurse Foley. 'Do you think she'll cope?'

'I've never known her not to.'

'The flying – the strange food – organising and remembering everything – above all, the thing of knowing – it's a lot to ask of her.'

'Prayer'll see her through. Everybody is praying.'

'Only time'll tell.'

Ben looked at his Grandma and then at Nurse Foley as they talked. They seemed not to look at each other. Nurse Foley stared down sideways into the fire. Grandma stared up at the frosted top pane of the window.

'Have you your own prayers said yet?' asked Nurse Foley.

'No – always straight after the tea. As you know,' said Grandma.

'Sure I'll join you since I have the beads with me.' She took out her rosary from her apron pocket and eased herself off the chair to kneel down.

'Call Tony,' said Grandma to Ben and held up her beads and rattled them at Granda.

They all began saying the family rosary. When Granda knelt at the chair his hearing-aid was useless. He said his prayers into himself because he couldn't join in the responses at the right time.

Tony knelt by the door so's he could escape immediately it was over. Ben made sure he was at the chair with the paper on the seat. He read an advertisement for Burberry raincoats while they repeated the Hail Marys over and over again. There was a drawing of a woman wearing a raincoat and striding through rain which was just black strokes all going the same way. The woman's leg, with its seamed stocking, was reflected in a puddle. Ben thought about washing a dead girl. The thought leapt into his mind and he couldn't get rid of it. A soapy flannel able to move anywhere. He tried to be good and put the thoughts out of his mind. He was getting a hard-on and if he allowed the thoughts to stay it would be a sin. In the middle of the rosary – it would be double the sin. He tried to concentrate on the prayer.

'Holy Mary Mother of God prayfrus sinners now and at the arovar death Amen.'

Beneath her armpits. Around her belly button. The wet face cloth moving down between her legs.

'Ben, can you not kneel up straight?' said Grandma. 'You're bent over there like a pig at a trough. The Second Joyful Mystery – The Visitation. Our Father who art in heaven . . .'

He turned his body away from her in case she would see what was happening to him and knelt up straight with his hands joined. He looked at the ceiling. He tried not to think of washing the body of a girl. Then he would definitely know whether they had hair hidden down there or not – or whether his brother was trying to make a fool out of him. Tony was smart. Tony knew everything. But Ben had seen marble statues in books with nothing obvious down there. What he did know was that they had hair under their arms. Last summer a French girl student had come into their class to teach for a while. On hot days she wore a summer frock and when she pointed out things on the blackboard they all saw the hair in her armpits.

He had to think of something different.

The worst thing he had ever seen in a paper was the air crash of the Busby Babes. The snow on the wreckage of the plane carrying Manchester United back from Munich. The thought of Duncan Edwards, his favourite player, lying dead. And all the others. It was beyond crying.

What if the plane bringing his Mum and Dad back from France crashed? That would make him an orphan. It was the first time they had ever flown and they'd seemed very nervous leaving.

'The Fifth Joyful Mystery – Jesus is Found in the Temple. Nurse Foley?'

Nurse Foley began giving out the prayer.

'Our Father who art in heaven . . .'

He thought for a while of being an orphan. Maybe it would be good. Everybody would make a fuss of him. Giving him extra things. But the thought of both his parents being dead was unendurable. Either one of them, maybe. Sometimes he made himself choose. Mum or Dad? Which was worse? Who would he miss the most?

After the rosary proper they said all the trimmings – right down to a prayer for a special intention. His Grandmother would never tell Ben what it was – it would ruin any chance of success if she said it out loud. And he noticed that when she said this prayer she clenched her eyes tight shut and moved her lips more than she usually did. When everything was finished Grandma blessed herself and kissed the cross of her beads and hung them on the handle of the cupboard. Tony left the room immediately and they heard him pounding up the stairs.

'I suppose Lord Duke McKittiax has better things to do than listen to us gabbing away,' said Nurse Foley, sitting back up in her chair and putting her beads in her pocket. Granda continued kneeling at his chair, not realising that the prayers had finished. Ben tapped the old man's shoulder and he looked up a bit startled. He smiled at Ben and said he was doing some extra praying – a wee prayer of thanksgiving for Celtic winning.

'That Charlie Tully's something else.'

Grandma had begun to clear the table, stacking the dishes up on the draining-board of the sink. The two women talked as Grandma went to and from the table. Granda fell asleep with his head lolled to one side and his mouth open. When Grandma had finished clearing the table she covered him with an overcoat to keep him warm. Nurse Foley asked,

'How's he keeping this weather?'

'He's rightly. The pains bother him a bit – but touch wood he's been fine today.'

'Surely they'll bring back some Lourdes water. You can put a drop of that on his joints.'

Grandma turned to Ben who was sitting pretending to read the paper.

'Ben, why don't you go into the other room and amuse yourself.'

'There's nothing to do.'

'There's those dishes to be done.'

'I'd better be on my way,' said Nurse Foley.

'Stay where you are. The dishes can wait.'

Ben lowered his head closer to the paper.

'I know there's nobody better than Our Lady when it comes to that kinda thing,' said Nurse Foley, '– but did they ever think of McHarg?'

'McHarg?'

'Seventh son of a seventh son.'

'Where's he?'

'Beyond Randalstown somewhere. It's nearer than France and it could do no harm.'

'I haven't heard of him.'

'It might be worth a try.'

Granda stirred in his sleep and made chewing noises. The coat began to slip off him and Grandma leaned over and adjusted it.

'His ears is beginning to flap,' said Grandma, nodding at Ben. 'Why don't you go and play some records, son?' Ben made a face and moved out of the room. As he closed the door he heard them lower their voices but did not listen to what was being said. He never listened at a door in case he heard something bad about himself.

He considered going up to talk to Tony but he would be reading or pretending to read. Going to Grammar school had changed him a lot – it had given him a big head about himself. He liked showing off – trying to scare everybody, quoting stuff like *Beware, beware the Ides of March* in a hoarse voice. Ben hoped to get his eleven-plus and be able to join him after the summer. It would be good if they had to walk to the College together.

In the sitting-room it was a grey summer's evening and the window panes were covered with rain. Away from the fire it was cold. There was a damp patch of wallpaper on the chimney-breast caused, so his mother said, by some cheapskate builder patching a hole with 'weeping sand' and it became more obvious on wet days. The noise of traffic passing was in that room all the time and somewhere a blackbird was singing. When a certain type of double-decker bus went past, the window pane vibrated, shaking the droplets of rain. There was a fly somewhere but he couldn't see it.

The chiming clock on the mantelpiece had stopped long ago because the key to wind it up had been lost. Ben stood staring at it. It had Roman numerals which turned more and more upside down the nearer they got to half-past.

He lifted the clock down and set it on the rug. There was a long hat-pin with a black pearl handle beneath where the clock had been and he took this and lay down. He opened the door at the back of the clock. Inside, a row of tiny brass hammers. The chimes were made of brass rods of different lengths. With the hat-pin he lifted and dropped each hammer onto its chime. The echoes went on and on and on – the different notes interfering with each other until the noise of traffic came back. It was the saddest sound he had ever heard. If he lifted all the hammers and released them slowly by withdrawing the hatpin then it sounded like a harp – unearthly. Like heaven. Deliver us from evil. He played the clock because there was nothing else to do. Once, when he was much smaller, a visitor had asked him if he played anything and when he said – the clock – they all threw back their heads and laughed. He smiled but he wasn't sure what was funny.

When he tired of the clock he went over and looked out at the street. The bluebottle flew into the window bizzing against the glass. The sound stopped and it climbed slowly. Ben folded a paper record sleeve so that the central hole became a bite out of one side. He folded it again so that the bite disappeared and it became a strap of paper.

After a while the fly zig-zagged back into the centre of the room and flew in squares around the light bowl. You could see a freckle of dead flies and moths in the bowl when the light was turned on. Eventually the bluebottle buzzed to the window again and Ben whacked it to the floor where he stamped on it. When he took his foot away the fly bounced against the pile of the fawn rug.

In the street a woman walked beneath her umbrella so that he couldn't see her face – just a coat and legs. He put his hands in his pockets. The face of a dead girl might be covered with a sheet – pulled up from her grey feet until only her face was hidden. Everything else he could see. He felt the beginnings of a hard coming and took his hands out of his pockets again. His eye kept being drawn to the dead fly on the carpet. He scooped it onto the record paper and threw it in the fireplace. Against the black of the grate he couldn't see it.

He went out into the hall and heard the voices still going on and on. His father had modernised the doors – hiding the panelling beneath hardboard – so that it made a double thickness. The voices were murmuring – indistinct. They were up to something. If he opened the door they would stop talking. They would look up at him waiting for him to give a reason for his being there. He hated that.

He went back to the front room and plugged in the radiogram. It was a huge unfinished affair being built by his father – 'a genuine piece of furniture'. The wood inside had not been varnished yet and smelt like freshly sharpened pencils. To the right of the turntable was a pile of records without their paper covers. They made zipping noises as he sorted through them. He played *Whispering Hope* very low – it wasn't the kind of thing he should be playing. Far too sloppy. If his brother caught him he would laugh at him and taunt him. Why do you play that when Johnny Ray's there? So he lay down with his ear very close to the black cone of the loudspeaker. His father had not got round to covering the speaker with material. *Whispering Hope* made him want to cry, it gave him a strange feeling in his stomach. Two voices, a man and a woman's, threading in and out of one another. Harmonising. Later he played Johnny Ray singing *Just-a-walking in the Rain* and turned the volume up loud.

Grandma banged the sitting-room door with her fist and shouted, 'Turn that thing down a bit.'

Nurse Foley opened the door and said at the top of her voice, 'That's me away.'

Ben turned the volume down. Nurse Foley stepped into the sitting room. Grandma stood behind her. Ben could see that they had both been crying.

'The spit of him,' said Nurse Foley. She reached into her pocket and produced a half crown and gave it to Ben.

'It's not seventy-five thousand but it'll get you some sweets.'

'What do you say?' said Grandma.

'Oh thanks –' said Ben.

'Don't look so surprised,' said Grandma.

'But what's it for? It's not my birthday or anything . . .'

'It's for being good,' said Nurse Foley.

JUST VISITING

The pub, almost opposite the hospital gate, had an off-licence attached. He waited a long time for the green man before crossing. The rain was falling constantly and the wind darkened the pavements as it gusted. He ran with his coat collar up. A bell chinked when he opened the door and a girl came out from the back to serve him. There was not a great range of Scotch in half bottles so he bought, not the cheapest – because that would look bad – but a middle-priced one. The girl began to wrap it in brown paper.

'Don't bother,' he said. 'It'll do like that.' He slipped the half bottle into his jacket, making sure the pocket flap concealed it.

In the lift to the wards a Sister with winged spectacles stood opposite him. He thought he heard the liquid clink in the bottle when they stopped at any floor but she didn't seem to notice. When the lift doors opened on the fourteenth floor he smelled the antiseptic – but there was another smell – a perfume he couldn't quite place. A sweet, intense – uneasiness. He walked along the corridor.

He hadn't seen Paddy for three years – not since he himself had moved to the city. Through the ward windows he could see men in various propped positions, in beds, on beds. A sign above one – NIL BY MOUTH. Was that him? How much had the illness changed him? Would he recognise him easily? A nurse in her forties sat at a desk mid-way along the corridor. She continued writing her report, then looked up.

'Just visiting,' he said. 'I'm here for a Mister Quinn. Mister Paddy Quinn.' She stood up and escorted him. The name tag on her lapel said *Mrs MacDonald*. Again he was aware of the liquid clinking in the bottle in his pocket.

'He's in a room by himself – he's still very weak after his operation. So please – if you don't mind – don't be too long.' She opened the door and called out, 'Visitor for you, Paddy.'

A figure lay flat in the bed with his back to the door facing the window. The visitor moved round the bed to face him.

'Paddy – how are you?'

The nurse closed the door. Paddy gave a groan and heaved himself onto his elbow.

'I hate that bitch, MacDonald. She is so fucking patronising,' he said. 'Good to see you, Ben.' Ben reached out and touched the older man on the shoulder. 'Watch me – or I'll fall apart.' Ben plumped up the pillows and wedged them behind Paddy's back.

'So – how are you?'

'Some fucker unseamed me from the nave to the chaps.' Paddy lay back on the pillows and blew out his breath. His beard and hair were now completely white. When he opened his pyjama jacket to display his wounds Ben tried not to let anything show on his face. There was an incision beginning at Paddy's neck which zig-zagged down his side to the bottom of his ribs.

'Jesus, it's like the map of a railway track.' There were junctions and off-shoots and either there was extensive bruising or else the whole wound had been painted with iodine.

'It's hand-stitched,' he said. 'Nothing but the best.'

'Is it sore?'

'Naw . . .' Paddy looked at him. 'What the fuck d'you think?'

Ben nodded, not knowing whether to smile or not.

'Did you manage to run the cutter?'

Ben glanced over at the small window in the centre of the door. There was no one looking.

'In my wash-bag,' said Paddy. Ben slipped the bottle from his pocket into the wash-bag, covered it with a damp face-cloth and zipped it up.

'Crinkle-free,' he said. 'The girl was going to wrap it but I said no. I didn't know the lie of the land up here.' The wash-bag was now stowed at the bottom of the bedside cabinet. Ben sat down on a chair. Paddy leaned back on his pillows.

'It's good to know that's there.'

'Are you not allowed *anything*?'

'Two cans of Guinness a day. Three if someone's brave enough to buck the system.'

'Slim rations,' said Ben.

'I'm on that many bloody drugs . . .'

'When did you arrive?'

'The night I phoned. They operated the next day.'

'I'm sorry I couldn't get up sooner but you know how it is.' Ben shrugged, making out he had no control over anything. 'So – how have you been since I last saw you?'

'Apart from cancer – okay.'

'Sorry – but you know what I mean. How's the town I love so well?'

'The terrible town of Tynagh. It's not been the same since you left. Morale has taken a nose dive.' There was a long silence. 'Where green peppers wrinkle on the Co-op shelf.' Ben rested his elbows on his knees and stared down at the terrazzo floor. Paddy stared at the white coverlet. 'What's the teaching like here?'

'For fuck's sake, Paddy . . .' Ben leaned back in his chair and appeared to concentrate on the ceiling. There was another pause – the wind buffeted the window and the rain sounded like hailstones against the glass. 'I mean – they wouldn't operate . . . to that extent if they didn't think they could . . . I mean the signs are *good*. My own father – they just took one look and closed him up again. Told my mother the only thing left was to take him to Lourdes. Are you getting radiotherapy?'

'Chemotherapy. They say it's worse.'

'But they wouldn't put you through all that if they thought . . . if they didn't think you had an . . . excellent chance.'

'Did she take him? To Lourdes?'

'Yeah.'

'And?'

'He died the week he came back. We were just kids – didn't even know he was ill.'

'Fuck it – pour me some orange juice. In that glass.' There was a carton on the grey metal locker and Ben stood and began to pour out of the torn spout of the cardboard. 'Stop – go easy. Just enough to colour it.'

'What?'

'The whisky.'

'Are you sure? Paddy, I'd hate to be the one . . .'

'I'll do it myself then.'

'Stay where you are.' Ben crouched and took the half bottle out of the wash-bag. There was a series of small metallic snaps as he broke the screw-top, then the hollow rhythmic clunking as he poured whisky into the tumbler of orange juice.

'Say when.' Ben kept his body between the tumbler and the door. He stopped pouring. Paddy said,

'When.'

He put the bottle back in the wash-bag and handed the glass to Paddy. Paddy sniffed at it.

'Terrible fucking smell – orange juice.' He raised the glass to his mouth, quickly tipped it back and swallowed half its contents. Then the remainder. He lay for a moment with his eyes closed. 'Oh that's good. What about yourself?'

'No, it's too early for me. Thanks all the same.'

'That's how it all started. Difficulty swallowing. It went on for a couple of months – and then it got so bad I went to Doctor Fuckin Jimmy. And now I'm here.'

'Doctor Fuckin Jimmy.' Ben shook his head, stood up and sniffed at the air. 'Maybe I'd better open that window for a bit.'

'Jesus, you'll have it as cold as the caravan in here.'

'It's the smell – if the nurse comes in.' The lower section of the window hinged in at the bottom. The wind gusted up into his face when he opened it. 'It didn't stop us having some good nights.'

'Plenty of internal central heating. Days in the *Seaview*, nights in the caravan.'

'Good times, Paddy.'

'Laughing to piss point.'

'*Mine's a whisky,*' said Ben, imitating Paddy's voice, '*and I'll leave the measure up to yourself.* And when it came to your round, you oul bastard – *What kind of beer can I buy you a half pint of?*'

'That's a lie.' They laughed and nodded.

'Do you still live in it?'

'The caravan? Yeah. If it hasn't blown away. It should be tied down a day like that. But I can't be bothered any more.'

'Come on Paddy . . .'

'The doctors were saying – when I get out the District will *have* to house me. They say they'll not release me *until* I get a place to recover in.'

'You see – they expect you to get better.' Paddy nodded but he didn't seem sure. He said,

'How's the wife and weans?'

'Fine – everybody's fine.' Ben looked at the racing grey sky and then down at the leafless trees in the grounds.

'I liked the kid who thought wind was made by the trees waving.' Ben looked round and Paddy was lying back on his pillows with his eyes clenched shut. 'Maybe I'd better go,' he said. 'Is there anything you want?'

'Yeah – you could run the cutter for me again. In fact, if you don't I'll break your legs for you.'

'Okay – okay. But it'll be Friday before I can come.'

'And close that fucking window.'

Ben snapped the wood frame back and snibbed it.

'The windows must be like that to stop you jumping out. When it all gets too much.' Just then Mrs MacDonald tapped the glass of the door with a fingernail. 'I'm overstaying my welcome here.'

'Fuck her. I remember seeing it written up in big six-foot letters once – on a wall. *Do what you're told – REBEL.*'

'So you keep telling me.'

'She's nothing but a saved oul bitch,' said Paddy. 'Before you go I want you to do something for me.'

'Yeah sure.'

It seemed important and he leaned forward to listen attentively. He thought of wills, of funeral arrangements, of last wishes.

'See the wardrobe – there's a dead man in my dressing-gown pocket. Dispose of it.'

On the way out in the main corridor he smelled the sweet intense perfume again. It was so strong it almost caught the back of his throat like cigarette smoke. Mrs MacDonald was now sitting at her desk in the light of an anglepoise. He stopped and waited for her to pause in her writing.

'Yes?' Mrs MacDonald looked up from her work and Ben felt he had to point vaguely in the direction he'd come from.

'I've just been visiting Paddy Quinn.'

'Of course.'

'And I wanted to give you my number – just in case. He hasn't anybody. Here, that is.' She wrote down Ben's particulars.

'You're a friend of his?'

'Yes – we've known each other for about ten years now. We were neighbours – sort of.'

'In Tynagh?'

'Yes – when I was teaching at the High School there.'

'Lucky you. What a beautiful place. It's my favourite seaside town.'

'How do you know it?'

'Mr MacDonald and I drive through it most years. On our way somewhere.' Ben nodded but decided to say nothing. He cleared his throat.

'How is he? I mean I know he's weak but . . . how is he?'

'Mr Milne – sorry, the surgeon – is convinced that he caught it in time. They are all quite hopeful.'

'That *is* good news.'

'But he's almost sixty – and hasn't treated himself as well as some.'

'Thank you – thank you anyway for all you are doing.'

Then he saw the source of the perfume – behind Mrs MacDonald's desk – two bowls of hyacinths. Big bulbs sitting proud of the compost, flowering pink and blue and pervading the wards and corridor with their scent. It was a smell he hated because he associated it with childhood, with the death of his own father. A hospital in winter brightening itself with bowls of blue and pink hyacinths – a kind of hypocrisy, the stink of them everywhere. His mother crying, telling them all to be brave.

It felt like the first day of summer – warm with the sun shining out of a cloudless sky and the trees in the hospital grounds in full leaf.

When Ben went into the ward it was empty. Mrs MacDonald said with a repressed sigh that Paddy was probably in the smoking-room. Ben walked to the far end of the corridor and looked through the small window of the door. There were four or five men inside. He went in.

'How're ya,' he said. Paddy was in his wheelchair sucking his pipe.

'On fortune's cap I am not the very button.' They laughed. After the treatment the hair on the right-hand side of his face had fallen out and gave his beard a lop-sided look. He was fully dressed in trousers and jacket and sat apart, looking out the window. The others were in a group, smoking cigarettes. 'Have you put on some weight?'

'According to the scales,' said Paddy. The room was bluish with smoke and smelled stale. There was a green metal waste bin quarter filled with cigarette butts. 'And how are you?'

'Great – the first week of the holidays. Like the first couple of hours on a Friday night.'

'You can hardly see out this fucking window for nicotine. Look at it.' The glass was yellowish, opaque. 'It hasn't been cleaned for months. Nobody *ever* sweeps the floor in here. The message is, if you smoke in this hospital we're gonna make you feel like shit because we're going to treat you like shit.' He knocked his pipe out into the bucket and began to crush some tobacco between his hands. Ben sat down. The white-painted window sill had tan scorch lines where cigarettes had been left to burn.

'Take it easy – maybe in a . . . a ward of this nature they have a point.'

'Fuck off, Ben. People get hooked on things.' He tamped the tobacco into the bowl of his pipe and began lighting it with a gas lighter. 'Addiction is a strange bastard. It creates a need where no need existed. And satisfying it creates a pleasure where no pleasure existed.'

Ben looked at the cigarette smokers. At least two of them looked like winos, with dark-red abused faces. They wore hospital dressing-gowns over pyjamas and had open hospital sandals. Ben stared down at their feet. They were black like hide with pieces of cotton wool separating the toes. Their toes looked dried, encrusted and brittle. His eyes flinched away.

'Let's go outside. I'll take you for a spin in the wheelchair.'

'Did you run the cutter?' Ben nodded and indicated his pocket. 'Let's stash it in my room first. And I'll get you the money.'

'Don't worry about it. It's a gift – this time.' Ben wheeled him along the corridor. Mrs MacDonald was on the desk and she spoke to Ben as they passed.

'He's fair putting on the pounds,' she said. Ben felt obliged to stop the wheelchair. He nodded.

'It'll be food – you must be giving him food.'

Paddy sat staring ahead.

'Why don't you go out – that lovely day. Get a breath of fresh air.'

'It's not fresh air I want,' said Paddy, 'but the good fug of a pub somewhere.'

'Don't you dare,' said Mrs MacDonald and Ben and she laughed. Paddy's knuckles were white on the armrests of his chair.

Ben slipped him the half bottle and Paddy stood up and went into the toilet with it. He tried to vary the places he stored it. Ben stood waiting, staring out the ward window. Mrs MacDonald passed the door with a slip of paper in her hand. She smiled and stopped. She put on a whispering voice.

'I'm serious about that.'

'What?'

'The pub business. It would be terrible to undo all the good work. I'm holding *you* responsible.' She grinned and walked away in her flat shoes, flicking at her piece of paper with her finger.

When Paddy came out of the toilet Ben smelled the whisky off his breath as he got back into wheelchair.

'How much weight have you put on?'

'A couple of pounds but I'm still lighter than when I came in. It's that fucking chemotherapy-therapy that goes for you. And the no drink laws. They stop you drinking and then ask you to put on weight – for fucksake. Drink's full of calories.'

'I've been thinking about half bottles – the shape of them. There's something Calvinist about them. They're made flat like that *for* the pocket. No bulge, no evidence. A design to fit the Scots and the Irish psyche.'

'Shut up and drive.'

*

There were many patients outside in the hospital grounds, sitting on benches in pyjamas and dressing-gowns tilting their faces up to the sun, or being wheeled about. A couple of female nurses in white uniforms lay on the grass. There was a blackbird over by the railway cutting singing constantly.

'It even feels like summer,' said Ben. They stopped at an empty bench beside a laburnum tree and Paddy got out of the chair onto the bench. He sat filling his pipe, staring at the cascades of yellow blossom.

'This bastard's poisonous. You've no regard for my health at all.'

'What was wrong with those guys' feet – in the smoking room?'

'Gangrene – smoking makes your legs drop off.'

'What?' They both laughed. 'That's crap. Why doesn't it happen to you?'

'I guess I'm just lucky. Naw – it happens mostly to cigarette smokers. It's called . . . some big fuckin name. It stops the circulation to your feet. They go black and drop off.'

'And those guys are still up there smoking?'

'You've never smoked Ben, so shut your mouth.' He lit his pipe with the gas lighter and exaggerated every gesture and sigh of satisfaction. 'It gives a selected few of us a little pleasure as we funnel our way down the black hole to oblivion. Speaking of which . . .'

'What?'

'Why don't we go for a drink?'

'Naw –'

'At the clinic where they used to dry me out they *taught* me to drink. They said . . .'

'Never drink on your own.'

'And now *you* are here. It can't be too far to the nearest pub, for fucksake. Isn't there one just at the gate?'

'Naw –'

'What the fuck's wrong. Are you on the wagon or something?'

'No – it's inadvisable. It's very pleasant here.' A train rattled through the cutting but they could not see it. The blackbird changed trees and began singing from the opposite side of the tracks. 'So – any word of a house yet?'

'No.'

'Or any word of them letting you home?'

'No.' His pipe wasn't going well and he knocked it against the spokes of the wheelchair. 'Fuck it.' He sucked and blew but couldn't free the blockage.

'There's no need to go into a huff, Quinn.'

'The first time in twelve fuckin weeks that I get a chance to have a drink without those nurses breathing down my neck – and you won't take me.'

'That's right.' There was an ornamental flower-bed with bushes and grasses screening them from the front of the hospital.

'Pull me a bit of that stuff,' said Paddy pointing to stalks of wheat-like grass. Ben glanced in the direction of the hospital then did what he'd been asked. Paddy pulled his pipe apart and pushed the stalk through the plastic mouthpiece. When it was cleared he blew through it and reassembled the pipe. He threw the grass stalk on the ground at his feet. It was black with tar.

'*WHY* will you not take me?'

'Because you're not allowed. The doctors do not allow you.'

'What doctors have you been talking to, for fucksake?' He turned away from Ben in irritation and looked towards the hospital gate. For a moment Ben thought the old man might attempt to make it on his own.

'They serve coffee on the ground floor. We could go over there.'

'What doctor said I wasn't allowed to go to the pub?'

'Look, Paddy – do you want to get better or not?'

'That is not what we are talking about – we are talking about going for a fucking pint and maybe a chaser in a nice atmosphere with maybe a barmaid.'

'Paddy – catch yourself on. Do you not think I know you of old? Nights spent in the terrible town of Tynagh. Once you get into a pub there's no way of getting you out.'

'You're chicken. A coward. A man who can't break the rules no matter *who* lays them down.'

Ben stood up and ushered Paddy back into the wheelchair.

'Come on. I'll buy you a coffee.

Paddy got unsteadily to his feet and almost fell into the chair. He was shaking his head in disbelief.

Ben got the coffees in wobbly plastic containers and brought them down to Paddy by the window. Outside was a small lawn with more off-duty nurses, both male and female, sprawled on it.

'Aw fuck,' said Paddy, staring out. 'Lift your knees a bit more, darling.'

'Stop it. Would you like a biscuit or anything?'

'No.'

The formica table-top was covered in brown sugar spilled from a half-used paper sachet. The plastic container was too hot for Ben's fingers and he left it to cool. A baby was crying somewhere and two children were running up and down between the tables chasing each other. A mother stood and called them to order. Paddy stared out the window, his hands joined across his midriff. Ben began wiping the spilled sugar into a neat pile with a paper napkin.

'I sometimes do what they told you not to,' he said.

'What? Who?'

'The drying-out clinic. I drink on my own. At night.'

'Thank God you fucking drink sometimes.'

'When everybody's gone to bed.'

'You mean your wife.'

'I *like* to relax with a dram.'

'It'll not do you a button of harm. There are worse things,' said Paddy. The nurses on the lawn got up simultaneously and moved back into the hospital. Paddy looked up at Ben. 'I believe you're the undercow of that wife of yours.'

'Nonsense, Paddy.'

'Do you drink more or less when she's there?'

'Probably less. But I only have one or two.'

'Or three? Or more? When you're drinking you can only count to three.'

Ben smiled.

'Sometimes it's frightening to see the level on the bottle the next day.'

'You're not too bad then – if there's any left in the bottle. But it'll get worse – you know that. You're no fool, Ben.'

'Thanks for the advice, Holy Father.'

'I want you to remember this – you can only give advice to fools.'

'I don't understand.'

'If you feel the need to give someone advice you're *assuming* that they are a fool.'

'That is advice.'

'What?'

'What you're giving now – to me.'

'It's not advice. We're having a fucking conversation.'

Paddy pulled out his pipe and lighter. He pressed the plug of tobacco deeper into the bowl and aimed the flame at it. Ben fanned his hand in front of his face to keep the smoke at bay.

'Problem drinking,' he said, 'is a thing that builds up gradually.'

'Problem drinking? What are you talking about *problem* drinking for?' Paddy laughed out loud. 'Drinking's the solution, for fucksake.'

'Paddy, you're right beneath a *No Smoking* sign.'

'Fuck it. People like the smell of a pipe.'

'In a hospital?'

'*Especially* in a hospital.'

Ben finished his coffee and made movements to stand up. 'Look I'll not be able to make it three times a week from now on. I have stuff for summer school. I'll come Tuesdays and Saturdays, if that's okay with you.'

'Yeah, sure. It's good of you to come at all.'

'Naw –. It's good to hear your crack again.'

'It's not the way it used to be. More's the fuckin pity. Ben, you're the best friend I ever had.'

'Easy on, Paddy. Statements are in danger of being made here.'

'No – it's true.'

'Okay – okay. But I've gotta go.' Ben stood up and spun Paddy round in the wheelchair and headed for the lift. There was no one else going up. When the doors closed Ben asked,

'Any dead men you want me to get rid of?'

'Naw – there was a fella got out yesterday. He took them away in his suitcase. They sent him home to die. But he took the empties all the same.'

There was snow on the hills which turned to sleet as Ben drove down into Tynagh. It was more a village than a town – a collection of shops, five pubs and as many churches all gathered around a harbour which had silted up over the past two decades. The school where he'd taught looked even more dilapidated and cement grey than he remembered. Because of the holiday the car-park and playground were deserted. On the football field in the drifting rain a flock of seagulls stood just inside the penalty area.

The hospital was on the far side of the town – on the outskirts. It shared a building with an Old People's Home. He recognised the nurse on the front desk; she had been a pupil of his. He remembered her as a bright girl – she had written a good argumentative essay on *The Nature of Tourism*. When she recognised Ben she blushed.

'Hello, sir. I presume you're here to see Paddy. He talks a lot about you.'

She led him down the corridor, speaking over her shoulder. He felt she was embarrassed at having made the slip and called him *sir*.

'So how are you liking the big smoke, then?'

'Oh fine – it suits me fine.'

She stopped outside a room and dropped her voice. 'They sent Paddy back here to . . . recuperate . . .'

'And how's he doing?'

'Not as well as we would like.' She gestured to the room and continued walking along the corridor. She had an Elastoplast between her Achilles tendon and her shoe.

Paddy was lying on his bed against a pile of pillows with his eyes closed. There was a drip above his bed and a tube taped to his arm. His cheek bones stood out and he was a very bad colour.

Hearing someone in the room he opened his eyes.

'For fucksake Ben, what are you doing here?' His voice was hoarse and he seemed to have difficulty swallowing.

'Visiting you.' Ben reached out and shook hands. He was aware of the sinews in the older man's handshake. The arm with the drip attached lay flat, wrist upwards on the covers. 'You're looking okay – for a man that's been through the mill.'

'Do you think so?'

'I *know* so.'

'Jesus, I don't feel it.'

'What's it like here?'

'Fuckin terrible.'

'But you're surrounded by people you know . . .'

'That's what I mean. Nosey cunts on zimmers.'

The room was on the seaward side of the hospital and the windows had been dulled by the salt blowing off the Atlantic so that the grey-green of the hills looked even greyer.

'Is your wife with you?'

'No – it's just a quick visit. I didn't know whether you wanted me to . . . y'know, run the cutter.' Ben tapped his jacket pocket and pulled the neck of a half bottle into view.

'All very acceptable,' said Paddy. 'The more the merrier. Put it there.' He indicated the open shelf on the bedside cabinet. Someone had brought him a basket of fruit which was still covered in cellophane. The white grapes were beginning to go brown. Ben reached over.

'Where?'

'Anywhere.'

It was only then that Ben noticed the full tumbler standing on the bedside cabinet. He bent over and sniffed it. It was whisky.

'They allow you it in here?'

'A little,' said Paddy. Then he smiled. 'As much as I can drink.'

'Is that a . . . That must be a good sign.'

'They say if it helps put on some weight it'll do no harm. Would you like a snifter?'

'Nah – Paddy. Never during the day. Anyway, I'm driving the car.'

'How long are you staying?'

'I'll go back tomorrow. All things being equal.'

'What the fuck kind of an expression is that? From an English teacher? *All things being equal.* When was any fucking thing ever equal?'

'Sorry. Sloppy speech.' Ben smiled. 'Any word of a house?'

Paddy shook his head. 'They say I've got to put the weight back on before I go anywhere.'

'Are you eating much?'

Paddy looked up at the drip and licked his lips. 'Lancashire Hotpot.'

Ben didn't know what to say. 'Sorry?'

'You remember we once talked about problem drinking? Well I've got it now.'

'What?'

'A problem drinking. My fucking throat's given up. I can't swallow anything any more. This is high protein, high fibre, high fucking God knows what – but it might as well be Molly Magill's pish as far as my weight's concerned.'

'Paddy – don't be so impatient. You're looking . . . okay.'

'Okay?'

'Okay is good enough – at this stage.'

'Angela says they put the apple tart and custard through at the same time as the hotpot. And a cup of tea.'

'Angela. That's it. I'd forgotten her name. Angela Stewart. She was a pupil of mine.'

'So she tells me.'

'Is there anything you want? Anything I could get you from the town?'

'Naw, thanks. When I was in the best of health there was nothing you could get me from this town.' He picked up the glass and took a tiny sip then lay back on his pillow. He held the whisky in his mouth but some of it leaked out at the corner of his lips.

'What brought you to this godforsaken dump in the first place?'

'It's where I ended up. After the war. As good a place as any. As bad a place as any.'

'Oh aye – the Morse Code business.'

'For the North Atlantic. The trouble with drinking cronies is – remembering what you've told them. *Drink is a great provoker of four things* – the one Shakespeare left out was amnesia.'

Ben had to lean forward a little to hear what Paddy was saying. He took the glass from Paddy's hand before it spilled and replaced it on the bedside cabinet.

'I still like the taste of it,' Paddy said. 'So you've met Angela?'

'Yeah.'

'She's a great kid. She does things for me. I suppose it's her way of telling the matron to get stuffed. The rules do not apply to a man in my position.' His breathing was becoming difficult. He reached out for his pipe which lay in a tin-foil ash-tray. He sucked the mouthpiece but did not light it. 'Could you maybe call her for me?' Ben rose quickly to his feet.

'Are you okay? Is anything wrong?'

'Don't fuss, Ben.'

He found Angela at the front desk and told her that Paddy wanted her. This time he made sure to use her name.

'I'm very busy,' she said. 'Tell him I'll be along as soon as I can.'

'Thanks, Angela.' Ben sat with Paddy for another fifteen minutes. The older man was tired or drugged and kept dozing off. Ben didn't like to disturb him and sat saying nothing. The hospital was full of noises – there was a distant rattling of dishes, someone whistling, a plastic door flapped shut, in the next room someone dropped a pair of scissors in a stainless steel sink. When Angela arrived breathless, Paddy said,

'Here comes the upwardly nubile.'

'Paddy – what do you want this time?' She turned to Ben. 'He's a terrible bloody man. You see what I've to put up with?' Ben nodded and smiled.

'I want to have a drink with my friend here,' said Paddy. He indicated the bedside cabinet.

'What do you take me for? A bloody waitress?'

'You know what I'm talking about, sweetheart. And I want you to pour one for that teacher of yours. A large one.'

'Honestly, Paddy, I've got the car.'

He sat bolt upright in the bed and his eyes bulged. His voice was as loud as he could make it.

'Fuck you and your fucking car.'

Angela winked at Ben and poured him a glass of whisky.

'Do you take water in it?'

'Indeed I do. The same again.'

The nurse handed him the glass and said to him, 'The toilet is on the left at the bottom of the corridor.'

'Sorry?'

'Just a little walk – for a few moments.' She raised her eyebrows and smiled.

'Oh yes – ?' He walked down the corridor and went to the toilet even though he didn't really need to go. When he came out Angela passed him, hurrying back to her post.

'He'll be in better form now,' she said.

Ben went back into the room. With one hand Paddy was combing back his white hair.

'There's your drink,' he said. Ben took it and toasted him.

'Cheers,' he said. He was looking for Paddy's glass to chink. The tumbler stood empty on the bedside cabinet. Paddy saw him looking and said,

'It's in the Lancashire Hotpot.'

Ben looked up at the drip. 'You old fuckin bastard.'

Paddy laughed. His eyes seemed brighter. 'All my life I've been looking for bad company to fall into and it's only recently I've realised I'm it.' They laughed a bit. 'I should've got Angela to fix one of these up in the caravan years ago. With a catheter out the window. You wouldn't have to budge for weeks.'

They talked about the good times – remembered the after-hours drinking, the windowsilling their way home, the parties with no food and 'the night of the starving fisherman' when they found bite marks in a bar of Echo margarine. When Paddy laughed it turned into a phlegmy cough which was difficult to stop so Ben tried to change the conversation and keep it as low-key as possible. After a while Paddy said,

'When you see people like her – Angela – it makes everything worth it. She doesn't give a fuck what anybody says.' He seemed to doze a bit, then jerk awake. He was beginning to slur. 'There was a thing about Wittgenstein on last night – on the radio – his last words were – *Tell them it was wonderful.* I think he was probably talking about the rice pudding.'

After about a half an hour Paddy felt into a deep sleep. Ben put his almost full whisky where Paddy's tumbler had been. Then he left on tip toe.

Ben walked along the school corridor into the carpeted office section. The red light was on outside the Principal's office so he went into the Secretary's room.

'Hi Ben.'

'Who's in with him?'

'A parent – I think.' She checked a notebook. 'Yes, Lorimer of 3D – his father.'

'Can I see him next?'

'Doubt it, love. There's a Revised Arrangements in Geography Higher Grade meeting at eleven.'

'Lunch time?'

'Come down again at one – I hope you had a good night somewhere, Ben?'

'Why?'

'You look like you're a bit hung over.'

'I was at home. I'll explain sometime.'

'Cheers.'

Ben wasted most of his lunch hour waiting for the red light to be switched off. He went again to the Secretary.

'Who's in?

'Nobody, love – just knock. He's probably at his lunch.'

Ben knocked.

'Come in.'

The room was filled with the scent of a single hyacinth in a pot by the window. It was that time of year again. The Principal was sitting behind his desk which faced the door. He was eating a sandwich and a cup of tea steamed on the polished surface of the desk. Beneath the cup was a wooden coaster, so crude it was obviously made by a pupil. The slats of the venetian blinds were half closed. Outside the harsh sunlight created a glare.

'Ben – what can I do for you?' The Principal was a dark silhouette. There was a distant yelling from the playground.

'Em – I got the news last night that a friend – a very close friend of mine . . . Well, that he died.'

'Oh, I'm sorry to hear that.'

'Yes, we got to know each other in the terrible town of Tynagh.'

'Oh yes – when you were teaching up there.'

'He was a great man.'

The Principal set his half bitten sandwich on a serviette on the desk. 'And . . .?'

'I just wanted permission to go to the funeral.'

'When is it?'

'Tomorrow.'

'In Tynagh?' The Principal considered this for a moment. 'What you're really looking for is leave of absence.'

'Yes.'

The Principal sighed, 'It's sad but you know the rules as well as I do. The Region will only allow it for *close* relatives.'

'This man was a close friend. Maybe he's the father I'd like to have had.'

The Principal folded the paper napkin over the sandwich. He put it in the desk drawer and closed it. He cleared his mouth of food.

'I'm very sorry, Ben. It's not up to me. I can only make recommendations to the Region. The decision is not mine. And I can only make recommendations with regard to *close* relatives. If you like you can submit a request to the Regional Director.'

'And if he refuses?'

The Principal lifted his shoulders in a long shrug. 'Then you can't go.'

'He was important to me. More than a relative.'

'I'm afraid it can't be helped.'

'What would happen if I went anyway?'

'If you went awol?'

Ben nodded. He was still standing in the middle of the floor. The faint yelling from the playground seemed to grow in volume.

'That would not be a good thing – at all. Because we are very short-staffed at the minute.' He looked up at Ben, then swivelled a bit in his chair. 'With this flu that is going about.'

'He was called Paddy Quinn. And he was one of the best read people I ever met. He was sharp and he had very little luck.'

The Principal stood up. 'They say it's not a particularly bad flu.' He went to the window and changed the tilt of the venetian blinds so the room was flooded with light. 'Ben, if you'll excuse me, I have a lunch to finish.'

The funeral service was at ten o'clock and there was to be a gathering in the public bar of the Seaview Hotel afterwards. A piper had been engaged and paid for by the owner of the hotel as a mark of respect for a valued customer and friend. There was no point in Ben sending condolences – who would he send them to? Paddy would understand – he never did have any regard for ritual or the niceties of any situation. He would have said, 'Fuck it – do what you want to do.' At 9.45 Ben set his third-year class a comprehension exercise to keep them quiet.

'Sir, why do we have to do this crap?'

'Lorimer – you are supposed to be on your best behaviour. You do it because I say you do it.'

Ben sat, glad of the silence he could impose. When it came to ten by the clock and the class were working quietly he got up and went into the book cupboard. Although he preferred whisky he had filled his hip flask with vodka – he knew it couldn't be detected on the breath – and he drank a toast to Paddy. Then another one. It was the first drink he had ever had during working hours and it made him feel good that he was, in some small way, giving them the fingers. He closed his eyes and leaned his head against a stack of *Art of English IV* and tried to visualise what was happening two hundred miles away in the town of Tynagh.

V
MATTERS OF LIFE & DEATH
2006

ON THE ROUNDABOUT

I suppose it's about doing something without thinking. But it was nothing really. Anybody'd've done the same.

We were driving back into Belfast – we could have been in Omagh or Enniskillen – visiting Anne's aunt maybe. But that's not important. It was the early seventies and that *is* important. Not long after Bloody Friday – nine dead, God knows how many maimed – all courtesy of our friends, the Provos. So everybody was a bit hyper.

It was beginning to get dark. I hadn't been all that long at the driving and I was feeling the family man – Anne in the passenger seat, the two kids in the back – like something outa Norman Rockwell. Seat-belts weren't compulsory but we were seat-belt kinda people. Clunk, click every trip – remember that? I'm thinking about what we have to do before we can relax – get the kids ready for bed – I remember all this very vividly, the way you remember just *before* a crash. Tell them a story maybe. They were the age for stories – wee Kate was anyway – at that time she made you get every word right. Any deviation and she'd have been up in arms. Sean was just talking and no more. The other thing was that the car radio was on and they were saying that the UDA were out in force in certain places – stopping and searching.

So I'm driving into that roundabout, the one at the bottom of the Grosvenor Road – the one that used to be Celtic Park – and there's this guy hitching, trying to get a lift before the cars go on the motorway. And there's a bunch of the UDA appear, about half a dozen of them, wearing khaki. And they go up to talk to the guy who's hitching. I'm about fourth or fifth in the queue onto the roundabout and I'm keeping an eye on the cars edging ahead and the UDA guys. You can never tell with them. There's one guy – he's wearing a black scarf – and he produces a claw-hammer. And he whacks the guy hitching in the face with it. And down he goes. And they start laying into him for all they're worth – boots, the hammer, the lot. There's only a couple of cars in front of us now and they scarper – away like the clappers – they don't want to know. And Anne is screaming did you see that? And her hands are up to her face. I put the boot to the floor, gunning the engine like, and before I know what I'm doing I'm driving up the pavement straight at the UDA. And they scatter. And they're laughing – I'll always remember that – laughing their heads off, especially the guy with the black scarf, the one with the hammer. I'm doing this before I know I'm doing it. But it's like we've rehearsed it. Anne pops her seat-belt, leans over and opens the back door. I get out and manhandle the poor bastard onto the floor of the back seat. He's not unconscious but he's not fully with it. He's bleeding all over the place. It's coming out of his eye and hitting the ceiling. Wee Kate is crying because she knows something's very wrong. The UDA guys are hanging back, still laughing. Maybe they think I'm the law or something. The Army maybe. Anyway I just want outa there. And I'm driving back onto the roundabout trying not to hit anything. I have a shammy for the inside of the windscreen and Anne's kneeling on her seat, leaning over, pressing it up against the guy's face trying to stop the blood spouting all over the place. And I'm lucky because without knowing I take the exit to the Royal. He keeps going unconscious and I'm shouting to Anne keep him awake, keep him awake. And she's yelling at him what happened? What happened? And both the children are crying now, yelling their heads off. And he says he was just hitching home to Lurgan and they said are you a Fenian and before I could even fucking answer them I'm on the deck. Anne's saying hold that there, hold it. To stop the bleeding. And he's falling about but he's still talking. He can't understand. A minute ago he was trying to get home. He says the funny thing is I'm Presbyterian. I start laughing at this, looking over my shoulder. A Presbyterian? Even he thinks it's funny. Jesus. Then he falls backwards and his mouth opens and there's blood inside that looks black in the street lights. He begins jerking and passing out. Anne holds him up trying to steady him, holds the shammy to his wound – a hole between his ear and his eye the size of a ten-pence piece. He comes round again shouting I'm dead – they've killed me. The cunts have killed me. By this time I'm driving up the wrong side of the road with my hand on the horn. Get out of my fuckin way – everybody thinks I've taken leave of my senses. Anyway we eventually get into the hospital and the staff take over.

It's only then I start to get angry. I try to give my name and address but the doctors and nurses don't want to know. There's a Brit soldier there with his gun and he doesn't want to know either. I've just witnessed an attempted murder and nobody wants to know. And Anne's carrying Sean and pulling at Kate. Come on, come on. She's looking ahead to me in the witness box facing the UDA across the court. We know your registration, we know your whole family.

The kids weren't affected. Sean doesn't remember a thing about it – he was too young – but wee Kate does. She was really scared and timid for a long time.

Anyway that's what Belfast was like at that time.

But about two months later there was a long letter in the *Belfast Telegraph*. The guy was outa hospital and he was trying to thank the Good Samaritan family who'd helped him on the roundabout that night. Wasn't that good of him? To tell the story.

THE TROJAN SOFA

It's dark – pitch black – and everything's shaking and bumping. I'm not scared – just have some what-if knots in my gut. What if they have a dog? That would be me – well and truly. Or a burglar alarm – with laser beams like they have in the movies. And when you walk through the beam, which you can't see, the alarm goes off in the nearest cop shop. But my Da would've asked all these questions when he was selling. My Da sells anything and everything, bric-a-brac, furniture, you name it. And he sells all over the place – fairs, car boot sales, a stall in the Markets – but quality stuff or as much of it as he can get. He's good – friendly – knows what he's doing.

'This is a good piece – worth quite a bit – as you well know.' And he'd laugh with the customer who had just paid up. 'If you'd more stuff like this you'd want to have an alarm in the house.'

'I don't like alarms,' or 'I've already got the best on the market.' And that'd be my Da clued in. 'You wouldn't want dog hairs all over good fabric like that.' 'I don't have a dog,' and that would be my Da clued in a bit more. He's a dab hand at getting people to tell him things.

I'm on my left-hand side – the side I sleep on at night – because I know there'll not be much turning round in the foreseeable future. My knees bent only slightly. I've all my bits and pieces.

'You've bugger all to do except keep your wits about you and open the door. In this case two doors.'

I'm in my first year at grammar school. Got the eleven-plus – no problem. Even though I hadn't reached eleven. That's good for a boy from the Markets. When my Da went up to the College the President told him I got the highest marks of anybody in Northern Ireland. Smart boy wanted. I can hear my Da's voice now talking to Uncle Eamon.

474

'Two flights of stairs and you're outa puff already?'

'It's the bloody smoking,' I hear Eamon say.

'Why don't you give it up? It was no problem for me.'

'Your right hand down a bit. Take it easy.'

I can hear the bumping of their feet on carpeted stairs.

'It weighs a fuckin ton,' says Uncle Eamon.

'Watch your tongue in front of the boy,' says my Da. I hear them both laughing.

He has very strong opinions, has my Da. A war is two sides, one against the other, he says. It's as simple as that. 'The wrong done to this country was so great that we can do *anything* in retaliation.' If it's done against the Brits it's OK by him. 'A broken phone is a British liability,' he says. 'So's a burnt bus. They're things that have to be replaced – by the English exchequer.'

That's why he likes to deal with the other side. I was there one time when he sold a three-piece suite to this guy – the most Orangeman-looking man I've ever seen. You could tell what he was from a mile away – the big fat jowls, the moustache, the accent. 'Your address, sir?' When he says the part of the town where he lives my Da looks at Uncle Eamon as if to say wouldn't you know?

'Yes – we can deliver free,' says my Da. So the next day I'm into the sofa with my gear and the hessian is stapled back onto the frame. It's usually an overnight. Next morning when everybody's away to work and the place is quiet I Stanley knife my way out and open the door. My Da and Uncle Eamon are sitting there in the van smiling. And in they come. The sofa's the first thing they lift because it has all the evidence in it – where I've bed and breakfasted. The modus operandi. Then they clear the place. And it's one up for old Ireland.

Before we did it for the first time my Da said to me, 'It's up to yourself. You can say yea or nay. I'd never force anybody to do something like this – never mind one of my own. But I must say it *is* for Ireland.'

'Ireland the Brave,' says Uncle Eamon from the sidelines.

What I'm in at the moment – so I've been told by my Da, the expert – is a Victorian sofa. It smells of dust, dry built-up-over-the-years dust. It's worse because we're on the move and everything's getting shaken up. Sneezing's a danger. There's a bump against something and I bang my head.

'Be careful,' says my Da to Eamon. 'The Major'll be none too pleased if his property comes damaged.'

'Niall won't be too happy either,' says Eamon.

That's me he's talking about. Niall. Niall Donnelly. Sometimes my Da calls me Skinny-ma-link. They set the sofa down and I hear a bell ringing in the distance. The door opens and a new English voice starts talking. This whole thing is like a play on the radio. You can hear everything but see nothing. And then a woman's voice joins in. There's a lotta bumping and angling so's they can get through the doorways – so much so that, when it goes upright, I have to hang on like grim death to the wooden frame. Like the ladder thing in the park you go hand over hand on.

'Here?' says my Da.

'There, with its back to the wall,' says the woman.

My Da rabbits on a bit with the Major and there's a lotta laughing while my Uncle Eamon goes for the clock. I can just see my Da, the way he throws his head back and opens his mouth wide enough to see his fillings. And Eamon smiling on his way down the stairs back to the van. He seems to take for ages. It's so bad the Major actually says, 'He's taking his time.'

'He'll be having a fly fag.' When Uncle Eamon does come back they all listen to the chimes and the Major sets it to the one he likes the best. He also chooses it to chime at quarter hours. They set the right time by their watches and there's the tickety sound of the clock being wound up. Eventually they go and I hear their voices getting weaker and the slam of the main door of the flat. I feel the vibration through the floor. There is silence now and I become conscious of my breathing – making sure my nose is clear. The man says something I can't hear to the woman. She laughs. I guess they are looking at the sofa. Then they go away.

I hear knives and forks and plates rattling in another room. A radio is switched on but it's posh music. They must be eating their tea. There's a great smell which makes me hungry. Bacon or meat of some sort. Or onions – I love fried onions.

It's very hard to know how much time has passed. My Da says I'm far better without a watch. You're more aware of time passing if you're always looking to check. Anyway I couldn't see a watch it's so dark. But it might be a kinda comfort to know how much longer I've gotta be in here. When I hear them actually talking in the other room I change my position. Move my leg a bit – change where the frame is biting into my backside – move my pillows around a bit. I'll eat my sandwiches in the middle of the night when they've gone to bed. My older brother says when I eat, it sounds like an army marching through muck. 'Keep your mouth closed.' Then I hear the clock chiming again. It does those chimes you hear on the news over a picture of Big Ben and Westminster. Then it bongs eight times.

My Da and Uncle Eamon had stopped the van out in the country to look the place over before they staple-gunned me in.

'How can you be so sure he's a Major?'

'Instinct,' says my Da. 'Maybe not a Major. But Army of some sort. All upper-crust Brits are. And they're as obvious as punks. Instead of a Mohican, a tweed cap. Leather shoes and that voice, that cut-glass voice.'

'If you were a Brit would you allow furniture in without checking it?' My Da didn't say anything. 'That's where they put fire bombs in the shops – down the sides of sofas.'

I'd gone over the hedge for a last pee – after drinking a can of Coke. I could see the house was a huge mansion with turrets and stuff, in among trees and gardens. It was about a mile away up a tarmac drive. My Da said the house had been turned into about ten flats by some developer. And he went on and on about the olden days and how could any one man have lived in such a place – to have it all to himself with servants tugging the forelock and kowtowing to him. Uncle Eamon spat out the van window.

When the Major and his woman finish their tea they switch off the radio and come into the room. Then the piano playing starts. Sort of rhythmic stuff. No point to it. Was it him or was it her playing? I was just glad there was something to listen to – to pass the time. I knew it was actual playing and not a radio, because sometimes the notes would stop and the same bit would be played again.

Better. After a while the playing stopped. Someone was clapping – pretend applause. Clap, clap, clap.

'Bravo,' said the Major. 'Play me the Mozart.'

The piano started again. And went on and on and on. With that kinda music, you know when the end is coming. It winds itself up. After that everything goes quiet.

I know they are in the room but I can't hear anything. So I start mouth breathing. It's quieter. I can sense someone sitting on the sofa, then getting off again. They're speaking very quietly – sorta murmuring. This goes on for ages and then they start exercising – sometimes on the sofa, sometimes on the floor. In school they have this crazy bastard of a gym teacher who has a yelpy voice. 'Running on the spot. Go!' 'Ten press-ups. Go!' And he reserves the highest and loudest note for yelping the word 'go'. Before the Major and his woman eventually stop the exercising and the gasping the penny drops. They're doing sex. Having a ride. Not two inches away. And I can't see a thing. And then they go back to the murmuring. I can't make out a single word. The clock chimes nine and the TV is switched on. The music is for the News. Somebody sits down on the sofa. The news is the usual boring stuff. When it comes to the Northern Ireland bit there are two murders. A prison officer who worked at the Maze tried to start his car and it blew up and he got killed. Boo-hoo. Lend me a hanky. The other was a drive-by shooting on the Antrim Road. A boy of seventeen had been shot and died on the way to hospital. If it's the Antrim Road he'll be one of ours. There was three explosions but nobody got hurt because there was warnings.

I'm feeling a bit sleepy but keep myself awake by sticking my fingernail into the back of my other hand. I don't think I snore. But you can't be sure. A comedy programme comes on because there's a lotta laughing from the audience. Canned stuff. It goes on for ages. When the clock chimes eleven the Major and his wife go to bed. I hear the click of the light switch going off and I'm aware that the darkness has increased. I hear them doing things in the distance – running taps, brushing teeth, kettles clicking off when they boil. A hot-water bottle for her, maybe. After a while everything goes silent. At last I can turn. And fix my pillows. I don't even risk a wee groan.

This must have been what it was like 'durin the war'. All the old ones at the stalls talk about 'durin the war'. They never stop. I reach out for my sandwiches – touch and rip the cling wrap. Ham and cheese. I normally like egg and onion but my Da said it's too risky – it would stink to high heaven. Give me away. Rosaleen made them. She lives with my Da now. I like her – she's a good laugh. My mother died of cancer when I was eight – right after my First Communion.

Chewing in the quiet like this is weird. The inside of your head is filled with noises, crunchings and squelchings – moving muscles and teeth-clicks and a roaring in your ears. And I think of myself as a mouse – the way other people hear a mouse. They sit up in bed at night and hear small noises, scratchings, pitter-patterings. 'There's the mouse,' they say. 'I must set the trap tomorrow.'

This is the third Trojan sofa I've done. The first was the worst. I was nervous and needed to pee a lot. Nearly filled the poly bag I had. Fresh piss is really warm. And – see – trying to get the knot outa the neck of the bag when it was half full when you wanted to go for a second and third time – that was awful. Anyway it all went fine. A cinch. It was funny being in a house with Union Jacks and pictures of the Queen on the walls. Really spooky.

On Saturday afternoons I help Rosaleen with her stall and she gives me a tenner. All the books are priced in pencil on the inside leaf so it's dead easy. I seen the Major that day. My Da's stall is about three over from Rosaleen's. There was no indication as to what or who he was. Nothing remarkable about him at all – heavy-set in a tweed jacket, open-neck shirt, wavy hair getting a bit grey – but my Da knew the voice. The voice is a dead give-away. He was interested in this old-fashioned clock for his mantelpiece, paid a lotta attention to it, listened to the different chimes it could do and all. Then he took the Victorian sofa as well. And now here I am lying in the back of it ateing sandwiches. I don't wanna wash them down. As little liquid as possible. So I just knock them around inside my mouth till they go away. It takes bloody ages. I don't bother with the crusts.

At this very minute my Da and Rosaleen'll be coming back after a night in the pub. He takes pints of lager, she has her vodkas and Coke. When they come home me and my brother hang around being nice. They usually bring a crowd back with them – maybe a couple of fiddlers who can play jigs and reels, or singers with guitars. It's a bit of a laugh and when he's in good form my Da's liable to put his hand in his pocket – but he never remembers the next day. So you can try and tap him again. Rosaleen hugs us and says things like 'Yis are not mine – but I love ya.' Then she'll punch my Da if he's beside her. 'My womb cries out,' she says and everybody'll laugh.

I start to feel really sleepy now. I think about having a piss but whatever way I was up-ended coming through the door I can't find the poly bag. It's probably down by my feet somewhere. And I can't bend. I must have dozed off because I waken up halfway through the Westminster chimes. I lie there counting all twelve of the strokes that follow the tune. Then I hear a creak of a door in the distance. Somebody on the stairs.

Jesus, maybe he's rumbled me. But how? What have I just done? Did I snore? Did I give myself away somehow? Did he hear me chewing? No chance. Wait. The light clicks on and I can see faintly around me after the blackness. It must be the Major because he clears his throat. A deep sound, not a woman. He doesn't come near the sofa. So it's a false alarm. He shuffles over to where I think the mantelpiece must be. He is doing something footery because he's cursing and mumbling to himself. Then he says 'Ha!' and goes out of the room. The light goes off and I hear nothing more. What was that all about? Maybe he was sleepwalking. Did people really do that? Walk about the place sound asleep? Uncle Eamon says he woke up one night and he was standing pissing into a suitcase. Maybe the Major's turned off the chimes. And I'll be able to get a bit of shut-eye. 'Thanks and praises be to God.' Rosaleen says that all the time.

I don't remember anything much of what my mother said. She smiled a lot – or did I get that from photographs of her? Sitting in the park. On beaches. With other girls on the wee wall outside Granda's. And the styles. Her hair and her clothes – they were just embarrassing. When she died she went yellow. I seen her in the coffin. It had the lid off before the funeral. That was a thing she said, 'Yella as a duck's foot.' I can remember that. 'So-and-so had the jaundice – he was as yella as a duck's foot.' I lie thinking about her for a while. My Da seemed to take a long time to get over it. If any grown-up on the street mentioned her to me – 'Aw, I knew your mother' – I just wanted to cry. And that went on for years. I don't have very many friends. Most of them are grown up – like Uncle Eamon and the ones who come back to the house after the pub. I don't really like the friends who are my own age. Danny Breen and Eugene Magee. I fight with them a lot. They're so stupid playing. They squabble and fall out about the rules for everything. And they cheat all the time. It's impossible to knock around with them. 'You do this.' 'No I don't.' 'Yes you do – for I seen ya.' 'Ya fucking did not.' Like politicians in Stormont.

I can't sleep because I'm still fairly uptight. But I'm relaxed enough to be able to think about the way things are. The second time we pulled the scam it was a woman who owned the flat. She was high up in the Civil Service at Stormont. My Da said it was a cover for something to do with the H blocks. But when I got out of the sofa I couldn't believe the place. It was the worst I ever seen. Everything everywhere. Newspapers and high-heeled shoes and magazines and half-drunk cupsa tea. Dirty knickers, dressing gowns, dresses and blouses flung all over the place. And tissues. I've never seen as many bunched-up tissues in my life. A fire hazard. And the only neat thing in the whole place was her manicure set and the ten wee nail clippings on a black coffee table – each one a wee arc. How will this woman know we've burgled her? She'll not know for a week. Unless she wants to watch the telly. Or play something on the video.

The smell of the dust inside the sofa for some reason makes me feel sad. It's not a bad smell. It's just sad. And it won't go away. The smell dries inside my mouth. I try to get in the habit of mouth breathing because it's quieter. And I begin to dream. I see myself dreaming in the darkness and then I wake up in the darkness. Not knowing where I am. And back to dreaming again. In one dream I'm in school and nobody in the class knows what 'onomatopoeia' is except me. But I can't put my hand up. I'm paralysed. Another dream is of me snoring. And jerking awake to stop me snoring. Rosaleen puts me in the bottom of a wardrobe and covers me with coats to keep the sound to a minimum. Then I wake up. Wide awake. I can sense it's light – morning light, not electric. I can make out areas and shades. I check where my Stanley knife is. It's one of those with a safety slide thing at the side for retracting and bringing out the blade. I should have been awake earlier. And I know there's something wrong. The first thing I hear is a man's footsteps walking away from the sofa. Quickly. I just know by the way he's walking that he's on to me. I hear him lifting the phone. He uses just one word. Police. Then he starts talking about an intruder in his house – trying to keep his voice down. I have to be quick. I get the Stanley knife and slide out the blade – stick it through the material above my head – out into the room. Then I pull hard. A kinda ripping sound. A thin line of light. A tent flap. And me getting out of it. Moving my stiff legs. Backing out. My feet are on the floor and I straighten up. My back feels like it's broke in two. I look down the hallway where the Major is on the phone. The door of the room is open and his eyes are watching me.

'Freeze.'

It's a scream that scares the shit outa me. The Major moves his arms upwards and now I can see he has a shotgun aimed at my head. The phone falls and swings on its wiggly cord. He starts to walk towards me. I see more and more clearly both barrels – two black holes – as they point straight at my face. He's as white as a sheet.

'Freeze you bastard.' My stomach swoops. Again and again. His voice is like the gym teacher's. Yelped. Because he's scared shitless. I could have been anything. So I do as I'm told. Try not to frighten him into doing something foolish. But I start to shake. I hope he doesn't notice me shaking. 'You fucking piece of shit. I've a good mind to kill you right now. Before the police arrive.' I'm still behind the sofa, between it and the wall. He walks past me and goes to the front door to check that it is firmly closed. My heart's beating like mad. Then the clock chimes – the whole Westminster followed by nine dings. He must have turned it back on earlier. When I was asleep. Now I can hear the clock ticking. Or is it my imagination. Myself breathing.

'Do everything nice and slow or I might just pull this trigger. Put that blade down.'

Very deliberately, with my thumb, I retract the blade into the handle and set it on the seat of the sofa. It's weird. I'm gonna be shot in the face and yet the thing that annoys me most is – the room isn't the way I thought it was. It's much, much bigger. The mantelpiece is on the wrong wall and the piano – a grand piano with a big fin sticking up in the air – is over by the bay window. I didn't even know the room had a bay window. Everything's in the wrong place.

'You're a bit young for this game.' The cut-glass voice. Like Prince Charles. 'Who put you up to this?' My hands are resting on the back of the sofa. It's velvety material – gives under my fingers when I press. I haven't a clue what to do. I've never been caught before. The only advice I ever heard was my Da's. 'Whatever you say, say nothing.' But he was talking about guys getting interrogated in Castlereagh. Guys getting tortured.

Another thing – I badly need a piss. Even more since he scared me. You can see the Major is delighted when he sees what age I am. He keeps moving about. Swaggering almost – like the cat that got the cream. He begins getting some colour back in his face. His wife must be away to work because there's no sign of her. He begins talking ninety to the dozen. Still with the gun levelled at my head.

'I was just thinking I'll try out my new sofa – read the paper. At first I didn't believe what I was hearing. I kept thinking there's someone else in this room. Breathing.' He shakes his head in disbelief. 'It wasn't snoring – just long breaths. Who are you working for?'

I don't want to say anything. Don't want to give anything away. I look down, like I'm in pain. I'm pressing myself hard against the back of the sofa.

'I need the toilet,' I say.

'Oh – it speaks, does it?' He kinda smirks. 'Go in the police station.'

'I'm gonna wet myself.' He just stares at me. 'I'm gonna wet the carpet.'

He thinks about this and stares at me. Like a teacher when he hears an excuse he doesn't believe. Like he thinks there's more to it.

'Please,' I say. 'I've gotta go now.' I grip the front of my jeans to stop myself and close my eyes – tight. As if every muscle was connected – even my eyes were contributing to holding it in. The Major now

sees it as a real threat. To his fawn carpet. He'd never get rid of the
smell. He waves me out from behind the sofa with the shotgun. He
goes in front of me and beckons me. He leads me into a panelled
hallway. There are various brown doors off it. One is open and I can
see office chairs in front of big drawing boards. Still my fist is bunched
at my flies. The Major indicates another door. I open it but it only
leads to another. In between there is a washing machine and a drier
and a big wash basket.

He holds the door open with the toe of his brown leather shoe. I
open the next door into the bathroom. He follows me in and nods
to the toilet. I'm still burstin but I don't like taking my thing out in
front of him. He sits down on the side of the bath and keeps pointing
the gun at me. So I half turn my back on him and take my thing out.

But being watched this closely nothing happens. I've gone into
some kinda block. I look at the wall in front of me. There's a framed
diploma. What a place to hang a diploma. It's for Architecture. For
somebody called Dunstan Luttrell. At the same time I'm trying to
think of a plan. To get away. There's a narrow frosted glass window
to my left but it looks well and truly closed. Anyway we're two floors
up which is a long way down. Then when the piss starts it nearly
drills a hole in the delph. It goes on and on and on – like it's never
going to stop, making an awful lotta noise in the bowl.

'You sound like a man on stilts after a night on the beer,' says the
Major. He's making jokes. There's no way this guy is going to shoot
me if I make a run for it. And he wouldn't be fit enough to catch
me. Fat bastard. Eventually I stop peeing and give myself a wee shake
and put it away. I give a wee shivery shudder because of losing my
central heating. I continue to stand at the toilet bowl. 'So you've been
in there all night.' I nod my head before I can stop myself. Give him
no information whatsoever. Maybe he's remembering doing the sex.
Maybe he's embarrassed about it. If I leg it this minute, I'll have time
to get down onto the road and into the van before the cops arrive.
Maybe the traffic is bad. He waves the gun towards the hallway. I
start to move past the mirror and the wash-basin. My face is too
pale. 'Wash your hands.' I don't know whether he's kidding or not.
The gun's pointing at me. I turn on the tap and wash my hands. It's

that soap with the wee label that never goes away. Imperial Leather. The last thing to go is the wee label. How do they make it do that? I reach out to get the towel and he screams again.

'Do not fucking touch anything in this house. Scumbag.' I shake my hands a bit, wipe them on my jeans. He is so angry I'm afraid he might pull the trigger by accident. He goes out the door with the gun still trained on me and he waits in the laundry bit and waves me through. I decide this is the time. If I'm gonna go – I have to do it now. He won't have the balls. I open the door into the hallway and pull it as hard as I can after me. It slams. I hear him shouting. And I run. His hands are full with the gun. As I race past the sofa I lift the Stanley knife and pocket it. I get to the front door of the flat. By this time the Major is out of the laundry room and putting the shotgun up to his shoulder. Which means he's standing still and I'm running.

'Stop or I'll shoot,' he screams. The front door takes two hands. My back quakes expecting to be shot. The lower handle and the Yale lock. I get both open – all the time waiting for my head to explode. But he can't do it – he doesn't have the guts. And I'm through the door and running down the central stairs about four at a time. Steadying myself with my hand on the banisters. And out the main door and leggin it across the lawn to get cover from some trees and bushes. The speed I'm going. It's a bright day full of sunshine with a blue sky. I'm high on adrenalin. And after a night with a mouth full of dust it feels great. I want to yell 'Fuck you, Major. Fuck the Brits.' I zigzag through the wood as far as the road, looking at where my feet land, avoiding tree roots, kicking dead leaves. The sunlight flickers as I'm dancing down dips and sprinting up slopes. I spot the white of the van in a lay-by about half a mile away. I hear a police nee-naw in the distance. By the time I get to the lay-by I'm completely knackered. My Da is in the driver's seat facing the house and Uncle Eamon's having a look through the binoculars at what he thinks is a sparrowhawk hovering over the motorway. The police Land Rover trundles past heading for the big house. I'm coming up behind the van and they don't see me. I bang the side.

Uncle Eamon opens the door and looks down at me.

'Where did you come from?'

'Niall,' shouts my Da.

I jump up into the van. I can hardly talk for panting. 'Get outa here.' My Da switches on, indicates and we start driving.

'He caught me.' And I tell them the whole disaster.

The next morning was Saturday and we were all standing about in the Market.

'What have they got on us?' Eamon says. 'What can they prove? Was anything taken? It wasn't "breaking and entering". For there was no "breaking". And no "entering". If anything the boy was "exiting".'

'And very fast by the sound of it,' said Rosaleen.

'I'm sure the Major's in Intelligence,' my Da says.

The next thing is the cops turn up. Out of an armoured Land Rover. Machine guns, flak jackets, the whole gear. They questioned my Da and he spun them some yarn about catching me drunk on cider and beating me and falling out with me and me running away to hide in the sofa he was repairing and falling asleep and then him stapling it up and delivering it with me inside. And them all laughing the way he told it – even the RUC men. Then the cops talked to me – Rosaleen had her arm round me the whole time – and I backed up what my Da said. 'Leave the poor wee guy alone,' Rosaleen kept saying. I also told them I was very anxious to get outa the Major's house. With that man threatening me with a shotgun. And me only eleven. The cops threatened to bring me in front of a magistrate but nothing ever came of it.

About the Markets the talk was of me being the only burglar to leave his victim richer by a bowlful of piss and a couple of crusts. The Major *did* turn out to be the famous English architect, Dunstan Luttrell, like on the diploma. Not long after that his photo was all over the papers for designing an oratory for some nuns. The Press made a big thing about it. English architect, Irish nuns. Protestant–Catholic co-operation. Still my Da said the architecture was a cover story – everybody in Intelligence work had one. They like to keep us in the dark, he said.

LEARNING TO DANCE

The boy sat on one of the divan beds for almost an hour without moving. At his feet the shopping bag with their pyjamas and things in it. His younger brother lay on a rug between the beds turned away from him. Nothing was said. Sounds drifted up from downstairs – the wireless was on, a mixture of distant music and talk. Doors opened and closed. Traffic hummed from the main road. At one point there was ringing.

'Telephone,' said the boy. His brother nodded. High heels clicked across the hallway and the ringing stopped and the doctor's wife spoke. Sometimes his younger brother made a noise like a pig – snuffing back and swallowing. It was revolting and he wanted to kill him. Then the boy heard someone coming up the stairs. The doctor's wife came to the half-open door and tapped it lightly with her fingernail.

'Can I come in?' The boy sat upright on the bed – his brother rolled around and looked over his shoulder. The doctor's wife stepped into the room. She leaned forward and put her hands on her knees so that her head was on a level with the boy's sitting on the bed. 'So – Ben and Tony – have you settled in?' The boys nodded.

'Do you want to go outside?' The boy on the bed thought it seemed somehow wrong.

'No,' he said. 'Thank you.'

'Into the garden for a bit. Get a bit of fresh air before lunch.' The boy had already made his decision and he felt it would be rude to change it.

'I'm OK.'

'Whatever suits. Also I was wondering if you had any likes or dislikes for lunch? Either of you. It's coming up to that time.' No. Both boys shook their heads. 'Some boys can be very picky. I have nephews who would run a mile rather than eat a soft-boiled egg.'

'Some eggs have elastic bands in them,' said the boy on the floor.
'Pardon me?'

'In the white bit – some brown rubbery things. Eucch.'

'Well the eggs we get here don't have anything like that in them.'
She laughed. 'So what would you like?' The boy on the bed raised
his shoulders in a slow shrug – he'd no idea. 'A boiled egg? With
plenty of hot buttered toast?' said the doctor's wife. The boys nodded.
When they had a boiled egg at home their mother spooned it from
the shell into a cup and mashed the bits up with some butter so that
the yellow and the white mixed evenly.

'Very well, then – it's too early, but let's go.' She ushered them out
of the room and down the stairs into the kitchen. They walked quietly
in their new surroundings. She sat them up on stools at a table and
bustled around putting on a saucepan of eggs, dropping slices of
bread into the shining toaster, setting salt and pepper on the table.
There was a refrigerator as tall as herself in the corner. Every so often
its engine shuddered to a halt and there was silence. She promised
they would make flavoured lollipops later on.

'What's your favourite flavour?'

'Orange,' said the boy.

His brother said, 'Milk.' The doctor's wife laughed, said it was
impossible to make a milk lollipop.

She was dressed as if she was going out for the evening – a silky
green frock, pearls around her bare neck, high-heeled sandal shoes.
She lit a cigarette from the lighter she used to light the gas and bit
down hard on the first intake of smoke.

'Dr D'Arcy and his wife – they're always immaculate,' their mother
had said. 'For all the world like Fred Astaire and Ginger Rogers.' Dr
D'Arcy wasn't their doctor – just a friend of the family. Ben and
Tony's father and Dr D'Arcy were both in the Young Philanthropists.
Their own doctor was Dr Gorman. Dr Gorman was the one who
came to the house when anyone was sick. And to the hospital after
you had had your tonsils out.

'Ice cream – and plenty of it,' was the medicine he prescribed.

The boy had seen photos of Fred Astaire and Ginger Rogers
dancing in the movies. His mother and father were very keen on

supper dances and would go to one or two every year – mostly ones run by the Young Philanthropists. For days beforehand the house would be full of excitement. On the night, the boys would be sitting in the kitchen with Grandma and Granda. Upstairs the bathroom would be going full tilt, the steam and the shaving and the powdering and perfuming all going on at the same time along with shouts of 'Are there no laces for these shoes?' 'Where are the cuff-links?' 'They'll be where you left them last year.' Dr D'Arcy would be picking them up by car, or a taxi would have been ordered and the ones getting ready would always be running late. And then they'd arrive into the room for the 'showing off' with his mother saying 'I'm as ready as ever I'm going to be.' And she'd swish and twirl around the kitchen, the dress and her petticoats taking up most of the small space. She'd touch the necklace at her throat and worry that it didn't match her diamante bag. His father would straighten his black bow-tie at the mirror by crouching his knees. It was set at the correct height for their mother. And because it was a special occasion they'd kiss the boys goodbye and tell them to behave and so on and not give Grandma any trouble. Their father smelt of shaving soap. And their mother would decide at the last minute not to wear a coat because it just made the dress underneath look silly – her wrap would be warm enough. And the doctor's car would be honking its horn outside and suddenly the door would rattle and slam and they'd be gone. Silence. And Grandma and Granda would be sitting opposite each other smiling, waiting to play cards. The next morning when the boys woke there would be balloons and paper hats and brightly coloured cocktail sticks shaped like tiny sabres on their bedside chairs.

'You poor things,' said the doctor's wife. Her long red hair gave the impression of being unruly – standing out as it did from her head. She fought a constant battle with it combing and sweeping it aside with open fingers.

'Four minutes?' she said. 'To be on the safe side?' She looked very tall and glamorous as she stood waiting for the toast with one hand on her hip and a cigarette in the other. Her fingernails were painted. Even her toenails were scarlet – peeping out the front of her high-heeled sandals. When the eggs were ready she set one in front of each boy. They stared at them but didn't move.

'Let me.' She sliced the top off each egg and set it on a plate beside the eggcup. 'No bits of shell,' she said. 'Clean as a whistle. And apostle spoons. What's keeping you?' The boy scooped a little egg white from the lid and put it in his mouth. His younger brother did the same. The doctor's wife took a seat on a stool and leaned her elbows on the table staring at her guests. She looked long and hard at them then smiled.

'I would just love two boys like you,' she said. There was a sound of crunching toast and chewing. She made a platform for her chin with her fists and looked from one boy to the other. The younger boy chewed his food with his mouth open. His brother watched in disgust as he rolled the mashed-up food around his mouth. Occasionally the younger boy stopped for breath – breathed in past the mush and then would continue chewing.

'So what would you like to do this afternoon?' The boys continued to eat and stare defiance at each other. 'We could do something in the garden.'

'Like what?' said the boy. He must have thought his reply sounded rude because he added, 'That'd be OK.'

'What games do you play at home?' The boys stared down at their eggs then looked at each other. The boy said with a smile, 'Cricket in the yard.'

'I'm afraid we have no yard here.'

'Slow-motion football,' said his brother.

'And what, may I ask, is that?'

The elder boy tried to explain – a round balloon – the pitch was the hall – the goalposts were the front door and the width of the stairs. His younger brother got off his stool and began to move in the kitchen with heavy limbs demonstrating to the doctor's wife. He was smiling, remembering. 'Like you're in syrup when you head the balloon – it's slow motion – like in the pictures.'

'I'm sorry but we have no real toys – not even a balloon.' The kitchen darkened and spots of rain appeared on the window pane.

'We'll have to think of something else. Would you look at that?'

She nodded outside. 'How I would love to live somewhere like Spain or Barbados. Somewhere you can depend on the weather.' The boy's brother took a spoonful of egg and looked down into the shell. He made a noise in his throat – he didn't spit – but he allowed the egg along with some half-chewed toast to tumble out of his mouth onto his plate. He drooled strings of liquid stuff after it. His brother turned away.

'Is anything wrong?' said the doctor's wife.

The younger boy was leaning forward, swallowing and swallowing. 'An elastic band,' he said looking down into his eggshell.

'No. There's no such thing.' The doctor's wife swivelled off her stool and came to see. The child pointed at a small brownish spot deep in the white of the egg and curled his lip.

'Would you like a banana?' She took the plate with the mouthful of mush and tipped it into the bin as if nothing had happened.

'Thank you,' he said when she set a banana on his plate. He peeled the skin back and scrutinised the white of the banana for flaws or ripe spots.

'I hope the rain's not on for the day,' said the doctor's wife. 'More tea?' Both boys refused. 'When you're finished in here – you can just wander about the place. Explore the house.' The telephone rang in the hall and she hurried out. They heard her talking for a long time. When she came back they had finished eating.

'You can go anywhere you like, boys, except the surgery. Dr D'Arcy sees his private patients in there. Need I say more? Needles and things.' She gave a little shudder. 'It's the only room we keep locked. Let me show you around.' She ushered them out of the kitchen and led them along a parquet hallway. She left wafts of lavender in her wake.

'Oh, this is what we call the dancehall.' She pushed the open door and the boys looked in. It was a yellow wooden floor. There was a large bay window which made the room seem very bright. They all walked into the room and suddenly there was an echo to every sound.

'This is a maple sprung floor – our one extravagance. It was put in by the same people who did the Plaza Ballroom. Feel it move with you.' She let her hand rest on what looked like a sideboard. 'The radiogram. The piano is for visitors who can play. Can either of you?'

They both shook their heads. No, they couldn't. They went to the next room.

'This is the library but not many children's books, I'm afraid.' She pointed to one side: 'Mostly medical stuff. Not very nice. Promise me you'll avoid that side.' The boys agreed. 'But the good Doctor likes the occasional detective story.' She waved her hand at a bookcase full of greenbanded paperbacks. 'Most of all, Agatha Crispy.'

'Christie,' said the elder boy.

'Just my little joke.' She smiled and pointed out some of her own childhood books, but they looked schoolgirlie. The telephone rang and she rushed to answer it shouting over her shoulder, 'I'll leave you to it.'

The boy and his brother stood staring at the detective stories. The older boy turned to the forbidden medical books at the other side of the room. They had titles he could barely read. Words that meant nothing to him – ologies and isms. There were *Lancets* and *British Medical Journals*, many books about 'the Catholic Doctor', shelves full of Maynooth and Down and Conor quarterlies, the yellow spines of countless copies of *National Geographic*. He took down a large book and opened it. It had some black-and-white pictures illustrating diseases. Misshapen men stripped to the waist. A person with a blackened hairy tongue thrust out. A bare woman with droopy chests covered in spots. Then babies stuck together – then things so horrible he slammed the book shut and put it back on the shelf.

He went into the dancehall, hoping to get away from such images. But they were in his head. He knelt down on the smooth floor to look at what records there were. They were neatly stored in heavy books which contained paper sleeves with a circular window so that the label could be read. Decca, Columbia, Parlophone and His Master's Voice – the rich red behind the white dog. The radiogram had a cupboard at one end and the door was not properly closed. The boy looked around then eased it open. Bottles and glasses. A bar stocked with gin and whisky and other stuff.

He turned round and his brother was standing there with his hands in his pockets. He pushed the cupboard door shut.

'What are you standing there for?' His brother pulled a face. 'Why don't you go somewhere else?'

'I'm all right here.'

'Why d'you always have to follow me?'

His brother didn't move for a while. Eventually he sidled off back into the hallway. It was good to be rid of him. His very presence was an annoyance – the way he spat out his food in front of the doctor's wife was terrible. But it wasn't just that – it was a continual thing. His sniffing. His mouth noises. He did sneaky farts. Sometimes you heard them, sometimes you didn't.

He went back to the library to look through the *National Geographics*. The rain had stopped ticking at the window and the sun came out. He sat down on the floor with a magazine. The light fell in warm squares on the flowered carpet. The wallpaper was strange and rich. He had never seen anything like it. It had a pattern of flowers – maroon against a creamy background. But the flowers were made of velvet. He reached out and touched the pattern with his fingers. It was soothing the way it gave when he pressed it. The words on the page seemed to move. He found them difficult to read. His eyes wanted to close. He was tired. He hadn't had much sleep. What with people running up and down the stairs all night. Sometimes loud voices, sometimes whispering outside his door. At one point he'd recognised the priest's voice. When he'd put his head out to see what was going on, his mother had pleaded with him to stay in bed. 'For me,' she said and her face had had a look he had never seen before. On anyone's face. So he stayed put with the eiderdown pulled over his head. His brother had slept throughout.

He put his head down on his forearm and closed his eyes. And he drifted in the warmth of the sun. When he awoke he smiled – then remembered and his face went solid again. He didn't know how long he'd slept for, but he had drooled on his arm. He rubbed it dry and looked around him. What must have wakened him was the slam of a car door because the back door of the house opened and a voice shouted, 'Hello!'

Dr D'Arcy, still wearing his hat, stopped at the threshold of the library and saw the boy lying on the floor.

'Hi,' he said. 'What a sad, sad day.' He came and hunkered down in front of the boy. The doctor reached out and touched him on the shoulder. Then patted him on the head as he straightened up. The boy did not know what to say. He was on the verge of tears but did not want to show it. 'You're making yourself comfortable, I see.'

'Yes.'

The doctor stepped back out into the hallway. His wife came to him and offered herself for a kiss. He took off his hat and kissed her. The boy looked away.

'Not lonely today, eh?' said the doctor.

'I have my hands full.'

'Where's the other boy?'

'In the garden.'

The doctor hung his hat on the hall stand. He was tall and thin and wore a dark pinstripe suit with a pink shirt and a maroon bow-tie. His thinning hair was Brylcreemed flat to his head. In high heels she was almost as tall as her husband.

'The weather's wonderful now.' The doctor's wife beckoned the boy. 'Let me show you the garden.'

All three of them went out the back door. The garden was surrounded by a grey stone wall, but the boy could see other gardens with hedges and apple trees.

'It keeps the heat in and the wind out,' said the doctor's wife. 'Do you like flowers?' The boy said he did. 'Dahlias and chrysanths are my favourites. I put so much work into my flowers.'

The doctor produced a packet of Craven A and he and his wife lit cigarettes.

'I suppose you're a bit young to start,' he said and they all laughed.

As they walked around the garden she pointed out various plants and told him things about them. 'Eternal vigilance when it comes to snails,' she said. 'Japonica here. And night-scented stock. Ummm . . .' She cupped a russet chrysanthemum and inhaled its scent while making swooning noises. The boy looked at her. The parting in her hair was straight. The skin of her scalp was blue-white shining beneath her auburn hair. The doctor walked with his hands joined behind his back.

Down behind a garden shed they came across the boy's brother.

'Is that where you are?' said the doctor's wife. The younger boy stood up and looked sheepish.

'It was nice and warm here,' he said.

'What age difference is there between you?' asked the doctor's wife.

'I'm ten and a half and he's twelve and a half.'

'I know what we can do,' said the doctor.

'What?'

'A little archery.'

'No.' His wife seemed taken aback.

'The boys can use your bow. They could draw that. Easily.' The doctor walked away towards the garage and came back with a bow and a quiver of six arrows which he gave to his wife. Then he went back and came out with a target which had cobwebs hanging from it. He walked past them and set it three-quarters of the way down the garden.

'Adult toys,' he said. Then he straightened his face. 'This is not a toy. People could get killed.' He dropped his cigarette and trod it with his toe into the grass. His wife took one more inhale and did the same.

'Ask King Harold,' she said.

'He got it in the eye,' said the boy.

His younger brother clapped his hand to his eye and staggered about gasping, 'Agghhh.'

'OK – enough. Enough. Who wants to go first?'

The boy shrugged and indicated his younger brother. The doctor's wife sat down on a concrete step and crossed her legs. The doctor talked them through the equipment in such detail.

'Watch carefully. Everything I say to your brother also applies to you. This groove at the bottom of the arrow is called the nock.'

The boys just wanted to be firing arrows. Eventually the doctor took one from the quiver and notched it onto the string. He pulled the bow and aimed at the target.

'Make sure the string touches your lips.' He released the arrow and it flew silently and stuck in the edge of the target. 'I'm not used to your bow, darling.'

'Nothing to do with the fact that we haven't shot for about five years.'

He laughed. Then fitted the younger boy up to shoot.

'At least move the target a little closer,' said the doctor's wife. Whenever the younger boy did shoot the arrow, it slanted into the grass well to the left of the target. His brother laughed and sneered.

The doctor noticed this and said, 'I hope you can do as well.' The doctor handed him the bow, then an arrow. The arrow had a brass tip which looked like a bullet. He notched it on the bowstring and drew the bow just as he'd been shown. There was a great feeling of power – like a spring wound as tightly as it would go. He shot the arrow and it ended up in a flower-bed at the foot of the wall.

'Not bad at all. Better distance,' said the doctor.

They continued practising for some time and they all cheered loudly when the older boy's arrow stuck into the straw at the outer edge of the target. The telephone rang in the house.

'Just a minute,' said the doctor and hurried away. It was the older boy's turn to shoot. The doctor called out to his wife and as she jumped to her feet the boy saw the white undersides of her thighs. She ran inside leaving the boys alone in the garden. The boy drew the bow and aimed at the target. He held fire. The thought in his head was that it was possible to kill his brother here – in this walled garden, away from everyday life. Then there would be two funerals. He could say it was an accident. At the pictures he had seen arrows thwack into the bodies of US Cavalrymen. He could see it now – this one in his fingers piercing his brother's pale blue shirt. The blood welling and gathering around the shaft as it protruded from his chest. He slowly turned the weapon on his brother. He stood there with his mouth half open, mouth breathing, squinting his eyes against the sun.

'You're not allowed to do that,' said the younger boy.

'Where's your brother?' asked the doctor.

'In the bathroom.'

'Good.'

'So everybody's hands are washed?' said the doctor.

'Including mine,' said the doctor's wife smiling.

The younger boy came to the table with the backs of his hands glistening where he had neglected to dry them. The doctor said grace and they all bowed their heads after the doctor's wife bowed hers.

'What are you interested in?' The doctor shook out his white linen napkin and looked first at the smaller brother, then the older boy.

The silence was there until the older boy felt he had to say, 'Dunno.'

The doctor spread the napkin over his lap.

'You're at the grammar school?'

'Yes. Going on to second year.'

'Have you any hobbies?'

The boy didn't want to say he didn't know again so he said, 'Yes.'

'What?'

The boy thought for a while. Then said, 'Painting by numbers.'

'That's interesting. How many have you done?'

The boy hesitated and the younger boy said, 'One. He's done one. But he never finished it. He only did up to four.'

'I did finish it. I did all the colours.'

'He only did two of the blues and two greys.'

The doctor's wife interrupted, 'Now boys I'm sure it's not worth fighting over. What was it of?'

'A garden.'

'How I would love to have this all the time. Bickering and refereeing. You are wonderful children . . .'

'Phyllis . . .' said the doctor and she stopped talking. She looked down at her plate. The doctor lifted his spoon from the white tablecloth and began his soup. The others did likewise.

'And you, little man? What school are you at?'

The younger brother sucked in the hot soup with a slurping noise.

'I'm not a man,' he said. 'I'm in Primary Seven.' The doctor's wife smiled. As did the doctor. There was silence at the table when the two adults refused to ask any more questions. Eventually the doctor spoke.

'Your father was a great man,' he said. 'It's so seldom one person can make a difference.'

All their spoons chinked against their plates and nobody said anything for some time.

In his single bed his younger brother began crying. But he tried to disguise it – keeping it in. This started the boy off too and he cried into his pillow trying to cloak the sound he was making – a silent kind of open-mouthed girning, with tears wetting his face and the pillow. He stopped to hear if his younger brother had stopped. Silence. Except for downstairs. There was music playing. He didn't know what time it was. It was still quite light. He didn't know if he had been asleep or not.

After dinner they had played cards. Knockout Whist, Old Maid, Beggar-My-Neighbour. Then the doctor had left to drive down to the boys' house to pay his respects. The doctor's wife said it was her duty to stay at home – not to babysit, they were far too old for that – but just to keep an eye.

The boy listened hard and heard the regular breathing of sleep coming from his brother's bed. He was thirsty. He'd have to get up. Did too much crying make you thirsty? Was there a loss of moisture? He didn't want to call out as he might do at home. And he needed the toilet. He got up and went to the bathroom. Afterwards he stood at the head of the stairs and listened down. The music had stopped long ago. Lights were on all over the place but he couldn't see anyone. Where was the doctor's wife? He could be down and get his drink of water from the kitchen and nobody would notice.

He began down the runner of carpet on the black staircase. The boards creaked a little but nobody came to see who or what was making the noise. In the kitchen there were glasses in the draining rack. He filled one and sipped from it. The refrigerator made him jump by quivering into life. With the glass in his hand he moved out onto the parquet tiles of the hall. There was a ticking noise coming from somewhere – not like the ticking of a clock, it was too slow for that. He walked towards the sound. It was in the room with the dance floor. He looked in and saw the doctor's wife sitting in a tall armchair – at least he saw her legs. Her back was to the door. The lid of the radiogram was up and a record was revolving slowly

– clicking in the overrun. The room was full of twilight from a yellow band in the sky. There was something about the way her legs were sprawled that looked strange. He walked towards her. Was she dead? Was it something to do with the light? He peered around the wing of the armchair. She was fast asleep, her mouth half open, her head slumped. She would wake with a sore neck if she slept like that for long. Still the record clicked regularly. He turned and with his right hand lifted the needle off. The noise stopped. Then she wakened. At first she looked glazed and bewildered, as if she didn't know where she was. Or who he was – a boy in pyjamas standing in front of her. She opened and closed her mouth drily several times.

'Oh, how thoughtful of you,' she said, taking the water from his hand. She gulped it down and sighed when she had finished. 'Thank you. Just what the doctor ordered.' As well as cigarette smoke there was a strange smell in the air. Not perfume – but like perfume. She set the empty glass down on a low table beside her chair. There were several bottles on it – a half-filled green bottle, a wine bottle – empty glasses, a half-filled ashtray. 'I'm such a mess.' She sat forward and had a double-handed scratch with her fingers through her hair.

'Where's Gabriel? Is he not home yet?' The boy didn't know so he shrugged. 'What time is it?' She squinted at her watch. 'Oh my God. A quarter to a lemon.' She turned to the small table and finished the drink in her glass and smacked her lips. She poured herself another drink and lit a cigarette. That was the perfumed smell. 'A gin is not a gin without ice,' she said and levered herself up from the armchair. She came back from the kitchen with her glass ringing and the cigarette in her mouth. 'I feel I want to dance. Will you do me the honour, Tony?' The boy didn't know what to say. 'Can you do a quickstep?'

The boy shook his head. He couldn't be rude to people who were looking after him. But he wanted to run.

'I thought not. But it's really quite easy.' She switched on a red standard lamp and stood in front of him. 'Right. To begin at the beguinning. That's hard to say at this time of night.' She went to the table and stubbed out her cigarette. She placed her hands on his shoulders and showed him the steps. Looking down she realised he was in his bare feet. 'I don't want to tread on your tootsies.' She unhooked her feet from her high-heeled sandals and kicked them to one side. Then she stood with her feet together and sighed. 'Ohh I have such bunions.'

She continued to teach him the steps and move him around. He felt ungainly and reluctant. His head was almost to the height of her shoulder and he could smell her perfume and another strange smell like onions. When he made mistakes with his feet she laughed uproariously – doubled over at times. He didn't see what was so funny. His face was hot and he was sure he was blushing. Once or twice she grazed his cheek with her breast. It was a soft feeling. It gave and he wanted to touch it again out of curiosity – like the wallpaper. 'Now music will sort the whole thing out. Listen to the music – really listen – and the dance will come to you.'

She turned away from him and played the record on the turntable. The music breathed out. '*Heaven, I'm in heaven.*' She began to sway in time to the singing voice. '*And my heart beats so that I can hardly speak; and I seem to find the happiness I seek, when we're out together dancing cheek to cheek.*' She laid her hands on his shoulders and pressured him into moving. 'No – don't look down,' she said. 'You're good – you're getting the hang of it. Move to the music.' She crooned the words along with the singer.

She said, 'Gabriel says dance is about not getting in each other's way gracefully.' Then she added as if it was an afterthought, 'I think it's about knowing – about knowing each other. And wearing gorgeous clothes. There is no sight in the world to beat a man in a dress suit. Love is everything.'

The boy tried to humour her. She made him attempt to dance again. His bare feet scuffed and bumped against the springy floor. He trod on her but she seemed not to notice. She seemed not even to be speaking to him. She said, 'For me dancing is a matter of life and death. Can you imagine what it would be like to be in an iron lung?' Somewhere a door closed but she seemed not to notice.

The doctor stood in the doorway of the dancehall room and switched on the main light which was shaped like a chandelier. She blinked and stared in his direction. He slowly removed his hat and hung it on the hall stand.

'Gabriel,' she said. 'I'm just teaching our guest the rudiments.'

'Ot-way are-hay oo-yay ooing-day?' he said.

'Othing-nay.' She took her hands off the boy's shoulders. The record came to an end and began ticking again.

'Oo-tay uch-may ink-dray.'

'No, only a little. I felt so sad when they went to bed.'

'My parents talk that language too,' said the boy.

'Of course,' said the doctor, smiling. 'I forgot – it was they who taught it to us. They said it was a code for talking in front of you.'

'But I got to know what they were saying.'

'We speak it even though we don't have any children,' said the doctor's wife.

'Ime-tay or-fay ed-bay. You have a difficult day tomorrow. Your mother sends her love.'

'Gabriel, dance with me. Let's demonstrate the quickstep for him.'

'Phyllis – you're being . . . The time is out of joint.' The doctor's glance went to the boy.

'Please,' she said. 'There's no time like the present.' She lurched to the side of the floor and got into her high-heeled sandals. From the window sill she took a box and sprinkled something from it whispering onto the floor.

'Lux perpetua,' she said and turned to the boy. 'Soap flakes – to allow the feet to glide.' She put the record on again. 'A bit more volume.' And raised her hand to invite the doctor to dance. He stared at her and nodded his head a little in disbelief. '*Heaven, I'm in heaven,*' and they were away across the floor, their bodies close, their feet in time. The doctor, when he turned, rolled his eyes to the boy – to let him know he was just humouring his wife who was being more than a little foolish. The fingers of their upright hands were interlaced. The doctor's hand at her back was cupped as if holding something precious. Their feet skimmed and her dress swished and outlined her thin body as she traversed the floor. The boy now knew the tune and knew where it was going. They moved as one person, their legs scissoring together to the music. They had variations – sometimes dancing side by side – sometimes swinging out away from each other and slingshotting back together again. She threw back her head and her red hair fell and swayed. The doctor's back was straight, his chin elegantly proud. The boy felt as if he was watching his parents. If they didn't dance like this – and he had never seen them dance at home because they had rugs on the floor and the room was too small – it is how they would have wanted to dance.

He felt he couldn't leave the room and go back up to bed because the doctor and his wife covered so much of the floor so quickly. He would be trampled or would at least cause them to interrupt their dancing and he didn't want to do that. So he stayed where he was and watched. He joined his hands behind his back the way he had seen the doctor do earlier in the garden and leaned back against the wall. The wallpaper in this room was also like velvet. The pattern was of green bamboo and moved beneath his hand. He caressed it behind his back as he watched the dancers.

Something moved in the doorway. It was his brother. The loud music must have wakened him. His face looked crumpled and sleepy and he stood with bare feet on the threshold.

'Dance with your brother,' shouted the doctor's wife.

'That would look stupid,' said the boy but not loudly enough for it to be heard. It was enough that at that moment he was glad he hadn't killed him in the garden earlier.

The music stopped. And the doctor and his wife ended their dance, he mock bowing and she inclining her head in gratitude for being asked. The only sound now apart from the ticking of the record was their loud breathing.

'I see we are all here now,' said the doctor looking at the boy in the doorway.

'I couldn't sleep.' The doctor, still panting, went over and squatted down before the boy standing on the threshold.

'I'm not surprised. At her volume,' he said and looked at his wife. 'Now boys you have a difficult day tomorrow. You'd better get some sleep.'

'I'll waken us at half eight,' said the doctor's wife.

'And I'll run all of us in for ten o'clock mass.' By now the two brothers were together at the foot of the stairs. The doctor was touching each of them on the shoulder. 'Oh, I forgot to say. Ben, Tony

– it is now definite. The Bishop *will* attend the funeral. Not many people that happens to. You should be very proud. Goodnights apiece.'

The boys began the stairs. When they were halfway up the elder boy looked round. The doctor's wife was in tears, watching them climb.

THE CLINIC

It was still dark. He was *never* up at this time, except occasionally to catch a dawn flight. He picked up his sample, his papers and the yellow card. The bottle was warm in his hand. He was about to go out the door when he remembered. Something to read, something to pass the time. In the room with the book shelf he clicked on the light. The clock on the mantelpiece told him he was running late. He grabbed a small hardback collection of Chekhov's short stories and ran.

It was mid-November. People's Moscow-white faces told how cold it was. Breath was visible on the air. The traffic was ten times worse than he was used to. He turned off into the hospital and got lost a couple of times before he saw the Diabetic Clinic sign. He parked ages away and half hurried, half ran back. He was breathless going through the door only to find that the place was upstairs. He was about eight minutes late and apologised. The receptionist shrugged and smiled, as if to say – think nothing of it. That made him mad too. He had been so uptight trying to get there on time and now, it seemed, it didn't matter very much. If there was one thing worse than worrying, it was wasted worrying. He was asked to take a seat.

The waiting room was half full even though it was only twenty to nine. There was a row of empty seats backing onto the window. He sat down, glad not to be close enough to anyone to have to start a conversation. A Muslim woman in a black hejab talked to her mother who was similarly dressed. The language was incomprehensible to him but he was curious to know what they were talking about.

All the men's magazines were about golf or cars. He picked up *Vogue* and flicked through it. Beautiful half-naked sophisticated women clattering with jewellery. But he couldn't concentrate to read any of the text.

His letter lay face up on the chair beside him.

> *Your family doctor has referred you to the Diabetic Clinic to see if you are diabetic. To find this out we will need to perform a glucose tolerance test.*

He remembered a crazy guy at school who had diabetes – who went into comas. But school was fifty years ago. Since being given his appointment he'd read up even more frightening stuff about your eyesight and how you could lose it. And your extremities – how in some cases they could go gangrenous and have to be lopped off.

His yellow outpatient card said *Please bring this card with you when you next attend.*

A door at the far end of the waiting room opened and screeched closed. It took about thirty or forty seconds to close, with its irritating, long, dry squeak. There was a damping device on the mechanism to make it close more slowly. But no sooner had it closed fully and the noise stopped than somebody else came through it and began the whole process over again. 'Collective responsibility is not being taken,' he wanted to yell. If he had diabetes and had to come back to this God-forsaken place then next time he'd bring an oil can. Recently in the newspaper he'd read that grumpy old men were more liable to heart attacks than old men who were not grumpy. He tried to calm down. To degrump.

He took out his Chekhov and looked at the list of contents. Something short. He did a quick sum, subtracting the page number from the following page number after each story. It was an old copy and the cheap paper had turned the colour of toast at the edges. The Vanguard Library edition – translated by the wonderful Constance Garnett. A nurse walked in and called people by their first names. She came to him.

'Hi, my name is Phil,' she said, 'and that's Myna at reception.' She explained what was going to happen. He had to drink a whole bottle of Lucozade and then, over the next couple of hours, every half hour in fact, he had to give both blood and urine samples. He nodded. He understood. He had grey hair, he was overweight, but he understood.

She took him into the corridor and sat him down in what looked like a wheelchair.

'Did you have any breakfast?' she said. 'A cuppa tea maybe? Some toast?'

'No. The leaflet said to come fasting.'

'Not everybody pays attention to that.'

'What a waste of everybody's time. Do people actually do that?'

'You'd be surprised,' she said.

It turned out not to be a wheelchair but a weighing machine. She calculated something against a chart on the wall.

'Did you bring a sample?'

'Yes.' He rummaged in his pocket and produced the bottle. It had returned to room temperature. *Spring water with a hint of Apple.* He handed it over and the nurse put a label on it.

'It might be a little flavoured,' he said.

'I'm not going to drink it.' She whisked it away into another room.

When he was back in his seat by the window she brought him Lucozade, a plastic glass and four lozenge-shaped paper tubs. She stuck a white label with a bar-code on each and wrote a time on the rim with her biro. He wanted to make terrible jokes about giving urine samples and her name. Phil. Phil these please. P for Phil. But he realised everybody must do this. He said, 'I hope these are not for blood.'

She laughed. She had a nice face – in her early forties.

'All at once now,' she said. He poured the Lucozade into the plastic glass and drank it. Refilled it, drank it. Halfway down he had to stop, his swallow refused to work against the sweet bubbles. Eventually he finished everything and childishly expected praise.

When she left him he tried to concentrate on his book. A story called 'The Beauties' looked feasible. Subtract one hundred and seventy-three from one hundred and eighty-three. It'd be hard with all this toing and froing – all the stabbing and pissing. All the people around him talking. He didn't think he'd read it before. That had happened several times with Turgenev – after fifty pages he'd said, 'I've read this before.' It went down so easily. Nobody gagged on Turgenev.

But Chekhov is Chekhov. He draws you in. He writes as if the thing is happening in front of your eyes. An unnamed boy of sixteen, maybe Chekhov himself, and his grandfather in a chaise are travelling through the summer heat and dust of the countryside to Rostov-on-the-Don. They stop to feed their horses at a rich Armenian's and the grandfather talks endlessly to the owner about farms and feedstuffs and manure. The place is described in minute detail down to the floors painted with yellow ochre and the flies . . . and more flies. Then tea is brought in by a barefoot girl of sixteen wearing a white kerchief and when she turns from the side-board to hand the boy his cup she has the most wonderful face he has ever seen. He feels a wind blow across his soul.

'The Beauties' had captured him. He knew exactly what Chekhov was talking about. He was there in that room experiencing the same things.

At precisely a minute before a quarter to the hour he lifted one of his cardboard pee pots and went to the technician's laboratory. The technician was a woman with long brown hair who smiled at him. She wore a white coat. Her breast pocket had several biro ink lines descending into it. She explained what she was about to do.

'You can choose to have it done on four fingers. Or you can have it done on one finger four times. That's the choice. Four sore fingers or one very sore finger?'

He chose his middle finger and presented it – almost like an obscene gesture. He looked away, anticipating a scalpel or dagger. There was a winter tree outside. Without leaves a crow's nest was visible. There was a click and the stab was amazingly tiny – like the smallest rose thorn in the world. He hardly felt anything. The technician squeezed his finger and harvested his drop of blood into a capillary tube the size of a toothpick. When she'd finished she nodded at his cardboard container. He lifted it and sought out the lavatory.

The sign on the door indicated both men and women. Inside there were adjacent cubicles and the mother of the woman in the black hejab was coming out of the ladies' bearing her cardboard pot before her like an offering. He smiled and opened the outer door for her.

Inside the men's lavatory was a poster about 'impotence'. A man sitting on a park bench with his head in his hands. How did he discover his condition in a public park? *Talk to your doctor*, said the words.

Conjuring up a sample so soon after the one in the house took a long time. But eventually he succeeded and left it in the laboratory. The technician was working near the window. Her long hair was down her back almost to her waist.

'There you are,' he said.

'Thank you.'

The nurse brought him a plastic jug of tap water and ice.

'You might be able to give blood every time,' she said, 'but for the other you need to keep drinking this.'

He swirled the jug and poured himself some. It sounded hollow compared to ice against glass. Sipping he tried to return to the Chekhov. A distant radio was far enough away to be indistinct but it was still distracting. At the moment the only other sound was of magazine pages being turned – the kind of magazines which were looked at rather than read – *Hello!* and *OK*. Flick, flick, flick. The nurse, Phil, came in and announced a name.

'Andrew? Andrew Elliot?'

A man stood and swaggered forward responding as if he had just been chosen for a Hollywood audition. In a music-hall kind of American drawl he said, 'You caalled for *me*, lady?'

Everybody in the waiting room laughed.

He tried to return to the mood of that hot, dusty afternoon in Rostov-on-the-Don but the smile was still on his face. He couldn't concentrate.

He was at that age when things were starting to go wrong. Knee joints were beginning to scringe. Putting on socks had become a burden. Pains where there shouldn't be pains. Breathlessness. Occasional dizziness.

An immensely fat woman came in. All her weight seemed to be below her waist. Her thighs and lower belly bulged as if she'd left her bedding in her tights. Sheets, pillows, duvets. The lot. After her, an old couple came through the doors, panting after the stairs. They sank onto chairs, incapable of speech, and sat there mouth breathing. They both had skin the colour of putty.

When he began to read again he found it awkward to turn the page because, like many people in the waiting room he had a piece of lint clenched between his chosen finger and his thumb.

The boy in 'The Beauties' when confronted with the girl in the white kerchief feels himself utterly inferior. Sunburned, dusty and only a child. But that does not stop him adoring her and having adored her his reaction is one of – sadness. Where does such perfection fit into the world? He hears the thud of her bare feet on the board floor, she disappears into a grimy outhouse which is full of the smell of mutton and angry argument. The more he watches her going about her tasks the more painful becomes his inexplicable sadness.

The first part of the story ends and Chekhov switches to another, similar incident when he has become a student. Maybe a medical student. This time he is travelling by train.

In the waiting room of the Diabetic Clinic the talk was of medical stuff.

'I have an irregular heartbeat . . .'

'Oh God help ye . . .'

'I'm just trying to keep the weight down . . .'

'Does the stick help?'

'It helps the balance . . .'

This is all in front of me, he thought.

But despite his age he felt good, felt ridiculously proud he had outlived his father who had died at the early age of forty-five. He didn't have a problem that would drive him to sit on a park bench with his head in his hands. So he felt good about that. He looked up at the clock above the posters. He picked up his pee pot and headed for the laboratory again.

This time when he looked away from the little machine which drew his blood he saw a crow settling in the branches of the tree outside. The thinnest of pinpricks and again she milked the blood from his finger into her glass capillary. This stranger was holding his hand. Her perfume radiated into his space – not perfume, but soap

– maybe the smell of her shampoo. Camomile, maybe. She clipped her capillary to a little sloped rack. There were two of them now, like the double red line he'd had to rule beneath the title of his essays at school. He provided another urine sample.

When he sat down again in the waiting room he finished his jug of water and asked for another. He returned to his book. And as he read, the room gradually disappeared. Somewhere in southern Russia a train stopped at a small station on a May evening. The sun was setting and the station buildings threw long shadows. The student gets off to stretch his legs. He sees the stationmaster's daughter. She, too, is utterly captivating. As she stands talking to an old lady the youth remembers the Armenian's daughter, the girl with the white kerchief, and the sadness it brought him. Again he experiences the whoosh of feeling and tries to analyse it but cannot. Not only was the student, Chekhov, watching this exquisite woman, she was being watched by almost all the men on the platform, including a ginger telegraphist with a flat opaque face sitting by his apparatus in the station window. What chance for someone like him? The stationmaster's daughter wouldn't look at him twice.

He was struck yet again by the power of the word. Here he was – about to be told he had difficult changes to make to his life and yet by reading words on a page, pictures of Russia a hundred years ago come into his head. Not only that, but he can share sensations and emotions with this student character, created by a real man he never met and translated by a real woman he never met. It was so immediate, the choice of words so delicately accurate, that they blotted out the reality of the present. He ached now for the stationmaster's daughter the way the student aches. It's in his blood.

He paused and looked at the clock. It was time again. He gave another blood sample and when providing the urine sample he splashed the label. He patted it dry with toilet roll and hoped that the technician with the long hair wouldn't notice.

In the waiting room he returned to his book. Was the story accurate? About such feelings? Was this not about women as decoration? Neither woman in the story said anything – showed anything of her inner self – in order to be attractive. Was this not the worst of Hollywood before Hollywood was ever thought of? Audrey Hepburn – Julia Roberts – the stationmaster's daughter.

'There's the water you asked for.'

'Oh thanks.'

He poured himself another glass. The water was icy. With his concentration broken he looked at the posters on the wall. He could barely bring himself to read them. They made him quake for his future. But he couldn't be that bad – his doctor had referred him because he was 'borderline'. The poster warnings were for the worst cases. *Diabetic retinopathy* – can lead to permanent loss of vision. Blindness. Never to be able to read again. *Atherosclerosis* leading to *dry gangrene*. Wear well-fitting shoes, visit your chiropodist frequently. Care for your feet. Or else you'll lose them, was the implication. Jesus. He drained the glass and poured himself another.

The door, which had been silent for a while, screeched open and a wheelchair was pushed through. A woman in her seventies, wearing a dressing gown, was being pushed by a younger woman. The screeching door must lead to the wards. When they came into the waiting area it was obvious the old woman had no legs. She wore a blue cellular blanket over her lap. She was empty to the floor. The woman pushing her sat down on a chair in front of her. From their body language they were mother and daughter.

Their talk became entangled with the Chekhov and he read the same line again and again. He needed silence.

During his final visit to give blood he tried to joke with the technician about there being no more left in that finger. This time there were two crows perched on either side of the black nest. In the lavatory he noticed that his last sample was crystal clear. The water was just going through him.

He sat and finished the Chekhov. It was a wonderful story which ended with the train moving on under a darkening sky, leaving behind the stationmaster's beautiful daughter. In the departing carriage there is an air of sadness. The last image is of the figure of the guard coming through the train beginning to light the candles.

The next thing he was aware of was hearing his name called out by a male voice. He was sitting with his eyes closed, savouring the ending of the story. He stood. The doctor smiled – he was not wearing a white coat. He had a checked shirt and was distinctly overweight – straining the buttons. He led him into an office and looked up after consulting a piece of paper.

'Well I'm pleased to say you don't have diabetes. You have something we call impaired glucose tolerance – which could well develop into diabetes. You must begin to take some avoiding action – more exercise, better diet. Talk it over with your GP. I'll write to him with these results.'

'Thank you.'

As he walked to the head of the stairs he heard the distant door screech for one last time. He will not have to come back. No need for the oil can. He went out into the November midday and across the car park. The sun was shining. He looked up at the blue sky criss-crossed with jet trails. People travelling. Going places, meeting folk. He thought of those people he had just left who daren't misplace their outpatient cards. Above him the crows made a raucous cawing. His middle finger felt tender and bruised.

He took out his mobile and phoned his wife, dabbing the keys with his thumb. He had seen her across a dance floor forty years ago and felt the wind blow across his soul.

She sounded anxious and concerned.

'Well?'

'I'm OK,' he said.

A BELFAST MEMORY

Our two rented houses faced each other across the street – my father's at seventy-three and Aunt Cissy's at fifty-four. There was another uncle, Father Barney, who used to call round most Sundays to Cissy's. In the evening they all played poker and Father Barney would drink whisky and do mock shouting and clowning. The others would roll their eyes. If the children were good and provided Father Barney wasn't 'beyond the beyonds' they were allowed to watch. My father always left early saying he had his work to go to in the morning. My mother said he just couldn't stand Uncle Barney any longer.

I knew my father's work had something to do with drawing and lettering. I'd found things in cupboards – small blocks of wood topped with grey zinc metal. If there was lettering on this metal it was always backwards, unable to be read. In cupboards there were pages of pink paper, thick as slices of bread, with lettering pressed into them and bulldog clips full of his newspaper adverts. At the moment he was illustrating a Bible for Schools. He'd shown me a drawing for the Cure at Capharnum and, as an exercise, made me read aloud the caption:

> 'They could not get in because the house was crowded out, even to the door. So they took the stretcher onto the roof, opened the tiles, and let the sick man down.'

I was about eight or nine at the time. It was dead easy.

It was a Sunday and felt like a Sunday. *Family Favourites* was on the wireless. My father sat beneath the window for the best light.
'What you doing?'
He held up the drawing.

'Abraham and his son, Isaac,' he said. A man with a white beard beside a boy carrying a tied-up bundle of sticks. '"*Where is the victim for the sacrifice?*" That's what the boy is saying.' My father put on a scary, deep voice and said, 'Little does he know . . .' He drew quietly for a while. The pen scratched against the paper and chinked in the ink bottle. He had a pad on the table and sometimes he made scratches on it. 'Just to get the nib going.' Sometimes the pen took up too much ink and he shook it a little. 'You're no good if you can't make something out of a blot.'

The hall door opened and footsteps came in off the street. My father stopped and looked up. It was my cousin, Brendan, who was a year and two months older than me. He was a good footballer.

'It's yourself, Brendy.'

Brendan stopped in the middle of the floor and said, 'Charlie Tully's in our house having a cup of tea.'

'Go on. Are you kidding?'

'No.'

My father gave a low whistle.

'This we will have to see.' He rinsed his pen in a jam jar of water and wiped it dry with a rag. He blew on his drawing then folded the protective tissue over it.

'Come on.' All three of us went across the road. The only car parked on the street belonged to Father Barney.

'Did Barney bring him?' Brendan nodded.

'And Terry Lennon.'

Terry Lennon was a blind church organist. He had a great Lambeg drum of a belly with a waistcoat stretched tight over it. He would sit in the armchair by the fire smoking constantly, never taking the cigarette from between his lips. A lot of the time he stared up at the ceiling – his eyelids didn't quite shut and some of the whites of his eyes showed. Now and again he would run his fingers down the cigarette to dislodge the ash onto his waistcoat. Aunt Cissy called him Terry Lennon, the human ashtray.

When we went in Terry Lennon was in his usual chair. Father Barney stood in front of the fire with his hands behind him. On the sofa was a man, still wearing his raincoat, drinking tea. His hair was parted in the middle. He was introduced to my father as Charlie Tully.

'You're welcome,' said my father. 'Is that sister of mine looking after you?'

Charlie Tully nodded.

'The best gingerbread in the northern hemisphere,' said Father Barney. 'That's what lured him here.'

'Where's the old man?' said my father.

'The last I saw of him was heading up to the lavatory with the *Independent*.'

'He'll be there for a week.' My father turned to the man in the pale raincoat.

'I bet he was delighted to see you Mr Tully – he's a bit of a fan.'

'Oh he was – he was.'

'So – how do you like Scotland?'

'It's a grand place.'

'Will Mr Tully have a cigarette?' Terry Lennon reached out in the general direction of the voice with his packet of Gallagher's Greens.

'Naw, he only smokes Gallagher's Blues,' said Aunt Cissy and everybody laughed.

'If you'll forgive me saying so Mr Tully,' said Terry Lennon, 'the football is not an interest of mine. You understand?'

'I do. You were making some sound with that organ this morning.'

'Loud ones are great.' Terry Lennon laughed. 'Or Bach. Bach is great for emptying the place for the next mass. The philistines flee.'

There was a ring at the door and Brendan went to answer it. When he came back he said it was Hugo looking for a drink of water.

'And run the tap for a while,' said Aunt Cissy laughing. 'Bring him in.'

'The more the merrier,' said my father.

'Wait till you hear this, Mr Tully. Our Hugo.' Brendan went into the kitchen and ran the tap very fast into the sink. He carried a full cup into the room and called Hugo from the door. Hugo edged into the room and accepted the cup. There was silence and everybody watched him drink. Hugo was a serious young man who was trying to grow a beard.

Father Barney joined his hands behind his back and rose on his toes. He said, 'So you like to run the tap for a while?'

'Yes, Father.'

'And why's that?'

'The pipes here are lead. And lead is poison. Not good for the brain.'

'The Romans used a lot of lead piping,' said Father Barney, winking at Charlie. 'Smart boys, the Romans. They didn't do too badly.'

'No – you're right, Father. But maybe it's what *destroyed* their Empire,' said Hugo. 'Being reared to drink poison helps no one.'

Father Barney sucked in his cheeks and rolled his eyes. 'I need a whisky after that slap down.' Aunt Cissy moved to the sideboard where the bottle was kept. 'Cissy fill her up with water, lead or no lead. Will anybody join me? What – no takers, at all?' He held up his glass. 'To Mr Tully here. God guide your golden boots.' Granda came downstairs and had to push the door open against the people inside.

'What am I missing?' he said.

'A drink,' said Father Barney. Granda looked around in mock amazement.

'He's getting no drink at this time of the day,' said Aunt Cissy. Granda was still wearing his dark Sunday suit and the waistcoat with his watch-chain looped across it. On his way to mass he wore a black bowler hat.

'It's getting a bit crowded in here,' Granda said, looking around the room. 'Reminds me of the day McCormack sang in our house in Antrim. There was that many in the room we had to open the windows so's the neighbours outside could hear him.'

'*Count* John McCormack?' said Charlie Tully.

'The very one.'

'How did the maestro end up in your house?'

'Oh, he was with Terry there, some organ recital.'

'And what did he sing?'

'Everything. Everything but the kitchen sink. "Down by the Sally Gardens", "I Hear You Calling Me".'

'It was some show,' said Terry Lennon, putting his head back as if listening to it again.

'Would you credit that?' said Charlie. 'I met a man who knows Count John McCormack.'

There was a strange two-note cry from the hallway: 'Yoo-hoo.'

'Corinna,' said Cissy and pulled a face. The door was pushed open and Corinna and her sister, Dinky, stood there.

'Full house the day,' said Corinna. She eased herself into the room. Dinky remained just outside.

'The house is crowded out, even to the door,' said my father.

'Is there any chance of borrowing an egg, Cissy? I'd started the baking before I checked.' Cissy went into the kitchen and came back with an egg which she handed to Corinna.

'Thanks a million. You're too good.' Corinna stood with the egg between her finger and thumb. 'What's the occasion?' She vaguely indicated the full room.

'Charlie Tully,' said Cissy. 'This is Corinna Boyle. And her sister Dinky.' Cissy pointed over heads in the direction of the front hall. Dinky went up on her toes and smiled.

'A good-looking man,' said Corinna.

'Worth eight thousand pounds in transfer fees,' said Father Barney.

'He's above rubies, Cissy. Above rubies.' And away she went with her egg and her sister.

'So,' said Granda, 'will we ever see Charlie Tully playing again on this side of the water?'

'Maybe.'

'Internationals,' said Hugo.

'But it's not the same thing,' said Granda, 'as watching a man playing week in, week out. That's the way you get the whole story.'

'There's talk of a charity game with the Belfast boys later in the year,' said Charlie.

'Belfast Celtic and Glasgow Celtic?' Granda was now leaning forward with his elbows on the table. 'There wouldn't be a foul from start to finish.'

'Where'd be the fun in that?' said Father Barney. 'Cissy, I'll have another one of those.'

Cissy went to the sideboard and refilled the glass. 'Remember you've a car to drive.'

Barney ignored her and pointed at my father. 'Johnny there would design you a programme for that game. For nothing. He's a good artist.'

'Like yourself Charlie,' said Granda.

'Is that the kinda thing you do?' Charlie said.

'Yeah sure,' said my father. Barney started mock shouting as if he was selling programmes outside the ground. Some of his whisky slopped over the rim of the glass as he waved his arms. My father smiled.

'Have you been somewhere – before here?'

'On a Sunday morning?'

Barney looked over to Charlie Tully. 'Johnny does work for every charity in the town. The YP Pools, the St Vincent de Paul, the parish, even the bloody bishop – no friend of mine – as you well know – his bloody nibs. Your Grace.' He gave a little mock inclination of the head. Cissy ordered Brendan out of his chair and told Barney to sit and not be letting the side down.

'So Charlie,' said Granda, 'the truth from the insider – is there no chance of Belfast Celtic starting up again?'

'Not that I know of.'

'We gave in far too easily. In my day when somebody gave you a hiding, you fought back.'

'Aye, it's all up when your own side makes you the scapegoat,' said Aunt Cissy.

'I mean to say,' Granda's voice went up in pitch. 'What were they thinking of?'

'The game of shame.'

'A crowd of bigots.'

'They came streaming onto that pitch like . . . like . . . bloody Indians.'

'Indians are good people,' said Hugo.

'. . . and they kicked poor Jimmy Jones half to death. Fractured his leg in five places. And him one of their own. It ended his career.'

'Take it easy, Da,' said Father Barney and slapped the arm of his chair.

'You were at the game?' said Charlie Tully.

'Aye and every other one they've ever played,' said Granda. 'I don't

know what to do with myself on a Saturday afternoon now. I sometimes slip up to Cliftonville's ground but it's not the same thing.
Solitude. It's well named.' Granda was shaking his head from side to
side. 'I just do not understand it. What other bunch of people would
do it? The board of directors,' he spat the words out. 'The team gets
chased off the pitch, its players get kicked half to death and what do
they do? OK, we're going to close down the club. That'll teach you.
In the name of Jesus . . .' Granda stopped talking because he was
going to cry. He looked hard at the top of the window and he kept
swallowing. Again and again. Nobody else said anything. 'Why should
we be the ones sacrificed? Is there no one on our side who has any
guts at all?'

'Take it easy,' said my father. 'They have the sectarian poison in
them.' He reached out and put his hand on Granda's shoulder. Shook
him a little.

Granda recovered himself a bit and said, 'It would put you in mind
of the man who got a return ticket for the bus – then he fell out with
the conductor so, to get his own back, he walked home. That'll teach
him.'

There were smiles at that. The room became silent.

'It was a great side,' said Charlie Tully at last. 'Kevin McAlinden,
Johnny Campbell, Paddy Bonnar . . .'

'Aye.'

'And what a keeper Hugh Kelly was.'

'Aye and Bud Ahern . . .'

'Billy McMillan and Robin Lawlor.'

'Of course.'

'Jimmy Jones and Eddie McMorran and who else?'

'You've left out John Denver.'

'And the captain, Jackie Vernon.'

'And yourself, Charlie,' said Granda. 'Let's not forget yourself,
maestro.'

Sometime later that year – which became known to Granda as 'the
year Charlie Tully called' as opposed to 'the year McCormack sang
in the house in Antrim' – I noticed drawings and sketches of my

father's lying about the house. They were of players in Celtic hoops in the act of kicking or heading a ball. Their bodies were tiny cartoons but their heads were made from oval photos of the real players.

It was many years later – half a century, in fact – before I would remember these drawings again. My father died when I was twelve and my mother was so distraught that she threw out all his things. If she was reminded of him she would break down and weep so every scrap of paper relating to him had to be sacrificed.

Recently I was in Belfast and I wondered if there might be a copy of the programme lying around Smithfield Market. I found a small shop entirely devoted to football programmes so I went in and told them what I was looking for – a Belfast Celtic v Glasgow Celtic match programme from the early fifties.

The man looked at me and said, 'Put it this way. I'm a collector and I've never seen one.'

I was disappointed. Then he said, 'If you do catch up with it, you'll pay for it.'

'How much?' I was thinking in terms of twenty or thirty quid.

'A thousand pounds. Minimum.'

I'm not really impressed by that kind of rarity value – but in this case I thought, 'Good on you, Johnny. After all the work for charity.' If that price is accurate I don't want to own the real thing – but I wouldn't mind seeing a photocopy. A photocopy would be good. Above rubies, in fact.

THE WEDDING RING

Ellen Tierney 1884–1904

Annie Walsh, a stout woman in her early sixties, stood at the ironing
board smoothing a white pillowcase. She liked to use two irons so
that she could work continuously – smoothing with one while the
other was heating. Her sister Susan, younger by twelve years, sat on
a stool by the kitchen range with a hanky in her hand. She had not
cried for some time, but it was at the ready because she knew she
would cry again soon.

'Will you be using the goffering iron?' she asked.

'Aye – a wee touch.'

Susan put the poker between the bars into the red heart of the fire.

'One more should finish it,' said Annie. The ironing board creaked
as she put her full weight on the material. Susan set the next hot iron
on its heel near her sister's hand. Annie picked it up and spat the
tiniest of spits onto its surface, testing it. The moisture fizzed and
danced on the black shine, then disappeared. Annie finished the
pillowcase and started on the nightgown. When she came to the lace
at the neck she nodded for the poker. Susan tried to withdraw it from
the fire but the handle was hot, even through the handkerchief. Annie
made an exasperated noise with her tongue. The poker was red hot
and when dust motes touched it they momentarily sparked white.
Annie quickly inserted it into the hollow tube of the goffering iron,
then grasped the moist lace in her hands and pressed it over the tube.
The material made sighing noises here and there as she worked her
way around it. When she was finished she held her work at arm's
length.

'Ready?' Her sister sat, not saying anything. 'I could still send for
Emily Mooney to help. But I feel it's something we should do ourselves.
Keep it in the family.'

Annie always wore a gold cross pinned horizontally to the dark material at her throat. If she wore it the right way up the top irritated the underside of her double chin. And she was forever looking down – at her prayer book or her embroidery. Even on other people. She was taller than most and bigger in girth. Mr McDonald, the boarder who had stayed with them longest, described her as 'a ship in full sail'.

'Some soap.' Susan lifted a bar of carbolic from the wall cupboard and sawed a slice off it.

'Is that enough?'

'Remember to wash that knife – or it'll taste the bread.' Annie picked up the pillowcase and ran her hand over its surface. 'The Belfast linen looks so rich.' You could see by her eyes that she had been crying too. But she had finished and was determined not to start again.

Susan thought her sister the strongest person she knew. Everything she did, she did with determination. The knock at the door at all hours of the day and night would be for her – to bring somebody into the world or to lay somebody out. And there were times the two things happened together. Their younger sister, Elizabeth Tierney, had died giving birth to her first child, Ellie. Five years later Ellie's father had died of consumption and the two of them had reared the child as if she was one of their own. All this as well as running a boarding house for three, sometimes four gentlemen.

Annie made a pile of the sheets and pillowcases and set the soap and face-cloth on top of the nightgown. Her white apron was stiffened with starch and it created small noises in the silence as she moved about her business.

'It's all about appearances, Susan – giving the right impression.' Susan washed the bread knife then filled the ewer from the steaming kettle and set it in the basin. She looked distraught.

'Be brave,' said Annie.

'I can hardly believe we're sisters,' said Susan.

'Is that water warm enough?' Annie cupped her hand to the side of the delft but pulled it away quickly. She picked up all her paraphernalia and began climbing the narrow staircase. Susan followed her to the return room carrying the ewer and basin.

The blind was down darkening the bedroom. Susan refused to look at the bed and set the ewer and basin on the marble-topped dresser. She stood facing the wall on the edge of tears again. Annie raised the blind. The light was harsh.

'Maybe keep it down,' said Susan. 'I know nobody can see in, but . . .' Annie thought, then shrugged and pulled the blind halfway down.

'I usher them into the world and I wash them on their way out,' she said.

'But this is Ellie – family – your niece.'

'Susan – you're forgetting – it was me brought Ellie into the world.' The figure in the bed was covered by a pink satin eiderdown, which Annie herself had quilted and sewn. She took a deep breath and pulled it back.

The girl's body lay straight and to attention. A pillow supported her chin and coins weighted her eyes. Annie took them off and the lids remained closed. There was a chink as she dropped the pennies into her apron pocket. The bedclothes fell quietly to the floor. Susan put both hands to her mouth and began whispering over and over again.

'Ellie – oh wee Ellie.'

'God rest her soul.'

'I thought she was improving last night,' said Susan, 'when she got up for a while. Said it eased the pain – sitting on her hot-water bottle – God love her.'

'And when she was anointed – that helped,' said Annie. 'It was more than good of Father Logan to come out so late.'

'The doctors said there was nothing they could do.'

'The kidney man from the Mater is supposed to be the best in the world,' said Annie. 'It's amazing what they can cure nowadays. Help me lift her.'

'Where's the best place for my hands?' Annie showed her. Ellie was cold to the touch. The two women raised the body and Annie pulled the nightgown off over Ellie's head and down the stiffening arms. They carefully laid her flat again. Susan looked shyly away from the body's whiteness and triangle of dark hair. Annie modestly covered it with a small linen towel. The material was dry and remained tented like cloth drying on a hedge.

Then Annie noticed a chain – a long chain around Ellie's neck. There was a ring on it.

'What's this?'

'I dunno.'

'A gold ring.'

'I can see that.'

'But why?'

'I know nothing about it.'

Annie turned the ring between her fingers. The fine chain holding it glittered as it moved. 'Why would anybody want to wear the likes of that? Instead of on your finger.'

'I've no idea.'

'Down her bosom?' Susan began folding the nightgown. 'A wedding ring too,' said Annie as she moved to the marble washstand to pour some hot water into the basin. She wetted and soaped a face-cloth and began washing Ellie's face, damping and pushing back the black hair from her forehead, making sure the eyes stayed closed. When she had finished the face she moved onto the body. Susan watched mesmerised by the way the skin moved, just as it would in life. The chain with the ring was in the way and Annie disentangled it and took it off over Ellie's head.

'You've never seen this before?' Annie wrinkled up her blunt nose and held up the chain.

'No. It's just a ring – all girls love to have rings.'

'But a wedding ring?'

'Especially a wedding ring.'

'Ellie could never have afforded this. You know how much one of these costs?'

Susan shook her head. No, she didn't. Sadly.

Annie was about to hang it on the bedpost when she paused.

'There's writing here. Inside. I can't make it out. It's too small. Susan, away and get me my specs.'

Susan left the room and creaked down the stairs. It was only recently that she'd needed glasses herself. Before that her eyesight had been good but now, definitely, she needed them for close work like darning or for reading a newspaper. Annie despite being so much older claimed she'd no use for them.

'Good light is all you need,' she said. 'You wouldn't miss much if you never read a newspaper. You have your eyes wore out, Susan.'

On the rare occasion she did need to see fine print she'd resort to a lorgnette which she kept in the drawer of the bureau bookcase. Susan, now with the lorgnette in her hand, climbed the staircase slowly as if it was the highest and longest staircase in the world. She knew what was coming and was filled with dread.

Susan passed the ring to her sister. Annie brought the lorgnette to her nose and focused on the inscription. '*For Ellie – my love – and* – I can't make out whether that's *life* or *wife*.' Annie moved closer to the window and held it lower to catch the light coming beneath the blind. 'What do you think?' She passed the ring to Susan who read it off almost without looking.

'*For Ellie – my love and life.*'

'In the name of God . . .' Annie stared at Susan perplexed. Susan handed the ring and its chain back. Annie hung it on the bedpost again.

'What's going on here?'

'How should I know?'

'Who would have given that to her – and her only twenty? Susan, why aren't you looking at me?' Susan raised her head and looked at her sister. 'You haven't been able to meet my eye since we came up here. What's wrong with you?'

'My wee niece has just died.'

'There's something else.'

'You're wrong. There's nothing.'

'I know you of old, Susan. You think I don't know when I'm not being told the whole story?' Susan's eyes went down again and she began to weep with her whole face. Eyes, mouth, chin, the wings of her nose. She did not wipe away the tears or knuckle her eyes. While her sister cried Annie continued to wash the body. Every so often she looked up to see if her sister had stopped. Eventually she did.

Annie dried where she had washed. She said, 'Nothing unclean can enter the kingdom of heaven.' She lifted the white freshly ironed nightgown. 'Let's get this poor girl respectable again.' Susan helped Annie insert Ellie into it.

'That was a favourite of hers,' said Susan, 'with its wee ruff of lace.'

'Where's her rosary?'

It was kept in the drawer at the bedside. Susan produced a purse. In it, dark knotty beads – and Annie bound Ellie's dead and waxy hands in an attitude of prayer.

'What I want to know is,' Annie looked up, straight at Susan, 'if Ellie couldn't afford a solid gold ring, then who on earth bought it for her. And put such writing in it?'

Ellie could carry three plates at a time – one in each hand and the third balanced between her forearm and the first plate. She swooped in and set a plate before each man. Mr McDonald, a whisky traveller from Elgin in Scotland, Mr Rinforzi a string player of Italian extraction from London, and a Mr Burns from Enniskillen who worked as a clerk on the railways. Mr Burns, in his mid-twenties, was their most recent boarder. At some point during the meal Annie always came into the room having taken off her apron and positioned herself with her back to the mantelpiece.

'Is everything to your pleasement, gentlemen?' They nodded, muttering little appreciations and continuing to spoon hot soup. In the few months he'd been eating with them Annie had noticed Mr Burns's habit of bringing the cutlery, either spoon or fork, into contact with his teeth. Each time it produced a metallic wet sound. She'd remarked to Susan that Mr Burns wouldn't be used to such accoutrements at home. Where he was from, the food came in handfuls.

Ellie dashed in to set more bread on the table. Mr McDonald had finished his soup and sat with folded arms. Mr Rinforzi was saying that he was a freethinker and that the only reason he went to mass was to hear the wonderful Carl Hardebeck play the organ.

'May God forgive you,' said Annie.

'He was one of the bishop's better appointments,' said Mr McDonald.

'The good Dr Henry Henry?' chuckled Mr Rinforzi.

'His mother suffered from double vision,' said Mr Burns. He laughed a little at his own joke and offered his empty dish to Ellie. When her fingers came in contact with it she winced and gave a little gasp. She put a finger into her mouth.

'What's wrong?' asked Mr Burns.

'A skelf. I got it earlier – out the back,' said Ellie.

'Let me have a look.'

'It's nothing,' she said and dashed out of the room.

'Such familiarity only embarrasses the lassie,' said Mr McDonald.

'Never a truer word,' said Annie, almost under her breath.

When he had finished his meal Mr Burns got to his feet and pushed back his chair with his legs.

'Excuse me,' he said with some gravity. 'But I will be back.' In his absence Annie sat upright on the edge of one of the dining-room chairs. She spoke quietly to Mr Rinforzi.

'Such talk of *freethinkers* is all very well between you and me but I'd appreciate it if you'd be more circumspect when younger ears are present.'

Before Mr Rinforzi could say anything Mr Burns returned with a small leather case in one hand and a magnifying glass in the other. Ellie was beginning to clear the table.

'We have all the equipment necessary, Miss Ellie,' said Mr Burns, 'to build the pyramids or take a mote from the eye of a gnat.'

'You'll not lay a finger on me,' said Ellie, laughing. She bunched her fists and held her elbows tightly in to her waist.

'Dr Burns at your service, ma'am.' He held the magnifying glass at some distance from his eye and regarded Ellie. The enlarged image of his eye made her laugh.

'That's horrible,' she said.

'Show me your pain.' Ellie smiled a bit. Then unfurled her middle finger. It was a cold night outside and the curtains had been drawn early to keep the heat in. 'Light,' said Mr Burns and moved her to the armchair beneath the Tilley lamp. He knelt before her, took the finger in his hand and examined it through his magnifying glass.

'I will draw the sting with my tweezers.' Ellie gave a sharp intake of breath when he touched the sensitive place.

'Do you know the story of St Jerome?' said Mr McDonald.

'Indeed you have me there,' said Mr Burns without looking up from his task.

'The lion with the limp,' said Mr McDonald. 'The saint saw what the problem was right away – a common or garden thorn. So he removed it and from that day onwards didn't the lion follow him about like a dog. Any picture of St Jerome – look in the background and you'll see our friend the lion.'

Ellie was tightening her mouth as Mr Burns worked at her finger.

'I'm sorry but I have to go against the grain,' said Mr Burns, 'to loosen it. Could someone hold the magnifying glass for me.' Annie was reluctant to move, to have any part in this performance. Mr Rinforzi obliged.

'Going against the grain may well get you frowned upon in this house,' said Mr Rinforzi glancing at Annie. But she was looking away from the tableau. Mr Burns cradled Ellie's hand in his and brought the tweezers close. Ellie closed her eyes and then yelped.

'There we are,' said Mr Burns. He felt he had to placate Annie and laid the skelf on the white tablecloth in front of her. She declined to look down.

'Small enough to be almost invisible,' said Mr McDonald. 'Large enough to cause considerable pain.'

'Like your whisky,' said Mr Rinforzi.

Ellie was sucking the bead of blood released from her finger. Mr Burns knelt on the floor putting the things back into his case.

'I'll send you my fee, Miss Tierney,' he said.

In the kitchen Susan, flushed with heat and work, had begun to stack dishes on the draining board. Annie came in and stood with her back to the range. Her fists were rolled into a ball and she was shaking her head.

'What's getting your goat?' asked Susan.

'Ohhh.' Annie refused to answer, keeping what she had, pent up. Ellie came in with some dirty plates.

'Make sure that door is closed,' hissed Annie. Ellie backed against it and it snapped shut. 'Have you taken leave of your senses, girl?'

'What?'

'That carry-on out there. Do you know how that looks? In front of rank strangers?'

'They're not strangers. They're our boarders.'

'They're not family and never will be. They are three gentlemen who are here as paying guests, and for you to be parading around – flaunting yourself . . .' Annie mimicked what she thought was Ellie's voice. "*Oh I've got a sore finger. Mr Burns would you like to hold my hand. Kiss it and make it better.*" I will not tolerate this . . . this sluttishness. If I see this kind of behaviour again from you Ellie I'll . . . I'll . . . You're not fit to be in the company of gentlemen.' Annie stormed out of the room and they could hear the carpeted stomps of her footsteps all the way up to her room.

Ellie stared at her Aunt Susan and her chin began to wobble. Then the tears came. Susan went to her, put her arms around her and whispered, 'She's in bad twist tonight. I could see it from early on.'

It was now much colder in the evenings and Ellie was lighting the fire in the dining room to have it warmed up in time for the evening meal. In the kitchen Susan was preparing a pie, cooking meat, chopping vegetables, rolling out pastry. Suddenly the door of the kitchen burst open and Annie strode in with her face like a clenched fist.

'What's wrong with you?' said Susan. Annie closed the door with a firm snap, made no reply and began pacing up and down. Her face was pale and her mouth drawn tight. She was arranging something inside her head.

'Has anything happened?'

Annie reached the pantry door and turned on her heel and walked back again. She looked as if she was rehearsing something – thinking through a game of draughts. Reliving old moves, anticipating new ones. Her index finger pointing things out.

'In the name of God answer me,' said Susan.

'I don't know whether I could. Or should.' Her voice was quiet, whispered, controlled. She now moved her head in the same way as she had moved her finger. Weighing, balancing, planning. She stopped pacing and put her face in her hands and remained like that for some time.

'I'm waiting,' said Susan. She was holding her chopping knife point up.

'About half an hour ago I sent Ellie to light the fire . . .' She stopped, realising this was the wrong way to begin. She began again.

'I have just seen . . . our Ellie . . . throwing herself at Mr Burns.'

'What?'

'Kissing him.' Annie almost shouted the words. Susan covered her mouth with her hand and widened her eyes. Annie began her pacing again. 'I have said or done nothing about it – because she didn't see me. Nor did he. His back was to me. She – she was so swept away, she had her eyes closed. I was in the hall – the door was open. Her eyes closed, I tell you. Her hands were that black with the coals, she was afraid to touch him – holding them up like this, she was. Not to spoil his jacket.' Annie demonstrated as if she were trying to stop someone in their tracks. 'That charlatan of a showman – Mr Burns – he's blotted his copy-book well and truly this time.'

'Maybe they're . . . they . . .' said Susan. She set her knife down on the chopping board.

'Maybe nothing,' said Annie. 'Men are only out for what they can get. Not one of them's any good – every one of them's after foulness and filth.'

'Och Annie, give us peace,' said Susan.

'And if it isn't foulness and filth they're after, it's a round-about way to lead up to foulness and filth. How dare he? I am going to ask that degenerate to pack his bags and leave *before* dinner. Him and his foul tongue. And foul ways. Did I tell you what he said at dinner last week?'

'No.'

'He didn't know I was coming into the room and he mocked your Brussels sprouts – *brothel sprouts* he called them. *Because that's what a brothel smells like*, says he. How does *he* know the smell of a brothel? And boasting about it too, into the bargain. That man makes me want to be sick.'

'Don't get yourself in such a state,' said Susan. 'You're too hard on them. They're only young. You see badness where nothing bad was meant.'

Annie sprang forward and flung the door open. She yelled at the top of her voice. 'Mr Burns! I want to speak to you right this minute. Mr Burns! And you too, Miss Ellie!'

After mass the crowds streamed out of the zinc Church of the Holy Family into the sunshine. From inside the organ boomed and warbled faintly. A parishioner stood on the steps holding a collection box for the poor. Aunt Susan and Ellie slotted some coins into it as they came down the steps into the chapel yard. They met Emily Mooney and chatted a bit. Ellie looked this way and that.

'And how's Annie?' said Emily Mooney.

'Fine. In the best of spirits. It's my week for this mass – otherwise you'd be talking to herself.'

'Give her my regards.' And she was away.

Ellie turned to Susan. 'Can I go and talk to Frank?'

'Who's Frank?'

'Mr Burns.'

'Oh, aren't we very friendly.'

'Och – Aunt Susan.'

'I'm sure Aunt Annie wouldn't . . .'

But before she had finished her sentence Ellie was away across the yard. Mr Burns, wearing a handsome Norfolk jacket, was standing by himself smoking a cigarette. He looked pleased to see Ellie, and touched his cap politely when she came up to him. They talked a little and Susan could see they were shy of each other because they moved a lot and laughed a lot. Ellie constantly fiddled with the drawstring of the little bag she carried on her wrist. Susan looked around to see if people had noticed the young couple. She strolled up and down, her hands joined at her waist. Inside the church the organ fell silent. Mr Rinforzi came down the steps, smiled and raised his hat to her in passing.

'Mr Hardebeck pulled out all the stops this morning, eh?'

The next thing Ellie was by Susan's side.

'Can we go home through Alexandra Park – with Frank?'

'But that would take ages,' said Susan.

'Yes.' Ellie smiled.

'Aunt Annie wouldn't be too pleased.'

'Please, Aunt Susan.'

'As long as you both walk with me.'

'Thank you, thank you.'

They walked down through the Limestone Road entrance to the park with Susan in the middle. To their left was the pond penned in behind waist-high railings. Swans moved quietly, looping their necks down into the water to feed, whereas the mallards and other ducks created an uproar of quacking and splashing. Mr Burns smiled and said, 'Acrimony among the duckery.' Ellie laughed.

Susan said, 'You do use such words, Mr Burns.'

'He makes them up,' said Ellie.

'Where do rooks live?' said Mr Burns defensively. All three smiled.

'Where do *you* live now, Mr Burns?' asked Susan.

'Got a good place now,' he said. Then quickly added, 'Not that there was anything wrong with my last place. I'm in the first house in Kansas Avenue. In every sense of the word.' They were strolling now – diverting to look at this bush or that flower-bed.

At one point Mr Burns said, 'Have you ever had a job, Ellie?'

'What do you call what I do? I'm never off the go – from morning till night – so's the likes of you can live like a lord.'

'That's family. What about a job – outside?'

'For a time she worked in Robb & Wylie's,' said Susan.

'Millinery,' Ellie added in a mock posh voice.

'So you know about hats.'

'I know *everything* there is to know about hats.'

'Why did you give it up?'

'They gave *me* up.'

'She was ill too often for their liking,' said Susan.

'You poor thing.'

'Ellie has to watch herself. She doesn't have a strong constitution.'

'I do so,' said Ellie. She pouted a little. 'How could I work the hours I do – lighting fires, cleaning, making beds, serving table, doing dishes? From morning till night? Maybe they discovered I was a Catholic – that would get you thrown out of a place like Robb & Wylie's much quicker.'

'They'd know what you were from the minute you walked into the shop,' said Frank. 'It's your halo that gives it away.'

Susan performed what she took to be a kindness for Ellie when she stopped at the board displaying the by-laws. The two young ones strolled on and Susan stood reading the multiplicity of 'Do Nots'. When she caught up with them again they were sitting on the grass, face to face.

'Come along, Miss Ellie – there's work to be done.'

On the way home Susan tried to reason with Ellie.

'I think he's unsuitable.'

'You make him sound like a job. I just love *him*. He's tender to me. I find him dear. And gallant. And sometimes he can be very funny.'

'Ellie you must remember that you are only nineteen.'

'How can I forget it when everybody always tells me.'

If the weather was fine this walk became a regular occurrence. On the Sundays when Ellie accompanied her Aunt Annie to the same mass they walked home by the quickest route. But with Susan the digression they took through Alexandra Park became a pleasure. Sometimes a uniformed band would be playing in the bandstand and they all sat and listened to the music.

When they arrived home Annie would ask, 'What kept you?'

Susan admitted to walking with Ellie. 'It's good for her constitution,' she said. But Susan made no mention of Frank Burns.

There was one weekend when Ellie was ill with her water-works. Cramps and pains so bad she had to take to her bed with a hot-water bottle. After mass Susan felt obliged to seek out Frank Burns and tell him that Ellie was indisposed.

On another occasion – after Susan had sat on a park bench for a considerable time as the two young ones strolled the perimeter of the park – she and Ellie were returning home by the Antrim Road.

'He seems so ardent,' Susan said.

'What's ardent?'

'Keen.'

'Yes, he's keen,' and Ellie smiled widely and swirled around so that her dress flared out at her ankles. 'Can you keep a secret?' Susan nodded unsurely. 'He asked me to marry him.'

'Oh child dear,' Susan clapped her hand to her heart and rolled her eyes. 'In the name of God. Ellie you *must* say no. Aunt Annie would have a fit. She'd kill the both of us. *And* Mr Burns. Promise me you'll say no.'

The two sisters faced each other across the body. Annie lifted the chain and ring from the bedpost. She spilled it from one hand to the other with a little metallic hiss. She continued to stare straight at Susan.

Eventually Susan said, 'How would I know who bought it for her?'

'All the times you were out together – she never gave you the slightest hint?'

'No.' Susan shook her head. 'Did she give *you* the slightest hint when *you* were together?'

'No. But as you say – we're very different. Ellie was your pet. She would confide more in you than me.'

'I don't know,' Susan wept. 'She got days off. How do I know where she went – or who she went with?'

'So she *did* go with somebody? Who? If you were to guess, Susan, *who* would you guess?'

Still Annie changed the chain from hand to hand. Susan stared down at the pink satin eiderdown on the floor.

'You are not going to like this,' she said. 'But I would guess Mr Burns. I know you despise him but . . . she was very fond of him.'

'I might have known,' Annie almost spat the words out. 'The one and only lodger I ever had to put out. I couldn't stand to be under the same roof one more night after that display of behaviour.'

'It was only a kiss.'

'She had her eyes closed. And for all I know, so had he. She would go for the likes of him because she *knew* it would annoy me. The most unsuitable man she could think of.'

'It wasn't like that.'

'So you know what it was like. How might I ask?'

'They were very fond of each other. Maybe more than fond.' Susan returned her sister's stare. She admitted that, after Frank Burns had been sent packing, the young ones had met in her company. Other times – they might've met by themselves, for all she knew.

'So he didn't move away.'

'He's in Kansas Avenue.'

'And you stood by and watched this pair?' Annie's voice rose in pitch.

'Yes. But not all the time. Maybe they *were* married, who knows – she talked enough about it – maybe they found a priest who did it for them. Mr Burns knew a curate in St Patrick's from his own part of the country. There's no give with you, Annie. The girl's dead.'

'Did she ever tell you she was married?'

Susan nodded her head.

'Sort of.'

'And you didn't tell me.' She dropped the chain and the ring onto the linen of the bed and buried her face in her hands. Then she took her hands away from her face and said, 'Susan you're a fool. An utter and complete fool. Poor Ellie's immortal soul . . . all because of your foolishness.'

'Yesterday – she only told me this yesterday – when she felt so ill she thought she was going to die.'

'She was a good judge of one thing, at least.'

'She said she wished she'd been really married.' Susan shook her head sadly. 'Maybe they weren't married – maybe they had only plighted their troth or something – maybe they were only playing at being married, playing at being man and wife.'

Annie stared at her sister and shook her head almost in disbelief. She said, 'Susan will you go down and get me a pair of scissors. The wee nail scissors.' Susan stared back at her, then did as she was told. She left the room and went down the creaking stairway. Annie shouted after her, 'They're in the sewing basket, I think.'

Susan went to the sideboard, crouched and found the pannier where the sewing and embroidery things were kept. She had to scrabble about hunting for the scissors. There was a green pincushion bristling with needles. Tiny hanks of embroidery threads in all the colours of the rainbow. Spools of white thread. Eventually at the bottom she saw what she was looking for. She trudged back up to the return room still on the verge of tears. She handed the scissors to Annie.

'She wasn't married. Not truly,' said Annie. There was a change in her voice. It had lost its note of worry.

'How can you be so sure?'

'I checked. Just now. For my own peace of mind.'

'You checked what?'

Annie said nothing but began to clean under Ellie's nails with the point of the tiny scissors. Then she gave her sister a look.

'Jesus Mary and Joseph,' said Susan.

The weather was unseasonable for the middle of June. Susan had to hold her hat on her head or the wind would have whipped it, hatpin and all, as she struggled up the Antrim Road towards Kansas Avenue. In her other hand was the small leather purse Ellie had used for her rosary beads. In it now was the gold ring and its chain – in her mouth, terrible tidings for Frank Burns.

THE ASSESSMENT

They're watching me. I'm not sure how – but they're watching me. Making a note of any mistakes. Even first thing in the morning, sitting on the bed half dressed, one leg out of my tights. Or buttoning things up badly. Right button, wrong buttonhole. Or putting the wrong shoes on the wrong feet. I don't think there's a camera or anything, but I just can't be sure. I know computers can do amazing things because Christopher tells me they can. It's his work, and good work by all accounts. He has a new car practically every time he comes home. Or he hires a new one. He's very good – comes home a lot – never misses. And sends cards all the time. Mother's Day. Birthday. Christmas and Easter. Mother's Day.

The nurses ask questions all the time – quiz you about this and that, but I don't know which are the important things. Some of them are just chat but mixed in with the chat might be hard ones.

'Did you enjoy your tea Mrs Quinn?' Any fool can answer that but 'How long have you had those shoes?' might be a horse of a different colour. Or 'Where did you buy that brooch?'

'It's marcasite. My son bought it for me. Look at the way it glitters.'

You wouldn't know what they could take from your answer. Before I came in here they wanted to know who the Taoiseach was and I told them I'd be more interested in finding out what the Taoiseach was. Then they realised I was from the North. Somebody out of place. I told them I took no interest in politics. My only real concern is . . .

Christopher would have something sarcastic to say. 'Mother, don't be such a fool – you'll be in there to see if you can still cope living on your own. A week, two weeks at the most. They'll just keep you under observation. Surely you've heard that. *She's in hospital and they're keeping her under observation.*'

'Don't mock me Christopher.'

I have every present Christopher ever bought me. I cherish them all – mostly for his thoughtfulness. I imagine him somewhere else, in some airport or city, trying to choose something I'd like. And I look after them. Dusting and rearranging. Remembering the occasion – Mother's Day or birthday, Easter and Christmas. A cut-glass rabbit, Waterford tumblers, leaded crystal vases. When the sunlight hits that china cabinet it's my pride and joy. Tokens of affection. Things you can point to that say . . .

I don't want to be a nuisance. That's the last thing I want to be. So I make myself useful. Looking after the old people in here. The rest of them just sit sleeping – in rows – I couldn't do that – I have to be doing.

It's such a strange thing to go to bed on the ground floor, at street level almost – although my room faces out to a courtyard at the back. All my life I've slept upstairs. Feel that somebody'll be staring in at me every morning when I open the curtains. Some gardener or janitor. Getting a peep. Giving you a fright. Maybe that's part of the watching – keeping me on the ground floor. If they find out something I'd like to be the first to know. Let me in on what . . .

I don't like this room. You can't lock the door. They say no locked doors. Anybody can come in. And has.

I'm glad I like Daniel O'Donnell because they play his songs all day long. After a while you don't hear them. In the TV room all the women sit in rows and sleep – me among them. A man hairdresser comes in to do everybody's hair and if you heard him – I say a man but he has this pansy voice. But everybody likes him. There's something about him that reminds me of Christopher – the way he turns. But Christopher's voice is all right. His voice is fine.

If there was a camera I think I'd notice. But I wouldn't notice a microphone – they can hide them where you'd never find them. They could be listening. Waiting for me to talk to myself. Mutter, mutter. So I'd better not. I'll not open my cheeper for as long as I'm in here. Maybe they've got something nowadays to know what you're thinking. I wouldn't put it past them. Holy Mother of God, the thought of it. They wouldn't be able to make head nor tail of what I'm thinking . . .

But they are watching me. Making a note of any mistakes. Half dressing myself. Or buttoning up something wrongly. Or putting the wrong shoes on the wrong feet. An old woman used to visit Mammy and the tops of her stockings fell down – like a fisherman's waders. That'll be me soon enough. A laughing stock. Nobody has enough courage nowadays to . . .

There are no rules here. Just get up when you like. Eat when you like. Sleep when you like. Christopher was a terrible riser – when he came home from university in England. He'd lie till one o'clock in the day sometimes. But he passed all his exams with very high marks. First-class honours. Must have been studying in his sleep.

The problem here is I don't know what you have to do to pass. Or what will fail me. So I'm stymied. It's like going into the kitchen and saying why did I come in here. So you just drink a glass of water whether you want it or not and forget about it. Or think . . .

The question is – what'll happen? If I pass I can go home and look after myself for a while longer. If I fail . . .

In here it's like an hotel instead of a hospital – with waiters, not nurses. There's a terrible tendency for the men nurses to grow wee black moustaches. I hate them. Always did. I said to Christopher if you ever grow a moustache, you needn't bother coming home again. But moustaches or no moustaches they're watching me and taking note of any mistakes.

My favourite is Gerard – he has suddenly appeared in front of me – a nice open face. He's kindness itself. It's funny that – to be thinking of someone and they just appear. Sometimes I think there's more . . .

'You wouldn't grow a moustache – sure you wouldn't, Gerard?'

'No chance, Mrs Quinn. I tried to grow a beard once and my mother said I was like a goat looking through a hedge.'

'Promise me you'll never do it again.'

'I promise. Now could you lift up a bit and I'll get this other leg sorted. And then we'll get the tablets into you.'

'You're very good, Gerard.'

'Once the tights are on and secured, Mrs Quinn, you can face anything or anybody.' His name is in big print pinned to the lapel of his white housecoat. He pours me some water and hands me my medication on a tray – three different-coloured capsules. I take them and swallow them down with the water. He smiles.

'Thank you. How long have I been in here Gerard?'

'Six weeks. But doesn't time fly when you're enjoying yourself.'

'If you find anything out I'd like to be the first to know.'

Old age is something you never get better of. I don't seem to have as many blemishes on my face as I used to. But maybe that's because my sight is failing. Like everything else. It's like on television when you find out that the head of the police is really the baddie. And you've told him everything. Where does that leave you, eh? That must be the worst feeling in the world – when you think somebody is on your side and he turns out to be on the other side. Like a penny bap in the window – you've no say in anything. What use is a bap in the window when all's said and done? Precious little . . .

Christopher must be very good at his job. It's thanks to him I'm in here. He moved heaven and earth to get me a place. They're few and far between in Dublin, so I'm told. Maybe if you refuse to answer any of the questions you'll pass. The only people who'll succeed are the ones strong enough to refuse to take part. But that's not me.

This is a strange place. The patients are all doolally except me. I'm the only one in here with any common sense. In the North it's called gumption. Down here it's in short supply. There's a notice on the front door which says it must be kept shut 'as residents may wander'. In more ways than one.

They don't like us Northerners. From the day and hour I moved here I sensed it. It's as plain as the nose on your face. They couldn't give a damn. The Troubles – that's something that happens north of the Border. Nothing to do with us.

And I hate the way they talk. Like honey dripping. Smarm and wheedle – like they can't do enough for you, like you're the Queen of the May – and all the time they're ready to stab you if it suits them. Probably when your back's turned. It's why that wee Gerard is my favourite – he's from the North. I feel at home with him. Comes from Derry. He doesn't smarm and wheedle like the rest of them. I never could stand that Terry Wogan – I don't know what anybody sees in him. He should have stayed in the bank.

I'd never have come south if it hadn't been for Vincent. He was from Galway, a different kettle of fish entirely. But his job was here in Dublin. And I was his wife.

Yesterday I was going to the toilet and I heard knocking. There was a glass door at the end of the passage and a woman was standing on the other side of it with her hat and coat on. She had one hand flat to the window and she was rapping the glass with the ring on her other hand. Tip-tip-tip. And she was shouting but I couldn't make out what she wanted. I could see her mouth and I thought she was saying let me out. I tried the door but it wouldn't budge. There were three or four other people standing behind her, standing there like Brown's cows – queuing, as it were. So I went and got one of the nurses, the one without a moustache – and says I to him – there's people wanting out down there and I pointed. He says, 'That's OK Mrs Quinn. That's just the special unit. Take no heed of them, God love them. They're being assessed for specialist treatment.'

'I'd prefer it if you called me Cassie.'

The next time I went to the toilet they were still there, the one with her hat and coat on, tapping the glass with her ring finger. Tip-tip-tip. Sometimes in here I want to cry but crying might lose you marks. So I don't.

They've done something to my ears. The time they removed the rodent ulcer from the side of my eye – just a local anaesthetic. But in the process they did something with my ears. They've never been right since. Black and as hard as bricks. And what's more it feels like they've put them on backwards.

My name is on my door to remind me which room is mine. It's very confusing when you come into a new place like this. Corridors with doors that all look the same. Like a ship. You think you're going into your room and it's a store cupboard or a toilet. That's the kind of thing they're watching out for. But Mrs Cassie Quinn in big letters on a wee square of paper pinned to my door – that helps.

*

I never did a test before. An exam. Except maybe for the Catechism. You had to learn it off by heart before you could make your first Holy Communion. And that wasn't today nor yesterday. I can still mind it.

'Who made the world?'

'God made the world.'

Or Oranges Academy. To do shorthand. And typing. But it didn't really feel like an exam – you knew what you could do, give or take a word or two, before you went in. You'd be a wee bit nervous in front of your machine – maybe one or two of the keys would stick. Or you'd go deaf. Or you would suddenly freeze up. My best was seventy-five words a minute. But I'm out of the way of it now. The fingers would never cope. Two words a minute, more like. And oul Mr Carragher teaching and talking and dictating away for all he was worth with cuckoo spit at the sides of his mouth. I'm too old for tests. Or maybe I'm just too old to pass them.

The peas they gave us for dinner last night were so hard you could have fired them at the Germans.

I suppose before our first Holy Communion was a test. Father McKeown came into our school and asked us the Penny Catechism. And woe betide you if you didn't answer up, loud and clear. Who made the world? God made the world. Very good. And who is God? You, yes you at the back. God is the creator and sovereign Lord of all things . . . Everybody laughed when he asked Hugh Cuddihy what do we swallow at the altar rails when we go to Communion and he said fish. But Father McKeown was furious. Shouting at us for not being able to tell right from wrong, silly from serious. I kept very still hoping Father McKeown wouldn't see me, wouldn't ask me a question. But he did. You, you – him pointing at me – how many persons are there in God? Three persons, Father, the Father, Son and Holy Ghost. Very good. Next? I remember I couldn't stop smiling. Very good, says he. To me. Very good.

It's funny how I remember all this from long ago but nothing from this morning.

'When did your husband pass away?' Gerard asks.

'Vincent died in nineteen fifty-four.'

'That's forty-seven years ago.'

'As long as that? Seems like yesterday. Vincent was the best husband and father that ever there was. The only thing – he was always very demanding. But he was a joker as well.'

'In what way?'

'If we'd a fallout he'd bring me a bunch of weeds from the front garden. Dandelions.'

Christopher said I was becoming very forgetful. Forgetting to eat. Forgetting to get up in the mornings. Forgetting to turn off a ring on the cooker and it blasting away all night. Just as well it wasn't gas, he said. All I could do was stare down at my shoes and him at the other end of the phone. Serves me right for telling him. I'd lost weight and it was nice to see he was worried about me. My next-door neighbour, Mrs Mallon, had phoned him, it seems. I was away to nothing. I wasn't eating. Wasn't looking after myself.

That's why they're watching me. Asking me all these questions. Making a note of any mistakes. Dressing myself like a doolally – maybe coming out of the toilet with your skirt tucked into your pants. Buttoning things up wrongly. Or putting on the wrong shoes. Looking out of place. Poor Emily McGoldrick used to visit us when she was old and the tops of her stockings fell down – like a fisherman's waders. We'd've got a clip round the ear if we'd made any remarks. Mammy was like that. Never let the side down.

I don't like this room. You can't lock the door. Anybody can come in. And did. One morning an old man in his dressing gown came in and started washing himself in my sink. I just stayed under the bedclothes. Didn't put my neb out till he'd gone. God knows what he was washing. I didn't dare look. Rummaging in his pyjama trousers and splashing and clearing his throat.

My only son, Christopher, wouldn't let me down. He's very good to me – he comes home a lot – never misses. Every November the car pulls up and he steps out of it smiling like a basket of chips. Just him – straight from the airport. Since I came in here he's taken to holding my hand like I'm his girlfriend. And he sends flowers at every turn-round. I call him my only son but that's not strictly true. I had a boy before Christopher – Eugene Anthony – but he died after three days. Not a day of my life goes past without me thinking of him at some stage or other. The wee scrap. A doctor told me later that he died for the want of something very simple. A Bengal light. They discovered that years afterwards. A Bengal light could have saved him, some way or other – don't ask me how . . . And that only made it worse, knowing that. I knew very little at the time – I wasn't much more than a girl. Lying in the hospital with my bump like some class of a fool. A baby started crying somewhere and I said is that my baby? I hadn't a clue. Not a clue of a clue kind. Sometimes I blame myself for wee Eugene. God love him. I think I was nineteen at the time. But I was well and truly married.

'Tablets.'

'Is it that time already, Gerard?'

'Your son'll soon be here.'

'What! How do you know?'

'He phoned. Last night. I told you, Cassie.'

'You did not.'

'I did.'

'Do you not think I'd remember something as important as that.'

'Here's a wee sup of water to wash them down.'

'I'd better tidy myself, if that's the case.'

Gerard opens the door and shows a man in. I swear to you I didn't know who it was.

'Christopher, what a delightful surprise.'

Aw – the hugs and kisses. He's very affectionate – kisses me on both cheeks. In front of all the others.

'How are you?'

'I'm rightly.'

'Did they not tell you I was coming?'

'I'm the last one to know anything in here. They tell me nothing.'

He likes to hold me at arm's length.

'I think you've put on some weight.'

'They're making me drink those high-protein strawberry things all the time.'

'You weren't looking after yourself at home. That's why you were down to six stone.'

He takes me for a walk in the walled garden stopping here and there to look at what plants are beginning to bud.

Christopher says, 'You're shivering.'

'It's freezing.'

'No, it's not.'

'It would skin a fairy.'

'I'll have to buy you a winter coat.'

'Don't bother your head. I wouldn't get the wear out of it.'

'I'm only joking.'

'The price of things nowadays would scare a rat.'

Sometimes of late I get a bit dizzy, become a bit of a staggery Bob. I bump into him coming down a step.

'Careful.'

He takes me, not by the elbow, but by the hand.

'Your tiny hand is frozen,' he says and laughs. 'I have a meeting with the doctors now.'

'Is that my window there?'

'No, you're on the other side of the building.'

'Do you ever hear anything of that brother of mine?' Christopher looks at me as if I have two heads.

'Paul's dead.'

'Jesus mercy.' I nearly fall down again, have to hold on hard to Christopher's arm. 'When did this happen?'

'Last year.'

'Why was I not told?'

'You were. He had a severe stroke.'

'Where?'

'At his home. In Belfast. I've told you all this many times.'

'Well it's news to me. Poor Paul. We were always very great. God rest him.' And then my chin begins trembling and I can't stop myself crying.

'Poor Paul.'

'Don't upset yourself so – every time.'

*

I keep myself very busy in here. I don't mind helping out. When they ask me to set the tables or make up the bed, I don't complain. If I see anything needing done, I do it. Makes me feel less out of place. The way some of them in here leave the wash-basins! And there are other things about toilets . . . it'd scunner you, some people's filthy habits. I draw the line at heavy work, like hoovering or anything like that, I'm not fit for it now but I don't mind going round and giving my own room a bit of a dust. I was always very particular. Or straightening the flowers. The others watch television all the time. They sleep in front of the television, more like. I don't see one of them doing a hand's turn.

But what really galls me, is I can't make Christopher a bite to eat when he comes. All the way from England. Not even a cup of tea. In my day I could make a Christmas dinner for ten. And a good one, at that. Holy Mother of God. And now I struggle to put on my tights.

Eugene Anthony was baptised not long after he was born – they suspected something, but they never told me. I was kept in the dark as usual. From start to finish. They've done something strange to my ears – that time they removed the rodent ulcer. My ears have never been right since. Black and as hard as the hammers of Newgate. It feels like they've put them on backwards too.

I'm sitting in the recreation room with the rest of them. They're nearly all sleeping. Chins on chests. There's a thing on the wall.

WELCOME TO EDENGROVE
TODAY IS FRIDAY
The date is 1st
The month is March
The year is 2001
The weather is cloudy
The season is winter

Christopher has let me down. Badly. Doesn't believe in God any more. That was the worst slap in the face I've ever had – as a mother. Said it to me one night in a taxi. Talk about a bolt from the blue. After the education I put him through. What a waste. With his opera and jumping on and off planes and all the rest of it. In one of the most Catholic cities in the world. It's a far cry from the way I was reared – but it doesn't matter what you get up to if you stop practising your religion. If you turn your back on God. What shall it profit a man if he gain the whole world and so shall lose his soul. Never a truer word. But, please God, he'll come round – before it's too late. I pray for him every night. What a terrible waste.

Another terrible slap in the face was the day I had to giveaway my niece's baby. In a sweetshop in Newry, of all places. That was where the priest had arranged the meeting. Among the liquorice allsorts and the dolly mixtures. And me having to hand over that wee bundle across the counter. All the more galling for me because of what happened to Eugene Anthony. The family counts at times like that. Everybody weighed in – driving and money and what have you. Of course she should never have had the child in the first place. And her not even considering getting married. I always said that. It was a sin – utterly wicked. So bad the whole thing had to be hushed up. There wasn't one of the neighbours knew a thing about it, thank God. She went to the Good Shepherd nuns for her confinement. Someplace they have on the Border. It's funny that, the way it doesn't show, sometimes – the way they can hide it. If they've done wrong. Something to do with the muscles – holding it in. There might be something else . . .

Maybe the best way to pass is to do nothing. That way you can't make mistakes. So just sit your ground. Take nothing under your notice. But that way they'll say there's something wrong – she's not in the same world as the rest of us. Doolally, in fact.

I sees a doctor and a nurse – it was wee Gerard without the moustache – come into the recreation room. And of all things! they have Christopher with them. That doctor looks too young. His hair sticks up like a crew cut.

'Christopher – when did you arrive?'

'We'll go to your room – it's quieter – for a chat,' he says.

'My name is on the door.'

I love it when he holds my hand like I'm his girlfriend. In my room we all get settled. And right away I get a bad feeling even though Gerard folds his arms and smiles at me. There's something about the way Christopher is clearing his throat.

'Well, we've come to a decision but we want to involve you in it,' he says. 'You know how you've been losing weight and not looking after yourself. And singeing the curtains with holy candles? You could have burned the house down, and yourself with it.' I just keep shaking my head. 'For six weeks or so the doctors and nurses in here have been building up a picture of you – and it's their opinion that it would be a danger for you to go back to living alone. Even with help and support. Now as you know it's impossible for me to come home and look after you. So the best option for you is residential care.'

'I wasn't born yesterday.'

'What d'you mean?'

'That's an old people's home.'

'It's not like that nowadays. Not like the old days . . .'

'The accommodation is state of the art,' says the doctor with the crew cut.

'They have their own hairdressers and chiropodists,' says Gerard. 'Cassie's a great one for the style.'

'Believe me, I've researched this.' This time it's Christopher talking. I'm getting confused about who's saying what. I keep looking from one to the other – watching if their mouth is moving, wondering if my backwards-on ears are playing me up. 'There are people who thrive when they go into such places. They've been alone at home – isolated and lonely – and find it's great to meet new people of their own age.'

'Not if they're all doolally, like in here. Who wants company like that?'

'I'll have a look around at the various options. Choose the best place or, at least, the best place with a vacancy. But we might have to wait a while. Dr Walsh here says everywhere is full at the moment. And you can't go home. It would be dangerous – you might set up another shrine and burn the place to the ground.'

'I would not.'

'I'm only joking, Mother.' Christopher smiles and puts his hand on mine. 'But it has to be your decision. We are not putting you in. We're telling you what the situation is and letting you decide. The doctors are saying you'd be best in residential care. And I think I agree with that. But the decision is yours.'

'Well, if it's for the best.' I hear the words coming out of me and they are not the words I mean to say. I go on saying things I don't mean. Why am I doing this? Why am I saying this? 'I don't want to be a nuisance. What'll we do if there's no places?'

'Not to worry, Dr Walsh says you can stay on here until we get somewhere.'

'People die,' says Gerard.

'Somewhere nice. Overlooking the sea – out at Bray. Or the North Side, Howth maybe.'

'The North Side – yes.'

It's dark. There's a strip of light under the door. If I turn to the wall I'll not see it. Away in the distance somebody's clacking plates. You can't lock that door. Anybody could come in. And climb into the bed. That oul man rummaging in his pyjama bottoms.

I want to be in my own house. With my own things around me. My china cabinet, my bone-handled knives and forks. The whole set's no longer there. But after so many years, what would you expect – wee Christopher digging with soup spoons. I'm like a penny bap gone stale in the window – I've no say. I don't want to be a nuisance. That's the last thing I want to be. I've no idea how long I've been in here. All I know is that I'd like to go home, if you wouldn't mind. Maybe my brother in Belfast could help. Paul is so methodical. Maybe – even better – if I got Christopher on to them he could sort it out – go and talk to the doctors. Convince them. And I could go home . . .

UP THE COAST

She came into the gallery the next day by herself. The bell chinked as she opened the door. The place was full of sunlight. The boy on the desk looked up. He recognised her and blushed a little. How sweet. He was in shirtsleeves. She asked if he'd gotten away at a reasonable hour the night before. He smiled and said it was OK. There hadn't been too much mess and nobody'd got *very* drunk, which was almost unheard of. And the wine had been a better choice than usual. It had really been a great opening. He had the loveliest eyes. Had she seen any reviews yet? She shook her head. No. She wasn't emotionally robust enough for that at the minute. Especially when her life's work was involved. One thing at a time. He smiled and nodded as if he understood. She was more apprehensive that there was to be a profile in the *Guardian* magazine. With a yet-to-be-taken photo. But she said nothing about this in case he'd think she was showing off.

He congratulated her on her sales. The fourteen works available to buy had all gone. Somehow last night there had been a feeling of stampede. Red stickers kept appearing and some people felt they were going to miss out.

'The hair may be turning grey but I'm not dead yet,' she kept saying to everyone. 'There's more to come.'

Last night had been so fraught with people that she wanted to have another, more contemplative look on her own. She hadn't selected the pictures for the retrospective herself nor had she had anything to do with the hanging. It had all been done by the gallery.

The three white rooms were empty and utterly quiet. In the first, the sunlight fell on the boards of the floor. They creaked a little as she put her weight on them. She took out her glasses to read the labels. Only one or two things had survived from Art College days.

And they were beside her grandchild series. So much for the chronological approach.

The second room was entirely devoted to the four large works to have survived from the Inverannich experience. There were others in various parts of the world but to have called them in would have been too expensive. She let her eyes traverse the space. They were good. All four of them. They each had something different to say. The stones took on a life of their own – like Plath's mushrooms. Strong, elbowing forward, butting for attention. Our story must be told. They had *become* the dispossessed, the abused – in contrast to the abject submission of the people of Inverannich as they'd left. The homesickness – the wrench from the land and everything dear to them. She'd read somewhere of the wailing and lamentation – the processions of people with a lifetime's paraphernalia making their way to the boats. It was a subject done by one of her favourite painters, William McTaggart, in the last century. Three times he returned to it – the emigrant ship. It waits in the distance as the departing boat rows towards it. Figures twisted with grief and loss merge with the rocks on the foreshore. In his last canvas, above the waiting ship is a barely perceptible fragment of rainbow.

Her almost abstract rendering of these same events in greys and greens, blacks and yellows brought her back to the anger at their making – the cross-hatching, the savaging of the paper surface. Always she wanted to be open to the accidental. These large works had been done from sketches and notebooks she'd retrieved from her camp the summer after. They were part of the healing process. Of the cat there had been no sign.

Alongside each was a framed picture with compartments. Every item – be it a grey stone or an oystercatcher's feather or a limpet shell or a page of a notebook – had a compartment to itself within the frame. They had the beauty of being themselves as well as the balance they achieved against or alongside one another. The cheap tear-off notebook pages with their pale blue lines covered in her dense, distinctive scribble had yellowed after so many years – changed colour like verdigris on sculpture – as they'd come to an accommodation with their surroundings.

Several works in the third room had been landscapes painted onto assemblies of these same writings and sketches – page after page after page, their content partly obscured by rough brush strokes – sea colours of Prussian blue and ultramarine. She approached one of the works and adjusted her glasses on the bridge of her nose to read the handwriting. Her handwriting. Her thoughts from so long ago made her cringe. Had she been so self-important? It was something about the tone:

Day 2.

I am amazed at the changes in the light here – not hour to hour, but minute to minute. So difficult to pin down. The landscape and seascape has such colour. I'd like to be able to do an Ivon Hitchens here but inhabited – highlighting the transience of people in such a place as this – borders and boundaries between one colour and the next, the shade and light. The balance between representation and allowing the paint its head.

When I get time to sit down and look around me this place is truly amazing. Yesterday was about practicalities. When I landed it was wet and blustery and the mountains, whose shape I knew from the April visit, had disappeared altogether. Shrouded, as they say. The black rocks in the bay spilled with white waterfalls after being swamped by wave after wave. Worst possible conditions for putting up a tent.

Today is what is required. The sky is blue and cloudless, the mountains magnificent. Green foothills become sand dunes, become the beach. Most black rocks are covered with lichen the colour of mustard. And the sea. It is such a presence continually roaring onto the beach. Waves are amazing things. Far out they rise as dark parallels. The best moment is when they break, the dark turquoise colour before the white spills curving down the face. Then the white spreads its length with a roar. On the gravel beaches to the north as the wave rushes in – the crest has such force it sets the tiny black stones hopping against the white foam.

It's always changing. Far out it is grey – it is blue – it is slate – it is shining like the bevel of a blade where it meets the sky. Was anything ever so straight as the line at the horizon?

From the maps the peninsula is about 30 miles long and at its narrowest about 10 miles wide. Where I am – the north-west – it's wild and virtually uninhabited – except for deer. I have a notion that it is only here, in solitude, that I might encounter my true self. With no interruptions I will become more and more conscious of myself and my place, however microscopic, in the universe. But then again I read somewhere about one of the medieval monks who refused to go on pilgrimage. 'If God was overseas, d'you think I'd be here?' Maybe it's the same with art. Maybe I should have stayed at home and worked.

The next morning he got up early and made himself some sandwiches. He buttered slices of white bread and filled them with the only thing in the fridge – cheese. He used his hunting knife to cut away the mildewed faces from the block even though there were plenty of knives in the drawer. He smeared the cheese with tomato ketchup.

The light was clear and harsh. It would be a good day. The sea was the right colour. He washed his blade under the tap, wiped it dry on a towel and returned it to its sheath at his waist. The sandwiches he wrapped in waxed paper from around the loaf. His Dad complained that bread went stale out of its wrapper. Fuck him, he could make toast. Anyway he'd still be too pissed from the night before to notice. Plus a hangover.

He walked down into the village, the sea on his right-hand side. Gulls squawked and screamed. After yesterday's storm there was no wind at all – smoke rose straight up from Loudan's chimney. Just as he passed the bastard came out his back door with a shovel in his hand and waved to him. Nod the head – that's enough for that cunt. The fishing boat must have sailed at first light or when the storm died down. There was a gap where it had tied up the night before. Brown seaweed had blown onto the road and there were strings of straw caught up on Loudan's wire fence.

He stopped at the hotel above the harbour and went round the back to see if anybody was up. Plastic crates and aluminium kegs were stacked beneath the kitchen window. Bottle caps of different colours were all over the yard and embedded in the mud at the back door. He arched his hand between the side of his head and the glass and tried to see into the kitchen. Empty stout bottles, a filled ashtray, a mug of tea not drunk from the night before. If he got anybody out of bed they'd tell him to fuck off. He sat down on the rim of an aluminium keg to wait.

After a while he heard a woman coughing. A lavatory flushed and the water rattled down inside the pipe at his shoulder. He stood and waited. Old Jenny came into the kitchen and put the kettle on. He knocked the frosted glass of the kitchen door.

'Who is it?'

'It's me,' he said.

Jenny drew the bolt and opened the door.

'Whatdya want at this time of the morning?'

'I need a couple of cans.'

The door swung open and he stepped inside. Jenny bent to light a cigarette at the blue flame beneath the kettle. She coughed and her face became red and pumped up. She steadied herself with her hand on the draining board until the fit of coughing was over.

'Aw Christ I'm dying.' She lifted the keys and went into the hallway. He followed her.

'Three Super lager.'

Jenny opened the bar. The place smelt of beer and stale cigarette smoke. The curtains were still pulled and it was almost dark. She switched on the light behind the bar and ducked beneath the counter. He watched her through the slats of the drawn shutters. She was still clearing her throat from the coughing.

'That was some night last night,' she said. 'Those ones from the north are wild men.'

'Aye – anyone off the boats is mad. And twenty Regal.' She put the cans in the pocket of her apron and came out bent double from beneath the counter flap. He could have got her like that – with a single rabbit punch. The oul girl was sticking her neck out. She straightened and set the things on the counter among last night's dirty glasses.

'It's a good day,' he said.

'I haven't had time to look yet.'

He tugged each can from its plastic loop and slipped one in each side pocket. The last one he zippered into his breast pocket with the sandwiches. The empty plastic loops he threw on the bar.

'Could you put it on the slate? The boss knows. He says it's OK.'

Jenny looked at him and shook her head.

'I'll tell him.'

You will too, y'oul hoor.

He set out at a good pace. His Ammo boots were very quiet for the size of them. Boots that big should've given more warning. After a couple of hours the road began to show a line of grass and weeds in the middle. He passed the last house, burned and left derelict some twenty years ago, and the road reduced to a track. The sun was becoming hotter and the effort of walking fast made him feel sweaty. His Dad would be up now – snarling and eating his toast. In the hotel Jenny would be adding water to the packets of 'home-made broth'. The track veered off to the sea. Sometimes farmers took a tractor-load of gravel off the beach but nothing had been up here for months.

He left the track and headed up the hill. His boots rattled through the heather and the sky was full of the sound of larks. He looked up but could see nothing. The hill was steep at this point and he had to lean into it stepping up like stairs – pressing on his thighs with his hands. Every now and then he would stop to get his breath back, breathing through his mouth. He should really give up the fags. There was a good view from here but it would be better from the top. When the noise of his breathing disappeared he heard a grasshopper. And insects came in, buzzing close to his ear, then away again. You never know. You never know what might happen. It was just luck there had been a storm and the fishing boat had been driven in to shelter. The crew had been good crack. He didn't remember everything they'd said – there had been too much drink taken – but he remembered enough. The boys off the boats had always plenty of money and bought drink like there was no tomorrow. You could be on the edge of company like that and get pished without them knowing you couldn't afford your round. He was always broke. But what else could he be? He was for the most part unemployed. Sometimes he did a bit of gardening – grass cutting and tidying up for cash. Occasionally, on account of his father, he'd get a day or two's work on a clam boat but he was prone to throwing up and began making excuses when he was asked. He tried the Army but it coincided with an appearance at the Sheriff Court for having a go at a cunt of a bus driver – he'd had a few drinks and the driver kept yapping on about not smoking, even though there was hardly anybody on the fucking bus. So he gubbed him. After that the Army didn't want to know – the bastards. So cash was a novelty.

It was the fishing-boat skipper who had told them about her. It was him who'd dropped her off a couple of weeks ago. Up here on the mountain – now – he was getting a hard-on just thinking about it. He put his hands down the front of his trousers and arranged it so that he was more comfortable. Not yet. He was only looking – sniffing around.

> *Day 6.*
>
> *Hadn't time to write anything yesterday. But there will be days like that. I am not going to oblige myself like some kind of schoolgirl to annotate each day. What is important is that I make things based on the nature of these ruins. That's the priority. Whether paintings or sculptures or photographs or notes towards such things. And yet the diary keeping is important to give a perspective of the overall project.*
>
> *The more I try to render these networks of tumbled walls – the danger is to make them not abstract enough – the more I feel the presence of the people who lived here a hundred and fifty years ago. They were me and the likes of me before they were driven out by hunger and landlords.*
>
> *I am outside in my sleeping bag because of the cold,*

sitting with my back to a stone wall writing this. The fire is cracking and hissing. The gathering of driftwood is one of my favourite chores. I walk the foreshore and spy dead branches and planks and whoop and pounce on them and drag them back. My Uncle would have been proud of me. It was him told me about this place. When he was stationed at the airfield during the war he came here many times. According to him in the mid-1800s the people of the village were evicted by the landlord, Lord Somebody-or-other, to make way for sheep. Or maybe they'd fled of their own accord in search of a better life, away from constant famine, leaving their homes to tumble. He said it was full of ghosts. Inverannich, he called it. 'A deserted village but you'll not find it on any map.' The ruins provide some shelter for my tent. The sea must have encroached since this place was built because it seems too close, too threatening. I can hear it now. On my doorstep, if a tent can be said to have a doorstep.

Day 8.

  Hot, idyllic weather. Blue sky and calm water. Tiny wavelets wash in – a kind of tongue roll – just one at a time. The sea is mirror flat reflecting the sky. Black and yellow bladderwrack breaks the surface between the dark rocks which are covered with tiny white pin limpets.

  Pools gather where they can on the black rocks and are edged with lettuce-green seaweeds. 'You would never want a nicer day than this.' I say it out loud to myself and the sound of my voice startles me. I realise I have not spoken for a week and have almost forgotten how to do so. I resolve to practise. At night, it being utterly clear, I look up at the stars transfixed. I say aloud, 'You would never want a nicer night than this.' My voice is strained because my head is back looking up. Pressure on the rusty vocal cords.

  I just adore the solitude this week so far. Not a manmade

sound, no smell of exhausts or cigarettes, not an artefact,
except that which is washed up – the odd light bulb, plastic
syringes, condoms, some trays each with an indentation to
rest your glass. One of which I rescued for my own use.
When you do lift your head here, whether it's rain or shine,
you see something worth looking at. Watching TV is a way
of not thinking. Being by yourself in this remote place forces
you into certain modes of thought and action. Work, apart
from the main purpose, is a way of entertaining yourself.
Making paintings passes the time. Indeed I know of nothing
better for that purpose. If you start to make a painting
after breakfast the next time you look up it will be supper
time. All the time you have been thinking, making decisions
– this or that? Darker or lighter? Is this line good enough?
How to incorporate the ghosts without actually showing
them?

I now know the surprise Robinson Crusoe must have
felt when he came across the footprint.

A little further on he came across a stream, rising up. If you looked
closely you could see pale flecks of sand rising and falling with the
force of the spring. There was nothing purer than that. The source
of a mountain stream.

Out of the corner of his eye he saw a herd of red deer. Property
of the fuckin gentry. They don't like you moving about on the hills
– warn you off. Not personally – but there's notices all over the place.
On gates, on fences. You're liable to be accidentally shot, they say.
There's more chance of being hit by a fuckin meteor. What they really
don't want is the dregs parading about their hills. Especially when
they've spent hours stalking beasts and suddenly some cunt like me
walks over the hill and they're off. Fuckin zoom, never to be seen
again.

He took out his binoculars and focused. The stag was out on his
own, away from the hinds. It had a good spread of antlers and just
as he watched it, it put its head back and barked. If he had a gun
– the right kind of rifle with a scope – he could bring it down from

here. No bother. A seven-millimetre Mauser snug between his cheek and his shoulder. The bastard would run for a bit, then crumple. Just like a chicken with its head chopped off. Or it would fall just where it stood – all legs and awkwardness, collapsing like an ironing board.

He had read in a magazine how to butcher a deer but had never had the chance to do it in practice. Rabbits he could skin, no bother – like pulling off a jumper.

The saw-toothed Bowie had arrived by post from the catalogue and he was surprised that it came up to his expectations. In fact it was bigger than he thought it would be. The blade was made of superb carbon steel which produced such a sweet ping when he plucked it with his fingernail.

He got up from his sitting position and broke the skyline. The herd galloped away. He climbed now with the determination that he would reach the top in one. Establish a rhythm. Pace the breathing. There was a pain barrier but once through that everything settled down. Sweat ran down his face and dripped from his chin. His thighs hurt but he continued stepping up. Over the top and then that view – headlands, islands and the Atlantic Ocean. Next stop America. He ran hop jumping down the other side. When he came to another stream he flopped down and immersed his face, then drank. The water was cold enough to make his teeth hurt.

Beside the spring was a kind of cliff face. He got his back against it. He smoked a cigarette and stared down at his tan boots. Here he could defend himself no matter what came at him. He liked the feeling he had in caves – with his back protected. That way there was no situation he couldn't cope with. He could light a fire, kill a rabbit, catch a fish, he could survive. He read in the papers of these people who died of exposure on mountains, hill walkers even. Accountants from Manchester, fuckin hippies from Leeds. It would never happen to him because he knew how to handle himself.

He put all three cans into the water twisting and embedding them into the gravel. The sun was hot for June. He stripped to the waist and spread his T-shirt on the rock to let the sweat dry. His tattoo caught his eye and he liked it all over again. The one word. Simple. The granite held the heat of the sun and was comfortably warm as he leaned his back against it. He had been on the move for about four hours now and was starving.

He took his knife from its sheath, unwrapped his sandwiches and cut them in two. He sat looking down at the coastline. There was no sign of her. But then he hardly expected to see her first thing. There would have to be a bit of stalking. He chewed each bite ten times to get the best out of it. The long waves rolled in as far as he could see.

He couldn't wait for the can to really cool down. He reached over and unstuck one and jerked the ring-pull. The lager exploded all over his face and chest.

'Aw fuck.' He laughed and held the frothing hole to his mouth. He drank until the lager was under control. A bite of the sandwich, a swill of the lager. The sun. This was it. Nobody to get on his wick. Just himself. When the can was finished he wondered if he should have another. Better not. They might come in useful. A can each.

When he had finished eating there was some cheese and tomato on the blade of his knife. He licked the food off then stabbed the blade into the sandy earth to clean it. It made the sound of the word sheath each time he drove it in. Sheath – sheath – sheath. He scanned the west side with his binoculars but could see nothing. He smoked a cigarette. Sometimes he thought the only reason he ate food was for the pleasure of having a cigarette afterwards.

Last night he'd been sitting – by himself as usual – on a stool at the far end of the bar when the skipper and his crew came in and told the story – said she had just arrived at the pier with a rucksack the size of herself and offered money to be dropped off by the deserted village at Inverannich.

'Was she . . .?' The barman raised an eyebrow.

'She made you pay attention – if that's what you mean.'

'She was a cracker,' said the youngest fisherman – and growled softly into his beer.

There was a slight breeze at this height which cooled him. He stood and unzipped his fly and pissed on the rocks and surrounding heather – like an animal marking its territory.

He did not want to pollute the spring. He retrieved his cans from the water and zippered them into the pocket of his anorak along with the T-shirt and the binoculars. He tied its arms around his waist and moved on, bare-backed, his hands free.

The journey down was so much faster. Parts of the hill were covered in scree and he ran down these in great leaping steps. The stones clicked hollow for the brief second his boots were in contact. Lower down the scree changed to peat and heather and tussocky grass. It was like dancing – the feet had to be just right – at the right angle – doing the right steps for the terrain. This way and that. A dog's hind leg. His eyes to the ground, watching for trouble. A zigzag.

He was in good shape – proud of himself. Lean and muscled. Like an athlete without ever having trained. But he was too white. His tan of last summer had gone. When he reached the bottom his instinct was to run and wipe the sweat from his face in the sea but he stopped. He would leave footprints the whole way across the sand. He wasn't ready to declare himself yet. So far it was only a bit of noseying – see what he could see, kind of thing. Nothing set in stone. Opportunity knocks. Whatever will be, will be. Kiss her ass, her ass.

This was easy walking – light, short grass growing out of sandy soil. He headed north keeping off the beach. The ground sprung beneath his feet. There were flowers all over the place. Blue ones, pink ones.

In the pub the youngest guy had said he thought she was game.

'She'd give you two dunts for every one of yours.'

The skipper wasn't so sure.

'That's the wee boy in you talking.' He put on a baby voice and said, 'The size of dick I want is a *big* dick.'

'Fuck off.'

They all laughed and ordered more drinks. He didn't know what was said next because he announced he was going for a crap. The barman winked and said, 'You're so full of shit it's coming out your arse.'

'Any more of that and I'll take my slate somewhere else.'

When he came back from the toilet the skipper was still talking about the girl.

'Naw,' he said, 'they'll be as happy as Larry on their own up there.'
'They?' said the barman.

'She took one of the cats with her – just as we were getting ready to go. One of the ones that hang about the pier. Anyway she grabbed a big kitten – for company, she says.'

'I told you,' said the youngest guy. 'She's lonely – up there all by herself.'

'He nearly missed the boat,' the skipper waved his thumb at the boy, 'running to get her cat food. To get in with her.'

Day 10.

Swimming in my swimming pool is a real treat. It's only about twenty yards away. There are a series of flat rocks jutting into the sea like a natural pier. The first one is like a slightly tilted raft which is great for sunbathing. At high tide the rock rises a couple of feet above the sea. The water is turquoise green because of its depth and the immaculate sandy bottom. I've seen grey fish moving down below – mullet maybe. It is also sheltered because the next outcrop of rock shields it from the open sea. The whole thing is a wonderful rectangular-shaped gully. If I was a geography teacher I'd take a photo as an example of a fault – you can see the strata. I might even put it on the classroom wall labelled – 'My fault'. You can dive straight in – it's like a diving board. I can't touch the bottom, even when I do. It's a freedom like no other – swimming in your pelt. I feel like an otter, a seal. The water cradles me, soothes me, caresses me, cleanses me. You feel clothed in it except for the fact that it's freezing. The first plunge is the worst. But that's the way it has got to be done – no testing the waters here – it gets all the pain over in an instant. If the midges get really annoying this is the best refuge.

He climbed the next headland and when he reached the top lay down. Beneath him the sandy bay was full of black rocks with cliffs at the back. His stomach tightened. There were footprints all over the place. Someone hadn't bothered to hide the fact that they were there.

He scanned the beach with his binoculars but could see no sign of movement. There was a river cutting across the sand and emptying into the sea. Further inland he saw a network of grey tumbled walls where houses had been. Suddenly in the lenses a flash of blue. He backtracked. A blue tent. Her place. A half-hour passed and still there was no sign of movement. He would venture down.

He walked on the flat table rocks. They were fissured and creased like old skin. He had to go the long way, leaping from rock to rock, so as not to leave his prints. When he reached an area where the sand had been churned up he left the rocks and moved as quietly as he could across the sand. Near the tent was a dead fire among some slabs. On a rock were three pairs of women's pants which had dried in the sun. They were the same shape. Two white and a black. Each was pinned down with a fist-sized stone.

The tent was pitched in the shelter of two old stone walls. Further back against another tumbled wall was a wind-break of the same blue material. There appeared to be no one about. He moved the flap of the tent which had been left open. He put his head inside. It was damp and smelt faintly of plastic and fungus.

There was a red rucksack with a sleeping bag rolled on top of it. A pot, a kettle, a large Winsor & Newton sketch-book, some tins of Heinz beans, some packets of dried cat food, a small Primus stove with blue canisters of gas. A used tin held paintbrushes and pencils beside packs of Polaroid film. He stepped outside and looked all around. No sign of anyone. Inside again he went to the rucksack. The zipper was already undone and he just flipped the top open. There was a black purse, which he opened. A handful of coins, bank cards wedged into their sections, a library card. In the wallet part there were three ten-pound notes which he folded and slipped into his pocket. He put the purse back where he found it – on top of a mauve jumper – and unzipped one of the side pockets. A box of tampons. Other pockets contained – a face-cloth, a book called *The Letters of Vincent Van Gogh*, a washbag with a toothbrush and stuff in it. The only thing of any interest was a half-bottle of brandy with very little out of it.

There was a hardback notebook. He spun through the pages with his thumb. It was blank except for the beginning pages. Here her writing was very neat and in straight lines even though there were no lines to guide the writing. The white paper took on a faint blueness from the tent:

> Day 12.
>
> I can hardly believe that three weeks ago I was in Art College. How awful that place was – spreading the new barbarism. They substitute randomness for creativity. They use the camera and the video now instead of brush and charcoal. The more clumsy and amateurish the result the better it's liked. Pass the responsibility for art onto the viewer (I know I have a Polaroid but it's useful for documenting work – they can even be works themselves).
>
> Mum and Dad were both painters so when I went to Art College I expected something better . . .

His eye trailed away from the words and he closed the book. He lifted the sketchbook and looked at the first page. It was fucking awful. So was the painting on the next page. And the next. Like somebody was cleaning different colours off their brush. Greens, purples, browns. If her mother and father were painters she was fucking adopted. Black scribbles were like what he'd done in school trying to wear down the lead of his pencil.

He set the sketchbook down where he found it and ducked outside the tent. The only thing stored in the wind-break was firewood, dry driftwood. He went back to the tent and unzipped the pocket of his anorak at his waist. He set a can of Super lager on an oval rock. She could take that two ways – either as a gift or else it would scare the shit out of her.

And he was away jumping from the churned-up sand at the campsite to the flat rocks and then up the hill to a position where he could watch for her coming back. It was late afternoon and there was a drop in temperature with the breeze coming off the sea. He spread his anorak on the grass and lay down. With his elbows resting on the ground the binoculars were steady and he could see much more through them. He kept his T-shirt off to get tanned by the breeze but after an hour or so he began to feel cold and put it on again. Various trails of her footsteps led nowhere in particular. He looked again at the knickers drying on the rock. He began to get a hard-on thinking about her. If he pulled himself off now it might spoil things. He had held off for so long he might as well wait a bit longer.

He imagined her walking up the hill behind him and surprising him when he was doing it. Might be good that – turn her on, maybe. He was hungry and tried to think about food to distract himself. New potatoes and butter. A fish supper. Wagon Wheels. Chocolate was good for energy in survival situations.

A pair of oystercatchers were creating a racket further up the beach – peep – peep – peep – peep. They were swooping and diving, going mad because somebody was approaching their nest. Something bad was going to happen. Was this her coming? He focused his binoculars on the birds, then on the landscape beneath where they were creating the fuss. Maybe it was a stoat or something like that. He saw movement and tried to keep the binoculars as still as possible. It was a black cat. Strolling out of the sand dunes. It was followed by a boy – walking – carrying a board or something. What the fuck was *he* doing here? Nobody mentioned *him*. He banged the binoculars down onto the grass. Keep watching – the girl is probably with him. In the vicinity. He looked again at the boy. About a mile away he looked young, around fifteen or so – walking barefoot carrying this board in one hand and his sandals in the other.

He tried to remember the conversation in the pub. He had been overhearing it – not taking part in it. Maybe he'd missed something important – one of the times he'd gone to the gents. Or had they said something he forgot because too much drink had been taken? Without the binoculars he watched the tiny figure and the cat approaching. The cat did not walk to heel like a dog but ran this way and that, towards the sea, into the dunes. It sat and got left behind, then caught up. The boy paid no attention to it. He approached the tent and set his board on a rock. Through the binoculars he could see the boy was wearing khaki shorts – bare-chested, his shirtsleeves knotted around his neck, his shirt protecting his back from the sun. He disappeared into the tent.

Almost immediately he came out again. He now had his shirt on. Then he spotted the can of Super lager. He looked all around, scanned the bay and the hills. He looked towards where he lay with his binoculars. The boy must have had good eyesight because he spotted him immediately and waved. Fuck it. Maybe the binoculars had flashed – maybe his stupid head had been sticking up. He felt he had to wave back.

He got up and slung his anorak over his shoulder and decided to go down. When he got there the boy was sitting on a rock sipping the can.

'Hi – was this meant for me?'

It was a girl. Jesus. Her red hair was cropped very close. He had been looking at her tits through the binoculars and hadn't even noticed – hadn't even paid attention to them. She'd been walking half naked.

'Hi,' he said.

'It was very thoughtful of you. Cheers.' She saluted him with the can. English, by the sound of it. He pulled out the other can and jerked off the ring-pull. It exploded but this time he had the can aimed away from himself.

'*Sláinte*.' He returned her salute.

'Oh yes – slanchay.' She smiled and tilted the can up to her mouth. He had a small tattoo on his forearm of the word *Mother*. The heart was red, the rest of the design, navy.

'So what brings you all this way?' he said.

She laughed, 'I'm an *artiste*.' She made fun of the word. 'Trying to be creative. And what brings *you* here? To the world's end?'

'I live here.' He nodded to the south-east. 'Over by.'

'What do you do?'

'As little as possible.' Seeing her look concerned he said, 'Naw – I'm on and off the boats – but it's not regular.'

She was in her early or mid-twenties. It was hard to tell exactly.

'That's miles away. I meant what brings you to this place.' She gestured all around her.

'They said there was an old village.'

'Yeah.'

'And that there was somebody here.'

'Where did you hear that?'

'In the pub. The guys in the fishing boat from the north.'

'Oh, did they come back?'

He nodded. 'They sheltered for a bit last night. Did you get that storm?'

'Yeah, for sure. Horrendous. My tent nearly took off.' She laughed. 'They were lovely – especially the skipper. They couldn't do enough for me. So friendly. And you came all this way . . .?'

'Yeah.' He stared at her.

'How sweet of you.' He looked away. She called the cat, 'Psh-wsh-wsh,' rubbing her fingers together. But the cat hung back.

'It's wary of you,' she said. 'Wary of strangers.'

'It's you that's the stranger.' She looked hard at him for a moment then smiled. He said, 'What's your excuse?'

'For being here?'

He nodded.

'Oh – a lot of reasons,' she said. 'I wanted to be on my own for a bit. Completely. And . . . I've just finished College. Art College. And . . . I wanted to do some work. And . . .' She looked all around her as if she couldn't believe what she was seeing. 'And to be in this place. It's the most beautiful place I have *ever* been.'

'Eh?'

'Yes – I never knew there was so much sky. If you live in a city you just never see it. And the stars at night. But I'm not here to do just landscapes,' she put inverted commas in the air with her fingers, 'but to register my *feeling* for landscape.' She smiled at him. He looked up at the sky. It was beginning to cloud over from the west. 'It's so remote. A great-uncle of mine was stationed up here with the RAF during the war – and he never stopped talking about it. He said this whole area was the most underpopulated land mass in the whole of Britain.'

'Because everyone living here's a bastard.' At first she smiled at this. He sat on a rock of his own. He took a long swill from his can of beer. 'English?'

'Born in England.' She laughed and shrugged her shoulders. 'Brought up in Edinburgh. You?'

'Here.'

'What's your name?' She waited for an answer but he just looked over his shoulder out to sea. Then he finished his beer and bent the can in the middle and set it on the rock.

'That was quick.' She was still sipping hers, barely tilting it. She pulled her knees up to her chin and encircled her legs with her arms.

'Do you have moles?' He was looking at her legs.

'No.' She laughed at the directness of his question.

'What's those?' He pointed. She looked down at the underside of her thigh and reached out a finger to touch the black thing on her skin.

'Not again.'

'Ticks,' he said.

'Nearly every day now.'

'There's another one.'

He pointed to the back of her ankle.

'I hate them.'

'You're their dinner. Any nail-polish remover?'

'Forty miles from nowhere? Does that kill them?'

'It gets them off your skin.'

'I just pull them off.'

'I bet they like that.'

'What do you mean?' She looked hard at him, not sure of what he'd said. Whether he meant it or not.

'Never mind. Doing that leaves the head in you. Then you get diseases and everything. They'll scar you for life if you do that. Want me to get them off so's they'll not leave a mark?'

She seemed unsure, but nodded. He pulled out his knife and watched her face.

'Relax,' he said. She became flustered and straightened her legs so that her feet touched the sand.

'It doesn't matter,' she said. 'They're no big deal.'

He came and knelt in front of her.

'Stand up then.' She balanced her can of beer on the rock beside her and slowly got to her feet. He was still kneeling.

'Turn around. Put your hands on your knees.' She did as he told her. He took a cheap plastic lighter from his trouser pocket. His hand was shaking badly. He tried to get it to light. She was conscious of him looking up her legs.

'I feel ridiculous,' she said and straightened up. 'What are you going to do?'

'Coax them out. Burn their arses off. Wait,' he said. 'Don't move.' He got the lighter to spark and turned the flame down. He held the jet close to the black bulb of the tick's body trying not to burn the skin of her thigh.

'Aaaah.' It was a cry of the fear of being burned more than anything else as she felt the heat. The tick moved and he pulled it away from her skin with his fingers. The touch was brief. Her hand came round her thigh to touch the place. There was a trace of blood on her fingers.

'They crawl up the grass and wait for something to pass – a deer – you – then they jump and hang on. Like grim death.'

'But in a place like this they could wait for ever.'

'Yeah – some of them can survive for years. Anything up to four years, they say.'

'You're a bit of an expert.'

'That cat is probably covered in them.' It was grooming itself on a wall near the tent.

His voice had a shake in it. She could see his knees shivering as he squatted behind her looking up. He held the lighter flame to the other tick behind her ankle. When it was out he rubbed the place. Her skin was hot.

'Is that it?' she asked. There was a long pause.

'I like the view from down here.'

She whirled round and stared at him.

'Did you say what I think you said?'

'Yeah.'

'Why don't you go for a swim and cool off?' She turned and walked quickly towards the tent, her limbs stiff and straight.

'Just kidding,' he called after her. The cat ran to her but she brushed it aside with her foot.

He pocketed the lighter and followed her. She was tidying up. She dropped his buckled beer can into a plastic bag. Then set the rest of her beer on the rock in front of him.

'Ta,' he said, swigging from it. 'I thought Art students were more broad-minded than that. Nudes and that kinda thing. Always in and out each other's beds.'

She didn't answer. The cat came to where she stood and began to criss-cross in front of her, rubbing its back to and fro against her legs.

'Anyway – nobody up here can swim. Nobody teaches it. The boys on the boats say if your boat goes down, it's better that way.'

She was busying herself doing nothing – lifting things, putting them in the plastic bag – moving items within her living space.

'I would like you to leave,' she said.

'I fuckin live here – you don't.'

She walked past him out of the tent and lifted her washing. Each rock, when she threw it away, bumped heavily on the sand. She rolled the pants up and stuffed them into a side pocket of the rucksack. Without looking at him she said, 'I thought I told you to piss off.'

'Huh!' He mocked her. 'Ladies don't use words like that.'

She refused to answer him again. Eventually he shrugged his shoulders in an exaggerated fashion and wandered off.

He found himself a seat in the sunlight on an outcrop above the beach facing her camp and sat watching her. She ignored him and, sitting outside the tent mouth, attempted to boil a small pot on the Primus. He took out his knife and began stabbing it into the mixture of sand and grass he was sitting on. Again the noise – sheath, sheath – as the blade sank in.

'Fuckin snobby ginger bitch,' he said. The bright flick of a reflection on one of the stone walls reminded him of something. He angled the blade to catch the sun and directed the beam into the open flap of her tent. A circle lit up the darkness of the back wall. As a child he'd done this with a mirror directing the sunlight into bedrooms along the main street – a disc flicking across flowery wallpaper – intruding into rooms – any room he wanted. What was odd was, even though the mirror was square, the light was always a circle. A woman might be taking off her clothes and see a bright spot on the wall and think nothing of it. But it was important to him, down on the street, directing the power of the light. Now he aimed the reflection into her space and the image was still round even though it came from a long narrow blade. He realised what he was seeing was an image of the sun. He had the power to aim the sun, to aim it into her tent – to flick it over the walls, at the girl's face, down between her legs – anywhere he liked. She became aware of the flash when it struck her face and she tried to wave it away like an irritating insect. He kept it trained on her. She looked at where it was coming from and pointedly turned her back on him to eat from her dish. The next thing she knew he was behind her.

'You really fuckin think you are something, don't you?'

She stood facing away from him. He turned her with a pull of her shoulder. The knife was in his hand, its point upwards.

Her voice had dried in her throat and no words would come out. She felt her legs turn to water.

Sometimes she ran, sometimes she walked. Always looking over her shoulder. Not believing. Checking. When she ran she clenched her fists. How awful. How utterly awful. The walking was mostly climbing the hills and the running was mostly on the down slopes, digging her trainers in so as not to go too fast and fall head over heels. To break a bone, to twist an ankle out here would be a disaster. She would probably die. Slowing herself down by planting her feet sideways against her own headlong downward rush. Sometimes to the left, sometimes to the right. Her arms out to the side, her hands splayed for a fall. This way and that – like herringbone – to slow her descent. What a nightmare. She had not slept but had kept the fire going all night. She'd sat or squatted, staring into its glowing heart, trying not to see the pictures it showed her. Her project destroyed. Her life wrecked. To have set out in the dark would have been too dangerous so she waited for first light. And when she rested from her running she cried. Her stomach was contorted, rigid and rippling with nerves. Full of gut knots. Stomach clenching. She had diarrhoea in the long grass. Afraid to look in case there was blood. It came, and she couldn't stop it coming. From nerves. Like the crying. She couldn't help herself. Too far from home to hold on. She remembered as a child wanting to cry – falling, or hearing something hurtful said to her – keeping it all in, holding her face straight until she got into her own room. Then letting it go. Always she kept going south, keeping the sea on her right-hand side. Sometimes it rained, sometimes the sun shone. And the whole time she tried not to think. Or to think local. Immediate. This is a hill. This is a descent. To think practical. Effort needs to be put into this particular climb. Agility needs to be the priority on these rocks. If I come across a sheep path it will get me to some sort of a track which will eventually get me to the tar road. Then a simple walk to the town. Oh fuck. She was so angry. She had never been as angry as this in the whole of her life. Had never used the word fuck, even into herself.

She didn't know how long it took her – most of the day – but eventually she came to the brow of a hill and saw in the far distance a smudge of smoke from the town. It was still a couple of hours away.

It was good to feel tarmac under her feet. On the road into town she saw a doctor's house. Set back off the road behind well-trimmed lawns. There was a brass plate on the railings. She read the surgery times and hesitated. Then walked on into the town. Down by the harbour she was aware that her knees were trembling. She didn't particularly want it, but she knew she needed some food. Her blood sugar must be low. The clock in the grocery shop said 6.30. The Sunday papers were just arriving. At six thirty in the evening? When she opened her purse she saw that the guy had robbed her. With what change he'd left her she bought a sandwich and an orange juice.

'The bastard.' She found a place with her back to the pier where she sat eating and drinking in the sunlight. She was amazed at how utterly changed she was and how it didn't show. In the shop she'd made sentences and spoken and asked for what she wanted. The elderly woman had listened to her and taken her money and smiled a little at the transaction. While she waited for her change she had turned her foot this way and that as if to admire her trainers and bit her fingernails and touched her ear lobe (as she had a habit of doing) and none of what had happened to her the previous day was apparent.

Something had profoundly changed and she had no way of showing it. She had no way of talking about it. The outside and the inside. They were not connected. And never would be again.

She needed a plan, needed to take charge of herself. All her drive so far had been focused on returning to the place she started from. That had been simple. Move south. Keep the sea on her right. But now she had to make up her mind what to do.

The doctor's wife cleared the plates from the table to the stainless-steel draining board. When it was just the two of them they ate in the kitchen. Her husband took what red wine remained in his glass to the other room to read the Sunday papers which had just arrived. The doorbell rang and his wife went to answer it. It was a girl.

'Yes?'

'Can I see a doctor?'

'It's Sunday evening. Can't it wait till tomorrow morning?'

'I'm sorry.' The girl was hesitant. 'I didn't know what day it was.' The doctor's wife smiled and began closing the door.

'Tomorrow morning – ten thirty,' she said. The girl shook her head in some distress.

'I need to see a doctor. I think it's an emergency.'

'What's wrong?' The girl was on the verge of tears and her hands were trembling. 'Are you on holiday?' The girl nodded that she was. 'Just a minute.' When the woman came back to the door she swung it open and ushered the girl in. Then asked her to take a seat in the surgery and left her on her own.

She tried not to think of anything. There was a desk against the wall. The chair she sat in was sideways on to it. On the desk, a blotting pad with leather corners. The room was silent. There were two framed prints on the walls – one of Matisse's abstract coloured-paper cut-out, *The Snail*, the other, Dürer's drawing of a hare. Made in 1502. The place was lit by a frosted glass window, the upper pane was normal. Blue sky, yellow clouds. She liked the way Dürer signed his initials, the way the legs of the A straddled the D. She could hear seagulls. In a distant part of the house, the click of plates and the rattle of a spoon on stainless steel. Against the other wall was a black examination couch covered with a fresh paper towel or sheet. The backs of her thighs were beginning to adhere to the leatherette material of the chair. They made a sound as she moved her weight. She stood when the doctor came in. He indicated that she should sit again, then lowered himself into the swivel chair at the desk.

'What can I do for you?' He was an overweight man in his forties with bushy hair beginning to go grey. His hands were podgy. She looked at his eyes – he had nice dark eyes – then down at her bare knees.

'I'm not sure.' She seemed not to know where to start. 'Just recently I graduated from Art School.'

'In?'

'Drawing and Painting.'

'Where?'

'Edinburgh.'

'My home town. How did you do?'

'Well. At least, I think so,' she said, then added with some hesitation, 'they gave me the Manser Prize as well as a qualification.'

'Congratulations.'

'But that is not what's important,' she said. He smiled, still waiting for her to come to the point. She shook her head – no. 'I wanted to get away from everything. To work. And I got a fishing boat to drop me off at the abandoned village up the coast at Inverannich.'

He nodded waiting.

'I have – I was – several times I was bitten by ticks and I wondered . . . some people say you can become very ill . . .'

He stared at her then stood up from his chair. The lids of his eyes were heavy.

'My wife said you led her to believe this was an emergency.'

'I'm sorry,' she began to cry, 'but I think it is.' The doctor extended his arm indicating the way to the front door.

'If you come back in the morning I'll see you.' Still the girl sat. She was quietly crying making small wet sounds.

'I've been raped,' she said. 'This guy raped me. But I don't want to go to the police.' The doctor was still standing over her. He touched her lightly on the shoulder and it made her crying all the louder. He gave a sympathetic sigh and sat down again. 'He had a knife – a kind of dagger thing . . .'

'Are you injured?'

'I don't know . . . I'm sore.'

'I'm very sorry,' he half shrugged, spread his hands. 'In your own time . . .' She heard him pluck several tissues from a box and they appeared beneath her downturned face. When her crying stopped she dried her face and said, 'I don't want a child out of him. Or a disease. So I came here.'

'I can help with both. Let me get some details first.' He put on a pair of half-moon spectacles and wrote down her particulars. Then he stood and took down a book and opened it flat on his desk. He studied it silently then said as he read, 'We have two daughters of our own, older than you no doubt. Both of them up and away. Can you undress and lie here?' He indicated the examination table. He reached into a cupboard and produced a paper hospital gown which he gave her. 'You may get dressed in this wonderful outfit temporarily.' He pointed to a grey canvas screen.

'Everything?'

'I think it's best.' Then he went out into the hallway and called his wife. There were lowered voices from outside the door.

Behind the screen she undressed, not daring to look into the clothes she took off, embarrassed and scared of what she might see. She put on the nightdress thing – shivering now, yet her armpits were wet with perspiration. She lay on the examination couch and felt it cold even through the paper sheet. The doctor came back into the surgery. He washed and dried his hands, put on latex gloves. The doctor's wife came after him with the colour supplement from the *Observer*.

'Would you like me to hold your hand?' she said.

'No, thanks. I feel not too bad.' The doctor's wife smiled and went to sit by the frosted window, her back to the room. The sound of her turning the pages made the silence of the room even more apparent. The doctor worked quickly – examining, taking samples, giving his patient commands and requests, asking her terrible questions, writing the answers on a pad on his desk. He gave her an injection in her hip which remained in her like a nugget of lead. Occasionally he went back to the desk and consulted his tome – as if it was a recipe book. He looked closely through his glasses at the bruising on her arms which she hadn't noticed before – then over his glasses at her face and the scraped bruise on her forehead. He warned her before he did things – like when he used forceps to pluck a few hairs from her head and some from her pubes. He asked her about allergies, then gave her some tablets.

'What are they?'

'Antibiotics. I'll prescribe the rest for you. It's most important you finish the whole course.' He handed her a small plastic tumbler full of straw-coloured water. 'Sorry about the state of the water but it is perfectly safe – it's just peat colouration.' She put the tablets in her mouth and swallowed them down.

'You've picked up another tick on the way here, I see.' With the forceps he slowly drew the creature out of a skin fold at her stomach and pressed a pinch of cotton wool to the pinpoint wound. 'That's the best way to remove them. You shouldn't burn them or put Vaseline on them. Just gently pull them off and treat the wound.' He wiped the black spot onto a tissue and put the forceps in a jar of disinfectant. He gave a sigh and looked up at her. He tapped his temple.

'We can perform effective damage limitation but the real hurt is in here. Very hard to get rid of. They say it keeps coming back. You have to work on the flashbacks. Where are you from?'

'Edinburgh.'

'Yes, yes of course – you said. I'll give you some helpful addresses to contact when you go home.' He touched his wife's shoulder. 'Thank you, love,' and she left the room. On the way out she touched the back of the girl's hand where it lay – gently with her own – almost covering it. Her touch was light and dry and motherly. The girl swung herself off the examination table and sat on the chair again, smoothing the strange textured paper garment beneath her.

'I think the best thing to do,' said the doctor, 'is to proceed as if the law *was* involved. That way you can change your mind later.'

'I won't.'

'Have you washed since . . .?'

'I've been in the sea.'

'Is that not washing?'

'It's swimming.'

'Do you have a change of clothes?' She shook her head – no.

'Not with me. I just ran first thing this morning.'

'These are what you were wearing at the time?' He looked over at the pile of clothes she had left on the table by the screen. She nodded – yes. 'I'd like to hold onto them. Would you have any objections to wearing some of my daughters' things?'

'I won't change my mind about the police.'

'Fair enough.' He looked her up and down. 'You and my youngest are of a size. She's in Australia.' He excused himself and left the room. He seemed to be away for a long time. She could hear someone treading the floorboards upstairs because they creaked. The ceiling light was a double fluorescent tube.

The doctor came back and put the girl's clothes into a brown paper bag.

'My wife will look after you just now.'

'Thank you.'

'Have you money?' She looked up at him startled. 'Sorry, I mean would you like me to order you a bed and breakfast for tonight?'

'Is there a bank I can go to in the morning?'

'Yes – several.'

She smiled for the first time since she'd come in.

'I thought you were going to charge me.'

In her presence he phoned a landlady from the town and booked her in.

'You'll like her – she's a very calm and comforting sort of person.'

The doctor's wife arrived with a pair of jeans, underwear and a maroon T-shirt which had been a handout at a conference on blood pressure.

'There's holes worn in the elbows of this sweater. But if it got cold you could push up the sleeves. That seems to be the style nowadays. You're welcome to have a shower first.'

'Then come into the other room for a cup of tea,' said the doctor.

'Or something stronger,' said his wife. The doctor stood up.

'Is that everything?' He went to the book on his desk and ran his eye down the page. He touched his pockets as if it would remind him of something. 'And what of him? The perpetrator?'

'I threw boiling water at him but it missed,' she said. 'All it did was make him more angry. Gave him more excuses. He had a knife – all I kept saying was I do not consent to this.' And again she was crying. Again he handed her tissues.

'Where is he now?'

'He just went on. To the north.'

'Did you know him?'

'No.'

'You're lucky to be alive, by the sound of it. Did you speak to him?'

'A bit. He said he was on the boats.'

'Everybody here's been on the boats. Except red-haired women.' The doctor put up his hands defensively when she looked up at him. 'Apologies. It's one of the fishermen's superstitions.'

Even though it was after eleven the bedroom was filled with a milky light. Things could be made out – the mirror reflecting the not-completely-dark sky, the Victorian picture of cattle drinking, the wardrobe and fireplace. There were still slivers of light in the west. It had been the longest day recently but she couldn't remember how long ago. The window was open an inch or two at the bottom and the net curtains furled and unfurled in the draught. The whisky was not doing the trick as the doctor had promised it would. Despite having had no sleep the night before she found it difficult to get over. She kept seeing him. Him. The fucking thug. To wrench herself away from such images was difficult. And the young men of the town did not help – gunning their engines and squealing their tyres as they cornered into the Square. When they drove off, in the silence which followed, she could hear the sound of geese. They were some-where in the sea loch and the racket they made was halfway between lamentation and laughter. She'd never heard anything like it. Images of him kept leaping into her head making her angry. Sick, as well. She kept swallowing hard, keeping things down. It was hard to get rid of. His eyes. That upper lip. His stupid boy's knife. The pain he caused her. Maybe the urge to throw up was the tablets – or the alcohol – she wasn't used to the taste of whisky. She remembered it from childhood – from her mother's remedy for toothache. Whisky painted onto the hurting tooth. The doctor had urged her to a second drink and she knew she shouldn't have taken it because he poured them large. But when she'd seen all the paintings on the walls – abstract landscapes by Barbara Rae, still lives by Elizabeth Blackadder and Anne Redpath – she felt at home, expected maybe to see some work by her own parents there. And all the pills he'd shoved into her. And that injection. What was it? When she closed her eyes the bed raced backwards and she had to snap them open again to stop the sensation.

No, she wouldn't tell her mother – not a word. It would be too distressing for her.

The way he undid his belt with a kind of smirk. And set his binoculars on a rock. She jumped out of bed and closed the sash window, pushed it down with both hands. Thud. The sound of the geese lessened, the curtain was still. She got back into bed again. She smelt of something she did not recognise. The T-shirt belonging to the doctor's youngest. It had been laundered but somehow when it was against the heat of her body it took on a smell of its own. A foreign smell – a maroon smell – a smell whose source was now at the other side of the world. It wasn't offensive, just someone else. A woman. Having been raped and finding herself wearing another woman's clothes she felt somehow representative. One size fits all. She endured the condition of women across the world. That buckle sound of the belt opening and her incredulous oh no, he's not after that. There is no shame about being raped. If somebody punches you in the mouth or glasses you in a pub you're not *ashamed*. You're injured. It's not *about* shame. As he was taking off his jeans she made a run for it but he easily caught up with her on the flat rocks by her swimming pool and dragged her to the ground.

Gut knots again at the very thought. The cigarette smoke from his breath, from his clothes – and afterwards the chlorine stink of his seed.

'We can do it again. The other way round.' And he did, just as soon as he was ready. She lay as still as she could in the hope that he would not hurt her beyond repair and kept repeating that she did not consent, she did not consent, she did not consent to any of this until he punched her violently on the back of the head and her forehead struck the rock so hard she nearly went unconscious.

'Just fuckin shut up.'

Then she just cried with the pain.

She must try and think positively. Practically might be easier. Later in the summer she could contact the skipper and get him to pick up all her gear and her work – the drawings and the paintings, the Polaroids and the notebooks. She should be able to salvage something out of this disaster. She had no fears for the cat. She'd seen it kill and eat – voles or mice, she didn't dare inspect them too closely. What she hated was the way it played with its catch – letting it almost escape so many times before killing it. At night it was breathtakingly fast catching and eating moths drawn by the light – once she was appalled to hear fluttering inside the cat's mouth before it chewed and swallowed. 'Oh cat how could you?' She'd never got round to giving it a name. When she'd left, it had been curled up by the fire, asleep. But would it get ticks in its fur – be weakened and eventually die? Or when she'd go back with the skipper would she meet this feral panther patrolling the place. Seeking whom it may devour.

The guy's face kept stabbing into her – the way he moved his upper lip as if he didn't believe a word she said. After the second time he got dressed and moved off by himself. He kept an eye on her from a distance. She cried herself out, then got dressed. What was she going to do? The stones which had pinned her washing to the rock were the right size but they were a long way off and there was nothing of a similar size here. And he was so strong and so fit. He would overcome her immediately. After a while he got to his feet and came closer, squatting in front of her.

'I bet you enjoyed that?' he said. She didn't say anything. He talked a bit. What amazed her was that he seemed to make so little of it. She hadn't consented – *at the beginning*, he seemed to say. What was all the fuss about? Why was she so bloody upset? Did she know how that made *him* feel? It was all natural – people fucked all the time.

Day in, day out. Implied that it should make them feel closer. She would consent the next time. That's the way it happened in the movies. How long would that be? How long had she got? He'd done the sneering lip movement when she asked if she could take a photograph of him. One side of his lip went up. A bit like Elvis.

'Fuck off,' he said. He smoked a cigarette as he stared at her. 'You must think I'm a stupid cunt.' Then the lip movement. 'But it doesn't work that way. All I have to say is you were dying for it. Out here on your own, for fucking ages. With nothing but your thumb. And then daaa-dahh! I arrive. You become a raving knob jockey. Fuckin Miss Posh panting for it. So yeah – take my photie. Readers' boyfriends. You're so fulla shit it's coming out your mouth. And by the way, your art's bum cheese – I could do stuff like that – fuckin dire, man. I hope you can take better photos.'

The souped-up cars roared back into the town and parked by the square, their stereos pounding. Bub-bub-bub. Wailing rock guitars. Heavy metal screeching. Getting deep into her. Almost hearing with her stomach. Then they drove off again bub-bub-bub and she heard the tyres yelp distantly as they cornered and zigzagged their way out of town.

The pillow was soft at her face. Sleep was close. Then all possibility of it disappeared.

'You fuckin stay where you are,' he said and walked back for the Polaroid.

'Don't think I'm going anywhere,' she said. Why did he think she could go anywhere? Her legs were like jelly and she could hardly move with the pain he'd left in her. But it might work. It would have to work. She was utterly convinced this guy was going to kill her when he finished with her.

He set the camera down in front of her. She got to her feet trying not to show her pain as she moved. She was sure she was bleeding at the back. He stripped off his T-shirt to show his lean and muscled upper body and stood with his back to the sea and sky, his knuckled fists on his hips.

'I like the body graffiti,' she said.

'What?'

'The tattoo.'

He turned his forearm to the camera and tensed it.

'I can do a close-up of that, if you want,' she said. 'Sit down.'

'Fuck – who's giving the orders round here?'

'Me,' she said. 'Put your top back on.' He put the white T-shirt on and sat down, leaning back preening himself. She went close to him, looking at him through the viewfinder. Would the blood show? But she kept her face simple. He lay back on his elbows with his knees wide open. She was shaking. She clicked the shutter and waited. The camera zizzed out a white print and she tucked it under her armpit.

'Lemme see?'

'Wait. The heat makes it quicker.' She counted. After about a minute she dropped it onto the rock in front of him. Head and shoulders with the blue sea behind him. He looked down at it but made no comment.

'Now one standing,' she said. He got to his feet and she moved in on him, close. 'To the left a step.' He did as he was told. She was giving him confidence in her. Hypnotising him. Holding up her hand for him to look at. She was trying out stuff she had seen other photographers do in the College. At one point she was doing so well she behaved as if she liked him. 'Eyes to the camera.' There was something terribly vain about him. Raising one eyebrow. She pressed the shutter and the camera expelled another print. She set it down on the rock to develop. Everything seemed to take ages.

'Why no armpit this time?'

'We've got all day.'

'You never spoke a truer word.'

When the print was ready he looked down at it.

'All right, man.'

'Now both of us,' she said. She set the camera on a waist-high rock and framed up the shot on him. 'Back a bit. Leave room for me. Watch the red light.' She clicked on the self-timer and began counting as she moved to where he stood. 'Ten, nine, eight.' His eye was on the camera watching the red light winking, arranging his face. The last couple of steps she ran. 'Six, five . . .' and she pushed him full in the chest with both hands. He grabbed onto her instinctively but she carried them forward with her momentum and they were falling. Toppling together. Both of them plunging deep into the water. She opened her eyes in the green depths to see where he was but saw only her own wake of white bubbles. Something touched her foot and she kicked out as hard as she could, scissoring her legs. The moment she surfaced she struck out to sea, swimming her fastest crawl. Then she turned and looked back. He must have kicked at the same time as the swell surged because his head and shoulders appeared and she thought for one horrible minute the sea was going to deliver him up onto the rocks again or that he had lied to her when he said that no one up here could swim and in fact he was actually a good swimmer – a strong swimmer. But the moving sea closed over his frantic head and he disappeared.

Next she was filled with a fear that he could swim to her underwater. And grab at her ankles. She waited treading water. The pain was still in her but now there was something else. The minutes passed. She continued to tread water – frog's legs. She waited and waited. He was nowhere to be seen.

'Yes,' she said to herself. She set out to swim to the beach.

On shore the first thing she did was to retrieve the Polaroid and the two pictures. There was a third picture hanging from the camera. It was of empty rock and sea. An absence. Two absences. Then she saw the binoculars. She flung them as far as she could into the sea. She left dark footprints and splashes as she moved over the rocks. She went back to the tent shivering. At this time of the evening the midges were beginning to annoy her. Her cheek-bones and the soft parts of her ears itched. To chase them she made the biggest fire she'd ever made and sat staring into it. She kept glancing behind her. If this was a Hollywood movie he would come back. Somehow he would be behind her the next time she looked around. Or the hand on the shoulder. Against all the odds he would have survived and would now be looking to punish her. Cut her throat. Sparks flew up into the sky and the burning wood cracked and spat.

Now, to do anything seemed the most enormous task. It took ages for her to unbutton her clinging shirt and take it off. She hung it on a stick. Steam began to rise from it almost immediately. She towelled herself dry and sat hunched and shawled by the fire, utterly weary. She felt she could not move. Even slightly. She daren't change any more. She daren't look to see if she was losing blood. She had ceased to exist from the waist down – except for the pain. Feed the fire. It'd get all the wood used up. She'd leave the next day. At some stage she summoned up enough energy to flick the two photos of him into the fire. They curled and burned with a pure blue fame. The picture of rock and sea and sky she kept. Towards morning she became cold and put on the dried shirt, and then was driven to get her mauve jumper and sleeping bag from the tent. The clothes she had on her were now dry partly from the fire, partly from her body. She remembered it as a night without sleep, yet she must have dozed with her head on her knees. Her memory of wakefulness and sleep became mixed with what was happening to her at present. Sleep was very far away, yet very close. Move a leg, rest her cheek on her forearm, turn on her left side. Towards the window, away from the window. A bed of soft nails. She might make the Polaroid the centrepiece of her exhibition – a picture with some rock and some sea and some sky. You never knew when sleep was close. Sleep was gradual. But it must be close because she hadn't shut her eyes for forty-eight hours. The human body needed sleep the way it needed food. Some shut-eye. It just could not be put off. Nobody died from sleeplessness. Lying there in your coffin with your eyes wide open. Able to die but not to sleep. Sleep and death were cousins. Shakespeare was always going on about it. Three layers – some rock and some sea and some sky. And nobody but her knowing the significance. Like that statement of the theme of a fugue. Variations to follow. Sky and sea and rock. Blue – grey – black. Solid – liquid – gas. And all stations in between. Light – half-light – dark. The doctor in his armchair after a few drams had apologised for being male – and his wife reprimanded him, saying it had nothing to do with gender and everything to do with misguided arrogance and brutality. Then they tried to pinpoint who the guy was. His age – on the boats – the knife. The doctor said his wife was also a doctor in the practice and knew more about the local people than he did. The boy she was thinking of hadn't far to go to seek his problems. She was almost sure she knew who it was. But then again, maybe not. How charitable. But the girl did not want to hear a name – it would have been too frightening to know a name. She wanted to get out of that sitting room before anything more was said. Before they became any more friendly. Moments came and went when she did not know whether she was asleep or not. Then she remembered the guy had seemed unable to smile – seemed not to know what it was to be amused – the muscles of his face were incapable of it. What a terrible thing to have happened. It had nothing to do with the remoteness of the place – that guy would have hurt a woman eventually – maybe even killed her, whether it was in a town or a city or a village like this. The doctor circling her, stooping and looking over his half gold-rimmed spectacles at her sex . . . a feeling not unlike blancmange or tapioca . . . a solution . . . an urgency . . . she was late for something . . . but the doctor's wife touched her hand, held it for her and said there, there love . . . however momentary . . . dreaming of insomnia . . . and blue sky and grey sea and black rocks . . . and blue sea and grey rocks and . . .

The doctor, with his wife in the passenger seat, was driving to the town at lunch-time. On the hill they met the funeral of the drowned boy walking behind the hearse to the graveyard. The doctor stopped his car and got out and stood to attention. His wife did the same by the passenger door. He recognised a few members of the family. Others were friends and neighbours. People in such a small place came out to show their respect. The father was pale – he was not crying but you could see he had been crying. Unsteady. He was being gripped under the arm and helped along by his brother. The father looked much older than he remembered him. The doctor had attended the house when the dead boy's mother was terminally ill with breast cancer. After she died the father had rolled up his sleeves and taken to the drink with some determination. Looking at him now some twenty years later it was remarkable how he had survived. But it was taking its toll – it was in his face. The doctor had warned him many years ago when he came to his surgery with an infected cut on his hand. And he had spoken to him on the day he had called to see his boy, sick with the measles and in danger of developing complications. In the middle of the day the curtains had been drawn in both the bedroom and living room – and the father was lying on the sofa in front of the television barely able to suck his thumb. With a sick only child in the house. At school the boy was not liked – other children feared him. Even the teachers were wary of him. A law unto himself – going to school when he liked – skiving when he had better things to do. Always getting into fights, and winning most of them. The doctor had inserted more than a few stitches for which the boy, and later the youth, was responsible.

Then there was a period of hope – after school when he talked about wanting to join the Army. People said it would straighten him out, give him a trade. But he was brought before the Sheriff Court for causing a row on a bus and the Army career fell through before it even started. It came as no surprise that such a boy should die young and in this tragic fashion. And then he remembered the girl who had come to him one Sunday evening in early summer to say she'd been raped. The doctor gave a little salute to the tail end of the cortege and climbed back into his car. His wife did likewise.

'Sad,' she said. 'The father looks poorly.'

'Yes.' He turned the key and started the engine. 'Did you do some forensic?'

'At Dundee – yes.'

'Hmmm.'

'Why?'

'How long do you reckon the boy was in the water?'

'Your guess is as good as mine. A month – maybe more. They say they relied on his tattoo for identification. He drifted thirty miles up the coast.'

'Yeah . . . but.'

'It depends on how cold the water is. Sometimes they don't resurface at all. But if you want to know when I think he drowned . . .' The doctor's wife trailed off. There was silence in the car.

The doctor said, 'The girl came to us in late June . . .'

'So what are you saying?'

'Nothing,' said the doctor. 'Not a thing.'

'I'm not saying anything either.'

He put the car into gear and his wife lightly covered his hand on the gear-stick with her own for a moment. She ended the gesture with a little pat. He moved forward down the hill. Through the windscreen they saw seabirds swing this way and that over the harbour. The masts of tied-up vessels criss-crossed and fenced as they wallowed and rocked in the choppy water of the harbour. In the rear-view mirror the funeral continued upwards to the graveyard.

Day 8.

Hot, idyllic weather. Blue sky and calm water. Tiny wave-lets wash in – a kind of tongue roll – just one at a time. The sea is mirror flat reflecting the sky. Black and yellow bladderwrack breaks the surface between the dark rocks which are covered with tiny white pin limpets.

She leaned forward, slightly crouched. The handwriting on the tear-off pages was partially obscured by her brush strokes. But she read the words as if they were new, as if the diary entry was today's. She expected to feel the lightning flash of fear again, the surge of adrenalin, but it did not come. Neither did the hand on the shoulder.

On the far wall were two of the series *Self-portrait in maroon T-shirt*. In one the face recognisable but smudged – in the other a further disintegration which she now thought too much like a Francis Bacon. Out of the corner of her eye she noticed something bright flit across the wall and ceiling of the gallery. She looked at what it was, full on. A bright disc shimmering. She moved her wrist and the disc of light traversed the painting. It was the reflection from her wrist-watch. She dismissed it – saw it as a good sign that she could remain calm. It was like the fairground attraction where you have to move a metal loop along a twisted wire from start to finish. If at any point the loop and wire touch there's a harsh electric buzz. Sometimes it was as if she was advancing the loop along her own jagged nerves waiting for the touch, the rasp of remembering. But now she was OK. She was capable of smiling.

The door of the gallery opened and the bell pinged. Voices. She was in the room with the Inverannich paintings and felt somehow guilty to be caught by strangers looking at her own work. The voices were American. An elderly couple. They approached the boy on the desk and wanted to know if they had to pay. He said no but invited them to sign the guest book. Were they on holiday? They answered, loudly now. They were not American but Canadian. From Halifax, Nova Scotia. Said that both their families were originally Scottish – how could they be otherwise with such names.

'My wife's a McKenzie. And I'm Campbell. Contrary to what people say,' the old man's voice had amusement in it, 'it was the brave who stayed.' They all laughed.

She stepped back and looked out at the desk. There was nothing remarkable about the tanned leathery faces and expensive spectacles. Both wore different tartan scarves. Souvenirs, no doubt.

They made their way into the rooms and began to look at the paintings. After each one the man stepped closer to read the painting's title aloud. As his wife gazed at the work she made disconcerting little noises with her mouth. The couple drifted into the room with the Inverannich works and the man blew out his cheeks. She hated being there, not declaring herself as the painter of these images. It was like overhearing herself being talked about. She had to get out. But they were friendly, wanted to declare their origins to anyone who would listen, wanted to acknowledge her, maybe share something with her in that polite North American way. The old man leaned towards her as she tried to sidle past him and said, 'Such images. Such vital images he's managed to capture.'

She looked at him.

'He?' The word was out of her before she could do anything about it.

'A woman painted these?'

'Yes – me.' She could have bitten off her tongue. He looked confused for a moment. Looked at his wife then back to the woman in front of him.

'They're your work? You're the painter?' She nodded but did not trust herself to confirm it by speech.

'That's wonderful.' He smiled.

'Yes, indeed,' said his wife. 'Wonderful work. You are to be congratulated.'

'Thank you.'

She began to make her escape, self-conscious that her block heels were making too much noise on the wooden floor.

VISITING TAKABUTI

Nora woke. Her mouth was dry. The glass of water had grown bubbles overnight. She washed down her tablets and afterwards listened hard but could hear no rain, nor signs of rain. Rain would spoil everything. She swung herself out of bed slowly. These days she was like eggs. Too sudden a movement and she felt something would give. She'd been feeling like this for months now – but hadn't had the courage to go to the doctor. What could she say? Last time, after checking her blood pressure, he told her she was showing signs of osteoporosis – effectively her inner scaffolding was dissolving.

She eased herself into her slippers. They waited left on the left, right on the right just as she had withdrawn from them the night before. Outside it was dry. December dull but dry. She sat on the side of the bed thinking about the day ahead. It would be good to have the boys. She knelt and said her Morning Offering.

On the way back from eight o'clock mass she took in the milk from the door. She made porridge, not forgetting the salt, and watched it boil – plopping into holes, blowing gouts of steam. When it was ready she tumbled it into her dish. Half a teaspoon of demerara sugar and the cream from the neck of the bottle. Porridge stuck to you – it set you up for the day.

Nora lived in a small flat above a dry cleaners overlooking the main road. She no longer heard the constant traffic. Occasionally she got the smell of the dry-cleaning chemicals but that was not unpleasant – a bit like petrol – but lately she had wondered if breathing this stuff, day in day out, could be good for her.

She put on her fedora-type hat, her good coat and knotted a cream silk scarf at her neck. Some strands of her white hair were sticking out and she tucked them in. On her lapel was a Celtic brooch of gunmetal and amethyst. She gave herself the once-over in the full-length mirror. She would do.

It was not far to her niece's place. She took her time, looking around her, nodding to various ones she knew.

'How do you do?'

'I'm grand. And yourself – how are you keeping?'

'Well – thank you.'

When she arrived she opened the door and walked up the hallway.

'Molly, it's only me.'

'Aunt Nora.' Her niece was at the kitchen table having a cup of tea and a cigarette.

'Where are they?'

'Out somewhere. I told them not to be long. And not to be getting dirty. Would you like a cuppa tea?'

'That would be lovely.' Molly made a fresh pot of tea.

'This is very good of you – taking them off my hands.'

'Don't mention it. Sure am'n't I the Aunt of Treats?' Every so often she would see something in the paper which would be suitable and would ask Molly if it was all right to take the boys. They'd gone to the pictures – to films she had previously viewed and approved. *Goodbye Mr Chips* and *Oliver Twist*. The older boy said he'd had nightmares about Bill Sykes and his horrible dog, that white snub-nosed thing. The one time it went wrong was when she brought them to Joyce Grenfell on stage. This actress was supposed to be very amusing but she was unsuitable for young ones. Thank God the boys were innocent and they came out none the wiser.

'I wouldn't do it if I didn't enjoy it.'

'There's a lot they can learn over there.'

'You never said a truer word. It'll teach them a thing or two.'

Molly poured the tea.

'I mind the day you brought me. I didn't sleep for weeks.'

'Isn't it only natural.'

'Natural can be upsetting. I wouldn't let them see their Daddy.'

Nora raised the cup to her lips and sipped. She nodded as if she understood.

'And how are you?'

'On the up and up.'

'I'm glad to hear it. Are you all set for Christmas?'

'The Widows' Pension doesn't run to big presents.'

'If you're short I've . . .'

'I'll be just fine.'

A door slammed and there was a blundering noise in the hallway.

'Here they are now,' said Molly. Aunt Nora drank off her tea just as the two boys burst into the room.

'Hellooo – you two. Are you all ready for your wee jaunt?' They grinned and whispered to each other. Then the younger boy said,

'Can we get sweets?'

'Who do you think I am – Carnegie?' Aunt Nora stood. 'So we're off to visit Takabuti.'

'Who?'

'Who's he?' said the wee one.

'Get your coats on.'

How she loved them – the both of them. And their wee upright-ness. With their grey socks and jumpers to match. Their mother scolded and wrestled them into their raincoats.

When their belts were tightened Aunt Nora held each of them at arm's length.

'Window models – would you look at them. Mr Burton would be jealous.'

As they stood at the bus-stop she talked to people she didn't even know – about the weather. The boys looked down.

'You're easy embarrassed.' And they smiled and continued to turn away. 'Don't they look well? Fine and dandy.'

'Is that their names?' People at the bus-stop laughed. The seventy-seven came, the only bus to go across town.

'Upstairs?' Aunt Nora pulled a face and nodded. The two boys dashed up ahead of her. She held onto the metal rails with both hands and hoisted herself up each steep step, complaining. The boys were together in a seat halfway up the left-hand side. Before she sat down the bell rang and the bus started. The back seat was empty and she

half fell, was half catapulted into it. When she got her breath back
she called out to the boys to ask if they were all right. They nodded
and went on talking to each other.

It had been years since she had travelled upstairs on a bus. You
could see so much more. Across the trees to the ponds in the
Waterworks, the green hills beyond.

'Boys – look at the swans,' she pointed and they turned. 'The man
swan is a cob and the lady is . . .?' The boys didn't know. 'A pen. A
female swan is called a pen.'

She wanted to add something about swans devoting themselves to
the same partner throughout life but thought it unsuitable for boys
of that age. And of no interest. She had retired from teaching some
twenty years ago – or was it thirty? If she'd married she would have
had to resign her post. That was accepted in those days. But she never
did marry.

Her own schooldays had ended at fifteen when she was asked to
stay on as a monitress. Then she'd gone to the newly opened St Mary's
Training College on the Falls Road. Her first school had been on the
north coast – in Ballintoy. It had been such an excitement – to be on
her own in digs. With the McBrides. Nicer people you couldn't meet.
She'd admired their youngest son, Arthur, almost from the beginning.
His manliness, the light in his eye, the comical way he said things.
'There's no use hurrying if you don't know the times of the trains.'
He had the north-east accent which made his sayings even funnier.
'A man's a man for all what?' he would say and laugh.

He was about the same age as herself and was working in a pharmacist's shop in Ballycastle. She smiled. *The Encyclopaedia of Primary
Teaching*. She'd talked so much about it he'd offered to buy it for
her. But she wanted to be independent. She saved everything she could
from her early wages and sent away to England for it. The best money
she'd ever spent. It came in three bound volumes containing methods
and lesson plans and 'pedagogical advice'. In a separate black box
– illustrations relating to the lesson plans. The pictures had a great
variety – some were famous paintings, *The Death of Ophelia* and
And When Did You Last See Your Father?, some were drawings –
Dürer's *Hands in Prayer*, others were diagrams – the best way to light

a camp-fire, a cross-section of a burial chamber in an Egyptian pyramid. In Ballintoy she had an easel at the front of the class on which she set such pictures. The children had walked to school in the rain, their clothes were grey, their slates were grey, as were the walls. The colours of the illustrations on the easel were vibrant, like stained glass.

The first time she had permitted Arthur McBride to kiss her was on the deserted and windswept beach at Ballycastle. The sand was racing, as was her heart, at the things he was saying. And they stepped into the lee of Pans rocks and he kissed her as she held her hat to her head. Such was his caution – she had been staying with them for almost a year – because he feared his action was too premature. If she did not feel the same way it would spoil his chances of walking out with her again. He later said he feared the loss of her company, more than anything. And she could not understand this – what else was there, apart from her company?

She had come this same journey two weeks ago to check that everything would be all right in the art gallery part of the museum. She had turned into one room and there in front of her was the most brazen picture she had ever seen. She had taken out her glasses and examined the label. *Somebody-or-other at her toilette.* The painter was French, of course. This bare-chested woman towered above her. Hester or Esther. She was stretching up to knot her hair, exposing even her armpits. The painting must have been six foot tall and it was done in the most realistic detail. She stared up in a kind of irritated amazement at it. A uniformed guard was pacing slowly around the room. He drew level with her.

'Is this on permanent exhibition?'

'Yes it is, ma'am.'

'Thank you.'

She would have to find another route.

By now others had come onto the top deck of the bus. A man in the seat in front of her read his newspaper. There was a photo of the Prime Minister on the front page. How could he take the country into war again so soon? Over such a thing as the Suez Canal. It had only been ten years. There should be no more wars – ever again. Because men will die and there will be widows and grieving sweethearts.

The bus was approaching Shaftsbury Square.

'How am I going to face those stairs?' Aunt Nora shouted to the boys. People turned. The boys' faces went red. She ordered them to ring the bell and go down the stairs in front of her 'to cushion her fall'. They were to take their time and on no account were they to let the bus move off until she was on the pavement.

She got down from the platform by herself and put her hands on the boys' shoulders.

'Holy mackerel. What a handling,' she said. The bus drove off into the traffic. She gathered them close, one on each side, to cross the busy junction.

The boys walked on in front, sometimes running and mock fighting, other times quietly in step.

'Would anybody like an ice cream?' The two turned. 'Cones or sliders?' They opted for cones. 'Watch you don't dribble on your coats – or your mother'll crucify me.'

They passed the University – red-brick gables set back behind green lawns. She felt the effect of such expansive and well-kept lawns was to hold the public at bay. How dare you – the grass said. The boys finished their ice creams and walked on the waist-high perimeter wall, their arms out for balance. It was tricky enough not to trip because there were still the stumps of metal railings which had been sawn off during the last war and never replaced.

'Careful,' she called out.

After the Great War she moved back to Belfast and taught in St Anthony's in Millfield, a poor part of the town. The windows of her classroom were of frosted glass except for the topmost pane and when the children had been set a task she would sit and stare through this pane at the battleship grey of the corrugated-iron roof of the parochial hall. Sometimes she cried – if she felt it coming on she turned her back on the class and pretended to look at the book shelf. She had developed the knack of weeping in silence. When it passed she removed her handkerchief from her sleeve, blew her nose and regained her composure. Only then did she turn to face the class.

The boys were setting a good pace on the wall and she began to feel a little breathless. She had worn too many clothes and was beginning to perspire a little. She liked 'there' journeys because they seemed shorter. 'There and back' journeys were a different thing. The farther you got from home the farther you had to go back.

In the middle of the driveway, in front of the University's main door was a memorial for the Great War – a winged female figure holding up a wreath which she is about to put on the head of a young soldier. Arthur McBride. All those years ago. He had enlisted without telling her. At the time it was the thing to do because the country was in a good mood and proud of itself. The place was flag mad – especially in Belfast. When he said goodbye to her, he took both her hands in his and kissed them. Adieu, he said to her left hand. Adieu to her right. Then her lips. Adieu. She often wondered why he had chosen the French. He was of a poetic turn of mind – very fond of Burns and had many of his songs off by heart. But to say goodbye that way? She told him that she loved him and only him. She promised never to love another.

In the Museum she made the boys hang their coats in the cloakroom. They'd feel the good of them when they went back out. She hung up her own coat but kept her hat and scarf on. In the middle of the entrance hall was a massive marble statue of a seated Galileo. The boys stood whispering in front of it. A statue of Robert Burns 1759–1796 was in the corner. 'Ae Fond Kiss' came into her head. 'And then we sever'. How cruel and clever of Burns to rhyme it with 'for ever'. Because Arthur never came back. His family got word that he was missing in action. And they told her because they knew what was between them.

'Aunt Nora. Where first?'

'This way,' she said.

The roller-ball clock was beautiful, glittering as it moved. The boys put their faces close to the glass case. It was an inclined metal plane with a shallow groove, along which a silver ball rolled, zigzagging from one end to the other. When the ball reached the bottom it struck a catch reversing the tilt and rolled back the way it had come. Each journey took a known amount of time and the hands moved on accordingly. She got her glasses out. When she snapped the case shut it popped too loudly and echoed. She read out the label for them. 'These clocks were not novelties but were serious attempts at time-keeping before the introduction of the pendulum.' The air was full of small mechanical sounds, tickings and scrapings.

She led them from room to room – pointing out what she thought would interest them. A one-hundred-and-thirty-five-million-year-old amethyst geode from Brazil – like a shark's mouth jagged with jewels instead of teeth. A ball made of rock crystal quartz 'for looking into the future' she said in a mysterious voice. Fossil sea scorpions that were four hundred and twenty million years of age – imprinted in shale.

'And you're only ten,' she said to the younger one, winking.

'Ten and a bit,' he said. 'Nearly eleven.' His voice was pitched high.

'So you are,' she smiled. 'So you are.'

The boys crouched to stare into the glass eyes of stuffed animals.

'How lifelike,' said Aunt Nora. Brown hares standing on their hind legs boxing. White hares in their winter coats, hiding in the snow. The boys straightened up and wandered the corridor ahead of her.

'Left here,' she called out. There was a sign for a café. 'Would you like a lemonade?'

She sat opposite them drinking her tea. They had bottles of lemonade with straws – two in each bottle for greater purchase – and were sucking hard, indenting their cheeks.

'Easy,' she said. 'No noises when you reach the bottom.' The boys looked at each other and tried not to laugh.

'No bottom noises,' said the wee one. Then they did laugh.

'It comes down your nose – the fizz,' said his brother.

'Oh don't . . . please.' There was silence except for the noise of spoons being dropped one after another into a drawer in the kitchen. 'Are you looking after your mother these days?' They both nodded. 'Good – because she needs a great deal of looking after. She's only a slip of a girl herself.' She blew a thin stream of air to cool her tea and sipped it.

'I liked the clock with the silver marble.'

'The hares were brilliant. Boxing.' The smaller boy bunched his wee fists and faced his brother.

'There's more,' said Aunt Nora.

'What?'

'Wait and see.'

When they were finished they set off again along polished corridors. She felt refreshed having taken the weight off her feet for a bit.

'Don't go running ahead,' she said. They walked beside her until they came to a doorway. She ushered them into a room where the blinds had been partially drawn. It was still light enough to see photographs on the walls – of the Sphinx with his lopped-off nose, the pyramids, boats sailing on the Nile. There was nobody else in the room. A glass case stood in the middle of the floor and Nora called the boys over.

'Meet Takabuti,' she said. The boys tried to see. 'She's been dead for two and a half thousand years.' There was some kind of black creature in the case. Wrapped in biscuit-coloured bandages.

'It's a mummy.' Both of them stared wide-eyed. The thing was completely wrapped except for its head and a withered hand. It wore a cape of blue earthenware beads. The hand, thin as a backscratcher, had stained the wrapping it rested on. Her lips were liquorice black but slightly open showing white teeth. The nose, a snapped-off beak.

'What's it made of?' the younger boy asked.

'It's a real dead person.'

'What?'

'Dust thou art and unto dust thou shalt return,' said Aunt Nora.

Lying beside the mummy was the decorated lid of her coffin. The idealised face – painted with gold and black and scarlet. Beside it – the dead thing.

'I don't like it.' The smaller brother pulled a face and walked away to look at something else. His brother followed him.

Nora was left standing by herself looking down into the case. She was so small. Shrunken almost. But she could have been a beauty once – with such white teeth, skin of alabaster. Walking in sandals by the Nile. She said a prayer for Takabuti, that she might be in heaven no matter what her faith.

She leaned her forearms on the glass and felt a great weariness come over her. The life she had lived now seemed barren and worthless. Everything she had taught would soon be forgotten. She had brought no children into the world. Maiden aunt to two boys was the most she could say. Today she had brought them to visit Takabuti and the lesson hadn't worked as well as she had hoped. They were not as shocked as she had been when she first saw her. The children's voices were now distant. Something was happening to the sounds. They were the way sound was when you listened to a shell. Distant seas. There was a sour taste in her mouth. Her heart skipped a beat and had to race to catch up again. She reached out and leaned her fingertips on the glass case for balance. Little haloes of condensation formed around each finger as she braced herself. She held on – until the dwam gradually disappeared.

The boy's voice was very close now.

'Mammy said we should get home before the rush hour.'

She looked at her watch. It was coming up to four o'clock. The light had almost disappeared. It was either night or the rain coming on. Or both.

On the way home the boys went to the upper deck – by now she was only fit for downstairs.

'Behave yourselves,' she had shouted at the disappearing legs. The conductor was standing by the stairs. She said, 'Old age is not for the faint-hearted.' The rush hour hadn't started yet so there were plenty of seats. The conductor came to where she was settling.

'Are you going far?' he said.

'All the way,' she said and laughed. 'And the two boys upstairs.' She paid the fares and arranged herself. It was warm inside the bus. The darkness and the rain were on the outside. The throb of the engine and the shudder was comforting. Warmth was a pleasure – whether it was in bed or beside the fire or with her hot-water bottle. The traffic lights changed and reflected their colours on the wet pavement. She began to feel drowsy and moved closer to the window.

She tried to think about the mummy and the gilded case. The container and the contained. And it made her remember the Irish story – of the soul that kissed the body. At the moment of death. She had first heard it from Arthur McBride at a wake in Ballintoy. His eyes were bright trying not to be moved as he told it. The soul leaves the body and tiptoes to the doorway. Then turns and goes back to kiss the body that has sheltered it all these years. Day in, day out. In sickness and in health. In grief and in joy.

And Nora imagines it happening at her own death. She sees it like cinema. The soul, in her own image, leans over and with tenderness kisses her empty body. Adieu. And each time the soul makes the journey to the doorway reluctance takes hold and it returns to kiss the body with its shrunken frame and its frail bones of honeycomb. Adieu. Three times in all. From one vital part of herself to another. Adieu.

When it came to their stop the two boys ran down the stairs. They shouted to their Aunt Nora on the lower deck but she seemed not to hear. The older boy went to her and she was still, her head in its hat pressed against the window, her skin a grey colour. The conductor came to see if he could help but there was nothing he could do.

WINTER STORM

He was wakened by the noise of the heated air rising from the vents in the bedroom floor. He got up and opened the curtains. The windows looked out into a wood of silver birch. Here and there were patches of snow which had not melted. Two squirrels were careering from one tree to another across the thinnest of branches. Up or across – it seemed to make no difference to their speed. From the other side of the house bamboo wind chimes created a faint but constant sound. Above the garage was a clock face with a single hand for temperature. It was twenty-two below.

It was amazing how folk had found ways to live in such inhospitable places. There was another bedroom where the owner had switched off the heating. For weeks now the windows had been opaque with patterned frost – on the inside. Each screw-nail in the wood frame had grown ice crystals as long as eyelashes.

On the wall above the bed was a modern painting by a Pawnee artist. There was Native American Indian stuff all over the place – wood carvings, a woven war shield and in the hallway a pair of snow shoes like bad tennis recquets pinned to the wall.

He checked that the telephone was firmly in its cradle. He picked it up and listened for the dialling tone then, on hearing it, replaced the receiver.

He was the only one at the bus terminus with grey hair. The others around him were Asian students. People his age and American students owned cars. When the bus arrived he got a seat by the window and flipped back his hood. The window seat mattered little because everything in the American Midwest looked the same. He found it hard to get a sense of history. The motor car dictated everything, swept everything aside. Businesses and shops had to have acres of parking space so that the town appeared spread out, flat, diluted – little more than a series of neoned fast-food places, telephone wires and car parks with the huge sky arched over everything. Buildings from the turn of the century were rare. People had told him of the prairies before the first colonisers came through. This was territory to be crossed as quickly as possible – the wet lands, the bogs, the seven-foot-high grasses. The air black with midges and flies. It was hard for him to imagine the place they described. Then one evening, as he stood waiting for his bus, he looked up high into the sky and saw countless thousands of crows, flapping slowly homewards out of the sunset. A huge flock with stragglers and outriders edging across the yellow sky. And he was aware that this was a thing that had happened every evening for thousands of years. He could have been – not a Scotsman at a bus-stop – but a Kiowa-Apache on horseback looking up, moving south, anxious to be away from such a winter.

Before the stop on the north side of the campus the girl beside him put on her mittens, covered her mouth and nose with her scarf and pulled her hood up. He got off behind her, tugging his black woollen hat well down over his ears. At home in Scotland he would be laughed at for such headgear. But here in Iowa, Midwest people seemed to wear anything in winter – even Norwegian knitwear. Which meant that he had difficulty lusting. It was hard to tell the sex of students from the eye-slit they left in their clothing. Bright colours were no indication that the wearer was female.

His room was on the south side of the campus, as far away from the bus-stop as it was possible to be – far enough away for him to classify it as 'exercise'. He burrowed down into his coat for the long walk. The university buildings were around the perimeter of a central green space, large as a public park. At least it was called a green space even though the winter grass was dead and biscuit-coloured.

Paths criss-crossed the park forming a lattice-work from one building to another. Between classes the central acres became thronged. The students reminded him of skeins of geese – moving Indian-file. At the intersection of several paths he always thought it remarkable that, like birds, they didn't bump into one another. Every time he came to a junction he was wary, measured his step, slowing down or speeding up as need be, to avoid a collision with another person.

The halyard on the flagpole clacked loudly as he passed and the Stars and Stripes stood out straight in the wind. It made a noise almost like rattling. The clock in the campanile chimed ten but he didn't look up because the icy wind was coming from that direction and it would sting his eyes. He kept his face turned away. At the halfway point he passed the emergency telephone.

As he entered his department building the first snow was beginning to blow in the wind. He cleared his throat. From past experience he knew his voice sounded peculiar when he didn't use it for a long time – it could shift a whole register or not come out at all. The last thing he'd said was 'Goodnight' to the girl in the office the previous evening.

'Good morning,' he said. The throat clearing had worked.

'And how's our Scottish poet today?'

'Professor to you.'

She smiled. It was she who had typed his name into a slot on his door – 'Professor Andrew Younger' – when he'd first arrived.

'Thanks for the promotion,' he'd said. His room was on the lee side and before he took off his coat he went to the telephone. He tapped in the voicemail code fully expecting to be told, as he had been told almost every morning of his stay, that he had no messages. 'You have one new message,' said the female recording. He had to sit down when he heard Lorna's voice as clear as anything from Scotland. She was sorry but she'd mislaid his home number – surely he hadn't changed houses again? The point was she'd been offered another subbing job at the same school – somebody else was pregnant. Whether or not it was because it was a Catholic school she hadn't a clue. But it was an offer she felt she had to seriously consider. The money was excellent. So it was a real possibility that she wouldn't be joining him in sunny Iowa. She had to say yea or nay by the end of the day. It could have been such an adventure. However she would see him when he came back in the summer. Maybe she would try and ring him later.

He sat in the chair for some time, then replaced the receiver. At the window the snowflakes rose and dithered. He took off his jacket and knitted headgear. He wore his hair in a pony-tail – had done since he could remember. There was a small oval mirror beside the door and he checked his appearance before going along the corridor to the kitchen beside the office. It was empty. He poured himself a coffee in a borrowed mug and dropped one of the larger coins into a basket – was it a quarter or a dime? This was the brush-off. How could she do this – after what they'd agreed? She was so obdurate. He'd said that to her one day, 'You are so fucking obdurate,' and wondered why she had laughed out loud in his face. Back in his room he sat down in front of his screen.

He switched on his computer and while it went through its warming-up noises he sat with his head in his hands. He had promised to write a CV for a campus radio show he was to be on. He gave a minimum amount of his history and listed the titles of his collections of poems – his 'slim volumes' as Lorna called them. 'Weight Watchers' poetry.'

Now and Again
Holidays of Obligation
Making Strange
Like Everything Else

How futile all this was. How was anyone to deduce his life from such fragments? He'd been married to a girl called Cathy for three years in the sixties. She'd worked for the Abbey National but it had all broken up when she went off with her branch manager, himself married. The only good thing was that there'd been no children. After that he'd had a succession of occasional relationships – until he'd met Lorna. She was widowed with two grown-up sons who were away at university – in Hull. Then in her early forties she herself decided to go to university. That was where he'd met her, one night in the bar after he'd done a reading. Andrew wanted to settle down with her but she was wary of commitment and wanted to keep her own place. And her own pace. So he visited a lot. And slept over. After a couple of years they began to become routine and still she wouldn't commit. She seemed to say, 'This is fine as it is – but don't push it.' When he was offered the poet-in-residence at Iowa State he hesitated but Lorna said he MUST take it. It was too good an opportunity to miss. Besides it was only for a year. Not even a year – September to May. Lorna had said it with such conviction that he wondered if she wanted rid of him – that this was the moment she'd been waiting for.

She was now a Modern Studies teacher but did mostly subbing because of the freedom it gave her. Her present contract was due to have run out sometime after Christmas and she had promised to give serious thought to following him to Iowa. Then they had this terrible falling out. Fights are never about what causes the fight. They are always about something else – something in the past, an irritation, a vengeance, a reprisal. He'd gone round to her place to watch *A Doll's House* on television. They'd settled with a glass of wine, she curled up on the sofa beside him. Then the cat had *wanted* out. That had to be made absolutely clear. And the other fact – that the outer storm doors were bolted shut because of the kind of night it was – is also relevant. If the storm doors were not closed against an east wind then the porch inevitably flooded. That wonderful actress Juliet Stevenson was in the lead role of Nora. It didn't seem like a long play but it was – and the only thing that distracted Lorna's attention was the rain against the windows. And the wind. She kept remarking it. Then the play ended with the boom of Nora closing the door as she left. Lorna went to look for the cat and, not finding her anywhere in the house, opened the front doors and it came streaking in, thin as a greyhound because of the wet.

'Did you know the cat was out?'

'Yeah, I let her out earlier.'

'Why didn't you let her in again?'

'We were watching the play.'

'She's been out for hours. In the rain.'

She got a towel and began to rub the cat down in front of the fire.

'You're shivering, pet.'

'Cats don't shiver.'

'Tell him. You're shivering, aren't you, darlin.' The cat's fur looked jagged. 'He's a bastard of a poet. Cares about nobody but himself. Here, love. Easy.'

'I hate the way you utterly sentimentalise animals.'

'Then you can fuck off. Back to your own place.'

He thought of Juliet Stevenson when he slammed the door on his way out. Before he left for America he'd tried to patch things up. But only with limited success. She seemed cold – couldn't care less whether they got back together again or not. As for him, he couldn't wheedle because . . . well, because it was wheedling. There were certain things couldn't be said out loud – 'I want someone to talk to, to share things with. I want sex and companionship. I want you, Lorna, to be with me. To complete me. You have all the things I lack.'

There was a knock at his door.

'Come in.'

It was the cleaner. Twice a week she excused herself and emptied his waste-basket. She was a Native American Indian woman, very big with a solemn leathery face. She had a trolley loaded neatly with brushes and shovels, sprays and polishes. She didn't smile when he greeted her but adjusted the muscles of her face to show him that she was returning his greeting. She reminded him of the tall Indian in the movie of *One Flew Over the Cuckoo's Nest*. The one who never spoke. She took his waste-basket to her trolley and upended it. Nothing much came out.

He said, 'It's *so* cold today.'

She set the basket back on the floor.

'You betcha,' she said and went out. Her metal shovels clanged like low-pitched wind chimes as she moved down the corridor.

He finished the CV and began to type up his notebook from the weekend. He'd written quite a lot. When he ate out he'd choose from the menu then jot things down until his food arrived. It was a way of having a conversation with himself. Writing in the notebook was a way of not being alone:

> *Shop at the Hy-Vee just as it's getting dark. The clear sky is amazing, almost like a tinted windscreen – pinkish rising to green then to navy. The evening star is low and as bright as a plane headlight coming at you straight on.*

Met a girl student today called Ellen Lonesome.

Walking down Hickory Drive I look up and see that in this country Cassiopeia has become an M rather than a W. And somebody has upended the Plough onto its handle.

Here people don't cook food, they fix it.

Remembered a phrase of rejection of my mother's today at lunch. 'The back of my hand to you.' If I failed to keep a promise to her or let somebody down and she was really disappointed she'd say it.

The snow fizzed as the wind whipped it at the window pane. He looked up but could only see the leaden grey sky. 'Will it lie?' In Scotland it was the first question asked when the snow came on. Here it always did.

At lunch-time he went along to the kitchen for another coffee. The last woman in the office was putting on her coat. All the others had gone.

'Didn't you hear the weather warning?'

'No.'

'Oh really?' she said. 'Campus Radio have been at it since morning. They don't expect it to quit until after midnight.'

He went back to his room and stood looking down through the window at the snowstorm. The paths were covered now. He sipped his coffee and sat down in front of the computer again. He checked the phone in its cradle. He should write to Lorna – put it on paper. Elegantly. To see if she could be tempted by words. But then it would be too late. Decisions would have been taken. He could ring her but she would be in class. And if there was one thing she hated, it was to be phoned at school. Trekking along corridors behind that stork of a school secretary.

He stood up to look out. Maybe he should go. He couldn't see to the ground and the trees outside his window were no longer visible. Yes, he should go. And not wait for a phone call. She'd only said 'maybe'. And if she was getting rid of him he wouldn't want to talk to him directly. He saved what work he'd done and snapped the Off switch on the computer. He put on his coat and zipped it up to his throat.

The only one in the corridor was the Native American cleaner mopping to and fro. Pulling an apologetic face he tiptoed over the wet floor.

'I'm off,' he said.

'You betcha.'

Somewhere there was the sound of a distant flush and a woman from Linguistics came out of the ladies' restroom.

'Hi – I thought everyone had gone,' she said.

'Not me.'

They walked together as far as the lift and she pressed the button.

'The University is officially closed this afternoon,' she said.

'Why's that?'

'That's why,' she looked towards the window at the end of the corridor. 'It's a rare event – to close down.'

Both of them turned from the window and stared up at the indicator lights.

'I think this elevator's bust,' she said. They went down the stairs. At ground level he turned off as she continued to the garage in the basement.

'You don't have a car?' she said.

'No.'

'Oh really?'

'The bus does me fine.'

'Are they still running?'

'I hope so.'

'Which side of town are you?'

'West – out by the river.'

'Oh – I'm the other side.' She hesitated. 'Can I offer you a ride?'

'No – no thanks. Not with the roads the way they are.' She nodded and jackknifed her hood up into place.

'Take care,' she said.

He waited until he was at the front doors before putting on his stupid hat and gloves. His boots squidged on the terrazzo. Even with the doors closed, papers swirled in the draughts of the hallway.

The snow had silted up the steps outside, evened them to a slope.

He wound his scarf around his mouth and nose, Bedouin style, and went down the steps. He breathed in and, at about the third breath, felt the hairs in his nose begin to stiffen and freeze. It was an odd sensation, a bit like having too much Coca-Cola. He turned left and headed along the path. In some places the snow was forming into drifts, other places there was no snow at all. The path in front of him was swept clean by the wind. It was so *bitterly* cold. He had never felt anything like it. At home in Scotland there was a damp cold that got into your bones and joints but this was different. This was thermometer cold. The wind ripped at the skin of his cheeks. He partially closed his eyes to protect them and kept his head down. Now the path disappeared into the snow. He couldn't tell where the edges were. So he just kept walking straight. Each time he put weight on his boot the snow creaked beneath his sole. He looked round to check on the direction of his footprints and noticed that he could no longer see the building he had just come from. It was a white vortex.

'Fuck me,' he said. His prints were fast disappearing as the wind evened them out. The snow was so fine it got everywhere – particles the size of salt. His wrists were feeling numbed. The wind got at the skin space between his gloves and his sleeves. He tried to put his hands in his pockets but it didn't help. With his eyes narrowed he now found difficulty in seeing. His eyes had begun to stick. His tears were gumming up his lashes as they began to freeze.

'Jesus . . .' He jerked his eyes open, widened them quickly so that the icing was broken. He'd had 'mucky eyes' as a boy and in the morning he'd have to open them with his fingers. It was like that now, hard to see into the wind with the ice on his lashes. There was also a terrible roaring of the wind around his head, cuffing him this way and that, probing his hood and the thin knitted hat. His boot sunk down to his knee in a rise of snow. His other foot followed and the drift covered his knee. It was getting deeper. This can't be right. It has only been snowing a couple of hours. He didn't want to look at his watch, to bare his wrist. He tried to calculate how long – four hours at the most. The snow was even, uninterrupted when he looked round for any sign of the path.

He heard a noise in front of him – a kind of stuttering – and for a moment he couldn't think of what it was. A rattling. Then he saw it was the flagpole. With its halyard vibrating in the wind. But the flagpole shouldn't be there. It was in the middle of the fucking green. How could it have moved to the path? He stopped and reached out and touched the metallic pole with his glove. He looked up but could only see glimpses through the driving snow of the flag at the top of it.

He knew the path was to the right of the flagpole so he headed back to join it. The wind had loosened the scarf protecting his face and it blew out in front of him. He tried to cover his face again and stuff in the end of the scarf at his neck. But his gloves were too big and insensitive for him to do it properly. He stumbled into a drift of snow and lost his footing. But he didn't fall far – this snow was up to his thighs and it was soft. He keeled over, more than fell. 'I'm too old for this kind of a caper,' he said out loud. 'What the fuck's going on here?' He clambered upright. Because of the fall, snow had got inside both his gloves and up his sleeves. As it melted his wrists were wet as well as cold.

Now the skin of his cheeks felt numb. He tried to protect himself from the wind by cupping his hands like horse blinkers at each side of his face. But this exposed his wrists again to pain. He looked back at his tracks and headed into the unbroken snow. Then he heard the gonging of the campanile. That must be the hour. Two o'clock. He had been out here the best part of fifteen minutes. Normally, at a good pace, it took him about eight minutes to cross from one side to the other. The sound was coming from his left, which was as it should be. Or *was* it coming from his left? The wind kept plucking and distorting it – was it an echo he was hearing? It was like trying to tune in an old radio. Then he heard another sound – distantly. The long slow hoot of a train. It appeared to be coming from his left also. But this could not be because he knew the tracks ran along the west side of the campus. He decided to keep going straight ahead. The sound could not be trusted.

The sheeting snow eased momentarily and he saw a clump of trees in front of him. Ah! He stepped into the shelter of one of the trees. Here the snow was over his boot mouth. Which particular group of trees was this? He tried to remember – there were groups of trees all over the place. Scots pines with the longest cones he had ever seen, evergreens with swishing fronds which he thought would do for whisking at flies if he stayed till the hot and humid summer, ornamental trees with burnished bark the colour of copper. But this was a group of trees he couldn't remember seeing – these were like silver birch. There was a bench of polished stone or marble in the middle of the copse which was still miraculously free of snow. Along the back of its seat the words:

AFTER TILLAGE COMES THE OTHER ARTS

Then in smaller gold lettering:

DONATED BY THE CLASS OF 1932

He sat down on it with his back to the wind – and thanked the class of thirty-two.

Fucksake, this was getting serious. He was completely disorientated and his cheeks were beginning to hurt or to go numb, whichever was the more dangerous. He was panting for breath and the tears in his eyes were freezing and icing his bottom lids to the top ones. He was too old for this kind of nonsense. He debated whether or not he should turn around and go back to the department. Maybe stay there till the thing had blown over. But the woman in the office had said the forecast was for it to continue snowing until midnight. There was a sleeping bag on the top of the book shelf in the room they'd given him. So it had happened before. He could stay the night. It was a piece of fucking nonsense that he couldn't get from one side of the quad to the other. He felt so tired. Tired out of all proportion. Maybe lie down on this marble bench. He took off his gloves to get a handkerchief to dry his face. He put his hand in his right pocket but he was astonished to find it full of snow. And it was frozen. He had not buttoned the pocket flap down properly. Somewhere beneath the snow he located the handkerchief, took it out and tried to wipe his face. But the hanky too was stiff and frozen and felt like sandpaper or broken glass on his skin. He put it away again. His left pocket was in the same state. He'd better get on, now that he'd got his breath back. Get the bus. Get home and make a cup of coffee. Turn up the heating. Maybe have a hot shower. Step out on the tiles with the underfloor heating. There was an enormous gust of wind which blew his gloves off the bench onto the ground. He grabbed at one but saw the other cartwheel away into the snow. Hand over fist. It was the right one he'd saved. The left one had disappeared completely.

'Jesus . . .' He cleared his left pocket of snow and put his hand into it for protection. The inside lining crackled and felt like cold tinfoil. He could maybe find the glove tomorrow. Or in the spring.

He hunched his shoulders and stood up. All he had to do was continue walking in the same direction – to walk in a straight line – across the diameter of the park – and he would get to buildings of some sort at its circumference. The snow in this place was so deep he was having to lift his knees to make each stride. Could this really be the path? Off the beaten track, for fucksake. It was laughable. Except that he hadn't enough breath to laugh. He was panting with the effort that was required of him now to keep going. He wanted to stop, to lie down. To curl up and sleep. The most bizarre things were coming into his head. He laughed. Where was the emergency telephone? What fucking use was an emergency phone if you couldn't find it? He had not thought much about it, assuming, because it was equidistant from all buildings, that it would be for violent situations at night – an assault or rape or something. It had a red push button and a built-in mouthpiece for speaking into. Yelling into, maybe. If he could find that he would definitely use it. He wouldn't feel shame-faced about using it – because now he felt he was in some difficulties. No, I'm not being raped – I'm just lost. Yes, somewhere in the middle of the fucking campus. Then he remembered someone telling him about the habit of Midwestern farmers in weather like this, who tied a rope from the house to the byre for fear they'd get lost going to feed the beasts. And another story about a father and son who tied themselves together in case they'd become separated in just such a storm.

He *must* be at the other side by now. The snow on the ground here was blowing, forming into ribs like sand at the seashore.

Something loomed up in front of him and disappeared just as quickly. He moved towards it. It was another flagpole. He leaned up against it. But he could only remember one – in the centre of the quad. There wasn't another one. Maybe he'd forgotten the second one. He looked up. This one was flying the same flag as the one earlier.

'Fuck it.' It *was* the same one. He must have walked in a circle.

He remembered a childhood game in which adult hands had grabbed and blindfolded him. Then they turned him round and round until he didn't know where he was. He'd stand, his arms outstretched, his fingers moving, listening to the breathing of the grown-ups. When they took the blindfold off he was always astonished at where he was in the room. And once memorably when he opened his eyes they had tricked him into a different room altogether.

He hunkered down to make himself less of a target for the wind and snow. He would have to try to extricate himself. But there was no guarantee that he wouldn't do exactly the same thing. In another fifteen minutes he could be blundering past this fucking flagpole for a third time.

He must conserve his energy. His feet were now totally numb and his left wrist was causing him pain. The scarf around his mouth had become saturated with his breath and refrozen so that it was white and brittle against his lips. Where any outer material came in contact with his skin, it was abrasive. His cheeks felt like raw meat and he wondered if they were bleeding.

If the flag was at the centre of the quad . . . He looked down but the prints he had made on his previous visit were completely obliterated. The wind direction was of no help because it was swirling and twisting . . . But neither could he take no action. Staying there was not an option.

If he found the emergency phone he would ask to be connected to long distance. Was it still called that? Lorna, get me outa here. I'm fucking lost. We can patch it up. We can make a go of it. I want somebody to share my life with. Somebody to come home to. His mother's phrase was now in Linda's mouth. 'The back of my hand to you.'

He got slowly to his feet. His gloved hand almost stuck to the metal of the flagpole. He arbitrarily chose a direction and set off. He was blundering now. Flutters of panic mixed with a couldn't-care-less attitude. Why was he so fucking tired? Monumentally tired?

He tripped on something and fell flat on the snow. He looked back to see what it was in the kind of stupid way you do. It was the path. The wind had cleared the snow and the concrete edge of the path was sitting proud of the snow. Ho-ho-ho – he now had a fifty-percent chance of getting to his destination. Follow the path. That way he would either end up at the department or reach the other side. Then he remembered that this is what he had done the first time. The path would disappear under the snow. He lay there wondering if he should get up. His face was against the snow. The carillon sounded. It must be a quarter past. Or was it half past? How long had he been blundering around out here? Surely to Christ a grown man could walk across a quadrangle – even if it was as big as a park. He looked to his left and saw a pair of boots. Then upwards to a padded coat. A hooded figure bent down and took him beneath his armpits, helped him to his feet.

'I must have slipped,' he said.

'You betcha.'

He tried to see the eyes behind the slit in the hood. He guessed it was a woman from the voice. She was tall and bulky or else she was wearing a lot of clothes. It was the Indian woman, the cleaner from his department.

At first she took his arm but, when she felt him walking steadily, she let it go. She looked closely into his hood.

'You from Scotland?'

'Yes.'

'You gotta phone call. Nobody else in the bildin.' She shouted above the howling of the wind, 'She said to tell you. She's coming.'

He sheltered in her wake as she walked the blizzard in a straight line to the buildings on the far side.